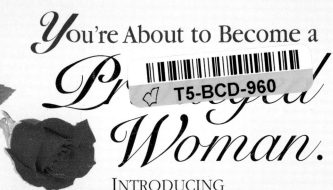

You're About to Become a

Pr~~*ivileged*~~ *Woman.*

INTRODUCING
PAGES & PRIVILEGES™.

It's our way of thanking you for buying
our books at your favorite retail store.

Get ALL THIS *Free*
WITH JUST ONE PROOF OF PURCHASE:

◆ **Hotel Discounts** up
to 60% at home and
abroad ◆ **Travel Service**
- Guaranteed lowest
published airfares
plus 5% cash back

$50 VALUE

on tickets ◆ **$25 Travel Voucher**

◆ **Sensuous Petite Parfumerie** collection

◆ **Insider Tips Letter**
with sneak previews
of upcoming books

You'll get a FREE personal card, too.
It's your passport to all these benefits– and to
even more great gifts & benefits to come!
There's no club to join. No purchase commitment. No obligation.

Enrollment Form

☐ *Yes!* I WANT TO BE A *Privileged Woman.*

Enclosed is one *PAGES & PRIVILEGES*™ Proof of Purchase
from any Harlequin or Silhouette book currently for
sale in stores (Proofs of Purchase are found on
the back pages of books) and the store cash
register receipt. Please enroll me in *PAGES
& PRIVILEGES*™. Send my Welcome
Kit and FREE Gifts -- and activate my
FREE benefits -- immediately.

*More great gifts and benefits to come like these
luxurious Truly Lace and L'Effleur gift baskets.*

NAME (please print)

ADDRESS   APT. NO

CITY   STATE   ZIP/POSTAL CODE

▼ DETACH HERE AND MAIL TODAY! ▼

PROOF OF PURCHASE

SAMPLE ONLY

Please allow 6-8 weeks for delivery. Quantities are
limited. We reserve the right to substitute items.
Enroll before October 31, 1995 and receive
one full year of benefits.

**NO CLUB!
NO COMMITMENT!**
Just one purchase brings
you great Free Gifts
and Benefits!
(More details in back of this book.)

Name of store where this book was purchased_____

Date of purchase_____

Type of store:

☐ Bookstore   ☐ Supermarket   ☐ Drugstore

☐ Dept. or discount store (e.g. K-Mart or Walmart)

☐ Other (specify)_____

**Pages
& Privileges** ™

Which Harlequin or Silhouette series do you usually read?

_____

Complete and mail with one Proof of Purchase and store receipt to➤

U.S.: *PAGES & PRIVILEGES*™, P.O. Box 1960, Danbury, CT 06813-1960

Canada: *PAGES & PRIVILEGES*™, 49-6A The Donway West, P.O. 813,
North York, ON M3C 2E8   **PRINTED IN U.S.A**

Before *or* after marriage, nothing can bring
two people closer than...

Making Babies

Ryder Braden isn't anybody's hero. But
Lauren Holt desperately needs his help and he
can't refuse. She's the mother of his child.

Just once, Jenna Bradford wants to see
the son she gave up at birth. But after
meeting Robbie's dad, she's tempted to
stick around a little longer.

Eve Triopolous had been paid to have another
couple's child. But when tragedy strikes,
Eve has to sort out her feelings for her
baby...and its father.

Making Babies

Not your average families!

Relive the romance...

*Three complete novels by your
favorite authors!*

About the Authors

Karen Young—Award-winning author Karen Young loves romance. "I like reading about it and I like writing about it. Every person I meet is potentially part of a book, part of a character." Karen's interest in people and diverse subject matters enables her to write books that keep readers glued to the pages. Karen lives in Louisiana with her husband, Paul.

Sandra James—Sandra James had always been a voracious reader, so it was only a matter of time before she decided to write a book herself. Now, several books later, Sandra's warm, family-oriented stories have made her a favorite among readers. After all, "commitment, family and marriage are what love is all about." Sandra lives in Oregon with her husband and three daughters.

Pamela Browning—Pamela Browning is a former nonfiction writer who decided to change genres one cold, rainy day when she was touring a dump for an article on waste reclamation. As the rainwater sluiced down her neck, she thought, *There's got to be a better way to get a story.* And there was! She's been writing romance novels ever since.

Making Babies

KAREN YOUNG
SANDRA JAMES
PAMELA BROWNING

Harlequin Books

MAKING BABIES

mechanical or other means, now known or hereafter invented, including
xerography, photocopying and recording, or in any information storage
or retrieval system, is forbidden without the written permission of the
publisher, Harlequin Enterprises Limited, 225 Duncan Mill Road,
Don Mills, Ontario, Canada M3B 3K9.

All characters in this book have no existence outside the imagination of
the author and have no relation whatsoever to anyone bearing the same
name or names. They are not even distantly inspired by any individual
known or unknown to the author, and all incidents are pure invention.

This edition published by arrangement with Harlequin Books S.A.

® and ™ are trademarks of the publisher. Trademarks indicated with
® are registered in the United States Patent and Trademark Office, the
Canadian Trade Marks Office and in other countries.

Printed in U.S.A.

TORONTO • NEW YORK • LONDON
AMSTERDAM • PARIS • SYDNEY • HAMBURG
STOCKHOLM • ATHENS • TOKYO • MILAN
MADRID • WARSAW • BUDAPEST • AUCKLAND

HARLEQUIN BOOKS

by Request—Making Babies

Copyright © 1995 by Harlequin Books S.A.

ISBN 0-373-20115-X

The publisher acknowledges the copyright holders of the individual works as follows:
COMPELLING CONNECTION
Copyright © 1989 by Karen Stone
A FAMILY AFFAIR
Copyright © 1986 by Sandra Kleinschmit
EVER SINCE EVE
Copyright © 1986 by Pamela Browning

CONTENTS

He was a stranger—
and the father of her child!

COMPELLING
CONNECTION

Karen Young

To Evan Marshall,
my agent and friend
who is the real Justin's daddy

PROLOGUE

1975

IT WAS EARLY, but Baby's Bar was smoke filled and crowded as usual. For once, conversation was possible, a circumstance brought about by the end of exam week. Like soldiers suffering battle fatigue after narrowly escaping disaster, weary students huddled around tiny tables. Over the rise and fall of hushed voices, the audio system pulsed with the rhythm of the Rolling Stones. Mick Jagger's wail blended with the muted clink of glasses and weary laughter.

Ryder Braden stared into his beer. *Thank God, it's over,* he thought. Graduation was only a week away. It had taken six years—six long, hard years—but now he could begin to reap the rewards. He savored his satisfaction for a long moment before lifting his head to look at his former roommate across the table.

Neil Putnam was finishing off his sixth beer. Or was it his seventh? Ryder hid a smile, shaking his head. Laid-back, low in his chair, he decided it didn't matter. It was over for Ryder but Neil, poor devil, still had three or four more arduous years of medical school to go followed by his residency. In spite of all that, tonight Neil still had the look of a man with cause to celebrate. Along with everyone else in the bar—Ryder included—Neil suffered from end-of-semester fatigue. But that circumstance was eclipsed by the momentous event which has just transpired. Tonight, Neil had become a father.

"Twins! Jeez, Ryder, I still can't believe it!"

Ryder chuckled, watching Neil gulp more beer. "These things aren't supposed to be a surprise to a man in your profession, buddy. Seems to me pretty difficult to keep two five-and-a-half-pound babies a secret. Didn't you have just a tiny hint from Patti's size?"

Neil ran slightly shaky fingers through his hair and shook his head. "There aren't any twins in either family," he said, looking dazed. "I haven't figured out how it happened yet."

Ryder laughed outright, drawing curious stares their way. "If you really mean that," he said dryly, "then we're having a serious talk...soon." The waitress appeared, and he ordered a refill for Neil, but nothing for himself. At the rate Neil was going, he thought, one of them would have to be sober enough to drive. Still smiling, he lifted his empty glass along with one dark eyebrow and acknowledged Neil's next toast.

He stretched out his long legs and considered his friend's proud look. Something akin to envy stirred briefly, and then he shook his head. Either the beer or the profound nature of the day's event was beginning to get to him. Before a man started thinking like that, he needed a home and a wife, neither of which were in Ryder's immediate future plans.

"I'm a father," Neil said, still awed and slightly drunk. He peered earnestly at Ryder. "You know something, Ry? At first I worried that we'd sorta jumped the gun. Hell, I've still got half a dozen years of med school and residency to go, but, by God, I forgot all that when I looked at the twins."

Smiling faintly, Ryder said nothing. Neil was beginning to sound a little fuzzy, but what the hell. A man didn't become the father of twin sons every day.

Neil inched his chair a little closer and brought Ryder into clearer focus. "You'd make a wonderful fam'ly man, Ry. Hell, I wish we were celebratin' the same thing."

Ryder's grin flashed again. "I don't know, buddy. Twins are pretty heavy. I think I'll start out a little more conservatively. Besides, there aren't any genes for twins in my family that I know of." He caught the eye of the waitress and signaled for coffee. While Neil was still mobile, they'd better wrap this up. The hour wasn't too late—probably about ten—but they'd left the hospital at three in the afternoon and had been drinking every since.

Neil reared back and studied Ryder solemnly. "You may not have twins in your genes, my man, but you've still got exceptional genes."

Ryder made a rueful face. "And you ought to know, roomie."

Neil looked momentarily gratified. He lifted his glass again and saluted Ryder. "It was a fine thing you did, my man. I told you how long we searched for a good match for that guy and you were perfect in every way." He sat up straighter, blinking. "Did I ever tell you just how well you matched up with Ho—uh...um, with the father?"

"Neil, why don't we change the subject?" Ryder suggested, shifting uneasily in his chair. He looked around impatiently for the waitress. Where was his coffee? He was always slightly uncomfortable talking about this subject. He just couldn't think of his sperm in scientific terms.

Ryder hadn't had any real objection when the topic of artificial insemination had first been broached. At the time, Neil had been studying infertility and was participating in a university-sponsored project at a nearby clinic. He'd approached Ryder, then his roommate, with the idea of contributing sperm. Ryder, it appeared, was an exceptional match for a particular infertile couple. He had refused at first, but Neil had encouraged him to think of being a donor as a humanitarian deed. After weighing the pros and cons and his own conscience, Ryder found he had no real objection to assisting a couple so eager to have a child. Such a child would be part of a loving relationship, truly wanted. But he had never quite managed to adopt Neil's casually sophisticated attitude. And he damn sure didn't consider his sperm something to discuss at Baby's Bar.

Neil screwed up his face, thinking. "Not that the, ah...recipient was the man you are, buddy."

Ryder groaned. "Neil—"

Neil studied him with a kind of alcohol-induced detachment. "'Course the similarities were there...brown hair, sorta like yours, blue eyes kinda like yours. That is, they're blue, but not as...blue," he finished, at a loss. "As for height..." he laughed shortly and shook his head. "He wasn't as tall or as tough, but who the hell is? The best way I can describe it, he was a sorta...pale imitation of you, Ry."

Ryder reached for the coffee which had finally been placed in front of him. "Yeah, well, I'm glad I was able to oblige. Now, could we drop the subject, Neil?"

"About the only place you two are equal is—Whoa!" Beer sloshed over the rim of his glass onto the table. Conscientiously Neil mopped it up with the tiny bar napkin. "Is intellectually. The guy's a genius, Ry."

Resigned, Ryder rubbed a palm over his face and swallowed more black coffee. He was definitely going to be the one behind the wheel of Neil's Corvette when they finally got around to leaving. Seated, Neil was still okay, but once he tried to stand, or when he hit fresh air... Ryder shook his head.

Warming to his subject, Neil screwed up his face again, concentrating. "His bloodline, now. It's interesting, too. He's from a very old family. Aris-to-cratic, you might say," Neil said, enunciating carefully.

Ryder rolled his eyes and decided it was time to go. He motioned to the waitress for the check. "Well, if that's the case, I'm surprised you guys at the clinic didn't throw out my contribution on a technicality, buddy."

Neil blinked and looked confused. "Whash that supposed to mean?"

Ryder stood up and tossed some bills onto the table. "Don't tell me you didn't notice the discrepancy in the subject's blood and my own." He shook his head and made a tsking sound. "I'm surprised it took, considering."

Neil struggled to his feet, frowning blearily. "Considering what, Ry? What're you talkin' about?"

Ryder grinned and wrapped an arm around him when it was obvious Neil's legs weren't cooperating. "You mean you didn't notice my blood was red and his was blue?"

Neil laughed loudly and hiccuped. He landed a playful punch on Ryder's shoulder and then slumped against his friend, who half carried him out of the bar. Neil continued to talk non-stop as Ryder struggled with him. "Nah, we didn't quibble over technicalities. Eyes and hair and brains and brawn seemed enough. Clay Holt better consider himself lucky that—"

Ryder looked startled. "Clay Holt? You mean the Holts of Mobile society? *The* Holts? That's who they gave my...uh, I mean, you're saying those people are going to be the parents?"

"Yessirree, they're the lucky ones," Neil said with satisfaction, stumbling a little. "And they're already parents. It's a boy!"

Ryder groaned again. "Hell, Neil, you weren't supposed to tell me that."

"Maybe I didn't really," Neil said, obviously addressing himself out loud. He leaned heavily against Ryder as they negotiated a path down the steps of the bar and through the parking lot.

"You did really," Ryder muttered beneath his breath, holding Neil upright. "But maybe you won't remember it in the morning." He propped Neil's dead weight against the passenger side of the sleek Corvette and put out his hand. He'd been right about fresh air. The proud new daddy was wiped out. "The keys," he demanded.

Obediently Neil dug in his jeans and pulled them out. Ryder took them and unlocked the car. "In you go, buddy."

Happily obliging, Neil crawled halfway in, then gave Ryder a happy smile when he bodily picked up his legs and stuffed them under the dash.

"Buckle up."

Hiccup. "Right."

Ryder slammed the door and stalked around the front of the car. As he was ready to pull out of the lot, he saw that Neil hadn't moved an inch. His seat-belt wasn't fastened and he seemed to be sleeping. Sighing, he leaned over and secured his friend.

"Thanks," Neil murmured, turning his head on the back of the seat to look at Ryder. "You're a great humanitarian, my ol' buddy, ol' pal."

"Don't mention it." The Corvette's three hundred horses roared to life.

Neil blinked gravely, his eyes on Ryder's profile. "No, I mean it. You helped that couple immensely."

"I was glad to do it," Ryder returned dryly.

"See," Neil said with satisfaction, "A great humanitarian. What'd I tell you?"

"I've got to get you home," Ryder muttered, turning out of the parking lot onto the street. "I hope you don't suffer brain damage. Patti would never forgive me."

He was barely a block from the apartment when Neil suddenly made an attempt to sit up. "Stop, Ry! We need to talk."

"No way am I stopping until I get you home, buddy," Ryder stated in a tone that was unmistakable even to a drunk. "But go ahead, talk anyway."

"I think the circumstances are such," he said, trying to sound stern, "that you should just forget that you are the natural father of Clay Holt's child."

Ryder threw him a wry glance. "Don't you worry, friend," he said grimly. "It's forgotten. It's history."

With great effort Neil kept himself upright as he considered Ryder's words solemnly, then nodded once. Bestowing a beatific smile on his friend, he relaxed in the luxurious depths of the Corvette's contoured seat.

After putting Neil to bed, Ryder prowled around the apartment feeling unsettled. *Too much coffee,* he decided, debating whether to just spend the night on Neil's couch or to go home. He turned the television on, flicking through all the channels before turning the set off. He wandered into the kitchen and checked the contents of the refrigerator. Nothing but rabbit food, he discovered, slamming the door with a disgusted mutter. Apparently Patti was still trying to reform Neil's eating habits. Finally he decided to go home even if it meant traveling on foot. He had his running shoes on, anyway. He went to the bedroom and checked Neil, who was passed out and snoring. No doubt exhausted from all that labor Patti went through, Ryder thought dryly. Daddy would pay for his celebration tomorrow with a world-class hangover. Shaking his head, he began turning out lights as he passed through the apartment heading for the door.

Outside, he checked the lock and stood a moment in the stillness of the spring night. The sky was clear and starlit. The beach was only a couple of blocks away, and the smell of the Gulf was heavy in the air. He swore softly but fervently, driving the fingers of one hand through his hair. Dammit! Why hadn't Neil kept his mouth shut? He didn't want to know the name of the couple.

The couple. That was the way he always thought of them. He never expected to know any details about them—certainly not their names! And that was the way it should be, the way he'd been assured it would be.

Ryder broke into a jog. His feet pounded rhythmically on the sidewalk, each stride on the hard concrete jarring him all the way to his teeth. He welcomed the distraction, hoping to push the events of the evening out of his mind. Until now he'd managed to convince himself that what he'd done was indeed a humanitarian act. Somehow, knowing the name of the couple and the sex of the child took the deed out of the altruistic never-never land where he'd mentally consigned it and made it all too real. Now he felt a stirring of curiosity, a sort of compelling interest in the lives of two people who, ordinarily, he would never have the slightest chance of meeting. At least in this life.

His laugh was short and humorless. No, in this life he'd never meet Clay Holt and his wife, whoever she was. His destiny and theirs were worlds apart. He thought of his interview with an international firm scheduled in just five days. If he got an offer, who knew where he would land—Saudi Arabia, Japan, Europe—the possibilities encompassed the whole free world. Meanwhile, the Clay Holts would stay in Mobile, Alabama, and enjoy a way of life almost extinct except in the Deep South, their little family complete.

He slowed suddenly as a new and good feeling stirred. Why was he having these second thoughts? His original reasons for donating to the clinic were unchanged. The only thing different was that he now knew the name of the couple, a couple who would otherwise have remained childless. Reflecting on his decision was a useless waste of time and energy. It couldn't be altered, and furthermore he discovered he had no desire to rewrite history. He was still confident the child would be loved and nurtured—probably even more than most. Smiling slightly, Ryder fixed his sights on a point high in the starry night. His own destiny was waiting.

CHAPTER ONE

LAUREN HOLT PAUSED a second with her palm on one panel of the massive double doors of the courtroom. She was dreading confronting the mob of reporters with their cameras and tape recorders on the other side. Maybe she should wait for Jake, she thought, frowning slightly, but she didn't think she could bear another moment inside the dark, oppressive chambers. When this ordeal was finally over—and please, God, she prayed, let it be over soon—she honestly didn't think she would ever enter a courtroom again. So far, all she'd ever heard from a judge was bad news.

Taking a deep breath, Lauren lifted her head and pushed the door open. She tensed, taking in the sea of bodies who turned as one toward her. Eyes straight ahead, her shoulders rigid, she moved forward, only dimly aware of the popping of flashbulbs and the intense light of a minicam zeroing in on her. There appeared to be dozens of reporters lying in wait for her. The questions were fired at her thick and fast.

"What was the judge's ruling today, Mrs. Holt?"

"Have you decided on your next move against NuTek-Niks?"

"Would you consider a settlement offer, Mrs. Holt?"

One overweight, rumpled reporter, chewing a repulsive cigar stub, shoved an expensive tape recorder in her face. "Are you ready to admit your husband was a lousy manager, Mrs. Holt?"

Lauren felt like crying. Instantly the firm hand of her attorney settled at her waist.

"No comment," Jake Levinson barked, shouldering aside a long-haired youth who was scribbling on a notepad. Jake turned Lauren so that his elbow struck the tape recorder and knocked it out of the hand of the fat reporter. "Sorry about that," he snapped, unaffected by the man's outraged reaction.

"Okay, let the lady through." Jake used his imposing height and a fierce look to part the crowd. To Lauren's relief he whisked her through the marble-floored foyer of the courthouse and down the steps without further delay.

Both were silent as they crossed the parking lot. Lauren matched her steps to Jake's and let him guide her to his car. He stopped at a dark green Mercedes. "You okay, hon?"

She inhaled a shaky breath. "I'm fine, Jake, just a little disappointed. In spite of everything, I'd counted on the judge seeing things our way."

Jake unlocked the door on the passenger side and seated her with the courtliness instilled in him by his Southern upbringing. Closing the door, he went around and got behind the wheel of the Mercedes. "We didn't provide enough evidence to convince him that Clay's designs were original. The attorneys for NuTekNiks argued that their engineers had been developing those procedures for a couple of years before Clay died."

"It's a lie, Jake. It's all lies. NuTekNiks pirated those designs from our company and I'm going to prove it somehow."

Jake started the car. "That's what it's going to take, Lauren—proof, solid evidence. Not a well-written brief stating our opinion that Clay's designs were ripped off, but proof from some source that they were so innovative nobody else could possibly have them."

Lauren sighed and rubbed her forehead. They'd played their last card by requesting the court to restrain NuTekNiks from the use of the systems that Clay had designed, but they'd failed to present a convincing argument. She knew they hadn't failed because of any lack of expertise on Jake's part. But he could only work with the information she'd furnished him. And she could only give him what she had from the company's records, records that were sometimes spotty and incomplete. Only Clay Holt fully understood his designs. And Clay was dead. She'd been a widow for over a year.

"What are we going to do, Jake?" She looked at him, her amber eyes troubled.

Jake reached over and gave her hand a reassuring squeeze. "Don't worry about it right now, Lauren. Between the judge's ruling and that scene at the courthouse, you've had a trying morning. Why don't you lean back and try to relax while I drive you back to your office? There'll be time enough when we get there to rehash everything. We need a new game-plan."

"But what else can we do, Jake? We've already—"

Jake gave her hand a little shake. "Forget it for a few minutes, Lauren. Trust me, we've just begun to fight."

Unconvinced, but too frazzled to argue, Lauren subsided. She didn't want any more battles. She'd never been an aggressive person, even though it seemed that all she'd done since Clay's death was fight.

Her husband had been an engineer with special abilities. Singlehandedly he'd developed sophisticated robotic techniques that simplified and streamlined a variety of manufacturing tasks. After struggling on a shoestring, the Holt Company had just begun to reap the benefits of Clay's research and development. But immediately after his death, NuTekNiks, a rival firm, began marketing equipment using exclusive designs that could only have come from Clay's confidential records. Lauren was shocked when she finally recognized what was going on. Industrial espionage was an ugly possibility she'd never expected to have to consider.

And she probably never would have had to if Clay hadn't died. Her own position in the Holt Company had been restricted to marketing and public relations. She'd enjoyed her work, but much of her energy and time had been devoted to her role as a wife and mother. Upon Clay's death, the reins of the business fell into her hands. After an initial period of panic and insecurity, she'd quickly adjusted to her new responsibilities and had discovered the surprising steel in her backbone. She was absolutely determined to protect the legacy left to her by Clay, not for herself, but for their son, Justin.

Again, Lauren was swamped with the familiar sense of pain and loss. Clay had been her best friend in all the world. Their relationship had been rich in so many ways. They'd come from the same social background, enjoyed the same friends, politics, music and books. Both had been born to old, once-monied Alabama families. Lately, however, the Holts and the Buchanans were rich only in tradition rather than wealth, a circumstance that didn't bother either Clay or Lauren. In fact Clay had often joked about it. All he'd really cared about had been Lauren and Justin and his work. In that order. A pang struck her heart. *Oh, Clay, I miss you so much.*

"Here we are," Jake said, pulling the Mercedes into the curved driveway of the Holt Company's front office.

Lauren uncrossed her legs and was opening the door to get out before Jake reached her. Smoothing her skirt down over her knees, she stood up, then passed one hand over the sleek fall of her hair and squared her shoulders. Her face reflected none of the uncertainty and fear she felt, as she fell into step beside Jake. Her people would have heard about this latest setback. When she went into her office, she didn't want to alarm them. Already the notoriety of the situation had given birth to a spate of rumors, which was understandable; three hundred employees were dependent on a successful resolution of the whole mess.

As they entered, Cheryl Biggs, Lauren's secretary, was chatting with a young receptionist. Both women looked up questioningly, but from Lauren's expression no one could tell how grateful she felt at the feel of Jake's firm grip on her elbow. She forced a confident smile and made her way down the hall, greeting the employees she met, heading straight for the sanctuary of her own office.

Turning the corner, she nearly collided with Michael Armstead, the plant's general manager. His clerk, Jimmy Johns, was with him. Michael was a tall, slightly built blonde with a pencil-thin mustache and a ready smile. Sometimes a little too ready, it seemed to Lauren. Then she chastised herself for the uncharitable thought. She didn't have to love Michael, she reminded herself. As the former chief of sales, he had done a super job. In fact the company's phenomenal growth of the past two years was due as much to Michael's salesmanship as to Clay's creative genius. No, she didn't have to love him, but she did know his value to the company and she appreciated it.

"Hello, Michael . . . Jimmy." She nodded politely to both men.

"Morning, Lauren." Armstead's pale blue gaze rested for just an instant on her breasts before he smiled into her eyes. "How did it go in court this morning?"

"Not well, I'm afraid."

"Anything I can do?" he asked sympathetically. Michael divided a look between Jake and Lauren. "Technical input, that sort of thing?"

Jake touched Lauren's arm to ease her away. "We'll keep that in mind, Armstead," he said, allowing Lauren to precede him into her office. He followed her inside and closed the door firmly.

Armstead stood for a moment studying the pattern on the door of Lauren's office, his eyes cold and hard. He reached into his pocket for a cigarette.

"Looks like the pretty lady doesn't need you anymore, boss." Jimmy Johns's knowing cynicism grated.

"She needs me, Jimmy." The sound of Michael's lighter was loud in the silence of the corridor. He inhaled deeply. "She needs me all right. She just doesn't know how much yet."

Jimmy glanced at the other man's hard features. "You ain't afraid that fancy lawyer'll upset your plans?"

Impatiently Armstead released a stream of smoke. "Nah, he's just doing his job. Things keep going from bad to worse around here, but Levinson doesn't know jack about the inner workings of the plant, so he can't help her." Smiling faintly he gazed at the glowing tip of his cigarette. "But I can. She'll turn to me because I'm all she's got."

Johns simply stared, impressed as much by his boss's audacity as by his arrogant self-confidence.

"And then—" Armstead's tone softened and his pale eyes took on an avaricious gleam "—I'll have it all right here in the palm of my hand, Jimmy-boy." He slapped Johns on the shoulder, and laughing together, they headed on down the corridor.

In her office Lauren went to her desk and sank into the chair that Clay had once occupied. She linked her hands together to keep them from shaking and looked up at Jake. "Okay, coach, what's the new game plan?" she inquired.

Jake seated himself opposite her. "We've got a major problem here, Lauren. The next time we go into court, we've got to have an expert witness whose credentials can't be questioned. It must be somebody who can state from a position of authority that Clay's designs were original state-of-the-art innovations in the use of robotics—designs that NuTekNiks couldn't possibly have formulated on their own."

Lauren laughed shortly and waved the fingers of one hand. "Sure, no problem. We'll just put an ad in the paper."

"Well, not exactly." Smiling, he shifted in his chair and propped one ankle on the opposite knee. "Actually we're in luck for once in the matter of the expert, Lauren."

Lauren gave him a puzzled look. "How, Jake? We haven't had any kind of luck except bad so far in this whole fiasco."

The lawyer leaned forward and Lauren sensed a sort of restrained excitement in him. "Lauren, does the name Ryder Braden ring a bell?" Without waiting for a reply, Jake continued. "It was about five years ago. That was when you met him, I think. At a New Year's Eve Party. Do you remember? You and Clay went with Clare and me."

"What?" Lauren said, momentarily thrown off track. As close as their friendship was, Jake *never* mentioned his ex-wife.

"A New Year's Eve party, five or six years ago," Jake repeated patiently. "Ryder Braden was there with Neil and Patti Putnam. He and Neil and I went to high school together and then he and Neil went on to college. They were roommates at Alabama. Anyway, Ryder graduated as an electrical engineer and was recruited by half a dozen companies. He went with a big international firm and his career took off like a rocket."

Lauren leaned back slowly in her chair. "And just exactly how does all this tie in with our problem?"

"He's a manufacturing expert and he's been in on the ground floor in the use of robotics since the concept was first introduced." He stared at her. "Do you remember him?"

"I remember him," Lauren said cautiously.

Jake hesitated at something in her tone, then went on. "Yeah. Well anyway, lucky for us he's still in town, has been for two or three months. Could be he's between assignments right now."

"Oh, Jake, do you really think he's the man we need?" Lauren stood up suddenly and walked to the window looking doubtful.

"Believe me," Jake said firmly, "he's an engineering expert with an impressive background in high-tech manufacturing. He'll be very convincing to a judge. Ryder's particular brand of expertise is exactly what we need at this point."

"I don't know, Jake."

"You don't know? What the hell does that mean? People with experience in robotics aren't exactly growing on trees, in case you haven't noticed, Lauren."

Lauren wondered how to explain. She was going to sound like an idiot. She remembered Ryder Braden all right. Vividly. She also remembered that New Year's Eve party.

Lord, was it five years ago? Lauren stared out of the window, blind to the lacy pink beauty of a crepe myrtle directly in her line of vision. Braden must have been "between assignments'' then, too. He'd been the star topic of conversation at that party, she recalled. He and Jake had been old friends and Jake apparently still thought highly of him, because he'd certainly grabbed the first opportunity to introduce him to Clay and her. Apparently everybody else in their crowd already knew him. Lauren, however, had already noticed him. Somehow Braden was the type of man who stood out, even in a crowd.

When Jake made the introductions she'd sensed a certain something in his cool acknowledgment as he'd looked into her eyes. When they danced—only once—he'd seemed literally wired with tension. He'd held her like a live coal and had been unresponsive to her efforts to make friendly conversation. When the music stopped, he'd walked her back to the table with almost indecent haste. She'd never seen him again.

For some reason that experience with Braden had been one that had stuck in her mind, a little glitch in her memory bank. It was like a close call on the expressway or a particularly embarrassing moment that one would dearly love to forget. The trouble was, Braden wasn't easily forgotten. Just the opposite. Lauren flicked the drapes with her fingertips and sighed. Jake seemed confident, but personally she wasn't going to count on Braden coming to her rescue.

She bent her head and kneaded her temples where a tiny ache nagged. She felt Jake waiting and inhaled deeply. ''I don't think you should count on Braden's cooperation too much, Jake.''

He searched her face, frowning. ''Why not?''

''This is going to sound stupid, but . . .'' She looked at him. ''Have you spoken to him yet?''

''Not yet, but—''

''I hope he doesn't remember me.''

Jake looked startled. ''Doesn't remember you? What—''

''I only met him that one time, but for some reason I felt that he . . . well, that he . . .''

''That he . . . what?''

''I told you, this sounds ridiculous, but I got the strongest feeling that the man disliked me.''

Jake looked at her. ''He disliked you. . . . Five years ago you met a man once and you think he disliked you on sight?''

''I told you it sounded stupid.''

Jake arched his black brows but said nothing.

Lauren sank back into her chair. "Everybody left the table and it was just the two of us. He had to ask me to dance and he acted as if I was Typhoid Mary."

"It must have been your imagination, Lauren. You're a beautiful woman. No man with half his hormones in working order could be indifferent to you. And believe me," Jake added dryly, "all Ryder's hormones are in excellent shape."

Lauren was unconvinced. "I didn't expect you to believe me, but I still remember it, even after all these years. I even mentioned it to Clay that night after we got home, and he brushed it aside, too."

"With good reason," Jake said, standing up suddenly. "I assume, then, that you haven't any real objections to my contacting Braden to sound him out?"

"Well . . ."

"We need him, Lauren."

"In the words of your own profession, Jake," she said with her usual good humor, "I think the question may be moot. The man's going to refuse."

THE TELEPHONE WAS into the ninth ring before Ryder Braden managed to climb down from the roof and drop onto the white pine boards of the porch. He moved quickly across the new floor, to the open window where he'd placed the phone. The sound was a jarring intrusion into the peaceful atmosphere of the old place. A few more months of nothing but his own company and he'd turn into a real hermit, he decided as he picked up the receiver.

"Hello?"

"Ryder?"

He shifted his weight onto one leg and squinted across the yard to the dappled shade under a pecan tree. "Yeah, who is this?"

"It's Jake Levinson, Ryder. How the hell are you, man?"

"Not bad, not bad. How 'bout yourself, Jake?"

"Fine. Still working on my first million."

"Hell, I thought you'd passed that point the last time I was home."

"Not quite." Jake paused a second. "I ran into Neil Putnam and he told me you were in town and that you'd lost your grandmother. I was sorry to hear that."

"Yeah, thanks. I'm going to miss her." Ryder could hear the creak as Jake leaned back in his chair.

"I never eat seafood gumbo that I don't think of her, you know that? Mama Jane sure had a way with shrimp. I remember how she'd feed about half a dozen of us after football practice and never complain." He fell silent remembering. "She was one sweet lady."

Ryder nodded. "She was that," he said huskily.

Jake cleared his throat. "So, I guess you're knocking around that big old house looking for something to do."

"I'm knocking around all right, but I'm sure not looking for something to do," Ryder said, eyeing the pile of old roofing shingles that had taken him two days to remove. "I've been doing some work on the house."

"Getting it in shape to sell, huh?"

"I don't know, Jake. Maybe, maybe not."

"Are you serious? You haven't got anything pressing in some far-off corner of the manufacturing world?"

Ryder eased down onto the windowsill and crossed his legs in front of him. "Not yet. I guess you could say I'm sort of on sabbatical."

Jake was silent a second or two. "In that case, this could be my lucky day. You suppose I could persuade you to take on a project here?"

Ryder swatted at a mosquito. "What kind of project? I didn't know you legal eagles were into high-tech manufacturing."

"I'm not, but a client of mine is and we need an expert witness before the next court date. We couldn't ask for anybody better qualified than you, Ryder. It's a great stroke of luck that you happen to be in town," Jake said with genuine feeling. "And it's about time Lauren got a break."

"Who?" Ryder had picked up a towel and was wiping sweat off his face and neck.

"Lauren Holt. You met her and Clay, her husband, about five years ago. He designed some pretty sophisticated robotics which you might be familiar with in your line of work."

Ryder went still, one hand on the towel. "Holt," he repeated.

"Yeah," Jake said, encouraged, since Ryder hadn't refused outright. "Clay was killed about a year ago in an accident at the plant. Lauren's had her hands full trying to hold everything together."

"Clay Holt is dead?" Ryder repeated blankly.

"Right, and his designs have been pirated by a rival firm, NuTekNiks. You haven't got any connections to them, have you?"

"No." Ryder absently smoothed a hand over his chest, his blue eyes fixed on the tips of his worn Nikes.

"Ryder? You still there, Ryder?"

"Uh, yeah. I'm still here."

"So, whadda ya say? Think you can take on a little project like this? It'll be a piece of cake for you, Ryder, but to Lauren it may mean the difference between keeping her company in one piece or losing everything to a bunch of thieves."

"I don't think so, Jake. It's like I said, I'm not locked into another assignment yet, and I don't think I want to be right now. The old place got run down these past few years and I've been spending a lot of time on it. I—"

"Ryder," Jake broke in, "we're not talking about a simple medical malpractice suit where I can call in any doctor as an expert. Not a hell of a lot of people know anything about robotics. Lauren's predicament is unique. You won't find a more astute businesswoman, either, considering the way she's had to pick up and keep going in a very sophisticated environment." He paused a moment before adding, "She's a great gal, Ryder."

"Look, Jake..." Ryder rubbed the towel across his face. "I'm sure Mrs. Holt is everything you say, but I'm just not the man for the job. Tell you what, I know some top-notch robotics people. They'll do a good job for you."

"But they're not right here in town, Ryder," Jake pointed out. "We'd have to fly them in, maybe more than once, put them up, pay them expenses. They'd cost an arm and a leg and Lauren just doesn't have it."

Ryder narrowed his eyes. "Is she in financial difficulty?"

"Well, yeah, didn't I mention that? With the rights to the designs on the street, her company's being screwed out of thousands in royalties."

"I don't know, Jake—"

"That's for sure, Ryder," Jake put in quickly. "You really don't understand what Lauren's going through. It isn't just the company's problems and the weight of knowing all her employees are counting on her. On top of all that, the case has become a media circus. I guess there's something about her and the situation Clay left her in that fascinates the public. Every little ripple in the case is splashed on the front page or aired on the evening news. Like today, for instance..."

"Today?"

"Yeah, the press was waiting for her outside the courtroom. I had to strongarm our way through; all the while they're yelling questions at her, some of them in pretty bad taste, I can tell you." He paused. "Well, hell, you can judge for yourself. Turn on the news tonight. You'll see."

Ryder's fingers flexed on the receiver. "It's really that bad, Jake?"

"It's that bad. She needs you, Ryder."

Ryder took a deep breath, wrestling with a multitude of thoughts that would have astonished his old friend if Jake had had an inkling as to what he was asking.

"Look, don't give me a definite answer right now," Jake said, shrewdly backing off. "Lauren's pretty strung out over this last setback. I wanted to give her the weekend to put the whole thing out of her mind, so I set our next appointment for Monday morning." He hesitated. "How does this sound, Ryder? Just meet her, get a fix on the problems she's up against, get a fix on Lauren herself. Then if you still feel reluctant, I'll understand."

"I'm telling you, don't get your hopes up, Jake."

"I hear you," Jake said amiably. "But Lauren Holt is a special lady, Ryder. You'll see."

Right up until a minute before six o'clock, Ryder planned to skip the evening news. It didn't take any special insight to figure out why, either, he thought, as he paced restlessly around his grandmother's outdated kitchen. He did not trust himself to see Lauren Holt's face again, not even on television. Once had been more than enough and even though it was over five years, he could still envision her with crystal clarity.

Damn it to hell! Why did Neil have to tell him? He raked a frustrated palm against the back of his neck, barely aware of the tense pain deep in his muscles. For the thousandth time, he cursed that night fourteen years ago when Neil had breached the confidentiality of the medical program. Now the woman was widowed and in trouble. And, heaven help him, Jake wanted him to be the one to run to her rescue. Ryder groaned and stared at the blank screen of the television. He'd never dreamed he'd be faced with a situation like this. He did not

want to get mixed up with Lauren Holt. Even the most super-
ficial association with her could become extremely complicated. Damn Jake for destroying his peace!

Almost as though someone else pulled the strings to manipulate his body, Ryder took a step forward and bent over to turn
the set on. The Middle East and Washington politics took up
the first ten minutes of the newscast. Bored, Ryder helped
himself to a beer and sat down, crossing his legs in front of him.
He was popping the tab when the words of the anchorman
brought him straight up in his chair.

"We'll be right back with the latest wrinkle in a local woman's attempt to challenge a company she claims has ripped off
of her dead husband's ideas," the newsman said. "Stay tuned."

With a sense of fate Ryder put his beer down and fixed his
eyes on the screen. Impatiently, he endured sixty seconds of
commercials. Then Lauren's face appeared and the muscles in
his stomach tensed. The minicam followed her leaving the
courtroom, catching every nuance of expression on her beautiful face. He sucked in a quick breath and watched her instantly besieged by a knot of reporters. *Jake should be with her,*
Ryder thought with sudden concern, feeling an unusual sense
of outrage at the reporters' callousness.

"What was the judge's ruling . . ."

". . . your next move against NuTekNiks?"

". . . settlement offer . . ."

"Mrs. Holt—"

"Lauren—"

In the chaos and distortion from the microphones, Ryder
couldn't hear the demands of the media clearly, but Lauren's
distress was obvious. In the artificial lighting of the minicam,
her expression appeared vulnerable, he thought, staring intently at her. Why had Jake allowed her to face the press alone?

"Are you ready to admit your husband was a lousy manager, Mrs. Holt?"

When he heard the question, Ryder was surprised at the
depth of his anger on her behalf. Was nothing sacred to those
vultures? He watched her as she fixed her gaze straight ahead
and attempted to make her way through the maze of bodies and
journalistic paraphernalia. Suddenly one reporter elbowed
aside his colleagues and thrust a microphone in her face. Lauren put out an unsteady hand to fend him off. Some emotion,
something deep and elemental, flared in Ryder. Abruptly, he

got to his feet to pace the length of the room, keeping an eye on the television screen.

"Where the hell is Jake?" he muttered, agitated. Then, to his relief, Jake's tall spare frame materialized at Lauren's side and began to sweep her through the crowd.

With swift strides Ryder reached the television and snapped it off. He gazed around the kitchen feeling a host of unfamiliar conflicting emotions. He cursed Jake for calling him and laying this burden on him. He damned Neil Putnam for his indiscretion fourteen years ago. He railed at fate for the uncanny trick it had played on him. The woman was not his responsibility, he told himself. Jake could find another expert. Then he remembered Lauren's circumstances and muttered an obscenity. Between her and Jake Levinson, they probably knew everybody in the state of Alabama who was anybody. Someone would come through for her.

The old screen door banged behind him unnoticed. He went to the edge of the porch and propped an arm on one solid heart-pine support. He groaned, wiping a hand over his face, and stared blindly into the night. He didn't want this.

Without warning Lauren Holt's classic features swam into focus, and on the heels of that another image tantalized him, one that was never very substantial, one that Ryder never allowed himself to dwell on.

The boy. His son.

He had no responsibility in this situation, Ryder told himself again fiercely. There was no shame in what he did all those years ago. The act placed no obligation on him. Only through a twist of fate was he even aware of any connection to this woman and her child. He should just pack up and leave town. Right now. Today. Everyone would be better off even though he might be the only one who knew that. He pushed away from the stout column with a motion that was slightly savage. Definitely the smart thing to do was just to forget this.

But how could a man forget his own son?

A FEW MILES AWAY, at the Holt plant, another man sat patiently at his desk waiting as the activity signaling the end of the work day slowed and then stopped altogether. When there was only silence, he looked at his watch. Six-fifteen. He would have plenty of time. She was only half an hour away.

He got up slowly and made his way to the bank of files against the far wall. The drawer opened quietly, but his own anxiety magnified the sound in his ears. With a quick, furtive look around, he began riffling through the plans and specifications until he found what he was looking for. Bending, he squinted at the color-coded tab and then straightened with a grunt. Mislabeled, as he'd known it would be. As he'd made certain it would be. He pulled out a set of prints and folded them into a neat square before slipping them under his jacket, making sure they were secure. It would never do to have them fall out as he was leaving the plant. No, that would never do.

He closed the drawer after making sure nothing appeared out of order, and then glanced at his watch. He had thirty minutes before he was due to meet her. For a moment he was still, his gaze unfocused. His hand unconsciously sought the plans folded tightly, securely, against his heart. Surely this would satisfy them. Surely this would be the last time.

Daydreaming of Anna, he left the building.

CHAPTER TWO

THE OFFICES OF Levinson, Rayne and Javits were carefully designed around three ancient live oaks. Natural cypress siding and the lavish use of smoked glass enhanced the rustic effect. Inside, no expense had been spared to create an atmosphere of confidence and comfort. The window where Lauren stood served as a frame for a shaded courtyard dominated by one of the moss-draped oaks. But the view was wasted on her, and the expensive decor failed to reassure her. She wrapped her arms around her middle and turned to Jake.

"I spent the weekend sorting through Clay's records trying to uncover something that might buy us a little more time, Jake, but I drew a blank." She gave her lawyer a bleak smile. "I know it sounds incredible. Clay was so special, a creative genius, but he apparently kept very little documentation. You'd think a scientist would be more conscientious about that sort of thing."

Jake rubbed a hand over his chin, silently acknowledging the truth in Lauren's statement. Why the hell had Clay been so cavalier about safeguarding his work? No man expected to die, of course, but with the prudent instincts of a lawyer, Jake couldn't help feeling put out with Clay for failing to secure the future of his wife and son, even if he was the proverbial absentminded scientist. His gaze was troubled as he studied Lauren. Her composure seemed far too fragile this morning. She'd shown extraordinary courage and strength so far, but weeks of unrelenting stress were telling on her.

She turned, plunging her hands deep into the pockets of her skirt. "So, did you have any luck contacting Mr. Braden?"

"I called him and filled him in on the situation," Jake said, wondering how to tell her that he'd struck out with Ryder.

"He refused, didn't he?"

Jake shook his head wryly. "I'll be honest, babe. He wasn't exactly eager."

Lauren's expression revealed nothing as she absorbed the news. She would not have to deal with Braden after all. She immediately dismissed the curious little pang of... something. Certainly not disappointment, she told herself.

"Well, I'm hardly surprised," she said.

Jake leaned back in his chair, his disappointment plain. "Hmm, it looks as though you read the situation correctly. He didn't give me a definite no when we talked, but since he hasn't shown up, I guess we'd better regroup." Jake glanced at the digital clock on his desk. "It's unfortunate. With his practical experience he would have made us a first-class expert. Here's a partial listing of his credentials." He pushed a paper across to her.

Lauren looked it over. "Surely there are others?"

"Well, yes. Ryder mentioned he'd give me the names of some qualified people. It'll take a little time, but . . ."

"But what, Jake?" Lauren asked just as the intercom sounded on the desk.

Jake lifted one hand to stay her, then answered the summons. After a couple of quick questions, he stood up and motioned toward a thermos decanter on a credenza against the wall. "Have some coffee while I take this call. It's confidential—No, no, don't get up." He waved Lauren back into her chair as she began to rise. "I'll take it in the other office. You wait right here. We've still got to map out some strategy. Back in a minute, I promise."

Lauren's brief smile faded as Jake disappeared. She was frightened. This morning, alone in the bedroom she'd shared with Clay, she'd faced up to the very real possibility that she might lose the company. She might not be able to ensure Justin's future, let alone banish the uncertainties of the three hundred employees who were counting on her.

Blindly she stared out the window to the courtyard, feeling none of the peace and satisfaction that the sight of the ancient, massive oaks usually produced. Wearily she kneaded the back of her neck. How long since she'd felt truly at peace? Lately time was measured in the number of days or weeks before some new disaster. Fatigue and the ugly reality of her situation washed over her and she felt the sting of tears behind her eyes.

RYDER HAD NO TROUBLE locating Jake's office. He reached the door and stopped, his palm flat against the sun-warmed surface, unable to explain the compulsion that had brought him this far, overruling his better judgment. One hand went to his sunglasses. He pulled them off and slipped them into his breast pocket. He could feel his heart thudding in his chest. He was as nervous as a boy on his first date. Again he realized the irrevocability of this meeting. He'd done some foolish and impetuous things in his time, but nothing to compare with this. He drew a deep breath and then pushed the door open.

Inside he was directed to Jake's office by a fresh-faced receptionist. The door was open. Ryder's gaze flicked over the unoccupied desk, going directly to the solitary figure at the window. It was Lauren Holt. Deliberately he studied her. Her pale gold hair was caught up and secured with a tortoiseshell comb, but several silky tendrils had escaped, giving her a slightly disheveled look. He frowned. He hadn't thought her the type to have a hair out of place.

She was simply staring out the window, shoulders slightly drooping. As he watched she brought one hand up and wiped at her cheek. It was then he realized that she was crying. Her cheeks were wet with tears even though she wasn't making a sound. Ryder's breath caught in his throat. Something about her weeping silently, alone, touched off a feeling that was both unfamiliar and disturbing. He had to consciously restrain himself from going to her. Where the hell was Jake?

His expression gentled as she suddenly drew in a deep breath and squared her shoulders. Sniffing, she wiped her cheeks with the heels of both palms. Ryder backed away from the door, his expression thoughtful. The last thing he'd expected to see was a vulnerable Lauren Holt giving in to a moment of despair. Her emotional reaction just didn't fit in with the way he thought of her—always composed, slightly aloof, more than capable of handling the stress in her world. He leaned against the wall, intrigued with his discovery.

A picture of Lauren's expression as she'd tried to fend off the reporters flashed in his mind, followed by a surge of protectiveness. Ruthlessly he closed off the feeling. He was not going to get personally involved with this woman. If his professional expertise could be helpful, fine—so be it. But that was where he drew the line. He wasn't even totally convinced that Lauren Holt needed him, no matter what Jake said.

So why am I here? he asked himself for the tenth time.

"Ryder! I'd just about given you up," Jake said, appearing from the opposite end of the hall. He put out his hand, grinning. "What are you doing out here propping up my wall? Come in, Lauren's already here." The attorney stepped to the open door and motioned Ryder inside.

Ryder tensed with anticipation at the prospect of once again facing Lauren Holt. In his travels he'd dined with royalty and parleyed with men who wielded enough power to change the destiny of nations, but he couldn't remember ever feeling quite this way.

Television didn't do her justice, he decided, looking at her closely. His recollection of her from that brief encounter five years before had always been colored by forbidden emotion. Her eyes were a pale, gold brown, fringed with long, dark, lush lashes; her features even; her makeup subtle. He wondered why she even needed it when her skin had the flawless look of magnolias. Except for a soft, vulnerable look to her mouth, he could detect no hint of whatever emotion had made her weep.

Jake made his way toward the credenza and the coffee carafe. "You remember Lauren, Ryder."

"Hello, Mr. Braden," she said in a low, husky voice. She extended her hand.

Ryder took it, bracing against the allure of that voice, determined not to be affected by it or the slight tremor he felt in her hand. "Mrs. Holt," he responded with a brief nod of his dark head, wondering at the clear, cold clarity of her eyes. He glanced at Jake, whose black eyebrows went up blandly before bringing his attention back to Lauren.

"Here we go," Jake said with determined cheerfulness, pouring coffee and offering it to Ryder. "Hot and black, Ryder. Unless you have a taste for something stronger?"

Ryder shook his head, managing to tear his gaze away from Lauren's face long enough to accept the coffee, then move to the chair Jake indicated. He waited for Lauren to sit first.

"Lauren's familiar with your professional background, Ryder," Jake said, leaning back and smiling at them. "Our case is more or less stymied unless we can convince the court of the originality of Clay's designs. I've assured Lauren that you're the man for the job."

Lauren met the look Braden sent her head-on, braced for more of the brusque, almost rude treatment he'd subjected her to the only other time they'd met. She still smarted a little from that, she realized with a start. She recalled feeling somewhat testy about it at the time. Now, she ran a dubious eye over his ancient Nikes and well-worn jeans. Even five years later, something about him still definitely put her back up.

His hair was a dark tobacco brown, thick and crisp looking, just a little too long. Sunglasses were casually anchored in the pocket of a white pullover, a color that emphasized his deep tan and the startling effect of his eyes. She gazed into them, expecting a conventional brown. Instead, she found them to be a deep, dark blue. His face was rugged and angular with high cheekbones and a strong chin. He had a tiny scar at the edge of one dark eyebrow. All in all, his features were too harsh for him to be considered handsome in the conventional sense of the word. His mouth, in contrast, was oddly sensual.

"Take a look at this," Jake said.

Ryder leaned lazily forward to accept the papers Jake handed him, and she caught the scent of soap and warm-blooded male. Ryder Braden might look laid-back and slightly worn around the edges, but he also looked powerfully, uncompromisingly masculine. Dangerous. Unconsciously she wrapped her arms around her middle.

Averting her gaze, Lauren edged back into her chair, feeling slightly stunned by her reaction to him. It had never occurred to her that she would be aware of him as a man. She thought about it, then decided it shouldn't surprise her that his appeal extended to women as well as men. Even Jake and his circle of friends—whom she considered sophisticated and discriminating for the most part—had reacted like starstruck boys, recounting Braden's exploits. She glanced at him, sprawled in the chair looking too confident, too at ease in the restrained decor of Jake's office. She felt certain that a law office in Mobile, Alabama, was as far removed from Braden's usual habitat as a zoo would be to a panther. He hadn't gotten that teak-dark tan behind a desk, that was for sure.

Was it safe to place the company's secrets in this man's hands? Her mouth compressed with sudden doubt. With that question in mind, Lauren concentrated on Jake's words as he briefed Braden on the status of their case.

Ten minutes later she had to admit that the man knew high-tech engineering. But still, when Jake sent a questioning look her way, she could not give him the nod of approval he sought.

Seeing her uncertainty, Jake confined himself to a discussion of a few problems he was having with some of the technical aspects of the case. Ryder's responses were concise and knowledgeable. Lauren decided that though he might drift from job to job, he seemed to be an expert, overall.

Lauren wondered about his personal life. Why was he still lingering in Mobile? According to Jake, it had been more than three months since his grandmother's funeral. She frowned, thinking back to something Jake had said. Wasn't he living in a ramshackle old house he'd inherited from his grandmother? It sounded as though he hadn't had enough self-discipline to manage the huge salaries he must have earned in the past dozen years if Jake's glowing professional assessment was to be believed.

Her thoughts were interrupted by the sound of Jake's intercom. After a quick word he stood up. "Another urgent call which I can take across the hall. You two have more in common than most of my clients," he added with total disregard for the fact that neither of the two people in front of him had spoken over two words to the other, "so I won't worry about leaving you alone together."

In the wake of Jake's departure, total silence filled the office. Ryder tossed the yellow notepad on the desk, his mouth twisted with the irony of the lawyer's casual remark. Purposely he hadn't allowed himself to think of what he and Lauren Holt *did* have in common. The moment he'd looked into those unique eyes, he'd felt the compelling connection pulling at him. Suddenly Lauren Holt was not just an appealing woman beset by a tangle of legal circumstances. And she was definitely not some unnamed female who'd received his sperm in some clinic. She was suddenly a very real, live, breathing woman whose destiny was linked with his whether he wished it or not.

He leaned back, extending his long legs and crossing his feet, his dark gaze intent upon her. For a woman who needed his expertise, she certainly wasn't going out of her way to charm him. He wasn't sure what he'd expected, but it wasn't this cool, deliberate assessment. It was as though he was a bug under glass. Had she taken a dislike to him? Feeling strangely affronted, he reminded himself that she needed him, not the other way around.

Rejection was a unique experience for Ryder, and under the circumstances, he could almost see the humor in the situation. Almost. But not quite. He was too aware of her—her subtle perfume, the near-perfection of her feminine shape, the sleek, satiny look of her skin. He was suddenly very curious about her reasons for choosing a clinical pregnancy.

"I suppose you've done this sort of thing often, Mr. Braden."

Startled, his eyes locked with hers. It took him a second to realize their thoughts were on different wavelengths. She was sitting very straight, her gaze clear and steady. "You mean the expert witness thing?"

Her mouth compressed with impatience. "What else?"

"I've done it a few times."

She inhaled deeply. "I understand you're a native of Mobile."

He withdrew his gaze from her long shapely legs. "Yeah, Alabama born and bred, like the song says."

She looked blank.

"It's a country song, Mrs. Holt," he drawled.

"Oh, I see."

She didn't, he knew. "Do you get back often?"

He stared intently into her eyes, intrigued by the way she had of looking at him while at the same time keeping him at a distance. It was almost as if a brick wall stood between them. "Not as often as I would've liked in the past few years," he told her.

"Your work must take you all over."

"I just wrapped up a job in Japan."

"How interesting," she remarked, managing to make it seem just the opposite. "Troubleshooting, didn't Jake say? How did you drift into that?"

Ryder stared into her beautiful eyes a beat or two, absorbing the subtle insult, watching as she had the good grace to color faintly. He couldn't remember when he'd been put down quite so ruthlessly, that is, without bleeding a little at the same time. This lady wasn't going to have any difficulty holding her own with the sharks who were trying to steal her precious husband's designs, he decided, torn between irritation and admiration. Jake must be totally dazzled by the genteel look of her to think anything else. If he hadn't seen her crying . . .

"I...ah..." She cleared her throat delicately. "I didn't mean that the way it sounded," she said.

"No kidding?" One dark brow arched skeptically. "Actually, instead of focusing directly on a single element, the bulk of my work for the past couple of years seemed to be getting the bugs out of my clients' operations. I guess I did, as you say, sort of drift into it."

"Would I recognize any of your clients?"

"It's possible."

When he didn't elaborate, she made a clicking noise with her tongue. "Well?"

"Jake has a list somewhere."

"Which *you* conveniently furnished."

His eyes narrowed. "Are you suggesting I lied?"

Lauren's gaze slipped from his. "No, of course not."

"Well, what then?"

"I just meant—"

He was still a second, waiting, before getting up out of his chair. "Look, maybe this whole thing is a bad idea. I guess you have a right to be suspicious of people considering what you've been through since your husband died. But I didn't volunteer for this, Mrs. Holt. Jake called me." He moved to place his coffee cup on the credenza, then straightened, pinning her to her chair with a look. "Or did you forget that?"

Disconcerted, Lauren could think of no ready reply. Then, fortunately, she didn't have to because Jake chose that moment to return.

"Okay, gang, ready to talk turkey?" He went directly to his chair, but when he glanced at the two faces before him, his smile faltered.

"I don't think Mrs. Holt is desperate enough to need me, Jake," Ryder said, reaching for his sunglasses. He shot her a piercing look. "Or maybe my credentials don't impress her. Whatever. I'll be seeing you around, buddy." He put on the sunglasses and, without glancing toward Lauren again, walked out.

Jake turned to her slowly, his eyebrows lifted in silent query.

"Please, Jake, not just now, okay?" The words came out low and slightly uneven. She stood up and set her coffee cup on the tray, hoping the tremor in her hands would go unnoticed by her sharp-eyed lawyer. Setting the strap of her bag on her shoulder, she walked quickly to the door. "Let me know when the next disaster occurs."

HOURS LATER, BACK at the old house, Ryder was still smarting from the encounter with Lauren in Jake's office. Standing in the middle of Mama Jane's outdated kitchen, he chewed thoughtfully on his bottom lip and wondered why. He reminded himself that he'd been reluctant to get involved in her affairs in the first place. But, hell, that was a dead issue now. She obviously didn't have any intention of retaining him even though she had been impressed with his professional knowhow. He knew that; he'd felt it as they talked. No, the problem was something personal. He felt that, too.

He stalked out of the house, slamming the screen door, and stood on the porch, his hand clamped at the back of his neck. Why did he care anyway? He had absolutely no obligation to assist her even if he was, by a strange quirk of fate, eminently qualified. He had made a respectable effort, and she had done everything except throw his offer back in his face. His duty was done.

Ryder stripped off his shirt and slung it over the porch rail. His body demanded physical release for the tension that was eating at him. He'd been tied in knots from the first moment he'd looked into her frosty, amber eyes. Now was the perfect time to rip out that section of the porch roof. He'd been thinking about it long enough. The old house could keep ten men busy. His renovation efforts had been on-going for months now with no end in sight.

Frustration and some other emotion he was unwilling to examine drove him to attack the porch with a ferocity that couldn't be sustained very long with the temperature nearing ninety. Doggedly, his thoughts went back to Lauren. For the tenth time he wondered why he was so bothered, because she obviously didn't want help from him. Scowling, he climbed up on a ladder to get to the aged joists of the porch roof. Hooking one leg over the top of the ladder, he sat for a minute, recalling how she'd looked, nodding in curt dismissal. He knew it wasn't reasonable, but something deep inside him leaped at the challenge of that gesture.

Ryder stared unseeing over the familiar territory that had once been Mama Jane's property. The sensible thing was to stick to his original plan and steer clear of Lauren Holt. Mutual avoidance would suit her just fine, judging by her attitude of that morning. Again he felt a stirring of some emotion he couldn't identify and knew that instead of washing his hands of Lauren, he was probably going to act like a damn fool. Muttering an oath, he grabbed a hammer and ripped at nails that had been in place more than sixty years. Somehow he couldn't forget how she'd looked when she was alone and crying.

Working with his hands eased the turmoil inside him after a few minutes. Actually he liked working on the old house with his own hands. It was the only home he'd ever known. He wasn't certain why he'd stayed on after Mama Jane's funeral except that the place offered some kind of anchor that he seemed to need in his life right now. Board by board, nail by nail, restoring Mama Jane's was a way of taking apart and examining the pieces of Ryder's own life: his failures, successes, losses, his loneliness and isolation. Ryder was almost forty years old, but hardly a soul would miss him if he disappeared tomorrow. It was a chilling thought.

He picked up a crowbar and began prising at a board. It was pure cypress, solid enough to weather another six decades. He ripped it from the overhead joists supporting the porch. Instantly half a dozen wasps swarmed in all directions. Swearing, he threw the board one way and leaped off the ladder, diving for the screen door.

Safely inside, he headed for the refrigerator and got out a can of beer, shaking his head. It would take a few minutes for the wasps to settle down before he could resume work. He drifted to the door and instantly Lauren Holt was back in his mind. The beer was cold and he was hot and thirsty. For several minutes he was still, thinking. Then he tossed the empty can into the trash and picked up the phone.

He punched out a number and slouched against the kitchen wall, waiting for an answer.

"Jerry? Ryder Braden." He tucked the receiver between his chin and shoulder and reached for a pad that lay on the counter, exchanging small talk with Jerry Lynch, the manufacturing manager at Hy-Tech Products, in nearby Pensacola, Florida. The company had retained Ryder as a consultant several times over the past few years.

"You're going to sub out some of the work on that job Hy-Tech landed to build electronic ignition assemblies, aren't you, Jerry?" He squinted through the window at the fierce noonday while Jerry responded.

"I've got about four possible suppliers," Jerry said. "The only drawback is distance. Most of them are on the east or west coast."

"Why don't you look into the Holt Company right here in Mobile?" Ryder suggested, running a finger down the pad. He stopped at a number. "I'll bet they could compete with the other sources, especially since they wouldn't have the shipping costs."

"Hey, sounds good," Jerry said, repeating the phone number Ryder supplied.

"You might ask for Lauren Holt," he said, shifting so that his weight was on one leg.

Jerry was silent for a moment, then asked, "That's the woman who's been in the news lately, isn't it? Legal trouble, something about claims against the competition, as I recall."

"Something like that."

Jerry cleared his throat. "We don't have to worry that the company might fold halfway through the contract, do we, buddy?"

"You don't have to worry," Ryder said.

"Okay, if you say so."

"I say so." Ryder looked up just in time to dodge a wasp that had followed him inside. Casually he added, "No need to mention my name, Jerry."

"Hey, no problem. Take care now, you hear?"

CHAPTER THREE

AFTER LUNCH LAUREN was back in her office trying to concentrate on the papers in front of her when a small sound at her door made her look up.

"Got time to take a little break?" Clancy St. James smiled into Lauren's eyes. Leaning slightly on a cane, favoring her left leg, the petite redhead entered the office without waiting for permission and sat down.

"Oh, hi, Clancy." Lauren pushed the papers aside. "Please. A break sounds fine, since I wasn't accomplishing much anyway."

"Well then, maybe you can understand how utterly boring my life has been lately." Clancy cautiously stretched out her left leg, revealing a knee wrapped with elasticized bandaging.

Lauren was sympathetic. "It's only temporary, Clancy. As soon as that knee can support the weight of your knapsack, you'll be off again." She waved a hand. "Where will it be next time—the Mid-East? El Salvador? Northern Ireland?"

"Uh-uh." Clancy shook her head. "I'm home for good, Lauren. I've covered my last political coup and reported my last bloody revolution."

Lauren glanced at the exotic black and gold walking cane resting across Clancy's lap. Ten to one she hadn't bought it in the continental U.S. "Remind me to throw those words back at you as soon as you can hobble around without that thing. Who're you trying to kid, Clancy? Reporting's in your blood."

"I'm not giving up reporting," Clancy told her. "I'm just staying home to do it from now on."

Lauren felt slightly alarmed. Clancy was a journalist with an impressive reputation earned during ten years of reporting from the world's trouble spots. After being injured on a foreign assignment somewhere in Central America, she'd chosen to recuperate at home. She was one of Lauren's oldest friends, but she was still a reporter, and Lauren had had her fill of the Fourth Estate lately.

Correctly interpreting Lauren's wariness, Clancy put out a hand. "For heaven's sake, get that look off your face. I'm not doing an interview. I've just been thinking over my options if I decide to stay in town. There's TV and the newspaper freelancing. But even if I were working again, surely you know you don't have to be concerned about privacy. You're one of the few friends I've got left at home, Lauren."

Lauren shook her head. "I'm sorry, Clancy. I guess I'm getting a bit paranoid lately. I was almost mobbed by reporters as I was leaving the courthouse yesterday."

"Where was your hero?"

"I assume you mean Jake Levinson."

Clancy's shrug was a little too nonchalant. "Who else?"

"He's my lawyer, Clancy, not my lover. Yes, of course he was there and he fended off the media. He even let me cry a little on his shoulder."

"Humph." Clancy made a face and looked unimpressed.

Lauren eyed her thoughtfully. Clancy and Jake Levinson had once been engaged, but that had ended ten years before when Clancy left for Washington. Although she'd been back in Mobile for several weeks, Jake had not appeared to notice. On the surface she appeared to be the same free spirit she'd always been. Suddenly Lauren wondered about Clancy's decision to settle down. She leaned back; an eyebrow quirked. "You just missed him."

Clancy busied herself suddenly by propping her injured leg on the seat of the chair beside her, arranging the folds of her denim skirt, positioning her cane just so. Hiding a smile, Lauren watched her, not fooled for a second by the studied nonchalance. Clancy was irritated by Jake's indifference.

"Well, aside from playing the hero to the hilt, did he do his job?" Clancy's tone had a little bite in it. "Did he conjure up a miracle?"

Lauren thought of Ryder Braden, engineer extraordinaire, adept and dark and dangerous. "He tried."

"No miracles, hmm?" Suddenly Clancy's attitude became one of genuine concern. "I was hoping you'd look a lot more optimistic this afternoon than you do. I'm almost afraid to ask, but how bad is it?"

"It's not good, I'm afraid," Lauren said. "As for Jake doing his job, as I told you, he tried. I'm the one who flubbed up, not Jake." She'd been feeling unsettled ever since her encounter with Braden that morning and no matter how she played and replayed the scene in her head, Lauren couldn't explain her reaction to the man. Or her behavior. Jake had persuaded Ryder to come around and talk, and she'd alienated him in two minutes.

"Whatever happened must have been upsetting," Clancy observed, looking at the hodgepodge of papers on the desk. "I thought I was the only one whose desk got in that shape. Can't you delegate some of that?"

Lauren shook her head. "I'm afraid not, but that's not the problem." She searched a moment for a way to describe her dilemma. Maybe telling Clancy would help her put the whole episode into perspective.

"A funny thing happened at Jake's office this morning," she said finally. "Our case needs an expert witness and Jake managed to locate someone here in town who's qualified."

"Well, great, what a lucky break. Anyone we know?"

"I don't think you know him, but I do. At least, I met him. Once."

Clancy looked intrigued.

"His name is Ryder Braden. We met at a Mardi Gras ball about five years ago."

"Ryder Braden." Clancy repeated the name thoughtfully. "No, doesn't sound familiar. He lives here, in Mobile?"

Lauren shrugged. "He doesn't appear to live anywhere, at least permanently. He manages a stop in Mobile every few years. Jake told me his grandmother died about three months ago which seems to be his reason for being here right now."

"A rolling stone, hmm?"

"Apparently, but one whose career makes him tailor-made for our expert witness."

Clancy leaned back and crossed her bad leg over her good one. "So what's the problem?"

Lauren hesitated before drawing a deep breath. "Clancy, have you ever done something that you looked back on later and wondered what had come over you?"

Clancy grinned. "No, never."

Lauren stared at her. "Do you want to hear this story, or not?"

The grin vanished from Clancy's face, but laughter lingered in her blue eyes.

Lauren's half smile was fleeting. She turned her gaze to the window, looking thoughtful. "I don't know why, Clancy, but I had my back up from the minute he sat down in Jake's office."

"That I can certainly understand," Clancy said dryly.

Lauren ignored her. "I practically picked a fight with the man over nothing. I was rude and arrogant and..." She brought her gaze back to Clancy who wore a look of amazement.

"*You*, Lauren Holt, the very essence of polite southern womanhood, were rude? I don't believe it!"

"It's true. I don't know what got into me, Clancy. He looked like some battle-scarred drifter who'd been around the block so many times that nothing much could shock him, and—"

"Wow, he sounds pret-ty interesting to me."

"Well, he isn't. I mean—" she hesitated and then smiled "—actually, maybe he is. Slightly."

Clancy's sandy eyebrows went up.

"The point is," Lauren continued, ignoring her friend's expression. "I'm not sure about turning the records of the company over to a man like that."

"You mean because he wasn't wearing a three-piece suit and carrying a briefcase?"

"No, of course not. But, we'd have to turn over all Clay's designs. Whoever the expert is will have full access to the company's files and records."

"He could hardly testify to their authenticity otherwise," Clancy observed, still looking a little baffled. "You said you'd met him before. Do you know much about him? I can't believe Jake would recommend him if he had any reservations."

"Oh, Jake's practically ecstatic over him falling in our laps like this," Lauren said wryly. "I didn't tell Jake, but some of the things I heard that night make me extremely nervous about putting the fate of our case in the hands of some vagabond engineer with a taste for life in the fast lane."

"What makes you say that?" Clancy carefully set her foot on the floor.

Lauren made a face, beginning to feel as though she was digging a hole and sinking in it. "It was nothing in particular.

Naturally I'm cautious about trusting someone with such a—such a colorful reputation."

"This is getting more and more interesting," Clancy responded. "Exactly what makes his reputation colorful?"

"Oh, Clancy—"

"Well, what?"

Lauren looked at her. "You'll probably love it."

"Try me."

"According to Jake, Ryder had an impoverished youth with few advantages except for an exceptional grandmother. He worked to pay for his own education and landed a plum job at graduation, then he launched a successful business as a troubleshooting consultant."

"So," Clancy nodded, urging her on. "I can't believe you have a problem with a self-made man."

"I don't. If anything, it's just the opposite," Lauren said. "I admire that kind of strength. Oh, I don't know what I think. Why in the world did I act like such a bitch, for heaven's sake!"

Clancy leaned back in her chair watching Lauren closely. "You know, Lauren, maybe you're looking at this thing from the wrong angle. Maybe you're trying to figure out a reason to reject this man professionally because your reaction to him was extremely personal."

"Don't be ridiculous, Clancy. I've only met the man once. Well, twice." But the minute the words were out of Clancy's mouth, Lauren knew they were true. There was something about Ryder Braden that put her uncharacteristically on edge. Deep down she trusted Jake not to turn over company secrets to a man he had any doubts about. No, her problem with Braden wasn't anything to do with the company or questions about his career. Far from it. He had somehow managed to disturb something deep inside her that had gone undisturbed for years. All the way back to her senior year in college.

She'd been engaged that year to a handsome, charming, intelligent, ambitious man. Unfortunately she hadn't realized how ambitious he was until he'd abruptly broken off their engagement a few weeks before their wedding. Lauren's family, the Buchanans, were an old and respected family. Old Buchanan money and connections would have been tremendous assets to his career. The problem was that at that time, Buchanan tradition and connections were still intact, but there was not much money left. The humiliation of his rejection still made Lauren's face burn.

She shifted suddenly, with a fervent wish that she'd never started this conversation. It wasn't like her to react so emotionally, let alone to tell anyone about it. Not even Clancy. Stress must be taking more of a toll than she realized.

Clancy rose, favoring her left leg. "Okay, babe, I'm out of here. Just one thing..." She grinned at the wary look in Lauren's eyes. "If this guy really is the perfect expert and he seemed willing enough before you...ah, insulted him, then maybe you ought to consider giving Jake a call and asking him to try and pour a little oil on troubled waters. Aren't lawyers good at that sort of thing?"

JAKE WASN'T HAVING any part of it. Lauren put down the receiver with a sigh and spent a fleeting moment remembering how uncomplicated her life had been before the responsibility of the whole company had landed in her lap. Her lawyer certainly hadn't hesitated to let her know how disgusted he was with her. She winced, recalling his words.

"What the hell happened, Lauren? I leave you alone for three minutes with the one man within a thousand-mile radius who just might possibly make a difference to our case. I come back and he's walking out looking like a man who wants to hit something."

"Do you think he might reconsider, Jake?" she'd asked, knowing she deserved Jake's displeasure. But how could she explain her behavior when she didn't even understand it herself?

"Hell, I don't know. He's not a man to forget an insult, Lauren."

"Maybe if you just called him—"

"No, Lauren," Jake had said emphatically. "You call him. You messed it up; you fix it."

"But—"

"I'm telling you, Lauren. He won't come around with a silly bread-and-butter call from me. He'll want to hear an apology from you. And then maybe, just maybe..."

Lauren stared at the phone number jotted on the pad in front of her. Jake was right. She had created the problem. Now it was her place to fix it. Shivering, she picked up the phone.

After punching out the number, she waited through five rings. Six. Seven. Maybe he...

"Hello?"

She licked her lips while something curled through her stomach and whispered down her spine. His voice sounded deep and impatient and she could hear him breathing as though he was out of breath. She wondered what he'd been doing, something physical, surely. He was definitely a physical person.

"Hello!"

"Uh, hello, Mr. Braden. This is Lauren Holt."

Silence.

"Mr. Braden?"

"Yeah, I'm here." The impatience was replaced with a cool formality that bordered on rudeness. He was definitely entitled, she thought.

"Mr. Braden..." Suddenly, Lauren could find no way to express the reason for her call. What could she say? That she'd taken a dislike to him because he brought to mind feelings and events that had caused her pain a million years ago? That she was too cowardly to take a chance on dealing with a man who reminded her of a time when she was so naive that she'd been an easy victim? That he was too...

"You said that."

"What?" She frowned.

"'Mr. Braden,'" he said and a hint of the charm for which he was famous crept into his tone. "We've established who we both are, haven't we?"

"Yes." She took a deep breath. At least he hadn't hung up. "Mr. Braden—"

He chuckled softly.

"Please," she murmured, struggling against her reaction to that sound. "I'm trying to find the words and you aren't helping."

"Words for what, Mrs. Holt?"

Lauren stared at a photograph of a broadly grinning Justin, which was propped in front of her. "Words to apologize for my unforgivable rudeness to you this morning in Jake's office. Words to try and explain what came over me so that I behaved like some kind of arrogant bitch. Words to say how sorry I—"

"Whoa." Ryder's voice was low and laced with amusement. "Why not just say, 'I'm sorry'?"

It was Lauren's turn to be silenced.

"And be done with it."

Lauren found she was holding her breath. "Is that all it takes?"

"I'm a reasonable man."

"And a nice one, too," Lauren said and wondered at the sudden lift of her spirits. "I'm sorry."

"Are you sure this is the real Lauren Holt?"

"It is, although I certainly can't expect you to believe it. I do sincerely regret that we got off on the wrong foot. I'm still not sure what came over me, but it won't happen again. You have my word on it."

"Your last one, I hope."

She laughed. "My last one, I promise."

"Finally."

Lauren laughed again. "Did I interrupt anything? The phone rang several times. Am I keeping you from something important?"

"I'm not on a schedule lately," he replied. "No, you didn't interrupt anything important."

She took another deep breath. "Mr. Braden—"

"Ryder, please."

"Thank you. Ryder, I know this sounds presumptuous, and you have every right to tell me no and just hang up the phone. But we still need you as an expert witness. I would be extremely grateful if you would reconsider."

So polite and gracious, Ryder thought, standing in the old kitchen enjoying the sound of her voice and—he admitted it—having the upper hand. He had no difficulty bringing to mind an image of Lauren behind her desk, her long legs crossed with ladylike grace. He'd bet his next consultant fee she wasn't used to apologizing, but she'd certainly done it with all the warmth and sincerity he could have wished for. He'd give a few thousand dollars to know exactly why she had reacted to him in a way that required an apology in the first place.

"Are you there, Ryder?"

"I'm here, Mrs. Holt."

"Lauren, please call me Lauren."

He smiled. "Thank you."

"'What about it, Ryder? Will you do it?"

"On one condition."

She hesitated. "Which is?"

"I'll need to familiarize myself with the disputed designs. Bring them out here tomorrow and I'll look them over. I'll give you my opinion just as soon as I can."

"Out there?" she said, sounding dismayed.

"Out here."

"But I don't know where your house is, Ryder. Wouldn't the plant be a better place? You may have technical questions, points that only our people in engineering are qualified to discuss."

"That's my condition, Lauren."

"Well, if you insist."

"I do. Now, do you need directions to this house?"

"No, Jake will be with me and he knows the way," she replied.

Ryder studied the look of his worn Nike running shoes. "Yeah, Jake knows the way," he said softly, hanging up the phone and wondering how he'd be able to think of anything but her for the next twenty-four hours.

LAUREN WAS MECHANICALLY navigating the rush-hour traffic on the beltline while her thoughts focused on Ryder Braden.

I can't believe I agreed to go to his house.

A strange dart of anticipation sliced through her. From the moment she'd hung up the phone, she'd been trying to understand how she'd let herself be so smoothly manipulated. Had he been serious? Would he have refused to reconsider if she hadn't agreed to come to him? Was it simply ego on his part? She inhaled deeply and turned off the main street and onto the curved, brick-paved driveway of her home, hoping that had not been his reason, but not quite willing to examine exactly what she hoped his real reason could be.

She pulled into the detached garage of the sprawling ranch house that she and Clay had bought about five years before. The neighborhood was fairly new, appealing mostly to newly established professionals, but she had never felt any special attachment to the house. Lauren had an appreciation for the history and tradition of old places. Both she and Clay had been reared in homes that were over seventy-five years old, but Clay barely knew the right end of a hammer to use, which made owning an old house impractical. One of these days she planned to find a little gem and restore it.

Justin would be her handyman, she thought, her expression softening as it always did when she thought of her son. He was as adept with his hands as he was at his computer. Smiling, she got out of her small Toyota and went into the house.

"I'm home!" Lauren laid her bag on the top of a Chippendale lowboy in the foyer and idly thumbed through a stack of mail.

"Lordy! Look who's home and it's only five-thirty in the afternoon."

"Hi, Hattie." Lauren smiled into the round ebony face of the woman waddling toward her. For thirty years Hattie Bell Brown had kept house and cooked for various Buchanans. Most of Lauren's childhood tears and fears had been soothed away on Hattie's expansive lap. When Justin was born, Hattie had announced to Pauline Buchanan, Lauren's mother, that her place was with Lauren and the baby, whereupon she'd packed her bags and moved over to the new house. Lauren knew how fortunate she was and couldn't bear to imagine life without Hattie Bell.

"I managed to get away at quitting time for once," Lauren explained, tossing the mail back onto the lowboy. She was used to Hattie's chiding criticism for the long hours she put in at her desk, and even though she'd like to spend more time at home, she simply didn't see how she could do so anytime soon. Maybe after the case was settled. "Where's Justin?"

Hattie smiled meaningfully. "Where do you think? If he isn't outside playing baseball or soccer, then he's going to be at that computer setup in his room. I tell you, Lauren, that boy is something else with all his energy. No telling what he'll grow up to be if he keeps on like this."

Lauren smiled. "Well, we have a few years yet to enjoy him, Hattie Bell." She turned her head at the sudden flurry of noise behind her.

"Hi, Mom!" Justin rounded the corner in the hall trailing a couple of yards of computer printout paper behind him. "Take a look at this. I had a heckuva time programming it." He pulled the paper around and stretched it out between his expanded arms.

Lauren leaned back to read an elaborate rendering of the words, All the Way, Bluejays! created with a million X's and O's. Besides his computer, Justin had two passions in life. One was baseball; the other was soccer. His Little League team, the

Bluejays, were in contention for the championship in their division.

"Very impressive," she said, reaching out and fluffing his hair, ignoring his longsuffering look. Motherly kisses were strictly forbidden, to Lauren's keen disappointment, and a hug was tolerated only under the most exceptional circumstances. Most of the time Lauren regretted the speed with which Justin was growing up, but there were a few compensations, she'd decided, if once he had matured, he'd let her touch him again.

She gazed down at him and felt her heart swell with boundless love. His blond head, so like her own, and those amber eyes, also like hers, were a combination of little-boy beauty and male promise that no normal mother could look at without a burst of pride, she told herself. Every day she thanked God that Clay had persuaded her they needed a child.

"What's for dinner, Hattie Bell?" Justin asked, carefully folding the paper streamer.

"Smoked oysters, brussel sprouts and beets," Hattie said, her black eyes dancing.

"Aw, Hattie."

"Well, it's pretty late," Hattie began, "but I guess I could make some cream of cauliflower soup with a spinach salad 'cause I know how you love—"

"I don't love any of that!" Justin announced firmly. "And you know it. I need real food, Hattie. How'm I gonna keep up my batting average with oysters and cauliflower?"

Lauren smiled. "Especially if you won't eat them."

Hattie braced her hands on gigantic hips. "Well, how about fried chicken and corn on the cob?"

Justin's eyes lit up. "Yeah! Now, that's more like it."

Hattie started toward the kitchen chuckling. "I'll see what I can do, my man."

Lauren put her hands on her hips and eyed her son, her mouth twitching. "Justin, I believe you'd like it if we had fried chicken or pizza every night. Don't you ever want any variety?"

Justin had the paper streamer folded into a neat stack. "Sure," he said good-naturedly, "hamburgers and french fries would be okay."

"Go wash your hands," she said, shaking her head helplessly.

A soft smile tugged at her lips as Lauren watched him disappear down the hall. He was getting so tall! His eleventh birthday had barely passed and he was already into teen-sized jeans and still growing. Intellectually he was far ahead of most of his classmates.

A troubled look entered her eyes. A threat to the company wasn't just a threat to her and the employees. It was a threat to Justin and his birthright. A swift, fierce rush of maternal protectiveness arose in her. If the case should be resolved, she could devote the time to Justin that he deserved. And Ryder Braden's expertise would definitely help.

A picture of Braden as he'd appeared in Jake's office took shape clearly in her mind. Something about him appealed to her as no man had for a long time. The cool, practical streak that had governed her most of her adult life was strangely silent, while something else, something entirely unexpected had come to life. It was as though her senses had been awakened after a long sleep. A feeling of anticipation made her pulse quicken.

This was ridiculous! She would wake up tomorrow and be her old self again. This strange attraction she felt would probably be gone, changed to the uncomplicated feelings she had for . . . Jake, for instance. Or any of the hundreds of men who worked at the plant. Tomorrow, this strange, compelling awareness of the man would surely pass.

Or would it?

CHAPTER FOUR

"HERE WE ARE, just around this bend." Jake winced as the Mercedes's front end was jarred by a deep rut in the road.

"Great." Lauren gazed at the uncut, sun-parched grass along the roadside and tried unsuccessfully to ignore the fluttery sensation in her stomach. Being on Braden's territory made her feel distinctly uneasy. At this rate, she thought, by the time she saw the man, she would be as nervous as a teenager.

"I hope we're doing the right thing, Jake," she said, focusing on professional problems rather than personal ones. "Turning everything over to Braden seems so... so drastic."

"That unexpected contract you just landed from Hy-Tech in Pensacola will help hold you above water," Jake said with patience, "but it's only temporary, Lauren. With Ryder's help, we're going to get out of the woods permanently. Trust me on this, babe."

"If you say so." Lauren sighed and resumed her tense contemplation of the countryside. "But I can't stay long. Justin's game is at four and I can't miss it."

Jake swerved to avoid a pothole. "Fine. That's over two hours from now. And after you've talked with Ryder, if you decide you simply can't trust him, then you can take Clay's files with you."

Lauren didn't comment. What was the point? It was obvious Jake didn't have a single reservation about his old buddy.

"Ryder isn't interested in grabbing anything that belongs to you, Lauren."

"So you've said," she muttered. "Ten or twenty times."

He grinned at her, not without sympathy. "I'll grant you've got good reason to be distrustful of some people lately, but Ryder Braden isn't one of them."

She gave up and tried to relax. It was useless trying to argue with Jake. He was firmly in Braden's corner.

"I still think dragging us out here was uncalled for," Lauren grumbled, bracing herself with one hand on the dash as Jake took a hairpin curve. "Why did the man insist on it? It's hot and dusty. I didn't have time for lunch and I'm thirsty. Honestly, Jake..."

Her words trailed off as the Mercedes turned abruptly into a lane formed by a double row of ancient live oaks. At the end, looking like something created from her own imagination, was a house. It had the graceful look of an early Victorian, complete with wraparound porch and gingerbread trim.

"Oh, Jake..."

"Yeah," Jake said, smiling. "I'd almost forgotten how beautiful this old place is."

"How old is it?" Lauren asked, taking in the twin turrets and double front porches, one at ground level and another directly overhead on the second floor. Over the front door was a beautiful leaded glass fanlight. And those windows, she thought, marveling at the varied sizes and shapes. The place was a treasure!

"Sixty...seventy-five years, I'd guess." Jake brought the car to a stop. Resting his wrists on the steering wheel, he studied the familiar lines of the place.

"No wonder Braden wants to restore this," she murmured. "Has his family always lived here?"

Jake shook his head. "I'm not sure, although I never knew him to live any other place. He was always pretty self-contained when we were kids. His grandmother raised him."

Self-contained. And nothing's changed, Lauren thought. He wouldn't have become any mellower in the years he'd knocked about the world. Just the opposite, she guessed, recalling hard, closed features and the fathomless blue eyes that revealed nothing. It was not difficult to imagine a man like Braden living a solitary existence. But burying himself in an old house like this in coastal Alabama was something else altogether, she thought, intrigued in spite of herself.

She was pulled out of her thoughts when Jake suddenly opened his door. Gathering up the rolled plans and her briefcase, she got out of the car, bracing herself to meet Ryder Braden again, face to face.

The front door was equipped with an old-fashioned twist bell which Jake rang half a dozen times before it became obvious that no one was in the house. "I know he's expecting us," Jake said, surveying the grounds with a frown. "Must be out at the barn." He started down the steps, saying over his shoulder, "Wait here while I take a look."

Lauren nodded, feeling the heat after the abnormal coolness of Jake's Mercedes. She put her briefcase and papers on the seat of an old rocking chair and blotted moisture from her upper lip with two fingers of her hand. There was no quiet like the stillness of a hot Southern afternoon. Even birds and insects retreated to whatever cool shelter they could find. In the glare of the midday sun, Lauren stared out over Braden's land. The line of woods toward the back was darker and greener, lush with vegetation, making her think there must be a creek or bayou marking his boundary line. It was beautiful and somehow primitive. She left the porch and followed a narrow brick path by the side of the house, drawn by the promise of a cool stream.

It was then that she saw him.

He was naked from the waist up. In the full heat of the sun, sweat glistened on his body, collecting in the dark curls fanning out over his chest and running down the center of his hard, flat middle. Faded cutoffs rode impossibly low on his lean hips. As he bent to pick up something on a workbench beside him, she could see a flash of the white waistband on his underwear.

Her mouth went dry and for a few lost moments, Lauren simply stared, more than ever aware of the tightness that had been in her stomach all day. What was it about this man that made her feel this way? The question resurrected old defenses. Why was he flaunting himself like a teenage boy who'd just discovered his muscles? He was expecting her and Jake. Why didn't he have the courtesy to at least put on a shirt?

She watched him glance at a paper beside him, and then measure a piece of lumber with a metal tape. He marked the wood with a pencil and lifted an electric saw, flexing the muscles in his arms with the effort. Raising one foot to brace the board, he carefully positioned the blade. Just before cutting, he cleared sweat from his temple with an impatient swipe of his shoulder. Then the piercing shriek of the saw rent the hot stillness of the afternoon.

A piece of the board fell away and he set the saw aside, holding on to the longer section. Straightening, he looked up directly into Lauren's eyes.

Neither of them acknowledged the other for a few seconds. And then it dawned on Lauren just how odd she must appear, walking up unannounced in his backyard, gaping as though she'd never seen a man working without his shirt. She cleared her throat and came closer.

"We rang but no one answered," she said, waving a hand vaguely toward the front of the house.

He nodded once, unsmiling. Tossing the wood onto the workbench, he reached for his shirt and unhurriedly pulled it over his head. Like his cutoffs, the garment had seen better days. The sleeves had been cut and the bottom hiked up, baring a tanned section of his midriff. Ryder looked grubby and hot and distinctly masculine. Everything about him should have turned her off, Lauren told herself, but yet he provoked all kinds of confusing feelings in her. And not all of them were negative.

He glanced beyond her. "Did Jake come with you?"

"He's looking for you in those buildings we saw on the other side of the property."

He started toward her. "Sorry about that. The time got away from me."

She gestured toward the materials spread out on the workbench. "What are you building?"

A rueful look came into his eyes. "Would you believe a birdhouse?"

She smiled, surprised. "What kind?"

"Purple martin."

"Declaring war on mosquitoes, hmm?"

"They say one martin eats his weight in mosquitoes every day," he said, falling into step beside her as she turned back, retracing the path toward the front of the house.

Lauren glanced at him through her lashes. "There's no accounting for taste, I guess."

He laughed. "Right. Although I'm not stopping with a single family unit. I figure I'll need at least a high-rise hotel."

She made a face. "Pretty buggy out here, huh?"

He surveyed the neglected grounds, squinting in the sun. "No more than usual, at least for this part of the country, I suppose. Being away so long, you forget—"

"Hey, here you are!" They looked up as Jake appeared at the corner of the house.

"Good to see you, Jake." Ryder reached out to accept the lawyer's outstretched hand. "Come on into the house where it's cool," he said, waiting while his guests climbed the steps to the porch. Lauren collected the material she'd left on the chair, and when Ryder pushed the door open wide, she went inside.

"There's iced tea or beer," he said, ushering them into the spacious front room. "What'll you have?"

"Beer," said Jake without hesitation.

"Iced tea," said Lauren. "Please."

He disappeared through a swinging door, saying over his shoulder, "You can spread the plans out on the dining room table. I'll look them over now, then tonight I'll study them in detail."

He was back with their drinks before Lauren had the plans out of their tubes. He handed Jake a beer and set Lauren's iced tea down beside her. "I'm a mess," he said, making a face and pulling at the sweat-stained sweatshirt with his hands. "Give me two minutes to get decent and we'll get down to business."

As soon as Ryder left the room, Lauren looked at Jake. "Maybe I should withhold a few of the designs until we're certain."

Jake shrugged. "It's your funeral."

"Oh, all right!" The plans landed with a thump on the table. She'd managed to stretch most of them out, anchoring them with ashtrays and other articles in the room that had probably belonged to his grandmother by the time Ryder reappeared.

Instantly Lauren felt the now familiar, intense awareness. He'd obviously taken a quick shower. He smelled of soap and warm maleness and nothing else. No after-shave, no cologne. His hair, dark and wet, had received only a quick swipe with a towel. It clung to the shape of his head, curling around his ears and the nape of his neck. Had he even bothered to dry off before pulling on his jeans? Was that why they molded his muscled thighs and outlined his maleness so faithfully? She cleared her throat and forced her gaze to the jumble of numbers and mechanical symbols on the plans and specifications before her. At least he wore a shirt. It was white and fashionably loose, subtly flattering. But wouldn't he look good in almost anything? Although her assessment had taken no more than five or ten seconds, his image was clearly imprinted in her mind. She

bent over the plans, determined to ignore the unsettling effect
the man seemed to have on her.

ALL OF RYDER'S ATTENTION was focused on the details contained in the jumble of plans that littered the top of his dining-room table. For the next half hour, as quickly as she answered one question, he fired another at her. Jake was no help. Lauren began to wonder why she'd insisted he come. He sat behind them, a silent observer. In her efforts to concentrate on technicalities that were hazy at best to her, Lauren grew more and more tense. Finally, in response to one of his questions, she pushed aside a schematic drawing in exasperation.

"I can't answer that, Mr. Braden. If you recall, I suggested that we meet at the plant so that there would be qualified people standing by who could answer your questions, but you—"

"Hey, hey..." He brought up both hands, palms out front, his smile slanted and loaded with charm. "It's okay. You did suggest that, Mrs. Holt, but I got so caught up in the designs that I forgot myself. I apologize. At any rate, you've answered most of my questions very respectably."

Jake stood up before the lively exchange between his two friends heated up any more. " 'Mr.' Braden. 'Mrs.' Holt," he said with exaggerated patience. "Are you two back to formal address again?"

Ryder looked into Lauren's eyes. "Are we?"

Lauren's smile began slowly and then bloomed. Watching it, Ryder felt an answering heat spread through him like warm honey. "That would be pretty silly, wouldn't it?" she said.

Ryder grinned. "That it would, Lauren."

The moment stretched out, deep and silent. Jake, amused, cleared his throat deliberately.

"Well..." Lauren looked away and focused blindly on the scattered plans in front of her. "We should get on with this since I've got to leave in time to get to the ball field."

"Ball field?" Ryder frowned, unable to picture Lauren interested in sports.

"Little League," she explained. "I've got to be there at four o'clock sharp. I've been chastised too often for missing the first pitch."

Ryder very casually unrolled a set of plans. "Must be some-body important playing," he said, the criss-cross of lines and angles now meaningless.

"Yes," Lauren said softly. "My son."

Still bent over the plans, Ryder closed his eyes and inhaled deeply. Then he straightened and looked directly at Lauren. "Your son."

She nodded, unable to hide the pride and love in her tone. "Justin, eleven going on twenty-one, the Bluejays' star catcher."

"That good, is he?"

She laughed ruefully. "Maybe I should have said the Blue-jays' only catcher. The team's not overmanned, I'm afraid."

Still holding her gaze, Ryder leaned against the table, cross-ing his ankles. "I can't see you as the mother of a jock, even an eleven-year-old jock."

"How about a computer whiz-kid?" Jake spoke up from behind them. "Justin's not exactly your average eleven-year-old. He's smart as a whip, but down to earth at the same time, a terrific kid." He glanced at his watch. "Lauren, we'd better get on with this if you want to stay in good with that terrific kid."

Looking thoughtful, Ryder bumped an empty cardboard tube against his thighs. At the first mention of the boy, his heart had actually jumped. Even though he knew it was a crazy idea, he wanted to see Justin. He swallowed painfully. *Justin.* Until this moment, he hadn't known his name. He told himself he hadn't wanted to know, but deep down, he knew better. Something inside him wouldn't be satisfied until he knew far more about the boy than just his name.

He looked at Jake Levinson. "Do you need to get back to your office, Jake?"

Jake glanced at Lauren. "Well, I—"

"I'd be happy to drive Lauren to the ball field." Ryder kept the expression on his face casual, sensing Lauren's wariness. "It's been a long time since I've seen a star catcher perform."

Jake grinned. "Say about twenty-five years?"

Lauren looked interested. "You were a catcher?"

"It's been a long time, but yes, I was once."

Jake turned to Lauren. "How about it, hon?" He swept a glance over the plans scattered on the table top. "It doesn't appear I'm making much of a contribution here. You have any objection if I head on back to my office?"

"I don't want to put you to any trouble," Lauren said to Ryder. "I—"

"It's no trouble," Ryder said quickly. "It'll be a nice break."

Still uncertain, her amber eyes searched his.

"Don't say no, Lauren."

He hadn't intended to say that. Or to sound like that. Feeling slightly embarrassed, he laughed softly and looked away, right into Jake's arrested gaze. He swore silently, imagining what the lawyer must be thinking. Not a week before, Jake had had to practically hog-tie him before he'd even consider Lauren's case and now here he was very nearly begging to take her to a kid's ballgame. Jake must be wondering whether he'd been out in the sun too long.

Two minutes later Lauren watched Jake turn the Mercedes around and then disappear down the oak-studded lane. Keenly aware of Ryder standing beside her, she raised her left arm and studied her watch. "If we're going to go through everything I brought with me and make the game on time," she said briskly, "then we'd better get on with it."

"Yes, ma'am."

Her eyes flew to his, tangling with a look so intensely blue that she had a ridiculous urge to fly down the front steps and call out to Jake before it was too late. Instead, she drew a calming breath and went back to the table. When Ryder didn't immediately follow her, she gave him a pointed look. Wearing an expression she didn't dare try to decipher, he pushed away from the door and joined her.

The man knew robotics. Even with her limited knowledge, Lauren recognized that. His experience was much broader and encompassed more than just the function of Clay's designs, she'd discovered. He talked with ease about product application and cost as well as prospective profits and markets. Provided the designs could be established as exclusive, she reminded herself grimly. Ryder, it appeared, could be every bit as valuable to the company and the lawsuit as Jake believed.

The next hour went quickly. She was startled when he began rolling up a set of prints.

"Time to wrap this up," he said, stacking everything neatly in the middle of the table and then turning to her. "What now,

Lauren? Do you want to take all this back with you or will you leave it with me? It's up to you."

She looked up at him, searching his face as though something there would give her the assurance she needed to place the company's destiny—and hers and Justin's—in his hands. Again she felt the pull of attraction, the lure of his deep blue eyes, and something else that she couldn't name. Suddenly she had no desire to hold out against him. "I'll leave it all with you," she said.

He grinned and reached for her bag. "Then come on, lady. We can't be late for that ballgame."

RYDER GOT OUT of the Blazer at the ball field, emotion pounding through him so fiercely that for a moment he couldn't move. He had never allowed himself to even imagine this moment. He had always believed no reason could be good enough or strong enough to overcome the complications inherent in a meeting between him and this boy. But then he had never intended to let himself get close enough to actually meet Lauren, either. Fate, five years before, had fixed that. As he slammed the car door behind him, his anxiety fell away, and only the inevitability of the moment was left, clear and sharp, in his mind. From the day of his return to Mobile, he'd been caught up in something so intense and compelling that nothing he did, no effort to keep his distance, no attempts at cool rationale, no struggle to deny his emotions had mattered at all in the end.

"Coming?"

Lauren was standing at the front of the Blazer looking at him expectantly. Feeling his stomach tighten in anticipation, he nodded and fell into step beside her.

He was barely aware of the friendly greetings called out to her as they negotiated the grassy perimeter of the ball field on their way to the sidelines. The place was alive with kids of all sizes—boys and girls, some in uniforms, some not. Frowning, his gaze swept quickly over them, resting on various boys who appeared to be the right age and size.

"There he is."

Heart hammering, he looked where Lauren pointed to a knot of boys outfitted in blue and white. His teeth, he realized in amazement, were clenched with the same tension that knotted his stomach. He had once faced a street gang in Tokyo with less trepidation.

"Hey, Mom!" One of the boys suddenly raised an arm and grinned at Lauren. Peeling off a catcher's mask, he tossed it aside and then broke into a run, his eyes on his mother. In seconds he pelted to a stop beside her, breathing hard from the exertion and yet laughing at the same time. "You were almost late!"

Something in Ryder twisted and turned his heart inside out. Justin was tall for eleven and skinny, all knees and elbows. His hair was light, exactly like his mother's. His eyes were Lauren's, too—clear amber—bright and intelligent. But his chin, Ryder noted wryly, had a stubborn shape to it and resembled the one he, Ryder, shaved every morning.

Lauren put a hand on the boy's shoulder and smiled up at Ryder. "Justin, this is Mr. Braden. Jake brought him in to work on the lawsuit with us. Ryder, this is my son, Justin Holt."

Ryder couldn't help it. The moment Justin's eyes met his, he felt a surge of pride and sheer possessiveness that was so strong, he wondered that it couldn't be read all over his face. He put out his hand. "Hello, Justin."

Justin cocked his head and studied Ryder for a few seconds before slowly extending his hand. His expression was slightly curious as he shook hands politely.

Ryder looked the boy over intently. *For what?* he asked himself. Some common trait, some inherited characteristic that would link him in some elemental way that only Ryder could ever recognize? Why? For what purpose? Pride? Ego?

"I didn't see you drive up, Mom," Justin said, but his eyes were fixed on Ryder. No dissembling there, Ryder thought, accurately interpreting the look, one male to another. The boy wanted to know what the hell his mother was doing with some stranger. *Good for you, Justin.*

Lauren's hand still rested on the boy's shoulder. "We just got here, Justin."

Justin eyed the vehicles parked on the other side of the ball field. "I don't see the car."

"I rode with Mr. Braden."

Justin looked at Ryder again with new interest. "Why?"

"Oh, uh…" Lauren appeared flustered momentarily. "Well, Jake had to go back to his office and Mr.—"

"Mr. Levinson just ran off and left you?" Justin demanded, suddenly sounding older than his years.

Lauren glanced quickly from her son to Ryder. "Justin, you'd better get back to your team. They're up next. I think Scotty's looking for you."

Justin turned his head and made a motion to two Bluejays who were beckoning to him impatiently. "I guess Scotty's mom can give us a ride home," he said, a hint of suspicion in the look he gave Ryder.

Ryder met the boy's eyes squarely. "Your mother needs to pick up her car at her office, Justin. When the game's over, I'll drive you both over."

His tone was laced with authority. Justin heard him out in silence, and then turned to go.

Lauren and Ryder watched the boy head back to his teammates, his spine ramrod straight. At some sound from her, Ryder glanced down. "What?"

She shook her head. "I don't know what in the world—" She put her fingers to her temples and laughed self-consciously. "I've never seen Justin act so...so..."

"Possessive? Protective?"

She shrugged helplessly. "Was that what it was?"

Ryder's lazy smile appeared. "Either that or jealousy, I'd say." His gaze roamed over her face. "Or a combination of all the above."

"That's ridiculous!"

Ryder lifted a dark brow. "Is it?"

Without another word, Lauren turned and headed toward the stands. Smiling, Ryder fell into step beside her.

For the next two hours, his eyes were fixed on Justin. He watched him leap and yell and crouch and stretch, performing all the familiar moves that he himself had perfected playing the same position when he was about Justin's age. He squinted through the late-afternoon sun as a fast pitch zipped across the plate. The ball made a solid *thwack!* into Justin's glove. In one graceful motion, he surged up, cocked his arm back and threw to the frantic first baseman, who triumphantly tagged the runner. A double play. Ryder found himself on his feet. Pride and something else fierce and deep burned inside him. He eased back onto the bleachers beside Lauren, filled with a confused jumble of impressions and emotion.

He had never felt entirely comfortable with the concept of artificial insemination, but he honestly believed that he had come to accept his role as an anonymous donor years ago. Why then this intense emotional reaction to the boy? Suddenly all his early doubts were back again. The impersonal contribution he'd made to secure Justin's birth didn't feel impersonal at all, he discovered, shaken.

Justin's team headed for the benches in high spirits. Unless they totally fell apart or the other team miraculously rebounded, the Bluejays were headed for victory. Ryder watched Justin's affected nonchalance as his teammates clustered around him. When Justin spotted someone walking across the turf and began waving enthusiastically, Ryder frowned. A tall man, slightly built with light hair and sharp features returned the boy's greeting. Ryder wondered who he was. Definitely a friend, he decided, watching the quick, easy way Justin launched into conversation with him.

"Oh, there's Michael," Lauren said, lifting her arm in greeting as Justin pointed toward his mother and Ryder in the stands.

"The team's sponsor?" Ryder guessed. "Michael" didn't look athletic enough to be a coach, but he kept that thought to himself.

"Not exactly," Lauren answered. "The Holt Company sponsors the team. No, that's Michael Armstead, general manager at the plant." She smiled as Armstead's gaze turned their way. In another moment, he left Justin and started toward them.

Ryder could see both surprise and speculation in Armstead's eyes as Lauren made the introductions. From the man's expression, Ryder assumed that Lauren wasn't usually accompanied at Justin's ballgames, at least by a male. Being linked with her gave him an inexplicable sense of satisfaction.

Armstead took the seat next to Lauren without an invitation. "You must be new in town, Mr. Braden."

"Not really," Ryder said, his eyes on Justin.

"Ryder's career took him away from Mobile," Lauren explained. "Actually he's a robotics expert."

"Oh?" Interest sharpened in Michael's pale eyes. "What company did you say you worked for?"

"I didn't." Ryder surged to his feet suddenly. "Now, Justin, *run!*"

Startled, Lauren turned her attention to the playing field just in time to see Justin seize a chance to steal home. "Yea, Justin!" she shouted, sticking up both her thumbs when Justin looked up in her direction, flushed and grinning.

"Way to go, Justin!" Ryder yelled. He turned to Lauren. "Did you see that? I thought for sure he was going to get tagged by that kid at third, but he dodged him and took off like greased lightning!"

For a second Lauren was caught by something in Ryder's expression. He was flushed, and his grin was every bit as wide as Justin's. Who would have thought he'd get so excited by a Little League baseball game?

"Justin can usually be counted on to make a couple of daring plays," Armstead said. "Remember last week when he set up the triple play that won the game, Lauren?"

Michael spent the next few minutes reminding Lauren of some memorable moments in Justin's Little League career, pointedly excluding Ryder. Next he mentioned a few social events they'd both attended, giving Ryder the impression that he and Lauren shared more than a working relationship. As if reading his mind, Lauren glanced at Ryder, whose attention appeared to be fixed on Justin. There was nothing personal in her association with Michael and she found she didn't want Ryder to think there was. Lauren frowned, wondering why she cared what Ryder thought about her personal life. As for Michael he had been spending time with Justin. More and more, lately it seemed. And with her, as well, she realized with a little start. She was chewing her inside lip thoughtfully when suddenly the game was over.

"Okay, that's it! Ten to four, not bad." Ryder got to his feet and stood aside while Lauren stepped around him and started down the tiers of bleachers.

"I noticed your car still at the plant, Lauren." Michael fell into step beside her, away from Ryder. "You'll need to pick it up. Why don't we run by now? I've got time and—"

"The situation's under control, Armstead," Ryder broke in, using the same tone that had curbed Justin earlier. "I'll see Lauren home and take care of her car."

"Lauren?" Michael's expression when he looked at her was definitely possessive.

"Thanks anyway, Michael," she said, not wanting to encourage him. "But there's no need. I stranded myself by not taking my own car to Ryder's place this afternoon."

Michael looked alert suddenly.

"Jake and I had an appointment this afternoon with Ryder," Lauren explained. "At his place in the country. He's agreed to act as a consultant for us in the lawsuit."

"I could have sat in if I'd known, Lauren," Michael said, faint disapproval in his tone.

"Nothing was definite until this afternoon, Michael." Just then she caught Justin's eye and motioned him over. "However, now that Ryder has Clay's designs, he will probably need to spend some time with various sections. I'll let you know if we need you."

Armstead started to say something, but just then the beeper on his belt sounded. He shut it off, looking irritated.

"Duty calls?" Ryder said dryly.

Ignoring Ryder, Michael turned to Lauren. "I've got a late shift working on that Hy-Tech contract," he explained. "I'll have to check in, I'm afraid. Will you tell Justin? I promised I'd see him after the game."

"Of course." A tiny frown formed between Lauren's brows. "If there's a problem, call me at home, Michael."

"Don't worry, I'll take care of it." Again he hesitated, about to speak. But looking from Lauren to Ryder, he appeared to change his mind. With a curt "Good night" he walked off.

Ryder was silent as he watched Armstead's progress across the turf. The fellow wasn't happy. He glanced down at Lauren. "Another jealous male looking out for you," he observed softly.

Lauren turned startled eyes up to his. "Not really," she said. "He's just a friend, as well as a dedicated employee."

They stood facing each other, the sounds of the ball field all around. Kids yelled, cars started up and then accelerated, a horn blew, brakes squealed. A soft night breeze suddenly stirred, disturbing the neat coil of Lauren's hair. Smiling faintly, Ryder reached up and captured a pale strand that blew across her cheek. He rubbed its silken texture between his fingers before tucking it gently behind her ear. Her heart jumped at his touch.

"That makes three, so far. How many more, Lauren?"

She moistened her lips, transfixed. "Three?"

"Three men looking out for you. First Jake, then Justin, now Armstead. How many more?"

His hand was warm. She could feel the heat. She would only have to turn her face a tiny bit to nestle her cheek into his palm. For a moment, she was wildly, crazily tempted to do just that.

"Jake is my lawyer," she said, her voice husky. "He's just doing his job. And Michael is only a friend. Justin is my son and sees himself as the only man in my life."

"And is he?"

"Yes."

Background sounds of the ball field, movement, people, all receded and became distant and insubstantial. Standing there, her gaze clinging to his, it seemed to Lauren that the appearance of this man in her life seemed suddenly fated. The confused tangle of emotion he evoked was no longer tension and wariness, but breathlessness and sweet anticipation. And much more, she was only just beginning to realize. How and why and exactly what weren't clear. Maybe that would all come later. Maybe later she would decide that she had been momentarily bewitched. But for right now, feeling strangely lighthearted, she fell into step beside Ryder, and for once in her life she gave herself up to the moment. Together they went to meet Justin.

THE MAN HUNG UP the telephone. Rigid and still, he stared at his clenched hands, forcing himself to breathe slowly. Otherwise how could he contain his outrage? He had bargained for none of this. God in heaven! He was not a puppet to be jerked by his contact whenever she conceived yet another maneuver to harass Clay Holt's widow. What would they have him do next? Had he not furnished every technical secret they required? He was a highly specialized professional, not a tale-bearing old woman!

Muttering, he fumbled with a drawer and pulled out a thick telephone directory. His contacts wished to play on the widow's vulnerability to the press. Why must he be the one to leak information? Such tasks were best assigned to the coarse types with whom his contacts consorted after hours. The widow's business was in jeopardy. With patience and shrewdness it would fall into their hands. But no. His contact had a vicious streak. She wished the widow to learn of a new development before the eye of the camera.

Adjusting his bifocals, he focused on the small print in the Yellow Pages. News dealers...news magazines...news service...the finger stopped. Newspapers. He found the numbers and scribbled them on a memo pad. With a heavy sigh he began to dial.

CHAPTER FIVE

"MOM! DID YOU SEE ME steal third, huh?" Justin ran up, triumphant and grinning.

"Did I see you?" Lauren gave his cap a playful tug. "Didn't you hear me cheering?"

Justin straightened his cap and made a face. "Aw, Mom, you always cheer, even when I mess up."

She shrugged, still smiling. "Well, what are mothers for?"

"The team looked good out there, Justin," Ryder said, catching the boy's eye. "And so did you. You made some fine plays. Are the Bluejays in contention for the championship?"

Justin's enthusiasm cooled slightly, but his reply was polite. "Yeah, we can win our division, no sweat, if Curtis Wainwright gets back in time."

Ryder exchanged a look with Lauren.

"On vacation," she supplied helpfully.

Ryder nodded with understanding. "Curtis is indispensable, I assume?"

"He's our best pitcher," Justin declared. "What a time to go to Disneyworld!" He kicked at a dirt clod in disgust.

Lauren dropped a hand to his shoulder and urged him toward Ryder's Blazer. "It's only for a week, Justin. Besides, I thought Freddie Preston did a good job today."

Justin looked doubtful. "Yeah, well, I just hope he can do it again Thursday."

"He'll do it," Lauren said, sounding cheerfully confident. "Meantime, let's get a move on, slugger. We've got to pick up my car. We don't want to monopolize Mr. Braden's entire evening."

"I can still get Scotty's mom to drop us off," Justin offered quickly.

Ryder heard the suggestion and realized that while Justin was tolerating him for his mother's sake, the boy was wary. Ryder

suspected it would take a while before Justin bestowed uncon-
ditional approval on any man who appeared suddenly in his
mother's life.

As they approached the edge of the field, Ryder put his hand
on the small of Lauren's back as she stepped over the low ca-
ble barricade at the street. They were only a few feet beyond it
when he felt her spine tense beneath his palm. She gasped.

A camera flashed directly in front of them.

"Mom!" The cry was wrung from Justin.

It took a second or two for Ryder to realize what was happening. A reporter stood squarely in their path holding a tape
recorder. At his elbow was a scruffy photographer. The camera's whirring sound was like a snake hissing before striking.

"Mrs. Holt, are you going to accept NuTekNiks's buy-out
offer or are you still determined to fight?"

Justin stepped in front of his mother, his chin set, his eyes
flashing.

"Is this your son?" The reporter made a gesture to his co-
hort. "Get a shot of the kid, Marty."

Ryder felt a hot surge of outrage and without thinking, he
reached for the camera. Stopping short of flinging it to the
ground, he settled for shoving it hard against the startled photographer's chest. Turning back, he saw the reporter moving in.
Impressions came and went on his brain like quick-stopped
images on film: Justin's eyes bright with tears, but his expression determined; Lauren's face wearing a trapped look; the
curious stares of Justin's teammates.

Quickly he took out his keys and gave them to Justin. "Take
your mother to the car, Justin," he ordered, giving the boy a
reassuring squeeze on his shoulder before pushing him on his
way.

His eyes were sharp with fury as he turned on the reporter.
"What the hell do you think you're doing?"

"My job, mister. The lady's news and I've got a deadline."

Ryder uttered an oath in a softly menacing tone and watched,
satisfied, as the reporter took a step backward. "Is nothing off
limits to you guys? Don't you ever rest?"

With a shrug, the tape recorder was pocketed. "Inquiring
minds want to know the facts."

Ryder looked him over, not bothering to disguise his disgust. "Well, I'd better not see you back at this ball field, buddy.

If you want a statement from Mrs. Holt in the future, call her office for an appointment. You got that?''

He watched both men stalk off before turning and heading for the Blazer. Still furious, he jerked the door open and got in behind the wheel. Ryder was aware of his two silent passengers, but for a moment, he didn't say a word. Emotions seethed inside him, and his thoughts were as tangled as the underbrush on his property. It seemed that ever since meeting Lauren, he'd been in a tailspin. He hadn't intended to get mixed up in her life. He hadn't counted on reacting so intensely upon meeting his son. What the hell had happened to his plan to keep his distance?

"Thank you."

Hearing her whispered words, he drew a deep breath and turned to look at Lauren. She was so beautiful. The breeze had ruffled her hair more now. It was loose at her temple, on her cheeks, her forehead. The effect softened the sculptured perfection of her features, enhancing her already considerable appeal. Again he had to forcibly remind himself of the deception that he was perpetrating just by getting to know her and Justin. It was one thing to work on the lawsuit with her, but he could not get emotionally involved. That would be crazy. Insane.

"Do you have to cope with that kind of thing often?" he asked, feeling renewed anger.

She touched her forehead with a shaky hand. "No, at least not until today. I couldn't believe it when that reporter appeared. I'm just glad you were there to hold them off until Justin and I could get away."

"We could have handled it, Mom."

Ryder glanced at Justin. The boy was positioned close to Lauren's shoulder, watching him. More emotion twisted through Ryder. Recalling the look on the boy's face when he'd stepped between the reporter and his mother, he was reminded of his own rebellious, scrappy adolescence. More than once he'd plunged recklessly into situations where he knew he didn't stand a chance. It would have been amusing if he hadn't totally lost his sense of humor.

"Is nothing private anymore?" Lauren cried as Ryder started the Blazer. "I thought I'd have a few days of peace after the court session Friday."

Ryder frowned. "What was that about a buy-out?"

Justin moved to the position between the two front seats. "That guy wanted to know if you'd decided to accept Nu-TekNiks's buy-out offer, Mom, or were you going to continue to fight," he said helpfully.

Ryder almost smiled. Justin was sharp as new nails. And spunky. As Jake said, a terrific kid.

Lauren looked at Ryder. "I haven't had an offer. I don't know what he's talking about."

Ryder down-shifted with renewed irritation. "That's just great. Now the media knows more about your business than you do."

Ryder wondered how the reporter had known she was at the ball field. And the information about the lawsuit was privileged. There were some things going on that needed looking into, he thought. Maybe he ought to have a few private words with Jake Levinson.

They were at the Holt plant within minutes. Seeing only one car in the parking area adjacent to the front offices, Ryder raised a questioning brow to Lauren. "Yours?"

She nodded and he pulled up beside it. Before he could get around to her side, she was out of the Blazer. Justin jumped out right behind her, jangling his mother's car keys. Smiling wryly, Ryder fell into step beside Lauren as Justin ran ahead of them, toward the car. "Now that it's summer, where does he stay while you're working?"

"At home with Hattie Bell," Lauren replied. "She spoils him rotten, but it could be worse. He's in his own neighborhood and Hattie Bell loves him almost as much as I do."

He smiled down at her. "Lucky kid."

She was silent a minute, watching Justin. "Truthfully we both spoil him, I suppose." Her voice took on a husky, loving tone as she added, "He's all I have. I worry about him."

"It works both ways, apparently."

She swung her eyes around to his. "What?"

"Justin feels the same sense of responsibility for you," Ryder said. "His reaction tonight when you walked up with a stranger and then again when that reporter approached you tells me that."

"He's just a little boy," she said, sounding distressed.

Ryder looked at her. "He's the man in charge, Lauren. That's the way he sees it."

"Mom, hurry up! Mosquitoes are everywhere."

"Well, get in the car, Justin," she told him, exasperated and amused at the same time. "You have the keys." She was smiling as her eyes met Ryder's. "You see? Fifteen minutes ago he was a tiger protecting me from pushy photographers and now he's whining about mosquitoes."

"As good an excuse as any to get you all to himself, again," Ryder murmured as they reached the car.

She glanced his way. "What?"

"Mom!"

Shaking her head, Lauren snatched Justin's cap off his head. Ignoring his indignant yelp, she gave him a playful whack on his rear and then pretended to cough and choke in the cloud of ball field dust that resulted. They were laughing together when she clamped the cap back on, turning the bill sideways. "Will you quit complaining and get in the car, Justin?"

"It's gonna be swarming with mosquitoes," he told her grumpily, his laughter fading as he met Ryder's dark gaze.

"Maybe we need to ask Mr. Braden to make us a birdhouse for the parking lot," Lauren suggested.

"You make birdhouses?" Justin asked.

"I'm working on one right now," Ryder said.

Justin studied him with his head tilted to one side. "You make birdhouses for a living?" His tone was filled with disdain.

"Justin!" Lauren put her hand on her son's shoulder, shocked at the boy's rudeness. "Mr. Braden is an engineer. He was building a birdhouse to put up on his property. Purple martins consume mosquitoes."

"I know all about purple martins, Mom," Justin said with longsuffering patience. "I just wondered about a man who spent his time building birdhouses, is all."

"I like to work with my hands," Ryder volunteered, feeling a mixture of fascination and delight with Justin. The boy was stopping short of outright hostility; his manners were too good for that. But he was still suspicious. And he refused to be intimidated. Ryder had to admire that kind of grit. Without conceit, he knew he could appear formidable. He had successfully vanquished men of power and position with a withering look. It pleased him to find that Justin could hold his own.

"Yeah, I like working with my hands, too," Justin said. "Maybe I'll build one myself."

"Justin—"

The boy waved away his mother's reaction. "I could do it in the garage."

"We don't even have a saw, Justin," Lauren pointed out.

"How would you like to check out the one I'm working on right now?" Ryder heard himself ask, seizing a chance to see more of Justin. He could set strict limits, he told himself, avoid getting too close or interfering in their lives.

"You could look over the plans," Ryder offered. "And then if you're still interested, you could try your hand at it. I've already worked up a material list."

"Ryder, I'm sure you don't—"

"Maybe you can't read a set of plans," Ryder said to Justin.

"I can read plans," the boy said firmly.

Ryder shrugged. "Then it's up to you."

Justin gave away nothing by the look in his eyes. "You mean go to your place?"

"Yeah, and since you don't have the tools, you could use mine."

Justin pursed his lips, thinking. "I don't know . . ."

"That is, if you decide you'd like to try it."

After another long, speculative look at Ryder, Justin nodded briefly. "I think I'll give it a shot."

Lauren made a strangled sound. "Wait just a minute, you two. I . . ." But her objection died as she eyed them both, Ryder, big and implacable, exuding confidence and male power. And Justin, exhibiting many of the same qualities tempered by his youth. Just now he looked inexplicably like the older man. She shook her head as if to banish the similarity.

"I'll pick you up tomorrow," Ryder told him. "How about eight o'clock? I like to get an early start . . . that is, if your mother has no objections." He looked at Lauren.

"No," she said faintly, then added, "if you're sure you have the time . . ."

"I have the time."

Ryder watched Justin get in the car on the driver's side and then shift over to the passenger seat. Holding the door for Lauren while she slid in behind the wheel, he waited until she looked up questioningly. "I want to study Clay's designs in more detail before making any recommendations," he said, adding when she nodded, "I'll take good care of Justin."

"Thank you," she said softly, her eyes meeting his.

They were both still as the moment stretched out. In the filtered glow from the streetlight, the delicate sculpture of her features was etched as if in moonglow. She was faintly smiling, her hair now hopelessly tangled by the wind, shining like spun silver. He wanted to touch her, Ryder realized. And more. To his chagrin, he felt his body stir and begin to ache. He straightened abruptly, tearing his gaze away. As she pulled out, he stood rooted to the spot until the taillights of her car disappeared into the night.

LAUREN WAS DRESSED and ready to go to work the next morning by seven-thirty, as usual, but she dawdled over her breakfast, took far more time over the newspaper than she ever did on a weekday morning and had three cups of coffee. Glancing at her watch for the third time in as many minutes, Lauren saw that it was finally eight o'clock. She got up then and, picking up the phone, called her office. She really had nothing pressing until ten.

She looked at her hand, still holding the receiver, and noticed the tiny tremor. Ryder would be here any minute. The uncomfortable feeling from yesterday had returned, stronger than ever. But this time she had no glib excuses. She knew the reason now—she was deeply attracted to Ryder Braden, and her time with him yesterday studying the designs, and later, at the ball field with Justin, had intensified that attraction. Replacing the telephone she began to pace the length of the room, admitting to herself that she was deliberately dragging out the time before going to work so that she could see Ryder. For the first time in her life she was waiting for a man.

She actually jumped when the doorbell rang.

Where was Justin? She'd counted on his presence to ease the subtle tension that seemed to hover like a palpable force whenever she was with Ryder. But Justin had been so excited that he had not brushed his teeth or made his bed, so she'd sent him back upstairs to do both.

The doorbell rang again.

"Mo—om! Will you please answer that!"

Lauren slid her hands down the sides of her skirt and opened the door. Standing in the sunshine with the fresh morning all around him, smiling that half smile of his, Ryder was more attractive than any man had a right to be.

"This is a surprise," he said, his expression unreadable as he looked her over. "I thought you'd be at work."

She stepped back so he could come in. "I would, ordinarily. I'm just a bit behind schedule this morning."

Dear heaven, now I've progressed to outright lying. It's a wonder lightning doesn't strike me where I stand.

As she closed the door behind him, Ryder made a quick inspection of the foyer and the stairs beyond. "Is Justin ready?"

"He will be in a few minutes. He's brushing his teeth and making his bed."

He lifted his eyebrows as though impressed.

She smiled. "Under duress."

For the first time since she opened the door, he smiled and Lauren felt suddenly breathless. "Would you like some coffee?"

He nodded. "Sounds good, if it's not too much trouble." Ryder followed Lauren as she led the way to the kitchen, accepting the cup she handed him. He looked out the double French doors that opened onto a patio and backyard while she turned to pour her own.

"Let's take this outside," she suggested, moving around him toward the French doors. "Justin shouldn't be too long."

"It's nice out here," he said, following her out into the clear, still-cool morning. He bent his head to avoid a hanging basket with bright pink bougainvillea cascading almost to the ground as they headed for a glass-topped table. Lauren took a seat, but Ryder refused a chair and leaned against a wrought iron support instead, crossing his ankles. "I used to like that first morning cup of coffee outside," he said.

"Was that when you lived with your grandmother?"

"Yeah, she'd always have biscuits or muffins for breakfast and they tasted even better outside." He focused on a carefully pruned wisteria alongside the patio. "There were flowers everywhere. And no gardener. I realize now how much work it must have been for her."

"Her garden was beautiful," Lauren said softly, recalling the old-fashioned flowers arranged in no particular order. "I fell in love with it—and the house, too." She studied him over the rim of her cup. "Were you born there?"

He smiled, cradling his cup between his palms. "I was born in a hospital."

"But did your parents live there?"

He looked down into his cup. "Not really."

She wanted to ask what that meant, but the look of him warned her off. "Did you have any brothers or sisters?"

His eyes lifted to hers again. "Uh-uh, there was just me. But I always wished I was part of a big family."

"Me, too," she said, letting her gaze drift beyond him to a bright red cardinal perched on Justin's bird feeder. "I always wanted brothers and sisters and aunts and uncles. I told myself when I had children, I would have half a dozen." Her tone became wistful. "Not only does Justin not have brothers and sisters, he doesn't even have any living grandparents."

"It's not too late," Ryder said, placing the empty cup on the table. "You're young; you can still have children."

Even as he spoke, Ryder rejected the thought outright. He moved beyond Lauren and stood looking out over the clipped and manicured perfection of her lawn, realizing that he hated the idea of Lauren having anyone else's children. The emotions clamoring inside him were strictly male, primitive and territorial. He was jealous. She made him feel possessive and protective and torn, as though she belonged to him. He closed his eyes. How on earth was he going to keep his distance if he was already thinking like that?

Justin's voice came suddenly from the upstairs window. "Mom, I can't find my baseball cap with Roll Tide on it!"

"It's down here, Justin," Lauren called back. Standing, she set her coffee cup down and moved toward shelves stacked high with Justin's personal junk. The cap was on the top, just out of her reach. Before Ryder could stop her, she stepped onto the bottom shelf. It boosted her a foot taller and she stretched an arm up to grab the cap. When she pulled it, several other articles were dislodged. Instinctively Lauren jerked back to avoid a baseball bat and lost her footing.

With a startled cry, she felt strong hands clamp around her waist and pull her backward. But it was not far enough. In one motion, Ryder turned her body into his as the avalanche of Justin's junk rained down around them.

The instant that his arms went around her, Ryder was aware of a host of sensations—the fresh, flowery scent of her, the soft, silky texture of her hair, the rapid-fire beat of her heart, her warm breasts pressed firmly to his chest, her thighs meshing with his. Her softness nestled snugly against him set up a throbbing ache that made him forget all the reasons he'd planned to avoid getting into just such a situation as this one.

Still he didn't let her go until he felt her stirring against him, bringing her hands to his chest. Another wave of her perfume filled his senses, and he inhaled deeply, his face buried in her hair. Instantly he was fully aroused. Lauren was soft and pliant and offered no resistance until she moved her leg and encountered the evidence of his desire.

A soft gasp came out of her and she looked up at him. He knew then that whatever the attraction was between them, she felt it, too. Her eyes were wide and startled. The clear amber of her eyes had darkened to a deep, smoky topaz. Ryder felt a mix of pleasure and pain. Her face was lifted to his, her lips, soft and moist, were slightly parted. The air between them seemed to throb with promise. He had never wanted to kiss a woman so badly in his entire life, he realized. With a soft groan he pushed her away from him, even as his instincts urged him to throw her down right here and now and satisfy the hunger that had plagued him from the moment he'd looked into her eyes in Jake's office. He was playing a dangerous game.

Moving quickly, Ryder went to the edge of the patio and stared across the bright green perfection of the lawn. His emotions were a chaotic jumble. The sensation was something utterly foreign to him.

Lauren's laugh, sounding soft and chagrined, came from behind him. He turned reluctantly. "I'm sorry about that," she said, indicating the chaos on the floor. "I've warned Justin a million times about throwing his stuff on those shelves." She picked up her coffee cup, not meeting his eyes.

"One of the hazards of living with an eleven-year-old boy, I guess," Ryder said, looking away uncomfortably when he saw the tremor in her hands.

They both turned in relief as Justin came through the French doors. He stopped short when he saw the mess. "What happened?"

"Justin, we have a guest," Lauren reminded him.

"Oh," Justin said, subdued. "Hello, Mr. Braden."

"'Morning, Justin." Ryder bent over and passed a battered baseball glove over. "If that look in your mom's eye means what I think it means, we're probably going to have to pick this stuff up before she gives us permission to leave."

"You are absolutely right about that," Lauren said, collecting Ryder's coffee cup and heading for the patio door. "I was almost maimed by that dumb baseball bat, Justin. Before you go to bed tonight, young man, I want those shelves as tidy and organized as Hattie Bell's pantry."

Justin glanced quickly at Ryder. He was in for a lecture and he didn't like having a witness. But when he encountered only shared male sympathy in Ryder's expression, he relaxed. Scrambling around, he loaded up his arms. "I've been meaning to clean out these shelves, Mom, but you know how busy I am."

"Spare me, Justin."

"Honest, Mom, I was gonna do it Sunday afternoon."

"I know, you promised on your word of honor," she reminded him.

"Scotty and Mike came by and interrupted me, remember?"

"So what happened Monday?"

"My computer—"

"Okay, that ought to take care of it," Ryder said, breaking in smoothly. He took the remaining articles from Justin and placed them on the top shelf. The boy's attitude was familiar. At the same age he had perfected every delaying tactic known to man with his grandmother. Mama Jane, however, had been as canny and determined as he. Unlike Lauren, who was too indulgent, too permissive. In another year or two, Justin would be rolling over her like a tank.

It was not his concern.

Lauren couldn't believe she was standing there bickering with Justin. Ryder was going to think her a complete failure as a disciplinarian. She turned abruptly and went inside, still a little shaken by that clumsy encounter with Justin's things. She hardly slowed down to drop the two cups into the sink with a clatter before heading for the foyer. What had caused her to melt like a besotted teenager the instant their bodies touched? The irony was, she thought as she shrugged into a raw-silk blazer, she'd never felt this way, even as a teenager.

Following silently, Ryder was behind her when she reached the front door. Before she had a chance to do it herself, his hand was on the doorknob, opening it for her. Justin darted around them and down the steps, making a beeline for the

Blazer. Wordlessly Ryder waited for Lauren and then followed her outside, pulling the door closed behind him.

"Thank you," she said quietly, using her key to turn the lock. "I didn't think to ask last night, but will it be okay to pick Justin up around noon? I can take a few minutes at lunchtime."

Ryder gestured for her to go down the steps in front of him. "It's not necessary. I'll drive him home sometime this afternoon," he said quietly. "Hattie Bell will be here, won't she?"

"Well, yes, but I don't want to put you to any trouble. It's enough that you've taken the time to give him this treat."

"It's no trouble," he told her, walking beside Lauren to her car and waiting while she unlocked it. He opened the door and she brushed by him and got in. Just that brief contact sent a quick tingle through her and she felt breathless again. He waited, while she smoothed her skirt over her knees and put her key in the ignition, before closing the door.

As Lauren looked up at him, she suddenly wished she had the nerve to do what she felt like doing at that moment. Ryder Braden was the most attractive man she'd ever met. What would he do if she just reached out a hand and touched that seductive mouth? Her fingers itched to trace the bold line of his eyebrow. She could almost feel the hard, uncompromising shape of his jaw against her palm. Oh, to just forget appearances and propriety. Oh, to be more like Clancy...

But she wasn't impetuous. She wasn't a risk taker. She would probably never feel Ryder's hands caressing her, his mouth tasting her. She would probably never hear him say things to her, sweet things, intimate things, things she couldn't even imagine because no man had ever spoken them to her.

"Take care," he said.

Her eyes clung to his for another timeless moment. And then, with a final soft tap on the roof of her car, he stepped back and she started her car and drove away.

Numbly, Lauren guided her car through her neighborhood and eventually out onto Spring Hill Avenue, which would take her to the Holt Company. For once her thoughts were not remotely concerned with work or its problems or her responsibilities. At a red light, she caught a look at her dazed expression and simply leaned back, closing her eyes.

What's happening to me?

How could she be so enthralled with a man she'd known only a few days? It was as though she'd been given a taste of something so intense and compelling that she had abandoned her innate caution, thrown it to the winds. It was as though a stranger had been lurking deep inside her, waiting to emerge after a twist of fate brought Ryder into her life. It was as though she was finally alive after... after what?

Lauren had spent years in a marriage with Clay Holt without feeling intense emotion. Clay had not been very passionate. The bond they shared was based on friendship, their backgrounds, similar interests. They'd married for all the right reasons, or so she'd always believed—compatibility, mutual respect, genuine affection. But not passion. There had been no breathless, intense *need* between them.

Only during her pregnancy had Lauren felt anything that came close to her feelings now. But something about the way she was feeling today brought back the emotional turmoil of those months. The sensual side of her nature had been carefully restrained most of her life. And her marriage to Clay was no exception. But when she'd carried Justin, there had been moments when she'd known there was more. Something, some element had been missing in her life.

Clay had been a scientist, a thinker. Logic and pragmatic action had been his way. When he discovered soon after their marriage that he was sterile, he immediately went about seeking a method to ensure that Lauren would not be denied the ultimate experience of childbirth. In expectation of the long life they would have together, he wanted her to have a baby and, he'd pointed out with a scientist's direct reasoning, modern techniques made childbearing possible through artificial insemination.

Lauren didn't think about her pregnancy often. It was just that somehow Ryder Braden brought back all those feelings. Why that should be so was as much a mystery as the medical miracle that had filled the void of a passionless marriage with the gift of Justin's birth. There was no connection surely, and yet... Lauren sat still, staring into space, knowing only that in her heart there was a very compelling connection.

CHAPTER SIX

RYDER DROVE THROUGH the mid-afternoon traffic, heading for the Holt Company. He was on his way to return Lauren's designs. As usual of late he was soul-searching, something he'd done more of the past few days than in all the rest of his life. After a day spent watching Justin, teaching him, enjoying him, Ryder was hooked. He'd been totally off the mark to think he could keep Justin at arm's length, spend a few casual hours with him here and there and then simply walk away. There was a link between him and the boy that could not be ignored. Walking away from Justin appealed to him no more than walking away from Lauren.

First the mother and now the son. A faint smile laced with a dash of self-directed mockery played at his mouth. For a man who didn't intend to get involved, his behavior was more than a little strange.

He pulled into the parking lot just as Jake Levinson was getting out of his car. Good, Ryder thought, he wanted to talk to Jake. The unexpected appearance of that reporter at the ball field still bothered him, plus the fact that the questions he'd fired at Lauren had been based on inside information. Maybe Jake could shed some light on the situation, otherwise . . . otherwise, he'd take care of it himself.

Ryder lifted a hand in greeting as he got out of his Blazer. When Jake spotted him, he waited, and Ryder fell into step beside him as they headed for the entrance to the business offices of Lauren's plant. Jake glanced down at the tubes under Ryder's arm that held the rolled-up designs.

"Did you get a chance to look them over?" the lawyer asked.

"Yeah."

"What do you think?" Jake reached for the door and waited for Ryder to precede him.

Ryder shrugged. "It's like everybody says—Clay Holt was a genius. The designs prove it." Using one of the tubes, he halted Jake before they reached the receptionist's desk. "And they're original, Jake. I'd stake my soul on it."

Nodding slowly, Jake smiled. "I'm relieved to hear it, especially from you." He studied Ryder for a moment. "And you're definitely going to help us?"

"Yeah, I'm in." Lauren's troubles concerned him in some elemental way; there was no use trying to deny the feeling.

Jake's smile widened. "Good, good."

"Jake—" Ryder hadn't moved. He looked past the lawyer down the hall where he assumed Lauren was waiting. His expression was troubled. "The designs are a gold mine, Jake."

Jake looked slightly confused. "That's what the lawsuit's about, Ryder."

"Except for one thing."

Jake stared at him, waiting.

The receptionist was watching them curiously and Ryder took Jake's arm and turned slightly, keeping his voice low. "Some of the designs are incomplete," he said. "Did you know that?"

Jake shook his head. "No. Are you sure?"

"The ones that were pirated by NuTekNiks are noted on the plans and they appear to be complete, workable designs. Others lack a couple of vital elements here and there, but the gaps are enough to make them unusable." He looked at Jake directly. "Did Lauren bring me everything, or are the originals in a vault somewhere?"

Jake was silent, thinking. "You're saying she purposely withheld the complete designs?"

"It looks like it."

Jake shook his head. "I don't think so, but there's one way to find out." Again, he attempted to walk.

Ryder put out a hand. "There's one more thing. Has she received an offer for the business?"

There was an immediate change in Jake. "Where did you get an idea like that?"

"Is that a yes?"

"You know that's privileged information, Ryder."

"Then maybe if I flashed a press badge, I could have the details," Ryder said, sarcasm in his tone.

"What the hell are you suggesting?"

Ryder studied the lawyer in silence and then made an impatient gesture with one hand, muttering something resembling an apology. He hadn't suspected Jake, not really, but years of corporate intrigue had made him a cynic. "Last night, a reporter just happened to find Lauren at the ball field," he explained. "One of the things he wanted to know was whether she was accepting NuTekNiks's buy-out offer. And since she knew nothing about a buy-out, I'm wondering how that reporter knew. Also," his tone took on a hard edge, "I'm wondering how he knew where she was."

Jake swore. "For the reporter, I can't say," he told Ryder. "As for the buy-out, that's what I'm here for now. I think she'll turn it down flat but they've made her an offer. I didn't receive it until late yesterday and I don't have any idea who leaked it."

"It would have to be damn generous to even come close to the value of those designs," Ryder said.

Jake met his gaze squarely. "That's for Lauren to decide," he said, then added in response to Ryder's skeptical look, "She knows the value of the business, man. She's not going to be suckered in by the sleazes at NuTekNiks."

"Damn right."

Jake's eyebrows rose. No two ways about it, that statement had a protective ring to it. Intrigued, Jake watched as Ryder's gaze strayed in the direction of Lauren's office. Unless he was very much mistaken, Ryder had the possessive look of a man with Lauren's welfare at heart. Very interesting, he decided suddenly, when not five days before, he'd had to practically beg to get the two of them together.

"How was the ballgame?" Jake asked. He'd wondered what could possibly interest a man like Ryder in a Little League game. Now it was coming to him. Lauren was a beautiful woman.

Ryder dragged his gaze from the hall back to Jake. "Uh, okay. You were right, Justin's a terrific kid."

"Uh-huh."

"His interests are at stake here, too," Ryder said after a moment.

Feeling better suddenly about Lauren's predicament than he had in a long time, Jake grunted and shifted the weight of his briefcase. Motioning Ryder ahead of him, he said, "So let's go hear what the lady has to say."

SHE SAID NO.

Lauren offered them both scotch and they drank it while watching her pace the length of her office reeling off all the reasons why she wasn't amenable to a buy-out. Ryder was silent, savoring his drink and the sight of her. Each time he saw her she became more beautiful, he thought, roaming the shape of her cheekbones and the delicate strength of her chin with admiring eyes. Without hearing the words, he watched her mouth as she told Jake exactly what he could report back to NuTekNiks. She moved her arms to emphasize the message and he caught a glimpse of the soft, white swell of her cleavage where her blouse came together. His body tightened involuntarily.

Jake tossed off the last of his drink. They'd already covered the matter of the incomplete designs and unless Ryder had totally lost his touch in judging when a person was lying or telling the truth, Lauren was as surprised as Jake had been.

With his hand on the doorknob, Jake turned, dividing a look between Ryder and Lauren. "Now that we've turned down NuTekNiks's offer, I expect them to try some other delaying tactic," he said. "The thing that would really clinch our case is to come up with something to prove outright theft of the designs."

Ryder nodded, acknowledging the message. After months of futile effort, it was obvious that Lauren and her present staff weren't going to be able to prove any such thing. From Jake's expression he appeared to believe Ryder might manage it. When the door closed behind the lawyer, Ryder raked a hand against the back of his neck and drew in a deep, resigned breath and accepted the inevitable. He was up to his neck in Lauren's troubles whether he'd wanted to be or not.

"I don't know what else we can do," Lauren said, sounding discouraged. "With so little documentation, it seems impossible to prove anything."

"Don't worry, the proof's around here; it's got to be." Ryder glanced around the office. "It's just a question of finding it."

Lauren heard the confidence in his voice and took heart. "I don't suppose it bothers you that everyone's been looking for that proof for almost a year and getting nowhere," she said.

"Not really." He folded his arms across his chest. "But now, it's time we got really serious."

She cleared her throat awkwardly. "You know, you don't really have to do this, Ryder."

"I need to see the complete designs, Lauren. The only way to do that is to turn this place upside down for the missing elements. Without them, any expert opinion is worthless." He smiled. "So, you see, I do have to do this."

In spite of the fact that she had Jake as her lawyer, and she'd never doubted his ability, Lauren had always privately feared that everything was slipping away from her—Clay's life work, the company he'd entrusted to her, Justin's inheritance—everything. She didn't know what it was about having Ryder in her corner that dramatically lessened her doubt and fear about her legal battle. But it did. Smiling at him, she found herself wondering suddenly how he and Justin had made out together. If her son had found him half as appealing as she did, then they'd gotten along like a house afire.

She studied him in silence for a moment and then nodded. "Okay, but will we recognize them if we do stumble on them?"

"I can read a set of specs, Lauren," he said dryly, then added, "and so can Justin, by the way."

"Oh?" Her pulse quickened with interest. "How did it go today?"

"Put your mind at ease," he said, smiling. "He hammered and sawed like a pro. If he chooses, he can be a carpenter some day."

"Really?" Lauren felt a little surge of pride that Justin had acquitted himself well in Ryder's eyes.

"Really. But from the way he talked, I'd say he's leaning more toward sports or computers."

"Tell me about it," she said with feeling. "Between Little League and soccer and that computer in his room, it's all I can do to get him to do his homework."

Ryder opened his mouth to tell her she was too easy on Justin, but with a quick shake of his head, left the words unspoken. The thought had come quickly and naturally, as though parental responsibility was something they shared. He looked at Lauren, thinking of the awesome bond they did share. Maybe he should tell her now. Maybe, before he got in any deeper, he should lay it all out before her. He didn't know what to do. Ryder raked a hand through his hair and tried to fix his mind on robotics and the missing designs.

His eyes fell on the computer terminal behind her desk. "What about the material stored in the computer?" he asked, walking around to examine it. "From everything I've learned about your late husband, he seems the type to fully utilize a PC." He turned and lifted a questioning brow. "Has everything that he stored in them been accessed?"

"Yes, Michael checked all that." Lauren came to stand beside him, smiling as she touched the keys. "You're right, of course; Clay loved computers. And he passed his fascination right on to Justin. As soon as he was old enough to comprehend the concept, Clay bought him a PC. Just like Clay, Justin took to it like a duck to water."

"We need to find the missing designs, Lauren," Ryder said abruptly. She glanced up quickly, looking puzzled at his tone, but he went on impatiently, "Clay must have stored them somewhere. Was this his office?"

"Before I inherited it, yes," Lauren said, wondering what had annoyed him. Had he underestimated her problems and was Ryder now wishing he was elsewhere?

"No vault or wall safe?" She shook her head. "Which areas of the plant are secure?" he asked. "Besides Research and Development, I mean."

Looking more and more dismayed, she told him none. Access to Research and Development was controlled with strict security, but there was nothing there that hadn't been scrutinized over and over again.

Frowning, he examined the interior of the office again. "What's behind those two doors?"

Lauren walked over and opened the first one, revealing a private bathroom. "The other one is an old storage room," she told him. "I never use it and neither did Clay."

He tried the knob and found it locked. "Let's take a look anyway," he suggested.

Lauren scooped up her keys and went to the door. She unlocked it and then, before going inside, flipped the light switch which was on the outside wall. Ryder followed, but failed to catch the door which swung shut behind them. When he tried the knob, it was locked.

"Don't worry," Lauren said, dangling the keys in front of him. "We're not locked in."

"I'm happy to hear that," he said, casting a quick look around the long, narrow room. There was no window and a fine film of dust lay over everything. There didn't appear to be any particular order to the stacks of boxes and documents. Some weren't even labeled.

"I'm afraid it may be difficult to find anything in here," Lauren said, echoing his thought. She began opening cabinet doors which appeared to be the only logical location in the room for anything valuable.

Ryder made his way down the middle of the room. Bending to examine a few of the boxes, he discovered the dates marked on them were too old to be useful. Looking around with a frown, he picked up a set of obviously old specifications and slapped them against his thigh, making a face when the dust flew. "Hope you're not allergic to dust," he said.

"Not dust or anything else that I know of," she said, closing the cabinet with a soft bang. "Are you?"

"No, only shrimp."

"Oh." She glanced up, smiling. "So is Justin. Isn't that—"

"No offense," he said, "but this place is a mess." He tossed the specs back where he found them.

The brusque note was back in his voice. Hearing it, Lauren was mystified. She looked around at the evidence of Clay's untidiness and smiled ruefully. "Looks like Justin inherited more from Clay than a propensity for computers. This place looks a lot like Justin's junk shelves on the patio."

When he didn't reply, she turned to look at him.

Somewhere in Ryder's mind, he registered the curious, arrested look on Lauren's face, but he didn't acknowledge it. He was too busy coping with the raw, frustrating effect of her words. *How could Justin inherit anything from Clay!* he wanted to shout at her. Maybe Clay had taught Justin, nurtured him, offered the fatherly guidance that had gone a long way toward molding Justin into the person he was today. But the boy didn't inherit anything from him.

"Ryder—" Suddenly, the lights went out, plunging the room into total, inky darkness.

Ryder froze. Calming his thoughts about being alone with Lauren in a dark room, he struggled to recall the layout of the storage area. The floor, he remembered, was an obstacle course. The walls were lined with boxes and junk, some of it stacked high and balanced precariously. Moving around blindly, they could dislodge something and it would all come tumbling down on their heads. On Lauren's head.

"Stay where you are, Lauren," he told her, instinctively moving toward the soft sound she made. "Where's the light?"

"It's outside on the office wall," she said, sounding disgusted instead of concerned.

"Great. Terrific," he muttered. He stepped around something in his path and stubbed his toe painfully on something else. "Ow!" He swore viciously.

"Wait," Lauren said, "I think I—" She gave a little cry when her elbow connected with a cabinet door that she'd left hanging open.

"Damn it! Just stay there, Lauren." Disregarding the debris littering the floor, Ryder plowed through the pitch blackness, homing in on the sound of her little moans. He reached her just as she straightened up and the top of her head connected with his chin.

"Ouch!"

"Ow!"

Swearing again, Ryder reached out blindly and hauled her into his arms. For a second, he couldn't tell much about what he was holding on to. In the total darkness that enclosed them, she could be backwards or upside down in his arms, he thought, just before he was swamped with sensation. Then there was only the sweet scent of her and the silky brush of her hair, and then her temple, against his mouth. In a sudden rush of heat and hunger, the softness of her and the womanly shape of her body were revealed to him. There was nothing blind or awkward in the way she fit. Her head was nestled in a spot perfect for her under his jaw. His hands curled naturally around the shape of her and everything in him urged him to pull her closer, tighter.

"Are you hurt?" he whispered thickly in her ear, his heart hammering so hard and loud in his chest that he could barely hear the sound of his own voice.

She must have whispered, "No," because he felt the small, negative toss of her head. He sucked in a deep, unsteady breath, flooding his senses with the intoxicating scent of her. Independent of his will, his hands moved over her back and the sweet curve of her spine, and then lowered to caress the soft, beguiling shape of her hips. His mouth skimmed her temple, her cheek, the corner of her mouth. A wave of longing washed over him, so deep and so compelling, that it was almost painful. Resisting that need was suddenly beyond him. Moving like a man in a dream, he breathed in deeply and covered her mouth with his.

It was nothing like a first kiss. They both fell into it headlong as though each was starved for the taste of the other. Lauren's lips opened under Ryder's and her body went soft against him. Her hands played over his back, then crept up until her fingers sank into his hair and held on as their tongues met. He groaned, muttering something, and tightened his arms so that she was crushed to him.

But one taste of her wasn't enough for Ryder. He craved more and more. Breaking the kiss, he turned his head to the curve of her neck and shoulder, grazing and nipping the sweet-smelling flesh. He stopped at the V of her blouse and with fingers that were unsteady, began to unbutton it. He found one breast and freed it, taking the weight in his palm, probing the nipple with his thumb.

"This is what I wanted to do this morning," he told her, in a voice rough with passion. She moaned and he raised his head to kiss her again, hotly, endlessly, fired by wild, hungry need that blotted out everything except how good she felt in his arms. How right...

Ryder came to himself with that thought and tore his mouth from hers, pulling away so abruptly that he castigated himself when he heard the soft, bewildered sound she made.

"Hell, I'm sorry, Lauren." His breath was heavy and labored. Desire still clawed at him, burned in him like a hot flame. He turned from her, sensing that she was still aroused, still willing. More than he'd ever wanted anything, he wanted to drag her back into his arms.

"This shouldn't have happened," he said in a low tone.

She was silent, but he heard the soft, rustling sounds as she adjusted her clothes.

"It won't happen again, Lauren," he promised. He knew she was feeling confused, and he squeezed his eyes shut, wishing he was somewhere else, anywhere else. She was probably cursing the day she'd ever laid eyes on him. He knew he was. He felt as though he'd been run over by a train—a part of him rejoicing the sweetly uninhibited way she'd responded and another part of him guilt-stricken for failing to exercise some control.

In the dark, Lauren's fingers fumbled with buttons. She was still reeling, not only from the explosion of passion between them, but also from the unexpected way Ryder had suddenly stopped. Lauren tucked the tail of her blouse back where it belonged and took in a long, unsteady breath. She was not a stranger to physical desire, but no kiss had ever, ever affected her this way. Surely he'd felt it, too?

"Lauren?" Ryder's tone was soft, husky with concern.

"It's okay," she said, backing away from him cautiously. He was easy to locate, even in the dark. She could feel the heat emanating from him, smell his musky maleness. "Stay where you are," she told him, keeping her voice steady with an effort, "and let me get the door. I've got the keys."

"No." The word was abrupt and she was startled. He must have sensed it because his next words sounded gentler, coaxing. "Please, just...just stay there and let me," he said his hand finding hers unerringly in the dark. He ignored it when she jumped as though jolted by a live wire. "Give me the keys."

She was reaching into her pocket when light suddenly flooded the storeroom making them flinch and blink, both temporarily blind.

"Lauren, are you in there?" It was Michael Armstead. He pushed open the door further and frowned as he took in the sight of Lauren and Ryder standing side by side in the litter of the storeroom. "What in the world are you doing here?"

"Michael." Lauren's mind went blank. Ryder touched her arm, urging her in front of him, and she moved forward into her office.

"How did you know anyone was in the storeroom?" Ryder asked, deflecting Michael's curiosity.

Michael pulled his gaze from Lauren to give Ryder a hard look. "I knew she hadn't left for the day. I came to her office looking for her and heard voices in the storeroom." He turned to Lauren again. "What's going on, Lauren?"

"I . . . we . . ."

"It has to do with the lawsuit," Ryder said smoothly, his tone discouraging more questions.

Michael's frustration was almost tangible as he turned back to Lauren. "Lauren?"

In truth she had almost forgotten the reason she and Ryder had originally been closeted together. She was still reeling from the kiss.

Michael studied the flush on her cheeks. "Is something wrong, Lauren? Are you sure you're okay?"

"I'm fine, Michael. Really."

Armstead hesitated, glancing at Ryder with cold suspicion before turning back to Lauren. "I don't have to remind you that I'm here anytime you need help, do I, Lauren?" When she merely gave him a brief, albeit polite smile, he added, "You know that, don't you? All you have to do is ask."

"I know, Michael," she said. "And I appreciate that. But you can help me best by doing exactly what you've been doing—staying on top of things here at the plant while Jake and I and—" she glanced at Ryder, not quite meeting his eyes "—Mr. Braden here, concentrate on our court case."

"If you're absolutely certain," Michael said, still reluctant. "But call me if you need me, will you promise me that?"

"I promise. And thanks, Michael."

"I think you hurt his feelings," Ryder said as the door closed behind Armstead.

Lauren didn't respond. She would have to be deaf, dumb and blind not to sense the male hostility that thrummed in the atmosphere whenever Ryder and Michael were in the same room together. A part of her was dismayed by it, while another part of her was pleased. But that brought her thoughts back to the few precious, magical moments in Ryder's arms. Had she only imagined the fierce, tender hunger in Ryder as he'd kissed and caressed her? Then why had he stopped?

"Lauren?" Something in his voice drew her eyes to his. "I'm sorry about what happened—grabbing you like that."

Lauren's gaze fell.

"I meant it when I said it won't happen again."

Lauren was amazed at her thoughts, amazed to discover how much she did want it to happen again. But she nodded mutely, her face turned from his. "There's no need to apologize," she said quietly. "It's forgotten."

With another long look at her, Ryder nodded once and then left.

"MAYBE HE'S MARRIED."

Startled, Lauren turned quickly to look at Clancy, who shrugged and leaned over, placing her wineglass on the low coffee table in front of the sofa. "It's been known to happen, sweetie."

Lauren gazed into pale gold Chablis and considered the possibility that Ryder was a married man. It was one logical explanation for the way he seemed to react to the growing attraction between them. It would also explain his promise not to touch her again. But somehow . . . She brought the wine to her lips slowly. "I don't think so, Clancy."

"What do you think?"

"I don't know." She leaned back against the cushion and recalled the rush of sensation that had flooded her body as Ryder's hands and mouth had worked their magic. "Whatever his reason, he forgot it in the heat of the moment and then when he remembered, he stopped cold. I don't think you forget a wife like that."

"Hmm," was Clancy's response.

"I want him, Clancy."

This time it was Clancy who was startled. She laughed. "I don't believe you said that. Is this the terribly proper, inhibited Lauren I know, lusting after a man and admitting it?" Clancy reached for the wine bottle and checked the contents. But it was still half full. "How much have you had to drink?"

"You see, Clancy!" Lauren came up off the sofa and began to pace the room. "If you'd said to me that you wanted a man, I wouldn't have batted an eye. You're honest and candid about your feelings, and you have been from the moment you first put on a training bra."

"I never owned a training bra," Clancy said.

Lauren whirled around. "That's just what I mean! I wore a training bra before I even needed one. My mother insisted."

"She meant well," Clancy offered.

"She was a tyrant."

"Steel magnolia is the term, I believe," Clancy murmured, sipping Chablis.

"I've been a good little girl all my life," Lauren said. "I've always obeyed rules, meekly followed directions, done all the things expected of me as a proper Southern woman. I've never taken chances, Clancy."

"You've never had to, Lauren."

"No. I've always chosen the easy way. Even when I married Clay, I did it because I knew it would be a comfortable marriage. There was no passion, but I overlooked that. I knew he loved me and would never hurt me."

Clancy watched her intently. "Ryder might hurt you, Lauren."

Lauren nodded. "He might, but I'm willing to risk it. I've been too inhibited all my life and too ready to place my destiny in the hands of other people. I need to be more assertive. I need to break the habit of relying on someone else to solve my problems. I know it won't be easy to change. But I'm going to."

"I think you're being too hard on yourself," Clancy said, her wine forgotten. "You could hardly handle your legal problems without a lawyer and you certainly needed help to run the plant. Why this soul-searching, all of a sudden?"

"It's a little complicated," Lauren said, frowning. "I like Ryder and I want him. But, true to form, here I am waiting for him to take the lead, to do all the running after me even though a relationship with him would make a major impact on my life."

"And your emotions," Clancy added.

"Exactly." Lauren stopped and looked at her friend. "You wouldn't hesitate to let the man you wanted see how you felt, would you?"

"Well—"

"You wouldn't, Clancy." Lauren's expression revealed her insecurity, but her chin was set, her mouth firm. "It might backfire on me. Instead of capturing his interest, he may be turned off."

Clancy smiled. "Or flattered all to hell and back."

"I mean it, Clancy."

"Hey, fine. All right. So... here's my advice." Clancy lifted her wineglass high. "Go for it!"

Lauren's smile was a little strained, but she finished off her wine, and then with a flourish sent her wineglass sailing across the room toward the brick fireplace. Clancy's mouth fell open as the crystal splintered in a shower of tiny fragments.

"I can't believe this," she said, studying Lauren as though she had sprouted a third eye. Suddenly she grinned. "This is a new twist. Usually it's you urging caution and me about to embark on some reckless venture."

Lauren nodded. "True, and look how interesting your life has been."

Clancy was shaking her head. "This really is too much. Here am trying for a little stability, getting ready to settle down and ounting on you to show me the way."

Lauren eyed her shrewdly. "For Jake's sake?"

Clancy sighed. "Is it that obvious?"

"Yes," Lauren said flatly.

Clancy groaned and then with a return of her natural optimism, she giggled. Copying Lauren, she lifted her wineglass. "Then I repeat, let's go for it!"

UNFORTUNATELY WHILE LAUREN had resolved to go for it, the object of her obsession had decided to do just the opposite. Ryder wasn't going to renege on his promise to appear as the expert witness in Lauren's court case, but he wasn't going to get involved in her personal life any more than he already had. Since he couldn't keep his hands off her, he resolved simply to avoid her. And for two weeks, he managed to do just that.

He was amazed how hard that was to do. Ryder thought of a dozen reasons to go back to her company. Or her house. He came up with so many creative ideas to spend time with Justin that he surprised even himself. But he didn't act on any of them. Instead he confined himself to a single visit to Jake Levinson in order to discuss the possibility of someone inside Lauren's company feeding secrets to NuTekNiks.

As it turned out, Jake suspected the same thing, he told Ryder, but flushing the informer out had proved impossible.

"Any idea who it could be?"

Jake shook his head. "Not a clue." He looked at Ryder. "You got any ideas?"

Ryder knew who he wanted it to be, who it might be. Michael Armstead was in a position to leak vital technical information. Lauren trusted him completely. But he was so visible that he made an almost too-perfect suspect. Just because Ryder had taken an instant dislike to the man didn't mean he was guilty of industrial espionage.

"What do you know about Armstead?"

Jake nodded slowly. "You, too, eh? I don't know, Ryder. It appears he's just exactly what he seems—a damn good salesman who worked his way all the way up to the top job. I've done some discreet background inquiries—without Lauren's knowledge, you understand—and turned up nothing." He looked squarely at Ryder. "He's got his eye on Lauren, o course."

"He seems to manage time with Justin, too," Ryder said a he got up and went to the window. "Justin's a kid; it's easy t fool a kid."

"I wouldn't say that," Jake murmured, "especially abou Justin."

Ryder laughed then. "Yeah, he's something else. I noticed it, myself."

Speculation sent one of Jake's eyebrows upward. "Bee spending some time with him, yourself, have you?"

"A little." *But not nearly enough.*

"Uh-huh."

Silence in the room stretched out while each man was occu pied with his own thoughts. Then Jake sat back in his chair.

"I've got an idea, Ryder."

Ryder's expression was impassive while he studied the law yer. He knew that look. He had seen it on Jake's face before but it had been years ago. He said as much and watched a wry smile spread over Jake's face.

"That was a long time ago, buddy," the lawyer said. "We were just kids then—high school kids pulling juvenile pranks. Besides, you always managed to pull everything together be fore the stuff hit the fan." He dismissed Ryder's objection be fore it could be spoken and leaned forward suddenly. "You know what Lauren really needs, Ryder?"

Ryder grunted. "You're gonna tell me, right?"

"She needs somebody on the inside looking out for her in terests."

"She's got Armstead."

"Yeah."

"You think I ought to go to work at the plant?"

"You picked up on my idea so fast it makes me wonder whether you've already thought of it."

"I know you too well," Ryder said.

"You would be perfect, Ryder," Jake coaxed. "Lauren could hire you as . . . as . . ."

"Production manager," Ryder supplied, leaving the win dow to begin pacing. "Not too elevated in the management hi erarchy so that I'd be alienated from the majority of her employees and not so low that I couldn't have access to sensi tive data."

Jake's eyes lit up. "Just enough authority to stick your nose into everything."

"Uh-huh."

"I see you have been thinking."

Ryder met his gaze with a bland look. "It'll screw up the expert witness thing," he reminded Jake. "No Holt employee would be acceptable to the court."

Jake shrugged. "So, we'll go with one of the other three men on your list."

Ryder went back to the window. "What if Lauren doesn't agree?"

Jake didn't even dignify that with a reply. Instead, he laughed. "You want to tell her or shall I?"

"You do it."

DRAWING A DEEP BREATH the man shifted in his chair, impatient for everyone to clear out. He stared at his watch, waiting. This time what she wanted was more difficult. He had tried to reason with her, but she was a hard woman. She never let up. Her promises meant nothing. Always it would be the last time, she said. A chill crept over him. What if all her promises were lies? What if everything he'd done was for nothing? Despair rose, almost choking him. No, he couldn't, wouldn't think like that. It could never be for nothing. The purpose he had was everything. His goal was as pure and perfect as his love.

He stood suddenly, realizing the plant was empty. In his hand was a plastic card. Getting inside the restricted area after hours was the biggest obstacle. He had to wait until he was certain everyone was gone. Once inside he knew his way around well and could take care of her latest demand. He made his way down the corridor. It would have been better if he could have stayed late. But he had to be seen leaving, just in case.

He could not afford to make any mistakes at this point. He was close. So close. It would only be a little while now and he would be happy again. What he was doing was dangerous, but the risk was worth the taking. He would do anything, dare everything, risk all for his Anna.

Looking once over his shoulder, he inserted the card, punched out the security code and waited. The door buzzed. He pushed it open and stepped inside.

CHAPTER SEVEN

"I DON'T KNOW WHAT to say, Jake." Lauren leaned back, her lunch forgotten. She hadn't seen or heard from Ryder for over two weeks and now suddenly he was applying for a job as her production manager. Delight and hope blossomed in her. "Are you sure you didn't misunderstand?"

"I didn't misunderstand, Lauren." Jake grimaced as he inspected the insides of the ham and swiss sandwich he'd bought from the snack bar's vending machine.

"I thought Ryder was going to be our expert witness. He can't do that if he's on the payroll."

Jake gestured with the sandwich. "No problem, he's already contacted a friend of his who's agreed to serve as our expert."

Lauren stared at him. "Why is he doing this, Jake?"

Jake pushed the sandwich away untouched. "He believes... We both believe that someone right here in your plant is feeding Clay's designs to NuTekNiks. As production manager, Ryder will be free to circulate. He'll get to know the employees, hear the scuttlebutt on the floor, be everywhere."

"I'm not arguing that," she said. "It's just that—"

"You're free to refuse, of course, but I've got to say I think it's the perfect opportunity to discover who's selling you out, hon."

She searched his face intently. "You didn't answer my question, Jake. Why is he doing this?"

She was never to know. Jake was distracted by a small flurry of activity across the room. He glanced past her shoulder with a startled look and then his expression was suddenly blank.

"Hi, Mom!" Justin called out. In jeans and sneakers with untied laces flying, he ran ahead of Clancy St. James, who was negotiating the crowded lunch tables with the help of her exotic cane. Shaking her head, Lauren watched her son twist through the tables at his usual breakneck pace. When he skidded to a stop beside her, she tweaked the bill of his treasured 'Bama baseball hat. "Hi, kid."

"No, no, don't get up." Clancy waved a hand as Jake politely started to rise, seemingly unaware of the guarded look in his gray eyes. With her cane, she hooked the leg of a chair and deftly pulled it around. Eyeing Lauren's yogurt and Jake's sandwich, she wrinkled her nose. "Wow, a gourmet lunch. You guys really know how to live it up," she said, sinking into the chair.

"Hi, Clancy." Lauren smiled and then glanced at her watch. "You two are forty-five minutes early, you know that?"

"Yeah, I know it and you know it," Clancy said, and playfully whacked Justin across the kneecaps with her cane. "But your firstborn here apparently wants to get an early start. I'm lucky I managed to hold him off till now."

Justin grinned and dodged just out of reach. "I didn't want to be late," he said, wide-eyed. "All that traffic and maybe a couple of accidents could have messed us up for hours."

"Give me a break!" Laughing, Clancy threw up her hands.

"Well, it's true!" Justin insisted. "Army Surplus could be closed by then."

"Army Surplus?" Jake repeated, looking at Lauren.

Shaking her head, Lauren waved Justin in the direction of the door with both hands. "The new hamburg-flipping robot is being tested in Research and Development, honey. Go check it out. I'll be finished here in a jiffy." Her smile lingered as she watched him dash off. She turned back to Jake. "In a couple of weeks, Justin's Boy Scout troop is camping out overnight and we're shopping this afternoon for his gear. He insisted on 'authentic' military stuff, hence Army Surplus." She smiled at Clancy. "Having camped out in some of the world's most desolate places, Clancy volunteered her services."

"For the shopping and the camping," Clancy put in. "I'm feeling magnanimous."

"And I really appreciate it. I'd probably embarrass Justin beyond words with the extent of my ignorance."

"No problem, sweetie." Clancy generously dismissed Lauren's inexperience. "Between Justin and me, we'll have you whipped into shape in no time."

"Don't they have men for that kind of thing?" Jake asked tightly.

"For what, whipping her into shape?" Clancy asked facetiously.

"For roughing it outdoors with a bunch of kids," Jake said evenly.

"You volunteering?" Clancy's blue eyes dared him.

Lauren cleared her throat hastily. "Clancy, have you had lunch? The ham and swiss is . . . interesting, right, Jake?"

Jake grunted and wordlessly passed his sandwich to Clancy.

Clancy just as coolly nudged it back to him before arching an eyebrow and dividing a look between her friend and her ex-fiancé. "So . . . you two still working on a strategy for flushing out the resident bad guy here at the plant?"

Jake's eyes narrowed, and for the first time he spoke directly to Clancy. "What's that supposed to mean?"

She shrugged innocently. "What? Wasn't I explicit enough?"

Jake looked at Lauren. "The less people who know about our suspicions, Lauren, the better our chances are of getting to the bottom of this," he said.

"Oh, for Pete's sake, Jake, stop sounding like a tight-assed lawyer!" Clancy said, exasperated. "Lauren didn't tell me anything. I'm reasonably intelligent *and* a journalist. Look into my baby-blues, man. I'm not blind. Anybody who can see beyond here—" she tapped the end of her freckled nose with her index finger "—can figure it out. Lauren's secrets are being pirated by a greedy-gus right here on her own turf."

She leaned back, eyeing them both speculatively. "So what do you plan to do about it?"

"It's none of your damned business what we plan to do about it," Jake told her through his teeth.

Lauren could count the times on one hand that she'd seen her unflappable lawyer ruffled, but at this moment, there was no mistaking the signs that Jake was tightly furious. All his attention was focused on the impudent redhead taunting him. Lauren might be his client, but he'd obviously forgotten her existence. It was just as well, Lauren thought. She had no desire to get caught in the crossfire between these two.

"I happen to consider it my concern if my best friend's business is being sold down the river," Clancy informed him.

The plastic spoon Jake held snapped in half. "Yeah, well, your concern's duly noted. We'll try to remember to send you a thank you note when you ride off into the sunset as soon as you can stand on that." He jerked his head toward her wounded knee.

"I'm not going anywhere," Clancy said.

Jake snorted. "I've heard that before."

"Well, you can believe it this time." Deliberately she turned to Lauren. "What happened with Braden?" Her eyes widened. "Don't tell me! Your new image must be work—"

"It's nothing like that," Lauren started to say.

Clancy was confused. "Well, what then? Isn't your super-duper lawyer here managing everything?"

"Well . . ." Lauren glanced at Jake and shrugged helplessly. "Ryder isn't the witness anymore; he's coming to work for me instead."

Clancy blinked. "Say, what?"

"Lauren, for Pete's sake!" Jake shoved his chair back but Lauren stopped him from rising with a soft touch on his arm.

"Jake, Clancy is my friend. I trust her."

"Thanks, sweetie." For a second the usual brashness in Clancy's blue eyes softened. "I thought this guy was a world-class executive. Why's he coming to work here?"

"I was just asking Jake that very question," Lauren said.

"And I was just trying to get a moment of privacy with my client to explain," Jake snapped.

"We need someone right here on the premises to expose whoever's stealing Clay's designs," Lauren said quietly.

"A plant in the plant!" Clancy looked delighted. "Great idea. Braden has volunteered?"

Lauren nodded. "Apparently."

"And you're going for it?"

Lauren hesitated and then nodded again. "I think so."

"Whose idea was it?"

That was something Lauren wondered about herself. She glanced at Jake. "Yours, Jake? Or Ryder's?"

"Both," Jake said shortly.

Clancy leaned back, looking pleased. "Well, frankly I can't wait to meet Mr. Wonderful. He sounds like my kind of guy, managing to shake you up, Lauren, and wringing a somewhat daring idea out of Jake, for a change." She shook her head and put her hand over her breast. "It's almost too much. Be still my heart."

"Clancy!" Lauren laughed helplessly.

"Look out, woman." Jake's tone was softly menacing. "You think you know me, but I just may decide to prove that you don't."

Clancy eyed him from beneath tawny lashes. "Promises, promises . . ."

Jake made a choking sound and Lauren quickly dipped into her yogurt. These two might come to blows before lunch, such as it was, was over!

"I've got an idea, Lauren." Looking thoughtful, Clancy tapped a forefinger against her lips. "One that goes hand in hand with your plan to put a spy in the plant."

"Leave Lauren out of your schemes," Jake told her flatly, "whatever they are. If I know you, it'll be some hare-brained, reckless idea with no chance of success and every chance of somebody getting hurt." He glanced pointedly at her knee.

"I got this when a car bomb blew up in front of a sidewalk café in Paris," Clancy shot back. "I was drinking coffee and reading the morning paper."

Jake's hand shook slightly as he crushed sandwich wrapping and a paper plate in one hand. "This doesn't concern you, Clancy."

"Look, isn't Lauren capable of deciding for herself if she wants to hear my plan?" Clancy demanded. "You're her lawyer, Jake, not her daddy."

"I'm warning you, Clancy—"

Lauren put a hand on Jake's wrist. "Just a minute, Jake. What do you have in mind, Clancy?"

Clancy hitched her chair closer to the table. "Look, we know somebody over at NuTekNiks is getting Holt designs; we're all agreed on that. You've already got Braden looking from this end. But what about from that end? If we cover the situation from both sides, we double our chance of success."

"How would we cover the goings-on at NuTekNiks?" Lauren asked. "We can't put a spy over there."

"I can't wait to hear this," Jake muttered.

"I thought maybe a little undercover work," Clancy said, ignoring Jake. "Have a couple of hangouts near NuTekNiks's plant under observation, see what we can pick up. After hours, of course. Guys talk about their work over a few beers." She sent Jake a sly look. "It's sort of a variation on the pillow-talk theme."

"Hmm." Lauren frowned, thinking it over. "You might have something there, Clancy. But how—"

"Nothing to it," Clancy said with a negligent lift of one shoulder. "Hang out a few nights, have a few beers, just like the guys. No telling what we'll pick up."

Jake's palm hit the table with a crash. "Absolutely not!" he roared. "I forbid it, damn it!"

Clancy glared at him. "I meant me, Jake, not Lauren. I'll go undercover. I've done it before. We're not going to harm a hair on the head of your client. Look, there's this place called the Blue Marlin. It's frequented by the guys at NuTekNiks; I've already checked it out. I'm bound to—"

"You're bound to get more than you bargain for at the Blue Marlin, you little fool," Jake said heatedly. "Be reasonable for once in your life, Clancy."

"There is nothing unreasonable or reckless about the idea, Jake," Clancy said. "It's just as rational as your own plan to put Ryder Braden in the Holt plant. In fact, there's absolutely no difference except in your head. You've got a man spying here at Holt. Why not have a woman at the other end spying on NuTekNiks? Or is your thinking so antiquated and chauvinistic that a woman simply mustn't be allowed to do that?"

"Looks like you're about to find yourself in deep water, my friend," Ryder said, coming up behind Jake. His slow smile included both Lauren and Clancy. "Lawyers—" he shook his head "—always ready to argue."

Jake laughed shortly. "Glad to see you, too, buddy. Take a seat and help me try to talk some sense into these two."

At the first sound of Ryder's deep voice, Lauren's heart had leaped wildly. It was the first time she'd seen him in anything except jeans. Even though he was outfitted exactly like a thousand other businessmen in town, as well as half a dozen of her own employees right here in the plant, no other man brought her senses alive or made her body burn with just one look. No other man very nearly took her breath away.

"Mr. Wonderful, I presume," Clancy said, her eyes dancing.

With a start, Lauren gathered herself and quickly introduced Clancy, who studied Ryder frankly, her head to one side. "I guess you know these two think you're a cross between James Bond and The Equalizer." She grinned when Ryder winced. "Frankly, it's about time somebody decided to actually do something to flush out the traitor in our midst."

Ryder glanced quickly at Lauren. "Jake told you what we discussed?" When she nodded, he continued, "What do you think?"

She looked uncertain. "I don't know what to think."

There was a moment of odd tension as Ryder studied her. "It was just a suggestion," he said, his eyes suddenly shuttered. There was an edge to his voice when he said, "You have more than enough help as it is."

"Maybe so," Lauren agreed. "But Clay's designs are still being compromised. If you're willing to pretend to be the production manager for the Holt Company, then the job and all its dubious benefits is yours."

Ryder hesitated for a heartbeat before the corners of his mouth lifted in a smile. "You've got yourself a production manager, lady." He reached for her hand and pulled her to her feet. "Now, come and break the news to my boss, whoever he is."

Before she could protest, Ryder's hand was at Lauren's waist gently but firmly nudging her along. "Clancy," she called hastily over her shoulder, trying to keep pace with his long strides. "If Justin shows up here before I run into him in the plant, tell him that something came up and I'll be back as quickly as I can."

"No problem," Clancy said, looking amused.

"Justin's here?" Ryder asked, slowing down once they were out of the snack bar. He liked watching her, listening to her, being with her. Now that he had Lauren to himself, he intended to prolong their time together, to savor her company. He had a legitimate excuse, he told himself.

"Hmm? Oh, yes. He's somewhere in the plant." She frowned slightly. "I don't know where Michael is at the moment," she murmured.

"He spends a lot of time at the plant?"

She gave him a startled look. "What kind of question is that? He's general manager, Ryder. It'll be understandable if he's a bit disgruntled to find out I've already hired someone without consulting him."

"I'm talking about Justin, Lauren, not Armstead."

"Oh." It was obvious that Ryder wasn't concerned about Michael's reaction, or anyone else in the plant for that matter.

'Clancy and I are taking Justin to get outfitted for a camping trip as soon as I can break away,'' she explained. ''He's probably entertaining himself just now at the expense of some poor engineer.''

''Asks a million questions, does he?'' Ryder pushed at a door and waited for her to precede him.

''And then some. I admit I feel slightly overwhelmed sometimes.''

''Who's taking him camping?''

She laughed wryly. ''Would you believe, me? And Clancy, thank goodness.''

Ryder arched one eyebrow. ''With an injured knee?''

''She swore to me it would be healed in two weeks.'' Lauren looked up into his face and laughed. ''When you're desperate, you tend to overlook niggling details.''

Her smile hit Ryder with the force of a doubled fist. He stared at her, feeling desire curl through him and settle in, heavy and deep. Two weeks away from her and he'd forgotten the immediate, intense reaction she triggered in him. How could he keep his hands off her if he saw her every day? But damn it, she needed him. And he needed to do this for her. And Justin.

As they toured the plant, Ryder kept a low profile, preferring at first just to observe. They weren't half through before he began to revise his thinking about what he'd stepped into. He had planned to make a mental list of employees who might be suspect, but after an hour it seemed nearly everyone Lauren introduced fell into that category. The company still operated with the close-knit harmony of a family owned and operated business. Security was a joke.

''This is our think tank.'' Lauren pushed a plastic card into a slot and punched out a security code. Ryder grunted, thinking that at least there'd been one area Clay Holt had felt compelled to safeguard. He followed as Lauren entered an all-white room where half a dozen technicians were bent over drawing boards.

''Clay, of course, was the driving force here. Fortunately his undeveloped ideas weren't lost. He recognized talent and creativity in others and encouraged the participation of his 'crew,' as he called them, in his experiments. We've almost perfected a robot designed to help a handicapped person. It isn't operated manually, but responds instead to voice commands. There are still a few bugs in it.''

Ryder listened to Lauren's detailed explanation of the problem and found himself revising his assessment of her as well. She must have put in countless hours after her husband died in order to familiarize herself with reams of technical material as well as the functional and administrative details of the company. According to Jake, her original career had been in marketing and public relations. Just holding the company together would have been a major feat, but she'd gone far beyond that, he thought, watching her use her hands to help explain a particularly complicated concept.

There was an air of vulnerability about her that he found almost irresistible. But she had shown remarkable strength and resourcefulness as a businesswoman. He wondered what other surprises were hidden beneath her cool exterior. It would be a delight to unveil her secrets slowly, one at a time. With just one kiss, she had turned to flame in his arms. He had been haunted ever since by thoughts of what it would be like to take her to bed.

The idea was so tantalizing that for a moment he was lost in the sheer pleasure of imagining himself entangled with those long, long legs, of losing himself in the sweet, warm depths of her body. Already he knew that loving Lauren would demand more of him than the quick, unemotional coupling of past sexual encounters. She would be— "Here's Michael now," Lauren said, and Ryder felt the tension that rippled through her as she looked beyond him to Armstead approaching them. "Good, it'll give me a chance to fill him in on what I've done."

Ryder wanted to shake her. "You sound like you've done something wrong, Lauren. The company belongs to you, not Armstead. You don't have to have his approval to make a management decision."

"He may see it differently," she murmured, moving a little closer to Ryder. "Michael, ah . . . I've just been showing Ryder around the plant."

Armstead looked at Ryder before silently lifting his eyebrows. *A classic tactic,* Ryder thought and wondered if the man often resorted to intimidation in his dealings with Lauren. He felt a surge of anger and barely resisted an urge to protectively place his hand on her waist.

"I've just been added to the payroll, Armstead," he said, issuing the statement flat out with a feeling of satisfaction.

"He's our new production manager, Michael."

Armstead's eyes narrowed. "I wasn't aware you were interviewing for that position, Lauren. Or any position, for that matter."

Lauren shrugged. "Well, Ryder is extremely qualified, Michael, and when I learned he was available, I knew we'd be lucky to have him." She appeared not to notice Armstead's lack of enthusiasm. "Production is scrambling to meet the terms of that new contract from Hy-Tech in Pensacola. Wasn't that what you said this morning? I assumed you'd appreciate all the help you can get."

"Of course." After a deliberate glance at Ryder, Armstead drew a deep breath. "The shipping department is having some difficulty." He turned to Ryder. "You can start down there tomorrow, Braden."

Ryder almost laughed. He had no doubt that Armstead would dearly love to bury him in the shipping department.

Lauren spoke up quickly. "To tell the truth, Michael, I've decided not to confine Ryder to one area. To begin with, I think it's best for him to be a free agent and sort of float around. His experience is broad based, and heaven knows, we can use all the help we can get." She gave Ryder a look of approval. "I thought we'd let him use his own judgment."

Ryder watched Armstead's jaw clench. He was beginning to understand Lauren's hesitation in going over his head. This was a man who did not cotton to any intrusion into his territory.

"Come into my office, Lauren. We can't talk here in the hall." Confidently Armstead stepped back to allow her to precede him.

"I'm afraid I don't have a minute right now, Michael," Lauren said politely. "Tomorrow morning at nine you can brief Ryder in my office on those areas where we're in trouble."

"I can see your mind is made up," Armstead said tightly, making a visible attempt to rein in his temper.

Lauren looked at Ryder, who gave her a slow, conspiratorial wink unseen by the other man. Her mouth twitched with an urge to smile, but she conquered it. "Yes," she told Michael softly, "my mind is made up."

He gave her a curt nod. "Then I'll see you both tomorrow."

Ryder felt Lauren wince when Armstead went inside his office and closed the door with a restrained snap. "A peach of a guy," he said dryly.

Lauren sighed. "Really, he is." When Ryder snorted, she felt compelled to defend Michael. "It's perfectly natural for him to be resentful. I hired you without consulting him and he's supposed to be the plant manager. How would you feel in his place?"

Ryder looked down at her. "The truth?" She nodded. "I would have been furious, too, but I wouldn't have stopped with a few mealy-mouthed objections. I'd have hauled you off to your office alone and given you an ultimatum."

"And I would have fired you."

He shrugged. "Maybe."

She stared at him. "Then why—"

"The fact that he didn't push you a little harder makes me more suspicious."

"It's because he's more than an employee, Ryder. He cares about the Holt Company and he cares about me."

He grunted and closed his fingers around her arm and guided her away from Armstead's office. The last thing he wanted to think about was Lauren's relationship with another man. "I think I've taken enough of your time today. Why don't you head on out?" he suggested. "Clancy and Justin are probably waiting. I'll cover the rest of the plant on my own and we'll talk again when you get back." He had another thought. "Better yet, why don't you do Justin's shopping and go home? I'll come by when I've had a good look around. Then we'll talk."

"Well . . ." It was tempting to turn everything over to him, Lauren discovered. There was something about him that awakened a feminine instinct to lean on his strength. But that was hardly in keeping with her new resolve to take charge of her own life. She hesitated, looking beyond him. "Oh, here's Justin now."

"Hi, Mom." Justin greeted his mother and looked curiously at Ryder.

"Hello, Justin," Ryder said with an easy smile. It still amazed him how much pleasure he got out of just looking at the boy. "How's your birdhouse project coming?"

"I finished painting it yesterday," Justin said proudly. "I'm going to mount it on a tall pole when it's good and dry."

"You need any help with that?" Ryder asked.

"Me and Mom can do it. I looked up in a book how you're supposed to anchor the pole in cement."

Lauren blanched. "Justin—"

His look stilled her protest. "We can do it, Mom."

Territorial rights again, Ryder thought. He breathed in deeply and replied patiently, "You'll want to be sure it's nice and sturdy..."

"I know that," Justin said.

"... because in a high wind, it could topple over."

"Well, sure..." The boy screwed up his face and considered that unthought-of possibility.

"There might be baby birds inside by then," Ryder reminded him.

Justin stared at Ryder. "Aren't the directions on those bags of dry cement you buy to do it yourself?"

Ryder nodded. "Uh-huh, all spelled out for you step by step. You're right, Justin. If you're careful, you can handle it." He glanced at Lauren, making a point to study her slender arms and smooth hands. "With your mother to pitch in and help hoist it, it'll probably be okay."

Following Ryder's example, Justin glanced at his mother as though considering for the first time her size and strength. Inhaling, he shifted his gaze back to Ryder. "I guess you've mounted plenty of birdhouses, huh?"

Ryder kept his expression neutral. "A few. I've had even more experience with dry cement."

"That stuff weighs a ton," Justin said, making a face.

"You're right there."

"How I know is I checked it out at the building supply place."

Ryder nodded. "You seem to have covered all the bases."

Justin chewed thoughtfully on the tender underside of his lip. "You could come over and check me out," he offered casually. "I mean if I start to do something really off the wall, you could stop me. I've noticed you're pretty good at showing how something's done."

Ryder savored the words, feeling a sweet satisfaction in earning a bit of respect from this boy. He was just beginning to realize how much more he wanted. "This afternoon okay?" he suggested. "After you get your camping gear, that is."

New interest quickened in Justin's amber eyes. Cocking his head to one side, he studied Ryder. "You probably know a lot about camping out, too."

Ryder hid a smile. "I've slept under the stars a time or two," he acknowledged.

"We've got two weeks before the trip," Justin said, favoring his mother with a tolerant glance. "Maybe you could give Mom a quick crash course. She's got guts but she's pretty much an indoor person so far." He turned to his mother. "Are you about ready to go to Army Surplus, Mom?"

"Justin—" Lauren sputtered.

"She'll meet you in a few minutes," Ryder told the boy, laughing at Lauren's outraged look.

With her hands on her hips, Lauren watched Justin dash off toward the snack bar, exasperation and amusement mingling on her face. Between the two, she was beginning to feel—

"Ah...Mrs. Holt..."

She turned, distracted. "Oh, Malcolm..."

A man, balding and permanently stooped, made his way out of a cluttered office toward Lauren. His threadbare lab coat was dingy and buttoned up wrong. Ryder judged him to be about sixty, easily the oldest employee he had met today.

"Did you...have you looked at my proposal?"

Lauren's expression showed regret and a touch of genuine apology. "I'm so sorry, Malcolm, I just haven't been able to manage it yet."

The man pushed at a pair of outdated spectacles. "I know you're busy, ma'am, but Armstead tells me you're the only one who can authorize more testing." The request was worded with respect, even a hint of subservience, but it was his fixed, intense gaze that made Ryder frown.

Lauren turned to Ryder. "Malcolm, this is Ryder Braden, our new production manager. Ryder, Malcolm Stern, an engineer who's been with the company since day one. Malcolm worked very closely with Clay."

Stern merely grunted in Ryder's direction before turning back to Lauren. "I've got Armstead's approval, Mrs. Holt. You talk to him; he'll tell you we should go on this one."

"Yes, all right, Malcolm." Lauren touched her temple with two fingers and closed her eyes briefly. "I'll try and look it over tonight, I promise."

The old man grunted again as though debating whether to push the issue. He muttered something, definitely nothing polite, and turned to leave. Ryder felt Lauren's distress as she watched Stern make his way back in the same direction he'd come.

"The resident absentminded professor, I assume," he said dryly, closing the door firmly on Stern and the slightly ratty work area he inhabited.

Lauren's laugh was forced. "Yes, actually. He was the first engineer Clay hired. I know he feels the company is going to wrack and ruin in my hands."

"Enough so that he would sell out to NuTekNiks?"

Lauren looked up, startled. "No! Absolutely not. It's true Malcolm resents me. I'm a woman and I'm not technically qualified to his way of thinking. But he's intensely loyal to the company and to Clay's memory."

"Yeah, maybe," Ryder said, but he was reserving judgment. So far Stern was the first person who didn't fawn all over her. Instead of feeling relieved, it made him slightly uneasy. Clearly the man had little patience in dealing with a woman, especially if she wasn't moving quickly enough on his pet project. Ryder had met Stern's type before. Eccentric, brilliant, single-minded. He glanced at Lauren and found her watching him. "What?" he asked.

"Nothing, just . . . did I remember to thank you?"

He shrugged. "Forget it."

Giving in to temptation, he curled his fingers around her arm. She was soft and warm, delicately feminine. He swore silently. Seeing her every day would be a little bit of heaven and a little bit of hell.

"I'm not going to forget it," Lauren said softly. "Thank you."

They stopped at the door to the snack bar. Ryder's smile as he looked down at her was wry. "The pleasure's all mine."

CHAPTER EIGHT

HOURS LATER RYDER was on his way out of the plant when he noticed the light beneath the door of Lauren's office. He stopped short, aware of conflicting urges—the first being to demand why she was back here working when she was already exhausted. But he was willing to ignore the first to indulge the second—the chance to see her alone, to be with her without the distraction of her friends, her lawyer, her employees, without any of the dozens of people who had claims on her time. He bent his head, shaking it slowly, feeling like a man going down for the third time, and pushed the door open.

"Why the hell aren't you at home, lady?"

Startled, Lauren glanced up into the midnight-blue eyes and tough, too-strong features that were growing ever more fascinating to her. He had discarded his coat and tie and rolled up the sleeves of his shirt. He looked big and slightly rumpled, incredibly sexy. "Ryder..." Even to her own ears, her voice sounded breathless. What happened to the poised professional woman she used to be?

He covered the space between them in a few lazy strides and glanced down at the papers that covered the surface of her desk. "What's so urgent that you had to rush back after promising me you'd go home with Justin and stay there?"

Lauren tossed her pen aside and pushed back in her chair. Sighing, she rolled her shoulders a couple of turns to relieve muscles that had tensed up. "I didn't *promise* to go home," she told him, sounding weary. "This is Malcolm Stern's proposal. I knew I wouldn't have a chance to study it tomorrow, so..." She shrugged. "It was either now or put him off again."

On impulse, Ryder moved behind her chair and put his hands on her shoulders. She tensed up instantly. "Relax," he murmured, finding the knobby bones of her spine with his thumbs while his fingers pressed into the strained muscles of her neck.

She responded with a faint whisper. "Oh, Ryder, that feels wonderful."

Lauren was suddenly pliant and yielding under his hands. Her head fell forward as though too heavy to support her neck. Caught in a snare of his own making, Ryder's senses reacted to the sight of her, relaxed and luxuriating in his touch, with a rush of unbridled desire. He stared at the silky, baby-fine hair at her nape and felt the shudder that rippled through her. He closed his eyes and imagined how it would feel to have her body beneath his while she was overtaken by another kind of trembling.

This was a mistake. Even if the slight, delicate feel of her bones and the warm satin of her skin was like no other woman's, this was crazy. Next he'd be wanting to touch more, and then he'd want to taste... He felt his body tighten, his manhood thicken. Fighting frustration and need, he inhaled and took his hands away.

Ryder swore and pulled the plans around. Somehow he managed to focus on them. Holding his rioting senses under some kind of control, he studied the papers. "Does this thing work?" he asked. A part of him wanted to take her to task for letting a thoughtless old man impose on her while another part of him wanted to take on all the excesses she was burdened with.

Still utterly relaxed from Ryder's skillful massage, she glanced up and gave him a dreamy smile. "Would you believe, yes, it does?"

He tore his gaze away and frowned over a detailed schematic. "How do you know?"

"Before I dug into the proposal, I went to Malcolm and he gave me a personal demonstration in the lab."

"This would be a godsend to a paraplegic."

"I know," she said softly. "A robot that will answer the doorbell, the phone, turn on a stove and the TV, to name just a few of the tasks it can perform. And all commands are voice activated. It can even transfer a person from bed to a wheelchair."

"True state-of-the-art robotics," Ryder murmured, squinting at the penciled notes made in Stern's wavering script.

"You want to see it work?" Lauren stood up.

"You think Stern's still on the premises?"

"It doesn't matter. I can show you what he's programmed it to do, so far." Lauren skirted around her desk, looking adorably flustered when she had to brush against him to get by.

His jaw clenched. "Lead the way."

"It looks like no one's here," Lauren said, hesitating when they reached the door of the Research and Development area. She reached for a switch on the wall and flooded the place with additional light before making her way toward the rear. Ryder followed. He had toured the area earlier, making a mental note to examine the half-dozen models in various stages of completion later in detail. Lauren passed them all and stopped finally before a unit that Ryder recognized from Stern's plans.

She swept out an arm. "Meet Hercules."

Ryder's eyebrow went up. "I could see Stern's interest in his pet project went beyond the norm, but ... 'Hercules'?"

Lauren shrugged, smiling. "You know how proud parents can be."

Did he ever. Ryder watched Lauren walk to the control board and touch a button. With a whirr and a few beeps the robot immediately came alive. "Malcolm put it through a few simple procedures," she murmured, frowning in concentration as she punched out a series of numbers. "I think I can recall a few, just to give you an idea of what ol' Herky can do."

"Be careful," Ryder cautioned, glancing at the long steel arm poised over her head. According to Stern's claims, the robot could perform a task as delicate as moving a chess piece or as impressive as lifting an occupied wheelchair. That kind of strength could be potentially dangerous. "Remember, when you give it a command, it's going to do whatever's programmed," he cautioned.

"Don't worry," Lauren said, still concentrating on the control panel. "It's only going to pick up that telephone." She waved vaguely at a telephone which had obviously been set up as a testing device.

Ryder grunted and moved to stand beside her. "Maybe, but let's not take any chances. Let me just check it out first."

"It's not necessary, really." She bent slightly. "Answer the phone, Hercules," she intoned, speaking into the built-in microphone on the control board.

It happened so fast that both were caught off guard. Instead of answering the phone, the robot's arm came around in a wide arc in the opposite direction. Lauren gave a startled cry as the steel bar connected with her waist and swept her inexorably backward toward the wall behind her. Frantically she tried to stay on her feet. It would crush her! Horror and fear rose in her throat as she felt the force of the cool steel pressing hard into her stomach.

With a harsh oath, Ryder lunged toward the control panel. His face wild, his hands flew over the instruments, pushing buttons, furiously punching out numbers. He swore savagely when the rote movements of the robot could not be interrupted.

"Don't fight it, Lauren!" he told her urgently. "Just be still until I find the code to cancel!"

Somewhere in her panic, Lauren heard him and stopped struggling. Desperately her eyes clung to Ryder's as though to a lifeline. The oxygen was being slowly squeezed from her lungs by the excruciating pressure tightening on her middle. Blackness dotted with tiny flashes of light swirled in her brain. She tried to call out Ryder's name but no sound came. Her hands lifted weakly in supplication only to fall back as she felt herself losing consciousness.

Ryder had never been so terrified in his life. If something happened to Lauren... He fought rising panic. There *had* to be a way to abort the command. He was aware of a slight sound and movement near the door. "Hey!" he yelled, glancing in that direction. "We need some help in here!"

There was no response. In a burst of fury and fear, he slammed a fist into the control panel. Short-circuited wiring popped and crackled and then the lights went out. Without power, the robot was suddenly lifeless.

"Lauren?" Ryder's harsh voice cut through the silence. The room was windowless and black as pitch. Cursing again, he kicked aside something obstructing his path and feeling his way, he started toward her.

"Hold on, sweetheart," he managed to say in a ragged voice. "I'm headed over there. Everything's fine." He thought she made a slight sound, but he couldn't be sure. *Please God, let her be all right, please just let her be all right.*

"Just hold on, love." He reached for her.

"Ryder..." Lauren made a soft, whimpering noise and his knees almost gave way in relief. Instantly he was running his hands over her hair and face, down her neck and shoulders. When he encountered the mechanical contraption that confined her, Ryder swore again. Then he silently cursed himself when she drew a shuddering breath and began to tremble all over. He took her face in his hands and nuzzled her temple and ear, then her cheeks, seeking to comfort her, crooning endearments, wishing he could take her fear and pain into himself. "It's okay, baby. Don't worry, sweetheart. You're okay now, I promise, you're okay."

"Get me out of this, Ryder," Lauren said, shuddering as she strained against the steel bar entrapping her.

She felt his hands moving in the dark, testing the pressure of the bar. "Do you think you could wiggle out if I can force the bar just a little?"

She drew a shaky breath and tried to control the panic that clawed at her. It was so dark! And she was trapped so completely. What was a mere mortal's strength against the steel jaws of a monster?

It was just the way Clay had died.

She must have said the words out loud, because Ryder's hands went back to her head. "Hush, Lauren!" Cupping her face in his palms, he held her so that she knew he was looking directly into her eyes even in the dark. "You're not going to die. This is no time to panic. Don't think about Clay or anything except getting free of this damned robot." He waited a second or two and then, satisfied that she was listening again, he nodded. "I can get you out of here, sweetheart. It would be easier if I had some light, but—"

Lauren shook her head vehemently.

"But I don't want to leave you to try and find a flashlight."

"Hurry, Ryder... please."

"I will." He hesitated, one hand on her shoulder. "Uh, Lauren, you're wearing a bra, right?"

"Yes, why?" She was nearing the line between sanity and blind panic. Why was he talking about her bra?

"It's one of those with a steel wire." It wasn't a question. Obviously he knew. "I think you should take it off," Ryder told her. "The bar is snug against your midriff, but when you try to work your chest past the barrier, you need to have as much flexibility as possible." He cleared his throat, sounding suddenly uncomfortable. "Without the underwire supports, your breasts will have room to, uh—"

"Flatten out," Lauren finished quickly. "Fine. It fastens in the back. Can you reach it?" In the dark he could hear the rustle of silk, sense the movement of her hands as she swiftly unbuttoned her blouse.

"I'm sorry," he said, reaching around her, his breath caressing her ear. Sliding his hands over the skin of her neck and shoulders under the silk blouse, he fumbled a second or two with the clasp of her bra before it suddenly gave way. With another murmured apology, he slipped the straps off her shoulders. Her breasts, free of the satin and wire restraint, burst forth, lush and heavy. He swallowed thickly.

"It doesn't have to come completely off, does it?" she asked, for the first time thankful for the pitch-black darkness.

"No." He sounded curt, but his hands were gentle, as caring as a lover's as he readied her for the ordeal.

Ryder's hands went to the steel bar at her waist again and when he spoke, it was in the patient, almost tender tone he'd often used when dealing with Justin. "Now...when I force this, like I said before, you just wiggle a little and see if it's enough to— No, not in that direction, baby." He laughed huskily. To Lauren the sound was reassuring, but his hands weren't quite steady as he touched her midriff to show her the way he wanted her to move. "Think of your body as liquid, Lauren, and just let yourself go. I think it'll be enough. Okay?"

She nodded. "Okay," she whispered.

"Now, Lauren!" He grasped the bar and pulled again with all his strength.

Banishing everything from her mind except the concept of her body liquified, Lauren raised her arms and began. It was going to work! Inch by inch, she worked her way down. As her breasts encountered the cold steel vise, she winced.

"What?" Ryder demanded urgently, the strain telling in his voice.

"It's okay," she assured him, knowing there was no way to avoid bruising her breasts. There! Now, one shoulder...then the other. She turned her head slightly and...she was free!

Her knees gave way as though they were in fact liquid and she collapsed in a heap on the floor. With a muffled sound, Ryder went down on his haunches beside her. In the dark, she couldn't see anything, but she could feel his warmth, smell the musky male scent of him. She wanted... A sob rose in her throat.

"Are you in pain, Lauren?" He put a hand out and touched her hair. "Tell me where, baby." His voice was uneven, raw with concern. She could feel his breath caress her cheek.

She reached for him. "Please, Ryder," she whispered, "just hold me."

With a groan, he put his arms around her and gathered her closely. For a long moment, he let himself savor the soft, feminine warmth of her while rage and a terrible fear coursed through him. It had been a close call. Without realizing it his arms tightened convulsively.

"I was so s... scared," she told him brokenly, the words muffled against his neck.

"I know, baby, I know." One hand cupped her head gently while he sat on the floor beside her, stretching out his legs, and then leaned back against the wall and pulled her into his lap. "Are you in pain? Are you hurt anywhere? I know your ribs are bruised—" he ran a hand down her ribs and around to her breast "—and your breasts. Did it—"

Nestling under his chin, she shook her head, sniffing. "I'm fine. Just shaken up."

"Hell." Weakly Ryder rested his head against the wall, but his insides churned with a consuming wrath. She shouldn't have to go through any more pain... She shouldn't have to be afraid anymore... She shouldn't be so vulnerable... She shouldn't be so beautiful... She shouldn't be the one woman he wanted most in all the world.

Lauren felt him shift slightly and bury his mouth in her hair. She had been terrified just seconds before. But now, held close in Ryder's arms, she knew only how safe and utterly content she felt. And how right it seemed to be where she was.

"I need to get you out of here," he told her. He drew himself up and got to his feet, pulling her up with him.

"Wait," she said, freeing her hand with a tug. "M... my clothes..." she reminded him in a breathless voice.

Ryder stopped and waited while Lauren fumbled with the straps and hooks of her bra. She was still numb with shock, her fingers awkward as she rebuttoned her blouse. As soon as he sensed she was ready, Ryder wrenched open the door, halting her with a touch on the arm while he made a quick, thorough search of the brightly lit corridor. His eyes were a dark, turbulent blue, still roiling with the aftereffects of rage and fear.

The corridor was deserted. Almost eerily so. Another tremor passed through Lauren. Ryder felt it and wrapped his arm around her, pulling her against him.

"Who was that you called out to when Hercules went berserk?" she asked, shivering again with remembered fear.

"I don't know," he said, his tone hard.

She drew in a shaky breath. Someone had been there and had chosen to ignore her cry for help. She didn't want to accept what that meant. "Surely they could tell we were in trouble."

"Yes." Ryder spoke tersely but his arm tightened around her reassuringly. Lauren leaned into him gratefully.

"I don't know what the hell's going on here," Ryder said grimly, "but as soon as I take you home, I'm going to start asking questions. Somebody had better have some damn good answers."

RYDER DIDN'T LINGER once he'd dropped Lauren at her house. He took a minute to explain to Justin that he would have to put off helping him mount the birdhouse for a day and then got back into his Blazer and headed for the plant. He suddenly craved a cigarette even though he'd given up the habit over two years before. Heaven knew he needed something to calm the tempest raging inside him. His stomach churned with a dozen violent emotions. Ryder had been in many tricky situations— some downright dangerous—but he'd always managed to come through unscathed. He knew now that until today he'd never been gut-deep scared before.

Had it been an accident? The robot was still in an experimental stage. Bugs were common, as in all computer-operated equipment. If it wasn't an accident, was Lauren the target? Or had she walked innocently into a trap rigged for another victim? For him, maybe? And who was behind it? He thought again of the furtive movement he'd noticed in the first panicked moments just after the robot malfunctioned. His eyes narrowed, fixed on the darkened street ahead of him. He couldn't shake a sense of urgency. But more disturbing yet was this feeling of impending danger.

It was the way Clay had died. He remembered the anguished cry torn from Lauren as the robot's steel arm crushed her. Ryder's face contorted and his hands clenched on the wheel as he recalled his helpless panic and mind-blowing fear that he might not be able to save her. Thank God, this time he'd been able to do something. Next time . . .

Tonight's near disaster made a mockery of his vow to distance himself from Lauren. He wiped a hand over his face, not a bit surprised to find himself in a cold sweat. In that split-second moment when he'd been so close to losing her, he'd realized just how much she meant to him. That alone was almost as scary as the experience he'd just been through.

What the hell am I going to do now?

He draped a wrist over the steering wheel and stared into the night. He couldn't walk away and he couldn't take a chance on revealing his deception. He was in their lives for better or worse. He thought of Lauren's passion, the taste of her kiss, the smell of her hair, the feel of her soft body. Groaning, he felt himself grow tight and hard and hot while his level of frustration climbed. Because as long as he continued to deceive Lauren, he couldn't have her.

WHEN THE MAN WAS CERTAIN the widow and her protector were out of the plant, he scurried out of the empty office where he'd secreted himself. He made his way through the work stations, heading for the window that overlooked the parking area. He watched the taillights of the Blazer disappear into the lowering dusk and then, grunting with satisfaction, he turned away, intent upon one final task.

The accident with the robot had been an impulse. He was not used to acting on impulse, but the widow must be discouraged from dropping into his area whenever she pleased. He was certain now that she would hesitate before intruding again. He was already juggling a number of projects which were known only to his contact. Now that the robot's tendency for unexpected behavior was known, no one would venture too closely. Consequently the other secrets he protected would be safe.

Shrugging into his suit coat, he frowned. The new man would not be so easily deterred, he suspected. But he would handle him when it became necessary.

He pulled a set of prints out of a folder that was conveniently wedged in the tight space between his desk and a drafting table. Quickly he slipped it under his jacket. His contact's appetite for Holt secrets was insatiable. He thought briefly of the death of Clay Holt. It was sad. Still, he felt no shame. Only impatience. And anxiety. What was a man to do? There was his Anna to consider. His course was set. There was no turning back.

CHAPTER NINE

LAUREN AWOKE THE NEXT MORNING to the muffled sound of Justin's voice, eager and excited. She opened one eye to read the time and blinked sleep away. *Six-fifteen!* Was he outside already? Good grief, was there no limit to the energy of an eleven-year-old male? Frowning, Lauren reached out to throw the sheet aside and immediately groaned as her bruised ribs protested. Last night's long soak in a hot bath had eased the aches and pains inflicted by Hercules-gone-amok, but she wouldn't move without feeling stiff and sore for a while yet.

Halfway to the bathroom, she stopped. That wasn't only Justin's voice she heard. Mixed with his boyish enthusiasm was a deeper, more maturely masculine tone. Grasping the flower-sprigged sheet, she covered herself and went to the window.

Ryder!

Her lips parted soundlessly. While Justin buzzed around him like a little worker bee, Ryder was calmly shovelling something wet and gray and gloppy out of a wheelbarrow into a hole in the ground. He was shirtless in the morning sun. And sweating. She drew in a breath and felt a sudden rush of heat. She could see the sleek, lean muscles contract as he thrust methodically into the goo and then lifted and deposited it into the hole. His movements were smooth and even, a study in earthy male strength and grace. She had never seen a man look that good.

Suddenly Ryder looked up and saw her. Instead of dropping the curtain and stepping back, Lauren stood rooted to the spot, caught in the intensity of his gaze. Her shoulders were bare, her hair was a mess, she was sleepy-eyed and heavy-limbed. She was tousled, trembling, breathless . . . But with his eyes locked on her, she had never felt more like a woman.

"Mom, come on down!" Justin spotted her and grinned, screwing up his face in the sunshine.

"What's going on?"

"The birdhouse," Justin explained, sweeping an arm toward a white painted pole lying off to one side. The birdhouse, she noted, was already nailed securely to the top. "Me and Ryder are almost ready to hoist this baby up."

Baby, huh? Had her son already adopted Ryder's pet phrases? A smile touched her mouth at Justin's exuberance. Any reservations the boy had harbored about accepting Ryder's help had apparently been forgotten. As she watched, Ryder shifted his shovel and leaned against it, thrusting his hips forward. Nearby, Justin struck an identical pose, propping on a board he'd been using to mix cement. Involuntarily her smile widened. Standing side by side looking up at her, they looked remarkably alike.

"Can you be down in ten minutes?" Ryder asked, his mouth tilted in a half smile. "If so, we'll hold up hoisting this baby. But hurry, otherwise the cement'll set and we'll be in trouble."

"I'll be right down."

Ryder watched the curtain fall back into place, obscuring the tantalizing sight of Lauren, flushed and sleepy-eyed. Turning, his hands weren't quite steady as they closed on the handle of the shovel. He wasn't sure why he was here this morning, other than the fact that when he had awakened at daylight, nothing had seemed as important as seeing her. It had been hard to wait until she woke up.

He was filled with conflicting emotions. With a mighty heave, he tossed another scoop of cement into the hole, hardly aware of Justin poking the board into the mess, conscientiously making sure no air bubbles survived as Ryder had instructed. Justin and Lauren had awakened protective instincts Ryder never knew he possessed. The more he was around them, the more complicated everything became. And now that he suspected Lauren might be in some personal danger, he was honorbound to stay and see her through. He pushed the shovel into the cement, caught in a trap of his own design.

At the sound of the glass door sliding open, he turned. She looked cool and early-morning sexy in a big white shirt and faded jeans. Her hair had been hastily caught up and secured with a red barrette. Her amber eyes smiled into his as she headed across the patio, balancing two mugs of coffee.

"How are you this morning?" he asked, accepting one. He wiped the sweat from his face in the angle of his elbow and took a big swallow, concentrating on not eating her alive with his eyes.

"Stiff, sore, black and blue," she told him. "But other than that, undaunted."

His gaze fell to the deep V of her shirt where the creamy skin and the soft swell of her breasts tantalized. He looked away hastily. "You should take the day off," he said, dropping his voice so that Justin couldn't hear.

"Did you find anything last night?" she asked quietly.

He shook his head. "Nothing. The place was deserted—unusual for R and D, but not unheard of. I found Malcolm Stern's home phone number and called him to report the damage to his brainchild."

"I'm sure he was upset."

"He seemed to be."

"Oh, Ryder, surely you don't think Malcolm would deliberately sabotage his own work? He's devoted years to developing Hercules."

For a minute or two, Ryder studied the tiny dimple at the corner of her mouth and then stared at a point beyond her shoulder. All that loyalty and trust lavished on her employees. When it was all over, would she have anything left for him?

"You can't afford not to suspect any employee, Lauren. But don't worry, I'll take care of it."

Justin scrambled over the pole and began dragging it toward the hole. "Mom, we haven't got time to drink coffee. This cement's gettin' stiff. Put your mug down over there while we get this thing in the ground."

To Ryder, she lifted her eyebrows helplessly, and reached to take his mug. "Aye, aye, sir. What can I do to help?"

"Grab the other end," Justin ordered.

"Nothing," Ryder said in a tone that rang with authority. He looked at Justin. "We can manage without your mother, Justin. She can stand back and tell us whether we're straight or not. You guide the end into the cement and I'll lift the top."

Smiling, Lauren obediently headed for the picnic table carrying the coffee.

"Okay!" Justin shouted as he rolled the bottom end into the cement base. Bearing most of the weight, Ryder raised it. "How does it look, Mom?"

"It's off ten degrees," Lauren reported.

"Which way?" Both males stared at her. Again she was struck by the similarity of their expressions.

"Left."

"How's this?" Justin demanded.

"Perfect."

"All right!"

Hattie Bell slid the patio door open and stuck her head out. "Breakfast!"

Giving the birdhouse a final proud inspection, Justin wiped his hands on his backside and dashed toward the patio. "Boy, Hattie Bell, you timed that just right. I'm starved!"

"When is he not?" Lauren murmured, watching him fondly over the rim of her mug.

"He's either hungry or in a hurry," Ryder observed dryly, giving himself a quick once-over with a towel and then tossing it aside. Picking up his mug, he finished off the coffee.

"Or giving orders," she said, looking at him from under her lashes. "Like someone else I know."

"Habit," he said shortly, wishing he could openly claim the host of similarities between him and Justin. He was only now realizing how many small mannerisms he shared with his son.

"Thank you for helping him," Lauren said, scooting over to make room for him on the bench beside her.

He didn't sit down, but leaned a hip against the table, crossing his ankles. "He would have managed without me," Ryder told her. "He's stubborn and resourceful."

"Hmm," she agreed, sipping her coffee. "But I would have been drafted and subjected to a lot of male ordering around, and the thing would still have listed a lot more than ten degrees."

She glanced up and her smile faltered as she caught Ryder frowning at a mark on her throat. He put out a hand and brushed her collar aside, then gently examined the bruise. A slow flush spread over her skin. He raised his eyes to hers and she drew back at the blaze of emotion she saw there. "I thought you said you were unhurt. This looks like it extends beyond your collarbone. Are you this badly bruised all over?"

"It's not that bad, Ryder, Lauren said. "I'm . . . My skin is pale. I bruise easily. I'm fine, really."

He pulled back and studied her. She didn't move or look away. She returned his skeptical look with grave amber eyes.

With one hand, he took her coffee and set it on the table, and then gently pulled her to her feet.

When he spoke, his voice was low and hoarse. "Is Justin occupied for a while?"

Lauren nodded, still mute, and then her lashes came down weakly as he settled his hands on her waist and flexed his fingers into her soft flesh. She felt a tremor go through him as he drew her close.

"I couldn't sleep last night," he murmured against her temple. "I kept remembering you begging me to free you. I kept hearing the broken little sounds you made trying not to cry." He drew in a rasping breath. "I felt like I was tied in knots. I wanted to hit someone, Lauren."

She kissed the skin under his jaw tenderly. "It wasn't your fault."

"I wanted to get up and come over here."

She smiled against his neck. His skin was damp and tasted slightly salty. "You could have."

He lifted a hand to her hair, catching it so that he could tilt her head to look into her eyes. Long seconds passed as though he couldn't quite believe what he'd heard.

She smiled. "You could have," she repeated softly.

"Lauren." he bent and kissed the corner of her mouth. "You're so beautiful, did I tell you that?" He ran his lips over her cheek, across her nose, and then touched her mouth at the other corner. She sucked in a quick breath and held it, wanting, willing him to do more. She whimpered as his hand came up to stroke the line of her throat and his thumb found the soft spot under her chin, nudging it up until only a whisper separated her mouth from his.

"Lauren . . ."

She opened her eyes and wanted to melt into the midnight blue depths of his.

"Lauren, I know this is crazy, but—"

She made a sound of protest and without another second's thought, discarded the inhibitions of a lifetime. Rising on her toes, she kissed him. His mouth was warm, his lips soft and giving. Her arms went around his neck, urging him closer. She had the initiative only for a heartbeat. He tensed and inhaled sharply, and then he caught her face between his hands, deepening the kiss hungrily. Desire so intense she thought she would surely die from it exploded in Lauren, filling her mind and her senses. The sun was hot, the sounds of morning were all around them, but she might as well have been on a deserted island for all the notice she took.

Ryder's fingers brushed past the smooth skin at the base of her throat, seeking the softness that had tantalized him earlier. He slipped a hand in the deep V of her shirt, trembling with the effort to be gentle, and curled a hand around one soft, full breast. She made a small sound and he tore his mouth away, resting his forehead against hers. A sweet weight still nestled in his palm.

"Did I hurt you, sweetheart?" He was breathing like a man who'd run a marathon. His thumb moved slowly back and forth, savoring the feel of her satiny flesh. "I'm sorry, I'm sorry."

She put a hand on his wrist when he would have withdrawn. "No, don't stop. You didn't hurt me."

Lauren, Lauren. Her name was a wild song in his head, her appeal an irresistible lure. She was so sweet, so desirable, the most desirable woman he'd ever known. He had to close his eyes to cope with the emotion surging through him.

And he had to stop. It was broad daylight. Any moment Justin might appear. Placing one last soft kiss on the curve of her breast, reluctantly he withdrew his hand, but continued to hold her close.

"One of these days," Ryder said, a huskiness lingering in his voice, "It's just going to be the two of us...alone, nobody else around. I'm going to be able to kiss you the way I've always wanted to." His mouth was at her ear. She felt the warm vapor of his breath and shivered. "I'm going to take a long, long time and savor every beautiful inch of you..."

One hand crept slowly around the back of her neck, then inched down, down her spine and came to rest at the small of her back with just enough pressure to let her feel the strength of his need. "One of these days..."

Lauren took a small step back, her shaky fingers going to the open front of her shirt. "I guess we should go in," she said, flushed and breathless.

He stopped her with a touch on her arm. "Lauren, stay home today, okay? I had your car delivered this morning and left the keys on that little table in your foyer. But you don't need to go in. I'll take care of Armstead."

She sighed, tempted to let him do what he'd suggested. But that was the reason she was in the mess she was in. Playing a passive role while the men in her life—first Clay, then Jake, Michael, now Ryder—smoothed the way for her.

She gave him a helpless look, wondering how to put what she felt into words. "I can't Ryder. I have things to do and I really owe it to Michael to personally explain my decision to hire you."

He looked grim, suddenly. "Don't tell him the truth, Lauren."

"Michael isn't selling Clay's designs, Ryder."

"How do you know that?"

"I just do. He's been too supportive, too—"

Ryder straightened abruptly and reached for his shirt. "Maybe that's the operative word." He shrugged into a white pullover. "Personally I think he's a little too everything, too smooth, too pat, too accommodating."

"Ryder—" Lauren put a hand out, not wanting him to leave feeling angry after the beautiful moment they'd just shared. She touched him on the arm and felt the tension in him. "Look, already you suspect Michael and even poor old Malcolm Stern. I value your opinion, Ryder, believe me. But you'll just have to accept that I don't agree with you on everything. I do still run the plant."

"Fine. Great." Ryder swept up his car keys and donned a pair of sunglasses. Gone was the concerned, gentle protector she'd kissed only minutes before. In his place was a grim-faced stranger. "I'm telling you, Lauren, if you keep seeing all your people as saints, you're in for an ugly surprise."

He saw the cool mask descend, but he knew her better now. No matter how she tried, Lauren couldn't control that vulnerable mouth. He stopped suddenly, dragging a hand through his hair. "I'm sorry, sweetheart. I know how you feel about this damn company, about the people in it. But somebody's eating your lunch, Lauren. Somebody's systematically selling you out, and you make it simple for him by refusing to face facts."

She reached out but didn't touch him. She knew his point of view was well reasoned. "It's not Michael," she said stubbornly.

She could not see Ryder's eyes for the dark lenses, but she felt the power of his look and knew he was wrestling with an urge to give her a good shaking.

"Maybe not," he said, his voice soft. "But in my book, nobody's home free yet. And that includes your precious Michael." He was halfway across the lawn to the patio when he suddenly stopped. Turning, he pinned her with a look. "And get Justin back out to clean up and put away those tools. He gets away with murder around here!"

Ignoring her outraged gasp, he stomped across the patio and disappeared.

"DO YOU THINK Justin is spoiled, Clancy?"

"Hmmph," Clancy mumbled, tossing popcorn into her mouth. Her eyes were glued to the Little League field, where play action was interrupted by an altercation between the Bluejays's manager and the pitcher's father.

She stared at Clancy. "Is that yes or no?"

Clancy got to her feet. "Get on with it!" she yelled. "Let's play ball!"

"Clancy—"

"They ought to outlaw parents on the playing field," she told Lauren with disgust, sinking back down in her seat. "Oh, shoot, I spilled the popcorn." She brushed salt and kernels off her jeans. "What do you mean is Justin spoiled? Of course, he's spoiled. He's an only child, too bright for his own good and surrounded by adults who think he's adorable. The kid's only human, Lauren. He'll survive it."

A week had passed since Ryder's provoking remark, but Lauren had been unable to forget it. Justin's welfare was her Achilles heel. She was sensitive about anything that had to do with him. And—she admitted it—she was supersensitive to criticism of her performance as a parent.

Play resumed on the field and Lauren watched Justin neatly scoop up a foul ball and tag a runner who was attempting to steal home. Her heart swelled with pride and love. "Maybe I am too indulgent, Clancy," she murmured. "But—"

"What brought this on?" Clancy asked, looking at her curiously. Her eyes narrowed suddenly. "Has Jake Levinson been advising you on parenting in spite of his total ignorance of the subject?"

Lauren laughed shortly. "Not Jake . . . Ryder."

"Hmm . . . What'd he say?"

"That I let Justin get away with murder." She looked concerned. "Do I, Clancy?"

Clancy was thoughtful. "Well, I wouldn't say murder, but the kid is pretty fast on his feet, and who of us wouldn't weasel out of a few chores if we could think of a way to do it?" She reached over and patted Lauren's hand. "My advice is to forget it. Justin's a good kid."

They watched the ball game a few moments in silence.

"What's interesting," Clancy said then, in a speculative tone, "is what provoked him to say something like that in the first place."

Lauren sighed. "Justin failed to put away some tools and clean up after he and Ryder put up the birdhouse."

"A few tools and a little trash," Clancy murmured. "Doesn't sound much like murder to me. I don't suppose anything else was going down at the time?"

Lauren's eyes remained doggedly on the field. "Such as?"

"Such as a little contretemps between you two."

"We were having a slight disagreement," she reluctantly conceded.

"Yeah, I wondered how things were going at the plant."

"Fine," Lauren said. "He's very good at what he does. Some of his suggestions involve major changes, but he manages people so skillfully that I've had few complaints."

"Understandable," Clancy commented. "The job would hardly tax a man with the kind of experience Ryder has. How's Michael Armstead taking it?"

"Not very well. He was offended that I hired Ryder in the first place and spent the first couple of days trying to persuade me to put some restraints on him." Recalling the scene enacted in her office that morning, a frown appeared. Although she'd expected a negative reaction from Michael, she'd been startled at just how angry he had been.

Clancy nodded knowingly. "It must have been a new experience for Michael when you refused."

"What choice did I have?" Lauren demanded wearily. "With Jake's encouragement, I agreed to the plan. I couldn't very well fold at the first sign of resistance."

"No, of course not," Clancy murmured.

"But I refuse to see everyone at the plant as a suspect the way Ryder does."

"He does have a point, Lauren. Until you know who's stealing Clay's designs, everyone is a suspect."

"I know, but I feel so disloyal letting Ryder in the plant under false pretenses."

"Don't, it's necessary." Clancy dismissed Lauren's misgivings with her typical pragmatism. "You can beg their forgiveness later when Ryder has saved the plant and Clay's designs and made everyone's job secure for the next thirty or so years." She flashed a thumbs-up signal to Justin as he tagged another runner out. "So, what's this I hear about you almost being devoured by one of your beloved robots?"

Lauren stared at her. "How did you hear about it?"

Clancy shrugged. "Jake."

Lauren was momentarily distracted. "Are you seeing Jake again?"

Clancy's gaze followed a high fly ball. "He dropped by my place a couple of nights ago."

"Oh, Clancy."

"We talked, Lauren, nothing more. He's still mad as hell at me for taking that job in Washington."

"He was hurt."

"It was ten years ago, for Pete's sake! I was just a kid with big dreams. I wanted to be a journalist. I wanted to see the world. It would have been wrong for me to try to settle down in a sleepy town in Alabama with all those needs unfulfilled inside me."

"You were engaged, Clancy."

"I wanted him to go with me. He was a lawyer. He could have stepped into a fabulous job in Washington, but he wouldn't leave Mobile."

"Everybody's different, Clancy."

"Yeah."

"I think he's scared to believe you've changed."

"I'm ready now, Lauren. I've seen the world. I've proven myself as a journalist. I'm home to stay." She picked at a speck of popcorn on her jeans and looked up suddenly, her eyes fierce. "And I'm going to make him believe me if it kills me."

Lauren hid a smile. Although a decade had passed, the chemistry between Jake and Clancy was still there. Sparks flew whenever they were together. It was sad that their differences were still keeping them apart.

Clancy propped her chin dejectedly on her cane. "It beats me how Jake can admire Ryder the way he does and yet he puts me down for the very same reasons."

Lauren glanced at her friend in surprise. There were indeed similarities between Ryder and Clancy. Both were stubborn and single-minded; both had pursued exciting careers that had taken them to exotic places. Both were risk takers, and both probably disdained the caution inherent in Jake's soul—her own, too, Lauren admitted wryly. Jake envied Ryder, so why did he reject those selfsame qualities in Clancy? Cheers erupted around her, but Lauren was caught up in her thoughts and barely noticed. That was where she, Lauren, and Jake differed. She was done with playing it safe. She was ready to risk her cozy, comfortable existence for the unknown delights she knew instinctively she could have in a relationship with Ryder. If he wanted her.

A thought caused her brow to knit in a frown. Were Ryder and Clancy afraid of commitment? Maybe. Probably. Ryder enjoyed a life-style admired and envied by many men. Lauren couldn't see him giving it up. As for Clancy, she was ready at last to link her destiny with Jake's, and before long Jake would realize it.

Clancy touched her arm. "Look who's here."

"Ryder," Lauren murmured, feeling her heart soar like a high fly ball. Looking neither right nor left, he was heading directly for Justin, who had already spotted him. A chain link fence separated the players from the spectators, but Justin ran up to it, grinning, and curled his fingers around the steel mesh. As Ryder approached, Justin began to talk nonstop. Lauren watched them with mixed feelings. Justin was hungry for the attention of an adult male. He missed Clay and the masculine camaraderie they had shared. But not just any man would do. He had rejected the attention of several of Clay's old friends. It had been months before Justin had warmed up to Michael.

Now, in less than four weeks...

She watched Justin enthusiastically describe a play to Ryder, who, smiling faintly, gave every indication of listening intently. It wasn't difficult to understand why Justin had fallen so quickly under Ryder's spell. The ease with which he'd won over the men at the plant would work equally well with an eleven-year-old boy.

Pain sliced through her. *Don't let him be hurt,* Lauren prayed. Ryder might genuinely enjoy Justin's company, but it could only be temporary. A man like Ryder would soon be off again to some obscure corner of the world, resuming a life-style that had no place in it for a boy. It was one thing for her to risk her own heart, but she must somehow safeguard Justin's.

CHAPTER TEN

"RYDER? RYDER BRADEN! Jeez, man, is it really you?"

Still smiling over Justin's play-by-play recap of the game's first two innings, Ryder turned, mildly curious, and found himself face-to-face with Neil Putnam. His eyes widened with surprise as Neil grabbed his hand, pumping it and grinning. "How the hell are you, Ryder?"

"Fine," Ryder said, grinning, too. "Couldn't be better."

"What's up, man? How long have you been in town?"

"A while. I called your office and they said you were out of the country on some kind of cultural exchange program. Mexico, wasn't it?"

"Yeah, I took Patti and the twins. We just got back this week." Neil stood back, subjecting him to a long, friendly inspection. "You're lookin' good, Ryder. How long's it been? Five years?" He shook his head. "Time flies, doesn't it?"

"Hi, Dr. Putnam," Justin said.

Still focusing on Ryder, it was a second before Neil glanced down at Justin. When he did he smiled vaguely, and then the realization dawned. Neil shot Ryder a keen look before saying to the boy, "Justin, hey, what's happening?"

Justin shrugged. "Not much, I guess. Where's Cody and Jace?"

"In the stands. Since they haven't made it to practice, they're benched for the time being."

Justin kicked the fence. "Aw, no, we really need them. Curtis Wainwright is still out and coach is playing Shirley Beecham!" His tone was filled with disgust.

"Maybe they can suit up next week," Neil told the boy sympathetically.

"Justin! You're up!"

"Gotta go!" he shouted and dashed off in the direction of the dugout.

A moment of heavy silence stretched between them before Neil spoke. "What the hell are you doing, Ryder?" he demanded.

Ryder's eyes were on Justin at home plate. He watched the boy make a few practice swings, then step up for the first pitch. He connected for a base hit, tossing the bat willy-nilly before charging in a dead run down the line to first. Ryder's eyes were fierce with emotion when he turned back to Neil.

He laughed shortly. "I've been asking myself that same question for the past month."

Neil stared at him and then turned to the bleachers, searching for Lauren. "My God, I never thought— What did Lauren say when you told her?"

Head bent, Ryder curled his fingers into the steel mesh of the fence and kicked idly at the red ball field dust. "I haven't told her. Yet."

Neil swore softly. "I don't believe this."

Mutely Ryder shook his head.

"Well, it won't be long until she guesses."

Ryder glanced up sharply. "Why?"

"Jeez, Ryder, he's just like you."

Ryder's face contorted as a mixture of joy and pain wrenched his soul. He ached to claim Justin as his son. For the past eleven years, he had roamed the world with no ties, no family, no roots, and no particular desire for them. When had his thinking altered so drastically?

Neil's troubled gaze strayed back to Lauren. "Are you involved with her?"

"Yeah, I'm involved." Ryder studied the toe of his shoe, shaking his head wryly. Funny that Neil should put it that way. It was the one thing Ryder had vowed not to do. But involved he was and in every facet of her life, it seemed. In all the ways it was possible, he was involved.

"How, Ryder? Why?"

"I don't know." He shrugged helplessly. "I damn sure didn't plan it. At first it was business. Jake asked me to consult on the lawsuit. You must know about it." He looked at Neil, who nodded. "I met with Lauren a couple of times. Her husband was dead. She seemed vulnerable somehow. I thought she . . . needed me. I knew it was crazy, but I couldn't help myself. Then I saw Justin." He laughed a little, unsteadily. "I tried to back off then, but I couldn't, Neil."

Neil shook his head slowly. "You're playing a dangerous game, Ryder. I guess you know that."

Ryder rubbed the back of his neck. "I know I ought to tell her. Hell, I've got to tell her. But when it comes down to it, I'm scared. I don't want to lose them."

"So, what are you going to do?"

"I'm not sure," Ryder murmured.

Neil's eyes narrowed. "What does that mean?"

What did it mean? Ryder looked at Justin and felt a rush of hunger and regret for all the episodes in the boy's life he'd missed. His first smile, his first step. Who had taught him to ride a bike? Had he cried when he left his mother on the first day of school?

He watched as Justin paced just beyond home plate waiting for his turn at bat. He was relaxed and confident, carelessly tossing the bat from one hand to the other. Someone yelled at him from the bench. He stepped up to home plate, laughing. No, he probably hadn't cried any more than he, Ryder, had cried on his first day of school.

Clay Holt and Lauren had done a good job raising Justin, but deep in his soul, Ryder felt proud of the obvious legacy he had bequeathed his son. Justin was healthy, intelligent, a born athlete. But more than that—he had grit and determination, an inborn fierce pride. What kind of man would he grow up to be? Ryder's eyes shifted from Justin to the bleachers where Lauren sat. How could he bear to walk away now?

"This is all my fault," Neil muttered, his blue eyes distressed. "I've kicked myself a thousand times for what I said that night, Ryder. It was an unforgivable breach of professional ethics. A damn stupid thing to do." He shook his head bleakly. "I'm more sorry than I can say, man."

Ryder's eye was on the playing field where Justin, now on third, was intent on stealing home. He danced tantalizingly out of range of the third baseman. Grinning, he ventured a little farther, ready to go for it. But the pitcher zipped one straight to third, forcing him to scramble madly back to the base, safe.

"Don't be sorry," Ryder told Neil softly, his eyes never leaving Justin.

Neil looked over at the bench where the twins, Cody and Jace, were on their feet yelling in unison for the Bluejays. After a minute, his expression thoughtful, he clapped Ryder on the shoulder. "Take it easy, buddy," he said, his tone gruff. "I'll see you around."

Ryder's brooding gaze followed Neil as the man made his way across the grass to the twins. Sandy-haired and blue-eyed, they were carbon copies of their father. He felt a twinge of envy watching the way they hurled themselves at Neil, laughing and jostling for position beside him like playful puppies. Ryder smiled slightly, remembering the night the twins were born. He'd been envious then, too, but only fleetingly. He had had places to go, things to do. That night—was it eleven years ago?—a family had been low on his list of priorities and a long way into the future.

When had that changed? When had he changed? A roar went up from the crowd. He turned, just in time to see Justin slide in to home plate and then scramble to his feet, flushed with success. He grinned at Ryder. It dawned on Ryder that he wanted the secrets and deception that clouded his relationship with Lauren cleared away. But how would she take it when he tried to explain? Would she even try to understand what he'd done and why? Or, once she knew the intimate connection they shared, would she order him out of her life?

She'd have to understand. He'd make her. Ryder clenched his fingers in the wire mesh of the fence, knowing if he really believed that he wouldn't be walking around with his stomach in a knot most of the time. Neil was right. He had to tell her. But first he would have to clear up the trouble at her plant. There was every possibility that Lauren might be in danger. That possibility took precedence over everything. Until he'd fixed the one, he couldn't do a damned thing about the other.

LAUREN SAT IN THE STANDS beside Clancy and felt her senses react as ever to the sight of Ryder, tall and broad-shouldered, making his way across the grass and then lithely taking the steps up the bleachers two at a time. Despite her best intentions she seemed helpless to control the butterflies that were suddenly doing aerobics inside her tummy.

"Wow."

Startled, she glanced at Clancy. "What?"

"Just 'wow,'" Clancy said, audaciously running her eyes over Ryder. "It's no wonder he has you ready to cast aside all your inhibitions."

Inhibitions. For a moment, Lauren thought how good it would feel to have Clancy's lack of them. Maybe then she wouldn't be walking around in a terminal state of nerves most of the time fantasizing about lovemaking techniques she knew little about and would probably be clumsy performing and not very skilled at, anyway. The brief taste of passion she'd had with Ryder only made her long for the whole feast.

"You're certainly not the only one smitten," Clancy said, patting Lauren's knee sympathetically. "From the way Justin was grinning all over himself talking with our hero, he's in love, too. What are they—bosom buddies?"

"Ryder spends a lot of time with Justin," Lauren said.

"Hmm," was Clancy's only response, but she had a thoughtful gleam in her eye that made Lauren distinctly uneasy.

"Clancy—"

"Sorry, excuse me...ah, pardon me." Ryder was making his way apologetically through the spectators in the stands, heading toward Lauren. People shifted obligingly to let him through.

"Hi," he said, stopping and looking directly into her eyes.

"Hi." She promptly lost the thread of her conversation with Clancy. Ryder, tanned and windblown, stole her breath away. Smiling slightly, outrageously male, he was indeed the kind of man to make any female heart flutter.

"Ryder," Clancy greeted him, inclining her head. Her eyes darted mischievously back and forth between the two of them.

"This is the cheering section for the Bluejays, I take it?" he asked, dropping down beside Lauren.

"It is," Clancy said, standing suddenly and balancing herself with her cane. "Here, take my seat. Our man behind the plate is having a super game. I think I'll just go down there and do like the rest of these pushy people—give the coach a few pointers."

Lauren looked alarmed. "Clancy—"

"Don't worry, I promise I won't embarrass Justin." She gave them a jaunty wave with her cane and started down the bleachers.

The bench was crowded, but Ryder shifted his shoulders, and Lauren found herself nestled snugly in the lee of his arm and chest. Instantly she was assailed by the scent of him—soap, she decided, and just plain warm maleness.

She hadn't spoken directly to Ryder since the morning he'd put up the birdhouse, but she had seen him every day at the plant. She was also kept well informed of his activities by everyone from the lowest ranking clerk to Michael Armstead. It seemed there was no way a man like Ryder could keep a low profile, especially in a plant the size of Holt with its family-oriented work force. That was the way they'd planned it, Jake and Ryder. But as the week wound down, remembering the kiss and her own part in it, she had found herself feeling the tiniest bit piqued by his failure to seek her out, even if it was only to inform her of any progress he was making. Her first effort to let a man know she found him attractive hadn't met with much success.

"I thought you might have found a minute to update me on what you've uncovered so far," she said coldly.

"When I know something for sure, you'll be the first to hear," he told her, his gaze on the field.

Why that statement should irritate her, she didn't know. "You mean the whole week's been wasted?"

"I didn't say that."

"Then you have found something..." She looked at him sharply. "Or someone. Who is it, Ryder?"

"I still only have my suspicions, Lauren." He gave her a deliberate look. "I've learned not to drop any names in front of you without hard-and-fast proof, so I'm still working on that. Besides, I'm not sure exactly what's going down at your plant."

Something in his voice and the grim line of his mouth made her forget everything else. "What is it, Ryder?"

"I don't know. The deeper I dig, the more tangled up I get."

She stared at him. "What on earth does that mean?" Her voice rose sharply, drawing curious stares from the couple sitting directly in front of them.

"This is no place to discuss it," he told her softly, squeezing her arm reassuringly. "Meet me at your office a little early tomorrow morning. We need to talk. You aren't the only one with questions."

The last thing Lauren wanted was to wait. If Ryder had something to tell her, she wanted to hear it. Now. Or rather, just as soon as the game was over. She would drop Clancy off and put Justin to bed and then Ryder could fill her in completely. She should have been getting daily briefings from him, she realized now, instead of tiptoeing around like a besotted teenager.

She was suddenly distracted by a flurry of noise and confusion at the Bluejays' bench. Beside her, Ryder caught her hand and hauled her to her feet.

"It's Clancy," he said, starting down the bleachers, sweeping Lauren along beside him. She craned her neck to see what had happened, and then drew in her breath sharply as she made out Clancy's petite frame lying face up in the red dirt of the dugout. Breaking away from Ryder, Lauren began running. Shooing Justin's team aside, she stared at Clancy.

"What happened?" she demanded, going down on one knee beside her.

"It's this damned—" Clancy's blue eyes swept over the whole Bluejays team that had gathered around and were now gazing wide-eyed at her. "Ah . . . this dadburn knee of mine," she amended sheepishly. "I was talking to the umpire, and suddenly I tripped and found myself flat on my back.

"You were yelling at the umpire, Clancy," Justin corrected, peering at her with the same wide-eyed interest as his teammates. "And then you started waving your cane right in his face. When he stepped back, you stumbled on those extra bats lying over there." Everyone, to a man, turned to look at the bats.

"Oh, Clancy, are you hurt?" Lauren ran a hand over the injured knee, jerking away as Clancy winced.

"I twisted it. It's nothing."

"It won't be 'nothing' in about fifteen minutes," Ryder said, bending down beside Lauren. "It'll swell to twice its size. Come on, I'll carry you to the car. Lauren can drive you home."

"What about Justin?" Clancy said, attempting to sit up. "The game's not over."

Lauren picked up Clancy's cane as Ryder bent and swung her easily up into his arms. Then he waited for Lauren to fall into step beside him. "Justin—" she began, glancing back.

"Don't worry," Ryder said. "You take care of Clancy, and I'll take care of Justin."

Wondering what he was up to, Lauren obeyed.

WHEN LAUREN ARRIVED at the plant the next morning, there were only two other vehicles in the parking lot. One she recognized as Ryder's Blazer, the other a black, low-slung powerful sports model she didn't recognize. She puzzled over it for a moment and made a mental note to find out who'd been conscientious enough to arrive so early.

Gathering up her briefcase, she climbed out of her car and promptly forgot about the driver of the black car. She hadn't had much sleep. For hours she had wrestled with unanswered questions and growing apprehension. Ryder had dropped Justin off, but had declined her invitation to come inside. In spite of her keen desire to question him, Lauren hadn't insisted. It was awkward trying to deal with the strong attraction she felt for Ryder while he was her employee. Not to mention the relationship that was developing between Justin and Ryder. She was frowning as she went up the steps to the entrance. Suddenly everything was so complicated.

To her surprise the main door was open. Shifting her briefcase, Lauren dropped her keys inside her purse. Ryder had probably left it unlocked for her. The sound of her heels echoed hollowly across the empty foyer. The area was usually filled with people and activity, but there was a strangeness about the area this morning that sent a little prickle along her spine. She turned the corridor to her office. Ridiculous.

Her door was slightly ajar, which meant that Ryder was already inside waiting for her. She felt a rush of anticipation and, taking a deep breath, she pushed the door wide.

What was that noise? A muffled thump—scuffling—and voices. Lauren's eyes quickly swept the interior of her office. It was too early to see without the lights. Why hadn't Ryder turned them on? Her hand went automatically to the switch, but never made it. There was another sound, and then a loud crash followed by a man's wrenching groan.

Her eyes flew to the storage room. It was brightly lit, the door wide open. Two men looked up, startled. Shocked, Lauren stared back. For a second or two, nobody moved. Both men had nylon stockings pulled over their faces. Someone lay on the floor at their feet. Her heart stopped. *Ryder!* He groaned and, raising one knee, tried to get up.

His movement seemed to galvanize the two. Without a sound, they headed directly toward Lauren. Her blood froze as she stared into features distorted by taut nylon. But the pair was bent on escape, not on attacking her. Brushing past her, they cleared the storeroom and then sprinted for the door of her office and were gone.

She started toward Ryder on legs that trembled and threatened to give way with every step. Sinking down beside him, she ran one shaky hand over his face. Blood came away on her fingers. "Ryder! Dear God, what did they do to you?"

Using his bent leg for leverage, he started to get up.

"No! Stay here, let me get some help."

He shook his head and got halfway up before groaning and clutching at his middle, his breath shallow. "I'm okay. They didn't have enough time to break anything." Ryder gave her a lopsided grin. "You arrived just in time to interrupt their fun."

Ignoring his attempt to put her off, Lauren slid an arm around his shoulders and helped him sit all the way up. His breathing was labored. Her amber eyes traveled over his face, darkening when she saw his mouth. "Oh, Ryder, you're still bleeding!"

He wiped it away with the heel of his hand. "I'm fine, Lauren. Really." He accepted the tissue she found in her purse and held it gingerly against his lip. "Did you get a look at them?"

She stared at him blankly. "What?"

"Did you see them?"

"Of course. They almost ran over me getting away."

"I mean, did you recognize them?" He began to get to his feet, wincing as he did so. Lauren scrambled to help him, putting an arm around his waist.

"No, those masks... Do you think anything's broken?" she asked anxiously, unconsciously stroking his chest through his shirt.

"Nah, just bruised. I've survived worse." He caught her hand in his and squeezed it. "I nearly died when you came through that door. I didn't know what they might—" He closed his eyes and leaned against an old filing cabinet.

Lauren's heart was in her throat as she reached up to touch his face. It was nicked and battered. His color was off. He turned his face into her hand. His mouth grazed her palm. Tenderness welled up in her along with another emotion far more intense and compelling.

"What's happening, Ryder? What was it all about?"

He pushed away from the file cabinet and, still holding her other hand, led her out of the storeroom into the outer office. Closing the door behind them, he headed for the leather couch

and sat down. When he tried to pull her down beside him,
Lauren refused. She was too shocked and upset to sit. Instead
she went to her tiny bathroom and found a cloth which she wet
with cool water. Coming back, she bent over him and touched
his lacerated lip, murmuring when he jerked his head away.

"Sorry," she said, concentrating on the wound, not the intense midnight eyes that were fixed on her own mouth. "I don't
think a bandage would help. Most of the damage is inside."

He raised his eyes then, and it was like looking into the turbulent, swirling waters of a stormy sea. She didn't get a chance
to be this close to Ryder often, and she seized the moment to
study him. His eyes, she thought, were oddly inconsistent with
the harsh masculinity of his face. The deep blue was enhanced
by a black ring and embellished with lashes that were lush and
slightly curled on the tips. A tiny cut by the corner of one eyebrow would probably be another lasting imperfection. She
found it strangely endearing.

"Somebody wants me to butt out of your business, Lauren."

She blinked. "What do you mean?"

"Those two thugs were waiting for me when I drove up this
morning. They've probably been watching me the last couple
of weeks. I get here early, before six, most days. They waited
until I was inside and then jumped me in the storeroom."

A chill feathered over her skin. Watching her, Ryder felt it
deep in his gut, along with an urge to gather her closely, to offer her his protection, to shield her from whatever the hell was
going on here. But that was just the problem, he thought,
frustration making him feel raw and powerless. He still didn't
know what the hell was going on here.

"Maybe they were just after the missing plans," she said. He
could feel her bewilderment, hear the fear in her voice. "I
mean, you and I were thinking they might be in that storeroom. Maybe that's what they were after."

"No. They had a message to deliver and they delivered it. Get
out of the plant and stay out."

"You mean they actually told you that?"

"They actually did," he said dryly. "And they were very insistent."

"I can't believe this," she whispered, sinking down beside
him. "What can we do? Shall we call the police?"

"Yeah, I think we should report it, but we don't have much to go on. I didn't recognize their voices and we don't have anything but their general physical descriptions, thanks to those stockings."

"I saw their car, but I didn't notice the license plate."

"How about bumper stickers, special equipment . . . anything?"

Lauren shook her head. "It was black and powerful. Fairly new, that's all . . . Seems like there was something on the back glass, but I can't . . ." Sighing, she looked at him. "I'm so sorry you were hurt, Ryder. I never dreamed anything like this would happen. But I sincerely appreciate everything you've done. Even though we—"

"Whoa, lady." He reached out and caught her chin between his fingers. "You sound like you're kissing me off, talking in the past tense like that." He gave her a little shake. "I'm not going anywhere, especially now that they've decided to use muscle. I'm in for the duration, sugar."

"But—" Her eyes swept his battered face. "If I hadn't appeared just when I did, Ryder, who knows how far they might have gone? I don't want any more violence. We'll pursue this through the courts just as we were doing before you and Jake came up with this . . . this scheme!"

Ryder got up from the couch, wincing only slightly. "It's not going to be resolved through the courts, Lauren."

"I know I stand to lose, Ryder. But it's a chance I'm willing to take. Besides, I won't lose the whole company, just the long-term royalties on Clay's designs. I can live with that. Justin and I—"

"Will you listen!"

Startled, she stared at him. He stood in front of her, his legs spread aggressively.

"It's not going to be resolved through the courts because I don't think we're dealing with a simple case of stolen designs. At least I don't think that's all that's going on here at your plant."

"What are you talking about, Ryder?"

He clamped a hand on the back of his neck and kneaded taut muscles. "I'm not sure." He moved over to the window behind her desk and stared outside. "I've been doing a lot of digging, Lauren. Things don't add up. Some of the projects going in Research and Development don't have a damn thing to do with industrial robotics." He turned back to her. "The Holt Company has never bid for any defense contracts, am I right?"

"No... ah, I mean yes, you're right." She shook her head, confused. "I assume you mean robotics to be used by the military on ships or airplanes, is that it?"

"Yeah, that's what I mean."

"No, never. Clay was a pacifist. He would never have consented to modifying his designs for anything other than peaceful, humanitarian purposes. He was an idealist in the truest sense."

"Somebody in the company doesn't share his philosophy, I'm afraid."

"Surely you..." Lauren shook her head. "No, it's impossible. Nothing like that could go on without my knowledge, Ryder."

"You said yourself you aren't technically qualified to run the company, Lauren. You can read a set of specs, but what if somebody is purposely keeping you in the dark?"

"But why?" she exclaimed, springing off the couch. "The company will never bid on a contract for anything other than peaceful purposes, I'd see to that. So what's the point?"

He faced her from behind her own desk. "I haven't figured that out yet. Frankly, I wasn't ready to tell you this much, since I still have more questions than answers. But because these people are beginning to play rough, it's time for you to know we're dealing with more than simple industrial espionage."

Lauren spread her hands helplessly. "To me, industrial espionage isn't simple," she said softly. "Anything beyond that almost boggles my mind."

He gazed at her a long moment. "I wonder if that's what they're counting on."

Her eyes clung to his. "Explain, Ryder. Please."

"You're harassed constantly by production breakdowns, late deliveries, a host of niggling problems," he reminded her. "Since I've been here, I've discovered other things. Last year, there was that fire in the old annex which caused a whopping increase in your fire insurance rates but conveniently didn't do any lasting damage to the main complex." He frowned. "Whoever's calling the shots has had it all his way—a woman alone struggling to cope with new, sometimes bewildering responsibilities and the added complications of a nasty court battle." He didn't say that he still had his suspicions about the accident with Hercules. In light of what had happened to Clay, he had gone over everything in grim detail, but had uncovered nothing.

Lauren was silent, considering Ryder's cool summation of the situation. "It does seem to make some sense when you put it all together that way," she murmured. She looked up suddenly. "Do you think NuTekNiks is in this all the way? I mean, not only Clay's designs, but the other military stuff as well?"

"It's hard to say, Lauren. There are plenty of unscrupulous types waiting to take advantage of a woman in your position."

The story of my life. If she had been more forceful, less passive, less willing to let other people lead her around, if she'd had a firmer handle on things, this probably wouldn't have happened, Lauren thought.

"You're right," she said. "If I hadn't been so naive, they never would have found the Holt Company so easy to sabotage."

He frowned. "That's not what I mean, Lauren."

"Let's face it, Ryder. If Clancy had been in charge of this company, she would have been on top of things from day one."

"What the hell are you talking about?"

"These people, whoever they are, have moved in because of me. You can believe that if I'd appeared more forceful or worldly wise, they would have had second thoughts."

Ryder leaned back, studying her thoughtfully. "No, I don't believe that. And I shudder to think of Clancy in charge. Only heaven knows if the company would have survived."

"Maybe so. But at least Clancy would have done something, not waited around for others to do it for her." Lauren drew in a deep breath. "Anyway, if you're right about these incidents over the past few months, whoever it is certainly won't welcome someone like you stepping in and having free run of the plant."

"Exactly. I'm surprised they waited this long to try and discourage me."

"And are you?" she asked, holding her breath.

His midnight eyes caught hers and held. "Am I what?"

"Discouraged."

Ryder's mouth was grim. "No, sugar. I told you, I'm in for the duration."

"I don't know what to say, Ryder. What if they try again? What if next time they do more than bruise a rib or two?"

"Don't worry, I don't plan to give them another opportunity. This morning, I was a sitting duck—the plant was deserted, I'd left the doors unlocked for you. I won't be that careless again."

Ryder moved from behind her desk and stood close beside her. Immediately Lauren felt reassured. Maybe it was his size and strength, or his innate masculine confidence—she wasn't certain. Whatever it was, she mustn't get too dependent on Ryder and his protection, she reminded herself bleakly.

He leaned over and picked up her telephone. "We both need a cup of coffee, but first the police." He punched out the number, slipping an arm around her waist while he waited.

Lauren leaned back and let him take charge, telling herself it was okay. This time.

THE POLICE CAME and Lauren gave her statement as calmly as she could manage, but she was still shaken. It was hard to believe the incredible things that were taking place in her world. Violence, industrial espionage, defense designs—what would it be next? She was relieved to see Ryder take charge as they prepared to dust for fingerprints and take photographs of the scene of the crime. The term made her shiver.

Handling her life on her own was her responsibility and no one else's, Lauren decided. The company was hers and Justin's. With that in mind, she picked up the phone and dialed the FBI. It was impossible to ignore Ryder's suspicions about clandestine defense work. She wasn't certain just how they would proceed to investigate such matters, but she was certain she should report it. She was also going to keep it to herself, she decided.

Michael Armstead was in Lauren's office minutes after the police departed. "Was that the cops?" He gave her a sharp look before striding over to where she stood watching Ryder and the two officers from her window.

Ryder had accompanied the men to their squad car. He wore his sunglasses, which concealed the scratches and cuts around his eye, but the damage to his lip—that full, sensual bottom lip—could be seen even from this distance.

Michael made a soft sound. "My God, he looks like he's been in a fight. What happened, Lauren?"

Lauren turned and studied Michael silently. His surprise appeared to be genuine. She didn't want to let Ryder's suspicions influence her. Was Michael a traitor and a thief? Could he be capable of the kind of betrayal—personal and professional— that appeared to be going on in her company?

"Lauren?" He was looking at her.

"Ryder was assaulted by two men early this morning, Michael." She waved a hand toward the storeroom. "In there. They had him down and were beating him and kicking him. If I hadn't happened along, there's no telling what might have happened."

Michael came closer, catching her shoulders. "Were you hurt? Did they touch you?"

She twisted slightly, so that his hands fell away, and retreated to her chair. "They didn't touch me. When I appeared, they ran away."

"Thank God." He was silent a moment. "What do you think it was all about?"

She looked directly into his eyes. "I don't know, Michael. What do you think?"

He turned away, thrusting his hands into his pockets. "I'm working on it."

She frowned. "What does that mean?"

"It means the whole company is down the tubes unless we find out what's going on and fast." He faced her suddenly. "It's plain to me that Braden's snooping in areas that don't have a damn thing to do with production. I know, I know." He waved her silent when she looked as if she might speak. "You gave him a free hand. Hell, let him go. I want to know who the sleazes are in our own house as badly as he does."

He paused. "But I'm not going to just sit back and wait to see what Braden turns up, Lauren. I'm going to do a little investigating of my own. I'm telling you up front so you won't freak out if I turn something up that you don't like."

Lauren sighed, knowing what was coming. She had little doubt his suspicions centered on Ryder, but what would be the harm in giving Michael approval to snoop all he wanted? She knew he wouldn't turn up anything about Ryder, but he just might throw some unexpected light on the situation. Every little bit counted at this point.

"Go ahead, Michael. Give it your best shot."

He stared for a second, obviously surprised to get her blessing without an argument. He came up to her, fixing her with a telling look. "Braden has played his cards close to his chest, Lauren. I don't have to tell you we didn't have this garbage going on before he got here."

"No actual violence, no," Lauren replied.

Seizing his opportunity, Michael eased into the chair in front of her. "Maybe you should reconsider giving him total access, Lauren. At least until we know more about him. See what the police come up with on this."

"Jake knows him, Michael," she said patiently. "He trusts him."

Michael drew a long breath. "Jake isn't infallible. He hasn't been around Braden in years, Lauren. Things change. People change."

"But I trust him, Michael." And, for the moment, that wouldn't change.

THE MAN STOOD at the window. The day had seemed interminable. He had waited apprehensively while the police came and went. A tic appeared at his left eye. The whole episode had been stupid and ill timed. He had tried to tell his contact so, but she had not listened. Her greed was such that she was starting to make mistakes. Most important of all, she'd underestimated Braden. He was not a man to be put off by the threat of violence.

He turned away, thinking of his options now, before it was too late. And then weariness and despair settled on him like a dead weight. He had no options.

Anna. Oh, my Anna.

CHAPTER ELEVEN

"I'M DOING IT AGAIN, Clancy," Lauren said.

From a prone position deep in the luxurious depths of the sofa, Clancy watched Lauren refill the two wineglasses on the coffee table. Stretching out an arm, she accepted one of them. "Doing what, Lauren?"

"Waiting to be rescued."

Clancy took a taste of pale, crisp Chardonnay. "You want to enlarge a bit on that?"

"I've already told you what happened today. It was Ryder who was hurt, not me, but he insisted that I go home early, well before the office cleared, with instructions to bolt the doors when I got home and not to let Justin out unless I know exactly where he's going and who he's with. If I had allowed it, he would have cancelled Justin's camping trip."

"Speaking of that . . ." Clancy shifted slightly, favoring her knee. "I feel awful about dogging out on Justin, Lauren. But there's no way I could have hiked in the woods with this knee."

"Don't worry, Justin wasn't exactly thrilled to be going with two women."

Clancy grinned. "You're right there. Tell me, what lucky suckers got saddled with the job?"

"Curtis Wainwright's folks," Lauren said. "But even then, I had a time talking Ryder into letting him go. Just listen to this. Until further notice, I'm not to stay in my office for lunch if I'm alone or go into any restricted area of the plant unless I'm with Ryder. I'm practically a prisoner until this whole thing is cleared up. All for my own good, of course," she added bitterly.

Clancy straightened up and put her glass on the table. "I can see his point, Lauren. The situation does warrant caution."

"What if it's not cleared up for weeks? Months?"

"I think Ryder will probably have the situation in hand before long," Clancy said. "He's not the type to tolerate anybody terrorizing you or yours. He'll take care of the problem. Soon."

"That's just it, Clancy. I'm expected to sit here and let him take care of the problem." Lauren came to her feet and began pacing the floor. "As I said, I'm being rescued again. If it's not Jake or Michael, it's Ryder."

"You can hardly strap on a weapon and become Ms. Rambette," Clancy pointed out. "I don't see that you have much of a choice."

Lauren finished off her wine and set the glass down with a clink. "Look at me, Clancy. I'm healthy, sensible and reasonably bright. Why am I waiting for my destiny to be decided by other people?"

"Is this twenty questions?"

"You remember I told you I've always done the proper thing, always made the safe choices?"

"This *is* twenty questions."

"I've been thinking about something you suggested the other day." She went to the bottle and poured herself some more wine.

A bit wary, Clancy watched her friend begin pacing again.

"What time is it?"

Clancy glanced at her watch. "Eight-thirteen."

"Justin's sleeping over at Scott's tonight, and we're going out.... We're going to the Blue Marlin, Clancy."

Clancy's eyebrows flew upward.

"You said yourself we could just drop in there casually and keep our ears and eyes open. Who knows what we might find out."

Clancy was shaking her head. "I didn't mean you, Lauren. You'd look as out of place at the Blue Marlin as...as..." Her eye fell on the pair of wineglasses—beautiful, fragile antiques—on the coffee table. "As those Waterford stems. Besides, somebody might recognize you."

"I plan to disguise myself."

Clancy was on her feet now. She propped both hands on her hips. "How?" she demanded.

"Makeup, hairstyle, a pair of glasses, clothes. You know yourself, Clancy, people only see what they expect to see. Nobody'll ever expect to see Lauren Holt at the Blue Marlin."

"I don't know, Lauren. I—"

"Please, Clancy. I'm going to do this and I'd feel a lot better if you came with me. After all, you said yourself you've done this before."

"That was in my past," Clancy argued. "The past I'm trying to put behind me. What if Jake finds out?"

"He won't. We're not telling anybody but Hattie Bell." She headed toward the kitchen. "With Justin camping out, I can't take a chance on being out of pocket in case there's an emergency."

"THEY DID WHAT?"

Holding Jake's gaze, Ryder's knuckles went white on the receiver as Hattie Bell repeated herself.

"Damn it to hell!" He slammed down the phone, pinning Jake with a black look. "Lauren and Clancy are at the Blue Marlin," he said. "Have you ever heard of anything as crazy as that?"

Jake resisted the impulse to relate a few equally reckless stunts Clancy had pulled that would make a Friday-night visit to the Blue Marlin seem like a Sunday School picnic.

"Come on," Ryder growled, grabbing up his keys. "We're going to get them."

They descended the steps of the old house two at a time. Ryder got in the Blazer and started it, waiting impatiently while Jake hurried around to the other side. Jake had arrived at his place a couple of hours before to discuss what to do next, now that the opposition had resorted to open violence. The last thing Ryder—or Jake—needed was for Lauren and Clancy to place themselves directly in the line of fire. Gunning the motor, Ryder tore out of the drive and down the lane to the main road driving like a man possessed.

"I didn't think Lauren would do anything like this," Jake murmured.

Ryder pointed an accusing finger at him and said in a tone that boded ill for somebody, "It was Clancy's idea, you mark my words."

"Probably." Jake clenched his jaw. He had just about had it with Clancy. It was just like her—tearing off without a thought for her own skin or Lauren's. If she was going to stay around Mobile as she claimed, she was going to get a glimpse of a side of him she hadn't seen yet.

Having his opinion confirmed seemed to pour more fuel on Ryder's wrath. He swore again and downshifted with a savage motion. "Why in hell can't you control your woman?" he demanded.

"She's not my woman," Jake said. "Yet."

"She sure wants to be!"

Jake grunted, his expression unreadable. "Nobody's ever been able to control Clancy. Me, least of all."

"Only because you refuse to see what's been planted in front of your face for weeks now," Ryder said, looking fed up. "When are you going to give the woman what she wants?" he demanded.

Jake leaned slowly back in his seat, his eyes on Ryder. "And what would that be?" he asked.

"She wants you, for God's sake! She's sashayed around you for weeks now getting about as much response as she could from a damned eunuch. If you'd act like the man I know you are, she'd melt like a snowball in hell. Instead, she's running around with time on her hands scheming up crackpot ideas, dangerous crackpot ideas. Damn it, Jake!"

Jake grunted again and thought of Clancy's fiery nature and how it would feel to have her beneath him, breathless and yielding, melting....

Ryder swerved around a pothole. "And now she's dragged Lauren into it with her! When I get my hands on—"

"Yeah," Jake said, his tone taking on a note of anticipation. "Me, too."

THE PARKING LOT around the Blue Marlin was crowded, forcing Clancy to circle twice before finding an empty spot. They were in her sleek little Mazda, since she had insisted on driving.

"We may have to make a quick getaway," she said in a tone that made doing so sound like a real possibility.

Lauren got out of the car, determined not to act as uncertain as she felt. Never in her life had she entered a bar without a male escort. And even with an escort, she'd never been inside a place like the Blue Marlin. Taking a deep breath, she headed for the entrance. But before they got there, she glanced back when a car, tires squealing, skidded to a stop a few spaces beyond them.

"Clancy!" Lauren's fingers closed on her friend's arm.

"What is it?"

"That car, Clancy..." She pointed to the low-slung, black Trans-Am. Two men were inside, but as yet they made no move to get out. A light flared when the driver lit a cigarette. Suspended from the rear window was a yellow sign.

"Three Fifty-seven Magnum Aboard," Clancy read aloud. She looked at Lauren. "Friends of yours?"

"No! I'm not sure, but I think it's the car that was parked at the plant this morning. I knew there was some kind of sticker or something on the back window, but when Ryder asked I couldn't recall what it said."

Clancy caught her arm and began to haul her back the way they'd come. "C'mon, we're getting out of here. Those guys aren't the type to be gentle just because you're female. They'll recognize you and—"

Lauren pulled her arm free and stopped. "You're probably right if their treatment of Ryder is anything to judge by," she said, her face thoughtful. "On the other hand, this is the first opportunity I've had to connect anyone with the trouble I've had at the plant, Clancy." She gave the other woman a pleading look. "If I leave now or delay long enough to find a phone to call Ryder or Jake or Michael, the opportunity may be lost. The company is my responsibility, not theirs. I can't quit now. I have to do this, Clancy."

Clancy was silent another moment, and then said reluctantly, "Okay, but just do as I say, you hear me?" She turned and they started back toward the entrance.

Lauren squeezed her arm. "Thanks, Clancy. We're going in that bar and we're just going to melt right into the crowd. Nobody'll recognize either one of us. Bars are always dark."

"Oh, sure. And of course you speak from a wealth of experience." Clancy looked at her. "How are you going to see through those ridiculous glasses?"

"I'll manage." Lauren adjusted the oversized tinted glasses that covered a generous amount of her face then she firmly tugged at the tail of her shirt, unaware of the fetching sight she made with her derriere tantalizingly outlined in acid-washed denim. Her outfit was so unlike anything she would ever dream of wearing except in her own backyard that she was certain no one could possibly recognize her. Just in case, she had set her hair with hot rollers and arranged it in a wild tangle of curls that fell forward at her forehead and temples.

They slipped quickly inside the bar. Lauren had an impression of men, lots of men, loud music and laughter. She wrinkled her nose at the smell of smoke and stale beer. Clancy moved confidently beside Lauren and, taking a bead on a spot toward the back of the bar, headed for it. Lauren's courage faltered as she looked around. It seemed as though every male eye in the bar was on them.

"Look straight ahead," Clancy said in her ear. "And don't stop for anything or anybody until we get to that table way over there against the wall."

"Hey, you ladies need a drink?" A tall, bearded giant stepped in front of them, baring a lot of teeth. His chest was so broad that he seemed like a brick wall to Lauren, whose nose barely reached the third button on his shirt.

"No thanks," Clancy told him. "We're meeting somebody."

He put out a hand. "Well, I'm somebody, darlin'."

Clancy dodged the hand and didn't slow down. To Lauren's relief the giant seemed to accept the rebuff with good grace.

"Change your mind, you know where to find me," he called, still grinning.

Quickly they found the table and sat down. Lauren kept an eye on the front door while the barmaid appeared making one or two swipes over the tabletop with a large wet cloth. She transferred a lighted cigarette from one side of her mouth to the other with her teeth.

"What'll it be?" she asked, squinting at them through smoke.

"Perrier and lime," Lauren told her and then winced when Clancy kicked her on the ankle.

"Two beers," Clancy said.

"Light," Lauren said quickly. "Make mine a light beer." Even so, it would be a miracle if she could drink it.

"Two light beers," the woman repeated. "Coming up."

As the waitress left, Clancy studied the crowd while Lauren concentrated on the front door. "Those men should be coming in soon, wouldn't you think?" Lauren asked.

"Not for a while," Clancy replied, shifting so that the barmaid could set the two beers down. As soon as the woman left, she said, "They're getting high in the car."

Lauren stared at her. "How do you know?"

"Did you notice they were smoking?"

"Yes . . . So?"

"That wasn't a regular cigarette, sweetie."

"Oh."

"You ladies want to dance?"

Startled, Lauren glanced up into the grinning features of a cowboy. At least, the man was outfitted like a cowboy, complete with Western shirt, jeans and worn boots. His silver and turquoise belt buckle was enormous.

Clancy laughed. "Both of us?"

Just then the jukebox blared out a new song, a blend of country and swing. "Sure, the Texas two-step," the cowboy said. "A pretty lady on each side of me is how I do my best work." he waggled his eyebrows suggestively. "Whadda ya say?"

"No, thanks," both "pretty ladies" said in unison.

"This might not have been such a good idea," Lauren muttered after they had finally convinced the cowboy to leave.

"No kidding," said Clancy, sipping her beer.

"Just sitting here, we're easy targets," Lauren said, frowning through the thick smoky haze. Behind them was a pool table. One lone man was just finishing a solitary game. After a final shot, he wiped the chalk from his hands and shelved the stick against the wall, where an array of pool cues were neatly racked.

As she watched, an idea came to Lauren. She turned back to Clancy. "Come on, let's go back to that pool table. If we're occupied, maybe they'll leave us alone."

After a moment of surprise, Clancy stood up. "Good idea. I forgot you used to play billiards with your daddy."

"And you probably learned to shoot pool in a place a lot like this one in some interesting corner of the world," Lauren returned with a smile.

"Germany."

"I knew it wouldn't be some everyday, ordinary place."

Clancy grinned. "It was the NCO club at an army base in West Germany."

Lauren saluted her with the chalk. "Rack 'em!"

In five minutes the crowd around the pool table was four deep and nobody was trying to come on to them—at least, not while the game was in progress. Clancy was obviously no shoddy player and Lauren found her own skill returning as they played. At first she was flustered by the audience, but after a few minutes she began to enjoy the men's enthusiasm.

"Bank the five and seven," advised one tough-looking dude.

"Nah, she ought to take that one straight," somebody named Joe countered.

"Whoo-eee! Did you see that shot?"

"Put some English on it, honey!" advised someone directly behind her whose gaze was fixed on her bottom.

"She's gonna run the table, hot *damn*!"

"Keep an eye on the door," Lauren murmured to Clancy as she neatly dropped the seven ball in a side pocket.

Pretending to chalk the end of her pool cue, Clancy leaned close to Lauren's ear. "They just came in."

Crack! The six ball went zinging across the table, striking a hair short of the corner pocket. A collective groan went up from Lauren's fans.

Getting into position for her shot, Clancy said for Lauren's ears alone, "Was that on purpose?"

Smiling enigmatically, Lauren allowed her gaze to drift beyond the crowd to the two men approaching the bar. There was nothing familiar about either one. Maybe if they wore stocking masks... She squinted through the haze, concentrating. But it was no use. Still she was certain the Trans-Am was the car she'd seen at the plant, and these men were probably the two who'd attacked Ryder. Fixing their features firmly in her mind, she turned back to the table.

"We can go now," she said softly.

Clancy nodded. "Nine ball in the side pocket," she murmured and then proceeded to do it.

"Game!" announced Joe. "Rack 'em up again. I'm gonna skunk this sweet thang." He winked at Clancy.

"No, you ain't!" The cowboy stepped up, pool cue in hand. "I already spoke to take on the winner."

"Oh, yeah?" Joe straightened up slowly. He looked the cowboy directly in the eye. "I don't think so."

The cowboy's fist shot out and connected with a thud, dead center in Joe's face. Joe grunted with the force of the blow. Shaking his head, he growled like an angry beast and charged at the cowboy, planting his fist squarely in the middle of the huge silver and turquoise belt buckle.

With the first blow, Lauren and Clancy began to back away hastily. But it wasn't fast enough. The cowboy crashed backward, sending them all to the floor in a tangle of arms and legs. Dazed, Lauren lay beneath somebody's thighs, vaguely aware of the pandemonium breaking out among the bar patrons who were still on their feet.

"What the hell?"

It was Ryder's voice. Lauren put a finger to the nose piece of her glasses, which were cocked at a crazy angle on her face, and straightened them. Looking up, she saw a ring of faces, all of them peering down at her. And Clancy. Blinking to clear the fuzziness from her brain, she focused on the man whose frown was the fiercest.

"Ryder," she said soundlessly.

Swearing, he reached out to pull her to her feet.

"Now just a damn minute," Joe began belligerently. "This little lady is with me. We—"

For the second time Joe was caught with an unexpected blow. Ryder's fist came out of nowhere and clipped him on the chin. He went down like a felled ox.

Without another word, Ryder took Lauren's hand and, turning on his heel, pulled her with him as he strode toward the door.

"What about Clancy?" she said, looking worriedly over her shoulder. She could see Clancy's red curls and—was that Jake?

"That's your lawyer's problem!" Ryder snapped.

JAKE SAVAGELY SHOVED the cowboy aside and pulled Clancy to her feet. "Of all the crazy, reckless, irresponsible—"

Her eyes wide and very blue, Clancy stared at him. "Jake—"

"Don't say a word, Clancy," he warned. Clamping both hands on her arms, he looked ready to explode.

"Hey!" The cowboy pushed Jake with a hand to the chest. "Don't be manhandling this little gal. Me and her gonna shoot a little pool. We don't need you, pal."

Jake was deadly quiet. Then he looked Clancy directly in the eye. "Is that right, Clancy? Do you have a date with this jackass?"

Eyes wide, Clancy shook her head.

"What?" said Jake softly.

"No. No, I don't have a date with this jackass."

Jake nodded and, moving her aside, turned his attention to the cowboy. "You heard the little gal."

Clancy put out a hand, suddenly worried. "Jake—"

Jake brushed her off with a twist of his arm. "You have a problem with that, cowboy?" His tone was still soft, but his gray eyes glinted with male challenge.

Cowboy put up both palms and backed off. "Hey, no problem, man. We were just gonna have a friendly game, but hell, we'll make it another time."

Jake's gaze never wavered. "Not with this woman, you won't."

He waited another deliberate second or two. Nobody made a sound. Jake's gaze passed over the men. Then, satisfied, he put his hand on Clancy's arm and guided her away from the pool table, across the tiny dance floor, through the chairs, past the bar and out the door.

"Where's your car?"

Clancy pointed toward the Mazda. For once in her life she was speechless. She stumbled slightly, having to stretch out her steps to match Jake's furious stride. At her car, she fished in her pocket for her keys. He took them and unlocked the car. She got in, but climbed across the steering console to the passenger's side. In Jake's mood, it was a given that he would drive.

Jake got in, closed the door and locked it, but he didn't start up the car. He still hadn't said a word. Turning in his seat, he looked through the back glass and located Ryder's Blazer. Lifting a hand, he signaled to Ryder, who waved in return. The Blazer started up, its lights flashing on. Ryder and Lauren were leaving. Jake grunted and, still without uttering a word, reached for Clancy.

Clancy let out a startled gasp as he hauled her over the console onto his lap and crushed her mouth with his. The kiss was hard and hot, wild and out of control. For timeless moments, Clancy was transfixed, stunned into uncharacteristic submission. But not for long. She was where she'd longed to be. With a glad cry, her arms went around his neck.

RYDER LEFT THE NEON LIGHTS of the Blue Marlin behind in a cloud of dust. If that was possible on a paved street, Lauren thought, swallowing an urge to giggle. He hadn't said a word since the moment his fingers, feeling like steel clamps, had fastened on her wrist when he'd hauled her out of the bar. His jaw, she noted, stealing a quick glance, looked as if it was made of steel, too. His gaze had not wavered once from the center-line of the street.

A little shiver went through Lauren. She was in for a lecture, she guessed. But she didn't intend to cave in simply because Ryder, and Jake too apparently, believed her place was at home or behind the safety of her desk waiting passively for them to solve her problems. He pulled up in front of her house with a squeal of tires.

Before he had a chance to start lecturing, Lauren had the door open and was halfway up the walk. In a few long strides, he was beside her. "Thanks for the ride," she told him, rummaging in her purse for her key, which she couldn't seem to locate.

"Would this help?" Ryder reached out and plucked the glasses from her face.

She grabbed them back and dropped them into her bag. Finally she found the key, and after fumbling with it, allowed Ryder to fit it in and open the door. When he pushed it open, she went inside, with him right on her heels.

"There's no way I'm leaving here tonight without getting a few things off my chest," he told her, taking her by one arm and shoving the door closed. "Where can we talk?"

"I don't need a lecture, Ryder. I went to the Blue Marlin tonight and—"

"How could you let her talk you into such a crazy thing?" he demanded.

"Who, Clancy?"

"Who else?" he asked impatiently.

Her laugh was short and harsh. "Of course, the whole idea had to be Clancy's," she said, speaking to the ceiling. "I'm a fully grown adult, but incapable of any decisive act, especially one that might hint of slight risk, even if the future of my company is threatened."

He stared at her. "I assumed it was Clancy's idea," he said, emphasizing each word, "because it *was* a risky thing to do. Not because I don't think you're capable of a decisive act.

You've proved yourself over and over, Lauren. But you don't have to do everything yourself. Staking out the Blue Marlin was a crazy thing to do. We're dealing with dangerous people. What if you'd run into one of them?''

There was a certain amount of satisfaction in the look she gave him. "I did. Actually, I ran into two of them."

He was silent for a second or two, his eyes locked with hers while the air crackled with his frustration. Then, catching her by the arm, he led her from the foyer to the living room. The soft glow of a single lamp was the only light. Shaking him off, Lauren sat down on the sofa and then watched him take a seat on the edge beside her.

"You ran into two of them."

His tone was even, but she sensed leashed emotion in him. For some reason, it gave her a feeling of power to provoke him. "I recognized the black car that was at the plant this morning. The two men who were in it came into the bar a few minutes after Clancy and me. I made it my business to take a good look at them."

It was a moment before Ryder could speak. And then his lips barely moved. "That idiot cowboy one of them?"

She laughed. "No, he was just trying to come on to us."

"And the other one," Ryder said, barely managing to keep from exploding into a jealous rage. "The jerk who was stupid enough to think he had some claim on you—what about him?"

She laughed again. "Oh, I think Joe was more impressed with my talent at the pool table than anything else."

"Guess again," Ryder scoffed. "A man doesn't go to fist city over a woman just to shoot pool with her."

"Oh, come on, Ryder. I—"

"You could have been hurt! What if you'd taken one of those punches!" He reached out and flicked a finger at her curls. "What if one of those bozos had recognized you?"

Lauren pushed her glasses back onto her face and gave him a saucy grin. "I was traveling incognito."

Shaking his head, Ryder slumped back on the sofa. "Didn't you believe a word I said today, Lauren? You took a chance going to that bar, getting tangled up in—"

She giggled and tossed the glasses aside. "I was tangled up all right." Leaning back, she turned her head to look at Ryder. "And so was Clancy. I was floored to find myself flat out with some big ape on top of me."

"How can you joke about this? Don't you know you scared the hell out of me? Don't you know you could have gotten yourself in deep trouble?" His eyes on hers were tormented.

Lauren's playfulness vanished under the hot, dark look. The air between them was suddenly charged. He reached for her with a purely male, animalistic sound and hauled her into his arms.

"Don't you know you're driving me crazy?" Ryder groaned, burying his mouth in her hair. "If that big stupid jerk had touched you, I would have killed him."

In a heartbeat, he caught her to him and covered her mouth with his in a scorching kiss that burned all the way to her soul. It began as a bruising, punishing declaration of his dominance, but soon it gentled into something more compelling. Lauren responded eagerly, letting all she felt for him burst forth in physical expression. His mouth closed over hers, opening wide, while his tongue swept fiercely into her honeyed warmth, possessing and devouring, staking a claim.

He groaned, murmuring something she didn't catch, and pulled her into his lap, renewing the wild ravaging of her mouth with his. His hands swept over her shoulders to hold her fast, locking her against him, letting her feel the hard male thrust of his desire.

Lauren wrapped her arms around him. Here was the promise of pleasure and satisfaction she'd longed for, and she welcomed it with her whole heart. She loved this man. She tore her mouth from his to tell him so.

"Ryder—"

"Don't stop…" His tone was raw, ragged. "God, don't stop, Lauren. I need this, I need . . ." His words trailed off as he ran his mouth over her cheeks, her nose, her hair, her temples.

Sweeping his hands down, he sank his fingers into her soft buttocks, holding her fast so that she rocked against him in a heated, rhythmic cadence. Her head fell back while her body shuddered and strained against his pulsing manhood. Ryder groaned, pushed to the edge of his control. Suddenly, with one decisive motion, he tumbled her gently off his lap and onto the floor, coming down beside her. Quickly he stripped her jeans away.

"I want to see all of you sweetheart." He pulled feverishly at her shirt, and Lauren willingly lifted her arms. His voice was low and intense as his hands readied her. "This is crazy, I know it. But it's either this or go stark-raving mad. I may feel like a bastard later, but right now all I can think about is how much I want you." The words rushed over each other, tumbling from him like leaves in a whirlwind. His breathing was labored and uneven as he looked into her eyes. "We'll work it out somehow, sweetheart. I swear it." His hands went to the snap on his jeans.

"Hurry, Ryder." Lauren's eyes, dazed with passion, clung to his. "I want you, too. I love you."

The words hung suspended between them. At first Ryder didn't take them in. At first. Dropping his head until he almost touched Lauren's chest, he drew in an agonized breath and held it. Lauren felt the deep tremors that shuddered through his body as he struggled to control the raging passion that had driven him blindly to this point.

Ryder looked down the length of Lauren's body, open and defenseless to his, and the full extent of his deception hit him like a blast of cold air, twisting bitterly inside him.

"Ry-Ryder... What is it?" Lauren said, staring up at him in confusion.

Cursing himself, he rolled off her and then reached for her shirt. Taking it, she felt her face flame. Suddenly she was scrambling to her feet, shielding her nakedness with the shirt.

Ryder got to his feet and reached for her, intending to help her put her shirt back on. Her hand flashed out to ward him off. Turning from him, she quickly put on the shirt, unaware that he'd turned his back.

He sensed when she was ready and gathered the courage to look at her. She was staring at him, her eyes more golden than amber, he noticed, and glittering with tears and some other emotion. *Outrage,* he suspected. *Well, she should be outraged.*

"What was that all about, Ryder?" she demanded in a voice that was low and intense and slightly unsteady.

He raked a hand across his face. "I'm sorry. I—"

"Sorry!" Her tone rose emotionally.

Oh, God, what should I do? Ryder wondered, closing his eyes against the bewilderment and pain in hers. What could he say? Was now the right time to tell her everything? But suppose she decided to shut him out of her life? He groaned, caught in a trap of of his own making.

"I can't figure you out, Ryder." Lauren stared at him, her lips trembling. "You barge into my company like some bigger-than-life corporate raider, you insinuate yourself into every facet of my life, win my lawyer's confidence, charm Hattie, captivate my son..."

She turned, closing her eyes, and wearily kneaded her temples with her fingers. "You're everywhere when I need you and I seem to need you often, no matter how I tell myself that I won't." She laughed hollowly. "This will probably amuse you. You're the first man I've met since Clay died who has stirred any sexual feelings in me, and I let you know it. It wasn't hard, because, although you seem determined to deny it, there is something special between us."

His eyes, meeting hers, burned with emotion. But before he could reply, she stopped him with a shake of her head. "No, Ryder, just don't say anything. I think your behavior tonight says it all. When you've made up your mind what it is you want from me, then we can talk. Until then, I'd like for you to leave."

Seconds ticked by as Ryder stood unmoving. Eight, ten, twenty. And then, without a word, he brushed past her and went silently out the door. Lauren closed it behind him and rested her forehead against it for a moment. Then she turned away, squaring her shoulders, and climbed the stairs. She had never felt more lonely.

On the other side of the door, Ryder wrestled with an onslaught of emotion. Lauren's words echoed over and over in his mind. Little wonder that she was confused and feeling rejected. In his attempt to behave honorably with her, he had hurt her. Looking upward in the night sky, his heart twisted. He had been afraid to tell her everything, fearing that she would shut him out of her life. He would lose her, Justin, the hope of a life together with them.

Standing stock-still, he absorbed his own pain. The last thing he wanted was to hurt Lauren. He loved her, he realized suddenly. He wanted her with an intensity that surpassed anything he'd ever known—beyond sex, beyond reason, beyond the secret that linked them. Shaking his head, he stood silently thinking of her. He had fallen completely and totally in love for the first time in his life and he would never be satisfied until she belonged to him in all ways.

Ryder shoved his hands in his pockets and reminded himself of all the reasons he should wait to claim her. He had a feeling it wouldn't be long before he unraveled the conspiracy threatening her company. What was a few more days, weeks? He pulled a hand from his pocket. In his palm lay the key to Lauren's front door. Fate again? He turned and stared hard at the polished brass lock winking at him in the moonlight. Reason and logic and even honor paled when every instinct urged him to open that door and declare himself. He would tell her everything soon. When the time was right, he would know it. Deep inside him, desire and love were tearing him apart, compelling him . . .

Like a man in a trance, the decision was made. He reached out and put the key in the lock.

Inside, he hesitated at the bottom of the stairs, and then took them, two at a time. At the top, he looked down the hall. All the doors were open except one. She was in that room, he knew it. None of his considerable experience with women had prepared him for the way he felt as he approached Lauren's bedroom. Taking a deep breath, he lifted a hand and knocked.

"Lauren?" he thought he heard a soft, rustling inside, but she didn't answer.

"Lauren, it's me, Ryder. Can I come in?"

Still there was no sound. He reached for the door and found it unlocked. He debated two seconds and opened it.

Lauren scrambled off the bed and stared at him, her expression wary. He didn't go to her, but simply stood there, feeling his heart pound. Emotion churned in his throat. He wanted to charge across the room and sweep her up in his arms. He wanted to kiss away her hurt, love away her misgivings. He wanted to feel her body, soft and warm, against his. He wanted to be inside her, to feel her passion, hot and fervent, surround him.

"Why are you here?" she asked, wiping tears from one cheek with her hand. "What do you want?"

His eyes swept over her hungrily. "You," he said simply.

CHAPTER TWELVE

LAUREN BEGAN TO TREMBLE. Suddenly it was hard for her to breathe. She searched Ryder's face, not daring to believe him or the look in his eyes.

He didn't go to her, but began talking, the words pouring out. "You were right when you said we have something special going for us, Lauren, but at first I really fought it. I've never felt anything like this before."

He closed the door behind him and walked over to her until she was only inches away. "I tried to keep away from you, but everything conspired against me. I was just going to be your expert witness and when the case was done, move on. And then there was the trouble at the plant. I couldn't just walk away then." He caught her hand and brought it tightly to his mouth. "And Justin ... I just kept getting in deeper." Sighing, he rubbed her knuckles against his cheek. It was rough with a day's growth, but to Lauren it felt delicious. "No matter how I tried, it was no good. The more I saw you, the more complicated my feelings became."

Listening, barely able to breathe, Lauren felt joy and hope spilling over inside her. His innate decency was revealed in every word as he tried to explain himself. She'd known all along Ryder was a man without roots, a man who couldn't stay long in one place. His relationships had been made up of brief encounters with no strings attached. She would surely have appeared unsuited for that kind of thing. Her heart filled as she realized he'd been thinking of her and of the eventual pain she would have when he moved on again when all she'd been thinking was how much she wanted him. He thought he knew her better than she knew herself.

He was wrong.

She drew in a shuddering breath and closed her eyes in relief and bittersweet joy. Maybe she couldn't have him forever, but the future and the illusion of security were not nearly as important as they once had been to her. She had chosen the ultimate in security when she'd married Clay and look what had happened. This time, she would risk whatever it took to know the joy of loving Ryder. If it couldn't be forever, then she could accept that.

He cupped her face tenderly in his hands. "I never meant to hurt you, sweetheart," he said, rubbing both thumbs over her lips. "Please believe that."

She made a soft sound and slipped her arms around his waist. He held her tightly, his mouth buried in her hair.

"I love you, Lauren."

Lauren felt as though her heart would burst. She'd waited so long just to know he wanted her the same way she wanted him. To hear him say he loved her...

"I love you, too," she said, holding him close, anchoring him to her to make the moment last and last.

"I want to show you how much," he murmured thickly, tunnelling his fingers through her hair. He brought her mouth to his for a kiss that was hot and hungry, rife with promise. It was potent and lavish and designed to make her crave more and more. Time was suspended as the kiss went on and on. When Lauren's body was melded to his all the way from her mouth to her toes, he finally broke off the kiss to urge her down onto her bed.

Ryder sat on the edge and reached for her hands. Bringing them to his mouth, he kissed them both. "I want to touch you all over, sweetheart. And taste... I want to taste you all over." His eyes flared when she shivered at the image his words conjured up. Lowering her hands, he took her mouth in a sweetly searing kiss. Her lips moved in instant, eager response.

"I'm going to love you in all the ways I've dreamed about," he promised huskily, putting aside his guilt and misgivings. "In all the ways it was meant to be with us."

They fell back together on the bed, and his kiss was suddenly no longer gentle. His mouth devoured her, sweeping over the curve of her brow, down her cheek to her parted lips. He kissed her with searing passion, his tongue plundering sweet, secret depths. His hand moved to her breast, holding it lovingly, and then she felt his breath, hot and heavy, through the thin knit of her shirt. She whimpered when he gently bit her nipple and then licked it soothingly. She caught his head and held him tightly against her, writhing and moaning, word-lessly urging him onward. She needed something...some-thing...

Ryder groaned, almost out of control. He'd meant to be tender, to prolong the pleasure for her sake as well as his own, but she was making it impossible, twisting and turning, on fire as much as he. He rolled off her and reached for her shirt. As soon as Lauren realized his intent, she scrambled to help him, lifting her arms so that he stripped the shirt away and then ripped open the snap of her jeans and unzipped them. Ryder pulled them down and off and tossed them aside, leaving her clad only in her brief ivory bikinis.

The blood rushed to his head. He had never felt anything like the emotion that welled up inside him. He stood to remove his own clothes. Made clumsy by his need and by the sight of her naked, her skin like creamy magnolias, Ryder's hands trem-bled, fumbled at his belt buckle. Lauren was following his every move, unguarded hunger in her eyes. Leaning back on her el-bows, her hair was a riot of swirling, golden curls, spilling softly onto the pillow.

He groaned and came down to her, feeling a fierce triumph as she reached for him eagerly. "If you keep looking at me like that," he told her, resting his head between her breasts and breathing hard, "it'll all be over in about two minutes."

For the first time Lauren felt something deeply feminine flowering inside her, nurtured by the knowledge that she could arouse him this way. She kissed his hair and hugged him to her breast. He drew in his breath sharply and buried his mouth in the soft, giving flesh of her abdomen.

"I don't want you to wait," she said, feeling a quick rush when his tongue explored her navel and then began to venture lower. Her bikinis were just a tiny scrap of silk with a lace flower inset over the mound of her femininity. Holding her hips in his hands, Ryder tasted that flower and sent white-hot heat searing through her, pushing her to the edge.

"You're so beautiful," he muttered thickly, drunk with the scent and taste of her. "I want you so much. I love you so much."

She arched against him, his name a strangled cry. The sound seemed to galvanize him to new heights of passion. Quickly he stripped her bikinis off and took his place between her thighs.

"I can't believe you're going to be mine at last," he said hoarsely. Almost hesitantly he bent and kissed her mouth.

"I am yours," she murmured against his lips. "Always, for as long as you want me."

Forever, he thought. He wanted her forever. *If only that could be.* With his hand, Ryder stroked the curve of her buttocks and down the smooth line of her legs, then up the delicate skin inside her thighs. He found the soft, intimate folds of her femininity and sank his fingers into her warmth. She was hot and ready for him. The knowledge filled him with fierce satisfaction. He anchored his hands at her hips, probing gently at her warm, creamy portal.

"Now, now," she urged, opening herself to him. "Take me now."

Ryder lifted his head and looked directly into her amber eyes. "What?" she murmured, sliding a hand along his hard jaw. She touched his mouth, her eyes sparkling with golden flame. "What is it?"

"I love you," he said, his voice unsteady, almost breaking. "Just promise me you'll remember that."

"I will."

"Promise?"

"I promise."

He nodded, everything he felt showing in his midnight eyes. And then, with a single hard thrust, he entered her.

He shuddered and went still, waiting for her body to accustom itself to his. She fit him perfectly. She was everything he'd ever dreamed she would be. He'd wanted her so long, waited so long. Could this really be happening? She stirred beneath him and his sex throbbed with its fertile burden. He squeezed his eyes shut and was flooded with feeling. He thought of that moment, twelve years before, when in a twist of fate their destinies became inextricably entwined. What would she say if she knew how fiercely he wished their child had been conceived this way, beautifully, naturally, lovingly?

"Come with me," he begged, breathless. Breathing deeply, he began to move in passion's instinctive, rhythmic dance. He gripped her hips, mounting a steady, loving assault that sent them racing toward completion. He felt the subtle ripples begin deep in her womb and it was like a gift from heaven. She sank her nails into the muscles of his back, making the small sexual sounds that had nearly driven him wild before. Hearing her moan now, as they surged toward mutual satisfaction, he felt the immediate, urgent response of his body and was helpless in the wake of its demand. Reaching as high as he could, he gave her everything.

WHEN LAUREN AWOKE, she was alone. It was not yet morning, but the lightening shadows at her window told her it soon would be. She stirred and passed a lazy hand over the space next to her. It was still warm. She moved over and buried her face in the pillow next to hers, inhaling deeply, and smiled. It smelled musky and male, like the man she loved.

She rolled over and sighed with pleasure. Never in her dreams had she expected to know the kind of joy that filled her heart. Ryder made her feel beautiful and cherished, wholly feminine. Not a part of her was left untouched or unkissed after their loving. Her body tingled and ached in new places to prove it. And to her delight, she now had the same intimate knowledge of his body.

After that first fierce coupling, when Ryder lay sprawled and sleeping—or so she thought—Lauren had slipped out of bed and into the bathroom. She was just sinking into the tub when he had opened the door. The corners of his mouth hiked in a sensual smile, Ryder had begun to move slowly toward her. He had been big and rumpled, lazily relaxed in the manner of a sated male. And naked, gloriously, beautifully naked. He hadn't even hesitated when he'd reached the tub. He'd simply stepped in, hauled her up into his arms and begun kissing and licking every drenched inch of her. Recalling the moment, Lauren smiled and felt a delicious expectancy, imagining pleasures yet to come.

Where was he, anyway? She glanced around the room. The bathroom was open and obviously empty. She got up and pulled on a deep blue silk wrap. In the hall, she saw the light in Justin's room. Curious, she walked that way.

OMIGOD, HERE IT IS. Ryder stared at the screen of Justin's computer. Everything fell neatly into place as he studied the complicated material displayed before him.

Who would ever have suspected? If he hadn't been curious to see the inside of Justin's room, if he hadn't been hungry to connect in a small way with Justin's everyday life, he might never have discovered this. But flipping through a box of diskettes, he'd found more than a boy's collection of video games. He'd stumbled on the missing schematics for Clay Holt's original designs!

Lauren was in the room before he became aware of her. She glanced curiously at the complicated material he had accessed, before turning her attention to him. He was wearing only his undershorts. Surrounded as he was by Justin's possessions and the youthful furnishings of the room, Ryder's body seemed even more rawly powerful than usual. Standing directly behind him, she slipped her arms around him and pressed a lingering kiss on the side of his neck.

"Oh, hi, sweetheart," he said huskily, but Lauren could tell that he was distracted.

"What are you doing in here?" she asked, wrinkling her nose at the monitor.

"Discovering lots of interesting things," he said, inclining his chin in the direction of the box of diskettes occupying the space beside the computer terminal. "See those?"

"Uh-huh." Justin's fascination with computers and all things electronic wasn't news to her. She certainly didn't find the subject interesting tonight.

"You'll never believe what I found tucked in among his video games," he said, tapping out a series of commands on the keyboard. To Lauren's amazement, up came something that looked like an electronic schematic. Even for Justin, it appeared complicated.

"What in the world?"

"Robotics," he said.

"Robotics?" She looked dumbfounded.

"Look here." Ryder shifted so that she could see the monitor over his shoulder. "You won't believe this."

Just then the air conditioner started up and Lauren shivered. Her silk robe was designed for beauty, not practicality. Idly Ryder slipped one arm around her, but his thoughts were obviously on the squiggles displayed on the monitor.

"I won't believe what?"

"All this time, we've been turning the plant upside down looking for the missing designs and they've been right here in Justin's room."

He reached over and flipped up the lid of the plastic case. "On these diskettes," he added, shaking his head. "The company's lifeblood carelessly tossed in among a bunch of video games, for Pete's sake."

Lauren stared. "Surely not."

"It's true. What the hell was Clay thinking about? These records are obviously vital, essential to the company's future."

She shook her head, mystified. Looking at the screen where the complicated schematic was still displayed, she tried to understand. "Clay was totally dedicated to his work," she murmured. "It doesn't make sense that he could be careless with so much at stake."

It made no sense to Ryder, either. Leaving the records of his multimillion-dollar business in the hands of an eleven-year-old, no matter how precocious, was just one more mystery in a whole string of them that didn't add up. His mouth was grim as he bent and switched off Justin's PC, determined to get to the bottom of things.

THE TELEPHONE WAS RINGING. Murmuring a complaint, Lauren awoke from a deep and dreamless sleep. They'd both gone back to bed. Reaching over Ryder's chest, she fumbled for the receiver, handling it gingerly, trying not to disturb him. But before she could carry it to her ear, Ryder's arms closed around her, pinning her close to his chest. She managed to get the receiver in place and was smiling into his eyes as she said, "Hello."

"Lauren Holt?"

Still smiling, she tilted the receiver up so that she could give Ryder a quick kiss. "Yes, this is she."

"The lady who owns the Holt Company?"

A tiny frown appeared, banishing her smile. "Yes, who is this?"

"I thought you might want to know that a bomb has been placed in the plant, Mrs. Holt."

She stared at Ryder, her face paling.

"Mrs. Holt?"

"What? What did you say?"

"You heard me, Mrs. Holt. There's a bomb in your plant and it'll go off in about—" he paused "—one hour and twenty-eight minutes."

Click.

"Dear God," she whispered, staring at the phone in her hand, unaware that she trembled with the fear and horror that suddenly coursed through her.

Ryder propped himself on one elbow, his eyes narrowed. "What is it, sweetheart? What's the matter?"

"There's a bomb at the plant."

"What!"

"It's going to go off in an hour and twenty-eight minutes."

Without another word Ryder grabbed the receiver from her and pressed the button to summon a dial tone. Swearing, he was on his feet and punching out the emergency number before she could scramble off the bed. In a few curt words, he explained the situation.

Behind him Lauren hurriedly riffled through a drawer and found both bra and panties, then quickly pulled on jeans and a shirt. When Ryder turned to her after hanging up, she was almost completely dressed.

"I'll just be a second," she told him, twisting her hair up and anchoring it with a sturdy clip.

"Would it do any good if I asked you to wait here?" he demanded, closing the zipper on his pants. His shirt was already on. He went down on one knee and found his loafers, then shoved his feet into them without bothering with his socks.

"Hardly." Lauren was already at the door. Impatiently, she looked back over her shoulder. He was at her dresser, sweeping up his keys and pocket change. "Hurry, Ryder!"

"I'm coming. But we need to tell Hattie to keep Justin close when he gets home from his sleepover. I don't like what's happening here, Lauren."

She nodded, still pale. Then, together, they went out.

A POLICE UNIT WAS WAITING when they got to the plant and so was Michael Armstead, along with his gofer, Jimmy Johns. He explained that he'd received an anonymous call about the bomb and, according to his responses to Lauren's questions, it appeared that the same individual had called both of them. Armstead appeared tense and grim faced. Watching him, Ryder had to give the guy credit. If he'd had anything to do with setting up the situation, he was covering it very well.

"I tried to call you at home," Michael said to Lauren, "but Hattie told me you had already left . . . with Braden."

Lauren barely heard him. Her eyes were on Ryder who was striding off to meet an arriving police van. *The bomb squad,* she thought, with a renewed sense of horror.

Armstead, too, was eyeing Ryder. "Braden seems pretty cool, considering the whole place might blow at any minute."

Startled, Lauren looked at him. "What are you suggesting, Michael?"

"I'm saying flat-out that he doesn't seem to be quaking in his boots." He shrugged, then added in a jeering tone, "Almost as though he knows something the rest of us don't. I'm still not convinced about Braden, Lauren. He acts like a con man, if you ask me."

Lauren struggled to hang on to her patience. "Your suspicions hardly constitute fact, Michael."

"Not yet, but—"

"You seem determined to concentrate on Ryder. Here's a suggestion, Michael. Check out the Blue Marlin where Nu-TekNiks's people hang out. Maybe you can turn up something more than innuendo."

"Uh, boss..." Jimmy Johns shuffled nervously at Michael's side. "Maybe we oughta go along with those bomb-squad guys while they check out the premises."

Lauren gave Michael a meaningful look. "Yes, maybe you should, Michael."

Armstead's jaw flexed in frustration as Lauren turned away abruptly and walked toward the growing number of people who were congregating at the entrance to the plant. In addition to Braden, the bomb squad and numerous uniformed cops, the press was also on the scene.

"Maybe you better back off bad mouthing Braden in front of the boss lady," Johns suggested.

"And maybe you better back off giving me advice!" Armstead snarled, more than ready to take his spite out on Johns.

"Okay, okay." Johns put up both hands. "It just looks to me like Braden's got the inside track right now, boss. She was ready to spit fire at you."

Armstead's eyes were on Braden and Lauren. "Yeah, it's going to take more than talk to shake her faith in that son of a bitch. He's managed to get her in the sack, Jimmy."

"A woman doesn't like to hear dirt about her lover," Johns observed sagely.

"Stupid, troublesome bitch," Armstead muttered, feeling another surge of frustration. "If we don't watch out, Braden's gonna move in and take everything. He's got to go, Jimmy. I didn't come this far to be robbed in the last inning." His expression was hard. "I just have to figure out how to make it happen."

THERE WAS NO BOMB. The search was abandoned that morning two hours past the eight o'clock deadline. The plant had been gone over with a fine-tooth comb and nothing suspicious had been uncovered.

The more Ryder thought about it, the more convinced he was that this event was just one more harassment calculated to annoy and distress Lauren, forcing her closer to a decision to dump the plant. But who was behind it and how far would they go? Would their next attempt be more personal? The questions came faster than answers in his head while his imagination supplied half a dozen ways a widow with a young son could be terrorized.

When Sunday night came, he was no closer to finding any solution. He paced the floor in Lauren's den, thinking about Clay Holt. He couldn't prove Clay had been murdered, but deep in his gut, he was convinced that the man's demise was just too timely, too convenient. Whoever was behind this mess hadn't stopped at violence then, and Ryder wasn't willing to take the chance that Lauren or Justin, or both of them, might also be victimized.

The press was on the scent again and making the most of it. When they'd returned to Lauren's house the day of the bomb scare, a reporter had been parked out front, waiting. Ryder had sent him packing. Later he had refused three telephone requests for statements. There didn't seem to be any end in sight to the media harassment.

"I don't like any of this, Lauren."

Lauren leaned back in her chair and rubbed her forehead. "Neither do I."

Ryder stopped behind her and put his hands on her shoulders. Instantly she relaxed against him, sighing as his fingers found her tight muscles and began to work the tension away. His own body stirred and started to throb. Ryder smiled and let himself enjoy the task, thinking how he'd like to have the right to take care of her always. Every day. Until they were both old and gray. And beyond.

"You know what I hate most of all?" Lauren murmured, tilting her head sideways so he could reach one especially painful spot.

"No, what?"

"The publicity. I hate being in the news again. I hate them calling me on the phone and waiting for me at my front door. I just hate that, Ryder." She leaned her head back and looked up at him. Her face was upside down to him, blurred with fatigue, but beautiful, so beautiful. He bent and kissed her lingeringly on her mouth.

"I've got an idea," Ryder said, inching himself into the chair and moving Lauren so that she gave him room before he pulled her onto his lap, breathless and flushed. "This situation has too many questions and not enough answers. Somebody is obviously harassing you, and so far has limited himself to tactics that haven't harmed anybody. I'm worried that he might cross the line."

Ryder touched her hair, idly sifting through the silky pale strands and then, catching her face in his hands, he dipped his chin so that he could look directly into her eyes. "I want you and Justin to come and stay with me at my place until this is cleared up."

Joy flooded her at the thought of sharing the intimacy of his home even for a short time. Lauren hesitated, searching his face. He wasn't talking about commitment, she reminded herself. It would be temporary, just until the trouble at the plant was over.

"If you're worried about what people will say," he said, misinterpreting her expression, "don't be. I mean for Hattie Bell to come, too. We need her for Justin, and besides she's part of your family. There's plenty of room."

"Are you sure this is what you want, Ryder?"

He'd never been more certain of anything in his life. To have her and Justin under his roof, to have the right to offer them his protection, was a chance he'd never expected. Ryder drew her back against his heart, tucking her head under his chin and thought about fate. Something had brought him here at just this time and in just this place and had thrust him into her life. He was not a spiritual man, but there must be some reason, he told himself. He knew now that no matter how everything eventually turned out, he would never be able to live his life apart from Lauren and Justin. Last night he'd claimed the one woman meant solely for him, thereby taking a step from which there was no turning back. Her troubles were now his. Everything he had and was, was hers.

"What do you think Justin will say?" he asked.

She laughed softly. "He'll say, 'how soon can we leave?'"

For a second his throat was too thick to speak. "And Hattie Bell?"

"She already thinks you need a female to take proper care of that old house of yours." Lauren tweaked a sprig of dark, curly hair on his chest. "Provided she gets the job, of course."

He caught her hand and brought it to his mouth, and then kissed her palm with languid thoroughness, making full use of his tongue. "She's got the job."

"Mom! Mom!"

Alarm flared in Ryder's eyes. He lurched out of the chair, setting Lauren on her feet. Justin was just beginning to trust him and he wasn't taking a chance on ruining everything now.

Lauren didn't appear to be concerned. Laughing, she went to the door. "In here, Justin," she called.

Justin rushed in, real distress bringing a glaze of tears to his eyes. "Mom, I was just fooling with my computer stuff and somebody has been in my room! My dad's diskettes are missing, Mom!" He caught her hand. "Come on, I'll show you."

"No, Justin, they're safe," she said. "I took them." Stricken, Lauren looked at Ryder over the boy's head. "I meant to tell you today, but in the excitement over the bomb threat, I completely forgot. I'm sorry, Justin."

Justin looked confused. "You took them? But why?"

Ryder went to stand beside Lauren. "Your mother and lots of other people have been looking for those diskettes a long time, Justin," he said quietly. "Where did you get them?"

"My dad left them there," Justin replied.

As always, when reminded of the casual way Holt behaved, Ryder became irate. No doubt the man had been brilliant, but he seemed to have been sorely lacking common sense. His carelessness in leaving those diskettes lying around might well have endangered both Justin and Lauren. "Did he tell you anything about them, Justin?"

Justin shook his head slowly. "Just that all diskettes should be kept closed up and all, so that they wouldn't get damaged."

He looked at his mother. "I'm real careful about that, huh, Mom?"

She ruffled his hair. "That's true, Justin."

"Once in a while I'd take a look at them," he continued ingenuously, "but I couldn't understand much when I displayed them, so I just put them in the back of the case."

Lauren stared at him. "You didn't once think that I might be interested in looking at them, Justin?"

"Not really, Mom."

She opened her mouth, but Ryder spoke before she could say more. "Does anybody else know about the diskettes, Justin?"

Justin shook his head solemnly, then looked anxiously from his mother to Ryder. "Did I do something wrong?"

Ryder put his hand on the boy's shoulder, smiling faintly. "No, you didn't. Don't worry about it, Justin. Sounds like you and your dad really enjoyed playing around with your computer."

"My dad was always fooling around with my computer," Justin told him proudly. "And when he took me to the plant, he showed me a lot of things his big one could do."

Ryder nodded absently, his mind still on the valuable design diskettes. "I'll bet your dad used your computer sometimes when he was at home, probably to review whatever he was working on. Maybe he forgot to collect them the last time he did that."

Justin shook his head. "No, he didn't forget them. The night he was using my PC, he had to go back to the plant for something and he told me if I turned it back on, to be careful and not damage his diskettes." He looked at his mother and then away quickly. "That was the night he had the accident . . . the night he . . . he . . ."

Ryder looked grim.

Lauren put her arms around Justin and hugged him tightly. "It's okay, love. We just wondered how they came to be in your room. And now we know. You've taken very good care of them."

Blinking back tears, she looked at Ryder, whose expression was troubled. She was glad to see that he was not insensitive to Justin's pain. She put out a hand to him and he took it, then pulled them both close.

CHAPTER THIRTEEN

THE NEXT TWO WEEKS passed in a blur of happiness for Lauren. It was the height of foolishness, she told herself, but loving Ryder and being with him all the time made it impossible to feel threatened and stressed out as she had so often in the past year. Besides, in that magical two weeks, nothing awful happened at the plant or in the lawsuit. It appeared that she was at long last enjoying a rare spell of peace and quiet, even prosperity.

She loved Ryder's house. Even though the place still needed a lot of work, it had so much potential that it was all she could do to maintain any kind of decorating restraint. It was exactly the kind of house she had always wanted. From her first glimpse of it that morning with Jake, she had appreciated its charm and grace. But now, more than that, it was special because it was the only home Ryder had ever known.

Getting to know Ryder was almost as satisfying as loving him. One afternoon, they took Justin and a picnic lunch and fishing gear and whiled away one whole afternoon beside the bayou that wound through the rear of Ryder's property. But Justin was the only one with enough energy to fish. Ryder sprawled out in the grass after propping his own fishing rod on the ancient boat landing and enjoyed Hattie's lemonade with real honest-to-goodness lemons in it. Hattie pampered Ryder outrageously and he loved it. Sitting beside him, sharing the peace and summer sounds of the lazy afternoon, Lauren couldn't resist a chance to learn more about him.

"You must have been very happy as a boy growing up here—woods, a bayou with fish in it, birds and animals everywhere," she said, looking around. "Did you know how lucky you were?"

He looked at her. "Lucky?" He leaned away and tossed out the ice from his drink. "I didn't have a lot of time to enjoy it. I had a job from the time I was nine years old."

She frowned, secretly shocked. "I thought you played baseball."

"I did. I worked the games and practices around my jobs, whatever they happened to be at the time. Mama Jane planned for me to get an athletic scholarship, but I broke my wrist in an accident on a job in a grocery store and that shot my chances in the big leagues."

Lauren felt a pang for the advantages he must have missed. "What about your parents?"

"What about them?"

She watched him squint out over the bayou. The set of his shoulders and the hard, grim line of his mouth told her his childhood memories weren't happy ones. She suspected his thoughts were as dark and held as many secrets as the murky bayou bottom.

"I was raised by my grandmother," he told her, his voice low and deep. "She worked two jobs until I got old enough to help out. As for my parents, I wouldn't know. I can't remember either one of them."

With a quick, unexpected movement, he tossed a pebble far out over the water. The peace of the afternoon had vanished.

"How old were you when they died?"

Ryder turned and looked at her deliberately. "If a kid doesn't have any parents at home, they must be dead—is that how neat and tidy your world has always been, sweetheart?" He shook his head, his mouth twisted in a humorless smile. "My parents aren't dead, Lauren, at least not that I know of."

Her voice was barely a whisper. "I'm sorry, Ryder."

"Apparently it was the age-old situation," he said dryly. "Pregnant teenage girl and immature youth forced into marriage. My mother had visions of becoming a country singer, so she split first. Took off to Nashville, I think. I was about eighteen months old, according to Mama Jane. But my old man..."

Ryder gazed at the wooden landing where Justin sat fishing. Lauren sensed he wasn't really seeing Justin, but was trying to conjure up a memory. Ryder blinked. "Yeah, my old man stayed a little longer. It was either Australia or Alaska he decided to try. He was a sailor with the sea in his blood." Ryder held Lauren's eyes. "That was a direct quote, in case you're wondering—Mama Jane's stock answer when I wanted to know where the hell my father was. I'm not sure how old I was when he left, about four, I guess. Some people claim they can remember things back when they were four years old, but I can't. Not even bits and pieces."

"Maybe it was too painful," Lauren said softly, feeling the sting of tears behind her eyes for an abandoned little boy. "Maybe you just blocked everything out."

Ryder rubbed his thumb against his chin. Lauren could hear the soft rasp of day-old beard. "You may be right," he said. "As a boy it was my father's desertion that bothered me the most. I had Mama Jane as a surrogate mother. She gave me all the nurturing any kid could ever need. But I wanted a father."

Lauren reached out and touched him. "You would be a good father."

He smiled softly and pulled her close so that he could nuzzle her hair. "What makes you say that?"

"The way you are with Justin," she told him. "And the way you are with his friends when they're over and at the ball field. You're a good role model. You teach by example when you can and you're tactful, caring of their feelings."

Watching Justin first, Ryder slipped a hand under her shirt and rubbed her stomach. "Their egos, you mean."

She smiled back, glad to see some of the shadows leave his eyes. "I'm happy to hear a man admit that the male even has an ego." She waited a moment. "Did you never want children of your own?"

His hand on her stomach went still. "My marriage was too rocky to risk bringing a child into it."

His marriage. Lauren felt a quick, sharp jolt and realized it was jealousy. And longing. Ryder had loved enough to marry once. She wished...

"How long...I mean..." The words trailed off, incomplete. There was so much she longed to know. She stared up at his profile, wordlessly urging him to tell her more.

"I got married about five years ago." He inclined his head so that he could see her face. "Do you remember the night we met? We danced..."

"I remember," she murmured.

"It was right after that. One of those whirlwind things. I was on a job in California. I met Stephanie. We got married."

Ryder closed his arms around Lauren and thought about Stephanie. She had been a lot like Lauren—pale ash-blond hair, warm hazel eyes, a cultured background. She'd even had a soft Southern drawl—from Texas, not Alabama. After the sexual heat between them had cooled, their differences started to cause problems. It had taken them only a few months to realize what a gigantic mistake they'd made. Stephanie had married Ryder to share his free-wheeling life-style, not because she loved him. As for Ryder, what he'd done was just now becoming clear to him. And why.

"What was she like?" Lauren asked softly.

"She was from Texas."

"No, I mean . . . what was she like?"

His tone was suddenly teasing. "Blond, hazel-eyed, five-four, a size eight."

She pinched him lightly on the arm. He kissed her on the neck. "She was a very nice lady, but it was just never meant to be."

"What happened?" Lauren whispered, closing her eyes as she felt his breath, hot and erotic, against her skin.

He lifted one shoulder. "Same thing that happens to one out of two marriages today. We got a divorce."

"But why?" she asked, distressed for him, for herself for reasons she didn't want to know right now.

She wasn't you. He had fallen for Lauren that night five years before, and he had married a woman who looked like her and talked like her—God forgive him—a woman who had soon sensed she did not have his heart. A woman who could never *be* Lauren.

"Ryder! Mom! I caught one. Look!"

Grinning, Justin stood on the landing holding up his line with a catfish dangling from it.

"Be careful," Lauren called. "A catfish has fins that—"

Ryder silenced her with a finger over her mouth. "He knows that, sweetheart. I showed him weeks ago how to get it off his hook without getting a fin stuck in his thumb."

Sure enough, Justin had already netted the fish. As Lauren watched, he flopped it on the pier and put one foot—safe in his Reeboks—on it. With a deft twist using a screwdriver or something—she couldn't tell what—the fish was free.

"He's too little!" Justin informed them and tossed it back into the bayou.

"Good job, Justin." Ryder settled back on one elbow, smiling at Lauren's chastened expression. "Cut him some slack, Mommy."

Staring at him, she allowed herself to dream for a moment. He was wonderful father material, whether he knew it or not. Her eyes roamed his rugged features, stopping at the tiny cut still visible beside his eyebrow. Now that she'd seen the two thugs in the Blue Marlin, she realized Ryder might easily have been killed that morning in the storeroom.

Impulsively she reached out and touched him, using one finger to trace the faint red line. "It's going to leave a scar," she murmured.

"Mmm, it sure won't be the first." He rubbed his cheek against her hand.

His shirt hung open, revealing a dark mat of chest hair. She slipped her fingers through it slowly. Ryder was like a big, lazy cat sometimes. He loved having her touch him and stroke him.

"You know what I thought that first day in Jake's office?" she asked softly, finding another jagged scar below his collar bone.

"Hmm..."

"You looked world-weary and battle-scarred," she said, her palm flat on his chest. "I thought you were the most beautiful man I'd ever seen." Her fingers moved lower. She felt his stomach muscles clench.

"Lauren—" Ryder glanced toward Justin, who was busy baiting his hook.

"And dangerous." Lauren's laugh was soft, self-mocking. "Of course, I denied it like mad." Careful to keep her back to Justin, she caressed Ryder through the heavy jeans.

A frustrated groan was torn from his chest. Ryder closed his eyes and fought to keep from surging against her hand like a wild man.

"How do you like the new, uninhibited me?" Lauren asked huskily.

His features were heavy and flushed and his breathing was uneven. "As soon as I get you alone," he told her in a rusty, rough tone, "I'll show you."

"WHAT'S THE MATTER, Justin?" Lauren pushed open the bedroom door and stepped inside. It was Saturday afternoon, and Justin and Ryder had spent most of the day working on the old house. Usually nothing short of a hurricane could dim Justin's enthusiasm for the renovation. Why was he up here lying on his bed?

"Nothing."

She hesitated, studying him a moment longer. Like hers, Justin's relationship with Ryder had flourished. They spent hours together—working or playing; it didn't seem to matter. Ryder's world travels were a source of wonder to Justin, and he was full of questions, which Ryder patiently answered. But what they both seemed to like best was working on the house. Ryder spent hours patiently demonstrating how to use a hammer, tear up and replace floorboards and how to replace wobbly railings. Sometimes the lesson would be how to caulk and paint properly. Or reshingle. There didn't seem to be anything Ryder considered beyond Justin's abilities. He even gave him a plumbing lesson when the ancient pipes in the bathroom began leaking from the strain of unaccustomed use.

"Weren't you going with Ryder to the building supply place this afternoon?"

Avoiding her eyes, Justin got off the bed. "I changed my mind," he said.

She didn't believe that for a minute. Maybe Ryder had decided he'd get more done without an eleven-year-old underfoot. "Well, maybe you'd like to give me a hand with the old pedestal table in the kitchen. I'm taking the finish off and it's turning into a messy job."

He shifted his weight onto one hip and looked dejected. "I don't think so, Mom."

She studied him shrewdly. Maybe he was simply bored with grown-ups. "You want to give Scotty a ring and see if he'd like to come over?"

He didn't answer, but sat back down on his bed. "Mom, what do you think Dad would say if he knew that you and me and Ryder were friends?"

A sharp pang went through her. Lauren had tried to shield from Justin the sexual nature of her relationship with Ryder. They were very discreet, but Justin was bright and perceptive. Did he suspect? Or was he simply worried about his own growing affection for Ryder?

She sat down closely beside him. "I don't think your dad would object to our friendship with Ryder," she said softly.

"Ryder is a good person, Justin. He's been helpful to me at the plant and he's opened his home to both of us when we needed a friend. Why do you think Clay would object to that?"

Justin plucked at a loose thread on one knee. "That's not what I mean, Mom. I know Dad would think that's okay." He looked at her. "I like Ryder a lot, Mom."

"So do I, Justin."

"He teaches me a lot of things."

"I know."

"He's almost as good at teaching me things as Dad was."

Her heart aching with tenderness, Lauren put her arm around his shoulders. Justin wasn't thinking she was disloyal. He was feeling disloyal himself. Staring at his firm little chin, she searched for the right words to reassure him.

"Your dad was blessed with lots of talent, Justin. He was an engineer and a scientist and an inventor. And although you were very young, he taught you many things, giving you as much information as you could understand." She caught his chin and turned his face so that she could look at him. She laughed softly. "But remember how he hardly knew a hammer from a screw driver?"

Justin's blond head bobbed up and down.

"Everyone has different talents, Justin, you must have noticed that." He nodded. "Then you must have noticed that Ryder handles a hammer and a screwdriver like a pro, right?" He nodded again. "He's an engineer, too, but his talents are different from Clay's. Still, Clay would want you to learn everything Ryder is willing to teach you, Justin."

"You think so?"

"I know so, Justin. I believe your father would think you've been lucky to find a friend like Ryder."

THE NEXT DAY was Sunday. Ryder invited Jake and Clancy over to cook steaks out on the grill. After they'd eaten, Lauren and Clancy took tall glasses of ice tea outside and sat down in the old swing in the backyard, grateful for the deep shade of a giant live oak tree.

"So, what's the latest at the plant?" Clancy asked. Using her foot, she gave a gentle push that sent the swing into motion.

Lauren shrugged. "Nothing. No incidents, nothing. Maybe whoever it is has decided there's too much risk involved."

"Now that you're under Ryder's obvious protection, you mean."

Lauren closed her eyes and felt color rise in her cheeks. "Oh, dear," she said faintly. "This is not what I meant when I said I was going to become less inhibited, Clancy."

"Don't look so shattered. Anybody who matters knows the circumstances, Lauren. Your safety—and Justin's—has been threatened. Besides, with Hattie Bell chaperoning, your behavior is perfectly respectable. Forget it, for Pete's sake. Let's enjoy the lull in hostilities, even if it's only temporary."

There was a lull, and for that Lauren was thankful. Another week had passed with no harassing incidents at the plant.

"What about those two goons in the Trans-Am?" Clancy gave her a wry look. "Or is the subject of that night at the Blue Marlin as touchy between you and Ryder as it is between Jake and me? I've had strict orders not to try my hand at covert operations again."

"I've been meaning to ask you about that," Lauren said, resting her glass on one knee. "When I saw Jake drag you into the car that night, he looked like a man getting ready to do something drastic. What happened?"

Clancy grinned. "Something drastic."

Lauren studied her friend in silence. She knew how much Clancy loved Jake. Had she finally overcome his doubts about her? Had Clancy convinced him that she was home to stay?

"You and Ryder missed it when he faced off the whole crowd at the pool table," Clancy told her, smiling at the memory. "I was busy planning how I could get us out of there in one piece, but he didn't need me, Lauren. He was terrific!"

"I've always known Jake was terrific, Clancy."

"Yeah, well—I don't mean that Southern gentleman stuff that you seem to bring out in a man. I'm talking physical stuff. To my amazement, not a one of those guys seemed willing to take him on." She shivered and looked like the cat who licked the cream. "Then he marched me off to the car and took out his frustrations on me."

"I can see how outraged you are," Lauren said dryly.

Wearing a dreamy expression, Clancy looked over in the direction of the men under discussion. "This may sound schmaltzy coming from a totally liberated woman, but Jake makes me feel one hundred percent female. It's like I've been looking for something for a long time and now at last I've found it.'' She looked at Lauren with a crooked smile. ''I tease him about being stuffy and overly conservative, but actually Jake appeals to me like no other man ever has. I think he's sexy as hell.''

''From what you say, he wasn't stuffy and conservative at the Blue Marlin,'' Lauren observed.

''Hardly. Here's the amazing part—I thought he was holding back because he was convinced that when the spirit moves me, I'd simply take off. That was only part of it. What he really feared was that he wasn't exciting enough for me, that I'd soon be bored with him.'' Clancy shook her head. ''I think he made that grandstand show at the Blue Marlin out of some crazy mixed-up notion that he had to prove to me that underneath he was as macho as…as Ryder, if you can believe that.''

Lauren *could* believe that. Hadn't she been thinking the same thing about herself and Ryder? How long would it be before Ryder moved on?

''I'm glad it worked out for both of you,'' she told Clancy, giving her a quick hug. ''You and Jake must be meant for each other, even if it took ten years to happen.''

Clancy bent over to place her empty glass on the ground. ''Speaking of 'meant for each other,' you and Ryder certainly are.''

''I don't know about that,'' Lauren murmured, her eyes on her lover. ''The time may be right for you to settle down, Clancy, but Ryder is still a vagabond at heart. Oh, I think he'll stay here until my troubles at the plant are resolved and the lawsuit is finished, but I'm not counting on a future with Ryder.''

Clancy looked distressed. ''I think you're wrong, Lauren. He loves you.''

But not enough to make a permanent commitment, Lauren thought. And because he wouldn't, she tried not to let herself dream the impossible. She tried to manage as much of the business independently of him—and Michael—as she could. She already accepted that the two men would never be able to work together. But getting along without Ryder at the plant was one thing. Getting along without him in her personal life was another.

''Well, we'll just have to see.'' Sounding brisk, she finished off her drink and set the glass down beside the swing. Deep down, she was anything but casual about her relationship with

Ryder and its tenuous nature, but the day was too beautiful and the company too enjoyable to dwell on it.

Clancy's eyes were on Ryder and Jake, who were sharing an intense conversation on the back porch. "I wonder what those two are talking about?" she murmured.

Lauren looked at the two men. "I was just wondering the same thing." Whatever it was, Ryder would tell her in his own good time, especially if it was something that might distress her. He was constantly trying to shield her. It was a daily struggle, trying to get him to treat her as the owner and CEO of the Holt Company first and his lover second—which didn't help in her campaign to control her own destiny.

"As for those two goons at the Blue Marlin," she said, "we know they work at NuTekNiks in the shipping department. Only we can't prove they were the two who attacked Ryder in the storeroom that morning." As she watched, Ryder reached into a cooler and got out a beer. He tossed it to Jake and then took one for himself. Still deep in conversation, the men came down the steps and started across the lawn.

"The only thing we have connecting them to the attack is my uncertain identification of the car. It's not enough."

"It was a good start," Ryder said, sitting down on the grass opposite the swing and stretching out his long legs. "Jake and I were just discussing the situation. We've got feelers out here and there. Some of them are beginning to pay off."

"Really?" Clancy perked up, her blue eyes going from one man to the other. "Like what? How? Is somebody staking out the Blue Marlin?"

Jake leaned back against the trunk of the big oak and crossed his legs. "Relax, relax, the deed is done."

"Well, tell us, for heaven's sake!" Lauren demanded.

Ryder grinned and saluted Jake with his beer. "My old buddy here has been enjoying happy hour at the Blue Marlin lately."

Clancy stared speechlessly at Jake and then at Ryder and then back to Jake.

"Can you believe this, Ryder?" Jake's mouth curled in a slow smile. "Clancy's struck dumb."

Everyone laughed as Clancy gazed at Jake with unabashed wonder.

A dull flush started at Jake's neck and spread upward. "What's the matter?" he demanded gruffly, "You think you're the only reckless fool around here?"

"Frankly, yes," Clancy said, still amazed. Suddenly she frowned. "Seriously, Jake, that's a rough place. We already know these people aren't playing games. I don't think you should—"

"Listen to this," Jake addressed the sky. "The original thrill seeker is giving me a lecture on prudence."

"I'm not kidding, Jake. Don't go back there. Please."

For a long moment, they seemed to forget Lauren and Ryder and simply stared at each other. Lauren could see that Clancy was truly shaken. Now that she had Jake's love and the promise of a future together with him, there was a new vulnerability about her. She wasn't as impulsive and free-spirited as she had been. The hint of a threat to Jake shook her. Lauren wondered what it would take to work some basic changes in Ryder. If he loved her...

Jake moved away from the tree and came toward Clancy. Taking her hand, he pulled her up from the swing and looped his arms around her. "Hey, what's this?" he teased. "I never thought I'd hear you urging caution. I thought you'd be impressed."

Clancy moved back so that she could see his face. "You mean after we knew first hand what a dive the place is and the kind of people that hang out there, you went anyway just to prove some macho principle?"

"No, I went for the reason we discussed when the idea originally came up."

"You said then that it was risky and you were right."

"Lauren is my client and I felt obligated."

Clancy's mouth trembled. "You could have been hurt!"

"But I wasn't." Jake reached out and gently touched her cheek. "What d'you say we go home and discuss this?" he suggested in a husky voice.

"Wow." Lauren's expression was a mixture of wonder and bemusement. She watched Clancy and Jake, oblivious to everything except each other, drift off toward their car after hurried goodbyes.

"Uh-huh." His eyes dancing, Ryder rose to his feet and brushed the grass off his cutoffs before sitting down beside her on the swing. Putting one arm around her, he brushed a kiss on her temple and then gave a shove that sent the swing gently in motion.

"I guess it's obvious what they plan for the rest of the day," she said, snuggling up against him.

"Hmm." Lazily he began unbuttoning her shirt. "Afternoon delight I believe it's called." One deft twist and he'd unsnapped her bra. Her breath caught as he touched her nipples and she shivered, closing her eyes.

"Come here." Ryder shifted in the swing and pulled her over onto his lap. As soon as he felt the softness nestled warmly against him, he groaned and moved urgently, searching for her mouth. Their lips parted and fused hungrily, tongues greedy and bold. For Lauren, the world and everything in it ceased to exist.

She clung to him, her body melting into his. When his mouth left hers, she whimpered at the loss until she felt him string a line of soft, open-mouthed kisses down, down, past her chin, her throat, then to her breasts.

He murmured something, rubbing his whole face against her, his beard sensually abrading her skin. Lauren, almost purring with pleasure, arched her body up, up...

"Nobody in the world could feel as good as you," Ryder whispered.

"Nobody but you," she said, straining against him, cuddling her softness against the hard ridge between his legs.

"I have a taste for afternoon delight myself," Ryder said, in a raw, rough voice. With a little growl, he pushed her shirt low on her shoulders and bared both pink-tipped breasts. Framing them between his hands, he renewed the slow, tantalizing seduction with his mouth. She felt dizzy and disoriented and it had nothing to do with the fact that she was being ravished in a swing. Her breath caught as his hand burrowed under the elastic waistband on her shorts and spread over the satin flesh of her stomach and then ventured lower to rake the soft, curly triangle. She arched, moaning, when he stroked the tiny core of her desire. Mindless, and thrumming with a thousand sensations, Lauren ached for more.

"Ryder, Ryder, let's go inside."

He made no move to stand. "Is Hattie Bell gone?"

"She's at the movies."

Losing all pretence of control, Ryder stripped off her shorts and panties, tossing them aside. Fumbling, breathing hard, he freed himself and positioned her so that she was astride him. Controlling her with his hands at her waist, he looked into her eyes and slowly lowered her, groaning as he sheathed himself in the warmest, farthest reaches of her femininity.

Lauren moved cautiously at first, unsure but eager for yet one more sensual lesson. But her wariness vanished with the quickening of Ryder's body and dissolved into shivering, mindless pleasure. She threw back her head and surrendered herself completely to the feeling. When Ryder found his own satisfaction, calling out her name hoarsely, she knew the deepest joy.

"I can't believe I did that," she murmured as soon as she could catch her breath. "In broad daylight, too, right out in the backyard, even if it is in the country." She was cuddled on Ryder's lap with her arms draped around his neck, still in the swing.

"It was awful, was it?"

She buried her face in his neck. "It was wonderful and you know it."

He chuckled softly, molding the curve of her hip with a languorous hand. "And you were the one who wanted to go inside."

"What do I know?"

"You know enough to make me the happiest man alive," he said huskily, closing his eyes and pulling her close against him.

The swing squeaked softly, the sound gentle in the lazy afternoon. The mockingbird that resided in the side yard was perched on a limb high above them, its song a clear, melodious tribute to the peace and beauty of the day.

"When's Justin due back?" Ryder asked after a while.

"Not until seven."

He frowned. "The movie can't be that long. He's with Scotty and Curtis, isn't he? What's the plan for afterward?"

"They're going from the movie to the plant to see a demonstration of the robot that flips hamburgers. Michael volunteered to—"

"Damn!" In one swift motion, Ryder was on his feet. "What in hell—do you mean to say he's with Armstead?"

"Yes." Lauren glanced at her watch. "He is by now." She sighed, knowing what was coming. "Ryder—"

"I thought I told you Justin's freedom was to be curtailed until we got to the bottom of whoever and whatever's trying to destroy you, Lauren! Didn't you hear me?"

"I don't take orders from you, Ryder."

He dismissed that with a wave of his hand. "Who's taking them?"

"Scotty's dad," she said coolly. "Michael was to meet them there at six." It was now past that time.

"*Damn it!* I don't believe this."

Without replying, Lauren turned on her heel and started toward the house. Ryder caught her before she'd gone three steps and whirled her around. "Do you know who Jake saw when he was hanging out at the Blue Marlin?"

"Take your hands off me," Lauren ordered.

He complied with an impatient look. "He saw your precious Michael Armstead, that's who!" Ryder said, his expression fierce. "Armstead was with a woman—the secretary to NuTekNiks's chief engineer, Lauren. Michael Armstead is the traitor in the Holt Company, the man who's masterminded all the grief you've suffered this past year, and now you hand him Justin."

"That's ridiculous, Ryder. How many times do I have to tell you that Michael is not the one?"

He stared at her incredulously. "What do I have to say to prove it to you? The man's a thief, a criminal, for heaven's sake, maybe worse!"

"He is not, I tell you!"

Unable to find words, Ryder swore savagely and started toward the porch steps, his pace literally eating up the distance. "I'm not wasting any more time trying to reason with you. I'm going to get—"

"You are going nowhere," she said, the words dangerously soft. "You have no right to dictate to me about Justin."

Ryder took the porch steps in a single bound. "We'll see about that."

Lauren had to run to catch up with him. She reached him at the door. "We won't see anything, Ryder. You're mistaken if you think you can dictate to me. I know I'm living in your house and I may have gone along with your suggestions at the plant, but none of that gives you the right to make decisions for me, especially concerning Justin."

Ryder didn't answer. He couldn't. Fear and frustration churned inside him. Armstead could be a killer. Clay Holt had almost certainly been murdered and everything, *everything* pointed to Armstead.

"Did you hear me, Ryder? You do not have any rights where my son is concerned."

Inside Ryder, something tight and hard suddenly gave way. He didn't stop to consider the consequences of his next impulsive words.

Angrily, he turned and looked straight into Lauren's eyes. "Oh, yes, I do have a right," he said softly. "He's my son, too."

CHAPTER FOURTEEN

LAUREN LOOKED AT HIM, her expression blank. "What?"

Ryder took a deep breath, gazing beyond her shoulder. His voice, when he at last spoke, was quiet. "I said, he's my son, too."

She shook her head, bewildered. There was something about the way Ryder looked that sent a chill down her spine. "Wh-what are you trying to say?"

She watched him rake his fingers through his hair, absently noticing that his hand was shaking. Apprehension grew, settling in her middle like a cold stone. He turned and his eyes, dark and compelling, met hers.

"Lauren, I know how Justin was conceived."

Her heart started to pound. "What . . . ? How . . . ?"

"God, there's no easy way to tell you."

Ashen, Lauren put a hand to her throat. "Tell me what?"

"Let's sit down over here first," he said gently. Unresisting, Lauren let him lead her to the ancient rocking chair. Her eyes followed him as he began pacing. "I was a student at Alabama twelve years ago," he began. "My roommate was in pre-med. He got involved in a research program that had to do with infertility."

He glanced at her quickly. Pale before, now she was as colorless and lifeless as a marble statue. Only her eyes seemed alive, and they were a bright, cold flame.

"What does this have to do with me?" Lauren whispered, her lips barely moving.

He looked away. "I donated sperm in that program."

She swallowed, trying to capture the whirlwind of her thoughts. What was he saying? *Dear God, what was he saying?* No one knew. *No one.* The doctor was dead. The records were supposed to be sealed forever.

"My roommate told me I was a good match for the...the father. I would never know his name or anything about him, I was assured of that. I was reluctant at first, but they finally persuaded me. I told myself a couple who wanted a child so desperately would be good parents. There would be an abundance of love for this baby, more so than some babies conceived naturally."

She stared at him in disbelief. What he was saying was so incredible, so overwhelming, that her brain sought frantically to deny it. She shook her head furiously.

"They never reveal who receives whose sperm."

He didn't quite meet her eyes. "Not intentionally, no."

"Then...?"

"I..." He swallowed hard. "Someone told me."

Lauren's eyes closed weakly. "That's despicable," she whispered, hardly aware that she spoke out loud. "As if the pain of being childless isn't enough. To think we were the object of snickering, behind-the-scenes gossip." Head bent, she rubbed her forehead with unsteady fingers. "I...it's..."

"No, you're wrong," Ryder said urgently. "It wasn't like that. It just happened. It wasn't a malicious breach of ethics. We were out celebrating the—"

"Celebrating." She sprang up from the rocker, her brain spinning with the sheer enormity of it. *Twelve years ago, it was Ryder's sperm that was used to impregnate her!*

"Lauren, if you'll just hear me out..."

"How much did you get paid?" she demanded coldly.

"I swear to God, Lauren, it was a purely humanitarian thing. It was just a fluke that I ever found out."

She lifted her chin, pinning him with a look. All of her strict, rigid upbringing was in that regard. "A thousand dollars, ten thousand? Twenty? Fifty?" Her voice dripped sarcasm and repugnance. "How much was your precious seed worth, Ryder? How much for you to sire Justin?"

He bowed his head.

She struck him on his shoulder to force his eyes to hers. "Because that is who we're talking about here, isn't it, Ryder? Not some nameless, faceless child spawned out of your *humanitarian* impulse to benefit a poor, sterile couple," she mocked him. "Hardly. We are talking about Justin Claymoore Holt, my son, aren't we, Ryder?"

"Yes."

"You bastard!" she whispered fiercely. "You lying, deceiving *snake*!"

Ryder felt real fear trace an icy finger down his spine.

"I can't believe this!" Her eyes, suspiciously bright, swept the ceiling.

"Lauren, listen—"

"Listen?" She laughed harshly. "To what? More lies, more deceit? I may seem like a simpleton to you, Ryder, but once I'm burned, I don't stick my hand back in the fire."

When he would have spoken again, she interrupted. "God, what a fool I've been," she said, regarding him with tortured eyes. "You must have been laughing your head off at me, the poor deprived, sex-hungry widow—so ready, so eager to fall into bed with you."

"Lauren . . ."

"I never had a clue," she said as if he weren't there. "I never dreamed it was all part of a . . . a mean, cruel plan."

Ryder came close and put his hands on her shoulders. "There was no plan, Lauren. I came home because of my grandmother's death. Jake called me about the expert witness thing, and then the situation at the plant heated up. It was almost as though fate brought me here and then one by one, things happened to involve me deeper and deeper in your life. In Justin's life."

"Fate." She shrugged off his hands, her tone derisive. "You're asking me to believe fate, not you, made you do it."

"No, I'm just saying it wasn't something I planned and plotted for. But once I got involved—"

"Does Jake know?"

Ryder shook his head. "No, he would never have contacted me in the first place if he had known."

Lauren considered that, realizing what he'd said was probably true. Jake would have no part in such a vicious deception. And how clever Ryder had been, manipulating her with his sexual technique, holding her at arm's length, letting her desire for him grow. By the time he'd judged her ripe to fall into his bed, she'd been literally panting for him. Fury and outrage and wounded pride mixed in her like a poison. The truth rose bitterly in her throat. He had not kept his distance for fear of commitment, or because he was too decent and too honorable to drag her into an affair that would go nowhere. Instead, every move he'd made had been part of a carefully orchestrated

scheme. *Get close to Lauren and thereby closer yet to Justin.*
It wasn't her he'd wanted, but Justin.

Fear now combined with other emotions, as the significance
of his parentage dawned on her. His real motive was to insinuate himself in her life and then seize his chance to take custody of Justin when the time was right. Reaching deep into
some secret well of strength, she drew a long breath. It was
Justin, not her pride, who was at stake here. Fortified by an
intense, almost primitive instinct to protect her son, she forced
herself to look at Ryder.

"It amazes me that I was too stupid to see the truth," she
said. "The physical similarities are remarkable. You stand
alike; you walk alike . . ." She thought of Justin's athletic ability and poor Clay's ineptitude at all sports. "You even smile
alike," she said bitterly.

He reached for her, but she moved away. "Don't touch me,
Ryder."

"Lauren, I know I have a lot of explaining to do," he said
urgently, "but right now I need to go to the plant and get Justin. It's unsafe for him to be with Armstead. Surely you see that
now."

"I see no such thing."

"Be reasonable, Lauren! I just told you that we've linked
him to the NuTekNiks people at that bar. You may be willing
to trust him with Justin, but I'm not."

"Michael was in the bar because I sent him there," she said
coldly, enjoying the incredulous look he gave her.

"When he insisted on doing his own investigation—with you
as his chief suspect, I might add. In fact, I suggested he check
out the Blue Marlin for starters. Apparently he decided to do
just that."

Ryder stared at her, his jaw clenched. "I don't believe this!"
he shouted. "If he is the informer, you've alerted him! Are you
crazy?"

"I must be, to ever have trusted you!" In her fury she, too,
was almost screaming.

"You don't know what you've done, Lauren."

"I know I'm still the owner of the Holt Company," she said,
"and as such I have the right and the authority to exercise my
best judgment in all matters." She lifted her chin imperiously.
"All matters, Mr. Braden."

Exasperated, he propped a hand on the porch railing and prayed for patience. "Then what would you say to the fact that someone in your plant is not only furnishing the sleazes at NuTekNiks with Holt designs, but that same individual is also passing more important, sensitive robotic secrets to a country in Eastern Europe."

Nothing surprised her anymore, but still the news hurt. Lauren put a hand to her throat.

"Yes, *Mrs.* Holt. One of your precious employees is a spy. A real spy." His eyes were cold. "The kind they charge with treason."

"It's not Michael," she said, her voice stony and unyielding.

"I don't want to waste any more time talking about this, Lauren. I'm going to get my son."

She caught his arm, her eyes flashing. "That's all this is about, isn't it, Ryder? Your son. You've planned and schemed and manipulated and . . . and cheated just to get your hands on Justin. There is no spy. Isn't that the truth, Ryder, or do you even recognize the truth when you hear it?"

"What about this truth! Have you forgotten that Justin told us Clay familiarized him with the computer at the plant? We've searched high and low for the key to Clay's records. What if Justin holds the key and doesn't even know it? What if he possesses information that could endanger his life if the wrong person finds out about it?"

"That's for me to worry about, not you!"

"Are you so blind you're willing to place Justin's life on the line, Lauren?"

She stared at him mutely, suddenly not certain of anyone's innocence, but unwilling to admit it to Ryder.

He took her hand from his arm. "We'll discuss this when I get back. Now go inside and wait for me."

"I'll do no such thing!" Lauren started down the steps, but just then the telephone rang.

He stopped. "Are you going to get that?" he asked evenly.

"No."

"It might be Justin," he snapped.

Without another word, Lauren turned on her heel and climbed the stairs, furious. The telephone was on the wall just inside the kitchen. She snatched it up. "Hello."

"Mom, could you come and get me and Scotty and Curtis?" Justin asked.

Through the screen door, she could see Ryder watching her, his mouth a straight, grim line. "Where are you, Justin?"

Ryder's eyes narrowed, and he started slowly toward the door. "At a pay phone. Get this, Mom, we caught a ride here with Scotty's dad after the movie just like Uncle Michael said, but he never showed up. Now we're stuck, Mom. You'll have to come here and get us, I guess." He paused, then added with undisguised hope, "Or maybe Ryder could pick us up." Fresh enthusiasm was infused in his voice. "Hey, he knows some stuff. He could show us the burger-flipper, couldn't he, Mom?"

"I don't know about that, Justin." She frowned. "Where exactly are you?"

"At the Timesaver on the corner by the plant."

"Stay there, Justin. Don't speak to any strangers and don't leave, don't take—"

"I know, I know, Mom. I'm not a baby."

"I'll see you in fifteen minutes, Justin."

"'Bye."

She replaced the receiver slowly, her eyes on Ryder, who was watching her from the open doorway.

"We'll go get him together," he said quietly. "And when we get home, we'll talk."

LAUREN SAT in stony silence as Ryder drove to the plant. It was just as well, he decided. There wouldn't be enough time for him to try and explain everything to her before they picked up Justin and his friends. And there would be no opportunity to talk once the boys were in the car, until after they'd been dropped off at their respective homes. Justin was already overly sensitive to his mother's moods, and Ryder had no intention of jeopardizing the growing affection or the trust the boy had for him. If Justin had a hint that his mother was angry with Ryder, he knew where the boy's loyalties would lie. Ryder didn't plan to let that happen. There was too much at stake.

He made an excuse when Justin asked him to demonstrate the burger-flipper and, though disappointed, Justin accepted the decision with good grace. He'd had a full day anyway, his mother pointed out. Ryder felt suddenly desolate. He wouldn't be spending any more time with Justin, if Lauren had anything to do with it.

He knew she was going to insist on moving back into her own house, and he was just as determined not to let her go.

Once Scotty and Curtis were dropped off, Ryder cautioned Justin not to mention that he had some knowledge of the computer at the plant. He had no desire to alarm the boy, but he had to make certain that Justin understood the seriousness of the situation.

"Your dad's ideas were very unusual, Justin. Some of them could be dangerous in the wrong hands."

Justin was occupying his favorite spot in the Blazer—in the middle directly behind the front seats. In the rearview mirror, Ryder could see him weighing the implications of what he'd just heard. Lauren stared straight ahead.

"You mean good ideas can be used for bad things," Justin said, looking at Ryder for confirmation.

"Exactly," Ryder replied.

"So we have to be sure nobody bad gets my dad's ideas."

"That's right."

Justin thought a moment. "So far nobody knows I can pull that stuff up on the big computer," he said.

Ryder swallowed hard, hearing the boy confirm his worst fears. Such knowledge was deadly. "Are you sure?"

"Nobody but you," Justin said brightly. "And Mom, I guess."

"Well, let's be sure and keep it that way," Ryder told him, resolving to take Justin to the plant himself and let the boy show him just how much he did know about the computer. Hopefully it wouldn't be much. It made his blood run cold to think that Justin might be the key to unlocking Clay's secrets.

"Okay," Justin said agreeably. "I won't tell anybody anything. Except you."

Trust was implicit in the boy's tone and the expression on his face. Ryder pulled up in front of his house and stopped. He had Justin's trust. Now he had to regain Lauren's.

"I'M GOING HOME." Lauren stood poised at the door, one hand on the knob. They were alone in the room that Ryder had converted to a den. Justin was upstairs playing video games; Hattie Bell was in the back of the house watching a Sunday-night special miniseries.

"You can't go home, Lauren." Ryder faced her, careful to keep some distance between them. From the look of her, it wouldn't take much to send her flying from the room and out of his life. "None of the reasons why you came here in the first place have changed."

"Don't bother trying to fast-talk me out of this, Ryder. I'm not staying under this roof with you another hour. Another minute."

"Lauren, stop thinking like a betrayed woman, for heaven's sake, and remember what's at stake here. It's just not safe for you and Justin to be alone in that house until this whole thing is cleared up and whoever's responsible is out of business."

"I'm not going to be at the house. I'm taking Justin and we're leaving town." She turned, fumbling at the doorknob.

"Leaving town?" Ryder felt a cold chill feather down his spine. "No, you can't take him—"

She rounded on him furiously. "I can take him anywhere I please, and don't you forget it!"

He put out his hands to try and calm her. "Okay, okay..." He cleared his throat. "Am I allowed to know where you're going?"

Lauren relaxed a little, her shoulders sagging. "Clancy's got a beach house on Dauphin Island," she said wearily. "I'm going to ask her if I can spend a few days there."

"Just the two of you, alone?"

"Yes."

"I know you need to think this over," he said hesitantly, "but won't Justin be bored and restless with no friends? Won't he be more of a distraction than you need right now?"

She looked at him. "What do you suggest, Ryder? That I let you baby-sit, and when I get back to town, maybe, just maybe my son will be here? Maybe you won't have decided to stake your claim and whisked him off to... to Saudi Arabia or some other godforsaken hole in the world?"

"You know I would never do that," he said quietly. "I would take care of him for you right here in my house."

"I wouldn't let you take care of my goldfish!"

He stared at her, anguished. "Lauren, I love you."

Instantly her eyes flooded with tears. "Don't—" she whispered, putting up a hand as though to hold him off. "Don't you dare say those words to me."

"I want to marry you, Lauren."

"Well . . ." She dashed a hand across her eyes and sniffed. "That would be the simplest way, wouldn't it?"

He reached for her again and she jerked away.

"What was it, Ryder? Were you like Clancy? Did you get lonely traipsing around the world alone, never having any roots anywhere, never anybody waiting for you at night, no one to care whether you lived or died? Did you wake up one day and discover it was time to have children while you were still young enough to see them grow up? What did you say—hey, I've got this readymade kid out there?" Her eyes shot daggers. "Almost as simple as ordering a baby right out of the Sears catalog, huh, Ryder? Was that the way it was?"

He stared at her, a million words, excuses, reasons trembling in him, but he knew nothing he said right now would make a difference.

"When were you planning to tell me?" she asked in a conversational tone.

"I don't know," he admitted with stark honesty. He thrust both hands through his hair. "A lot of what you said is true. I have felt for a while that my life was empty. I was lonely and bored. And when Mama Jane died and I came to Mobile, I just stayed. I don't know why. I didn't know Clay had died. I didn't know your company was in trouble. Once I did know, I'd intended to keep my distance. I knew the complications that would arise if I told you who I really was. I never intended to fall in love with you, Lauren, but I did."

"I don't believe you."

He expelled a tired sigh and just looked at her. "I didn't tell you at first, because I was going to help you out, as Jake suggested, and then get right out of your life."

"The old rolling stone maneuver," she said, nodding with heavy sarcasm. "It's probably gotten you out of a few tight scrapes before."

"And then I met Justin." He clamped a hand against the back of his neck. "I told myself I'd just spend a little time with him, get to know him, and then I'd move on. What could it hurt?"

"Oh, sure. What's another loss in his life? His father—" she emphasized the word "—a year ago, and you this year?" Her eyes accused him. "But who's counting? He's a tough little kid."

Ryder closed his eyes, stung by the lash of her words, feeling her pain because it was his own. "It just snowballed from there. I didn't tell you then because I was afraid of what you'd do. I was afraid you would never trust me again, that you'd send me away. Everything I ever wanted was in the palm of my hand—the woman I loved, my son, a real honest-to-goodness home." He stared earnestly into her eyes. "Can you understand that? To tell you the truth meant I might lose everything. Is that really so wrong?"

"You were right about one thing," she told him coldly. "I can't trust you, and I'm not staying in a house with a man I don't trust."

"Lauren, don't do this... please."

Ignoring him, she walked to the telephone and, turning her back, deliberately punched out a number. Clancy answered and she went right to the point, foregoing the usual small talk.

"Clancy, is that offer to let me use your beach house still good?"

"Sure, just say when, and it's yours," Clancy replied.

"How about now, tonight?"

Clancy laughed. "You and Ryder ready for some much-deserved privacy, hmm? No problem. The key's with an agency there on the island. I'll give them a call right now and all you have to—"

"Ryder won't be going, Clancy."

Clancy was silent a beat or two. "Umm, you're going to the beach alone?"

Sighing, Lauren squeezed the receiver a little tighter. "I'll be taking Justin."

Another short silence. "What does Ryder say about this, Lauren?"

"Why should he say anything?"

"He's just letting you go?"

"I don't need his permission."

"Wait a minute," Clancy said. "Am I talking to the same woman who entertained me this afternoon at Ryder's house..." There was a significant pause. "The same woman who's under Ryder's protection, who's madly in love with Ryder—and as long as we're being frank—sleeping with Ryder. A woman who hasn't had a thought or said a word in the last three weeks that isn't somehow connected to Ryder? Is this that same woman?''

Oh, Lord, she's right. Am I that hopelessly infatuated? Lauren clenched her teeth. "May I use your beach house, or not, Clancy?

"Had a little spat, hmm?"

"And would you please give Jake a message for me?" Lauren continued. "Tell him that I'll be back on Friday, in plenty of time for the deposition he has scheduled with the expert witness."

"Tell him yourself. He's right here."

Lauren wilted suddenly as it dawned on her what she'd probably interrupted. "Oh, Clancy, I'm sorry, I didn't think—"

"Don't apologize, you ding-a-ling. Jake's not going anywhere." In the background Lauren could hear the low rumble of Jake's voice. And soft laughter. His and hers. Had it been only half an hour since she and Ryder had been exchanging the same loving sounds? Lauren felt a clutch of pain.

There was some shuffling on the other end and then the sound of Jake's familiar voice. "Lauren what's this about you leaving town? You can't leave town, babe. I thought Ryder would have laid down the law since he tends to take his protective instincts to the max when it comes to his ladylove."

Ladylove. Lauren's mouth trembled suddenly. Turning from Ryder's sharp gaze, she closed her eyes.

"If he hasn't said anything, the phone's not the place to discuss it," Jake continued.

"If you mean Michael and the spy and the lies and the security breaches and who knows what else, he's already told me." Her voice was trembling.

Jake was silenced momentarily. "Well then, you understand. You can't leave town, babe."

"But Jake, I have to," she whispered urgently.

"Not this time, love," he said firmly. "It's not safe and it's not smart. Just stay put. You're in good hands right where you are."

When Jake hung up, Lauren stayed at the desk with her hand on the telephone until the line began to beep its electronic re-

minder. She replaced the receiver slowly and turned to face
Ryder.

"Jake seems to think I should stay in town," she said quietly. "But I won't stay here."

"You and Justin can't stay alone in your house, Lauren," he
argued desperately. "Just think. He knows too much. Somebody else might suddenly put everything together and come to
the same conclusion we reached. He's full of energy and a
child's innocence. If you'll just stay here with me, I'll hire a
couple of men—"

"Bodyguards?"

He nodded. "Yes, bodyguards. Don't worry, we won't alarm
Justin. We'll tell him they're professional associates of mine or
something."

Looking at him, Lauren was reminded of her first impression that day in Jake's office. She had thought then that there
was probably nothing much life could dish out that would in-
timidate Ryder. And soon she'd turned herself and Justin over
into his keeping without a doubt that he would keep them safe.

But that was before!

He moved close to her. "Please stay, Lauren. I won't touch
you, I swear. I'll stay out of your way. You won't have to see me
except at the plant."

She covered her face with her hands. "Oh, God," she whispered, "I don't know what to do."

He put a hand on her shoulder, aching to take her fully in his
arms, knowing that it might be a long time before she would
welcome him again. If ever. "You can't go, sweetheart. You
have to stay."

Without a word she turned from him and walked to the door,
her chin up, her eyes dry. It opened soundlessly. Only last week,
the door and several boards in the stairs had been so squeaky
that she'd teased Ryder and Justin about the resident ghost.
Ryder had oiled the hinges and braced the stairs that very day.
She climbed them now slowly, trailing a hand along the beautiful old banister, polished to a gleam by her own hands. And
then she was in her room, the one she'd taken so much pleasure in fixing up at Ryder's insistence. Her eyes swept over the
Queen Anne desk she'd refinished, the rocker that had been
Mama Jane's own and the big brass bed with the elaborate
curlicues where she and Ryder had loved . . .

Only then did she let the tears come.

ON MONDAY Lauren got up, determined to get a handle on whatever it was that was going on. The sooner she did, the sooner she would be free of Ryder. The problem was—who could she trust? Her self-confidence had been badly damaged. She'd been taken in completely by Ryder. As for Michael, she'd tried to call him Sunday with no luck after the broken appointment with Justin, but it worried her that he was out of pocket. The FBI agent she'd contacted after the attack on Ryder had turned up nothing on Michael or the men who worked closest with him. Michael himself was hell-bent on finding something incriminating in Ryder's past. If that's what he was doing, he had his work cut out for him. Ryder's career had taken him around the world.

At the plant Cheryl met her with word from Michael. He was on to something, the message said, but it would take a few days to get all the details. He didn't say where he was, but he remembered to apologize for failing to honor his appointment with Justin and the boys at the plant. He would explain everything when he got back.

Ryder was skeptical, as usual.

"I don't want to argue with you about Michael anymore," Lauren said wearily. "He isn't the informer."

She seemed so positive. It was almost enough to make Ryder doubt his own instincts. "What makes you so sure?"

Some of the starch seemed to go out of her, as though the battle was just not worth the struggle. "I think it's Malcolm Stern."

His eyes narrowed. "Malcolm Stern? The old guy?" he laughed incredulously. "The father of Hercules?"

"When you mentioned your suspicions about the clandestine Research and Development work, I requested a background check on the employees I felt had enough technical qualifications to be suspect. The information on Malcolm is extremely incriminating."

"Such as?"

"His wife and son are being politically detained in East Germany. He's been trying to get them out for years."

Ryder was stunned. "Who did it for you? Who else knew about it?"

"The FBI. Who else do you call if you suspect espionage? And nobody knew except me." She looked at him, her chin slightly lifted. "If someone in my employ is engaged in research for hostile purposes, it is my responsibility and mine alone to find him.''

''But Malcolm Stern . . .'' Ryder was still trying to take it in. ''Can you prove anything?''

''Not yet, they told me they would handle it.''

THE CLOCK on Malcolm Stern's desk told him the hour was late. But still he sat staring at the small framed photograph. Anna, himself and their small son, all smiling. The intricate scroll-work decorating the frame was worn smooth in places from the many hours he'd handled it, touching, stroking, caressing. Poor substitute for the warm, vital flesh of his beloved Anna.

God willing, the waiting was almost over. Although—he frowned. What they planned next was foolhardy, a venture destined to fail. The widow's protector, Braden, was a threat to the entire operation and must be eliminated, so said his contact. Whether to drive him away or to kill him outright was a decision not yet made. *Fools,* he thought contemptuously. Had they not yet discovered the kind of man Braden was? He would not be intimidated once he was set on a course. Braden loved the widow. There was only one way he would leave her unprotected. He would die first. Stern shrugged. It was not his concern.

Carefully he replaced the photograph in the small, velvet-lined box that was its special place. He had carved the box himself of the dark, strong wood from the famed Black Forest of his homeland. As he did, more and more frequently now, he let his mind drift back to happier days. Anna, his beautiful Anna, beckoned. And the boy . . . smiling. He moved toward them, his arms wide.

The clock, a marvel of German craftsmanship, ticked on.

CHAPTER FIFTEEN

SIGHING, LAUREN SHUFFLED another file over to the "hold" stack on her desk. Another decision she'd make . . . tomorrow. Tossing her pen aside, she made a face. Her desktop overflowed with an accumulation of paperwork. She was finding it more and more difficult to concentrate, when her thoughts kept straying from her work to the situation with Ryder. Without opening another file, Lauren turned her chair slightly and stared out the window.

The past four days had been miserable. True to his word, Ryder kept out of her way at his house, though he always found time for Justin, she noted bitterly. They hammered and nailed and sawed and painted just as though nothing was wrong. Ryder was always excruciatingly careful never to take Justin out of her sight. Why did that fact, instead of making her feel perfectly justified and reasonable, make her feel mean and ungenerous?

Lauren wasn't sure when he ate or slept. At mealtimes he was never around. In the evenings he was in his study and he stayed there after everyone else was in bed. If they bumped into each other in the hall, he treated her with the same courtesy he showed Hattie Bell. Or Clancy. Or Murphy or Jannsen, the bodyguards he'd hired, who had taken up permanent residence in two spare bedrooms in the rambling old house.

The idea of bodyguards for Justin had appalled Lauren, but Ryder had them in residence bright and early Monday morning. He told Justin they were carpenters hired to speed up the job of restoring the old place.

She rubbed her forehead wearily. Surely everything would be resolved soon. She might have been able to bear up a little better if she weren't living and working with Ryder every day.

How could you miss someone when you were living right in the house with him? And how could two people seem like strangers when they spent the whole day working together? And most disturbing of all—why did Lauren feel as though she had somehow been unreasonable and unfair?

She missed him. With a deep, dark longing that reached to the bottom of her soul, she missed him. Even knowing that he had lied and deceived her, that he'd only been with her so that he could get to know Justin, even then, she missed him.

THE WEEK FINALLY wound down. Almost. The expert witness's deposition was scheduled for mid-afternoon Friday. Lauren and Jake were already in her office waiting for him, a man named Collier Steele, recommended by Ryder. Jake had also asked Ryder to sit in.

Jake leaned back in the deep leather couch, placed at an angle to her desk, and studied her for a few seconds in silence. "I'm trying to decide whether to mind my own business or stick my nose in something that could very well cost me a client and blow a perfect friendship at the same time."

Lauren was immediately wary. Jake knew her well, but even a stranger could tell that something was wrong with her lately. There were circles under her eyes, and she appeared as thin and fragile as hand-blown glass.

"Hmm, sounds serious," she said, trying for a light note.

"You and Ryder haven't patched it up yet, hmm?"

"It can't be patched up, Jake," she said. "Just be satisfied that yours and Clancy's story has a happy ending."

"You want to tell me about it?"

She stared down at her hands. "It's...personal, Jake."

"Is it so dreadful—whatever he's done—that you can't forgive him?"

For one wild crazy moment she imagined telling him everything. *You see, Jake, Clay could not have children and so Justin was conceived by artificial insemination. Ryder just informed me a few days ago that it was his sperm that was used to impregnate me. Ryder is Justin's natural father. Isn't that amazing, Jake?*

"It's too bad." Jake shifted on the couch, resting one ankle on his knee. Lauren blinked, then scrambled mentally to pick up the thread of the conversation. Watching her intently, Jake said, "Justin will miss him."

Pain ripped through her so sharply that she actually made a small sound.

"Amazing how they took to each other, Justin and Ryder, wasn't it?" he said.

Her nod was barely perceptible.

Jake studied his shoe. "A lot alike, those two."

Lauren's head came up and she stared at her lawyer. "What are you getting at, Jake?"

He met her gaze directly. "Does your disagreement with Ryder have anything to do with Justin?"

She looked at him speechless. *Did Jake know, too?*

"I have some legal files which Clay left with me for safekeeping," Jake said, "in the event a problem should ever develop regarding Justin's trust fund. It was established at his birth. The details of his conception and birth are there, Lauren."

Lauren put a hand to her throat.

"Stop me if I'm butting in or offending you, and I will drop the subject," he told her softly. "I give you my word, we'll never speak of this again, Lauren."

Her eyes were wide, smoky with emotion. "No, it's...it's all right."

"Does Ryder know any of this?"

She cleared her throat. "Yes," she whispered.

"Ryder is the donor, isn't he?"

He watched her turn to gaze distractedly out of the window. She nodded her head mutely.

"And is that a problem?" He went on when she didn't answer. "Ryder loves you both—it's obvious to anyone who sees you together. I know lawyers are the original cynics, but when I put it all together..." He stopped, shaking his head. "By God, what were the chances?"

"Ryder knew," she said bitterly. "He's known all along, Jake, from the moment of Justin's birth."

His eyes narrowed. "Are you sure?"

"I'm sure. He came here knowing, and when he thought he had Justin and me dependent on him, then he told me who he really was."

Jake frowned. "Is that what this is all about?"

"Isn't it enough?"

"He didn't ever have to tell you, Lauren."

She got out of her chair abruptly. "And it would have been a thousand times better if he hadn't."

He thought that over. "Why? Because then you'd never have to wonder if he really loved you, or if he just deceived you so that he could be with Justin forever."

She regarded him with eyes filled with pain. "Can you blame me?"

At the sound of voices in the outer office, Jake started to get to his feet. "This is not just your own hurt and wounded pride at stake here, Lauren," he said. "You'll be throwing away Justin's chance to know his natural father. Just remember that."

ALL THROUGH the deposition Jake's words kept going round and round in her head. Was it just her own pain, her own wounded pride that made it impossible for her to believe Ryder? Suppose he hadn't come to Mobile for the express purpose of insinuating himself in her life. Suppose he really *hadn't* meant to get involved. It was easy to believe that once he'd seen Justin and gotten to know him, he couldn't have helped but love him. Had he kept his secret for fear of losing what he'd just found? She tried to imagine his dilemma. Would he want to marry her if she weren't Justin's mother? God help her, she wanted to believe that more than anything. Over and above the technical dialogue of the deposition, she was intensely aware of Ryder's brooding gaze on her, his dark eyes saying to her... what?

She had found no answers by the time they started back to Ryder's place. The beltway was crowded with Friday traffic. Lauren watched Ryder's hands on the wheel of the Blazer. He drove with the same competency that he brought to most things. But just then he made a turn with a little less finesse than usual, and she glanced quickly at his face.

"I'm going to have these brakes checked this weekend," he said quietly. "They seem a little low."

They exited the beltline then and headed south. Soon they were off the main highway and on the winding country lane that led to Ryder's property. Out of the traffic the Blazer picked up speed. They'd be home in a few minutes.

Home. Lauren turned her head on the seat and idly watched the passing scenery. How quickly she'd learned to think of Ryder's place as home. And so had Justin. And Hattie Bell. They'd moved in without a backward look at the house in town. It was as though they'd all finally come home.

She felt urgent and unsettled suddenly. She and Ryder needed to talk, she decided. She wanted to hear everything and this time she would— She heard the startled sound Ryder made and then became aware that he was having trouble steering the Blazer. She saw with alarm that they were nearing a dangerous hairpin curve and that he was not slowing down.

"The brakes are gone!" he told her, glancing quickly to see that her seat belt was fastened. His was not, she noted, and felt horror clutch at her throat.

It couldn't have taken more than fifteen seconds, but the whole world and everything in it seemed to de-escalate to slow motion. They approached the curve, tires screaming on the worn asphalt. The first quarter of the turn they made, just barely. But then they hit a pothole. At that speed the wheel was wrenched out of Ryder's hand. The Blazer began to slide. Moving sideways, it hit the edge of the pavement and soft shoulder, out of control.

Lauren was frozen with terror, but her brain registered the deafening sounds, topsy-turvy scenery, the gut-wrenching jerk of her seat belt, glass shattering. And Ryder coming toward her, his arms reaching out for her, his body covering hers, shielding her. And then—truly in slow motion, it seemed to Lauren—the Blazer rolled, end over end, and came down with a bone-jarring crunch.

The cessation of all noise was shocking to her rattled senses. Stunned, she was incapable of any thought for a few seconds. She was not unconscious. She stirred and became aware that she was trapped somehow.

Ryder. Ryder was on top of her.

Moving cautiously he lifted his head until he could look into her eyes. Never, Lauren thought, if she lived a hundred years, would she forget the expression on his face at this moment. Urgent, terrible, fearsome. Wild, turbulent emotion churned in the blue of his eyes, turning them almost black.

"Are you all right?" he asked hoarsely, lifting his weight only slightly from her.

She wiggled a bit experimentally. "Yes, I think so."

His eyes were anxious, searching her face. "Are you sure?"

Her hands were trapped against his chest. She pulled them free and threw them around him, hugging him close to her heart. "I'm not hurt."

"Thank God, thank God." His eyes closed and he leaned his forehead against hers, while a deep, convulsive shudder shook his whole body.

She ran her hands over the heavy masculine shape of his shoulders and back. He didn't move except for the clenching of his hands anchored around her. She swallowed thickly. Maybe he was hurt. Maybe he couldn't move. "Ryder..."

"I'm okay," he said, his voice muffled against her temple.

She breathed a silent prayer of thanksgiving and relief and humility. They could so easily have been killed, Ryder especially, since his seat belt had not been secured. It had been crazy of him to throw himself over her like that, shielding her with his body. He should have— Light dawned, and her thoughts went flying. Using his body to protect her had been the instinctive act of a man whose first thought had been for her, not himself. Amid the dusty, steaming wreckage, she drew a deep, unsteady breath, not daring to believe what that meant.

"I have never been so scared in my whole life," Ryder said in a shaken tone. He lifted one hand and began stroking her hair. Lauren could feel the fine tremors still racking him.

"All I could think about was how would I get you to a hospital? This road is so isolated. If I had to leave you to run to the house, how long would it take? But then I knew I couldn't leave you—" He made an anguished sound and buried his face in her neck.

"You thought all that, while we were tumbling all over the road?" Smiling softly, she threaded her fingers through his hair and kissed his ear. "You are a remarkable man."

He lifted his head, then, and stared at her. His gaze seemed to go right through her to the very gates of her soul. "No," he said slowly. "Not remarkable. An ordinary man who just came too close to losing the person who matters most to him in the world."

"Ryder..."

"I love you, Lauren." The words were low and urgent. "I know you don't believe me, but just now I have to say the words or else go crazy. I love you so much."

Without giving her a chance to say anything, he suddenly straightened up. "No, just be still until I get you out of this, sweetheart." His voice was still not back to normal. He fumbled with the lock on her seat belt, finally releasing it. Then with a word of caution to her, he pushed open his door and came around to her side. After letting her out, he moved back, watching her as she straightened her clothes and smoothed a shaky hand over her hair. "You're sure you're not hurt?" he demanded anxiously.

Her knees were a little rubbery, but she gave him a reassuring smile. "I'm fine. No lumps or broken bones, maybe a couple of bruises, that's all." Her smile faded. "Thank you.'"

"For what, for God's sake? I almost killed you."

"For using your own body to protect me. If the window had shattered, you could have been cut seriously. Or worse." She shivered, turning away as though to block out the thought.

When he didn't say anything, she raised her eyes and looked him over more closely. Particles of glass clung to his clothes and his hair, but she didn't see any blood.

"Let's go," he said, turning away to check the deserted road for any sign of life. Her gaze fell to the back of his jeans, midway down his left thigh. Her eyes widened.

"You are hurt! There's blood all over, Ryder."

Raising his arm, he stretched backward, trying to see it. "I don't think it's bad. When we get home, I'll see to it."

Lauren didn't even bother to reply to that. She reached into the Blazer and rummaged under the front seat for the box of tissues she knew was there. Grabbing a handful, she told Ryder to turn around. The tear in his jeans was long and jagged. She shivered at the thought of the damage it could have done to his neck or a vulnerable artery. Thank God for tough denim.

There was a lot of blood, anyway. She located the cut and pressed the tissue to it. "I'm scared to press very hard," she told him, her whole attention centered on the wound. "If there's glass still inside, I could do more damage than good."

"Don't worry," he said, touching her hair. "Fortunately we're only two or three minutes from the house. No one's likely to come along to give us a lift, so we'd better start hiking."

Chewing her lip, she had to face the fact that they had no choice but to start out on foot. Using the belt from her skirt, she secured a thick fold of tissue over the wound, and then fell in step beside him as he turned toward home.

"It was rigged; I guess you know that."

"I was just thinking the same thing," Lauren said, wrapping her arms around herself to control a shudder.

"You know what it means."

She clamped her jaw hard. "These people mean business, Ryder."

"Yeah." His mouth was a grim line.

Ryder felt the intensity of her gaze. She'd been sending those little looks his way every thirty seconds since they started walking. He kept his eyes straight ahead. Otherwise, no power on earth could have stopped him from turning to her and closing his arms around her and promising her the moon and the stars, anything that would take that bruised, vulnerable look from her face. But she would know his promises weren't worth spit, because he couldn't fight shadows and suspicion. And that was all any of them—the FBI, Jake, the police—had to go on.

They were entering the tree-lined lane that led to the house. With every step he took, Ryder's rage had risen a notch. He didn't care a damn for the scratch he'd taken. What incensed him and scared him to his toenails was how quickly and finally Lauren could have been taken from him. For days he had guarded against doing anything that would have made her shy away. He knew she was having a tough time dealing with his deception. But he hoped she would come around. He had been telling himself that, every hour on the hour, for days now. Everything that made his future worth living she held in the palm of her hand.

He touched her elbow as they started up the front porch stairs. The problem was he didn't know if he could keep his emotions in check after what he'd just been through. He just wanted to put his arms around her and never let her go. Instead he opened the door and, without touching her, waited for her to step inside.

"First we need to call the sheriff's office," he said, steering his thoughts in another direction. Sounds came from the backyard, Justin's yell and the deeper tones of Murphy and Jannsen in a game of touch football. Just as well, he thought. He didn't want Justin alarmed. He headed for the telephone.

"Ryder, your leg—"

"In a minute, sweetheart."

It wasn't a minute. It was more like three hours later, when Ryder allowed Lauren to hustle him into the bathroom to tend to the cut on his leg. First the wrecked Blazer had been towed, then the Sheriff notified, the FBI advised, Justin's questions answered and Hattie Bell calmed down. The house was finally quiet.

"What if it has glass in it?" She watched him shrug out of his tattered shirt, shuddering at the sound of tiny particles of the Blazer's windshield tinkling to the floor. "And your hair! I can see the glass in your hair, Ryder."

"I'm going to take a shower," he told her, popping the snap on his jeans. "That'll take care of it. It's also the most efficient way to clean the cut. Just give me a few minutes, sweetheart."

"Well—"

Sensing a subtle change in him, she raised her eyes to his. "Unless you want to get in that shower with me, lady, you'd better run."

She didn't. At least not right that minute. Instead she subjected him to a long, long look. Heat shafted through Ryder like lightning splitting a pine. He could see her fear, her doubts, her desire, her love. He could no more have prevented himself from reaching for her than he could have stopped a lightning bolt.

But she slipped past him in a twinkling and he was left staring at the wrong side of the door.

In the bathroom adjoining her bedroom, Lauren had her own bath while Ryder showered. She didn't take the time to luxuriate in the steamy tub, because when Ryder finished, she wanted to see for herself that his wound was truly nothing to be concerned about. Hurriedly she put on an ivory silk caftan and, still pulling the sash around her, made her way down the hall to the master bedroom.

He was just coming out of the bathroom. He was damp and steamy. His hair was dark and still wet and clung to his head. He was naked except for a towel that rode low on his hips. Her breath caught at the sight of him, because he would always take her breath away. He had already bandaged the cut. White gauze laced with surgical tape circled his left thigh.

He stopped short and stared at her. She glanced at his thigh. "Was it bad?"

"No."

"All the glass is washed away?"

"Yes." His gaze caught her and held her with its intensity. "Lauren—"

"While you were with the sheriff, I called Agent Sommerfield at the FBI," she said, her tone husky.

It took a moment, but his brain finally clicked into gear. "I wonder if the Feds' right hand knows what the left hand is doing," he muttered, thinking that that pale silky thing made her look virginal and innocent and vulnerable. He had a hunger for all three. "I've been dealing with an agent named Whitman."

"I guess I should have told you when I called the FBI." Her hands fluttered as though she was having trouble finding a place for them.

"You didn't quite trust me," he replied, and then held his breath for her answer.

"It wasn't that. I just felt I needed to take full responsibility. After all, I knew you'd be leaving."

For the first time in his life, Ryder let his heart show in his eyes. "I won't be leaving unless you tell me to go, Lauren." He looked away, ran agitated fingers through his hair and looked back at her. "I know I promised not to touch you, but..."

Without even thinking about it, she was in his arms.

He caught her up close, crushed her to him as though he could absorb her very essence through his body. For long, timeless moments it was enough just to have her in his arms again. He knew exactly what he needed: the feel of her softness giving way against him, the brush of her hair on his face, the scent of her.... Ah, the scent of her.

Somehow he had her pressed against the wall, and his hands were in her hair. His mouth covered hers; hers yielded, opened, blossomed inside his. Every cell in him was alive to the smell and taste and feel of her. Hoarse sounds came from deep in his throat. She must think she'd unleashed a wild man, he thought.

But if so, she seemed undaunted. Her hands were eagerly fumbling with the fold of the towel. It gave, and her hands went around him, pulling him into the inviting softness below her waist. He groaned, and his mouth left hers to skim down her throat to the soft hollow there. He kissed it, open-mouthed, his tongue hot and hungry. Lauren clung desperately, melting with feminine need. He felt powerful, with her in his arms, invincible, ready to leap tall buildings. Without her, he had discovered how bitter *lonely* could feel, how bottomless *empty* could be.

He was aching, swollen, throbbing with his need for her. His hands swooped down the delicate curve of her spine and fanned out over her soft buttocks. She was sleek, silky smooth warmth. She whimpered, wordlessly encouraging. The sound tore through him. He wanted—needed!—to touch the hot, sweet treasure that was so close, needed to bury himself in that most vulnerable, secret part of her.

"Lauren, Lauren . . ." Her name was an agonized cry as he tore his mouth from hers. Breathing like a man who'd run a marathon, he leaned against the wall. "We can't do this here, Lauren."

Her nose was buried in the curls on his chest. She laughed shakily, warming him all the way through. "I know. The bed's only a few steps that way, darling."

For a second he couldn't speak. Then he swept her up in his arms, his own laugh a little unsteady. "I may make it."

"Lauren?"

"Hmm?"

"Does this mean you've forgiven me?" Ryder raised his head high enough to look down at her.

Her gaze was soft as she regarded him. "Yes."

A groove formed between his dark eyebrows. "You're sure?"

She smiled at him. "Yes." He lay back and she resumed her place, snuggled close against him, her arm draped across his chest, their legs entwined.

His arm went around her waist. "I do love you."

"I love you, too."

"I meant it when I asked you to marry me," he told her, and she heard the faint tension that laced his voice. His muscles felt taut beneath her cheek. "Say you will, Lauren."

She smiled against soft, curly hair. "I will."

He relaxed a fraction. "Can I tell you something?"

"Yes," she said dreamily. For a moment nothing disturbed the deep, quiet stillness of the night. It was late, and they were drowsy, love-laden, sated in the afterglow of passion.

"Five years ago, when I met you at that party, I felt like I'd been hit by a truck. There was something about you—I still don't understand it." He dipped his chin so that he could see her, could judge her reaction.

She was quiet. She hadn't forgotten his strange behavior that night.

"I knew the name of the couple who'd had my child, but until that party, I'd never seen you." He stared earnestly into her eyes. "And I never intended to, I swear that, Lauren."

"You were so cold and abrupt that night," she murmured, her eyes smoky as she recalled the way he'd held her when they danced.

"One look," he said, settling back. "Just one look and I ran like hell. I left the party and Mobile that same day as if I was being chased by a demon. You were happily married to a good, decent man. Justin had exactly the life I'd imagined he would have. After that, I didn't come back to Mobile until Mama Jane died."

He took a deep breath. Intense emotion made his voice rough. "They say everything has a purpose, Lauren. We were meant to be together with Justin. I was here; you needed me. It wasn't my plan, Lauren, but it was someone's plan. It was meant to be. I believe that."

Listening to him, she felt her throat grow tight and achy with emotion. At last he was telling her what her heart longed to hear.

"And something else, Lauren. I want to know about Justin, about his babyhood, everything. I want to see pictures of him when he was christened and when he went to kindergarten and in his pee-wee uniform and when he lost his front teeth. I want to know all those things I missed even though I know I don't have any right to ask." He turned his mouth to her temple. "I have so many years to catch up on. Tell me you understand, Lauren."

She brushed a kiss under his jaw. "I do."

He pulled her up until their lips touched, parted, touched again. Whispering incoherent things, his mouth skittered over her face. Her hair fell forward, forming a golden curtain enclosing them. Lauren made a soft sound, seeking the full satisfaction of his kiss. His tongue spiraled deep into the warmth of her mouth, questing and seeking, tender and wild. Instinctively her hips began the rhythm. Ryder stretched out his legs. Lauren arched and bent her knees. They came together, his hardness to her softness.

She gasped his name.

He sighed hers.

LAUREN WAS IN Mama Jane's garden when Michael Armstead drove up the next morning.

"I thought I'd find you here," he said, looking oddly excited.

Slowly she began to pull off her gloves. "It's no secret where Justin and I are staying, Michael. And Hattie Bell, too," she tacked on pointedly. She could also have mentioned Murphy and Jannsen, she thought sardonically, but it wasn't important. She didn't need to justify anything to Michael. However, he did owe her some answers.

"Where on earth have you been, Michael?"

"Florida, for starters," he told her. "And then New Orleans. I ended up in Denver."

Her mouth fell open. "Denver?"

"We've been operating in a hotbed of intrigue, Lauren."

She was in no mood for drama. "Please, Michael. Between the FBI and bodyguards and robots running amok, I've just about had it. Now, please tell me what you came to say."

"Malcolm Stern is in love with a woman who works for NuTekNiks."

"What?" Lauren squeaked, holding back laughter with an effort.

"He's the one who's been selling Holt designs to that lousy outfit."

That could well be true, she thought, but Malcolm...in love? No, it was too much. "Malcolm Stern, my...our Malcolm?"

"The inventor of Hercules, yes."

"How did you find that out, Michael?" she asked faintly.

"After that incident with you and Hercules, I was suspicious of him." He paused, meeting her eyes. "It was too similar to what happened to Clay. I decided to follow him one night."

"To the Blue Marlin?"

"No, he didn't go there; the woman did."

Lauren looked confused.

"She and Stern met at a restaurant, but left in separate cars. It was odd, but I didn't realize the significance of it...then. The next night, I did as I told you I would. I went to the Blue Marlin and she was there. Imagine my surprise when I discovered she was the secretary to Jonathan Green."

"NuTekNiks's president?"

"The same. I had to drink a lot of beer and listen to a lot of macho bar talk, but I found out she's his secretary."

She sighed. He was truly enjoying playing private detective. "And what does that prove, Michael?"

"We know they're getting our technology some way. It has to be Malcolm. He's doing it for love of a woman," Michael said, his contemptuous tone revealing his own opinion of that. "Selling us down the river for sex."

She drew in a deep breath. "I appreciate you making such an all-out effort on this, Michael, but what you've told me doesn't really prove anything." She rubbed her forehead. "It's pretty incredible to think of our Malcolm nursing a grand passion." What about his wife and child in East Germany? she wondered. Was the FBI on the wrong track?

"That's not all I discovered, Lauren."

"What else?"

"Braden is not the sterling character you believe him to be," he said.

"Oh?" The tone of her voice cooled noticeably.

"I know you trust Jake Levinson's judgment. He found Braden and persuaded you that he was trustworthy." He was suddenly defensive. "I definitely think some of the blame for this belongs at his door."

"Get to the point, Michael."

"Do you remember the contract that so conveniently fell into our laps the same week Braden showed up?

"Hy-Tech in Pensacola?"

"Yes. Braden's been on their payroll for years. I checked. Throwing that contract to our company was a shrewd move on his part. It was a way to line his own pockets at Hy-Tech and get a firsthand look at sophisticated Holt designs and techniques."

"Next, he talked you into setting him up as production manager where he'd have access to anything else he might decide he wanted. He's an expert in the field and uniquely qualified to siphon off anything he had a buyer for."

Lauren stared back at him wordlessly.

"Where is he, anyway?" Michael inquired, seeming to recall suddenly that he was on Braden's property.

"He's . . . he went to the sheriff's office."

He frowned. "Sheriff's office?"

"To file a report." She waved a hand vaguely, speaking through lips that barely moved. "We had an accident in the Blazer last night. Someone cut the brake line. He discovered it this morning."

"My God, were you hurt?"

"No."

"Well..." He seemed distracted for a moment. "What do you plan to do about all this, Lauren?"

She pinched the bridge of her nose, feeling as old as...as Malcolm Stern. "I don't know, Michael."

He cleared his throat and moved slightly closer. "Lauren, we never get any time together anymore, but I've been doing a lot of thinking about your situation."

Oh, no, she just wanted him to go. Her head was throbbing, trying to absorb everything he'd turned up about Ryder.

He caught her hand. "Lauren, you need someone to turn to who you can trust now. We're good together, and you know how I feel about you. Ever since Clay died, it's been you and me together, when you get right down to it."

She pulled at her hand, and reluctantly he let it go.

"Braden just happened along at a time when you needed someone with his experience," he told her with a smile that did nothing to reassure her. "It was a mistake to let him take over like he did, but fortunately we found him out in time."

"I didn't let him take over, Michael," she said coolly.

He hardly heard her. "Forget him, Lauren. You and I can make a go of this plant, and we can do it as man and wife."

She stared at him, totally repelled. Why today of all days had Michael decided to propose? "It's not a good time, Michael. I'm upset and worried. Ryder—"

"Didn't you hear me, Lauren? Braden's got irons in the fire from here to infinity! Pensacola and New Orleans are just the beginning. He's hooked up with some outfit in Denver and if I'd had more time, I could have chased down leads in L.A. and Honolulu."

"He's a consultant, Michael."

"Consultant!" He swore. "He wants your company. Are you too hung up on him to see it?"

He sliced the air with one hand. "Forget Braden! Don't be a bigger fool than you've already been. Is he so fantastic in bed that you're going to hand him the plant?"

She froze him with a single look. "I think you'd better leave, Michael."

Instantly he realized his mistake. "Lauren, I'm sorry. I shouldn't have said that."

"But you did, and now I know your true opinion of me personally and my judgment and my ability to run my company." She mustered her tattered dignity and looked him directly in the eye. "I'll just say this. I don't need you or Ryder Braden or any man to help me hold my life together. And if you plan to keep your job, I suggest that you remember it."

She forgot Michael and his clumsy attempt to manipulate her almost before his car disappeared. The real challenge was not to panic over what she'd learned about Ryder. Deception and a betrayal of trust had nearly destroyed her relationship with him once before. She paced restlessly, longing for him to return. Everything Michael said was so *plausible*.

Her head spinning, she thought back to the day when the Hy-Tech contract had come to them. As Michael pointed out, it was right after Ryder had come on the scene. Was he getting money under the table from Hy-Tech? Was he managing production in her plant so that he could get his hands on all the designs, instead of just the few that NuTekNiks had stolen? She thought about the first night they'd made love, how she had awakened and found him gone from her bed. She'd found him in Justin's room, jubilant over finding the lost designs.

She cringed with a growing sense of foreboding. What if she'd been worried about the wrong thing all along? What if he didn't really care anything about Justin? A searing, twisting pain caught at her heart. After all, he had known about him for eleven years and had done nothing. Her thoughts raced ahead, darting first one way, then another. Did he care about his son? Or her? She sat down, feeling sick. Dear God, was it her business he'd wanted all along? Did he want the Holt Company? She had to have some answers.

WHEN RYDER CAME from the sheriff's office, she was waiting for him. He was dusty and tired looking and utterly appealing. She hardened her heart, watching him cram his sunglasses into his shirt pocket and head toward her. He was going to kiss her; it was in his eyes.

"Why didn't you tell me about your connection with Hy-Tech?"

He stopped, the kiss forgotten. Something—a frown, a flare of surprise, she couldn't be sure—came and was then gone from Ryder's face. "Hy-Tech?" he shrugged. "I guess because it never came up in conversation. I've consulted for them for years. Why, Lauren?" His tone was quiet, not a bit like a man with something to hide. "Why do you ask now?"

She was put off momentarily. "Did you get—" she waved a hand, trying to come up with a term that wasn't too offensive "—ah, anything from Hy-Tech for arranging that contract with my company?"

He eyed her narrowly. "You mean personally?"

She met his look squarely. "Yes."

"No."

For the life of her, she couldn't think what to say to that. She could believe him, or not. But he was a man who had secrets; she already knew that. She needed to know more.

"I knew they had the work going," he told her. "And it was no secret your plant needed work. I put the two of you together."

"You could have accepted a gratuity from them," she said. "A finder's fee . . . or something."

"A kickback," he said bluntly.

Oh, she was no good at this. Since Michael had left, all she'd done was chase chaotic thoughts round and round in her head. Her first impulse had been to pack and leave, but there was too much at stake. Maybe he could explain everything. If he couldn't, and he really wanted the company, instinct told her that barring him from the plant would cause him more dismay. Now she just didn't know. It wasn't that he couldn't explain; it was that her trust in him was too shaky, untried. He'd deceived her before. Was he deceiving her again?

"Ryder, why did you take the job as my production manager?"

Ryder turned from her and went to the window. She would hardly believe the truth, he thought, feeling the pain of disappointment and deep hurt. Everything he had done since coming into her life he'd been compelled to do, compelled by something beyond logic, beyond rational thinking. His heart had sought to seal the connection between them. Would she believe that?

Still not looking at her, he said, "Why do you think I did?"

"I don't know!" she cried. "You're overqualified, you don't need the work...you tell me. Clay's designs are valuable. Only a few people could understand them even if they saw them. You could. And you have the connections to market them."

A tiny muscle moved in his jaw. Still he didn't turn.

She swallowed around the tightness in her throat. "Or you could marry the widow and have it all," she said.

He closed his eyes. "I see you've done some thinking since I left."

"Please answer me, Ryder."

He turned and looked at her. "Don't forget Justin. I could have you and the company and Justin."

She had been pale before. Now she looked like a ghost.

"What happened, Lauren? Last night I thought we reached an understanding. I told you that I love you. I want to build a life with you and Justin. When I left this morning, you were a happy, satisfied woman. Now you're full of suspicion and accusations."

"Michael came while you were gone."

"Michael."

"He'd been doing some...investigating. He told me about Hy-Tech."

"Did he also mention the FBI is looking for him?"

She frowned. "No."

"They're on their way to pick up Malcolm Stern right now. The evidence against Armstead is inconclusive, but not for long. Where did he go?"

"I don't know. To his apartment, I guess."

He regarded her steadily for a long moment, before moving abruptly from the window and striding across the floor. At the door, he turned. "I've just about had enough of your precious Michael." He reached into his pocket and pulled out some keys. "I'll have to use your car since the Blazer is wrecked. Stay put," he ordered, heading for the porch steps with Lauren at his heels. "And keep an eye on Justin. Murphy and Jannsen are off for the weekend."

She caught his arm. "Ryder, I...I may not be here when you get back," she told him.

He pinned her with a look. "Then you'd better find a good place to hide," he told her grimly. "Because you and I have unfinished business, lady."

"MOM . . ."

"I told you, Justin, go to your room and pack your things."

"But why? Won't Ryder wonder why we up and left like this?"

Lauren set her jaw.

"Mom, I heard you and Ryder fighting."

"It's rude to eavesdrop. I've told you that." She unsnapped the clasp on a piece of luggage and flipped the lid open.

"Don't you love him anymore?"

Her hands hesitated, but only for a second. How did he *know* these things? "You're too young to understand, Justin."

"I like living here with Ryder, Mom."

She closed her eyes. "Go pack, Justin. I'm not telling you again."

Only after Lauren was ready to go, did she realize she didn't have a car. Hattie Bell didn't bother to conceal her relief.

"You're making a big mistake running away like this, honey. You haven't done anything this silly since you were a teenager."

"I know you think Ryder has no faults, Hattie, but there are things you don't understand." She ran a distracted hand through her hair. Was she making a mistake?

"I understand he won't be happy when he comes back here and finds you and that boy gone," Hattie muttered darkly.

Clancy. She could call Clancy and ask her to pick them up. Of course, she would be subjected to a third degree. She hesitated, her hand hovering over the phone. Maybe it would be a good thing. Having to justify her decision to Clancy would force her to think it over. Her whole life was at stake here, her future with Ryder, Justin's relationship with the one single man in the world who was the perfect father for him. She picked up the phone.

Busy! Damn it, was everything going to go wrong today? She slammed the receiver down and looked around for Justin. When she couldn't locate him in the house or up in his room, she went outside. After calling him several times and searching the immediate area, she felt a tiny tremor along her spine. Panic wouldn't help, she reminded herself and hurried inside to find Hattie Bell. Together they began calling and searching in earnest.

She tried to tell herself he would be just around the next bush or the next tree. Although it wasn't like him to flagrantly disobey her, it was possible she'd pushed him too far. He wasn't leaving Ryder's place willingly. She put an icy-cold hand to her throat.

She called his name again. But all she heard were crickets and early night sounds. It was getting dark. Her mouth dry, she forced herself to think where he could be. The place was so isolated, he couldn't have walked to the nearest neighbor. Besides why would he? She refused to think the word that hovered on the edge of her mind.

"Lordy, do you think he's been kidnapped?" Hattie Bell moaned, putting both hands on her cheeks.

"Oh, Hattie..." Lauren took a deep breath. His bike. Was his bicycle gone? Hurrying around the corner of the house, she saw that it was missing from the bike stand Ryder had made for it. Her heart pounding, she sank down on the porch steps. It was dark, and the only road out was long and lonely. Where was he? Was he alone? Was he hurt?

"We gotta tell Mr. Ryder!" Hattie Bell said, heading for the phone.

Oh, Ryder, I need you now.

AT THE PLANT Malcolm Stern shuffled down the hall heading for the data-control center. This was his last mission. If he failed he would never see Anna and his son. His contact had been most emphatic about that. Authorities were closing in, she informed him. So be it. He would make this last effort and then... He patted his pocket where the gun weighed heavily. He was very tired.

If he had any regrets, they were that he hadn't acquired all the access codes from Clay Holt before arranging the accident. Muttering to himself, he made a mental review of the particular design that his contact demanded from him not later than tonight. How much simpler all his tasks would have been this past year with the access codes. Maybe then, Anna's release could have been arranged.

Hearing a noise, he stopped abruptly. There should be no one remaining in the plant, especially in the computer room. He had waited until everyone authorized to work on Saturday had departed. Even the janitors were in another area. Frowning, he peered through the small window in the door. He blinked in amazement. It was Clay Holt's young son seated before the monitor. Stern's gaze narrowed suddenly at the screen. The boy was not playing one of the silly video games. The schematic displayed on the monitor was familiar. Stern himself had been privy to Holt's early work on the design. Soon after, Holt had become more secretive with his work, an attitude that had made Stern's mission very difficult.

He stepped back from the door, his face thoughtful. He remembered the frequency with which Holt had brought his son into the plant. Always the boy had gravitated to the computers. He was intelligent. On the occasions Stern had spoken to him—always in the company of his father—he had been impressed. Did the boy posses the precious access codes?

There was only one way to find out. His expression intent, Stern pushed open the door.

CHAPTER SIXTEEN

Armstead had not been at his apartment. Fed up with Lauren's right-hand man and the horse he rode in on, Ryder's temper was simmering just shy of hot, as he pulled up at the plant in a squeal of tires and spraying gravel. Right behind Armstead's fancy Jag. He didn't know what the creep was doing here on a Saturday night, but he intended to make it his business to find out.

He was out and halfway up the steps when a car pulled in off the street and stopped. Frowning, he watched as the passenger door was flung open and Lauren scrambled out, before the driver, whom he could see now was Clancy, had a chance to open her door.

Lauren felt a moment's uncertainty as Ryder stared at her from his position on the steps. Would she always feel this overwhelming instinct to fly into the safety of his arms when she was frightened? A feeling of relief and rightness suddenly bloomed deep inside her, and she knew she would. Always. Who else could understand the depth of her fear for Justin except Ryder?

"Ryder, Justin's missing!"

He started toward her, concern etching a sharp line between his eyebrows. Automatically he opened his arms as she reached him and caught her up hard against him.

"Wait, calm down, sweetheart." His tone was soothing, the words spoken against her temple. She knew he could feel her trembling, but some needy part of her that had been as cold as death sought the warmth and reassurance only Ryder could give her. He caught her face in his hands and made her look at him. "Now, tell me."

"Oh, Ryder, I got ready to leave, and he didn't want to. I told him we had to, that there were things he didn't understand, and you know how he hates to be told that. It was only a few minutes later that I came to my senses, but by then he was no-where around." Her eyes clung to his, frantic. "Nowhere, Ryder. Oh, God, please don't let this happen."

He pushed her head against his chest and held her there for a second or two. "Don't cry, darling. And don't panic. We'll find him." He started up the steps with his arm around her and remembered Clancy.

"Go get Jake," he told her. "Tell him to get Whitman at the FBI." Clancy nodded and without a word turned and ran back to her car.

"Now, when did you last see him?"

"It was when I told him to go and pack." Desperately she tried to think back. "It was a good hour and a half ago, Ry-der. Oh, what do you think could have happened to him?"

"Did he say anything that might give us a clue?"

"No," her voice rose. "Nothing, nothing."

He hugged her again, his hand warm and reassuring at her waist. With an effort, she tried to keep her teeth from chatter-ing. "He couldn't have gone far," he said, thinking out loud. "The place is deserted and—"

"His bike was gone."

"Good." When she started and glanced up at him, he ex-plained, "That means he meant to leave. If he'd been taken against his will, they'd have hardly bothered with his bike."

A rush of complicated emotion was released with his state-ment: relief that he hadn't been kidnapped; fear that he'd started out on that deserted road alone; guilt that she'd caused her son to run away from home.

Standing on the steps in front of the plant, Ryder thought of the possible places Justin would go. Scotty's or Curtis's, maybe. His gaze drifted over the small landscaped area where the flagpole and the iron bench were. His eyes stopped and flicked back again. Justin's bike was leaning against the flag-pole.

"Lauren . . ." He touched the soft underside of her chin and turned her head gently in the direction of the bike. "He's here."

For a second she simply stared. And then she slumped against him with a cry.

"He's inside with Armstead," Ryder said in a tone laced with menace. "Stay here."

"No."

"I mean it, Lauren. Let me handle this."

She put both hands on his arms. "I'm not arguing about your rights where Justin is concerned anymore, Ryder. But I have some rights, too. I'm not waiting out here."

They entered the plant quietly and did not turn on any lights, at Ryder's insistence. Outwardly Lauren still staunchly defended Michael, but Justin's disappearance and the accident in the Blazer and Michael's new hostility had shaken her. There were depths to Michael she had just glimpsed.

They headed directly for the data center. While they were still in the hall they heard voices. The place was brightly lit. The door was wide open. Ryder put out a hand to caution Lauren. She looked up at him and nodded. Urging her to stay slightly behind him, they peered in between the door and the doorjamb.

Justin was sitting at the keyboard. Michael Armstead was standing a few feet from him. At his shoulder was Malcolm Stern. Stern had a gun and it was pointed at Armstead.

Ryder heard Lauren's involuntary gasp and quickly covered her mouth, frowning at the evidence before his eyes. He was startled to discover that Armstead wasn't in league with Stern, but that wouldn't help Justin, whose cheek, he noted with a grim hardening of his jaw, was bruised. All of his years of survival rushed to the forefront of his mind, readying him for the supreme challenge—to protect and defend his son. Standing flush against the wall, he restrained Lauren with one arm. He could feel her whole body quaking. Quickly he reviewed his options.

Armstead was speaking. "You're making a big mistake, Malcolm. Let the kid go. He's accessed the stuff you wanted, and you've got a printout. They're on to you, believe me. I'm not making this up."

Stern looked defeated suddenly. "It does not matter. I am committed for this last mission."

"Haven't you done enough? Clay was supposed to be your friend, man. You've sold his designs to NuTekNiks; you've sat back and watched them practically push the plant down the tubes. His widow's been hounded and harassed. Give it up, for God's sake."

Neither man appeared aware of Justin seated between them, listening.

"One moment, if you please." Stern gave a short bark of a laugh. "You speak as though you yourself have the interests of the widow at heart, Armstead. Do not bother to lie. My contacts are aware of your petty attempts to, as you say, hound and harass—a bit of arson, shipping mix-ups, malfunctioning equipment."

"You're crazy, Stern!" Michael gave Justin a quick look.

Malcolm Stern nodded slowly. "Well, we shall see. Nevertheless, we must proceed here." He made a gesture with the gun. "I know what I have to do, and nothing you say can persuade me otherwise."

"And what is that, Malcolm? What do you have to do?"

A spasm of emotion twisted Stern's mouth. "She promised, this one last time. She promised."

Michael shook his head. "Who, Malcolm? Who promised what?"

"Evelyn . . ."

"Jonathan Green's secretary? Your lover?"

Stern's laugh was pitiful, but his eyes were wild and unfocused. "Lover? I have no lover. There's just my wife." His face crumpled suddenly. "My wife, my Anna."

Michael's eyes narrowed suddenly. "You killed Holt, didn't you?"

Stern seemed to focus his mind on the question. He straightened a bit, still pathetic in his dingy lab coat. "I arranged an accident. He was an impediment that had to be eliminated."

"Impediment? He was a genius!"

"He would not be reasonable." He gave Michael a simple look. "My contacts demanded his designs in exchange for Anna's release."

Michael stared. "You did it for some dumb broad? You are crazy!"

"Stay there!" Stern brandished the gun menacingly and forced Michael back against a row of file cabinets. He turned to Justin. "Now, boy." He nudged Justin's shoulder with his free hand. "You must print out that document you located in the index."

Justin turned his face up to Stern. "I don't know whether I can call it up or not, Mr. Stern."

Stern put out a finger and touched the bruise on Justin's cheek. "I do not want to cause you pain, boy," he murmured, looking regretful. "But if I'm ever to see Anna and my own son again, you must obey me."

Lauren had never felt such terror. Malcolm Stern was obviously a deranged man, a traitor and a murderer. The things he said were muddled and incoherent, but he was desperate. It wouldn't take much provocation to push him over the line. And Justin could be the victim. She looked up at Ryder, her eyes full of anguish and a mother's fear.

He bent to her. "Don't make a sound," he whispered. "I think I can slip inside behind those files and then work my way over to them." She started to object, but he caught her arm and squeezed it with sudden authority. "Do as I say, Lauren. Justin's life is at stake here. Now, go into that little office—" he hiked his chin to indicate the door across the hall "—and don't come out until I say you can. Okay?"

She gazed at him a moment, torn, instinctively feeling a mother's reluctance to walk away from her child. And then she looked at the deadly little scenario across the room, where Justin was at the mercy of a crazed man.

The decision was taken from her when, incredibly, something prompted Justin to turn slightly and see them. He stared directly for a second or two, and then without a flicker of an eyelash he turned back to the computer console.

"Mr. Stern, I have to go to the bathroom," he said a moment later. *Cool, Justin,* Ryder thought, swamped with pride and admiration at the boy's courage. He would have to come through the doors where Ryder and Lauren waited, to get to the bathroom.

"Not now, boy." Stern adjusted his bifocals to focus on the monitor.

"I'm sorry, Mr. Stern, but I really have to go."

Michael cleared his throat. "I think you'd better let him," he suggested.

"I'm not playing games, young man!" Stern admonished, holding the gun up as a reminder.

Justin looked properly chastened, but undaunted. "If I don't go, I don't see how I can keep my mind on this stuff."

Stern sucked in an exasperated breath. "Then we will all have to go." Justin stood up quickly. Stern jerked his head toward Armstead. "You go after the boy and remember, I will use this if I have to."

Michael warily stepped behind Justin, but when he would have put a reassuring hand on the boy's shoulder, Malcolm Stern uttered a sharp objection. Michael obeyed, but he was clearly prepared to use Justin's tactic, somehow. If Armstead caused a hair of Justin's head to be hurt, Ryder vowed the man would wish Stern had used the gun on him.

Ryder touched Lauren's shoulder and urged her toward the small room. With a last, agonized, backward look, she went. He flattened himself against the wall and waited, while Justin calmly led the group of three to him.

Justin's karate yell startled everyone, Ryder included. But mostly it was Malcolm Stern who was rattled. The old man's nerves simply couldn't stand up to a martial arts cry. Justin quickly dropped to the floor, rolling into a ball that Michael Armstead couldn't avoid. They both went down in a tangle of arms and legs. Stern bellowed once in rage, pointing the gun at the downed pair. Ryder stepped out and delivered one sharp chop to the back of Stern's neck. He dropped like a puppet whose strings were suddenly cut.

There was an instant of quiet as they all stared at Malcolm Stern. Sprawled on the floor, he looked old and pitiful. The gun had flown out of his hand and lay against the baseboard where it had landed.

Justin blinked once or twice, his valor all used up. And then he scrambled to his feet and launched himself at Ryder, whose arms opened to receive him. Eyes closed, throat tight, Ryder could do nothing for the sheer power of his love for Justin. Wordlessly he treated himself to another second or two of the joy and relief of having his son, unharmed, in his arms, and then he let him go.

"Where's Mom?" Justin asked with eyes suspiciously bright.

"Right here." Lauren fumbled with the door of the tiny dark office and rushed out. Justin ran to her, and she swept him up, her eyes closed in heartfelt thanks. *She could so easily have lost him!*

"Are you hurt?" she said, her voice tight with emotion. Leaning back she inspected his face, wincing when she saw the bruise.

"I'm okay, Mom."

Michael was on his feet again, favoring his elbow which was skinned and bleeding from the tumble in the hall. He was watching them warily. "Umm, how long have you been here?"

Ryder gave him a hard look. "Long enough."

"Well..." He gestured to Stern. "He came in and found Justin at the console. He knew Clay and Justin had spent a lot of time here together. He decided to use Justin to get all the files, once he discovered he had such complete knowledge of the system.''

Not a muscle moved in Ryder's face. "Clear your desk, Armstead. You're fired.''

Armstead sent a challenging look to Lauren. "Are you going to let him do that, Lauren?''

"We heard everything, Michael. Do as he says.''

Everyone turned at the flurry of sound down the hall. "That'll be the FBI," Ryder said. "A little late.''

Michael frowned. "Why are they here?''

"For starters," Ryder said with obvious satisfaction, "to pick you up, Armstead.''

"What!'' he blustered. "Now look here, Braden. The Feds don't have a thing on me and neither do you. I—''

"Tell it to them," Ryder said, taking Lauren's arm and putting a hand on Justin's shoulder.

"Are you mad at me for leaving the house without telling you?'' Justin asked, looking warily at his mother and Ryder.

Lauren put a hand on his shoulder. "Not mad, Justin. But you certainly gave us a good scare. Striking out in the dark on your own was very dangerous. Why did you do it?''

Justin dropped his eyes. "I knew what was causing the trouble between you and Ryder. It was all that missing stuff—my Dad's designs and the secrets in the big computer at the plant....'' He looked at Ryder. "And maybe a little bit Michael Armstead. I couldn't do anything about Ryder disliking Michael Armstead 'cause I didn't like him much myself.''

Ryder felt a little spurt of satisfaction. It might be unfair, but still it was gratifying to know that Justin shared his disdain for Armstead. He glanced at Lauren, who refused to look his way.

"I knew you would probably be mad, Mom," Justin said. "But I figured if I was able to do any good with the big computer, maybe you wouldn't stay mad at me very long.''

One look at his anxious, bruised face and Lauren forgot the stern lecture he deserved. Since Ryder was so eager to exercise his parental authority, she'd let him take it from here.

Ryder shot her a wry look, unwilling to scold his son when the sight of Stern's gun pointed at him was still fresh in his mind. Besides, he was too busy feeling pleased over how far Justin had been prepared to go to fix things between his mother and Ryder. He cleared his throat. "You meant well, Justin, but next time remember the house rules—you don't go anywhere without asking permission.''

"Yes sir.''

Some disciplinarian, Lauren thought, secretly amused.

"Can we go home now?'' Justin asked, stretching his legs to match Ryder's strides.

"Yes.'' Ryder squeezed his son's shoulder and pulled Lauren into the place that seemed designed for her under his arm.

"Your place?'' Justin inquired, dividing a look between his mother and Ryder.

Over his head, their eyes met. "Yes,'' they said together.

Outside, they lagged behind when Justin dashed toward the car.

"Poor Malcolm,'' Lauren murmured, thinking of the old man with his broken dreams. "Michael was right in a way. He did do it all for love. For his wife, Anna.''

"And his son,'' Ryder put in. "Evelyn, the woman, was his contact to a communist agent. She promised him papers for Anna and his son in exchange for Holt secrets.''

"Incredible.''

"But she was greedy,'' Ryder said. "As secretary to NuTekNiks's president, she recognized the overall value of Clay's designs. She had Malcolm hooked, anyway. She simply coerced more and more from him.''

She had probably ordered Clay's death, Ryder thought, but he kept that idea to himself. Later he would talk to the authorities. Right now, he was worried about Justin and Lauren. He wanted to take them home, where they could talk about Clay and the way he had died.

"Jonathan Green was in it with her,'' Lauren said, marveling at the audacity of people.

"Yes.'' Ryder hugged her to him suddenly. "Your lawsuit will be dropped, all the harassment that NuTekNiks instigated here in your plant will end, and you'll have to look around for somebody to replace me as your production manager.''

She paled. She had known all along that he was not the settling down kind, but . . .

"What's the matter?'' he asked, tipping her face up.

She licked her lips and watched as something flared in his eyes in response. "You're resigning as my production manager?''

He angled his head back, and she got a look at the devil dancing in his eyes. "Well, I kind of thought I might be in line for a promotion. Now that I finally managed to get Armstead booted out, how about making me general manager?"

Her lashes fell. "I'm not sure I can afford you."

"We can probably strike a bargain." He squinted, looking at her with his head to one side. "The price might have to be negotiated, but I'm a reasonable man."

She smiled. "Okay, what's your price?"

He didn't hesitate. "Marriage, sugar. You promised and I'm holding you to it. I want you and Justin and Hattie Bell set up permanently in that big old house. Work as long as you want to at that plant, but I'm betting you're going to be a very busy lady at home."

Pale pink color stole into her cheeks as joy stole into her heart. "Doing what?"

"Making babies."

She made a soft, faint sound.

He added emphatically, "The old-fashioned way."

She came to see her son—
and stayed to marry his father!

A FAMILY AFFAIR

Sandra James

CHAPTER ONE

THE STILLNESS of the night was broken only by the quiet murmur of the sea. Gently undulating waves lapped the Gulf Coast shoreline. Soft as a sigh, a salt-tanged breeze wrapped its way around the solitary figure roaming the sandy stretch of beach.

There was a sensual fullness to the tall and graceful form, from the curve of rounded breasts beneath the pale blue cotton top, to the coltish legs clad in dark blue slacks. The woman ceased her restless prowling and slowly closed her eyes, lifting her face to the sable canopy that stretched endlessly above. Hundreds of diamond-bright stars wove a meandering pathway through the night-dark sky. The moonlight shone down on her profile, etching in silver the small straight nose, the full mobile mouth, the wavy hair that flowed like silk halfway down the proud lines of her back.

To a casual observer, she might have appeared much like the serene moonlit Texas night of which she was so much a part. But only the moon, the stars and the sky were there to bear witness to the turmoil in her mind—and her heart.

No, there was little comfort to be found in the solitude of the night for Jenna Bradford. And for the third night in a row, she was very much afraid she would find sleep just as elusive.

A sudden burst of wind sent her long black hair whipping around her face. Eyes that were normally a vivid shade of green turned dark with uncertainty as she opened them and lifted a slender hand to brush the wayward strands from her face. Wrapping her arms around herself to ward off the sudden chill, she retraced her steps with a long-legged stride that soon carried her to the rear of a long string of apartment buildings dotting the shoreline. Once on the flagstoned terrace, however, she made no move to enter her home. Instead she settled herself on a lounge chair and gazed out at the glasslike surface of the Gulf.

Jenna smiled a little ruefully as she pulled a blanket over he shoulders. Neil would have a fit if he could see her now. He late-night excursions would have to stop once they were mar ried; he would never stand for it. Perhaps Neil was a bit over protective, but he had compensating qualities, she hastened t remind herself. He was concise and articulate, not only in hi manner of speaking but in his way of thinking, as well. Sh suspected this stemmed from his years in law school. With hi oftentimes serious, intent look, she occasionally teased him tha he reminded her of a wise old bird. A pair of owlish glasses wa all that was needed to complete the picture. Yet, even thoug she admired his sound reasoning and judicious nature, she wa beginning to wonder if he wasn't rather...ambitious.

And somehow, Jenna wasn't quite sure how she felt abou that.

But now was a time for joy, a time to love and be loved, a time every little girl dreams of. She should have been deliri ously happy, she told herself for what seemed the thousandt time that day. Well, perhaps not deliriously so, since that wasn' her style. But certainly she had every reason to be thankful.

Again her eyes grew troubled as she gazed at the lumines cent moon riding high in the sky. *Thankful.* It was, perhaps, a odd word to describe a woman who was to be married to successful Houston attorney in six weeks' time.

Prewedding jitters. Could that possibly be what this vagu uneasiness about her future husband could be? She breathed a uneasy sigh. She wasn't sure, and a twinge of guilt shot throug her. Neil, her wedding, her future with him, should have fillec her thoughts to the exclusion of all else. Instead the past fev days had found her looking over her shoulder, unable to es cape the specter of the past.

No, it wasn't Neil who dwelled in her thoughts so much as...Robbie. *Robbie.* Again she felt that elusive tug on hei heart, like a fish caught on a hook and struggling to be free.

It was hard to believe the evening three days prior had started so innocently. Jenna shook her head. Her feelings, capped tightly in storage for nearly four years, had suddenly escaped, like a burst of steam from a kettle, and now she was being forced to deal with them. The only problem was how. Her heart gave her only one choice, but her mind urged caution. Three days of searching and she still wasn't sure. But was her choice the right one? For her? For him? For all concerned?

Her doubts had started Monday night, just a few days after she'd stopped working. It had been ages since she'd taken a vacation, and with so many details to be taken care of before the wedding, she had decided to take a short leave of absence from her nursing job in the Galveston Hospital Emergency Room. She and her mother had spent the day in Houston shopping for a wedding gown, and when her mother had headed home late in the afternoon, Jenna had met Neil for an early dinner. Later, when the nose of his car pointed toward Galveston, she glanced over in surprise as he exited the highway for a suburb twenty-five miles from the city. He drove straight to the heart of a residential district, finally pulling over to the curb on a wide, tree-lined street.

"Well, what do you think?" With the characteristic energy that was almost his trademark, Neil was at the car door and opening it for her before she had a chance to turn in her seat.

Out on the sidewalk, Jenna could only stare at the large Cape Cod-style house in front of her. Dense foliage edged the house before giving way to a velvety green lawn that stretched to the curb. Tendrils of ivy hugged the base of the huge oak tree in the middle of the front yard, lending a homey ambience that she found immensely appealing.

"Why are we stopping here, Neil?" she asked curiously as he pulled her toward the house. "I thought you were taking me home."

A slight breeze ruffled his thick brown hair, and he grinned openly at her. "How would you feel about calling this place home?" Pulling her toward the front door, he laced his fingers through hers.

Stunned, Jenna turned slightly to stare over his shoulder. Her gaze encompassed the house and surrounding expanse of lawn before she turned her tentative look on him.

"Well, don't you have anything to say?"

A niggling feeling of suspicion traced its way up her spine. "Neil," she began, "are you trying to tell me—"

"I bought this place?" he finished for her, smiling. "Not exactly, but I think we should think seriously about it. Even the location is perfect—halfway between Houston and Galveston. It's no more than a thirty-minute drive to work for either of us." He grabbed her hand and pulled her along behind him. "Come on, I'll give you the grand tour."

Jenna was speechless as he produced a key and led her through the house, exclaiming delightedly over the extensive use of wood and brick throughout, the polished oak and parquet floors, the crisp starched curtains hanging at the windows. When they were standing in what Neil informed her was the master bedroom, he wrapped an arm around her and tipped her face up to his. "Tell me the truth now. Do you like it?"

"I—I love it," she told him breathlessly. "But I had no idea—"

"I know." His mouth curved in a self-satisfied smile. "I wanted to surprise you. You don't mind, do you?"

"Mind! How could I mind living in this lovely home?" Her fingers traced his cleanly shaven jaw. "You're a treasure, Neil. You know that, don't you?"

He laughed and pressed a kiss in the palm of her hand before his eyes roamed around the room. "You're the one who's a treasure. I wish I'd found you years ago. Long before I ever met Anna." He shook his head. "Marrying her was the worst mistake of my life. Thank God the marriage lasted only two years."

Jenna smiled. "Marrying her was probably the *only* mistake you've ever made in your life," she teased gently. "And you did find the perfect woman eventually."

"A woman after my own heart," he said, looking down at her. "Just as dependable, efficient, stable and practical—"

"As you are," Jenna finished, laughing. "I've never been much of a believer in the theory that opposites attract."

Neil drew her body firmly against his. "We are a lot alike, you know. Anna used to prattle on incessantly. I think your reserve was one of the first things that attracted me to you."

"I didn't think you even noticed," she recalled dryly. "The night we met you were too busy talking about the job offers you'd had and which one you were going to accept."

His smile was a little sheepish. "What can I say? I was fresh out of law school and I guess it went to my head."

On reflection, she could see why. Neil had worked hard for his law degree. His parents had farmed a small piece of land in west Texas that had seen drought after drought for many a year, and his childhood hadn't been the easiest. After a stint in the military, Neil had been nearly twenty-six before he'd been able to scrape up enough money even to begin college. But despite juggling his classes with a full-time job, he had graduated from

aw school with honors. As a result, he'd had offers from sev-
ral prestigious law firms. He had finally accepted a position
as legal counsel for Citizens for Texas, a watchdog land con-
ervation group that had become a force to be reckoned with
during the past two years.

"You told me once you thought I was rather stand-offish,"
she remembered suddenly.

"You do come across that way at times," he said, raising an
eyebrow. "You're not shy, just rather conservative. Not that
there's anything wrong with that." A rare twinkle appeared in
his eyes. "But I certainly never thought I'd have an Amazon in
my bed."

She smiled in spite of herself. "You may never have one in
your bed if you keep this up," she warned him with mock se-
verity. Neil was usually so serious and businesslike; she enjoyed the few times he teased her. But the fact that she didn't
wear her heart on her sleeve was no indication that her feelings
weren't as strong as the next person's. And as for her height,
she *was* tall for a woman—five-nine in her bare feet. Secretly
she was glad she didn't have the large bone-structure that
sometimes went hand in hand with such height in a woman. As
a child, she'd hated towering over her schoolmates, boys and
girls alike. It wasn't until Jenna was thirteen, when her mother
finally convinced her to throw back her shoulders and make the
most of her slender gracefulness, that she'd gotten over her self-
consciousness. And, she had to admit, it was certainly no liability for a nurse to have a strong back.

She lifted her hands to Neil's shoulders and glanced up at
him. "When Mother and I were shopping today, I found the
most fantastic wedding dress at Neiman-Marcus." Touching
her lips gently to his, she smiled up at him. "You should see it,
Neil—yards and yards of ivory satin and lace, a high Victorian
neckline . . ."

A half smile tipped his lips. "Are you trying to tell me I'm
marrying an old-fashioned girl?"

"I thought I was marrying an old-fashioned guy," she retorted pertly.

"You are." Gently he untangled her arms from around his
neck. "Come on, I'll show you the rest."

There were four bedrooms upstairs, a country-sized kitchen,
very spacious living room and a small den downstairs. Though

the house was old, it had obviously received a great deal of tender loving care.

"Has it been on the market long?" she asked as they stepped into the dining room. Her voice bounced off the walls of the empty room.

Neil shook his head. "The owner was transferred out of state. I don't think it will take long to sell once it goes into multiple listing. Mark Henderson tipped me off about it."

"Mark?" She glanced over in surprise. A big, sandy-haired man with a booming voice, he was an acquaintance of Neil's. "I thought he was an insurance salesman."

Neil nodded. "He's taken up real estate on the side." Blue eyes alight, he clasped both her hands in his. "Well, what do you think? Should we buy it?"

Jenna frowned. "What about the price?" she asked cautiously. "You're not a struggling young attorney anymore, but can we afford it?"

A faint line appeared between his eyebrows. "You said it yourself, Jenna. I'm not a struggling young attorney. Do you think I'd even consider it if I thought it was beyond our reach?"

It was, she decided, a silly question, after all. Neil was perhaps the most organized person she had ever known, always planning ahead. Her smile reappeared. "Does that mean no more peanut butter sandwiches for lunch?"

He seemed to relax. "No more peanut butter sandwiches," he assured her, then kissed her briefly on the mouth. "The owners are eager to sell and they're asking less than market value. I think we could make this place a home, Jenna." Slipping an arm around her narrow waist, he walked her into the living room, glanced sideways at her and said lightly, "I can see it already—coming home from the office into your arms, the smell of fresh-baked bread drifting through from the kitchen, the pitter-patter of little feet upstairs...."

"Whoa!" Jenna wrinkled her nose at him. "I might be a little old-fashioned, but homemade bread? Not unless you'd like a few broken teeth. Yeast and I just don't get along. And as far as the pitter-patter of little feet..." She shook her head. "There's no hurry, remember? We've already decided to put that off for a while."

"I know. But I've been thinking." He gave a shrug. "We've got money in the bank and we're financially able to support a child. Why wait?"

Jenna stared up at him for a few seconds before gently pulling away from his arms. "But we already agreed," she protested. "We were going to wait at least a year."

Neil frowned. "What's the matter, Jenna? I thought you liked children."

She half turned away from him, aware of the displeasure in his tone. "I do," she said earnestly, then hesitated. "But there's plenty of time...."

"*This* is the perfect time." Neil's face softened as he caught her by the shoulders and turned her to face him. "And *you* are perfect in every way for me, Jenna. You'll be a perfect wife, a perfect mother." He bent to take her lips in a brief kiss. "That's why I'd like to buy this place. My apartment in Houston is no place to bring up a child. Here he or she will have room to run, room to grow."

Jenna grew suddenly stiff in his arms. "You want to buy this house because you think it's the perfect place to bring up a child? I thought you wanted it for *us*."

The minute the words were out of her mouth she realized how selfish they sounded. But Neil didn't seem to notice.

"I do. For all of us. And now that I've been giving it some serious consideration, I like the idea of having a child right away. After all, I'm a man on his way up and I won't be at Citizens for Texas forever. And I have an idea being a family man could be a big plus for my career."

"A man on his way up..." Jenna could hardly believe what she was hearing. His tone was matter-of-fact, but laced with a touch of something she found oddly disturbing. "I thought you liked your job," she said slowly. "I thought you believed in what Citizens for Texas stands for. Environmental law is your specialty."

"That's not the point, Jenna." There was a slight tinge of exasperation in his voice. "The experience has been invaluable, but who says I have to be locked in to one organization for the rest of my life? In fact, I've been putting out a few feelers lately and it looks as if I might be in hot demand. We're going places, lady!" he said almost gleefully. "I have big plans, Jenna. Plans for me, plans for you, plans for *us*." His blue eyes gleamed as he squeezed her waist and grinned down at her.

Jenna felt almost sick. There was nothing wrong with a little ambition. After all, Neil had had so little as a child and he'd come such a long way. But she couldn't shake the feeling that he was being greedy, that he wanted too much too soon. She had to struggle to find her voice. "And those plans include starting a family right away?"

"The sooner the better. In fact, even six weeks is too long to wait." His expression changed as he bent to take her lips in a hungry kiss. "I wish we were getting married tomorrow," he whispered against her mouth. "And don't say you weren't warned—I don't intend to let you out of bed for an entire week after we're married."

And that should accomplish what he wanted quite effectively, Jenna reflected with some resentment. Unable to feel her usual tingling response at his touch, she pulled away from him to gaze out the window. Darkness was settling, and pink and purple clouds hovered on the horizon. Love and family and children were what marriage was all about, so why was she feeling such a burning sense of betrayal? Neil was a strong-principled man, staunch and firm in his beliefs. He was close to his parents and two sisters, perhaps not as close as she was to her mother and father, but they kept in touch and spent many holidays together. And yet . . . here he was talking about making a home, having children and his *career* in the same breath.

She clenched her hands. She was overreacting, she told herself frantically. Putting too much into his words, looking beyond them. But that didn't explain her strange reaction to the mention of a baby so soon in their future.

Jenna's skin grew cold and clammy. Suddenly she knew what was behind this vague feeling of doubt she was experiencing, and it could be summed up in a word.

Robbie.

"Jenna, what's wrong?"

She could feel Neil's puzzled look on her face and shook her head quickly. There were some things better left unsaid and—God, but she hated to think it—forgotten. Buried in the past, where they belonged.

She forced a smile. "Nothing. Nothing at all."

And she went through the evening with a curious feeling of hope in her heart—hope that the matter would work itself out

and things could go back to the way they were before. But it was
a sense of blighted hope, as she soon discovered.

They had finally agreed to put off making a decision about
the house and give it a little more thought, but again and again
over the next three days she recalled his wish for a child, and
soon the words hung over her like an oppressive shroud. He
wanted a family right away. Regardless of Robbie, regardless
of Neil's reasons, the idea shouldn't have bothered her so
much. They had discussed children soon after their engagement six months ago, and she'd known the first time they'd
touched on the subject that she was going to have to deal with
it eventually. But now that the prospect was baldly staring her
in the face, she was aware of a nagging restlessness inside her,
and she wasn't sure why.

Still, she tried to delude herself. She even tried to picture
herself as the mother of Neil's child. Would he or she have
Neil's rich brown hair and her green eyes? Or would he have her
dark hair and Neil's blue eyes? Or would their child be a carbon copy of him—or her?

But that was when the trouble really started, because no
matter how many times she tried to envision herself with a baby
in her arms—*Neil's* baby—all she could see was another.

She drew a deep, unsteady breath as she continued to gaze
vacantly at the Gulf. There would come a day when she could
remember Robbie without this hurting, empty ache inside, but
when? *When?*

She couldn't hide things from Neil any more than she could
continue to deceive herself, and the matter had finally come to
a head a few hours ago. Neil had come for dinner, and it was
after they had cleared the table that he drew her down beside
him on the couch.

His fingers slid beneath her hair to knead the taut muscles of
her shoulders. "Something's bothering you, Jenna," he remarked softly. "Tell me what's wrong."

Jenna sat silent for a long time, her fingers clasped tightly in
her lap. For an instant she considered telling him the truth—
"the whole truth, nothing but the truth." The phrase rang like
a death sentence through her mind. Still, given the same set of
circumstances again, she knew she'd have done exactly the same
thing as she'd decided before. But would Neil understand?
Would he forgive her? Yet what was there to forgive? She'd
done nothing wrong; she had nothing to be ashamed of. She

had given two people what they had desperately longed for, all they'd ever wanted in the world, and it was a gift more precious than gold.

She had once promised herself there would be no regrets, no dwelling on the past or on what might have been.

"You've been acting strangely ever since I showed you the house." Despite his soothing touch on the muscles of her shoulders, there was a trace of impatience in his voice. "I thought you liked it."

A sigh escaped her lips and she smiled weakly. "I love the house, Neil."

When she hesitated, he pressed on. "Then what is it?" His eyes on her averted profile, he frowned, and then comprehension suddenly dawned. "It's what I said about having a baby, isn't it?"

Jenna nodded, then hesitated. "I'm not sure we should rush into it right away," she said slowly. "It would be nice to have some time to ourselves for a while."

"We've known each other for two years already, Jenna," he reasoned calmly. "And we'd have almost another year even if you got pregnant right away."

She turned away from his eyes, unable to bear his piercingly direct regard. Somehow she realized she'd secretly been nursing the hope that his desire to have a baby so soon was perhaps a moment of whimsy, a fanciful notion. After all, they'd been standing in what he hoped to see as their home, looking into the future.

She shifted uneasily on the cushions. "Yes, that's true, but . . ." She stopped, unsure of what she wanted to say, unsure of what was driving her. She and Neil were about to start a life together. Why was she suddenly plagued by doubt and senseless fears? What was wrong with her?

"I don't think you realize how strongly I feel about this, Jenna," he told her with a hint of obstinacy. "So I'd like to have a baby. What's the problem?"

"That's all well and good, Neil," she said in a carefully neutral tone. "But you seem to be forgetting I have a voice in this, as well."

Neil drew back from her abruptly. "I'm not trying to force you into anything," he said coldly. "But I'm thirty-six years old. I want to have a family while I'm young enough to enjoy it. I want to be able to run and play with my children—I don't want to be resigned to sitting on the sidelines because I'm too damned old to have a little fun.''

Jenna prickled like a cat at his sharp tone. "You're exaggerating," she countered swiftly. "You're as fit as any twenty-year old—and you're making it sound as if you're about to fall over dead any day now!"

His mouth tightened angrily. "I suppose it never occurred to you that not only would I like to be around for my children, but I'd like to be here to see my grandchildren, too!"

Her lips puckered with annoyance, she stared at him as he paced around the room. He was being completely unreasonable—wasn't he? How many couples did she know who elected to have a baby right after they were married? Surely not many. If it happened, more than likely the baby was on the way before they were married. If only he hadn't mentioned that a family could be a boon to his career. If only...

But suddenly she realized she was only making excuses. No matter what his reasons, she should have had no reservations about carrying Neil's baby, whether it was now or ten years from now. Creating a child together was the ultimate expression of love between a man and a woman, wasn't it? The thought of having Neil's child should have held no doubts, no uncertainties, but—God help her—it did. And she didn't know why.

She knew only that in some twisted, jumbled way deep in her soul it had something to do with Robbie. She closed her eyes as a feeling of hopelessness rose inside her.

"Well, don't you have anything to say?"

Jenna flinched at Neil's angry bark, opening her eyes to stare at him. His arms were crossed over his chest. She could see frustration warring with anger in his dark blue eyes, and something else, as well. The harsh and implacable look she detected on his face stunned her.

Her mind whirled giddily. She had the strangest sensation that she was seeing him for the first time...and he wasn't the earnest, thoughtful man she had come to know at all, but a stubborn one. Unyielding. She felt helpless, suddenly drained, suddenly...so very empty inside.

Slowly she shook her head, her eyes dark and cloudy as she looked at him. "I'm sorry, Neil," she said quietly. "But this is something I'll have to work out for myself."

A tense silence settled over the room. When Neil finally spoke, his voice was curiously flat and hollow sounding. "So this is where we stand. You go your way and I go mine." He paused. "Is this any way to start our marriage, Jenna?"

EVEN NOW, hours later, his words caused an empty ache and a feeling of frustration to well up inside her. Jenna stirred on the chair and glanced at the luminous dial of her watch. It was nearly midnight. She rose and stretched her cramped muscles. In the time that she had known Neil and they had started to date, they'd had the usual heated exchange every so often. But he had never—*never*—walked out on her. She was sorely tempted to call him....

As if on cue, the telephone rang. Jenna hurried to answer it, her voice rushed.

"Jenna. Were you asleep?"

Neil. "No. I was just outside...thinking." Her tone was carefully neutral as she eased into a chair. Was he still angry? Upset?

"Outside? You were outside at this time of night?"

She nearly laughed at his sharp tone, reminded of her earlier thoughts. "I'm fine, Neil," she said softly.

He surprised her by pressing no further. Instead he said in that brisk, no-nonsense way of his, "I had to talk to you, Jenna. I called to apologize." When he cleared his throat, she had the feeling that for once he was at a loss for words. But when she made no response, he went on. "You were right, Jenna. Having a baby is something we should decide together. When we make up our minds to go ahead with it, I want it to be something we both want. So..." He seemed to hesitate. "We'll put the idea on hold for a while until you make up your mind."

Jenna sat quietly through the brief speech. Perhaps she should have been relieved; she had won, hadn't she? He wasn't going to try to force something on her she didn't want or wasn't ready for. Neil had come through, after all.... As she had known he would? She *hadn't* known that, and the thought was jarring.

"I love you, Jenna."

Jenna opened her mouth—but nothing happened. Her throat constricted tightly against the words uttered so easily up until

hat moment. They simply refused to come, and it was several
econds before she finally found her voice. "I—I love you,
oo."

"Then I'm forgiven?"

Her fingers tightened on the receiver. "Y-yes."

He didn't seem to notice the almost imperceptible hesita-
ion, and they went on to talk for several more minutes. But
while she was on the phone with Neil, the hazy shroud of doubt
hat had plagued her these past few days at last began to slip
away, and she finally felt able to see her way clear through the
ıncertainty, the shadow of the past....

Her thoughts were a strange mixture of hope and fear as she
:umbled into bed that night. Later. Later she would sort out this
jumble of emotions about Neil, but for now it would have to
wait. Her marriage would have to wait. *Everything* would have
:o wait. And she could only hope that Neil would understand,
because she had the feeling he would never have brought up the
subject of a child if he'd known what it would trigger.

Because in the past few minutes Jenna had come to a very
important decision and a startling realization about herself. She
had once promised herself she would never look back, but she
couldn't go on any longer as she had been—floundering in
limbo, caught somewhere in time, trying to forget and never
quite being able to, not wanting to go back and yet afraid to
take that first step forward to sever all ties.

She was trapped and there was only one way out. In her mind
there was no right, no wrong, no past and no future. There was
only *now*....

And an overpowering need to see her son once more.

CHAPTER TWO

THE DECISION finally made, Jenna was left feeling oddly at peace with herself. She slept the sleep of the dead that night, awakening the next morning feeling far more refreshed and revitalized than she had all week. She had never been one to wallow in indecision for long; once her mind was made up, she wasted no time making clear her intentions. "Willful" was what her mother called her. She smiled a little as she showered and slipped into jeans and a pale yellow T-shirt. Her father wasn't one to mince words. "Pigheaded" was how he often referred to his daughter.

She made several quick calls to the florist and caterer. But once she sat down to address the wedding invitations she'd started a week earlier, her brief respite of peace began to shatter once more. She had to force herself to plod through the remainder of the guest list. It was well after lunch when she drove over to the post office, but once there, she stood before the big blue mailbox outside for a full minute before slowly dropping the bundles of envelopes inside. Without being consciously aware of it, she found herself at her parents' house a short time later.

She glanced up warily at the threatening purple storm clouds gathering overhead as she switched off the car engine. A gusty wind blowing in from the Gulf rattled the leaves of the huge cottonwood tree bordering the sidewalk as she hurried toward the white two-story house, wrapped on three sides by a wide porch. Jenna had come to live in this house when she was five years old, and even though she had been on her own since she'd finished her nurse's training, this was the one place in the world she would always think of as home.

A drenching sheet of rain began to fall just before she reached the shelter of the porch. Mindful of her wet feet, she ran around to the back entrance and slipped off her sandals.

"Whew! Just in time!" she muttered, stomping into the kitchen. She reached for a towel and smiled at her mother as she wiped the moisture from her face.

Marie Bradford looked worriedly from her daughter's rain-spattered cotton blouse to the moisture trickling freely down the windowpanes. "Oh, dear," she murmured, "your father will be dripping wet by the time he gets back."

"Dad's gotten lazy since he retired," Jenna said with a shake of her head. "I suppose he's out fishing again."

Her mother nodded. "I'll have to dig out the hot water bottle before he comes home. His circulation isn't what it used to be."

"Oh, come on, Mom," she said softly. Already she could feel herself relaxing, and her lips twitched as she held back a smile. "Can't you think of a better way to keep him warm?"

"Like what?"

"Like body heat, for instance," she murmured. "If it were my husband out there getting soaked to the bone, that's the first thing I'd recommend. And as a nurse, I can't think of a better remedy."

Marie Bradford turned to face her daughter with her hands planted squarely on her hips. "I know what you're trying to say, young lady, and I don't think I need to remind you that you and Neil are half our age!"

Jenna didn't miss the amused glitter in her mother's brown eyes. She sat back and eyed her as she bustled around the kitchen, wiping the counter and spooning fragrant grounds into the coffee maker. Her mother was in her mid-sixties, and if it hadn't been for the snowy white hair that she wore in a loose bun on her nape, she might have been taken for a woman twenty years younger. Her skin was smooth and free of wrinkles, her brown eyes snapping and vivacious.

"I hope Neil and I are as happy as you and Dad have been all these years," she said suddenly, last night's argument with Neil abruptly jumping into her thoughts. Her parents had been married for forty-five years, and she couldn't help but wonder—would her own marriage last that long?

There was a hint of wistfulness in her tone, and Marie looked at her in surprise. "I'm sure you will be," she said softly, moving to sit across from her daughter. "Dad and I were happy and content before you came to us, but there was something missing. I'll never forget how you looked the first time we ever saw you. You were so tall and straight, and you tried to look so brave—'' She shook her head in remembrance. "But I could sense how lost and alone you were." Her eyes lifted to Jenna's and a soft smile lighted her face. "And I knew then how much joy you'd bring into our lives."

Jenna's thoughts drifted fleetingly backward. When she was four years old, her parents had been killed in a collision with a train. Miraculously she had emerged with barely a scratch. With no family other than an eighty-year-old great-aunt in Maine who was too old to be burdened with a small child, custody had been given over to the state. Her memories of that time were few: stark white walls, hard narrow cots, being shuffled from foster home to foster home for over a year. She had been too young to understand the whispered excuses...*too quiet, too withdrawn*...but old enough to understand the loss of warmth, the absence of love from her young life. Two people whom she had loved and depended on had been wrenched from her and there was no one to replace them. No one who willingly gave what her tender four-year-old self craved so desperately: a warm pair of arms to hold her, the solid strength of a shoulder to lay her head upon.

Not until Jerry and Marie Bradford had entered her life.

She smiled across at Marie, her heart filled with tender emotion for this unselfish woman who had given her so much. She reached across the table and squeezed her mother's hand. "And you brought love back into mine," she said softly. Their eyes met and held, but suddenly a troubled light entered Jenna's.

"Mom—" She traced an idle pattern on the tablecloth, trying to find the right words. "What you said before...were you trying to say that children have a way of bringing people together?"

Marie shrugged. "I suppose so. Some people—the *right* people." She paused. "Not that I think it's a way to cure a troubled marriage, but I know that my own marriage to your father wouldn't have been nearly as meaningful without you."

Jenna took a deep breath. "I suppose a lot of people feel that way. People like—like Megan and Ward Garrison." Her fingers closed tightly around her coffee cup.

Marie regarded her steadily. "There's nothing wrong with that, Jenna."

"I never said there was," Jenna said quickly. She hesitated, then blurted out, "Neil . . . he—he'd like to have a baby right away."

For a long moment her mother's eyes remained riveted on Jenna's carefully controlled features before drifting to the white-knuckled grip of her hands around her cup. After all these years, there was still so much that Jenna held inside. . . . Marie offered a quiet statement. "And that bothers you."

There was a tight little silence. "Yes and no," she finally admitted, her tone carefully neutral. Fingers that weren't entirely steady traced the rim of her coffee cup. "We—Neil and I had decided to wait a while before we had a baby, but now he's changed his mind." She hesitated. "And nothing would make me happier . . . eventually. But right now . . . right now it brings back so many memories, and I can't help but think of—" She broke off, stung to the core by her suppressed pain.

"Robbie," her mother finished for her softly. Again her hand reached out to cover Jenna's.

She nodded slowly, drawing both strength and comfort from the touch of her mother's hand. "Tomorrow I'm going to Plains City to see him, Mom," she said quietly. "Even if they won't let me touch him or hold him." Her eyes seemed two huge pools of longing in her pale face. "I have to do this, Mom. I *have* to." She looked across at her mother, somehow not surprised to see a kind of gentle comprehension reflected in the soft, brown depths. Instantly the years fell away. . . .

IT WAS A NEWSPAPER article that had first caught Jenna's eye nearly five years earlier. "CHILDLESS COUPLE SEEKS SURROGATE MOTHER" was how the headline in the Houston newspaper had read. Since her adoptive mother had been unable to have children, Jenna was intrigued by the unique approach to the problem of infertility. On reading the story, she discovered that Megan and Ward Garrison, a couple who lived in northern Texas, were actively searching for a woman to bear Ward's child. Married for fifteen years and puzzled by Megan's inability to have a child in all that time, both had undergone a battery of tests several years earlier, only to find that Megan's fallopian tubes were blocked by scar tissue and she could never become pregnant.

Jenna was working as an office nurse for a physician with a family practice in Texas City at the time, and both the receptionist and the bookkeeper could talk about little else.

"You wouldn't catch me offering to have this guy's baby," Vera, the bookkeeper, declared later that morning. She flicked a disdainful finger at the newspaper. "My sister was sick for weeks on end when she was pregnant—and she looked like a cow from the time she was two months along!"

Marsha, the mother of a ten- and a six-year-old and infinitely more mature than Vera, held a different viewpoint. "Your sister also had twins," she pointed out. "And some women love being pregnant—"

"Not me!" snorted Vera.

Marsha had simply smiled and shaken her head. "Wait until you're married," she said with a smile. "You might feel fat and ugly and you might be so sick you feel like you could never hold your head up again, but the minute you hold that tiny bundle of life in your arms, it's all but forgotten."

Vera cast a wary eye at the older woman. "That might be," she sniffed a little indignantly, again waving a hand at the newspaper, "but if you ask me, this is a little weird. I'd say that any woman who volunteers for this is doing it strictly for the money!"

"I'm not sure," Marsha said thoughtfully. Her eyes skimmed over the article. "It says here that the man is an engineer, and I doubt if they make all that much money. And though it says all hospital and legal expenses will be taken care of, it doesn't specify how much the fee is."

"It would have to be one heck of a lot before I'd do it," Vera snorted.

Jenna and Marsha exchanged a glance that seemed to indicate Vera needn't worry about the possibility. Marsha glanced down again at the newspaper. "It also says that any woman applying will be tested physically *and* psychologically." She frowned, then said slowly, "I guess that makes sense. I suppose that they would want to make sure she really knew what she was getting into, and after all—" she shrugged "—if a person went to all that trouble and expense, I guess they'd want the mother to be reasonably intelligent."

"Good Lord." Vera looked disgusted. "Imagine having to *apply* to have a baby—just like applying for a job!"

"It wouldn't be easy giving up a baby," Jenna put in pensively. "I suppose if you looked at it in terms of a job right from the start, it might make it a little less traumatic when the time came to hand over the baby."

"And that's not all," Marsha added. "It says here that single women are preferred. Apparently both the couple and their lawyer seem to think a woman who's never had a baby wouldn't be as likely to have second thoughts about giving it up."

"Well, they can count me out!" Vera's voice rang out loudly. "I might be single, healthy and intelligent, but there's no way I'd get involved in anything like this!"

There was a pause, and then two pairs of eyes simultaneously turned to Jenna.

"Don't look at me!" She held up her hands and laughed. "I tend to agree with Vera. It's a little too bizarre for me." The plight of these two people was rather sad; she felt a small stab of pity that they were so desperate for a child of their own, and the fact that they were willing to go to such lengths even made her admire them to a degree.

But beyond these thoughts, the realization of the heartache these two people were going through didn't hit home until several days later, when she walked in on her mother watching a local talk show that featured this same couple. More out of courtesy for her mother than any vested interest, she sat down to watch.

Seeing the actual faces of those two, instead of merely reading names in a newspaper, made the situation all the more real and all the more heartrending. Her first impression of Megan Garrison was that of a woman in intense pain. She was very blond, and small-boned and fragile-looking. Her husband, Ward, was as dark as she was fair, good-looking in a rough sort of way. There was something in the quiet tautness of his tone that caught Jenna's attention as they pleaded their cause, but it was his wife she responded to. She listened as they related how a previous attempt at locating a surrogate had ended in heartbreak: after carrying the baby to term, the woman had changed her mind at the last minute. And adoption was all but ruled out; the waiting list was seven years long at the least—they had been waiting years already.

Jenna's heart turned over in her chest as she heard the woman say, "I die a little inside with every day that goes by, and I see the hope that someday I may hold a child in my arms grow dimmer and dimmer. And hope is all I have—'' Her voice broke tearfully, and long painful seconds ticked by before she was able to speak again. "Hope is all I may *ever* have."

The desperation, the fear, the despair, the realization that the woman had only this one small thread to cling to, touched something deep inside Jenna's soul. She longed to reach out and comfort Megan as her husband was doing, to wrap her arms around her and tell her that it was only a matter of time before her hope became a reality.

When it was over Jenna turned to her mother with a murmur of sympathy on her lips, only to find her doe-soft eyes swimming with unshed tears.

Jenna rushed to her side. "Mom, what is it?" Her tone was anxious as she pressed a handkerchief into her hand.

Marie attempted a watery smile. "I'm all right." She dabbed at her overflowing eyes and leaned her head back tiredly. Concerned, Jenna sat on the arm of the chair and searched her mother's face.

"I'm fine, really," Marie said again. She set aside the handkerchief and turned to Jenna with a sigh. "It's just that seeing that couple brought back so many memories." She lapsed into silence, but again her eyes grew red.

Jenna sat very still. She knew that she had been adopted because of her mother's fierce desire for a child, but for a moment she was almost stunned at her mother's heartfelt reaction to the plight of two people who were, after all, strangers. Instinctively she said, "You know exactly how that woman feels, don't you?"

"Oh, yes—*exactly*." Marie dashed at her eyes, and Jenna patiently handed the handkerchief back to her. "I wanted a child so badly I could taste it. Everywhere I looked—the grocery store, the drugstore, the doctor's office—there were mothers with children, mothers *about* to have a baby. And there I was, helpless, frustrated, hating myself for being jealous and wanting what they seemed to take for granted." A pained expression flitted across her face. "No one knows how worthless the inability to have a baby can make a woman feel—except perhaps a woman who's been through it herself." A pensive smile curved her lips as she looked up at Jenna. "But your father was wonderful through it all. He was the one who suggested adoption." She reached up a hand to cradle Jenna's cheek in her palm. "You'll never know how much of a blessing you were. Like a day of sunshine after a storm."

Jenna's throat felt raw. She tried to speak, but the sound refused to pass through her throat. She could only grip her mother's hand more tightly. Her eyes turned toward the television screen, where a newscaster's voice now droned on and on. She chastised herself for being the most insensitive clod ever to have been born. And yet these two people weren't the only ones involved.

"I hate to say this . . ." She hesitated. "But finding someone to bear a child for them seems so—so drastic." She slipped onto the carpet in front of the chair, laced her arms around her legs and rested her chin on her knees. "Another woman is going to have to give up nine months of her life for these people. How many women would be willing to do that?"

"Oh, Jenna." The raw emotion in Marie's tone brought Jenna's eyes to her mother's in a flash, and they were held there by a depth of intensity she'd never glimpsed before. "What are nine months compared to a lifetime of loneliness? Some women can go through life without a husband or child, but there are others who can never be fulfilled unless they can share their love with a husband and family. Women like Megan Garrison—and me." She paused, her eyes now shining luminously. "It would take a very special woman," she said softly. "A woman who isn't afraid to give all of herself." She shook her head, a wistful smile on her lips. "I can't imagine being able to give anything more precious than the gift of life."

The gift of life. Almost with a sense of awe Jenna absorbed the words. Her parents had taken her into their home and their hearts, freely bestowing all the warmth and love they were capable of giving. She knew, beyond a shadow of a doubt, that their love for her was no different from what they might have felt for a natural child, had they been able to have one. And during the past few minutes, somehow all the long lonely years her mother had struggled through were poignantly brought to life inside Jenna. She could feel the same intense longing, the empty ache inside, that both her mother and Megan Garrison lived with day after day. But there was one difference.

She rushed to find a pencil and pad. Her fingers shook as she scribbled down the name of the Garrisons' Dallas attorney. It might be too late, or they might not want her, but by heaven, she was going to try. Her heart fluttered almost painfully in her chest as she looked up at her mother with shining eyes, her heart bursting with emotion.

She, Jenna Bradford, was determined to have the child these two people wanted so desperately. For herself, for Megan Garrison—and for the woman before her, who had given her own life so much meaning. The woman who had taught her how precious love really was.

"JENNA." A gentle voice prodded her back to the present. "I understand what you're going through, but I have to ask this. How are the Garrisons going to feel about this? Have you talked to them yet?"

"No." She shook her head quickly, stilling the sudden pitter-patter of her heart that the words evoked. "I know we all agreed to make a clean break," she said quietly, looking straight at her mother. "But I think Megan will come around fairly quickly."

"And Ward?"

Jenna frowned. She took a sip of her coffee, grimacing at the cold, bitter taste. Carrying the cup to the sink, she emptied the contents, pondering the question while she poured a fresh cup. She had sympathized with Megan even before they had chosen her for a surrogate, but it had come as a surprise to find how much she really liked her when they had finally met face-to-face. Ward, on the other hand, was a different story. He was sweet, warm and tender with his wife, and though he was gracious enough the few times the three of them had been together, he wasn't nearly as easy to read as Megan who was much more vocal. In fact, one of the last times she had seen him had left her feeling rather shaken.

She'd been in her sixth month of pregnancy at the time. Ward was in Houston on business, and Megan had come along with him. She'd met with them briefly at their hotel, and Megan was absolutely delighted at feeling the baby's vigorous movements inside her.

"Come and feel this!" she'd beckoned to Ward. Wasting no time, she snatched one large hand in hers and guided it to Jenna's protruding tummy. "He's doing somersaults in there!"

Jenna had laughed a little self-consciously, but at the sight of that dark hand lying so intimately on her belly, she'd felt an odd tightening in her chest. It really brought home the fact that it was this man's child she was nurturing inside her, but before she had time to analyze the feeling, the baby moved. Ward's hazel eyes flitted to hers in surprise before an oddly shuttered expression came over them, and then he abruptly snatched away his hand. The incident had hurt for some unknown reason, and she was left feeling just a little bit wary.

She turned to face her mother. "I'm not sure how Ward will feel," she admitted. "I didn't do it for him, you know. I did it for Megan." She mulled a moment longer. "But I think if Megan agrees, he will, too."

Marie nodded, then smiled. "I already know what your father will say."

Jenna resumed her place at the table and shook her head fondly. "He'll boom and bluster the way he did when I told him what I was up to in the first place, and then he'll say in that gruff way he has—" she drew her brows together over her nose and stuck out her lower lip wrathfully "'—you'll do what you want, anyway!'"

They both ended up laughing at a time when they very much needed the release. "You obviously see through him just as I do." Marie laughed one last time, then looked at her daughter. "How long do you plan on staying?"

Jenna's smile drooped a little, but she kept it firmly in place. Surely Megan and Ward couldn't deny her if she was practically camped on their doorstep. She refused to think beyond that.

"As long as it takes, Mom," she responded with false lightness. "As long as it takes."

"Then that leaves just one person to contend with, doesn't it?"

Her mother's voice was so quiet Jenna almost suspected she knew. Her fingers tensed in her lap. She took a deep breath. "It's his problem if he doesn't understand, Mom. Because I'm going to do it, anyway."

Marie darted her a surprised look. "That doesn't sound like you, Jenna. Surely you and Neil aren't having problems already? Heavens, you're not even married yet!"

Jenna could tell the laugh she gave was forced. Suddenly her thoughts darted back to the time when she was a lanky thirteen-year-old and had just discovered that their neighbor, Darren Phillips—the boy who threw stones at her and boasted he was the better baseball player simply by virtue of his sex—

wasn't such a disgusting creature, after all. A ghost of a smile tipped her lips. Intent on proving him wrong, she'd spent many an evening with her father pitching a ball to her and giving her tips on her stance and swing. She'd broken the kitchen window twice with some very nifty line drives. And then the day came when Darren had given her her first kiss and she'd decided it was time to shelve her ball and bat. She had breezed in from outside, dropped herself at the kitchen table and *promptly* asked her mother how a *woman* knew when she was in love.

She'd never forgotten her mother's reply: "If you ever have to ask yourself if you're in love," she said with a secretive smile, "then you're probably not."

Suddenly Jenna couldn't help but recall the moment last night when she hadn't been able to tell Neil she loved him.

Marie reached out a hand to cover Jenna's. "You're not having second thoughts, are you, dear?"

Her reply was a long time in coming. "Neil is everything a woman could possibly want in a man. He's mature, nice-looking, attentive, and he has a very good job...." Yes, he was a prize catch, according to her friends in E.R.

"That doesn't tell me much, Jenna. You say Neil is everything a woman could want in a man, but is he everything *you* want? You know I like Neil," Marie said slowly, "and I'll be more than happy to have him as a son-in-law, but we're talking about your happiness. And what you just said sounds strangely like an excuse." Her mother gave her a long, thoughtful look. "None of us needs excuses for loving, Jenna. Do you?"

Jenna looked down to where her hands rested in a white-knuckled grip in her lap. This time she didn't answer—though not because she didn't want to. She couldn't.

All of a sudden she didn't know.

THINGS DIDN'T FARE well at all with Neil that night. The changing expressions on his face would have been rather comical if the situation hadn't been quite so serious. Jenna could almost see the wheels turning in his head. At first he looked totally blank when she mentioned the term "surrogate mother." An extremely brief look of amazement came next, followed by disbelief and then what she really hadn't expected to see—a cold-faced fury. In fact, if the truth were known, she had been much more worried about Megan's and Ward's reaction than Neil's.

"Damn it, Jenna! How could you do something so hare-brained, so foolhardy, so thoughtless?" Neil slammed his fist down on an end table and glared at her. "You, of all people!"

"Why, thank you. I'll take that as a compliment!" Her voice dripped icicles as she watched him pace around her living room. "It wasn't thoughtless, Neil," she countered harshly. "I knew exactly what I was getting into."

"And did you think about how you might feel five or ten years down the road? Did you ever think about how you're feeling *now?*"

When he threw her another furious glance, Jenna dug in her heels and prepared to do battle. Good Lord! Did he think she had gone into the arrangement blindly? Even if she had, the Garrisons' attorney, Ron Brewster, would have enlightened her in no time flat! Over and over he had stressed that they wanted someone who fully understood what she was getting into. And she had spent months and months preparing herself *not* to feel the way she did right now.

So what had happened?

She brushed aside the disturbing voice as quickly as she did Neil's accusations. "Of course I did," she told him tautly. "I didn't let myself think of it as *my* baby—it was *their* baby. All I did was give Robbie a temporary home."

"Robbie? The baby was a boy?"

Her chin held high against his accusing voice, she nodded.

"How old, Jenna? How old is he?"

"He's nearly four years old," she said quietly. "He has a birthday in January."

Neil dropped into a chair. He sat there, his hands dropped on his knees, his forehead supported by his fingertips. When he finally looked across at her, his eyes had lost some of their fierce glitter, but his voice was bitter and flat.

"Damn it, Jenna, I can't believe it! A stranger! You had a stranger's baby!"

"They weren't strangers, Neil. Not from the minute I saw them, and especially not after I met them."

"And that's supposed to make a difference?" Anger hardened his features. "You got all cute and cozy with the husband and that makes it all right?"

Jenna could hardly believe his outburst. "I didn't sleep with him," she said sharply. "Artificial insemination is about as cold and sterile as you can get! You're an attorney—you should know how it works!"

"I know all I care to know, and believe me, you just took the words right out of my mouth. 'Cold and sterile' is exactly the way I see this whole thing! How much did they pay you?" he demanded.

"Very little!" she shot back hotly. "I was off work for less than six weeks and I accepted only what I lost out on salary. And the fee didn't even play a part in why I did it! Just the other night you were spouting off about wanting a home and a family, but *you're* the one who's cold and unfeeling! Is it so hard to understand that someone else has that very same need?"

His eyes remained locked with hers endlessly. Then finally he shoved an agitated hand through his hair. "All right, you've made your point. But we're getting married in less than six weeks, and besides, I can think of a dozen reasons right off the top of my head—moral, ethical *and* legal—why this shouldn't be a proving ground for childless couples."

"I'm not saying it's the answer for everyone." Her tone was quiet as her anger began to abate. "But it was right for them, and it was right for me, and I'm not sorry I did it." She hesitated. "Only I have to see Robbie again."

His eyes locked with hers, probing, questioning—and still angry.

"I'm not sure I can explain exactly why," she said with a feeling of helplessness. "I only know that it's something I have to do." She swallowed uneasily before forcing herself to go on. "And then—then you and I can go on with our lives together."

The harsh, grating breath he drew was the only sound in the room. "I think you're asking for trouble, Jenna. I'm not even sure I should let you do this—"

She shook her head quickly. "You can't stop me, Neil." Her voice was very quiet, yet there was an unmistakable ring of finality to it. "No one can." She paused. "Please, try to understand—"

"I don't understand," he cut in abruptly. "And even if I could, I think you picked one hell of a time to go running off! In case you've forgotten, we're getting married six weeks from

Saturday!'' He whirled around and headed for the front door. ''If it's not too much trouble—'' he threw the clipped words over his shoulder ''—give me a call when you get back.''

With that, he walked out on her for the second time that week. Silently Jenna made her way over to a chair and sank into the cushions. It was, she realized shakily, perhaps a good thing that she was leaving for a few days.

It would give her some time to think about Neil—something she realized she desperately needed to do.

CHAPTER THREE

THE DRIVE NORTH filled one of the longest days of Jenna's life. Anxious to arrive in Plains City, she'd felt the long hours stretch out endlessly, particularly the last half-hour after Waco. Her muscles were cramped and aching from the hours spent in the driver's seat, and her frame of mind nose-dived even farther when a fan belt broke just outside of Abilene and there was a two-hour wait trying to find a service station willing to repair it. And the matter wasn't improved any when her little Datsun became testier yet and she had a flat tire a mere half-hour after she'd finally gotten started again. Tired and frustrated, she finally arrived well after ten o'clock. She pulled into the first motel she saw and crawled into bed, exhausted.

She shielded her eyes against the bright glare of the sun when she stepped out of her motel room the next morning, looking up and down the main thoroughfare of the sleepy little town. There was a market, a hardware store, a feed supply store, a barber shop and a café.

It was in the direction of the café that Jenna guided her footsteps. She had awakened ravenous, since she'd been too tired the previous night even to bother searching for a place to eat. Stepping inside, she glanced around the matchbox-sized interior. There was room for perhaps half a dozen people at the small counter, and three well-worn booths lined the wall. The fragrant smells wafting from the kitchen sent hunger pangs growling anew in Jenna's stomach.

She sat down on one of the stools near the counter, waiting her turn while a threesome in one of the booths was being served. She looked up when the waitress, dressed in a crisp blue uniform and jaunty cap, approached her.

"Hi." Fresh-faced and open, the woman flashed a wide smile. "What can I get you?"

Jenna smiled back and eyed the hand-lettered menu before making a quick choice. "How about coffee and a cinnamon roll to start with?"

"Comin' right up."

Her eyes widened when the waitress placed a Texas-sized roll in front of her and a cup of fresh hot coffee. Pulling the warm, fragrant roll apart with her fingers, she savored the spicy taste of the cinnamon and gooey icing, resisting the impulse to lick her fingers.

"More coffee?" The waitress returned a few minutes later with the carafe in her hand. Jenna placed her hand over her cup and shook her head quickly. "How about another roll?"

"No, thanks." Jenna smiled and indicated her stomach. "It was delicious, but I couldn't take even one more bite."

"Not many people can handle more than one of Herb's cinnamon rolls." She grinned. "Fact is, he makes the best rolls in town."

Jenna nodded politely and commented, "It's so quiet here. It's hard to believe that Abilene is less than thirty miles away."

"It's not always like this," the waitress said with a wink. "After dark, things tend to liven up a bit. You know how some men are about dropping in for a few beers after work....." She shook her curly head and grinned. "They talk about women being no better than a bunch of cacklin' hens when they get together, but I'll never believe it."

The waitress took advantage of the lull in customers and returned the coffee carafe to the hot plate, then came back to Jenna. The look she gave her was amicable but inquisitive. "You stayin' at the motel across the street?"

Jenna nodded.

"Just passing through, I'll bet."

"Yes and no. Actually, I hope to be staying a few days." She hesitated, but couldn't help responding to the woman's friendliness. "I'm here to see the Garrisons—the Ward Garrisons. Do you know them?"

"Not personally." The woman shook her head, and a shadow passed swiftly over her face. "Don't see much of him anymore since...well, that's beside the point." She eyed Jenna curiously. "Are you a friend of the family?"

"A friend of the family?" For some reason the term sent an unexpected pain shooting through her heart. On blood ties alone, she was practically a *member* of the family. She resisted the impulse to laugh hysterically. Instead she gathered herself quickly under control and nodded. "Megan and I...were good friends some time ago. But I'm afraid I've lost the address after all these years." She tipped her head to the side and smiled encouragingly. "I don't suppose you happen to know where they live?"

The waitress shook her head apologetically. "Sorry—no. Wait a minute!" She snapped her fingers, already heading toward the kitchen. "I'll bet Herb knows. He's lived here forever.

"Take the first road to the left heading north out of town. Turn left again at the first intersection," she announced, bustling through the double doors a moment later. "It's the house at the end of the gravel road. Only one there, so you can't miss it."

"Thanks so much. I'll just be on my way, then." Jenna smiled gratefully and paid for her breakfast. Glancing back, she saw the waitress gazing after her with an odd look in her eyes. Jenna sent a little wave over her shoulder as she exited the tiny café.

She quickly walked across the street to where her car was parked in front of her motel room. She inserted the key in the lock, but suddenly she stopped, one hand poised on the dark blue roof as her mother's words from yesterday came back to her. How *would* Megan feel about her dropping in without any warning? It could be quite a shock, she suddenly realized. For a moment she hesitated, temptation almost overruling reason in this instance. Then, with a sigh, she turned and trudged the few steps to her room.

Inside, she sat down on the double bed and reached for the phone. The Garrisons' phone number popped into her head without conscious thought, and for a moment she sat stunned. Why was it that she remembered it after all this time? Was it because she hadn't *wanted* to forget? Her hand gripped the receiver as she recalled the last time she'd telephoned, to let them know her labor had started. Once again she could hear Megan's ecstatic voice coming over the wire.

"Oh, Jenna, I can't believe it! It's finally about to happen! A baby—our very own baby! We'll be there as soon as we can."

The memory was both poignant and sweet, and Jenna took a deep, shuddering breath to force back the odd sensation gripping her heart. She punched out the number with steady hands, aware of a faint flutter in her chest as she eased back on the bed and waited.

The phone rang once, twice and then again. Jenna felt her heart beating crazily.

"Hello?"

She couldn't prevent a note of breathless excitement from entering her voice. "Megan?" She sat forward on the edge of the bed, her body taut as a bowstring. "Is that you, Megan?"

There was a long silence, and then a female voice demanded, "Who is this?"

Recoiling from the sharp tone, she shifted uneasily as she realized it wasn't Megan who had answered. "I . . . my name is Jenna Bradford." She heard a soft gasp but paid no mind. Her tone was cautious but hopeful as she spoke to the woman on the other end of the line. "I've just driven all the way from Galveston and I was calling to see if I might be able to see—" *Robbie.* She stopped the word from slipping off her tongue just in time. "Megan," she finished hastily. A little puzzled by the awkward silence that followed, she bit her lip. "I'm sorry . . . I must have dialed the wrong number."

"No. No, this is the right number."

The admission came readily enough, but there was something in the tone . . . it was brusque, even a little hostile. Jenna's words were polite but guarded. "If I have the right number, then who are you?"

Again there was a long empty silence before the unknown woman spoke. "Eileen. Eileen Swenson." She seemed to hesitate. "I'm Ward's sister."

Ward's sister. No wonder the surprise at her name. "Then you know who I am," she said softly.

"Yes—yes, I do. And I think I know why you're here."

There was no denying the challenging note in Eileen Swenson's voice. If this was any indication of how Megan or Ward would feel . . . She could only pray it wasn't. She prickled a little but said politely, "If it's not too much trouble, could you put either Megan or Ward on the phone?"

There was a seemingly endless silence. "Megan's dead," the woman finally said quietly.

Dead . . . Megan was *dead.* Her mind reeled. It didn't seem possible. She'd never known her, not really. Was it possible to mourn someone's death without ever really knowing that person? But certainly Jenna knew all she needed to know. Megan was a warm, vital woman whose capacity for love went far beyond any ordinary measure, if indeed love could be measured. A dozen questions tumbled around in her brain. How had Megan died? And when? She couldn't suppress a burning feel of resentment against Ward for not letting her know, even while the rational part of her argued there was no need for her to know.

But suddenly she remembered Robbie. Megan was gone, but did that change anything? Her reason for being here? No.

"I'm sorry," Jenna said softly. "When ... ?"

Eileen Swenson had no trouble understanding. "About a year and a half ago."

She twirled the cord around her finger and thought a moment. "Mrs. Swenson, I'd still like to talk to Ward—"

"He isn't here."

Jenna took a deep breath. "Then could you give him a message for me?"

"I'm sorry. I—I don't know when I'll see him again."

The woman was beginning to sound a little agitated. "Look," Jenna said evenly, choosing her words carefully. "I'm really not here to cause trouble, but don't you think you should let Ward decide whether he wants to talk to me?"

"I'm not lying," the woman defended herself. "He isn't here and I couldn't say when he'll be back. I only stopped by this morning to check on the house while he's away."

"Where is he?"

"New Mexico. He's working on an irrigation project there."

New Mexico ... Lord, and she'd come so far already. Her muscles tensed with an emotion she wasn't yet ready to name. "I see," she said slowly. "Is Robbie with him?"

"No. He's staying with me. But please don't ask to see him. I couldn't possibly agree without Ward's permission."

Jenna's body went limp with despair. "I understand." Her voice sounded as hollow as she felt inside. She wasn't such a fool that she didn't know that engineering projects sometimes lasted weeks, months even. But suddenly there was a glimmer of life inside her. Surely Ward wouldn't leave Robbie for weeks at a time. "Do you expect him back soon?" She made no attempt to disguise her hopefulness.

There was a heavy sigh on the other end of the line. "I'm really not sure. Early next week maybe, but as I said before, I'm not certain." It was obvious the admission was made with great reluctance. "I'll let Ward know you're here . . . if you decide to wait around that long. Where are you staying?"

"I'll be here," Jenna promised in a low voice. "I'm at the Sundowner Motel." She paused. "Mrs. Swenson . . . ?"

"Yes?"

"I—thank you. Thank you for telling me."

The moment stretched out into a taut silence. When Eileen Swenson finally spoke, her voice sounded oddly strained. "Don't thank me yet. For all I know, you may have made the trip for nothing."

Jenna stared pensively out the window after hanging up the phone. The shimmering sunlight outside seemed a stark contrast to the dark emptiness of her mood. Apparently, all the odds were stacked against her. It had all started with her vague, restless feelings about Neil, and then he had warned her against coming. Then her car had broken down, and now—this. Megan was *dead*, and Jenna had been so certain she would let her see Robbie. It would be days before Ward returned, a hollow voice inside her protested. Better to go home now and forget she had ever come, forget she had even tried to see Robbie, forget he had ever been born.

But she couldn't. Dear Lord, she couldn't.

Refusing to give in to that tiny voice, Jenna got up, grabbed her purse and walked outside. Dispiritedly she walked the few blocks to the town's business district. There was more to the town than she had originally thought; she noticed at least three drugstores, a steak house and several more small cafés, one small but complete department store, one clothing shop, even a movie theater and a playhouse. All the amenities of a city, Jenna thought to herself halfheartedly, but without quite the variety to choose from.

Her steps eventually took her back to the motel, and Jenna found herself driving toward the Garrison place. The directions she'd been given earlier unconsciously guided her. Before she knew it, her car was parked in the gravel drive and her feet were carrying her toward the front door. Her footsteps echoed emptily as she mounted the steps, and for a fraction of a second, she stopped before lifting her hand to the brass knocker.

Silence greeted her.

After a long moment of almost fearful waiting, she turned and trudged slowly down the steps, her emotions so tangled that she felt unable to sort through them.

Taking a deep breath, Jenna forced her attention back to her surroundings. Beyond the cross-fenced boundaries of the small acreage the plains stretched for miles, rolling and dipping endlessly, glinting yellow in the bright September sunlight. In the distance she could see the sun-baked, gently rolling hills to the west. Settling herself under a towering cottonwood tree, she turned her eyes once again to the two-story farmhouse.

The yard was well kept, and the white clapboard exterior of the house looked newly painted. Although it was quiet outside, there was a warm, homey look to the house itself. A wide swing hung from the porch rafters near the front window. Jenna could almost visualize the inside, cheerful and cozy, a comfortable sofa laden with pillows in the living room, thick braided rugs covering the floor and knickknacks and treasures strewn throughout. The urge to scramble to the window and peer through the sheer curtains was so strong that she almost succumbed. Only the feeling that she would be spying, intruding where she had no business, prevented her from doing exactly that.

The thought sent a chill through her. Why had she come here? she agonized silently. Despite what Eileen Swenson had told her—that Megan was dead and Ward was gone—had she really believed it? Had she really expected the door to be thrown open and to be welcomed with open arms? She shivered. No. She could never expect that from Ward. She didn't know how she knew, but she did.

What if he said no? What would she do then? Could she deal with it, or would she handle it the way she had handled it all this time, sweeping her feelings under the rug once more? Denying the hopeless longing to see her child, to hold him, to *know* him? All these months—years!—she hadn't let herself think of him, but no matter how hard she tried, the memory was always there, lurking in some distant corner of her mind. Denied but never forgotten. For the first time, she realized how desperately afraid she was that Ward would refuse to let her see Robbie.

But her need outweighed her fear by far.

"Oh, Robbie," she murmured faintly, fervently. "I'm so close...." Slowly she closed her eyes, unable to stop a wave of despair from sweeping through her. She heard words spinning through her brain—words she couldn't speak. *So near and yet so far.*

Her entire body trembled as she stumbled to the car and started the engine. She drove back to the motel in the same trancelike state she had left it. Outside, the small town went about its business while Jenna shut herself away in her room. Neil . . . Megan . . . Robbie . . . Faces whirled through her imagination, the features obscure and blurred. The squall of a newborn infant resounded in her subconscious and she flinched.

Finally she stumbled over to the bed and lay down, her body curled in a tight ball. She knew she desperately needed an outlet for all the pent-up emotion inside her, but as always, the tears refused to come. All the pain was tightly locked up inside her, and her heart was an unbearable weight in her chest.

IT WAS NEARLY DARK when the wheels of the small Cessna touched down in a perfect landing on the small airstrip just outside Plains City. Skimming across the smooth surface, the plane gently glided to a stop in front of the metal barn that served as a hangar. Moments later, a lean figure emerged from the building and strode toward the house. Though the man was rapidly approaching forty, a rangy, muscled hardness to the six-foot-three-inch frame had not yet been softened by the years.

Though Ward Garrison was tired and weary to the bone, a kind of hurried impatience marked his long-legged stride as he took the porch steps two at a time, heading with intent toward the den.

The room was paneled in knotty pine, and sparsely but comfortably furnished. Bookshelves lined nearly every available wall space. The only decoration was a pair of old flintlock rifles mounted above the stone fireplace. Near the window stood a worn leather armchair that had seen many years of use. A massive desk dominated the room, and Ward directed his steps toward it.

The chair behind the desk creaked a protest as he sat down. He made no move to reach for the phone; instead his hazel eyes rested on the framed photograph that occupied a place of honor on the desktop. A shuttered look came over his face as he picked up the oak frame, studying the fragile features in the photo as if to memorize them. But there was little need. Even without the reminder of those laughing blue eyes and silky blond hair, the image was printed indelibly on his brain. She looked so happy and carefree.... And it seemed like a lifetime ago that *he* had felt that way.

"Megan," he said aloud. And then he wished he hadn't, as the familiar tightening began to build in his chest. He took a deep, shuddering breath, but long minutes passed before he set aside the photograph and leaned back in his chair.

"Oh, Meg," he murmured faintly. "Sometimes it's still so hard to believe you're gone...." She had been a part of fate, a moment in time ... and she was no more.

His eyes flitted to a smaller picture, but one no less dear to his heart. He felt a surge of pride and possessiveness. His son. His own flesh and blood, the one bright spot left in his life. The son Megan wanted so badly but wasn't able to have. Despite the brief time allotted to them, no one could have been a better mother to Robbie than Megan. She *was* his mother, the only mother he had ever known.

Ward's eyes grew unusually soft as he reached out a finger and traced the outline of the miniature features so like his own. Robbie had his bold nose, the same square jawline. But his eyes ... those vivid green eyes could belong to only one person.

The reminder was one he had learned to live with. Not that he was ungrateful...but there were times when he was strangely resentful of the woman who had given him his son, as well as of the fact that his own wife could never hope to conceive...while it had been so *simple* for her. And there were also times when Robbie would look up at him, his eyes unusually serious and urgent, yet so full of life and expression, and he felt a brief surge of anger jolt through his body, because he looked so *damned much* like her.

Ward reached for the phone and punched out a number. "Eileen?" He swiveled around in the chair to stare out the window. "It's me."

"Ward!" Mild surprise was registered in his sister's tone. "Are you home already?"

One side of his mouth quirked upward. "I pushed the crew as hard as I pushed myself so we could finish ahead of schedule."

"Well, thank heaven you don't do near as much traveling as you did five years ago." There was a brief pause. "It's hard on

Robbie with you gone, as young as he is. He tries not to let it show, but I can tell."

"I know." There was a bitter edge to his smile. "You wouldn't believe how much I miss him. But with Tyler breaking his leg and laid up in the hospital, I had no choice but to fill in for him." He lifted a hand to smooth his rumpled dark hair. "Is Robbie still up?"

"No. I put him to bed right after dinner." Eileen's voice was full of apology.

Ward's smile was halfhearted at best, but he disguised his disappointment. "Well, don't bother waking him. I'll be over tomorrow to pick him up."

"Don't hurry on my account." Eileen laughed. "You know Robbie—always where the action is. And if there's nothing going on, he creates a little excitement of his own. But he keeps me busy and I love having him around. The house is so empty with Tim and Katie away at college." She stopped for a second. "But I'm really glad you came back early. Frank's going to a cattle auction in Amarillo on Monday, so maybe I'll go along and do some shopping."

He nodded. "I'll see you tomorrow, then...."

"Ward, wait! There's something you should know—"

The sudden urgency in Eileen's voice stopped him from hanging up. Frowning, he spoke into the mouthpiece again. "Yes?"

"Ward..." Her voice dropped, and she seemed unsure of something. "I was at the house today to pick up the mail, and...someone called."

Something in her tone brought his tired senses fully alert. He leaned forward in his chair and asked in a clipped voice, "Who?"

It was a full minute before Eileen spoke. He could scarcely make out her muted tones. "Jenna Bradford."

"Jenna Bradford!" Ward sat back disbelievingly, his fingers tensing around the phone. "What did she want?"

Eileen was silent, hesitating just a moment too long, but somehow he already knew. "Robbie."

His insides were suddenly tied in knots. Why now, after all this time...? "What else did she say?"

"Nothing really." Eileen sounded just as confused as he felt. "She just said she didn't want to cause any trouble—but wants to see Robbie. And she's staying until she talks to you about it."

"Staying? You mean she's *here?*" He felt as if he'd been struck.

"Yes. She's at the Sundowner Motel in Plains City." An empty silence hung in the air as their thoughts veered in the same direction. "Ward, do you think . . . ?" Eileen swallowed, almost afraid to say the words aloud. "Do you think she wants him back?"

"If that's the case, she won't be long in discovering she'll have one hell of a fight on her hands," he said grimly, "because I'm not about to let *anyone* take my son away from me. And the sooner she finds that out, the better." On that unrelenting note, Ward slammed down the phone and walked out the door.

There was no point in putting it off—he intended to find out *exactly* why Jenna Bradford was visiting.

THE EVENING stretched out emptily after Jenna finally roused herself. She must have fallen asleep, she thought vaguely, switching on the bedside lamp. Sitting up, she glanced at her watch. It was just after nine. A dull ache throbbed in her temples, and she stumbled to the bathroom to splash some cold water on her face. As she dried her hands, she studied her reflection. She looked strained and rather drawn, her eyes the only splash of color in an otherwise pale face.

The lateness of the hour rather than hunger reminded her that she hadn't eaten since lunch. Rummaging through a small bag from a convenience store where she'd stopped on the long drive yesterday, she found a half-eaten package of tiny sugared donuts. She nibbled on one, but the sweet taste was unexpectedly cloying. The few bites she took sat like a heavy stone in her stomach, and she pushed aside the package distastefully. Suddenly she felt as if the walls were closing in on her, and she knew she couldn't remain in the stark motel room any longer. After running a brush through her long dark hair, she grabbed her purse and a light denim blazer and went outside, intent on getting a breath of fresh air.

Darkness had already settled over Plains City, but the parking area of the motel was lighted by the bright glare of the sign near the office. Jenna was in the process of closing the door behind her when she noticed a dark maroon Blazer pull to a halt in one of the stalls. As a man got out, something in his lean, muscular bearing caught her eye. He was tall and broad shouldered, and a faint breeze ruffled his thick dark hair as he dropped his keys into his pocket. The sharp blade of his nose bespoke arrogance, the thrust of his chin determination. She registered the deeply chiseled features with a prickly sense of unease as she watched him slam the car door shut with almost vicious intent. Hazy spears of light shone down from the streetlamp, falling full on his face for a moment, as he moved away from the car.

Jenna froze.

Dressed in a plaid shirt, jeans and boots, the man could have passed for just another cowboy, one of the many who seemed to populate the town. As if he were caught in the same current of awareness as she, the man slowly turned to face her. Jenna couldn't tear her eyes away from his as a flicker of recognition passed between them.

Ward Garrison didn't bother to smile; he didn't bother to tip his hand in greeting. He just stared at her for what she suspected was the longest moment in her life. Then he began to move toward her.

Jenna's breathing grew almost painfully shallow as those hazel eyes stared unwaveringly into hers. Her heart thumped as she watched his face grow colder with each step that brought him nearer.

She had the feeling that the battle for Robbie was over before it had even begun.

CHAPTER FOUR

THE PREMONITION held her pinioned where she stood for what seemed an eternity. She'd thought of little else but this meeting for the past few days, but now that the moment was úpon her, she knew with an unswerving sense of certainty that it wasn't going to go at all as she'd planned. She'd intended to pave the way smoothly so that there were no surprises for any of them, to be calm and reasonable and persuasive, but above all—civilized. Becoming argumentative had been the last thing on her mind, but in the face of those cool and slightly hostile hazel eyes, she felt an unmistakable surge of anger.

She moistened suddenly dry lips. "You came here . . . to find me." Almost defiantly she waited for Ward to speak.

He inclined his head, his eyes never leaving hers. "Yes."

His even tone didn't fool her. She could feel his eyes on her, weighing her. Again she was aware of a forceful undercurrent rippling between the two of them, as if . . . as if they were both preparing to do battle.

As indeed they were. The thought was a jolting one, but she instinctively summoned all her pride. It took effort, but she met his gaze unflinchingly. "We need to talk." One hand still rested on the doorknob behind her, and she turned slightly to open it. "Shall we go inside?"

There was an uneasy silence as Ward breached the few steps between them. Again Jenna felt a debilitating sense of apprehension invade her body as he brushed by her and stepped into her motel room. For a moment, she was tempted to give in to it, to let herself face the truth and be done with it, to admit once and for all that the man at her side had no intention of letting her see her child. Not now—not ever. Not entirely to her surprise, Jenna found that her hands were shaking as she closed the door behind them. She quickly crossed to switch on the light above the long, maple-veneered dresser, then turned to face Ward.

He was still standing near the doorway. To Jenna, he appeared big and powerful and more than a little intimidating. It took no stretch of the imagination to realize that beneath the flannel shirt he wore there lurked a number of extremely well-developed muscles. Her stomach gave a peculiar lurch as her eyes rested briefly on the dark thatch of wiry hairs emerging from the opening of his shirt. He seemed to tower mere inches from the ceiling, and the unruly dark hair falling over his forehead, mussed from the wind, only emphasized the impression of strength and power. The faintly uncompromising look on his face as his gaze met hers did little to dispel the notion that she was coming up against a brick wall.

Jenna made a nervous gesture with one hand. "Please, have a seat." She indicated the chair nearest the doorway, then sat down in one of the two chairs flanking the tiny round table near the window. Once there, she laced her fingers tightly in her lap and dropped her eyes for an instant. Now that the moment was actually upon her, she wasn't sure what to say. A tremor ran through her body. Should they exchange a few civil words—though from the look on his face she doubted that was possible—or simply get down to business? God, how cold that sounded! What might have been a business transaction for some women had definitely *not* been one for Jenna, despite the contracts and legal mumbo jumbo between her and the Garrisons all those years ago. She had done it for Megan, and how she wished it were Megan she were facing right now!

Finally she cleared her throat and looked up at him. "I talked with your sister today. I—she told me you weren't expected back for some time."

He made an impatient gesture with one hand. "We finished ahead of schedule."

"I see," Jenna said carefully, her eyes meeting his for a fleeting second. "I—I was also at your house today. It seems a very nice place to—" her gaze slid nervously away from his for a moment "—to bring up a child."

"Is that why you're here? To see if Robbie is being provided a proper home? If that's all that concerns you, I'll set your mind at ease. My son is being raised in a normal, stable environment and there's no need to worry—"

His tone wasn't openly hostile, yet Jenna felt her temper rise at the faint bite in his tone. She hadn't even asked to see Robbie yet—as if it weren't already apparent what his answer would be! But she wasn't about to be pushed out of the arena when she'd done nothing wrong.

"I didn't come here because I was worried about Robbie!" she said sharply. "And I'd hardly call it a normal, stable environment when you decide to go riding off into the sunset and dump Robbie at your sister's! In fact, it makes me wonder just how often that happens!"

"I have to make a living and my job demands that I travel." The words were clipped, but inside Ward felt a wayward twinge of guilt. The extensive amount of travel was the only thing he disliked about his work, but both he and Megan had known what he was getting into. If anything, it had made the time they spent with each other all the more valuable. Nevertheless, that was the reason he'd decided to obtain a pilot's license and do his own flying. He preferred to schedule his own time rather than arrange it around commercial flights. He'd hated the hours spent hovering in and around airports. Over the years he'd moved up in the firm, and his trips away from home had decreased enormously since he was now a consulting engineer. Still, he couldn't help but remember how, in the first months following Megan's death, he'd thrown himself into project after project, welcoming any and every opportunity that took him away from his home and away from the painful reminders. No, he hadn't seen much of Robbie then, and he still regretted it to this day.

But he didn't need anyone, and especially Jenna Bradford, throwing it up in his face. Robbie was *his* son, and he wasn't about to stand on the sidelines and watch someone jeopardize that relationship—not when that person was the only one on earth who could come between them. And she was a threat. Of that he was convinced.

"I don't see the need to explain my actions to you," he said gruffly. "Robbie is my son, not yours. I would think that you, more than anyone, would be aware of that."

For an instant Jenna had regretted her carelessly flung words, knowing they weren't fair. But his, quiet though they were, stabbed at her like the point of a knife.

She could only stare at him. This, then, was what she was up against, the hidden fear she'd be afraid to give voice to lest it be true. Ward Garrison resented her presence, probably wished she had stayed in Galveston, forgotten by all concerned. After all, he and his wife had their lives, and she had hers. And the two had been intertwined for so brief a time. But she couldn't forget....

She forced herself to meet his eyes. "All I want," she stated with quiet deliberateness, "is to see Robbie. Is that so terrible?"

For just an instant Ward hesitated. Once...*once* he might have been able to appreciate her request, perhaps even honor it. But how could he now? He'd already lost Meg. That thought kindled a moment of pure panic. What would he do without Robbie?

He couldn't afford to let Jenna see his fear, he suddenly realized. He couldn't stand it if he lost his son.

He made a vague gesture with one hand. "You shouldn't even be here," he said in a very low voice. "Your part in Robbie's life is over and done with—finished. Can't you see that?"

Jenna drew a deep, uneven breath. "I'm not saying I want to be a part of his life. I know that's not possible. All I want is to see him again. Just this once."

Ward's mouth tightened. "You're here. Don't you think that counts for something? How can I believe you'll stop at just once?"

She thought quickly. "All right." She bit her lip guiltily and looked away quickly. "I'll admit...I thought I'd stay a few days and—and I could see him while I was here."

"No."

The single word was like a cold blast of wind from the Arctic. Jenna felt a shroud of iciness steal around her heart. When she had come here she'd had so much hope...and he was shattering it as surely as if he'd taken her heart in his hands and crushed the life from it.

"Please..." She had to force the word past the unfamiliar dryness in her throat.

"Damn it, I said no! I can't take that chance!" He made a sudden movement, then abruptly checked himself.

Jenna caught the motion, watching as his hands balled into fists at his sides. Oddly, she wasn't intimidated by either his size or his actions. Still, she couldn't prevent her eyes from locking sharply on his face. Before she'd almost had to strain to hear his low, clipped responses. Now the sudden harshness in his voice startled her. His expression conformed with his voice, dark and brooding. But as she stared up at him for an intense moment, she became acutely aware of something else.

He looked—and sounded—almost bitter. And yet for a fraction of a second, she could have sworn she glimpsed something else in his eyes, and she wasn't sure she could put a name to it. Pain? Fear? No. Surely not fear. He had no reason to be afraid of her.

Little did she realize that was exactly how Ward was feeling. He was furious with himself for nearly letting his emotions get the best of him, but also angry with Jenna for precipitating this ungodly situation. His thoughts in turmoil, he turned away. He'd had no choice when Meg was wrenched from his life, but now he did. He wouldn't stand by and let this woman snatch away the only thing he had left in this world. He loved Robbie so much. A life without him was something he couldn't even bear to think about.

So why was he feeling so all-fired guilty about protecting his own interests?

"Why?" he muttered. "Why did you come here? Damn it, *why?*"

It slowly dawned on Jenna that this wasn't any easier for him than it was for her. There was a muscle twitching in one lean cheek, and she watched him close his eyes as if in pain. For a moment a part of her wanted to reach out to him, to soothe away the hurt, whatever the cause.

But she knew instinctively that the gap between them was miles wide, particularly at this moment, and would not be so easily bridged.

She stared at the unyielding strength of his back, the muscular width of his shoulders, and wet her lips nervously. "Look, I know what you're thinking—"

"Do you?" Slowly he turned to face her. "I don't think so, or you wouldn't be here."

Jenna lifted her chin proudly. "I think I do," she refuted quietly. "It was never my intention to barge in and turn everything upside down. I know we all thought it best to each go our own ways after the birth, and I'm not aware of any reason we still can't do that. Seeing Robbie now isn't going to change a thing. And I've kept my promise to stay out of your lives—"

"Until now."

Ward's voice was low and controlled, yet he seemed to be looking right through her. Dear Lord, she could almost believe he hated her! Why—*why* did he think it was so wrong for her to want to see Robbie?

Denying the cold feeling of dread that was creeping through her body like a slow and deadly poison, she spread her hands beseechingly. "I-I'm getting married soon and...and I'll be having my own family eventually. I swear I'll never interfere again...." She shook her head quickly, feeling she was making a terrible mess of this whole thing but not sure how to set it right. She drew a tremulous breath before going on. "Please. Surely you can understand that I *need* to see him—even if it's only a glimpse! As much as I need air to breathe...."

The silent plea in her eyes cut into his soul. Those eyes so like his son's held no secrets, and he could see the fear, the longing, the desperation. And he could only thank heaven that Jenna didn't know he was just as scared as she.

"I'm not sure I can." He studied her. "Are you trying to say that after nearly four years you're finally having second thoughts? That you actually care about him?"

Jenna straightened with an indignant gasp. "Of course I care about him! I cared about all of you. And you can't accuse me of having done it for the money, because you know very well that had nothing to do with it!"

Damn! Why couldn't she just let go? She was leaving him with no other recourse. God, but he hated himself for what he was about to do! "Of course you do," he echoed firmly. "You cared so much you didn't even want to hold him when he was born!"

Jenna felt the world whirl giddily around her. Raw pain splintered through her, until she felt she would break apart from it. Dear God, why did he have to remind her? It wasn't because she *didn't* care that she hadn't wanted to hold him! It was because she *did*. And she hadn't realized just how much she'd grown to love that life that had bloomed inside her until she'd actually seen him. She'd been afraid that if she touched him, if she held him...

Seconds passed. Seconds that became long, intolerable minutes in which a mantle of gloom slowly descended over her. There was no movement in the small, stark room, no sound to break the deathly silence. How could she make Ward under-

stand that it was love that held her back, love that brought her
back now?

Her jaw wouldn't work properly. "For God's sake, there's
not a child on earth who was more wanted than Robbie. And
not just by you and Megan, but by me! He was yours. I knew
that—I've always known that. But that doesn't mean I never
cared about him. That I never stopped thinking of him...."

Her voice trailed off. She couldn't go on anymore. Who was
she trying to convince? Ward? Or herself? She did love her son,
the son she had never really known, would *never* know. But it
was less than a week ago that she had finally owned up to the
truth—that no matter how she tried, she couldn't forget,
couldn't erase the memory as easily as chalk on a blackboard.
All these years it had always been there, like a pebble in her
shoe. Dear heaven, what a comparison! For an instant, she almost hated herself. He was her son. Her child. Yet she wouldn't
know him if she came face-to-face with him at this very moment!

"It won't do any good." Dimly she heard Ward's voice.
"The answer is still no. I won't let you see Robbie."

Slowly Jenna raised her head to look at him. For a moment
her mind was unwilling to believe her ears. But beside the cold
finality of his words, she was stung to the core by the look of
unyielding harshness in his face. His eyes were cold, totally de-
void of any feeling. In that moment Jenna hated Ward Garrison, hated him fiercely, with every ounce of feeling she
possessed. She wondered wildly if she could ever get through
to him. If anyone could get through to him. He seemed so different from the man she remembered, the man who had been
so protective and loving with his wife. She sensed a hardness,
perhaps even a ruthlessness in him that she was sure hadn't been
there before.

"Megan would have let me see him, and you know it," she
told him in a low voice. Her hands curled into fists at her sides
as the rush of emotion inside her began to swell. Both anger and
resentment fueled her attack, forcing the words from her.
"You're not the same man you were—not the loving, tender
husband she thought the world of, the man I thought she was
so lucky to have. What happened to him, Ward? Did he die
along with his wife?"

For an instant Ward couldn't believe his ears. An agonizing
pain ripped through him before he acknowledged that she was

probably right. Megan would never have denied her. Couldn't he have let Jenna down easier? He wasn't sure. He couldn't afford to give her any encouragement. There was too much at stake.

His jaw hardened. He met her defiant gaze from across the room, inexplicably wanting to hurt her as much as he'd been hurt these past few years, even while something inside stabbed at him and pricked his conscience.

"I won't deny it. Meg would have let you see him," he said flatly. "And since you know it, you might as well know this, too. It won't do you any good to stick around in hope that I might change my mind, because I won't." His eyes drilled into hers. "Robbie is my son. As far as I'm concerned, he no longer has a mother. He lost the only mother he had when Meg died."

He turned and strode from the room. The door slammed behind him with a resounding bang. His footsteps pounded the pavement, not faltering until he wrenched the car door shut beside him.

Once there he blew out a long, harsh sigh. It was over. Done. No doubt Jenna Bradford thought he was a bastard. A cold, selfish, unfeeling bastard who didn't give a damn about anyone or anything but himself. Well, perhaps it was best. He'd made sure she would never again try to see Robbie. He'd succeeded in crushing her hopes, smashing any dreams she might have had of reuniting with Robbie. The look in her eyes before he whirled from the room told him more clearly than words that he'd succeeded.

But even then the tight knot of tension that sat like a stone in his stomach didn't begin to ease. If anything, it curled even tighter, slowly moving upward, until he felt as if he would choke on it. There was a bitter taste in his mouth, a gnawing feeling that clawed at his gut.

He knew this night would prey on his mind for a hell of a long time. He stared into the stark blackness of the night, suddenly seeing her face again, that look in her eyes—haunted, full of anguish, dark with pain and helpless frustration. Oh, yes, he knew that look. He'd seen it often enough in the mirror. How many days had he awakened in the morning to that very same image? How often had he seen it eating into his soul?

With a muttered curse he slammed his hand against the steering wheel and shoved the keys in the ignition.

JENNA WASN'T AWARE how long she stared at the closed door. It could have been minutes, hours, or it could have been seconds. She began to shiver, whether from reaction or the coolness of the room she couldn't be sure. Wrapping her arms around her body, she got up and switched on the heat. But just as suddenly, she felt as if she were being smothered. The walls were closing in on her, and it was hot, oppressive.

Unable to stand the silence, she turned on the television. The newscaster's voice droned on in a dull monotone, but the sound was faintly reassuring. Somehow she didn't feel quite so alone. It wasn't until she had settled herself in the middle of the bed that reality began to set in.

She should have known Ward wouldn't let her see Robbie. She was an outsider, an intruder, interfering where she had no business. Now she remembered vividly the day she, Meg and Ward had signed the contracts in Ron Brewster's office.

"Please don't get me wrong," Ward had said, looking directly at her. "We realize how much you're going out on a limb for us. And I can't tell you how grateful we are to know that we're finally going to be blessed with our own child." He'd exchanged a tender look with Megan, who sat at his side, before turning back to her. "We're not dealing with money here. We're dealing with feelings. This is a very complicated situation and there's so much at stake. Though we've tried to think of all the problems that might occur, the one thing we don't want is for any of us—the baby included—to be hurt unnecessarily. That's why we both think it best if we stay out of one another's lives after the baby is born. No cards, no pictures, no phone calls. We hope you'll agree that this is the best way. The *only* way."

Megan had looked a little contrite, rather uncomfortable, Jenna recalled. Though Ward's voice had been rather quiet, his look had been piercingly direct and there had been something totally unyielding in those hazel eyes. But it wasn't as if she minded—at the time.

No, she had wholeheartedly agreed with his stance. It was the only practical way to approach the experience. No messy, sloppy or sentimental feelings to clutter up the issue. Any maternal instincts she might have had had been swiftly suppressed. They simply didn't belong, she'd told herself. It didn't matter that she was doing it for love. She couldn't afford to love this child, because it really wasn't hers. Her whole being at the time was geared toward giving this couple what they wanted. A

aby, *their* baby, and nothing else mattered, including her own
eelings.

But that was before, and this was now, and how cold it all
eemed at this moment.

It was all too much. Too much, and all at once. She leaned
ack against the pillows, suddenly unbelievably tired. She ig-
ored the tight knot of pain that sat on her chest like a viper
eady to strike and forced herself toward the bathroom to un-
ress for bed. She really should call her mother, she thought as
he slipped a thin cotton nightgown over her head, but she
idn't have the energy. All she wanted to do was crawl be-
ween the sheets to nurse her wounds in private.

Tomorrow. There was always tomorrow, and then she would
ecide what to do. But for tonight, all she wanted was to
leep... and mercifully find forgetfulness.

DESPITE HER FATIGUE, Jenna's sleep was fitful and disjointed,
roken by dreams of a harsh male voice that jabbed and ac-
used. Dreams. More like nightmares, she thought as she swept
side the sheet and padded toward the bathroom early the next
norning.

Even a hot shower didn't revive her. She felt as if she were
ighty-eight instead of twenty-eight. A wry smile touched her
nouth. "Good Lord," she told the face in the mirror, think-
ng back earnestly, "you haven't felt this bad since...since the
irst few months you were pregnant." She was one of those
ortunate enough to be rarely sick, but she'd been sick often
hen; hardly a morning had passed during her first trimester
hat she hadn't been plagued by nausea. And tired—God, how
ired she'd been, no matter how many hours of sleep she got.

The smile faded. The memory of last night came flooding
back. What was she going to do about Robbie? Should she
eave, or try to see him on the sly, perhaps? No, she couldn't.
That idea was almost as unpalatable as leaving without seeing
Robbie. It simply wasn't in her nature to go behind Ward's
back, no matter what the cost. But was there any other way?

After dressing in jeans and a short-sleeved jersey pullover of
jade green, she opened the drapes and stared out the window.
The day was bright and sunny, and huge puffy clouds were being pushed by a steady wind overhead. An occasional car
whizzed by, but Jenna's mind was elsewhere.

Exactly what kind of response had she expected from Ward
Garrison, she demanded of herself impatiently. A little wariness, a bit of uncertainty, maybe—somehow they hadn't come
as a surprise. Her mind delved further. Gratitude? Maybe. But
certainly not what she'd gotten! If he had thought to deal her
a low blow, he'd certainly succeeded. She shivered as she remembered his words. "Robbie lost the only mother he had
when Meg died."

Still it was his right to say no, to deny her request. But did he
have to be so cruel? So ruthless? Was that what grated her so?
Partly, she acknowledged with a weary slump of her shoulders. But that wasn't all. It hurt to admit the truth, but she had
to face it. When Ward had walked out the door last night, he'd
taken a part of her with him, a part she could never hope to regain. But it wasn't fair, she cried silently. It simply wasn't fair
that she had to leave before she'd even had the chance to say
hello.

Jenna had always prided herself on being in control. It wasn't
ego that told her she was a good nurse. Her composure was one
of the things that made her so. But where Robbie was concerned, that was something over which she had no control, and
she couldn't help the wave of helpless fury that surged through
her. There was no choice to be made. Ward Garrison had seen
to that, she thought bitterly. She would head back to Galveston this morning as soon as she was packed. There was no reason to stay. She wouldn't see Ward again. She simply couldn't
stand to go through this yet another time.

A wave of despair swept through her, so intense it bordered
on pain. The harsh knock at the door was almost welcome.
Jenna opened the door wide without a thought as to who her
early morning caller might be. She stood frozen as she saw who
was on the other side.

For a moment she couldn't speak. Disbelievingly her eyes ran
over the tall figure filling the doorway. Just as he had last night
he wore boots and a pair of jeans, but they were topped by a
camel-colored sweater. He was hatless; his jet black hair tossed
freely in the breeze. His lips were set in a straight line, though
and the curve of his jaw seemed just as unyielding as it had been
last night.

A surge of resentment poured through her as he brushed by
her and stepped into the room. The door closed with a silent

lick behind her. Her hands still curled around the knob, Jenna
urned to face him.

"Come to kick me while I'm down?" Her chin lifted defi-
ntly as his eyes swiftly toured the room. She had the feeling
hat nothing escaped his notice, not the rumpled unmade bed,
r her robe and nightgown tossed carelessly over one of the
hairs. She gave a silent thank-you to herself that she hadn't yet
ifted her empty suitcase onto the bed to pack the few things
he'd brought. She might regret it later, but she couldn't resist
dding tightly, "I might be down, but I'm not out, and I'm not
eaten. So if you came to gloat—"

"Do you still want to see Robbie?"

The clipped, quiet words almost slipped by her completely.
Jenna stared at him, convinced she hadn't heard right. "Are
you serious?" she finally breathed.

His head barely moved as he nodded. "But you have to understand—this is the only time I'll let you see him."

Jenna's eyes were fixed on his face. There was nothing soft
n his expression; those hazel eyes were unerringly direct as he
ooked at her. "I—" Her voice cracked as she tried to cope with
is sudden appearance. He'd changed his mind? It seemed too
good to be true. "Yes, of course...of course I still do!" She
sounded breathy and excited. Her hand came around to fiercely
atch onto the other in front of her.

"He's still at my sister's. You can come with me to pick him
up if you want."

Already he was brushing by her on his way out. Jenna's eyes
were wide and disbelieving as he stepped out on the sidewalk
and turned to face her. Under any other circumstances the
curtly given invitation would have grated on her like a fingernail scraping a chalkboard. But right now the world could have
come down around her ears and somehow she didn't think
she'd have known. Her heart began to soar within her chest as
she hurriedly slung her purse over her shoulder.

Robbie. At last she was going to see Robbie.

CHAPTER FIVE

UNFORTUNATELY the exhilaration skittering through Jenna's veins proved to be rather short-lived. She couldn't stop herself from studying the expression that met her glance for an instant over the roof of the Blazer. Ward looked every bit as unapproachable as he had last night. She felt her excitement dampened more than just a little.

Only one small thought kept her heart from plummeting straight to her feet. Ward had yielded enough to give his consent to let her see Robbie. She didn't know what was behind his change of heart, and since she suspected he was far too complicated a man for her to figure out, she didn't bother trying. She found herself wondering if she dared hope he would unbend even further and let her spend a little more time with Robbie.

Once Jenna had purchased some take-out coffee and they were on the main highway heading north out of town, she risked another glance at Ward. "Is it far?" she asked presently.

His response was more a growl than an answer. "What?"

Jenna wiped the palms of her hands on her slacks. What was it about him that set her so on edge? She'd never felt quite so ill at ease around anyone before—and somehow she suspected it wasn't just because of all the friction between them now.

"Is it far to your sister's?" she repeated. "The drive—how long will it take?"

"About twenty minutes." The answer seemed to come grudgingly, as did his next words. "She and her husband have a four-hundred-acre ranch. They raise beef cattle—and a few horses, as well."

Jenna spoke without thinking. "I'll bet Robbie likes that. Most kids are fascinated with animals." An unconscious smile curved her lips as she let her mind wander, despite the disturb-

...g presence at her side. At nearly four years old, a little boy's ...orld probably consisted of sleep, eat and play, though not ...ecessarily in that order. What were his favorite toys? Cars? ...rains? Books? And what was he like? Quiet? Robust? Sud...enly her mind was filled with questions. How old was he when ...e learned to crawl? To walk? When had he first laughed? And ...alked? What was his first word? Mundane matters, to be ...ure—but ones only a mother could express such a profound ...nterest in.

Forgetting herself for a moment, she turned to Ward, curi...sity overruling caution. Question after question formed on her ...ps. But the sight of his face, taut and grim, and his lean fin...ers clenching the steering wheel, stopped her short. Too late ...he realized her mistake. She shouldn't even be thinking of ...erself as Robbie's mother. Already her mind—or was it her ...eart?—had begun to trespass on forbidden territory.

Her fingers tensed in her lap. Lord, and she hadn't even seen ...im yet. She was going to have to do better than this, or she ...vould only end up getting hurt.

Instead she asked quietly, "Does he stay there often? With ...our sister, I mean?"

Their eyes met as he flashed a quick, sidelong glance at her. ...There was a hint of annoyance in his eyes. "He only stays with ...Eileen if I'm going to be out of town." He sent another swift ...glance at her before stressing, "Which isn't all that often any...more since I'm a full partner now. Otherwise he goes to a sit...er in town."

Jenna frowned. "Isn't your office in Abilene?" When he ...nodded and said that the sitter was in Plains City, she added, "You're a partner now? You weren't before, were you?"

"No. I was offered the partnership about a year ago."

So it was after Megan had died. She would have been proud ...of him, Jenna suspected. She almost voiced the thought aloud, ...but his tone was clipped and abrupt, and she was left with the ...feeling that he wanted nothing more than to be left alone.

That was something Jenna was only too willing to do. She ...turned her head to the side. Idly she saw that the terrain had ...changed slightly. They were leaving the flat plains behind and ...the road followed the dips and curves of gently sloping hills. ...Homes were few and far between. Cattle grazed in the dis...tance and fields of wheat rippled in the wind.

Though she tried to content herself with the sweeping Texas landscape just outside the window, the strange sort of tension that had sprung up between them last night was in full force once again. Maybe it was because she didn't understand him. She couldn't even pretend to comprehend his hostility last night, or his abrupt about-face. But was it only that? No, there was something else.

More and more Jenna found her gaze touching on that strong, masculine profile presented to her. Ward's eyes were focused straight ahead. His nose jutted out forcefully and there was a faint bump on the bridge that made her wonder if he'd broken it once. The firm contours of his mouth pressed together in a straight line. Didn't he ever smile? She shifted uncomfortably on her seat. She didn't like looking at him, yet he drew her gaze like a magnet.

Her eyes slid downward. His hands were big and very strong-looking, the fingers long and lean, not in the least bit fleshy. One hand lay carelessly over the top of the steering wheel. The other was curled firmly below. She drew in a soft breath of surprise. How long had his sister said Megan had been dead? A year and a half. Her eyes lingered on the smooth band of gold that still encircled his wedding finger.

Her attention drifted back to his hands. Bristly black hairs covered the wide backs. The sleeves of his sweater were pushed up to his elbows, and Jenna's gaze followed the muscular definitions of his forearms. They, too were coated with a thick layer of dark hairs. Was he as hairy as that all over?

She caught her breath again, but this time it was for an entirely different reason. Warmth tainted her entire body, and she had the sinking feeling that a tell-tale trail of red was creeping into her cheeks—she, who hadn't blushed in years. *This drive is going to last a lifetime,* she thought to herself uneasily. She didn't like Ward Garrison and she definitely didn't like the strange way he made her feel.

"When are you getting married?"

The question, out of the blue as it was, gave Jenna a start. It was the first time Ward had spoken of his own accord. For a moment she was unable to speak. "In November," she finally responded. Neil . . . her marriage. They both seemed a lifetime away. "The first week. We—Neil and I have been engaged for six months now."

Ward took his eyes off the road long enough to study her for
a moment. She was looking silently out the window. Meg had
really liked Jenna, he remembered. She'd been impressed by
that fleeting, almost shy smile and her quiet levelheadedness.
She'd decided almost on sight that Jenna was the one.

"She's perfect!" Meg had told him enthusiastically. "Perfect! She even looks a little like you!"

He had agreed that she was the best choice, though not until
after they'd interviewed her. Ron Brewster had really grilled her
on her reasons for wanting to carry a baby for nine months and
willingly then give it up. Her responses had been quiet, almost
serene, but there was a world of emotion in those vivid green
eyes. No one could doubt her sincerity after looking into those
eyes.

But now Ward did doubt—for the first time. At this moment, he couldn't respond to her calm demeanor the same way
he had when they'd first met. She was quiet, almost too quiet,
as she gazed at the passing countryside. What was going on inside her head? Was she plotting? Scheming of ways to take
away his son?

With a harsh sigh he leaned back against the seat. Damn it,
he was letting his imagination run wild. Or was he? He didn't
know. That was the whole problem. He just didn't know. Meg
would have had his hide for being so suspicious; in those days
he hadn't been. In fact, he hadn't been until now.

But Jenna *was* getting married, he reminded himself reluctantly. Although he tended to view her as a noose around his
neck right now, after this one day she would be out of his life
again. But for how long? He pushed away the nagging voice
and instead found himself wondering about her future husband. Did it bother him that she was a woman who had vol-
untarily carried another man's child? Probably not, he decided,
a wry twist to his mouth. Today's morals weren't exactly Victorian, and she was, after all, a very attractive woman.

The observation surprised him, as did the realization that he
didn't even have to look at her to recall the slender curves of her
body. She was so small boned for such a tall woman. The jeans
she'd worn this morning had outlined her narrow waist and the
flare of her hips. Once again he visualized the gentle thrust of
her breasts against her top. Ward shook his head and his jaw
tightened. Damn! He was suddenly almost painfully aware that
this was the first time since Meg had died—since he'd known

Meg, in fact—that he was actively taking note of a woman's appearance. An odd twinge shot through him and his mouth twisted.

Somehow it went against the grain to admit that the first woman he was even remotely conscious of was Jenna Bradford. He could understand the attraction if she reminded him of Meg, but they were nothing alike, not in personality and certainly not in looks. And she was the one woman on earth who stood to harm him the most.

The realization hardened his voice. "What does your intended think of your visit here? I assume he knows why you've come."

Jenna grabbed at the armrest as Ward made a swift turn off the highway onto a narrow side road. They bounced along for several seconds before she spoke.

She tilted her head to look at him. Her quiet voice seemed to hold a challenge. "I didn't need his permission."

"Then I suppose he's behind you all the way."

Jenna bristled at the insolent tone. She had the feeling he was goading her. "My fiancé," she ventured again in forceful but carefully measured words, "is well aware of my reasons for being here." Certainly it was the truth, yet she knew a niggling sense of guilt. Neil had probably known very well he couldn't stop her, but while he was aware of her reasons for coming here, he didn't understand them. He hadn't been at all as supportive as she'd hoped, but even while she told herself this, Jenna knew that even if his objections had been far more strenuous, it wouldn't have made one whit of difference.

But she couldn't be one hundred percent honest with Ward, considering this strange unnamed battle they were having. She didn't quite understand why, but they were adversaries, each on guard against the other. To admit that Neil didn't want her here would be akin to handing an arsenal of weapons to an army.

A dark shadow passed across Ward's face as Jenna fell silent. Meg would have laughed at him if he'd ever have said he had a tough-guy image, callous and hardhearted, but he had the feeling Jenna Bradford thought of him that way. Last night he'd wanted her to think that. Hell, he'd acted like a mother hen rallying around her chicks, but with all the noise of a raging bull. But this morning...this morning was a different story.

He'd slept little the previous night. Her image had danced behind his eyelids all night long. He couldn't forget her expression when he'd left her. Even as he stared at the winding ribbon of road in front of him, the vision in his mind blurred and repeated itself. In her face he'd seen his son's tiny features staring back at him again, crushed and shattered, without a shred of hope to cling to.

He couldn't help but wonder—who was he hurting more? Jenna? Or Robbie?

No, he could have stuck to it if it hadn't been for that. He hadn't been able to live with his decision even one night—he couldn't say no! What if she were the one denying him the chance to see his own son? It was something he didn't want to think about, and for an instant, he hadn't been able to stop putting himself in her place.

Yet he despised himself for being so weak, and he hated the fact that she had put him in this position. It was one neither he nor Meg had given any thought to once Robbie was safely in their possession.

But he had no one to blame but himself, and like it or not, he would stick to his word and let her see Robbie.

The rest of the trip was made in silence, with Ward grimly giving his attention to the road ahead. Jenna stared pensively out the window, both afraid and excited. She was a bundle of nerves by the time the Blazer turned onto a narrow access road, and she began blotting her hands nervously against her thighs as she spied a house in the distance. Her heart was pounding so furiously she could feel the rapid rise and fall of her breasts against the soft jersey of her blouse.

She marveled that her legs even held her as they drew to a halt. Opening the car door, she had to force her attention to her surroundings. She was standing in front of a modest ranch-style house, nestled into a grove of trees. It was tranquil-looking despite the cluster of outbuildings and randomly parked pickup trucks several hundred yards away.

Ward gave her a cursory glance as he got out. "Eileen's probably inside," he said shortly. Just as he rounded the front fender, a flash of red and blue careered around the corner of the house.

"Daddy!"

In that instant, Jenna felt her heart stop beating.

It resumed with thick, uneven strokes as the small figure raced toward them as fast as his chubby, three-year-old legs would carry him. They came to an abrupt halt, and the boy, squealing with excitement, was snatched high into a pair of arms.

Transfixed, Jenna could only stare at him. So this was Robbie. This was her son. *Her son....*

"I missed you, Daddy. I missed you this much!" The little boy spread his arms as wide as they would go, then latched on to his father's neck once more. Tanned, chunky arms peeped out from a short-sleeved bright red polo shirt over which a pair of bib overalls was worn. On his feet were a pair of red canvas sneakers. "Did you bring me a present?" he asked eagerly.

"I missed you, too, champ." A warm kiss was pressed on one dirt-smudged cheek, and Ward drew away to gaze at his son. His lips curved upward as he winked. "And yes, I brought you a present."

So he can smile, after all. Despite the fact that Jenna's whole being was focused on her son, Ward's voice was so full of warmth, his eyes filled with such love and gentleness, that for an instant she was almost stunned. The harsh, unyielding man she had glimpsed last night might have been a stranger, a figment of her imagination.

But the shadow of the stranger was back when he turned to her—reluctantly, it seemed. She collected herself quickly as she saw Ward's smile fade.

"Robbie, there's someone I'd like you to meet." His arms tightened around the boy. "This is Jenna."

Eyes round with curiosity, the little boy wiggled in his father's arms to stare at her, but he didn't say a word.

That he didn't was beyond Jenna's comprehension. Again she felt the breath wrenched from her lungs as a rush of the sweetest, most delightful sense of pleasure shot through her. Robbie's mop of fine, almost black curls could have come from either her or Ward, but those vivid green eyes surrounded by bristly black lashes could belong only to her. *Her!*

In the space of a heartbeat, her joy was shattered as she realized how much of an outsider she really was. She was his mother, but she didn't belong in this tightly woven circle of love between father and son. Jenna was overcome by a rush of emotion so intense she almost cried out with it. Was it possible to feel both joy and pain at the same time? It was, indeed. The moment was both poignant and heartwarmingly precious.

"Hello, Robbie." Her greeting came out as a whisper, and she found herself unable to tear her eyes from that small cherubic face.

"Hi," he finally whispered back. Then he promptly turned and shyly buried his face in the strong column of Ward's neck.

Cast in the unlikely role of rescuer, Ward set the boy on his feet, then ruffled his thick dark hair. "Where's Aunt Eileen?"

His shyness forgotten, Robbie beamed up at him. "In the barn," he responded happily before dashing off.

Ward started off after him, then paused for a second and glanced back at her over his shoulder. Though her insides were still quivering at her first sight of Robbie, her legs felt as if they were leaden poles beneath her when she moved to where he was waiting for her.

The day was sunny and rather warm, lighted with brilliant patches of sunshine. Jenna shivered as they stepped into the barn. The temperature inside was noticeably cooler, so cool that she slipped into the denim blazer she'd removed against the warmth of the car's interior. The odor of fresh, sweet-smelling straw permeated her nostrils and mingled with the aroma of leather and horses. Beneath massive overhead beams, she kept apace with Ward's long-legged strides as he followed Robbie.

"Look, Daddy! Misty's gonna have a baby horse!" Jumping up and down, Robbie pointed toward a stall.

Jenna heard a feminine chuckle as they halted, and then a cheerful voice announced, "Looks like you're just in time, Ward. Misty Moon is about to drop a foal."

Jenna peeked around Ward's broad shoulder. The voice came from a woman with hair as dark as Ward's, worn in a crisp, no-nonsense hairdo that waved neatly back from a friendly, likable face. Eileen Swenson, she assumed. She guessed her to be in her early forties, perhaps slightly older than Ward.

Eileen was kneeling near the flanks of a horse. Jenna drew in a soft breath of surprise. There on a fresh bed of straw lay a beautiful chestnut mare, her golden brown coat glistening with sweat, velvety nostrils flared.

At the small sound, the woman looked up to where Jenna stood slightly behind Ward. Jenna saw the friendly expression vanish as Eileen's eyes darted from Jenna to where Robbie had come to thrust one dimpled hand into Ward's, then back again. Intercepting the look, Ward gestured between the two women and gave a curt introduction. "Eileen, this is Jenna Bradford. Jenna, my sister Eileen."

Aware of the closed expression on Eileen Swenson's face, Jenna murmured a polite greeting. Eileen nodded briefly. Then the mare's sides began to heave and she whinnied, a low sound that spoke of pain.

Moments later a much smaller version of the chestnut mare was awkwardly trying to stand. Inspecting the baby, Eileen announced it was a colt.

"What's a colt?" Robbie piped up.

Busy attending to the mare, Eileen looked up at him and smiled. "A boy. A girl is called a filly."

"Does he have any teeth?"

Eileen shook her head. "Not yet, but he will very soon. By the time he's six months old, he'll have almost as many as you."

Robbie moved a few steps closer. Eyes as wide as saucers were riveted on both mother and baby. "If he doesn't have any teeth," he persisted, "how will he eat?"

Eileen hesitated and looked at Ward, who took up where she left off. He glanced down at his small son. "Well, Robbie," he said, his voice very gentle, "his mother is going to take care of that for him for a while."

Almost as if he knew he was the subject under discussion, the spindly-legged colt finally made it to his feet and unsteadily moved to nuzzle his mother's belly. The mare whickered softly and looked back at her offspring with velvet-soft eyes.

Somehow the gentleness in Ward's voice was Jenna's undoing. She had watched the foal's quick birth silently, but at the sight of mother and baby, her lungs constricted painfully. Suddenly feeling as though she were suffocating, she stumbled out of the stall and ran toward the wide double doors.

High in the sky, the sun shone down on her still figure as she stood motionless near a whitewashed fence. Several horses grazed peacefully in the paddock near the barn. Beyond, the wide sweep of prairie seemed endless. The land was a rich golden color, fields of wheat swaying in tempo with the gentle breeze.

Jenna saw none of this. Her lungs ached with the effort it took to breathe. Her head hurt. And her breasts; her nipples tingled and she crossed her arms across her chest as though to stop the milk that had never been allowed to flow.

She had declined the shot that would have dried her milk, she remembered vividly. Stubbornly, willfully refused it. She had elected instead to let nature take over the drying of her milk, stoically enduring the slow-going painful process as if . . . as if by doing so she could purge herself of the memory of the tiny being she had nourished and given life to for nine long months.

She grabbed the wooden railing tightly for support. Still, the memories lingered. And then, as now, the pain in her breasts was nothing compared to the pain in her heart.

Sensing she was being watched, Jenna drew a deep quivering breath and slowly turned. Robbie was standing several feet behind her, small hands clasped behind his back and one sneakered foot toeing the sun-baked dust.

The cobwebs of the past floated away like a dew-kissed mist before a softly sighing breeze. With a feeling strangely akin to relief, she noted he was alone.

"Hello again." She smiled reassuringly at him and inclined her head toward the barn. "Are Daddy and Aunt Eileen still inside?"

Wordlessly he nodded, his eyes huge in his small face.

She took a step forward, stopping when he retreated a step in response. "I'll bet you like the baby horse, don't you?" She deliberately didn't call it a foal, wanting him to feel they were on the same level.

Again he nodded.

"Do you know what Aunt Eileen is going to name him?" she asked coaxingly. Wanting desperately to hear his voice once more, she sighed when another nod was all she received. The green eyes studying her were thoroughly childlike in their curiosity—and their wariness.

She tried again. "You'll probably get to ride him when he's older. Won't that be fun?"

There was an answering sparkle in Robbie's eyes for a second. Seeing it, Jenna slowly moved toward him. She sank down on her knees before him and dug into her coat pocket, remembering the small packet of candy she'd purchased during the long trip from Galveston.

"Do you like jelly beans, Robbie?" She held out the cellophane package in her hand for his inspection. Her eyes ran over his babyish features as if to memorize them for all eternity. Being so close to him, she could see that his cheeks had the bloom and texture of a ripe, fuzzy peach. She longed to reach out and stroke the downy curve, knowing instinctively his skin would be as soft as it looked.

She smiled at him. "I like the red ones," she said. "I have since I was a little girl—not much older than you." She opened the package and poured a few of the candies onto her hand, then slipped the package back into her pocket. There was a look of longing in his eyes as she slipped one into her mouth. "Mmm, they're really good," she told him. "Are you sure you wouldn't like one?"

He hesitated for so long Jenna thought he would finally relent, but then he shook his head. Up until that moment, she'd always thought she had a way with children. She couldn't help but be disappointed that he wasn't responding as she'd hoped. She was just about to rise to her feet, when he smiled at her. It was a tiny, shy smile, but a smile nonetheless.

Jenna thought her heart would bubble over with joy. Suddenly she wanted to reach out and touch him, run her fingers through his silky dark curls and hold him to her breast, capturing the moment and holding it close to her heart forever. Trying not to move so quickly she would frighten him, she did indeed stretch out her arms to fold him close.

Her hands got no farther than his shoulders. At her first faint touch, his eyes widened and his lower lip began to quiver. Feeling as if she were a hot air balloon that had just been deflated by a mere pinprick, she felt her hands fall limply to her side. Slowly she rose to her feet as, with another fearful glance, Robbie turned on his heel and ran toward the house.

"Is everything all right?"

Ward's voice behind her startled her. She pivoted to face him, aware of a burning resentment building inside her. No, everything was not all right, she wanted to tell him bitterly. *Nothing* was right. Her eyes hardened for a fraction of a second as she let the bitterness take hold. This man ... *this man* was all that stood between her and Robbie. If it weren't for Ward Garrison, Robbie would be hers and hers alone.

She was immediately ashamed of the thought. It wasn't fair, any more than were her angrily flung words last night. She summoned a wan smile. "I'm fine," she murmured. She looked up at him, vaguely surprised to see a hint of compassion in those dark eyes.

Her reaction to the foal's arrival was silly, she decided. She had embraced the situation awkwardly. Birth, like death, was but one of life's everyday occurrences. One was a miracle and the other was something to be dealt with but not dwelt upon. She was, she realized, experiencing a kind of delayed reaction over her forfeiture of Robbie. Perhaps if she had forced herself to deal with the pain of her loss at the time of his birth, she wouldn't be feeling so desolate inside right now. And maybe she had expected too much of Robbie, of the moment. But now...before...what did it matter? The ache in her heart was there, and it was real.

Ward moved closer, studying her quietly. There was a shadow of pain in those luminous green eyes, and it took no stretch of the imagination to know that it had to do with Robbie. His unexpected sense of helplessness when she ran from the barn surprised him. He'd known instinctively that she'd been thinking of Robbie's birth. Especially in light of his feelings about her presence, the stab of pain he'd felt was unexpected, as well. But he couldn't help remembering the long and difficult labor she'd endured. Hours and hours of pain while he and Meg had sat waiting. Hoping. Anticipating. Talking in hushed, excited whispers about the baby they would soon hold in their arms.

It made him cringe to be suddenly reminded of what Jenna had gone through to give him his son and how he had repaid her. He had emerged from the barn in time to hear her say jelly beans were her favorite candy. Then when Robbie refused them, his throat had tightened oddly at the look of hurt that flashed across her face. Robbie loved jelly beans.

But the fact remained: Jenna's simple request to see his son wasn't simple at all. If he ever lost Robbie, he didn't think he could bear it.

"You'll have to forgive Robbie," he said finally. "He's a little leery of strangers."

For an instant Jenna's eyes collided sharply with his. But there was no hint of malice in either his tone or his expression, and strangely enough, she sensed his words were meant to be reassuring. She moved to step into the shade of a cottonwood tree, absently running a hand over the pale rough bark. "Don't apologize," she said in as light a tone as she could muster. She leaned against the tree before turning to face him again. "He's not too young to learn that he shouldn't take candy from someone he doesn't know." And she should have known better than to try to bribe him with it, she added silently.

He glanced over to where Robbie now played happily with a truck on the sidewalk in front of the house. Jenna's eyes followed, but when her eyes met his again she was stunned at what she saw. There was a flash of pride as he looked at Robbie, but the look changed completely as he turned back to her. Again she glimpsed the same elusive emotion she'd seen in his eyes last night. Fear? Something wasn't right. She almost sensed he was somehow afraid of her. *Of her?* No, that wasn't possible. He had nothing to fear from her; she could do him no harm. The ball was in his court, as it had been all along.

Both of them were lost in thought, and so neither of them heard Eileen come up silently behind them. Glancing uneasily between the two of them, she cleared her throat. "Will you two be staying for lunch?"

CHAPTER SIX

JENNA LOOKED AWAY quickly, leaving it totally up to Ward, as it should have been. She didn't want to influence him one way or the other. On one hand, she was admittedly reluctant to leave just yet, having only had a mere glimpse of Robbie. But she suspected the less time spent with both Ward and his sister the better.

Her thoughts proved to be right on target. Eileen insisted on preparing the light lunch of chicken soup and tuna sandwiches herself, and Jenna was left feeling awkward and out of place.

The jelly beans had left a sticky mess in the palm of her hand, and when she emerged from the bathroom and walked back to the living room, where she'd been ushered in to wait, the sound of voices carried through from the kitchen.

"You're making a big mistake, Ward." Eileen sounded tense, agitated. "Don't you realize the trouble you've invited?"

Jenna stiffened. There was no doubt in her mind what—and whom—Eileen was talking about. The deep sound of Ward's voice was muted, so she couldn't make out his reply.

She glanced around the room, trying to take her mind off the conversation in the kitchen. The overstuffed sofa and matching wing chairs looked inviting, but Jenna was too tense and restless to sit. She stared at the array of photographs hanging on the pale gold of the living room wall. There must have been at least twenty. A boy, a girl—at various ages. Indoor poses, outdoor poses. The same print of a waterfall in three different sizes on the opposite wall. That was all she really registered.

"I still can't believe you went ahead and did it. I thought you weren't going to let her see him."

Eileen's voice again. If she was trying to stifle her words, she wasn't doing a very good job of it. Or perhaps they were meant to be heard. In any case, the conversation didn't make for the best atmosphere when Eileen finally announced lunch.

They all seemed edgy and nervous as they gathered around
the butcher block table in the big, roomy kitchen. All except
Robbie and Frank Swenson. Wearing a battered Stetson and
dusty boots, Frank arrived at the table a few minutes late after
washing up. Barrel-chested and muscular, he had a thatch of
graying blond hair and bright blue eyes in a rugged, tanned and
weather-beaten face. Robbie chuckled delightedly when he sat
down and proceeded to tickle his ribs, and he even succeeded
in earning a reluctant smile from the other three adults at the
table.

As for Robbie, he could hardly sit still. Jenna could see that
he was a very active little boy who, in spite of his reticence with
her, was possessed of a sweet and loving nature. He ended up
spilling his milk, and the few bites he took of his sandwich were
punctuated with an excited, "Can we go see the baby again
before we leave?" And then those big green eyes would turn
hopefully in the direction of his father.

Ward finally relented. "All right. One more time before we
head for home."

Frank went with them, leaving Jenna and Eileen alone. The
silence that settled over the room was stark and uncomfortable. Jenna at last folded her napkin onto her luncheon plate,
rose and carried her dishes to the cupboard beside the stainless
steel sink. When she walked back to the table, Eileen cleared
her throat and looked up at her.

"Robbie's quite a little boy, isn't he?"

Jenna gathered up the other cutlery and placed it on a plate.
Surely this wasn't an overture of friendship, not after what
she'd said to Ward. Eileen had been polite but no more during
the meal. "Yes," Jenna agreed in a noncommittal tone, then
looked directly at her. "But, then, you're in a much better position to know that, aren't you?"

The woman blanched and her tentative smile faded. At her
stricken look, Jenna felt a stab of guilt. The episode with Ward
last night, and even today's events, had left her defensive and
prickly. "I'm sorry," she said quickly. "I shouldn't have said
that."

"No." Eileen took a deep breath. "No, I probably deserved
it." She paused, indicating that Jenna should take a seat. When
she was sitting across from her, she studied the younger woman
for a moment. "You heard, didn't you?"

Jenna hesitated. "It was hard not to."

"I'm sorry. I honestly didn't mean for that to happen."

Jenna silently eyed Eileen for a moment. What could she say? That it was all right? It didn't erase the feeling of hurt she'd felt. First Ward and then Eileen. But she looked so deeply contrite that it was hard to doubt her sincerity.

"Look, I'll be honest with you." Eileen leaned forward in her chair. "If it had been my decision to make, I'd have decided against letting you see Robbie. But since it wasn't, I think you should know that Ward's been through a lot since Meg died. Sometimes I think the only reason he's gotten through it all is because he's had Robbie to think of and Robbie to hold on to." She shook her head. "I just don't want to see him hurt any more."

Jenna lifted her eyes. "And you think that's what I'll do?"

Eileen made a vague gesture with one hand. "You seem like a very nice person, but, yes, that's exactly what I'm afraid of."

"Please don't be." Jenna spoke softly, imploringly. Her dark hair swirled around her shoulders as she shook her head. "I don't want to hurt anyone. Not Ward and certainly not Robbie. All I wanted was to see him—" how she kept the quaver from her voice she was never quite certain "—and now that I have, I'll be going home."

JENNA REPEATED those words over and over in her mind late that day. Though it was early afternoon when Ward headed back to Plains City, the day's sunshine had given way to a dark covering of threatening purple storm clouds. They seemed to penetrate her soul as they hung over the earth. The meeting had been such a letdown, she acknowledged wearily. Robbie was shy and hesitant with her and refused to let her touch him, though Ward, surprisingly, encouraged him. Jenna was under no illusions about the softening of his manner. She had the feeling it was only because of the presence of his sister. What saddened her the most was that she felt Robbie would have come around—in time.

Yet time was the one thing she didn't have. The one thing she would *never* have with her son.

"Here we are." Ward pulled into the parking lot of the motel. He found an empty space next to her car, then switched off the engine. Turning slightly, his eyes drifted to his slumbering

son, strapped between them in his car seat, then on to Jenna.
"Will you be leaving right away?"

If I don't, will you run me out of town? The words were on
the tip of Jenna's tongue. She had to fight to bite them back.
She stared out the window, at the wind relentlessly pushing the
clouds across the sky.

"Tomorrow, I think. It's a long drive." Her tone was almost curt as she tucked a long strand of hair behind her ear.
"It's too late to leave today."

Ward nodded. "I suppose you have to be back at work
Monday morning."

In spite of herself Jenna felt a skitter of excitement. He *had*
yielded enough to let her see him this once.... She sensed he was
as ill at ease as she was. And why the small talk unless... "No."
She rubbed damp palms against her jeans. "I've taken a short
leave of absence."

Out of the corner of her eye she saw him rub a hand against
his jaw. "You were working for a doctor before, weren't you?"

She nodded. "He closed his practice and moved to Michi-
gan. I've been working in the hospital emergency room for almost two years now." She held her breath and waited, waited
for him to say he was willing to let her stay as long as she
wanted.

She waited in vain. The small spiral of hope inside her died
as quickly as it had risen when the words didn't come. One
hand fumbled for the handle of the door before she turned in
her seat, her throat constricting tightly.

Her eyes moved unerringly to the small boy at her side,
adoring him, memorizing the tiny features to hold them close
to her heart for all eternity. His lashes were dark and bristly,
fanning out thickly on plump, pinkened cheeks. Her eyes soft
with emotion, she ran the tip of her finger around his small
bow-shaped mouth.

She drew a deep, quivering breath. She would never be able
to hold him, or touch him, or do all the things a mother should
do for her child. No longer caring that Ward was watching her
she slid her fingers through the silky dark curls on his smooth
forehead and bent to kiss his cheek. "Goodbye, Robbie," she
whispered softly. "I'll always love you." Her lashes fluttered
shut as she kissed him again, her heart full of silent wishes and
hopes ... and a fleeting sense of despair.

A hot ache filled her throat and it took a moment to control it. When she finally lifted her head to look briefly into Ward's eyes, she had schooled her features into a mask of composure. What she had set out to do had been accomplished. She had wanted to see her son and she had. Now it was over, and she could ask no more of this man.

"Thank you," she said quietly. "Thank you for letting me see him."

Her legs were unsteady as she got out of the car and made her way into the motel. Inside the room she stretched out on the bed, but for the second night in a row, the tears refused to flow.

THE EMOTIONAL EVENTS of the previous day had drained her, but Jenna woke up in the morning feeling as if she'd slept little more than an hour or two. She dragged herself out of bed toward the window. Parting the thin material, she noticed that the leaden gray cloud cover still remained, dampening the morning sun's arrival.

Several large raindrops spattered the car windshield as she stepped outside a short time later and loaded her suitcase into the trunk. After dropping off her room key and settling the bill at the office, she crossed the street to the little café where she'd breakfasted on Friday.

Despite the fact that it was Sunday morning and church services were undoubtedly going on, every booth was filled. The same friendly waitress who had served her a few days ago bustled over when she slipped onto a stool at the front counter.

"So you're still with us." The woman gave a beaming smile. "How about another cinnamon roll today?"

Jenna shook her head. "No, thanks. Just coffee."

She lingered over several cups, trying to shake her listless mood. Finally she glanced at her watch. It was nearly eleven o'clock. If she didn't leave soon, it would be dark by the time she arrived home.

The waitress came back over, wiping the counter with a spotless white cloth. "Looks like we're in for a downpour, doesn't it?" She nodded toward the swirling turbulence of the ever-darkening clouds outside.

Forcing a smile, Jenna agreed. "If I were home, I'd say we were due for a hurricane."

"It's that time of year, all right." The woman eyed her curiously. "Where's home?"

"Galveston." She lifted the brown ceramic cup to her lips.

She didn't see the figure at the end of the counter move until he sat down in the stool next to her. Pretending not to notice his interested absorption, she stirred more sugar into her coffee.

"I couldn't help but overhear you say you're from Galveston." When he paused briefly, she could feel his gaze lightly resting on her profile. "I hope you don't mind my saying so, but I spent a good many years in Houston myself."

The voice was well modulated and pleasant, but the line was a come-on if ever she'd heard one, and a very bad one at that. She didn't mind small talk from the waitress, but she wasn't in the mood for unwanted attention from a male admirer. Her eyes flickered briefly in his direction. "Really," she commented in as polite a tone as she could muster.

From the corner of her eye she saw him nod. "I went to medical school in Houston," he added. Her mind deliberately ignoring him, she turned to deliver a suitably curtailing remark that she hoped would send him back to his seat at the end of the counter. When she did, her hand was seized in a brief warm clasp. "Steve Reynolds here. And you are . . . ?"

His words finally penetrated, and the blistering comment on the end of her tongue never came. "Jenna Bradford," she said faintly. A frown etched itself between slender dark brows as she withdrew her hand. "Medical school? You're a doctor, then?"

Smiling, he nodded. Jenna finally took the time to examine him thoroughly. She guessed he was in his early forties, and with his long legs awkwardly tucked beneath the counter, he appeared thin and gangly. His hair was a sun-streaked shade of light brown, with a few threads of gray, as well, and he had the gentlest pair of brown eyes she had ever seen.

Her apprehension melted away beneath his warm smile. "A general practitioner?"

He nodded, cheerfully adding, "I've even been known to look at a few dogs and cats over the past ten years."

Jenna smiled. "What a coincidence, Dr. Reynolds. I happen to be an R.N."

"You are?" His eyes lighted up with surprise, and it wasn't long before the two were engrossed in conversation, comparing notes on their medical backgrounds. Dr. Reynolds,

eemed, had also served a brief stint as an E.R. physician years
before.

"Can't say as I miss the hectic pace," he finished, several
cups of coffee later. "I didn't mind all the stress back then, but
it's a different story now." He laughed. "Don't think I could
pry my wife and kids away from this town now if I tried." One
shaggy eyebrow lifted as he studied her, a distinctly speculative look in his eyes. "I don't suppose you're ready to give up
all the excitement of a big city hospital just yet. My nurse quit
last week and I haven't found a replacement for her yet. I could
use a good office nurse, if you're interested in a change of
pace."

Jenna shook her head, declining with a smile.

Dr. Reynolds sighed and pushed his cup and saucer away. "I
don't suppose you have any family in town who could entice
you into staying."

"No. As a matter of fact, I was here for the weekend visiting—friends." How quickly she was falling into that lie.
Friends. She and Ward were more like divine enemies. His
hostility suddenly vaulted into her mind and she shifted, feeling rather uncomfortable. Plains City was a fairly small town.
If the friendly atmosphere of this little café was anything to go
by, it was the type of town where everyone knew everyone else.

Apparently Steve Reynolds's thoughts were following the
same vein. "Oh?" He glanced over at her curiously.

Jenna nodded, feeling compelled to elaborate. "Uh,
yes . . . Ward Garrison."

"Ward? He and his wife were two of my very first patients.
I've known him for years." He looked at her intently for a
moment, a flicker of concern in his eyes. "I've been telling him
for months it was about time he pulled his head out of the sand
and started looking ahead again. There's no sense living in the
past."

Her heart began to thump unevenly. Megan. He was talking
about Megan. Eileen, Ward and now Dr. Steve Reynolds . . . they had made no bones about telling her that Megan
was dead, but she was beginning to wonder *how* she died. "Yes,
I—I quite agree."

She held her breath and waited, hoping he would say more.
But instead his features relaxed and a slow smile spread across
his face. "Now that I've seen you," he added with a wink, "I
can understand why a pretty lady like you would be enough to

turn his head. If I weren't already very happily married, I might be giving him a little competition.''

Competition? For a minute Jenna drew a complete blank. Then she realized what he was thinking. She and Ward? Good Lord, the idea was ridiculous. But all of a sudden she remembered the look of those strong, intensely masculine hands curled around the steering wheel and she couldn't prevent the rush of heat that coursed through her body. She started to tell Dr. Reynolds that he was totally mistaken, but he was eyeing her quizzically, a faintly puzzled look on his face.

"Now that I think about it," he said slowly, "you look rather familiar. Are you sure we've never met before?''

"No," she said quickly. "I'm sure we haven't. I've never been to Plains City before.''

"Well." He studied her for a moment. "You sure you won't reconsider the job offer? My receptionist is already complaining I'm running her ragged. And after all—" a twinkle appeared in his eyes "—Plains City is a lot closer to Ward Garrison than Galveston.''

Jenna smiled and opened her mouth to decline once more, but suddenly the impact of those words left her feeling giddy. "Plains City is a lot closer to Ward Garrison than Galveston.'' Not Ward, but Robbie. *Robbie.* Perhaps she could accept his offer, after all, even if it were only for a few days or a few weeks. As long as it took him to find someone permanent. There was really no reason for her to hurry back to Galveston. She'd taken care of all but the final wedding preparations, and there was nothing that needed her immediate attention. This job would give her the perfect excuse to remain here and see Robbie again. Why couldn't she stay?

The answer was like a tidal wave coming down around her, crushing her hopes with the same driving force. Ward. She flinched, remembering his adamant refusal. She had already pressed her luck with him once. Could she risk it again? Her shoulders slumped dejectedly. No. Ward would never let her.

She shook her head and forced a smile. "I'm sorry, but tempting as it sounds, the answer is still no.''

Steve Reynolds looked disappointed, but they chatted for several more minutes before Jenna got up to leave. Her car was still in the motel parking lot, and she pulled up the collar of her Windbreaker against the steady pelt of the rain as she ran back across the street.

"Say, aren't you Jenna Bradford?"

She nearly ran headlong into the motel manager as he poked his head out the door. "Yes!" She had to shout to make herself heard above the driving force of the rain and the howl of the wind.

"Got a phone call for you!" he yelled back, motioning inside.

Puzzled as to who might be calling her here, she lifted a hand to her face to wipe away the rivers of moisture rolling down her cheeks and picked up the phone on the counter. "Hello?"

"Jenna, is that you?"

It was Ward. One hand tightly gripped the receiver while the other curled tightly at her side. He sounded rather strange. "Yes."

"Thank God you're still there! Can you come out here right away?"

She could think of only one reason for him to sound like this. "Ward, is Robbie—"

She got no further. "He's sick, Jenna! He was burning up this morning! Will you come out and look at him?"

"I'll be right out," she promised. Neither the impatience nor the urgency in Ward's voice was lost on her.

Childhood illnesses were many and varied, and Jenna knew she couldn't even hazard a guess as to what was wrong with him until she had seen him. Once there, she took the porch steps two at a time. Before she even had a chance to knock, the door was yanked open.

Ward looked so relieved to see her that if the circumstances had been otherwise, Jenna might have enjoyed a self-indulgent laugh. As it was, there was barely time to breathe before Ward grabbed her elbow and practically dragged her into the living room.

Clad in jeans and a Dallas Cowboys football jersey, Robbie was sitting on a braided rug in front of the fireplace, surrounded by a dozen Matchbox cars and trucks, playing quite contentedly.

She slid a sideways glance at the tall figure next to her. The hard, self-possessed man of yesterday was gone. Now his expression was harried. The blue denim shirt he wore looked as if it had been shoved hurriedly into his belt, but his hair... She tried very hard not to smile as she passed him. The thick, dark strands were standing in a dozen different directions, no doubt from his running his hands through them the way he was doing right now.

Stopping in front of Robbie, Jenna studied him for a moment. His cheeks appeared slightly rosier than they'd been yesterday, but he didn't look all that sick. When Ward finally dropped down in a gold upholstered chair next to her, she looked up. "What's wrong with him?" she asked softly.

Ward ran a hand over the bristly line of his jaw. "He's sick!"

Jenna's lips quirked a little. "Sick . . . how? Other than the fever, of course," she added on seeing his mouth open. "Not eating, or vomiting . . . what?"

"He's covered with spots!" Again he ran his hand through his hair. "I don't know. Maybe it's measles or something."

Spots? Jenna could see no such indication. It was clear Ward was in no condition to offer anything more substantial than what he already had, so she knelt down in front of Robbie, then curled her legs beneath her.

"Hi, Robbie," she said softly. "Remember me? My name's Jenna."

He avoided her eyes and wheeled a tiny truck in a slow circle, but he finally nodded. "Smart boy," she praised, hoping to gain his confidence and trust. "Do you know what a nurse is?"

He hesitated, then shook his head.

"That's okay," she said with a smile. "A nurse is someone who helps people who are sick. Did you know I'm a nurse?" There was a barely imperceptible shake of his dark head. Jenna glanced briefly at Ward, then back at Robbie. "Daddy says you're not feeling well, and I'd like to help you. Can you tell me where you hurt?"

"Don't hurt anywhere." His words were muttered into his shirt front, and Jenna had a hard time understanding him.

Ward leaned forward in the chair. "He said his head hurt this morning when he woke up," he told her in a low voice. "I gave him some Tylenol about an hour ago."

Jenna nodded. "It's probably taken effect by now." Moving slowly so she wouldn't startle him, she lifted the back of her hand to Robbie's cheeks, then lightly felt his bare arms. He was slightly warm to the touch, but certainly not "burning up" as Ward had said.

"Do you have a thermometer around?" she asked Ward. When he rose and went in the direction of the hall, she couldn't resist calling after him, "You might want to look for a comb, too." At the startled look he sent over his shoulder, she smiled and added softly, "For yourself."

His black brows drew together in a frown, and she half suspected he would bite her head off for even making the suggestion. But when he returned, handing her a fever thermometer, she noticed his hair was once again in order.

"Now," she said to Robbie, "you just pretend this is a straw, and don't bite, so we can take your temperature." Surprisingly, he obediently clamped his lips around the thermometer and held it there.

Watching from the chair again, Ward commented, "I wanted to take it earlier, but he'd just had something to drink."

As Jenna suspected, Robbie had only a very low-grade fever. Replacing the thermometer in the case, she looked at him. "Can you show me your spots, Robbie?"

Robbie frowned heavily, then looked at his father. When Ward nodded encouragingly, he lifted his shirt. Jenna leaned closer. There were probably a dozen tiny, reddened blisters on his rounded tummy and back.

"What's wrong with him? Was I right? Is it measles? Is it serious?"

Typical parental overreaction, Jenna thought with a silent smile. Ward seemed to have calmed down for a few minutes, but the anxious alarm was back in his voice.

"No, it's not serious," she said soothingly. She rose and sat on the couch across from him while Robbie went back to his toys. "But you were close. It's not measles. It's chicken pox. His fever is very low and shouldn't last more than a day or two. It's hard to say how many more blisters he'll get, but they'll begin to dry up after a few days. The itching is probably what will give him the most discomfort, but baking soda baths will help."

"Chicken pox!" Ward looked half relieved, half aghast. "Damn! That's contagious, too!"

Jenna nodded. "One other thing. You'll have to keep him away from other kids. If you don't, every child in Plains City will end up with it."

"How long is it contagious?"

"Well . . . at the very least a week." She frowned thoughtfully. "Probably not more than two weeks."

Ward rose and began to pace around the room. To Jenna's mingled surprise and confusion, his expression again grew more harried by the second.

"Ward—" her tone was very gentle "—it's really not that bad. Except for the rash, I doubt you'll even know Robbie has it. There's no need to worry so about him—"

"I understand that." He drew a deep breath and stopped in front of the fireplace.

"Then what's the problem?" Puzzled, Jenna tilted her head to the side. Instead of looking relieved, as she had expected, he still looked as if the world were about to come to an end.

He made a helpless gesture with one hand. "You just said he shouldn't be around any other children."

"Yes, but . . ."

"His baby-sitter takes care of two other kids and has two of her own. She won't be able to watch him. I can't afford to take even one day off right now—let alone a week or two—because the firm is negotiating a deal to oversee a dam project in Oklahoma."

"I see," Jenna said slowly. Her fingers clenched the nubby fabric of the couch. One of the trials of single parenthood was child care, and finding someone to take care of a sick child could make things doubly difficult. She hesitated. "What about Eileen?"

Ward ran a hand through his hair, undoing all the neatness so recently restored. "She and Frank left for a cattle auction in Amarillo today. They won't be back until Wednesday." The response came absently. "Damn!" he muttered. "I've got meetings all day tomorrow and Tuesday and there's no way I can get out of them. What the hell am I going to do with Robbie?" He stared out the window, where the wind furiously lashed the tree branches and rain poured freely down the windowpanes.

Jenna's heart skipped a beat. The solution was obvious. Sitting in the very same room with him, in fact. Her mouth opened, then clamped shut in a tight line. She wasn't going to humble herself by offering to watch Robbie for him and having him fling it back at her. But if he chose to ask her, then that was another matter entirely.

"I see your point," she agreed blandly. "It might be wise if Robbie were at home, particularly the first week or so. Is there someone you could get to stay here with him during the day?"

"Not on such short notice." Jenna held her breath almost painfully. She saw his expression change, his eyes narrow thoughtfully as he turned to her. Jenna looked at the russet brick of the fireplace, the polished oak extending beyond the mantel, the smaller shelves beneath laden with pitchers and leafy green plants. Anything to keep from looking at Ward and conveying the silent plea she knew would be reflected there.

"I don't suppose—"

She could hear the hesitance in his voice before he broke off abruptly. She stilled the shaking of her hands by clamping them around her knees and then forced herself to meet his gaze. "Yes?" How she managed to quell the quaver in her voice, she was never sure.

"When did you say you had to be back in Galveston?"

Jenna could scarcely believe her ears. "There's no hurry. I can stay as long as I want." Or maybe a better choice of words would have been as long as she was needed, she added to herself.

Ward was silent for so long she began to give up hope. "I don't suppose," he said finally, "that you might be able to stay with Robbie." He considered for a moment, his expression guarded. "You'd be doing me a big favor and—it would give you the chance to get to know him a little better."

She wanted to jump for joy. She could almost see the wheels in motion in Ward's head, but she wasn't so naive as to believe Ward actually wanted her there. It was merely a matter of convenience to him.

But it didn't matter. Nothing mattered but the chance to be with Robbie. And if that meant putting up with his father, then so be it.

"I'd be glad to," she said softly. Suddenly she frowned, thinking out loud. "Except I've already checked out of my motel." She sighed. "I guess I'll have to go back and—"

"There's no need. You can stay here, if you like." The words were uttered with grudging reluctance. Nevertheless the offer came as a surprise. When her startled, uncertain gaze met his, he added, "There's plenty of room. And I wouldn't feel right if I put you to the extra expense of a motel just so you could watch Robbie for me."

The opportunity was heaven sent. By some miracle, she'd been granted more precious time with her son. She'd be a fool to say no. She *couldn't* say no.

And she didn't.

"Are you sure it won't be a problem?" she asked softly.

"No." He looked away from the gentle probe of her eyes. "No problem."

Outside it was still dark and dismal as they hurriedly collected her luggage from the trunk, but Jenna felt as if a ray of golden, glorious sunshine had burst inside her.

She only hoped that she and Ward didn't kill each other inside of a week.

CHAPTER SEVEN

JENNA FULLY EXPECTED Sunday to be the worst day for all of them. But as it was, once Ward seemed to have assured himself that chicken pox wasn't as deadly as the plague, he excused himself. "I'll be in the den, catching up on some work, if you need anything," he said, glancing at Robbie, then back at her. "Maybe you two should spend some time alone together so Robbie won't be surprised when he's left with you tomorrow."

The observation surprised her. She had the uncomfortable feeling she was walking on very thin ice when she was around Ward, and somehow she'd expected that he would spend the afternoon keeping an eagle eye trained on her while she acquainted herself with Robbie. As for tomorrow, Robbie would be forced to rely on her no matter what, but at his tender age, she agreed that the fewer surprises in store for him, the better.

She spent the next few hours playing with him, while he dragged out first one and then another of his toys from his room. While he rebelled slightly at having her touch him as she longed to do, more and more she found herself on the receiving end of his shy, sweet smile. By the evening she was certain that she would have very little problem with him the next day.

Ward, on the other hand, was another story. She was uncomfortably aware of him when they were in the same room. When he looked at her, it was hard to believe he was the same man whose eyes softened with warmth and love each time they rested upon his son. While his manner toward her wasn't precisely aloof, she did sense a definite coolness.

The bedroom he'd shown her to was light and airy. The white wicker accents, garden-fresh pastels and mellow pine furniture lent the room the charm of a country inn. Yet even when she was alone that night she couldn't escape his presence. Exactly what role, she pondered quietly as she slipped into the wide double bed, other than that of a live-in baby-sitter, was she to take? He had very effectively coped with dinner, a delicious casserole she couldn't have topped herself. After dinner, he had briefly discussed his son's routine with Jenna, then hustled Robbie into the bathtub. A short time later, the youngster was neatly tucked into his bed and sound asleep.

He was indeed a very capable man. The thought was strangely irksome, but suddenly remembering how tired he'd looked that evening, she realized for the first time that his role as a single parent couldn't be easy.

She finally decided sleepily to play it by ear. She could—if she wanted and if he would let her—make life a little easier for him. And after all, she had no doubt that if he had any objections, he wouldn't hesitate to tell her.

On that note, she rolled over and went to sleep.

SHE NEEDN'T HAVE WORRIED, however. Always an early riser, she awoke just past dawn and showered, then padded downstairs to start breakfast. She pulled out a frying pan, then cracked an egg into a bowl and began to whip it. Sensing she was being watched, she looked over her shoulder to find a pair of very bright, watchful green eyes peeping around a corner of the swinging door.

"Well, hello there! How are you feeling today?"

"Fine," he whispered shyly.

"No headache today?"

When he shook his head, she nodded. "Good." Crooking a finger at him, she grinned and beckoned him closer. "How would you like to help fix breakfast?"

A pajama-clad Robbie eagerly ran across the room, clambering onto the chair she pulled up to the cupboard for him. "Here you go." She neatly broke several more eggs into the bowl and handed him the whisk. "Think you can beat these while I set the table?" His smile revealed two rows of tiny, pearly-white baby teeth. It was coming her way more and more often, she thought with glowing satisfaction.

Between the two of them, they managed to have breakfast on the table a very short time later. Robbie grinned happily as she lifted him into his booster chair, and while she grinned back at him, Ward walked into the room.

Jenna felt as if someone had wrapped a huge rubber band around her chest. She stood stock-still, and for an instant she couldn't breathe. Compared to the ragtag figure she'd glimpsed yesterday, the man before her could have graced the pages of a fashion magazine. His dark hair waved crisply away from his tanned forehead, and the three-piece suit he wore was molded with ease to the lean lines of his body. Yet for all the imposing figure he presented, it was the air of raw virility surrounding him that caught her unawares.

A restless shiver snaked down her spine as she straightened. She was far too conscious of Ward as a man, far more conscious than she should have been...and the thought was strangely unnerving.

"Good morning," she said.

He nodded curtly to her greeting and started across the room. "Would you like some breakfast?"

"Daddy never eats breakfast," Robbie piped up.

Standing at the stove with a plate in her hand, Jenna glanced over in surprise. "You really should, you know," she admonished gently. "Breakfast is just as important for you as it is for Robbie."

There was a sheepish look on his face as he poured himself a cup of coffee. "I usually don't have time," he admitted, sitting down at the table, "what with dressing and feeding Robbie and getting him to the baby-sitter's on time."

"Sometimes Daddy doesn't hear his alarm." This latest offering from Robbie was made with his mouth full of scrambled eggs.

Jenna smiled at the embarrassed look that flitted across Ward's face. Walking over to the table, she set a plate heaped full of bacon, eggs and toast in front of him. "But you don't have to worry about that for the time being, do you?"

Strangely, the gesture seemed a kind of peace offering. She had reached out a hand, and though for a minute she thought he might slap it away, he didn't. Instead he reached for the fork she extended to him, and though he didn't smile when he took it, there was something in his eyes that hadn't been there before—at least when he looked at her.

It made her feel warm all over, both inside and out. She found her lips still curving upward when Ward finally left and she carried his empty plate to the sink.

She turned back to Robbie and loosened the strap on his booster chair. "Since you're such a fountain of information when it comes to Daddy," she said with a wink, "maybe you can tell me what to fix for dinner tonight."

His eyes sparkled up at her. "He likes berry muffins."

"Berry muffins!" Jenna laughed. "You mean blueberry muffins?"

Robbie nodded vigorously and scrambled down from his chair. With her hands on her hips, she grinned down at him. "Sometime this week we'll have blueberry muffins for breakfast, but I think we'd better come up with something else for dinner."

LATER THAT MORNING she made a much belated call to her mother.

"Mom? How are you?"

"Jenna! Thank heaven you finally called! I was beginning to worry about you!" Marie Bradford's voice was tinged with relief, but her next words were cautiously optimistic. "How are things going, Jenna?"

Twirling the telephone cord around her finger, Jenna sat down at the round maple table. Hazy streamers of sunlight poured through the window, and she turned so that the warmth caressed her shoulders and back. The rain-sodden landscape of yesterday was gone, leaving behind a world of glistening brightness. A gentle breeze ruffled the starched yellow tablecloth, and she smoothed it with her fingers before finally responding.

"Things couldn't be better." She smiled against the mouthpiece. It was good to hear her mother's voice. She had wanted to call sooner, but she'd been wrapped up in trying to inspire Robbie's trust so he wouldn't be frightened of being alone with her. When she had finally remembered, it had been rather late. Ward had already gone to bed and she didn't feel right about using the phone while he was asleep, even though she intended to charge the call to her home number in Galveston.

There was a smile in her mother's voice, as well. "I take it you've seen Robbie, then."

"Yes, oh, yes. He's beautiful, Mom. The sweetest little boy you could ever imagine." She laughed, a clear, tinkling sound that was as lighthearted and carefree as she felt inside. Sensing he was being talked about, Robbie looked up from the color-ing book he was absorbed in across the table from her. "Even though he's covered with chicken pox this morning!" she added.

She went on to tell her mother of Ward's dilemma, includ-ing Megan's death, though she purposely eliminated the fact that it hadn't been an easy task to get her foot in the door in the first place.

"Jenna—" Marie's voice was a little dubious "—I'm glad that things have turned out as well as they have, but please re-member that this is only temporary."

Her smile faded. Her mother was warning her not to get too involved. But Jenna knew the score. She always had. At least she wasn't foolish enough to disillusion herself that times such as these with her son could become a habit. And as long as she kept that firmly in mind...

"I know that Mom," she said lightly—perhaps a little too lightly.

"I hope so, Jenna. I hope so." Once again Marie sounded faintly worried, but she changed the subject. "Does Neil mind that you're staying a few more days?"

Neil. She felt an unwelcome pang of guilt. She had hardly given Neil a second thought since she'd arrived. And though Robbie was her first and foremost reason for being there, she'd told herself it would be a good time to hash out her feelings for Neil.

At her silence, Marie sighed. "He doesn't know yet, does he?"

An uneasy twinge shot through her. "No."

"Have you even talked to him since you left?"

Jenna bit her lip. "No, I haven't," she admitted in a small voice.

"Jenna, you know I'm the last person to lecture you. Heaven only knows I'm grateful you've been the kind of daughter who's never needed it," she interspersed gently, "but this is the second time you've come to me before going to Neil. And soon you're going to have to realize that some things are best told to your mother second and your husband *first.*"

It was on the tip of Jenna's tongue to blurt out that Neil wasn't her husband yet. But having already had a similar con-versation only a few short days ago, she knew what her mother was trying to say. She smiled a little wistfully to herself. What wisdom was it her mother possessed that she knew when to prod and not pry?

"I know." Jenna sighed. The truth was, she wasn't looking forward to the conversation. She was afraid Neil was going to be less than thrilled with her decision. "I'll call him today."

She chatted with her mother a few more minutes before hanging up, then dialed Neil's office. When his secretary perfunctorily announced he was out of the office, she left Ward's number and asked that he return the call.

Her smile was back in place, however, when she turned her attention to Robbie. This was her one chance in a lifetime, and now that he was beginning to warm toward her, she wasn't going to let *anything* stand in the way of this special time with her son.

Later she would wonder how a day that started out so right could possibly end up so wrong.

TO BEGIN WITH, Robbie woke up from his nap fretful and feverish, and all of Jenna's attempts to soothe him were met with his further withdrawal. The Tylenol she gave him reduced his fever, but he lay on the living room sofa, quiet and unmoving, with a picture book in his lap that was never opened. Jenna's heart ached for him as much as it did for herself. He didn't feel well; he wanted his father and he was stuck with a stranger, instead.

It was nearly six when she finally managed to coax a tenuous smile from him. During his nap, more blisters had appeared on his arms and chubby, reddened cheeks. As he took one look at himself in the bathroom mirror, his eyes widened to the size of saucers and the makings of a smile appeared.

Taking advantage of the moment, Jenna moved to sit beside him on the couch, telling him about her own bout with chicken pox when she was six years old. "And as my dad constantly used to tell me, covered with spots the way I was, I had a face only a mother could love!" She pinched his cheek lightly. "So what do you think, Robbie? Is this a face only a mother could love?"

At that precise moment Ward walked through the front door. Jenna's smile faded as she watched his expression tighten—as if a curtain were slowly being closed until not even a sliver of light remained between the folds.

She had said the wrong thing...at the wrong time...and perhaps worst of all, in front of the wrong person.

From that point on things went from bad to worse. Without a word, Ward walked straight to Robbie and began talking to him in a voice too low for her to hear. Jenna felt shut out, betrayed. The feeling persisted through dinner, when Robbie insisted that Ward, not Jenna, pour his milk and cut his meat, and continued when Ward finally carried him up to bed. That afternoon before his nap she'd persuaded him to press a damp and hasty kiss on her cheek; tonight all she got was a mumbled and disinterested good-night over his father's shoulder.

The strained silence hung in the air like an ominous rain cloud when Ward finally came down the stairs. The fragile peace that had existed that morning was gone, almost as if it had never been. Jenna tried to interest herself in a paperback she'd brought along for the trip, but she was so tense she actually jumped when the phone rang a few minutes later.

"It's for you," Ward announced curtly from the kitchen.

Startled, Jenna looked up. "For me?"

He nodded and held out the receiver. When she got up and took it, he walked back into the living room. When he was gone, she spoke into the mouthpiece. "Hello?"

"Jenna. Sorry I couldn't get back to you sooner, but I just got back into the office. I've got the most fantastic news, sweetheart!"

Neil. She'd completely forgotten about him calling. Yet even knowing he probably wouldn't be pleased about what she was about to tell him, she knew a faint sense of relief at being allowed this small respite from Ward. The tense silence in the other room was about to strangle her.

She laughed a little shakily. "I've got some news for you, too, Neil."

"You go first, then."

She hesitated. "No, you first. Mine can wait."

Neil didn't waste a second. "Jenna, you're not going to believe this! Remember I told you I've been putting out a few feelers?" There was barely time to grasp what he meant, when he plunged on excitedly. "Bates-McKinnon Oil has offered me a job as a lobbyist. Can you believe it?"

Could she believe it? She was stunned. "Bates-McKinnon Oil?" She frowned. "But Neil..."

"I'll be making double my present salary, Jenna. Double! Do you know what that means for us? I'll have an expense account that's out of this world, and on top of it, they're throwing in a company car, a *luxury* company car. From now on, where we go and what we do, we do in style! And that's not all, babe!" He laughed exultantly. "That house we looked at last week? I called Mark and told him it just wouldn't do. We've got to have something bigger and better, especially with all the entertaining we'll be doing. In fact, that's where I was this afternoon. I found the perfect house, Jenna. It's beautiful—lots of high ceilings and glass. We can make it into a real showplace!"

Jenna's head was whirling. All this talk of showplaces, and entertaining. She liked the house they'd looked at. It was cozy and homey, much like Ward's house with its charming nooks and crannies. She took a deep breath. "Neil, I can't believe you'd actually take a job like that! After all you've done for Citizens for Texas ... it's like going over to the enemy camp!" The oil companies had been a particularly troublesome spot for Citizens for Texas, but when she mentioned the fact to Neil, he brushed it aside.

"I'd be a fool to turn down an opportunity like this, Jenna. Bates-McKinnon is one of the biggest independents in the state. This could open up a whole new career for me."

She flinched at the cold disapproval in his tone. "Aren't you going to at least give it some thought?"

"I *have* thought about it, Jenna. I'm doing what I think is right—for both of us."

"For both of us?" Her voice rose shrilly. "Only last week you were telling me how much you wanted a family! I'm beginning to wonder if a family even fits in with your plans!"

"Of course it does," he said impatiently. "That doesn't change a thing."

"I still think you should think about it, Neil. Have you already given them an answer?"

He was silent for a moment. His voice was rather sullen when he finally spoke. "No, but I'm going to have to very soon, or they'll start looking elsewhere." He paused. "I never expected this from you, Jenna."

"What?" Her mouth tightened. "You never expected me to interfere?"

"Well, yes...now that you put it that way." He sounded defensive.

By now Jenna was furious. "Let me put it to you this way, Neil. Just in case you're interested, Robbie is sick and I can't say for sure when I'll be home." Hastily she slammed the receiver down.

Her anger dwindled as rapidly as it had erupted. Numbly she made her way back into the living room. Neil said things hadn't changed—but they had. She wondered if he was marrying her because he thought she would sit passively in the background, bear his children, do his bidding without a second thought. It was true that Neil didn't have much when he was growing up, but at least he'd always had his parents' love. Now she couldn't shake the feeling that he was trying to make up for his lack of material comforts, that he wanted too much, too soon.

He had said she would be the perfect wife, the perfect mother...and now he wanted a car, a house, a child, a family. Everything proper and in its place, she concluded miserably, everything contributing to the image of a young, successful attorney well on the way to the top of the corporate ladder.

Suddenly Neil seemed a stranger, someone she'd never really gotten to know at all. And on top of it, Neil hadn't even asked about Robbie. Somehow that hurt more than anything.

"Is something wrong?"

She jerked her head up. In her preoccupation with Neil, she'd nearly forgotten about Ward. He was peering over the top of the newspaper at her. "Everything," she wanted to shout. Instead she muttered, "No."

"I take it that was your fiancé who called." Raising a dark eyebrow, he added, "I also take it that all is not well in paradise."

Jenna glanced at him sharply. Something in his tone set her on edge. "What makes you say that?"

"You were shouting." He set aside the newspaper and looked at her. "I wasn't eavesdropping, but I got the impression it was something to do with his job." He paused. "What does he do?"

Jenna lifted a hand to massage her aching temples. "He's an attorney," she answered distractedly.

A dark shadow passed across Ward's face. He'd been waging a battle with himself all day, rallying first to one side and then the other. He hadn't been in the best of moods when he'd awakened that morning, but when he'd arrived downstairs to find Jenna and Robbie waiting breakfast for him, he'd found his tension easing.

Yesterday he had rationalized letting her stay with them to nurse Robbie through his chicken pox because he had hoped it would satisfy her and perhaps avoid trouble in the future. Yet his dark side had invaded once again when he'd arrived at his office. No matter what Jenna said, what if she decided this one time with Robbie wasn't enough? He wanted to believe and yet he couldn't. If he lost Robbie he'd never forgive himself. What if she made these visits a habit? What if she wanted to see him every year? What if—God forbid—she decided a yearly visit, a monthly visit, wasn't enough? What if she decided she wanted him as her own?

It was a gut-wrenching fear. Unfounded, perhaps. Unwarranted. Who could say? But the very fact that she had come in the first place counted for something. He'd told her he couldn't take any chances. And he couldn't.

Face the facts, mister, he told himself harshly. *You're working without a net. If you take a dive, you've got no one to blame but yourself.*

But there was one thing he could do, and that was to be prepared for the worst. Be one step ahead of Jenna. The law was on his side—he hoped. And it was then that he had decided to place a call to Ron Brewster.

Now he found himself driven by the demon that had plagued him since he'd learned Jenna wanted to see Robbie. He might as well have been punched in the stomach when he'd come home earlier. Her smile had faded the minute he'd walked in the door, and seeing those two dark heads spring apart at his entrance, he'd felt like an interloper in his own home...as if he'd ruined their fun. Hell!

"Knows his stuff, does he?" Ward asked, suddenly curious about Jenna's fiancé.

Though her mind was still in a muddle over Neil, there was something in Ward's tone that caught her attention. "He's been fairly successful," she answered guardedly. "He's been at it for about four years."

He stopped directly in front of her. "I see," he said coldly. He paused, then added very deliberately, "Did he tell you you don't have a prayer in the world if you plan to take my son away from me?"

The words hit her like a blast of frigid air. Jenna's mind reeled. She looked at him, stunned to see that the cold mask she was only too familiar with had once again fallen over his features. "How—how do you know that?" she gasped.

Hot anger swept over Ward. He was right—she *was* after Robbie—and this from her own mouth! He pounced like a vulture. "Because I checked with my lawyer this morning, that's why! You signed away every hope of that the day you handed him over! Your name isn't even listed on his birth certificate as his mother anymore! Robbie is mine and mine alone, legally and every other way that counts!"

His words sliced into Jenna's brain like a whip. She recoiled, pressing herself back into the chair. For a full minute she sat stunned, not wanting to believe that he'd actually gone so far as to contact . . . She wanted to run and hide, but she could retreat no farther.

God only knew what lay behind his reasoning, but there was no question in Jenna's mind that he fully believed she was capable of wanting to wrest Robbie away from the only home he had ever known without any qualms whatsoever.

The thought sickened her. She felt cold—cold inside and out—and empty. God, how empty! Ward thought she was insensitive, selfish. How could he, after what she had done for him—for both of them? Megan. If Megan hadn't died this wouldn't be happening! Jenna hugged herself as if for warmth, her thoughts a mad jumble inside her brain.

"You're wrong," she announced suddenly. The sound broke the tense, waiting silence. "Wrong about everything. The other night you accused me of not caring about Robbie, and now—now you're accusing me of trying to take him away." She looked at Ward then, all her anger and resentment bubbling to the surface like water gushing from a well. It seemed that she was damned in his eyes, no matter what she did—or didn't—do. "Make up your mind," she told him, her voice shaking with emotion, "because it can't be both. If you'd think for a minute, you'd realize I would never try to take him away unless I *didn't* care about him—and I do. I would never uproot him from his home and his family because *I* know what it's like to wake up and have everything and everyone you love just disappear before your very eyes!" Her jaw jutted out stubbornly as she sent him a fulminating glance. "I don't give a damn about what your lawyer says. Robbie *is* a part of me as much as he's a part of you. And that's something no legal document can ever take away from me. And just for the record, Neil is an environmental attorney who probably doesn't know much more than I do about child custody!"

Ward blinked a little and ceased his restless pacing. He stared at her before she ran across the room and out the front door. The last words were fairly flung at him. In fact, the entire speech was. Somehow he hadn't expected such an outburst. Yet he knew he was making her miserable. Was it because she made him think of Meg? Her memory had been with him all day long, all day yesterday, just under the surface. After all the long, lonely months, just when the ache inside had finally begun to ebb, Jenna had reappeared in his life, and it was back again, as powerful and as painful as ever. *Admit it, Ward,* he told himself grimly, *you wanted to lash out at her and hurt her the way you've been hurting.*

And apparently he'd succeeded.

In the moment before those defiant green eyes had clashed with his, there was no denying what she was feeling...the hurt and the vulnerability. He could recognize those feelings easily, being so familiar with them himself. She reminded him of a hunted animal, totally defenseless and at his mercy.

Taking a deep breath, he opened the front door and stepped onto the porch. The sun had set in an amber blaze of glory, with lingering wisps of pink-tinged clouds hovering just above the treetops. The autumn air was faintly cool as a gentle evening breeze whispered through the trees. From the corner of his eye, Ward could see Jenna sitting motionless on the wide wooden swing, her face drawn as she gazed at her hands, clasped tightly in her lap.

He swallowed. Damn! What the hell could he say? He felt guilty as hell and yet . . . Taking a step forward, he grasped the railing and stared straight ahead.

"I'm sorry."

Jenna's head shot up. His words were bitten off. That was supposed to be an apology? She stared at him, mouth tight. "Are you?" She couldn't contain the bitter edge that crept into her voice. "I wonder."

"Yes. Yes, damn it—I am!" Straightening his shoulders, he turned to face her. "I had no right to assume that he might have offered any kind of legal advice."

"Even if Neil specialized in family law, it's an issue that would never have come up—" her chin lifted proudly "—because I wouldn't have brought it up!"

She almost dared him to refute the statement. His eyes met hers, then slid away so quickly that she was left believing he was as angry with himself as he'd been with her earlier.

And much as she wanted to stay angry with him, she couldn't. Because suddenly she could define what she hadn't been able to until now, that elusive something she'd glimpsed in his eyes the night he'd come to her motel room and at the ranch when he'd held Robbie in his arms.

It was fear. The fear that she might somehow snatch his child from him. Compassion surged through her, but there was no denying the feeling that she'd been wronged.

The words came out almost unconsciously. "But if you had it to do over again, you would make the same choice, wouldn't you?" she asked in a very low voice. "You'd have checked with your lawyer to make certain that I . . . that Robbie could never be taken away from you." She glanced up at him, and she knew, even before she finished, that she was right.

Ward looked away from her steady gaze. When he finally gathered the courage to look back at her, he saw that her eyes were cloudy with pain. She looked so wounded that for an instant she reminded him of Robbie when he came running into the house after a bump or scrape. Only she wasn't crying. And she wasn't looking to him for comfort, as Robbie always did.

But that didn't stop him from reacting in much the same way. It had grown too dark for him to see the uncertainty that plagued her, yet he could sense it, knowing they had been at odds ever since her arrival. And it was his fault. He had to fight a crazy urge to take her in his arms, to stroke that silky, dark hair away from her forehead and soothe away her pain. The only thing that kept his hands at his sides was the certain knowledge that the only thing she wanted from him was his son.

He eased himself down into the swing, next to her, but not touching her. "Would you like to tell me why you were so upset about the phone call?"

Jenna hesitated. He caught the look and frowned. "You don't have to. I just thought it might help to talk about it."

"Maybe . . . maybe it would," she said slowly, and haltingly she began to tell him about Neil's job offer and her doubts about the move. Ward didn't offer any judgments, any solutions, and she expected none. It was, after all, something only she and Neil could work out. But oddly enough, it did feel better to talk about it.

"You said you knew how it felt," Ward said suddenly, "to have someone you loved taken away from you." He hesitated, then asked softly, "Your parents?"

Jenna nodded.

"Weren't you adopted?" He peered at her in the darkness, not sure where the memory had come from.

"Yes," she answered quietly. Then, in a low voice she began to tell him about the accident that had claimed both mother and father. Ward listened quietly, intently, while she spoke. She was lucky, she said, to have found two people to replace her natural parents, two people she loved with all her heart and who loved her the same way.

Lucky? he reflected with a touch of cynicism. She had been a child, innocent and alone, lost in a world without love . . . for over a year. She, too, had known grief and pain, loneliness and despair.

But what about him? Would he ever love again? He was unaware of the tightening of his hand around hers.

Jenna glanced down in surprise. Her fingers were twined tightly in his, resting against her thigh. The fingers of his other hand brushed gently across the inside of her wrist in a gentle caress. She didn't remember him reaching out to her . . . but he had. His skin was warm, his grip sure and strong. It was strange, she mused. Two days ago she wouldn't have thought it possible. She and Ward didn't trust each other—she didn't even think they liked each other. Yet the eyes looking down at her were warmed by compassion, by understanding.

She spoke softly. "You're thinking about Meg, aren't you?"

A flicker of pain flashed in his eyes. Slowly, almost reluctantly, he nodded.

His fingers tightened, then relaxed, but he didn't pull away. Reassured, Jenna looked at him. Moonlight spilled down from the sky, etching the strong, proud features in silver. "Ward, what happened to her? How . . . how did she—?"

She never got the chance to finish. Ward lurched to his feet so suddenly she felt her nails rip into his flesh as he pulled his hand away. He took a single step away from her, leaving her staring at his broad back.

"I think it's time you went inside," he said flatly. "It's getting cool out here."

Jenna swallowed and got up slowly. She moved so that she could see the rigid set of his jaw. He had removed his jacket after dinner and rolled up his shirt sleeves. His shoulders were stiff with tension as he grasped the railing, the muscles of his forearms knotted.

"Ward—" She reached out a tentative hand and moistened her lips. "Please, I'd like to kn—"

"Just leave it, Jenna. Please, just leave it."

There was such a world of agony in his low whisper that Jenna felt her heart contract. Deliberately she laid her hand on his bare arm. She felt his muscles tighten at her touch and her heart sped up fiercely in response, but she kept her hand there until she felt him relax.

She turned slightly so that she could see his face. With the moonlight and the small pool of light slanting through the window from the living room, it was nearly as bright as day. Each had caused the other too much pain and suffering already, she thought sadly. Some was unwitting, and some was not. But it couldn't go on. For either of them. "I think," she said softly, "you and I could both use a friend...a truce. Shall we call off the dogs—on both sides?"

His eyes searched hers for a long moment. What he found there must have satisfied him. A tiny smile hovered at his mouth as he asked gravely, "A new beginning?"

Her gaze never wavered from his. "Yes. A new beginning."

Something flickered in his eyes. "Jenna..." He paused. "I really am sor—"

She shook her head swiftly. "No more apologies, either. Agreed?"

Ward smiled then, and she felt as if something inside him, something that had lain dormant for a long, long time, had suddenly come alive. His lips quirked faintly. "Do I have a choice?"

A warm feeling flowed through her. "No." She tossed her hair back over her shoulder and laughed lightly. "As my dad always tells me, I am one very stubborn lady."

Ward smiled. His eyes roved over her face in the moonlight, touching on the faint mauve shadows beneath her eyes. "This very stubborn lady looks tired. Maybe it's time you turned in."

She started to shake her head in denial, then realized he was probably right. It had been a long day, and from the look of Ward, not an easy one for him, either. Even in the silvered light she could see the deepening grooves of fatigue etched around his mouth. Suddenly she ached with the need to lift her hand to his face, to smooth away his tiredness with the gentle touch of her fingers.

The urge left her feeling a little shy and awkward. Taking a deep breath, she turned away. "You're right. It's late." She took several steps toward the door, then paused and glanced back at him.

His eyes bored into hers for a moment. "Good night, Jenna," he said very softly. Then, before Jenna was even aware of it, he crossed to where she stood. He kissed her gently on the cheek and then brushed by her to go inside the house.

When he was gone, she found herself smiling. Her hand stole up to cradle the cheek he had kissed. For an instant, she was reminded of her fierce avowal never to wash her hands again after the first time she and Darren Phillips had ever held hands.

She was still smiling when she went to bed that night.

CHAPTER EIGHT

IF ONLY THE PROBLEM with Neil were as easy to solve as the antagonism with Ward, Jenna mused pensively four days later. He had called again on Wednesday night, and much the same angry scenario had been repeated. Jenna simply couldn't understand his dogged determination to take the job with Bates-McKinnon Oil, and Neil was just as determined that it was the right career move for him. Only this time it wasn't Jenna who hung up on Neil—it was the other way around.

Did most brides-to-be experience cold feet? She breathed an uneasy sigh and opened the refrigerator to pull out several chops. This impasse was more than cold feet, and it was time she admitted it. More and more she was beginning to wonder if marrying Neil was right for her. Every time she thought about it, she felt a tiny frisson of doubt and as a result she found herself burying the subject in a far corner of her mind. But the fact remained: she was going to have to make up her mind when she returned to Galveston.

That, too, was something she wasn't yet ready to face. After six days with Robbie, he was just really beginning to trust her, to show signs of genuine affection for her. His case of chicken pox was mild; the fever and headache had long since disappeared. She could tell that he was tiring of being cooped up inside, and tried to come up with as many different activities as she could for him. Unfortunately he came up with a few of his own—including trying to paint the pale blue of his bedroom walls with white shoe polish. Ward returned on more than one day to find her practically dropping on her feet.

But no matter how tired she was at the end of the day, how naughty or mischievous Robbie was, she loved every minute spent with him.

"Will you draw me a picture, Jenna?"

Waving a piece of paper at her, Robbie skipped over to the kitchen table clutching a handful of fat crayons. There was still time before lunch, so Jenna pulled up a chair and sat down.

"Sure," she said cheerfully, then cocked an eyebrow at him. "I'm not much of an artist, though, so don't expect too much." She picked up a crayon. "What do you want me to draw?"

"Soupman!" he replied promptly.

Jenna laughed. "Soupman! What—or who on earth is Soupman!"

His small brow pleated into a frown. "Don't you know who Soupman is? Daddy does!" he informed her staunchly.

"Well, Daddy will just have to enlighten me," Jenna said with a chuckle. "I can't draw Soupman if I don't know what he looks like, so what else would you like?"

Robbie's eyes lighted up and he began to bounce in his chair. "Matman! Or Wonder Worm!"

Jenna blinked. Soupman. Matman. Wonder Worm! His childish pattern of speech was adorable, and she'd had no trouble figuring out that the hem was coming out of his jeans the day he'd come to her complaining they were "broke," but this time she was at a complete loss.

She choked back a laugh. "Robbie, where have you seen these people?"

"They're not people. They're heroes—superheroes! And I see 'em on TV all the time!"

Jenna was finally able to grasp that he was talking about cartoon characters, and convinced him to let her draw something else. He settled for a man, a woman and a child. Jenna glanced doubtfully at the drawing—she wasn't exaggerating about her artistic ability—the characters were little more than stick people—but Robbie was thrilled.

"That's you and me and Daddy!" he exclaimed delightedly. "Can I draw one, too?" he asked eagerly.

"Of course." She ruffled his silky curls and helped him with his drawing. She smiled a little crookedly when Robbie insisted on clamping them both to the refrigerator with tiny banana-shaped magnets. To her nondiscriminating eye, it was hard for her to tell which was his and which was hers.

While Robbie napped that afternoon, Jenna, on a whim, turned on the television. A silly little grin curved her lips as she tuned in a cartoon channel, but at the end of an hour and a half she was completely baffled. There was no sign of Soupman,

Matman or Wonder Worm. She frowned a little. Robbie had been so adamant....

Robbie had just awakened from his nap, when a knock sounded on the back door late that afternoon. Jenna heard a cheery, "Anybody home in there?"

Robbie ran across the floor to open the door. "Aunt Eileen!" he cried. Eileen Swenson bent to hug the small body, then smoothed the unruly curls from his forehead. "Good heavens!" She laughed, eyeing his blistered cheeks. "What happened to you?"

"Pox!" Robbie declared. He nearly poked his eye out in an attempt to point to his roughened cheeks.

Eileen laughed again and whirled him around. "Where's Daddy? I didn't see the Blazer outside."

Standing behind the doorway, Jenna knew Eileen wasn't aware of her presence. She stepped forward, saying lightly, "Hello, again. Ward's working late tonight. He won't be home until later this evening." She paused. "Did you just get back from your trip?"

Eileen nodded and set Robbie on his feet. Her face still registered stark surprise and Jenna could almost see the questions tumbling around in her head. "How did you know I was in Amarillo?" she finally asked, breaking the taut little silence.

A ghost of a smile curved Jenna's lips and she glanced at Robbie. Eileen looked just as uncomfortably uncertain as she, but they both knew what the real question was. "Why don't you sit down?" Jenna waved a hand toward the table.

Eileen was quiet while Jenna explained that her reason for being there was merely an issue of expedience—for Robbie's sake and Robbie's sake alone.

At length, Eileen's eyes lifted to Jenna's. "So you're staying here, then?"

Jenna nodded, sensing something in Eileen's tone. "You probably think it's not wise under the circumstances," she stated calmly.

The older woman frowned. "I'm surprised that Ward asked you," she finally admitted. "But I'm a mother myself . . . and now that I've had the chance to think about it, I can understand your need to see Robbie."

"I meant what I said last week," Jenna said quickly. "I don't want to hurt anyone—"

"I know that." Eileen reached out a hand to lightly squeeze Jenna's. "I guess we're not so different after all." She leaned back and shrugged. "And it's not as if there isn't room. This is a big house."

Jenna was touched at the gesture, and smiled gratefully, but suddenly her breath caught in her throat. It had never occurred to her until now how it might look to someone else. "I'm sleeping in the room next to Robbie's," she began quickly.

To her surprise, Eileen laughed. "Good Lord, don't look so guilty. Ward still hasn't gotten over Meg—" she frowned thoughtfully "—although maybe that's exactly what he needs...."

Her voice trailed off so that Jenna could barely hear. But the gist of her words wasn't lost on Jenna; now that she thought about it, she remembered Steve Reynolds's having said something to the same effect. And recalling Ward's pained reaction to the mention of Meg's name, it was very obvious that there was still a very deep attachment. She sighed. It was really rather sad....

But while Ward might be oblivious to any and all women including her, Jenna was certainly not as unaware of him as she would have liked to be. Her palms grew damp as she remembered the sandpaper roughness of his cheek against hers, and she thought of how he had looked that very morning. As usual, he was still sleeping when she had awoken. The bedroom door was ajar and she'd caught a glimpse of him in bed as she'd tiptoed past his room. She'd tried to look away, and found herself staring, instead. The covers were pushed down to his waist—thank heaven he'd been no more exposed than that—revealing strong shoulder muscles that flexed when he turned on his side. His chest rose and fell evenly in sleep, and was literally covered with dark, wiry-looking curls. She'd been rather dismayed by her reaction, and had been trying to vanquish the memory all day long. In the course of her job as a nurse she'd seen literally hundreds of men—both young and old—and many of them more good-looking than Ward. Yet she had never been quite so conscious of one man's body. But she'd never created a child with any other man, either, a niggling voice reminded her.

The sound of Eileen's voice dragged her mind away from that last disquieting thought. "How are all of you getting along?" she was asking.

"So far so good," Jenna quipped lightly, then crossed her fingers. There had been a few times she'd caught Ward looking at her with a wholly unfathomable expression in his eyes, and her heart would speed up for a second, but when she looked again, it was gone. Certainly their manner toward each other couldn't be called easy and carefree, but with each day that passed they seemed to grow more comfortable with each other. And at least they hadn't crossed swords again.

She glanced down at Robbie, playing on the floor between the two women with a box of bristle blocks. Eileen's eyes lighted up suddenly as she followed Jenna's gaze. "You know," she said, looking down at Robbie with a sparkle in her eyes, "I think this is a moment that should go down in history."

Robbie jumped up immediately. "Are you gonna take a picture at me, Aunt Eileen?"

"I certainly am going to take a picture 'at you,'" she said with a chuckle, echoing Robbie's words. She reached down from the bag she'd carried in and pulled out a .35 millimeter camera. While Robbie preened and hammed it up, Eileen must have taken a dozen pictures, including one when Robbie threw his arms around Jenna's neck and smacked her soundly on the cheek. Jenna looked at her in amazement when the camera clicked and whirred for the last time. "I thought you were going to take *a* picture!" She laughed a little. "He probably won't thank you for this when he's older—not with his face all covered in chicken pox!"

Eileen laughed. "All the more reason to take advantage. Believe me, this is par for the course. And I love taking pictures of Robbie. Tim and Katie always groan when they see the camera come out. 'Here we go again,' they always say. 'Our life in living color!'" She laughed once more and looked at her. "Haven't you seen the albums yet? I've been at it since I was fifteen years old, and Meg kept every picture I ever took of Robbie and Ward. There must be hundreds."

"No, I haven't." She paused. "Tim and Katie are your children?"

Eileen nodded. "Tim's twenty and Katie's eighteen. They're both students at San Angelo State," she said proudly. "Tim is studying drafting and Katie's enrolled in a preveterinary program. This is her first year."

Jenna noticed the wistful look in her eyes. "And Mom misses them both already," she teased gently.

"Well..." The other woman grinned rather sheepishly. "It's been less than a month since the semester started, but with Katie gone, too, breakfast for two after twenty years of eating with the kids can get a little lonely. Already I have the feeling I'm going to have a lot of time on my hands this year. That's why I don't mind having Robbie." Hearing his name, Robbie grinned up at his aunt. She winked back at him. "He keeps me out of trouble."

"Doesn't the ranch keep you busy?" Jenna asked curiously. "I mean, you were so good with the mare the other day."

"I don't mind helping out with the horses, but when it comes to cattle—" she rolled her eyes heavenward "—that's Frank's department, and that's the way I intend to keep it."

Jenna smiled. "Sounds to me like you need a job, then."

By the time Eileen left a short while later, Jenna was surprised but pleased at the outcome of the encounter, especially considering the shaky foundation that had resulted after their first meeting. She liked Eileen's warmth, openness and frankness, and she was glad that Eileen was a part of Robbie's life. Much as the thought pained her, Eileen was, after all, the closest thing to a mother the little boy had.

When Eileen was gone, Robbie pulled a chair up to the counter and clambered up beside her. She had learned very quickly that no activity was complete without his "help," and he seemed to derive a great deal of satisfaction in the small tasks he was able to perform. Jenna smiled at him fondly when he asked if he could help with dinner. She handed him the silverware and watched, amused, as he carefully arranged it beside the two plates.

The afternoon wore into evening, and soon the clock on the mantel chimed eight-thirty. She had been reading aloud to Robbie from a book of bedtime stories, and when she felt his small body sagging limply against her, she glanced down at him. He drowsily smiled up at her, but his long-lashed eyes drooped heavily.

She leaned down to brush his hair off his forehead. "I think it's time you were in bed, young man." Upstairs she undressed him and put him in a pair of lightweight pajamas. Jenna smiled, thinking she could have dressed him in a hair shirt and he wouldn't have minded. But tired as Robbie was, Jenna had no more than slipped his small body between the sheets than his huge green eyes opened wide. "Daddy," he whispered plaintively. "I want my Daddy."

She lifted a hand to stroke his cheek. "Sweetheart, Daddy had to work late tonight. He still isn't home yet." His lower lip began to tremble, and she sighed. "How about if I have Daddy come in later and kiss you good-night—as soon as he gets home. Will that be okay?"

Robbie nodded, and apparently satisfied, he turned on his side, tucked a fist under his cheek and closed his eyes. Jenna stayed with him for a few more minutes, fingering his soft dark curls, brushing his dimpled arm, savoring the petal-soft feel of his skin and tucking the sensation away in a corner of her mind for the time when she would be with him no more.

Her heart was heavy when she finally drew the blanket under his chin and crept softly from the room. She had been with him for six days now. Six days. How many more would she have with him? Only a handful. Soon. Soon she would have to leave. She had carried him beneath her heart for nine months, nurtured him and given him life—she had secretly carried him *in* her heart all this time—and these few, precious days with him would have to last her a lifetime.

She had avoided the room next to hers up until now, but found her footsteps directed there beyond her will. She cautiously stepped inside, noting the pale yellow wallpaper and the serene pastoral scenes framed on the wall. Studiously avoiding the huge four-poster in the middle of the room, she walked quietly to the pine desk on the opposite wall. She scanned the shelves above the desktop. Then with a sigh she turned, and her eyes rested on the framed photograph staring back at her from the dresser.

Tentatively she reached out and picked it up. "Would you have approved of my being here, Meg?" she whispered. "Would you have minded my being a mother to Robbie?"

The laughing blue eyes that looked back at her were full of warmth and life, yet Jenna had never felt so cold inside.

She found what she was looking for downstairs in Ward's den. The picture albums Eileen had spoken of. She hesitated before reaching for one of the heavy leather-bound books, feeling as if she had just broken into a place that was forever barred from her.

Switching on a lamp, she sat down on the oval braided rug in front of the fireplace and tucked her legs beneath her. Eileen hadn't been exaggerating, she thought dumbly. There were hundreds of pictures. Literally. There was Ward as a fuzzy-cheeked boy, openly adoring an equally loving Megan, who wore a bouffant hairstyle that had gone out when bell-bottomed pants had come in. Jenna would have laughed if it hadn't been so damnably sad. Just yesterday she had noticed a few fine threads of gray in Ward's thick dark hair. Even when he was laughing and playing with Robbie, she occasionally glimpsed in his eyes a fleeting expression of sadness that made her ache inside.

Her throat tightened as she turned a page. There was Meg, flashing an engagement ring; later, her face was wreathed in a glowing smile beneath a lacy veil as she walked down the aisle in a flowing ivory wedding dress.... The years passed as the pages turned. Meg was still smiling, but those delicate Dresden features looked haunted.

Then Jenna stared. Her fingers traced the features of a tiny infant cradled lovingly in Megan's arms. Ward stood beside her, one arm curved protectively around his wife and newborn son, beaming down into her radiant face. And there was so much more: a bare-bottomed Robbie sprawled on a blanket in front of the fireplace; Robbie crawling across the room; then later, Robbie spreading his arms wide for balance as he tentatively raised a foot. Jenna made a faint sound as she imagined those first tottering steps forward.

A rush of joy swept through her, so intense she was totally unprepared for the shattering pain that followed. Yet it wasn't the first time she'd felt that way. It had happened before...the moment she had felt her baby's first faint quickening inside her womb and later, his more vigorous movements at his birth when she had first glimpsed his soft down-covered head and wrinkled red body.

And as before, she knew she couldn't afford to love Robbie now...any more than she could then.

She hugged the book to her breasts and brought her knees to her chest. The haloed lamplight began to swim before her eyes as she blinked rapidly, her heart so full of emotion she thought she would burst.

That was how Ward found her. At first he thought she was asleep. She looked cold, huddled on the rug, her forehead resting on her upraised knees and her arms wrapped around her legs.

"Jenna?" He set aside his briefcase. Loosening his tie, he threw it aside and walked across the polished floor. Bending over her, he gently shook her shoulder. "Wake up, Jenna."

Slowly she raised her head and stared up at him. Ward went absolutely still. The torment in her eyes was almost unbearable, and touched a corresponding chord deep in his soul. He looked down and saw that she was clutching a picture album. Easing it from her white-knuckled grip, he held it before him and focused on the photograph of Meg bending over Robbie, the child's face smeared with ice cream and frosting from a huge layer cake. It had been taken on Robbie's first birthday. Ward's chest tightened. It hadn't been long after that ...

Slowly he closed the album and replaced it on the shelf, wishing that both he and Jenna could close the door to the past as easily. Once he had told himself that time would heal all wounds, that time would ease the ache in his heart. But at that moment, he wondered if there would ever be peace for either of them.

"Jenna." His hand curled lightly around her shoulder. "You shouldn't be here. You should be in bed."

The gentleness both in his voice and in the touch of his hand was almost her undoing. She had to struggle to find her voice past the tightness in her throat. "Why...why are you always trying to pack me off to bed like—" she attempted a feeble, quivering smile "—just like a child?" She took a deep breath and tried to gather some control.

Ward smiled a little at her valiant attempt at normalcy. Then, driven by some emotion he didn't fully understand, he pulled her up to her feet and reached out to trace the soft curve of her cheek. "What's wrong?" he asked softly.

Jenna's insides were so knotted she could scarcely speak. She shook her head helplessly, unable to look at him. "I...are you angry?" was all she could say. The quiver in her voice was unmistakable.

Ward brushed a tendril of hair from her cheek. "Because you were looking through the albums?"

She nodded. "Eileen was here today and—she told me about them."

He hesitated. A week ago he would have been angry. A week ago he might have felt she was intruding, interfering where she had no business. Hell, who was he trying to fool? He *would* have. But this week had softened the blunt edges of his volatile

emotions around Jenna. Seeing how warm and patient she was
with Robbie—she could barely tear her eyes away from him
when he was in the same room. Even if Ward had been angry,
he couldn't have stayed that way after coming in and seeing
Jenna so upset.

"No," he said finally.

"I didn't mean to pry."

His hands squeezed hers. "I know."

Spurred on by the warmth of his fingers, lightly grasping
hers, she met his gaze shyly. "I—I feel as if I've missed so
much," she said in a low voice. "I wanted for once not to be on
the outside looking in...."

"And?" His voice was cautious. His shoulders tensed.
Somehow he knew what was coming.

"And now I feel that way more than ever." There was such
a wealth of sadness in her voice that Ward closed his eyes
against it. When he opened them, she was gazing at him
searchingly. He started to shake his head and speak, but she
stopped him. "Please understand—" she lifted her shoulders
helplessly "—I don't regret anything, even coming here. But
there's so much I don't know." She paused. "Will you tell me,
Ward? Will you tell me about Robbie?"

Ward let out a deep sigh, moved as much by the quiet plea in
her voice as the look of blind trust in her expression. His voice
rough with emotion, he asked, "What is it you want to know?"

Jenna made a vague gesture with one hand. For a moment
she was afraid he might close her out as he had the time she'd
asked about Meg's death. "Anything. Everything." The eyes
she lifted to his were suddenly eager and shining once more, so
much like Robbie's that he caught his breath. "Was he a good
baby?"

Ward waited only a second before pulling her toward the
small love seat across from his desk. It took a minute for him
to gather his thoughts. "Did you know," he began with a
thread of laughter in his voice, "that after all the horror stories
I'd heard about a newborn's 2:00 A.M. feeding, that Robbie
slept the whole night through his first night home?"

Jenna listened quietly, attentively, thriving on every word.
She learned that Meg had stayed up with him at night nursing
a croupy cough on several occasions, and that later, at the age
of seven months, Robbie had crawled into the bottom shelf of
the pantry and removed every single label from the canned

goods stored there. Ward laughed a little as he recalled how many surprises they'd had at dinner after that.

By the time he finished, they had moved closer to each other, though neither one really seemed aware of it. A long arm curled lightly around her shoulders. It seemed the most natural thing in the world to nestle trustingly into the hollow below his arm, and that was exactly what Jenna did before glancing pensively up at him.

"It hasn't been easy for you, has it? Trying to raise Robbie on your own, without—" she almost stumbled over the word "—without a mother." She held her breath uncertainly, almost afraid he would lash out at her again. She had noticed how his voice became edged with pain at the merest mention of Meg.

He looked down at her with a frown. "We've managed." Then, surprisingly, one side of his mouth turned up in a wry smile. "Robbie and I ate a lot of burned oatmeal, peanut butter sandwiches and frozen casseroles from Eileen before I discovered what a cookbook was for."

"Ward..." Suddenly aware of just how close they were, she drew back slightly. "Now that Eileen is back, would you prefer that I...I mean, do you want me to—"

"Leave?"

The utter calm in his voice made her faintly uneasy. She nodded slowly.

"Is that what you want?" Ward asked quietly.

Jenna closed her eyes and half turned away from him. "Do you really have to ask?" she whispered.

The room was so silent Jenna could hear her heart pounding in her ears. She waited almost painfully for his reply. It was a long time in coming.

"If you left, I'd have to go back to eating burned oatmeal for breakfast. You've got me spoiled in less than a week, Jenna." His light tone disguised the sudden churning of his stomach. He was playing with fire, but as he caught a glimpse of the naked vulnerability in her eyes, he knew there wasn't a damn thing he could do about it.

Jenna gave a silent prayer of thanks that she was sitting, because she knew her knees would have gone weak with relief otherwise. The smile she offered was tremulous. Impulsively she laid a hand on his arm. "You've done a wonderful job with Robbie," she said shyly. Long dark lashes feathered down over her eyes and she hesitated. Her eyes darkened to the color of jade.

Ward caught the painfully acute look and frowned. "What? What is it?"

Her voice was a halting whisper. "I know that when I leave here, I won't be a part of Robbie's life anymore. But knowing that he'll be loved and taken care of here with you will make up for a lot." Her voice broke treacherously. "But Meg only had a year with him, and it seems so unfair..."

Yes, it was unfair. And it was also unfair that for a fraction of a second, as Ward stared at the tears that welled in her eyes and slid slowly down her cheeks, he wondered if it was a ploy. A ploy to gain his sympathy.

He dismissed the idea almost as soon as it entered his head. And suddenly he realized something else, realized it with a shattering certainty that nearly snapped the fragile network of emotions he had spent the past eighteen months learning to control.

Slowly he leaned forward and extended a fingertip to trace the watery trail of a glistening tear down her cheek. "For Meg?" he asked softly.

Her dark hair fell in a silken curtain around her face as she nodded, her head bent. She felt too full of emotion to speak. It was almost a shock to acknowledge that she was crying. Now, after all these years.... She had wanted to...wanted to so badly the day that Robbie was taken from her and she knew she would never again see her son. But she hadn't. She hadn't because she was afraid that once the tears began to flow, they would never stop.

But now the well inside her had finally been released. Jenna was helpless as the tears rolled freely down her cheeks—for Meg, for herself, for the son she would never see grow straight and tall.

With a muttered groan, Ward pulled her into his arms. His eyes were dark with remorse as he tucked her head beneath his chin, gazing off into the shadowed corners of the room. How blind he had been. How wrong he'd been to utterly mistrust this woman. But Meg had known. Meg had seen what he hadn't been able to. Until now, he hadn't realized just how caring a person Jenna was—how much giving there was inside her.

He was touched beyond words; the sobs she choked back tore into his heart like a knife, bringing back poignant memories of the many nights he had lain alone in his bed after Meg had died, the empty ache inside as deep and dark as a bottomless pool. For long moments the storm of emotion overtook them both.

It wasn't until Ward felt the moisture in his own eyes that he eased back from her. "Jenna." His voice was a hoarse whisper. "For God's sake, this isn't doing either of us any good." He gave a forced laugh, trying to lighten the intense situation. "If you don't stop crying, you'll drown us both."

Jenna blinked back a fresh supply of tears and wiped the moisture from her cheeks with the back of her hand. "This is crazy, isn't it?" she said shakily. "I can't remember the last time I shed a single tear." She looked up at him through misty eyes. "I'm sorry—"

Two fingers pressed gently against her mouth stifled the words. "No apologies, remember?" There was a faint twinkle in the dark brown eyes that moved over her tear-stained face. Then with a sigh, Ward slowly folded her still trembling body in his arms once more.

Incredibly tender fingers smoothed damp tendrils of hair away from her flushed cheeks, then slid through the long shimmering tresses to knead the tense muscles of her shoulders. Feeling exhausted, drained, Jenna wrapped her arms around his waist and sagged against his strength. Ward's touch was warm and caressing through the thin fabric of her blouse, a soothing balm to heal the raw edges of her emotions.

Somehow the effect carried through to both of them. His heartbeat was slow and strong beneath her ear. The pale blue shirt he wore was open at the throat, and beneath the skin, with its fine covering of silky dark hair, the pulse at the base of his neck echoed the gentle rhythm. Of their own volition, her fingers crept up to measure the slow, steady cadence, while the wiry hairs tickled her skin.

It was inevitable, perhaps, that she should be reminded . . . she and this man had created a child together, a sacred bond they would share through all eternity. And yet it was the first time they had touched, *really* touched.... It was incredible. It was beautiful.

It also made her achingly aware of Ward in a way that she couldn't quite control. Suddenly she was only too conscious of the intimacy of their bodies. Her breasts were crushed against the solid breadth of his chest. Somehow her legs had become entangled with Ward's, and she was half sitting on his lap. She was helpless to prevent herself from wondering what it would have been like had Robbie been conceived in the normal way....

Ward felt the slight stiffening of her body. "It's all right, Jenna," he murmured against her forehead.

"No. No. I—I'm tired and—I'd like to go to bed." Even to her own ears, her voice sounded high-pitched and nervous.

She would have pushed away from his shoulders with her hands, but he prevented her intended motion by wrapping his arms around her more tightly. His brows drew together in a frown. "Are you all right?"

Jenna gazed into the deep brown of his eyes, unable to move, mesmerized by the tiny flecks of amber and gold she noticed, yet aware of a fleeting sense of alarm. Something of her distress must have shown in her face, for he brought a hand to her face. With the pad of his thumb, he brushed away the shimmering dampness on her cheekbones. "Jenna, what's wrong?"

His tone was so incredibly gentle. Yet she thought, irrationally, that his cold, angry words were almost easier to bear than his concern, his comfort, his closeness. She shook her head, unable to speak for the churning of her insides.

She would have pulled away then, if it hadn't been for the look in his eyes. He was staring at her intently, and for a heart-stopping moment, Jenna could see the same shattering awareness in him that had seized her only seconds before. His fingers slid down her cheek, over the curve of her jaw and down her throat. For a timeless moment his fingers rested on the frantic throb of her heart, his touch burning through the thin material to the bare skin beneath.

"Jenna..." There was such torment, such desperation in the sound of her name on his lips, that she wanted to cry out in sympathy for him. Again he touched her face, her eyelids, her cheeks, her mouth....

When he finally lifted his hand away, Jenna felt the desolation of her own loss. And then her senses were spinning, swimming, awash in a tingle of expectancy as he resettled his hands on her waist. His mouth was a mere breath away, and she knew with delicious certainty that he was going to kiss her.

And she knew she had never wanted anything so much in her life.

CHAPTER NINE

THE TIGHT ACHE of anticipation grew, until Jenna wanted to scream with frustration. She could sense Ward's uncertainty and see the conflicting emotions warring in his eyes. She wanted desperately to take his face in her hands and cover his lips with hers until nothing else mattered. But something held her back, kept her hands at his shoulders, curled tightly into his flesh.

Somehow this made the moment, when at last it finally came, all the more precious ... all the more exciting.

A sigh of relief escaped her lips when Ward lowered his head, claiming her lips with such sweet tenderness that Jenna felt herself caught up in a whirlwind of emotion unlike anything she had ever experienced before. Her hands slid up to tangle in the thick darkness of his hair, urging from him what she herself craved with an intensity that left her breathless.

Ward's response was instantaneous. His mouth moved over hers almost fiercely, filled with such hunger that for a moment Jenna was totally overwhelmed. Yet her mouth opened beneath his, yielding to the gentle demand of his tongue. Searing pleasure licked along her veins and consumed all but the heady sensation of his lips against hers.

"Ward ..." There was a note of wonderment in her voice. Her fingers glided down the fluid lines of his back, delighting in the feel of muscle and bone. She moved closer, molding her softly cushioned breasts against the hardened contours of his chest.

Suddenly Ward froze. He tore his mouth from hers. "Oh, God, Jenna, what are we doing?"

Stunned, Jenna looked up at him. The words were wrenched from deep inside him. There was a faint glitter in his eyes, a lingering ember of desire, but the look was compounded with remorse and anger.

She felt as if she'd been slapped in the face. Her breasts tingled from the rousing contact with his chest, and there was a yearning ache in the pit of her stomach. Her hands still rested on his shoulders, and she shook her head, as if in denial. She felt her eyes glaze over with the unexpected sting of tears, but then she stilled.

She fixed on a point just beyond his shoulder, where a pair of very accusing green eyes were leveled at Ward's back.

Ward caught the look and glanced back over his shoulder at the same time a disgruntled voice charged, "You didn't come up and kiss me good-night! Jenna said you would!"

Inexplicably Ward found himself torn between the trembling woman he held in his arms and the small pajama-clad figure in the doorway. Pressing her head down against his chest, he spoke over his shoulder. "Why don't you go back upstairs and wait for me, Robbie? I'll be up in a minute."

The little boy doggedly stayed where he was in the doorway.

Ward gave an exasperated sigh, and Jenna's throat constricted tightly. She realized her eyes must have been puffy and swollen from her tears, and her cheeks felt flushed, as well. She drew in a deep breath against his chest, feeling the steady thud of his heart beneath her ear. Ward didn't want Robbie to see her like this, to know that she'd been crying. It would hurt Robbie as much as it had hurt her. But she knew, just as certainly, that concern for her as much as for his son had prompted Ward's oddly protective gesture.

"Go ahead, Ward." Her voice was muffled against his shirt front. "I'll be okay."

"You're sure?"

She nodded. Ward drew back—reluctantly, it seemed. He looked at her for a very long time, his eyes deep and dark. He seemed on the verge of saying something. Then, without a word, he gently disentangled her from his arms and went to his son.

When Ward and Robbie had gone, Jenna drew another deep, steadying breath, straightened her clothes and, with careful, concise steps, made her way up the stairs to her room.

SHE WAS GONE by the time Robbie had been tucked into bed for the second time that night. Ward paused at the door to his den, not realizing how tense he was until the knotted muscles in his shoulders eased when he looked inside and saw that the lamp had been extinguished. He felt a niggling sense of shame at his relief that he didn't have to face her.

When he'd settled himself in the living room with a good stiff drink, he leaned his head against the back of the easy chair and tried to relax. Thoughts of Jenna invaded in spite of his attempts to resist. What the hell was he supposed to say to her, he wondered grimly. He had no explanation for his behavior—just as he had no explanation for her uninhibited response. And somehow he found her reaction just as unsettling as his own.

His hand tightened around the glass before he took a long draft. He would have liked to tell himself that the kiss had evolved out of a very natural desire to comfort, but he knew this wasn't true. He recalled her sweet fragrance, the velvet softness of her hair, the honeyed taste of her mouth. Damn! Who was he trying to fool? Gradually, during the past week, his feelings of resentment had faded, replaced instead by something far different.

He hadn't looked at another woman since Meg had died. And the thought of touching someone other than Meg had never even crossed his mind, even after she was gone. And now that he had, he couldn't help but feel guilty... as if he had somehow betrayed her. Betrayed her memory. But it was only a kiss, he argued with himself. Only a kiss....

Still, there was no denying that he was attracted to Jenna. Maybe it was because she was living here with him. Wasn't it to be expected with a woman in the house again? Or maybe it was simply because it *had* been so long since he'd acknowledged the physical ache inside him.

Or maybe it was because she was the mother of his son.

Ward squelched that thought as swiftly as he downed the rest of his drink. That was one subject that was best left alone—as Jenna herself was best left alone, he advised himself sternly. She was, after all, engaged to be married, and it was that realization that finally permeated his brain. Thank God things hadn't gone any farther! But from now on, he was going to have to keep his eyes, and especially his hands, to himself. Sitting up, he rubbed the back of his neck, suddenly reminded with startling clarity of what she'd said earlier about his always trying to hustle her off to bed like a child. He snorted derisively. Like a child?

There wasn't much chance of that, he thought grimly, picking himself up and heading for the stairs. Not much chance at all.

NINE O'CLOCK the next morning found Ward and Robbie putting the finishing touches on the last of the breakfast dishes. Robbie looked up as Ward lifted him down from the counter where the youngster had been sitting to watch him stack cups and plates.

"Where's Jenna?" the little boy asked.

From his worried tone and the way his fine dark brows puckered in a frown over his small nose, he reminded Ward of a small, wizened old man. He ruffled the dark curls and set him on his feet. "Still sleeping, I guess."

"Can we go see?"

A reluctant smile pulled at the corners of Ward's mouth at his eager tone. "No, we can't go see."

"Then can we wake her up?"

"Not yet." Especially if she hadn't slept any better than he had, he added silently. But Robbie's face crumpled, and Ward found himself yielding with a sigh and a grin. "I'll tell you what. If she isn't up by the time *Superfriends* is over, you can go up and wake her. Now is that a deal or what?"

"Deal!" Robbie slapped his tiny palm against his father's much larger one and giggled.

Ward's eyes softened as he bent over to pick up his son. "You like Jenna, don't you?"

Robbie's eyes brightened further. "She plays Leggos with me," he said with a vigorous nod. "Don't you like her, too, Daddy?"

"Yes," he said slowly, unaware until that moment how true it really was. "Yes, I like her, too."

"And she's pretty, too, isn't she?"

The sudden vision that appeared in his mind of flowing dark hair, creamy translucent skin and glowing eyes triggered a stab of awareness in his body.

"Isn't she, Daddy?" a little voice repeated insistently.

Ward was silent for a moment. "Yes," he agreed reluctantly. "She's pretty, Robbie. She's *very* pretty."

Robbie grinned delightedly and Ward couldn't help but grin back.

"Good morning."

The quiet voice from the doorway caused both males to look
a that direction. "Looks like I interrupted a man to man talk,"
enna added with a shy smile.

Man to man? More like heart to heart, Ward thought,
watching her advance a few steps into the room. She was
wearing dark slacks that hugged the flare of her hips entic-
ngly, not too tightly, and a simple scoop-neck pale yellow
-shirt that gently molded the curve of her breasts. Ward had
o force himself to look away, remembering suddenly how his
fingers had charted those slender curves.

Robbie was wiggling in his arms, anxious to be free, and
Ward, feeling very ill at ease, let him down. He ran immedi-
tely to Jenna, who scooped him up in her arms.

Ward cleared his throat. "Would you like some breakfast?"

Pleasurably intent on the small snuggly body in her arms,
enna laid her cheek against Robbie's. "No, thanks," she an-
wered absently. "I think I'll just have coffee."

The sight of those two dark heads nestled together had a very
trange effect on Ward. He felt something that was half plea-
ure, half pain, stir deep inside. In spite of himself, he smiled
wryly. "I seem to remember someone telling me just a few days
go that breakfast was just as important for me as it is for
Robbie. Don't you practice what you preach?"

There was something almost intimate in his tone, and Jenna
glanced up in surprise. The mild amusement in Ward's eyes
kindled a like response in hers, but not before she felt her heart
lutter strangely in her chest. "Well, then . . . I'll have what-
ver you're having."

"We already ate," Robbie piped up, crawling onto her lap
when she sat down at the table.

Jenna smiled at his cheery tone. Then her eyes slid to Ward.
"Not burned oatmeal, I'll bet."

Their eyes met, and he smiled again. "No, not burned oatmeal," he returned softly. "I've progressed to bacon and eggs
by now. Sound okay?"

She took a deep breath. "Sounds fine," she murmured.

While Ward busied himself at the stove, she watched him
from the corner of her eye, and some of her tension dissolved.
She had dreaded coming face-to-face with Ward that morn-
ng, and she'd given a silent prayer of thanks that Robbie was
with him in the kitchen. She had scarcely slept the previous

night, thinking of what had happened between her and War
She'd found herself reliving the moment when his lips had fir
touched hers, wondering if he'd felt the same explosion insi
as she. The next minute, she was telling herself it would be wi
to simply forget it had ever happened—because surely
wouldn't happen again. But as he didn't seem to be dwelling o
the incident . . . well, then, neither would she.

"You're up early today," she remarked as he set a steamin
plate in front of her.

A grin tugged at his lips as he removed Robbie from her la
and settled him on his own so she could eat. "It was worth
not to have to take a cold shower this morning."

The fork she held in her hand stopped midway to her mout
"Cold shower?" she stammered.

Ward smiled at her wide-eyed surprise, aware of what sh
was thinking. "This is an old house, Jenna. It could use a bi
ger water heater. You've beaten me to the shower every day th
week, and I've had to pay the price."

Jenna was utterly warmed by the genuine amusement in h
voice. "I'm sorry, I didn't know," she began. If only . . . if on
she weren't so completely aware of him as a man, a very a
tractive man, she could be completely at ease with him.

"Daddy thinks you're pretty," Robbie interjected sudden!

She held back a grin at the embarrassed look on Ward's fac
"Does he now?" she asked. A pang of sheer pleasure swe
through her.

"Uh-huh." He stopped playing with the buttons on Ward
denim shirt to look at her. "Do you think Daddy's pretty?"

Jenna looked startled. "Uh . . . well, Robbie . . . men are
usually called pretty—"

"What are they called, then?"

"Well . . . handsome—"

"Do you think my daddy is handsome?"

Jenna felt herself go crimson. From the look on Ward's fac
he was obviously deriving an enormous amount of pleasu
over his son's bald-faced questions. "I suppose he is," s
muttered gruffly.

"There are no secrets with a three-year-old in the house
Ward commented, chuckling.

Jenna let herself fall in with the light mood. It felt so rig!
so good, to be sitting there in that house, enjoying the bant
ing among the three of them.

She smiled good-naturedly as Robbie scampered off toward the living room. "Speaking of secrets..." She raised her eyebrows and looked at Ward. "Your son seems to think I was born in the Middle Ages because I don't know who Soupman, Matman and Wonder Worm are. Would you believe I watched cartoons all yesterday afternoon and the closest I could come up with were He-Man and the Masters of the Universe." She shook her head and laughed. "I'm not so old that I don't remember my childhood years, but whatever happened to Casper the Ghost and Mighty Mouse?"

She felt an eddy of pleasure whirl inside her as he laughed. "Casper the Ghost and Mighty Mouse are alive and well and featured in living color on Saturday morning TV," he intoned gravely. "As are *Super*man, *Bat*man and Wonder *Woman*...." There was a decided twinkle in his eye as he added, "Otherwise known as Soupman, Matman and Wonder Worm to one Robert Edward Garrison."

There was a stunned silence. "You're kidding," Jenna said with a burst of laughter. "And I thought..." She tilted her head and looked at him. "Last night he asked me to frost his teeth. He was a little put out because I didn't understand him. What exactly—"

"*Floss* his teeth," Ward supplied with a chuckle. "How on earth have you two managed all week without an interpreter?"

She got up to carry her plate and cup to the sink. "I'm beginning to wonder," she said dryly over her shoulder.

Ward's eyes followed her as she moved back across the room, admiring the lithe grace of her movements. He enjoyed the low musical tone of her voice and the lilting sound of her laughter; he liked the way the smooth strands of her hair flowed over her slender shoulders....

He was still thinking about her when he walked upstairs half an hour later. The sounds of Robbie's delighted squeals drifted to his ears, and he glanced idly into the bathroom as he passed by. What he saw made him feel as if he'd been hit in the stomach with a cannonball.

A waterbug from the time he was born, Robbie loved his bath time and considered the extra baths to relieve his itching chicken pox a special treat. Jenna was kneeling by the side of the bathtub, and just as Ward looked sideways, Robbie

sprawled headlong into the soapy water, drenching Jenna fro
the waist up in the process.

"All right, young man, you've had enough," she a
nounced, laughing and wiping the moisture from her cheek
"One more dive like that and there won't be a single drop
water left in the tub. It'll all be on me!"

It was already, Ward thought, totally nonplussed. Her T-shi
was plastered to her body with a thoroughness that left abs
lutely nothing to the imagination. Her breasts lifted beneath th
clinging material as she reached for Robbie's small squirmir
body. Ward stood rooted to the floor, unable to tear his ey
from the gentle, swaying movement those soft curves made
she briskly rubbed his son's body dry.

When she was finished, she wrapped the towel around Rol
bie, trailing her fingers lightly across his bare shoulders. It w
then that she became aware of Ward watching her from th
doorway. "He's so soft," she murmured, casting a slight
embarrassed look at him from the corner of her eye. "Touc
ing a baby's skin is like . . . touching a feather."

His eyes moved slowly upward to linger on a faint bloom
her cheeks. And *hers* had the same dewy softness and textu
as a rose petal, he thought to himself. His fingers tingled as
vividly remembered the feel of her beneath his hands, the tas
of her on his mouth. An odd twinge shot through him, a twin
not unfamiliar to him, but dimly recalled nonetheless. It to
a moment before he recognized it for what it was. Desire. D
sire so strong he almost shuddered from the force that c
through his body. Compulsively his eyes slid downward on
more.

God, how long had it been? he wondered achingly. How lo
had it been since he'd made love? . . . Too long. Not lo
enough. He knew some people, particularly other men, mig
say he was crazy, but there had been no one since Meg. The id
of making love—even going through the motions with his bo
and not his heart—sharing himself in that way with anyone b
Meg, left a vile taste in his mouth. It was something he had
even thought about.

Until now.

He tore his eyes away from her breasts, aware of his brea
coming jerkily "You'd better go change," he muttered. "I'll
Robbie dressed."

His tone wasn't really rough, but there was an edge to it that
aught Jenna by surprise. When she glanced up at him, his terse
od indicated her clothing. Aware of its sodden state, she
arted to comment laughingly about Robbie's "bath" man-
ers. But when she looked down she noticed her shirt clinging
etly to her body as if it were a second skin. The skimpy little
ra she wore did nothing to disguise the pucker of her nipples
rough the thin material.

She hugged her breasts defensively and gave a forced laugh.
Yes, I suppose I should.''

Ward stepped aside so she could pass, dragging his eyes from
er figure as she went toward her room. It was, he thought,
roaning inwardly as he pulled a polo shirt over Robbie's head,
oing to be a very long weekend.

HERE WAS A VERY definite change in their relationship after the
cident the previous night, and Jenna wasn't sure who was
ore keenly aware of it, she or Ward. That night, and the fol-
owing morning, as well, they had shared something—a kin-
hip, a feeling of togetherness. For that brief time, Robbie
asn't *his* son, or *her* son, but *their* son. Regardless of how
uch either one of them wanted to skirt the issue of his birth,
here was no denying it.

And somehow that acknowledgment set the pattern for the
ays that followed. The time spent with Robbie was precious.
enna knew with a poignant sweetness in her heart that these
ilded days of sunshine would have to last her a lifetime. But
ist as precious were the moments when her eyes met Ward's
a glimmer of shared amusement over something funny Rob-
ie said or did; the feeling of utter peace that swept over her as
ley tucked Robbie, who now insisted that Jenna assist with his
ightly routine, into his bed; the warmth that flooded her as she
atched Ward and Robbie tussle on the floor after dinner. Nor
ould she forget the day Ward, realizing she'd only brought a
mited amount of clothing with her, handed her a neatly folded
ile of laundry, several items of which were lacily embroidered
ras and panties.

If only he hadn't kissed her. What had seemed so right at the
me later took on monstrous proportions in Jenna's mind.
egardless of her trouble spots with Neil, she was engaged to
im, only a single step away from a lifelong promise to love,

honor and cherish. And yet the minute Ward touched her, Ne
momentarily ceased to exist. She almost wished she could for
get... almost, but not quite.

Along with their newfound closeness grew another element
an element that stemmed solely from that not-so-innocent kiss
an element that magnified tenfold when they were alone. By th
simple act of walking into a room, Ward precipitated a reac
tion in her that she was totally unable to control and—which
was even more frightening—wasn't sure she wanted to. Sh
couldn't deny the sheer pleasure she derived from observing th
rugged male beauty of his face and body. Yet her heart race
dangerously, vying fiercely with her thundering pulse. Ther
was no way she could attribute the reaction to the unease she'
experienced when she'd first arrived in Plains City. After the
first tense days together, he seemed to have accepted her pre
ence in his house with an alacrity that continued to surprise he

Still, it was almost a relief when Monday came and she wa
left alone with Robbie. She needed some time to sort throug
her cluttered thoughts. She was at a total loss to explain th
very strange attraction to Ward, especially when she was s
closely tied to Neil. If only she knew more about Ward... an
Megan, as well.

The perfect opportunity arose that very afternoon whe
Jenna answered the knock on the back screen door. Eilee
stood there, dressed in a neatly tailored cinnamon-colore
blazer and slacks that added deep tones of russet to her da
hair. Despite the crispness of her attire, her shoulder bag wa
pulled haphazardly over one shoulder and she looked ready
keel over with the slightest breath.

Jenna opened the door wider. "You look," she said with
smile, "like a woman who has just blown her last dollar on
all-day shopping spree." She glanced at Eileen's station wago
sitting in the driveway. "Don't I get to see any of the loot?"

Eileen walked in and promptly collapsed on the neare
kitchen chair. Hearing voices in the kitchen, Robbie ran in fro
the dining room, where he'd been playing, gave his aunt a hu
and kiss and promptly dashed out again.

"I wish," Eileen said glumly after he'd gone, "that I ha
been shopping. At least I'd have something to show for my e
fort besides two aching feet."

Jenna pondered the weary set of her shoulders. "Would yo
like some tea? I was just about to make some." Eileen nodde

ratefully. After setting the tea kettle on the stove, Jenna looked
ver her shoulder. "If you haven't been shopping," she ven-
ured curiously, "what have you been doing?"

"Job hunting," came the grim response.

Jenna pulled down two cups from the cupboard. "Job
unting?" she echoed. "With no luck, I take it?"

"Exactly."

Their conversation of last week came back to Jenna in a flash
and she gasped. "Surely not because of what I said—"

Eileen waved a placating hand. "Oh, don't feel bad. It's not
our fault. It's just that I hadn't considered how difficult find-
ng a job in a town of less than two thousand people might
e. By noon I'd hit every business in Plains City and Silver
alls—" Jenna knew that the Swenson ranch was midway be-
ween Plains City and Silver Falls "—so this afternoon I de-
ided it wouldn't hurt to try Abilene, instead...." Her voice
railed off, and Jenna didn't need to ask to know how she had
ared.

"Have you worked before?" She placed a cup and saucer
efore Ward's sister.

"Actually, I've never been trained in anything." She looked
ather sheepish. She shook her head and gave a rueful smile. "I
uess if anything ever happened to Frank I'd be a classic model
or a displaced homemaker. I haven't had a job since before
rank and I were married, and that was clerking in the drug-
tore on Main Street."

Jenna reached out to cover her hand. "It's nothing to be
mbarrassed about," she said gently. "My mother would have
een in exactly the same position." She paused. "What does
rank think of the idea?"

"Of my getting a job?"

Jenna nodded.

"Oh, he's all for it." A smile flitted across her tired face.
"And so are the kids. They called this weekend." She laughed
little. "Of course it might be a different story if I told them
ack of training was the problem and that I was gearing up to
nroll in college along with them."

"They shouldn't knock it," Jenna observed with a wry smile.
"It's been known to happen." She patted Eileen's hand com-
ortingly. "I wouldn't be so discouraged so soon, though. What
ind of job did you say you were looking for?"

"I've done a little typing and bookkeeping for the ranch. I
hought I'd try to find something in that area."

Jenna's eyes narrowed thoughtfully. At the look, Eileen prompted with a laugh, "What? Go ahead and spit it out. I'm open to any and all suggestions."

"I was just thinking of all those photographs at your house—the ones on the living room wall. You took those, didn't you?"

Eileen looked puzzled. "Yes, but . . ."

"I didn't give it a second thought at the time. I just assumed they were taken by a professional."

"A professional!" Eileen gasped, then laughed. "I've taken some classes in technique and developing and have a dark room at the house. And I have some good equipment. But photography has always been just a hobby. Good heavens, a professional—"

"No, really!" Jenna interrupted, beginning to gather enthusiasm herself. "You're good, really good—at least *I* think you are. And as long as you're looking for a job, why not make it something you like?"

For the first time there was a genuine spark of life in Eileen's eyes. She looked at her in amazement. "You really think I should?"

Jenna spread her hands. "That's entirely up to you, but as long as you don't actually need the money, you're not really out anything by looking. And if nothing turns up, you can always try something else."

"Jenna—" she reached across the table and hugged the younger woman "—you are a lifesaver."

Jenna was touched by the spontaneous gesture. She smiled back at Ward's sister, and it was then that Eileen's gaze dropped to where Jenna's hands were curled around her tea cup.

"I didn't know you were engaged."

Jenna flushed, a little puzzled at the odd look in Eileen's eyes as they lingered on the engagement ring.

"When's the big day?"

"The first Saturday next month," Jenna murmured, suddenly very uncomfortable.

"Next month! My goodness, that's so soon!" Eileen sounded shocked. Their eyes met for the briefest of moments and Eileen looked away, visibly embarrassed. "It's just that . . . when I think of the last few weeks before Frank and I were married . . ."

Jenna had no trouble deciphering Eileen's thoughts, or picturing a younger Eileen, glowing and radiant, in a trailing white
wedding gown with a lacy veil. She would have been wildly ecstatic . . . and not hundreds of miles away from her fiancé.

Suddenly the tiny gold band with its sparkling chip of dia-
mond seemed to weigh heavily on her finger. If Neil were to
walk through the door at this very moment, how would she
feel?

She didn't know, and the realization was more than a little
disturbing.

Oddly, the thought of her own marriage only brought her
around to the subject of Ward and Meg. She took a deep breath
and eyed Eileen assessingly. "Eileen, would you mind telling me
about Ward—and Megan?"

For just a moment Eileen was startled. Jenna could see it in
her eyes. "It's funny you should put it like that," she said
slowly. "After all this time, I still find it hard to think of one
without the other. Meg and Ward. Ward and Meg."

Jenna hesitated. "I feel awkward about asking you, but
Ward—"

"I know." Eileen nodded understandingly. "He doesn't talk
about Meg to anyone, not even me. He'll mention her name in
passing once in a while, but that's as far as it goes." Her eyes
darkened. "Except for once," she added softly, so softly Jenna
could hardly hear.

"Are you sure you don't mind telling me?" she asked tentatively.

"No. Not at all." Eileen shook her head firmly. "I think I
actually wanted to dislike you, but I couldn't—I mean I can't."
She waved a hand in the air and laughed a little shakily. "It's
crazy, but how many times have we met . . . three? I guess what
I'm trying to say is, I feel as if you're family."

"It's not crazy at all," Jenna said quietly, oddly touched by
her honesty. "Because I feel the same way."

Those were the only words necessary as they smiled at each
other. Then Eileen's tone became brisk again. "Well. What is
it you want to know?"

"Anything. Everything." Jenna's head began to whirl. "You
said it was hard to think of one without the other." Her shoulders lifted. "Why?" she asked simply.

Eileen gazed through the window, where a restless breeze
tossed the branches of the trees. Watching a faraway look come

into Eileen's eyes, Jenna could almost feel her sifting back through her mind.

"Our family lived in town then," she finally began. "I was nine and Ward was six when Meg's family moved next door early one fall. From that day on, Ward carried Meg's books to school for as long as I can remember. They were inseparable. Where one was, the other wasn't far behind." Her smile grew wistful. "My parents used to tease each other and say those two were exactly like Mary and her little lamb—and they were."

"So they were childhood sweethearts," Jenna murmured.

Eileen nodded. "I think I could count on the fingers of one hand the number of girls Ward dated during high school and college and still have a few fingers left over. It was the same way for Meg. We all knew they would get married eventually, and they did, right after Ward graduated from college. They had the kind of relationship that was almost too good to be true. They were the couple with everything—a fantastic marriage, a nice home, stable career...." Her voice grew very soft. "And in fact it *was* too good to be true. There was only one thing missing. And other than each other, the one thing they wanted most was the one thing they couldn't have."

Jenna knew Eileen was talking about a child.

Eileen touched her arm gently. "You'll never know how much happiness you brought to Meg—to both of them."

Jenna's throat constricted tightly. Oh, she knew. But it wasn't without a loss of her own. Through a haze of pain she heard Eileen's voice.

"Robbie has been Ward's only salvation," she said quietly. "The day of Meg's funeral, Ward told me he felt as if he'd lost a part of himself forever, a part he knew he would never regain."

"How long had they been married when...?"

"Fifteen years," Eileen said quickly.

Jenna wet her lips. "Eileen..." She had wondered so often, and she knew, now more than ever, that she couldn't ask Ward. Her voice was a tiny thread of sound. "Exactly what happened?... I mean, *how* did Meg die?"

The silence stretched out endlessly. Jenna held her breath and waited...waited in vain.

Eileen shook her head sadly. "I'm sorry, Jenna," she said quietly, "but if you asked Ward and he didn't tell you...well, maybe it would be better if it came from him." She paused briefly, then gazed across at her. "Is there anything else you'd like to know?"

Jenna shook her head quickly. In some ways the day had brought the answers she sought. But in other ways... She had wanted to know about Ward, and now she did.

She no longer wondered why he still wore his wedding ring, though somehow she had known all along. Ward was still very much in love with his dead wife. She sighed, her mood a soulful contrast to the bright and cloudless day outside. She didn't even wonder why the knowledge hurt so much.

She only knew that it did.

CHAPTER TEN

THE MOON CAST a pearly glow against the enveloping darkness when Jenna slipped outside several nights later after a brief phone call to her mother. Lacy patterns of ebony and silver disappeared and reemerged as a smoky cloud wandered across the crescent that lighted the night-dark sky.

She lifted her face to the soothing caress of the breeze before crossing silently to the swing. The days had been filled with warm, brilliant sunshine. But the crisp, chill October nights foretold the waning of summer and nature's silent entrance into autumn.

And with each evening that passed, she was reminded that soon she would have to leave; Robbie was almost well. *Soon....*

"Beautiful night, isn't it?"

She turned her head to find Ward's form outlined in the doorway. Nodding silently, she watched as he came toward her and extended a mug identical to the one he had. She congratulated herself when her heartbeat fluttered only slightly before settling down to a normal rhythm as he sat down beside her.

She smiled as her hands closed around the warm cup and the tang of sweet-smelling chocolate drifted to her nostrils. "Is this a hint, Ward?" she murmured teasingly. "You're trying to bundle me off to bed again so you can work late?" Just this week Ward had told her about the roadblocks his firm had been running into with the project in Oklahoma. Consequently, it had been after midnight when he'd finally emerged from the den and gone past her room last night.

"Not at all." There was a thread of amusement in his voice. "Though I did hear you tossing and turning all last night."

Jenna looked away. She and Neil were still going around in circles, and her thoughts regarding him were a muddle of confusion, at best. Yes, there were reasons for her fitful sleep, the least of which was her budding awareness of her growing feelings for the man sitting beside her. She sipped her chocolate. "If you heard me, you must have been awake, too."

Ward stifled the urge to groan. If only she knew.... "Score one for the lady in blue," he said with a chuckle. His eyes swept over her, resting for a moment on the gentle thrust of her breasts beneath the thin sweater she wore. A now familiar ache swept through him, and unable to resist, he reached out to gently touch the downy curve of her cheek.

"You must be getting stir-crazy by now," he commented softly. "Plains City must be quite a change from life in the big city."

Ward's tone implied that she must be bored stiff, but that wasn't the case at all. Her cheek tingled pleasantly as she glanced at him in surprise. "A change, yes—but definitely a change for the better," she said firmly. "It's peaceful and quiet, and I can't honestly say I miss the hubbub of the city at all. I'm not the kind of person who has to be constantly on the move to be happy."

Somehow he had known that even without her saying so. "But surely you must miss your fiancé."

Jenna's fingers stilled around the smooth surface of the cup. He knew. She didn't know how, but somehow *he knew*. She gazed off into the distance. Just beyond the slatted boundaries of the property, wheat fields undulated gently beneath the starry sky.

"Did Robbie settle down all right after I left you two alone?" she asked, changing the subject. She knew Ward was aware of her ploy, and deliberately looked away from his strong features.

He was quiet for a long time. "Yes," he said finally. A wry smile suddenly curved his lips. "I suppose by the time I finally get used to being greeted in the evening with, 'Daddy, I itch!' Robbie will be over his chicken pox."

Jenna smiled wanly. "Probably," she agreed, though her heart wasn't in it. She was still disturbed by Ward's mention of Neil. She sensed he was trying to get at something—but what?

"He loves you, you know."

The oddly gentle tone, as much as the words and the freely given admission, stirred something deep inside Jenna. Coming from him, did he know how much that meant to her? She felt Ward reach for her hand and clasp her fingers lightly in his. "The feeling is mutual."

And how do you feel about me? Through the silvery darkness, Ward studied her delicate features. Her head was bent and her lips were clamped together. She was gazing downward, her feathery lashes veiling her eyes, the one thing he wanted most to see. The question echoed in his mind. If he were to ask and she were to look at him, he would know what was in her heart.

There had been something between them almost from the beginning, and he knew he wasn't the only one to feel it. Yet these past days he'd fought a constant battle with himself. Though he had wanted to, there was no way he could ignore the fact that she was a very attractive, desirable woman. Robbie's frequent baking-soda baths had seen to that. His mouth turned up fleetingly. The last time he had resigned himself to cold showers in the morning, found the toothpaste tube squeezed from the middle instead of the end, or folded women's underclothes while doing the laundry was when Meg was alive.

The reminders of Meg were many, the actual similarities between the two women few. He liked having a woman in the house again, and it had nothing to do with being relieved of some of the household burdens. But not just any woman, he corrected staunchly. Jenna. He liked her warmth, her sweetness, her quiet, loving nature. It was, perhaps, a very good thing that Jenna was involved with another man.

He expelled a harsh breath. No, it was Meg who complicated his attraction for Jenna. Meg who made him feel as if he were torn in two and unsure of himself for the first time in years. His eyes were drawn to Jenna, the slight vulnerability in her parted lips, the warmth of her hand lying trustingly in his, the dark uncertainty in the eyes that finally lifted to his face.

And he knew that he was growing weary of the battle.

He passed a hand over his face to clear away the fog, and felt her hand tense slightly in his.

"Robbie—" Jenna wet her lips tentatively "—Robbie doesn't remember Meg, does he?"

It was a moment before he shook his head. "No. No, he doesn't." He paused. "You've seen how Eileen is with her camera...I've tried to keep her memory alive to him that way...." His voice drifted off. It was oddly gentle, yet there was something in it she couldn't define.

She hoped it wasn't meant to be a warning. "Ward," she began hesitantly, "did you and Meg ever intend to tell Robbie about me?"

The air had been alive with the sounds of the night. A gentle breeze sighed through the trees; an owl hooted in the distance. The stillness seemed to drag on forever. Jenna could feel her blood thrumming in her ears.

With a sigh of dismay she blinked back her disappointment. She pulled her feet beneath the swing and began to rise.

"Don't go...." He spoke so low that if the wind hadn't momentarily abated, she might never have heard.

Her mouth dry with expectation, Jenna sat back down. The ensuing silence was so awkward that she almost fled once more; only the light, reassuring squeeze of Ward's fingers against her own stopped her.

Ward hesitated. No matter what he said, it would hurt her. He knew this and hated his inability to prevent it.

"I don't want to hurt you, Jenna. You know that, don't you?"

Her throat constricted at the intensity of his voice. His concern moved her beyond words, but it didn't erase the need in her heart, the questions in her mind. Her thoughts about Meg were a tormenting mixture of gratitude and pain. Megan had taken another woman's child—no matter that it was also her husband's—taken that child and raised him as her own, *loved* him as her own. Why—why did the idea hurt so? Because she had always thought of Robbie as *her* son. She'd never said the words aloud, but she'd felt them in her heart...so many times. And now more than ever.

But Megan was gone—and Robbie did have a mother. And Jenna didn't want to be relegated to a nameless, faceless person.

Slowly she raised her eyes to his. "I need to know, Ward. I *have* to know."

Moonlight silvered her features, accenting her vulnerability. He ached with the need to fold her into his arms and ease her uncertainties. But he knew he didn't dare.

"Meg wanted to tell him about you when he was old enough to understand..." he said slowly.

Jenna tensed at his hesitation, sensing what was coming. She forced the words from her lips. "And what about you?"

He let out a harsh breath and looked away. His voice sounded strained. "I thought it was best to let him think Meg was his natural mother." He shook his head. "We thought we had plenty of time to decide . . . nothing was ever really clear-cut. . . .''

He was trying to soften the blow. She understood that and could even appreciate it in an anguished kind of way, but it didn't stop her from resisting his attempt to slip an arm around her shoulders and draw her to him. Gently but firmly she withdrew, gathering her tumultuous emotions like a cloak around her shoulders, as if to shield herself from the pain of her world splintering around her. If he touched her. . . if he touched her she would shatter into a million pieces.

She drew a steadying breath. ''I think I'll say goodnight now,'' she said carefully.

Upstairs in her room she prepared for bed mechanically, but the minute she slipped between the cool sheets, her numbness began to wear off. She stared at the shadows dancing on the ceiling. These past few days she had felt, little by little, that she wasn't on the outside looking in, that she was a part of her son's life.

But what did it mean, she cried out silently. What was the use? She had come here, filled with an all-consuming need to know who he was, where he was, what he was. But what would he know about her? Nothing. Ward would never tell him about her—never. She felt helpless, betrayed, shut out, almost as if she had never existed.

She turned over and clutched her pillow to her chest. Much as she would have liked to, she couldn't be angry with Ward. He didn't deserve to be hurt anymore. Even now she ached to go to him, to seek solace in his arms and forget the storm in her heart. And she knew that it could happen.

Despite the kiss they had shared, she'd been telling herself for days that Ward wasn't interested in her as a woman. But wasn't there something—a flicker, a spark—whenever their eyes met? Always . . . always one of them would quickly look away. Whatever the feeling was, it was happening to both of them.

But the realization only complicated an already complex situation. If she weren't pledged to Neil . . . and if only he weren't still in love with Meg. . . .

JENNA AWOKE to the sound of a childish giggle. Prying open an eyelid, she looked straight into a pair of impish green eyes. She felt the dark mood of the night before disappear the way a dewy morning mist might evaporate under the bright rays of the sun.

"Hi, sport." Delighted, she propped an elbow on the pillow to confront her visitor. Robbie still wore a pair of light blue pajamas but looked amazingly wide-awake.

Smothering a yawn with the back of her hand, she sat up and glanced at the bedside clock. "Six-thirty!" she groaned. She was sorely tempted to bury her head beneath the pillow and sleep an hour longer, but another shy giggle from Robbie stopped her.

Instead she reached out and lifted him to the side of her bed. "You little rascal!" she said with a chuckle. He squealed happily when she began tickling him on his tummy and sides. Jenna laughed aloud herself, feeling gloriously alive and light-hearted.

"Can we make berry muffins this morning?" he asked eagerly after their horseplay, throwing chubby arms around her neck.

Jenna laughed and hugged him tightly, breathing in deeply of his delicious baby smell. "You've already learned I can't say no to you, haven't you?"

The fragrant aroma coming from the kitchen lured Ward downstairs an hour later. Jenna wasn't aware that he had entered the room until she heard Robbie's squeal of greeting and a deep, "Good morning," behind her. She turned, an over-sized hot mitt still on one hand.

"How are you this morning?" He lifted his cup to his lips and gave her a faintly questioning look over the rim.

Jenna managed a tentative smile. "Fine," she murmured, turning around once more. He looked almost unbearably attractive, but there were faint lines etched in the tanned skin around his eyes. She felt her heart go out to him.

"What's for breakfast this morning?"

"Berry muffins!" Robbie's voice sang out before she had a chance to respond. Jenna grinned as she piled half a dozen warm muffins onto a plate.

"My favorite," Ward remarked beside her. His look was full of wry amusement as it traveled from his son to Jenna. "Do I need to ask how you knew?"

The three of them sat at the table and the muffins disappeared at an amazing pace, though Robbie didn't eat more than a few bites of his. She was just about to comment on this, when

Ward carried his plate over to the sink. He turned back with smile.

"Which of you do I thank for breakfast?"

"I helped!" Robbie shouted, beaming.

Ward laughed. "I'll just bet you did." He lifted Robbie fror his chair and pressed a kiss onto his forehead. "Now Jenna!" Robbie demanded. "She helped, too!" He squirmed in h father's strong arms to point at Jenna.

Jenna felt her cheeks flush as she discerned his meaning. Sh watched Ward lower Robbie to the floor, then move to wher she sat.

"With pleasure," he conceded softly. Her eyes widened as h bent over her and she saw that he actually meant to kiss he Fingers knitted tightly in her lap, she turned her face slight and raised her cheek, expecting a chaste, perfunctory kiss.

What she got was something else entirely. A finger beneat her chin tipped her face to his, and her heart began to poun furiously as his gaze dropped to her mouth. His touch wa warm and sure as his knuckles brushed the curve of her jaw. H was so close their noses almost touched, and for a moment sh sat breathlessly awaiting his next move. Her lashes flutter shut when at last it came and his mouth brushed gently acro hers. The smell of his after-shave whirled around her as his li returned, pressing the kiss firmer, deeper. Every cell in her bod reacted to his nearness in a totally intoxicating way that wa both confusing and alarming. She was helpless to stop t melting sigh that escaped her lips when she reached up to tang her hands in his thick hair.

The sound of two small hands clapping delightedly final broke them apart. Shocked at the urge to let herself be swe away by her feelings—and in front of a three-year-old child, r less!—her mortified gaze sought Ward's. He grinned a litt sheepishly as he slipped into his coat, ruffled Robbie's hair ar then walked out the back door, leaving her staring after him.

Her legs felt like two heated wax candles beneath her. Sh was thankful she was sitting. Because if she hadn't been, sh was very much afraid she'd have fallen into an ignominiou heap on the floor.

SHORTLY AFTER Ward left Eileen dropped in. She had been frequent visitor during the week, and Jenna found she liked h

nore and more with each day that passed. Eileen was throw-
ng herself wholeheartedly into launching what she laughingly
called her "career," and that morning she brought along a
portfolio of photographs she had taken to see what Jenna
thought of them.

The house was very quiet after she left, and after a quick call
to check in with her mother, Jenna walked into the living room
to find Robbie curled up in a chair with a book. Despite his
early morning enthusiasm, it became increasingly obvious as
the day wore on that Robbie wasn't feeling well. His eyes lacked
their usual luster; he picked at his lunch and crawled listlessly
into her lap early in the afternoon. By the time he awoke several hours later, she could feel the heat emanating from his
small body.

He turned lethargically in her arms, snuggling his face
against her breast. His dark hair clung damply to his forehead. His chicken pox were gone except for a few scaly blisters
on his arms and legs. She studied him when he opened his eyes
to stare up at her. Though his complexion was clear and un-
blemished once more, his cheeks were flushed with fever.

"You don't feel good, do you, sweetheart?" she asked gently.

Robbie shook his head. His lashes fluttered closed once
more, fanning out darkly against his pale skin. Jenna eased him
gently onto the sofa and retrieved the thermometer from the
medicine cabinet in the bathroom. Minutes later, her suspicions were confirmed as she pulled the thermometer from his
mouth. His temperature was 104 degrees.

"Robbie—" her fingers smoothed the matted hair from his
forehead "—can you tell me where it hurts?"

Mutely he opened his mouth and pointed inside. Jenna could
see from the brief glimpse she was afforded that the tissue at the
back of his throat was fiery red.

Jenna went immediately to the phone, thumbing through the
small directory nearby until she found the number for Dr. Steve
Reynolds's office. A moment later she hung up, uttering a silent prayer of thanks when the receptionist informed her she
could bring Robbie in right away. She wasted no time in bun-
dling Robbie's limp body into her car and driving hurriedly into
town.

There were several patients ahead of them, but it wasn't lon
before the receptionist called Robbie's name and they were le
into one of the examination rooms.

Steve Reynolds's brows lifted in surprised recognition whe
he opened the door and entered the small room. "Well, hell
again!" He glanced from Jenna to the small boy nestled in he
arms. "Isn't that Ward's boy?" When Jenna nodded and stoo
up, his sharp eyes went over Robbie. "Not hard to figure ou
which one of you is the patient," he murmured. "Just gettin
over chicken pox, is he?"

Jenna nodded. "His throat is red as a firecracker, though
doesn't look like his tonsils are affected."

Dr. Reynolds held out his arms to Robbie. "How about if w
take a look, young man?"

Despite the doctor's warm, kindly manner, Robbie refuse
to leave her arms, so Jenna sat on the small rectangular tab
with him while Dr. Reynolds checked his throat, glands an
ears.

Finally he straightened up. "I think we'd better do a throa
culture to check for a strep infection."

Jenna sighed. "That's what I was afraid of. It's not unusu
with chicken pox, is it?"

"No, it's not," he confirmed. After swabbing Robbie
throat, he sat down at the small desk in the corner, then hande
her a prescription. "We won't have the results of the culture f
a few days, but I think we should start him on antibiotics rig
away." He handed her a prescription, then gave her an inqui
itive smile. "Didn't you tell me you were heading back to Ga
veston?"

"Yes . . . well . . ." Jenna could feel herself flushing.

Steve Reynolds laughed. "No need to explain," he sai
waving a hand. "As I said before, I think it's the best thing f
Ward—"

"I'm afraid you've misunderstood," Jenna broke in hu
riedly. "It was really Robbie's chicken pox that kept me her
I've been taking care of him, you see. Actually, I knew Mega
and Ward. . . ." Suddenly an idea began to blossom in her min
She had wondered so often about Megan's death. Wa
wouldn't tell her about how she'd died, and neither would B
leen.

But Dr. Reynolds had said that Meg and Ward were two
his first patients. Glancing down, Jenna noticed that Robb

had fallen asleep. The moment couldn't have been more opportune. She felt a little guilty at her deceit, but other than asking point-blank... She took a deep breath and plunged ahead. "It was so unexpected when Meg died. We were all so shocked...." She let her voice trail off, hoping he would pick up the conversation and tie up the loose threads.

His face was suddenly grim. "It was certainly the last thing in the world I ever expected. I diagnosed her infertility in the first place, you know." Jenna nodded, and her arms tightened around Robbie. She hadn't known that, but she let him go on. He shook his head. "Who can say why it happened? It was God's will. I tried to tell Ward that. There was no reason for him to feel responsible—there was no way anyone could have known it would happen—but I often wondered if my talk did any good. I think he still blames himself."

He shrugged dismissively and stood up. "We'll call if the results of the culture are positive. You'll be at Ward's?" When Jenna nodded, he shook his head and winked at her. "I still haven't found an office nurse. Let me know if you change your mind."

Jenna stopped at the pharmacy to have Robbie's prescription filled, but her thoughts were a mad jumble on the short ride home. She didn't really know any more about Meg's death than she had before, except that Ward blamed himself for some reason. What could possibly have happened that everyone was so reluctant to speak of it? She bit her lip thoughtfully, ruling out natural causes. Meg hadn't been that old, and as far as Jenna knew, she'd been healthy except for her infertility. And besides, Ward would never have held himself responsible for that. An accident, perhaps?

She sighed and reached out a hand to touch a lock of Robbie's dark hair. Her confusion was like a maze with only one way out: Ward. And yet, he had already been through so much she couldn't find it in her heart to ask him again.

His Blazer was already parked in the driveway when she arrived back at his place. She checked her watch briefly. Almost five-thirty. As she unbuckled Robbie from his seat belt, she noted that he seemed a little cooler. Thank heaven, she thought, cradling his limp body over her shoulder. He roused slightly when she lifted him, and she stroked the back of his head as she climbed the steps.

"Ward?" She looked around and stepped into the living room. Robbie smiled drowsily up at her when she put him on the sofa. "I'll be right back, sweetheart," she told him. "I'm just going to find Daddy and tell him we're back."

Ward wasn't in either the den or the kitchen. Maybe he was outside, she thought with a frown. She was standing near the stairway, so she decided to run up and drop her purse in her room.

That was the last place she expected to find him. "There you are!" she murmured with a soft laugh. "Were you looking for me—" She stopped short at the expression of stark relief in his eyes when he turned and saw her. He was standing just inside the doorway. The look on his face puzzled her for a moment—but only for a moment.

His eyes flitted quickly from the empty suitcase that sat near the closet door to where she stood in the hallway, and comprehension washed over her in an icy wave. For an instant she refused to believe . . . refused to believe that *he* could believe . . .

"Have you been home long?" she asked in a low voice.

"No." He shook his head and dropped his eyes before the silent accusation in hers. "I just got here."

"I see." Her voice shook with the effort it took to control her anger. "And I suppose the first thing you noticed was that my car was gone."

Ward closed his eyes and swallowed. He didn't bother to answer. She already knew.

"And when you came inside to an empty house, with both Robbie and me gone, you just *assumed* that I . . . that I . . ." Bitterness choked her. She couldn't say the words—she couldn't even *think* them. How *could* he? "I'm surprised you trusted me enough to stay with him all this time!" she flung at him. Anger and hurt combined to wrench the words from her. "Is that why Eileen has been dropping in so often all this week?" she lashed out furiously. "Checking up on me to see that I haven't run off with *your* son?"

"Jenna . . ."

She ignored the hand stretched toward her, the silent plea in his eyes, the despair in his voice. His features were twisted into a dark mask of pain. He made no effort to conceal the agony that lay just beneath the surface. But there was no way Jenna could respond to it then.

"In case you're interested, I took Robbie in to Dr. Reynolds's office this afternoon," she informed him icily. "He may have strep throat." She spun around on her heel.

Ward was beside her in an instant. "Is he all right?"

"He will be," she said flatly, moving past him toward the stairs. "He'll be on antibiotics for a few days, but he'll be fine."

Dinner that night was a grim, silent affair. Robbie ate no more than she and Ward. The pall that hung over the table was like a heavy mist that entrapped the earthly world beneath. Exactly as she was trapped, caught between father and son.

She glanced at where Ward held a pajama-clad Robbie in the living room, rocking him to sleep. Robbie looked up at his father with quiet adoration. Though all she could see of Ward was the back of his head, the loving way he touched the child's cheek and his dark curls was more eloquent than words in describing his feelings for his son.

Her anger melted beneath a rush of sensations so strong they made her feel giddy. There was no denying the charged awareness that sizzled whenever she and Ward were alone together. She could see that now more than ever. He made her feel . . . strange. But it was an exciting feeling, a feeling she had never experienced with Neil. Neil, whom she was supposed to love, but who existed in a dark, shadowy corner of her mind. Not like the flesh and blood man before her.

She wiped her hands on a dish towel. Her eyes lingered on Ward, trying to understand the conflict in her heart, the tumult in her mind. What was wrong with her, she wondered silently. Ward was just a man, a man like any other man. But he wasn't, a voice insisted. He was the father of her child, the child she had nourished within her, given life to. The child she loved now more than ever, who was as much a part of Ward as he was of her. The child they had created together.

The sterile atmosphere in which this small child had been conceived was of little or no consequence. The bond between her and Ward was as constant and unchangeable as the tide that washed upon the shore.

But they were paradoxically tied by the one thing that stood between them.

The thought brought a wealth of sadness in its wake. She couldn't have said how long she stood there, staring at Ward and Robbie, before Ward carried his son upstairs. The next thing she was aware of was a gentle touch on her shoulder. With a gasp she looked up to find Ward standing in front of her.

"Who called?" At her blank look, he frowned. "The phone rang while I was putting Robbie to bed. Didn't you hear it?"

"No. I—I'm sorry. I didn't." Nervously she got a grip on herself and squared her shoulders.

"It doesn't matter," Ward said softly. "Whoever it was will call back."

For a long moment their eyes clung. Hers were dark with uncertainty as she remembered her bitter words to him not so long ago. His weren't quite so easy to read, but she could see a muscle working in his jaw.

"Did I tell you I have to go to Tulsa the week after next?"

Jenna shook her head. As casually as she could, she dropped her gaze and moved past him.

"I was just thinking—" there was a trace of hesitancy in his voice "—maybe before I leave we could go somewhere, just the three of us. Maybe a picnic the Saturday before, if the weather stays warm. There's a place just north of Abilene . . ."

"Just the three of us"? What about the two of them—he and Robbie? Jenna was standing near the dining room table, and her hands gripped the back of one of the chairs so tightly her knuckles showed white. She hated the bitterness that crept into her soul, but she couldn't help it. Only a few short hours ago he had thought she'd kidnapped his son! Was this his way of making amends?

"You will stay, won't you? At least until I get back from Tulsa?"

Despite what had just happened, how could she refuse? Silently she nodded.

"Do you think Robbie will be up to a picnic?"

"I don't see why not, since it's over a week away." Her voice sounded hollow. "His chicken pox are nearly gone, and his throat should be better by then."

"Shall we make it a date, then?"

His tone was light. She didn't have to look around to know that he had moved nearer. She swallowed. "If you like." He was standing next to her, so close she could feel his breath stirring her hair. Simply to have something to do with her hands, she reached for the small paper bag on the dining room table. "What's this?"

"Something for you." There was a slight pause. "I stopped at the candy store on the way home."

Her hand stopped in midair. "For me?"

Ward nodded, his eyes on hers. "Open it."

Hesitantly she reached for the sack. Inside were jelly beans—dozens and dozens of shiny red jelly beans. How had he known— Of course. That day at the ranch. She hadn't thought he'd been listening then. The gesture was silly, sentimental . . . and so sweet. Jelly beans. Blueberry muffins. She felt as if a giant hand were squeezing her heart when she realized that he had done this and then come home to an empty house and believed that . . .

"You'll have to share them with Robbie, I'm afraid. The red ones are his favorite, too."

For a moment she couldn't speak. Her throat tightened as she shook her head, unable to look at him. "You said he'd come around," she whispered.

"And he did, didn't he?" Ward's touch, like his voice, was very gentle as he tucked her hair behind her ear so he could see her face. "You know what they say—like father, like son. In this case, it's like son, like father."

Jenna closed her eyes and turned away. What was he trying to say? She was almost afraid to think about it. Her body trembled. Last night—and now. All the signs were there. She should go home, home before this charade went any further. If she stayed, there would only be more heartache. It was inevitable. She was blind if she couldn't see what was coming.

"Jenna . . ." Strong arms came around her and drew her up against him. Ward could feel the tenseness radiating from her body. He lifted a hand to stroke her hair, over and over again. When he finally felt her relax against him, he closed his eyes and rested his chin against her hair. "I'm sorry, Jenna. God, I'm sorry!"

She stiffened against him, but he held her firm. At his words, all the hurt she'd felt earlier came rushing back. "I thought you trusted me," she whispered brokenly. "How could you think I could actually do that to you . . . to Robbie . . . ?"

He drew her yielding body up closer to his and spoke above her head. "What can I say, Jenna? Somehow I always seem to be apologizing to you. Hurting you is the last thing I want, yet it seems to be what I do best." His voice held such anger, such self-contempt, that she gazed up and saw a face that mirrored her own anguish. "When I arrived home and you weren't here, I panicked. I thought..." He expelled a harsh breath and shook his head. "God knows what I thought." His eyes looked deeply into hers. "If there's any way I can make it up to you ..."

Her eyes misted over with tears. "Hold me, Ward," she pleaded with an ache that penetrated clear to his soul. "Please, just hold me."

He did. There was no force on earth that could have stopped him. He gathered her fiercely against him and held her close to his heart as if he would never let her go. But in spite of his attempt to communicate his regret, her eyes were still dark with pain when he finally tipped her face to his.

Her lashes were long and spiky, wet with tears, before her gaze fell and her eyes were hidden from him again. The curve of her cheek was damp, as well, gleaming in the muted lamplight. But the sight of her soft lips, trembling ever so slightly, tore right into his heart. He caught his breath as his gaze dropped to her mouth.

And he could think of only one way to stop the quivering.

CHAPTER ELEVEN

HIS LIPS WERE WARM, undemanding, and brought such a storm of tenderness rising within Jenna that she almost cried out. With a helpless moan, she twined her arms around his neck and let her body melt into his.

Ward felt something snap inside him the minute she molded herself to him. The cushioned softness of her breasts crushed against his chest was driving him wild, and he yearned to mold her gentle curves to the shape of his hand. He longed to touch every square inch of her delicate skin. With a muffled groan his hands stole down her back, tracing the curves and hollows of her spine. She fitted him perfectly. He knew he should stop, knew he should put her from him that instant and forget he had ever held her in his arms. But she was too soft, too pliant in his arms, and he was like a man starved for the taste of her.

"God, you're sweet," he murmured huskily against her mouth. He gathered her closer still. "So sweet . . ."

A soft sigh emerged from her throat at the feel of tautly muscled thighs against hers. A welter of excitement skidded through her body as the kiss deepened to a heady intimacy. His tongue gently traced the shape of her lips before sliding within. Jenna could feel his heart pounding wildly in a feverish tempo that matched her own.

Her eyes flicked open to stare directly into Ward's. His were smoky with desire and spoke of hunger long denied; his wordless message sent the blood rushing hotly through her veins.

He kissed her again, his body silently communicating his longing. She was almost painfully conscious of the firm swell of arousal pressing into the hollow of her stomach.

His fingers tangled in her hair and he drew back slightly to gaze down at her. The muted lamplight behind him softened the harsh planes and angles of his face, but Jenna was aware that his warm chocolate eyes were smoldering with passion. "I want you," he whispered intensely. "I want you so much."

His hands tightened on her waist, as if he were waiting...as indeed he was. He was giving her the chance to pull away. Now, while there was still time. There was an agony of emotion tossing in her breast as she silently held his gaze, and desire—God, yes, desire!—pounded along her veins in a torrent so strong she felt consumed by it.

"Ward..." She murmured his name in a soft sound of protest. She knew, in some distant corner of her mind, that there were many reasons this shouldn't be happening...and all were forgotten in the storm that followed. Every muscle in Ward's face was taut. He looked as if he'd been carved in stone, and she could sense the control he was exerting over himself. But his eyes...one glimpse of the tightly leashed passion in those smoky brown depths was all she needed. She couldn't fight it any longer. She wanted him, she realized breathlessly, wanted him with an all-consuming passion that left no room for denial. She lifted her hands and drew his face to hers to ease the yearning ache in his eyes. This was the moment she had waited for, wanted without even knowing it, and nothing else mattered.

When next she spoke his name it was a whisper in the dark, a promise in the night. How they came to be in his bedroom, standing next to the huge four-poster, Jenna could never have said. The moon was rising to the east, spilling silvered pools of light through the windows. Ward's face was highlighted as she reached for her, undid the buttons of her blouse and slid the material from her shoulders. Her flimsy lace bra followed, and soon she was naked.

Entranced, she watched as Ward threw his own shirt aside and reached for his belt buckle. When at last he stood as naked as she was, he looked bigger, more powerful than ever before. His sinewy chest was matted with curly dark hair that arrowed downward; his legs were long, supple and strong. Moonbeams gilded his flesh, and she was unable to take her eyes from his stark masculine beauty.

An evening breeze rippled through the sheer lace curtains. She shivered, but it had nothing at all to do with the cool caress of the wind.

"Cold?" Ward's voice was tender. He reached for her, and Jenna met him willingly, eagerly.

"Not anymore," she murmured. With trembling fingers she reached up and smoothed the sensuous curve of his lower lip, loving the feel of his beard-roughened skin beneath her sensitive fingertips.

Ward groaned softly and slid his fingers into her hair, lifting her face to his. Her hair was smooth and silky against the bare satin of her shoulders. In one smooth fluid motion he lifted her and laid her on the bed, smiling tenderly as he joined her.

The smile faded as his gaze roved over her slender body, bathed in moonlight. Never had he seen anything so incredibly beautiful. His throat ached at the sight of her firm ripe breasts with their dusky crowns. He reached out a trembling finger to touch the swelling flesh he worshipped with his eyes.

Jenna thought she would die from sheer pleasure at the feel of his hands on her breasts. A tight ache began to build inside her, swirling and gathering force as he pulled her to him so that their bodies were touching from head to toe and his hands searched out and learned the secrets of her body. His mouth took hers with a searing hunger that amazed as well as pleasured her in a way she had never even dreamed of. She clung to him, exploring, hazily aware that soon there would be no turning back for either of them.

And Ward knew it, too. Desire licked through his veins like a raging inferno. He knew he couldn't hold back much longer. It had been too long, far too long since he'd made love to Meg... *Meg*...

Suddenly he froze.

The seconds ticked by while Ward fought a silent inner battle. But the more he admitted how much he ached to share himself with Jenna, the more his guilt magnified in his mind.

"I can't do this," he muttered hoarsely. His face was buried against the smooth column of her neck. "I can't..."

Jenna glanced at his face...and bit back a cry of pain, a cry of frustration, at the turmoil she saw in his eyes. His body was still hard and warm where it covered hers, but Jenna suddenly felt as if she were bathed in a sheet of ice. And she knew...

She wanted to rage at how unfair it was, but all the pain was tightly capped inside her. She struggled to be free of him, and though he rolled aside, he refused to let her leave the bed. His arm shot out across her waist to hold her pinned to the mattress.

"Let me go, Ward," she cried desperately. "Please . . ." She glanced down at where his bronzed forearm rested across her stomach, but all she could see was her own nudity, stark and glaring. The earlier pleasure she had experienced might never have been. Now she felt ashamed and exposed.

Ward saw the look and gently pulled the sheet up over both of them. He no longer touched her, but his arm still banded her body. "Please, Jenna. Let me explain."

Jenna looked everywhere but at him. The ceiling, the walls, the bureau. Her eyes suddenly riveted on the photograph there, and the room seemed to close in on her. Her breath came jerkily. She was in Megan's house, Megan's bedroom, making love with Megan's husband. *Megan, Megan, Megan.* Her thoughts were wild, disjointed, the name a silent scream that echoed in her mind. And to think she had actually felt guilty about being able to be with Megan's husband and son! She felt hysteria rising up inside her.

Strong hands shook her. "Jenna, for God's sake, don't look like that! It's not the end of the world—for either of us!"

Wasn't it? His world had ended when Meg died. She struggled to choke back the words, realizing she hadn't succeeded when Ward stared down at her, a muscle tightening his jaw.

"You're wrong," he said slowly, taking a deep breath. He reached over and flipped on a lamp. "At one time I did feel I'd lost everything when Meg died. . . ." He hesitated. "But now, more than ever, I know I haven't. . . ." He sat up and ran a hand through his hair. "We need to talk, Jenna," he said quietly. "Clear the air."

Jenna shook her head. She slumped back against the pillows, suddenly drained. "There's no need," she said in a small voice.

Ward made an impatient gesture with one hand. "There's every need. Look, I don't want you thinking it's you—"

"Don't you think I know that?" The words were torn from her. She felt as if her heart were breaking in two. "There's been no one since Meg, has there?"

There was a seemingly endless silence. "No," he said quietly.

Her fingers curled tightly around the sheet. "And there's no one *but* Meg—not for you." She swallowed, wondering how she could speak at all for the pain and misery churning away inside her. "Don't you see, Ward? It wasn't me you wanted to make love to—'' her voice broke treacherously ''—but Meg...*Meg*.''

''I wish it were as simple as that,'' Ward said heavily. He stared across the room. He wanted to say—so many things. But how could he explain what he didn't fully understand himself? ''The thought of making love with my head and not my heart leaves me cold. If it's no more than physical release, it's not love, it's an act. A biological function. In a word—lust,'' he said flatly. The expression in his eyes softened as he looked at her, hating himself for the naked vulnerability in her eyes and knowing he had put it there.

''You're the first woman I've touched since Meg died,'' he said quietly. ''The first woman I've *wanted* to touch.'' He drew a deep, unsteady breath, feeling as if he were baring his soul to her. ''I do want you, Jenna,'' he said fervently. ''I want you so much it scares me. The way you make me feel scares me—'' his voice faltered uncharacteristically ''—because I never thought I'd feel this way again. And—I'm still trying to get used to it.'' His eyes were cloudy with pain. ''But somehow the fact that it *is* you only complicates things even more.''

The emotion in his voice shook her. A part of her rejoiced when he said he wanted her, but the agony in her heart still festered.

''I'll never forget the day at Eileen's when you first saw Robbie again,'' Ward continued. ''And the night you said you didn't give a damn about what my lawyer said—that Robbie was a part of you just as much as he's a part of me. That statement haunted me for days afterward, because I've always thought of him as mine—and Meg's.''

Jenna nearly cried out. Why was he doing this? Couldn't he see how much this was hurting her? Every word he spoke was like salt on an open wound. She turned on her side to hide the torment she knew was reflected on her face, silently praying that he would stop.

But he didn't.

He hesitated, wishing he could see her face. Then he touched the curve of one bare shoulder gently, closing his eyes when she flinched.

''Do you remember that day in Houston when you were pregnant? The day Meg insisted I feel Robbie move inside you?''

Jenna nodded, a barely imperceptible movement of her head on the pillow. How could she forget, she cried silently. He had placed his hand on her abdomen and then snatched it away abruptly. It was as though an invisible glass wall had dropped between them. She had felt his withdrawal then as acutely as she had felt it only moments ago.

"That haunted me for days afterward, as well," she heard him say in a voice she didn't recognize. "It was a shock to see you and know that a part of me was curled up inside you. Then, when I felt Robbie move . . . you were carrying my baby inside you and I felt—I felt it should have been Meg, not you." His voice dropped to a pained whisper. "I was tied to a woman I barely knew in a way I had never been tied to my wife. I wasn't prepared for it, and crazy as it sounds, I felt as if I'd been unfaithful to Meg. I resented you for it. For a while I think I almost hated you, even while I knew I had every reason in the world to be grateful."

Somehow that hurt more than anything. She'd suspected his feelings toward her were far from friendly, but she'd never suspected . . . "Ward, don't . . . don't say any more." She threw off the sheet and reached blindly for her clothes. Her hands shook, but somehow she managed to dress.

But when she would have risen from the bed, she felt Ward's arms go around her from behind. "Jenna, please . . . please." His voice was a throbbing whisper. "I—I have to say this, not only for you but for me. Please listen and try to understand."

On the verge of struggling, she felt herself go slack.

Ward released her, resisting the urge to take her in his arms. He swallowed with difficulty. "When you came back, it was all there again . . . the hurt, the resentment. Because of you, I found myself thinking of Meg, bombarded with a million memories just when all the hurt inside had finally began to go away. But these past few weeks, all that's changed. She's been on my mind less and less and—and that's good." His hand touched her arm gently. "Instead I've found myself thinking of you."

"Good! How can that be good? You feel guilty, Ward. Guilty!" The words were a cry of anguish she could no longer hold inside. "Because of me! How do you think that makes me feel?"

"I *know* how that makes you feel," he said fervently, and this time he did take her into his arms. His heart turned over as, with a muffled cry, she nestled her face against his shoulder.

"And it doesn't make me feel any better to know how much I've hurt you—yet another time." There was a ragged edge to his voice as he slid his fingers through her hair. "I may feel guilty, but it doesn't change how much I want you. And I want you so much it hurts inside."

The rhythmic sound of his heart beating beneath her ear was faintly soothing, somehow giving her a measure of courage. "I'm sorry," she whispered. The hair on his chest prickled her cheek. Her mouth barely moved as she spoke. Then, without her being aware of it, she pressed her lips against the skin stretched tautly over his collarbone.

Ward's fingers stilled in her hair. "Sorry that it happened?"

There was something in his voice that drew her eyes to his. Lines of strain were etched around his nose and mouth, and Jenna couldn't help but feel responsible.

Miserably she nodded.

"Oh, Jenna," he groaned softly. His fingertips stroked gently over her cheekbones, and then he took her face between his hands and looked deeply into shimmering green eyes. "Don't be sorry, because I'm not." At her faintly puzzled look, he went on. "It shouldn't have ended the way it did, but I'm not sorry it happened."

Stunned, she looked at him. "I don't understand. You're tied to the past—"

His hands dropped away from her. "And you're tied to another man." His quiet tone was like a bomb dropping in the stillness of the night, and his eyes, which had darkened momentarily, were suddenly harsh and accusing. "Does that explain what happened here tonight? Does it change anything? No!" He answered the questions with an anger that stunned her. "You don't love him and you know it! If you did, you'd never have let me lay a hand on you—"

"Don't! Don't say anymore!" It was a plea for mercy. Didn't he see what he was doing? Neil...oh, God, was this why she and Neil had never made love? He had pressed her occasionally, but she had always put him off, preferring to wait until they were married, saying she wanted the time to be right, for it to be perfect. What a change that was. How had things turned around so quickly between them?

It *would* have been perfect with Ward. She knew it as surely as night followed day.

The thought was like a knife to her heart. She drew a deep, shuddering breath, devastatingly aware of the warmth radiating from Ward's body. She wished he would move. As if he sensed her thoughts, she saw him from the corner of her eye get up and shrug into a robe. But it didn't make any difference. She still couldn't think with him so close.

The mattress sagged as he sat down next to her. Sitting on the very edge of the bed, her toes curled and bare feet poised on the floor, she looked like a frightened rabbit ready to flee. She had precipitated this entire ungodly situation by coming here. It had been a mistake, a mistake from start to finish. And wasn't this where it ended?

"I can't stay here any longer, Ward," she decided. Her voice was high and tight. "Robbie—Robbie's chicken pox aren't contagious anymore. You could take him back to his babysitter's. I should leave—"

"So you can forget about tonight?"

She swallowed. His voice was sharp and she knew an unwarranted twinge of guilt. There was no need to answer. He already knew.

Ward's eyes narrowed on her ashen face. "I can't forget and neither can you. And I don't want to."

No. She couldn't accept that. They were both tied to the past—he to Meg and she to Robbie—and neither was willing to let go just yet.

"Ward, please—" She could feel what little control she had mustered slipping away from her. "How can you say that when just seconds ago you admitted to feeling guilty about Meg?"

"I can say that because I feel it here." She watched as he touched his hand to his heart. His voice had dropped almost to a whisper. His eyes never left her face. "All I need is a little more time, Jenna. Time to adjust."

"Why? So you can ease your conscience about Meg?" If she did as he asked, what then? She would be leaving soon, anyway. Picturing Ward with Meg, let alone another woman, hurt too much to even think about. Her response was wild and a little panicky. It was her only weapon against the sensual magic of his voice. "Then you'll be totally free again, Ward. A bachelor once more. Free to go where you want, when you want, with whomever you want." The spiteful words had no sooner left her mouth than she wished she could recall them. They simply weren't fair to him. And they weren't worthy of her, either.

A taut silence reigned for a moment. "I didn't have that kind of life before Meg and I were ever married," he said curtly. "I don't want it now." He paused and his voice softened. "Don't leave yet, Jenna. Stay...a little longer. At least until I get back from Tulsa."

Time. He was talking about time, and that was the one thing she'd been trying so hard not to think about—the fact that her time with her son was rapidly drawing to a close. Didn't he know she was living on borrowed time already?

It was a stark reality she couldn't hide from any longer. Still, the thought triggered a burning ache in her breast.

Without being aware of it, she had moved to the doorway. She stood wavering on the threshold, as if that single step into the hallway would take her out of his life.

It was a step she found herself unable to take.

Ward came up behind her and drew her back into a secure embrace, cocooning her with his strength and his warmth. "I don't want you to go yet," he murmured into the dark cloud of her hair. "Please stay, Jenna. Robbie needs you...." He could feel her indecision in the tautness of her body. Did she realize what he was asking? His arms tightened around her; his lips pressed gently against the soft skin of her temple. "*I* need you," he whispered.

Jenna sighed at the ache in his voice. Her hands lifted to tear his arms from where they were nestled around her waist; instead her fingers closed around his muscular forearms, loving the feel of the crisp dark hair beneath her skin, gently gauging the shape and feel of him. He was tense as a thin metal wire, she realized suddenly, and felt her resolve crumble.

Little by little his warmth seeped into her. There was no easy way out, no matter what she did. Would another few days really make any difference? Her mind seized on the thought. A few more days, a few more memories to hoard in her heart for the empty days she knew stretched ahead of her.

And Ward . . . he'd said the thought of making love with his head and not his heart left him cold. Her breath caught in her throat. She would be leaving—*leaving*—and neither one of them could afford to become involved with the other.

But weren't they already involved? Wasn't tonight proof of that?

It was a question she refused to answer. They were both so vulnerable, each in his or her own way. Her shoulders sagged wearily as she gently disengaged herself from his encircling embrace.

"I don't want either one of us hurt anymore," she whispered haltingly. "I think—I still think it would be best if we both put tonight out of our minds and—and go back to the way things were before."

"You'll stay, then?" His eyes, dark and intent, were riveted on her face. Yet there was nothing in his expression to indicate what he was thinking.

She nodded slowly. "I'll stay."

THE DAYS THAT FOLLOWED were like a roller coaster ride for Jenna, full of highs and lows. Each day that Robbie crawled into her arms, his small body warm and sweet-smelling, and she rocked him to sleep, she felt her heart swell with happiness. Sometimes she caught Ward looking at her with a strange light in his eyes, and she sensed some tension in him, but on the whole, he seemed more relaxed than she had ever seen him, and for that she was glad. And though he scarcely touched her, except in the most casual of ways, she was as quiveringly aware of him as she had been that night they had lain together with nothing between them. There was an undeniable warmth in his eyes when they rested on her, a warmth that disturbed her even while it excited and frightened her. Could she hold on until Ward left for Tulsa? She hoped so, because if she didn't leave soon, she was afraid she might do something foolish, something very foolish, indeed.

She tried to counter her riotous emotions by telling herself she would have a lifetime with Neil. But the truth was, she didn't *want* to leave. She wanted to pretend this was a part of her life that could last forever. Yet she was invariably reminded that never again would she hold her sleeping son. Never again would her eyes meet Ward's across the table in silent amusement over something Robbie said or did. *Never.* She would have to bear that terrible finality for the rest of her life.

Jenna was glad for Eileen's company during that time. She dropped in nearly every day, even if it was for a few minutes. It was nice to feel that Ward's sister liked and respected her for herself, and she and Eileen had become fast friends, even though Jenna didn't feel quite comfortable in discussing her feelings about Ward. And much as she hated to admit it, those feelings blossomed with each day that passed. Frank and Eileen had stayed for a few impromptu dinners, and it was obvious that the two shared a very special relationship, a relationship much like her own parents'. They were friends as well as lovers, and she felt a stab of envy. More and more Jenna was beginning to feel that she and Neil could never share that special kind of closeness.

On Thursday, since Robbie was feeling better, Eileen asked Jenna and him to accompany her while she drove into Plains City to run some errands for Frank. Jenna was thankful for the opportunity to stop at a ladies' wear store and add a little to the weekend wardrobe she had brought with her. After coming out of a feed supply store, Eileen suggested they stop in somewhere for lunch. Robbie insisted on sitting next to Jenna in the booth, and Eileen pretended righteous indignation at his decision.

"You're a fickle little man," she accused laughingly, "deserting me like that at the first pretty face that comes along."

Robbie giggled when she reached across the table and tweaked his button nose, but when his squeals turned into shrieks of delight both women looked around in embarrassment and tried to shush him.

"That'll teach me to keep my sexist remarks to myself," Eileen said with a laugh after promising Robbie a chocolate milk shake. She winked at him and added, "You just cost me another dollar, young man."

Jenna eyed her over the menu. "That reminds me. How did the job interview go yesterday?"

Eileen grimaced. Her interview had been with a firm that specialized in school and sports pictures. "What interview?" she said dismally, unable to hide her disappointment. "After I got there, I was politely informed that someone had already been hired for the job and they'd neglected to get in touch with me." She frowned into her coffee cup. "I've been thinking about checking with a few photo processing labs in Abilene."

"That's not really what you want, though, is it?"

"Not really," Eileen said with a shrug. "But it's a start."

"Have you ever thought of opening your own studio? Children's pictures, family portraits, that kind of thing?"

Eileen nodded. "I might yet," she admitted. "And I wouldn't mind that, but actually I'd like a little variety." She smiled rather wanly and picked up her napkin when the waitress delivered their sandwiches. "Pretty picky for a lady who doesn't even have a job yet, huh?"

"You've only been looking for a few weeks," Jenna pointed out.

"In other words, don't give up yet."

"Exactly." She smiled a little at Eileen's glum expression. "I'm sure it's only a matter of time."

"Actually, I like doing candid shots. Catching people by surprise, that sort of thing." She grinned a little sheepishly. "Tim and Katie always hated that, but I loved it."

"Too bad this isn't New York or Los Angeles." Jenna reached over and poured a generous amount of catsup near Robbie's French fries. "You could work for one of those scandal sheets."

Robbie's eyelids were drooping heavily by the time they finished lunch and walked out to Eileen's station wagon. As Jenna fastened the seat belts around herself and Robbie, her engagement ring caught the sunlight.

Her eyes rested on it briefly. She had adored the ring when she and Neil had picked it out, but the jewel's flash in the midday sun suddenly seemed cold and artificial. She couldn't help but recall the conversation she and Eileen had had the previous week when she'd learned of Jenna's marriage, now a mere three weeks away. Jenna hadn't been the blushing bride-to-be Eileen seemed to expect then any more than she was now. And perhaps it was time she stopped lying to herself.

In three weeks' time she wasn't sure she would be a bride at all.

CHAPTER TWELVE

THE SATURDAY MORNING before Ward was to leave for Tulsa, Jenna found him in the kitchen, standing over the stove.

"Chicken? For breakfast?" She peered at the contents of the frying pan and raised her eyebrows. "You and my dad would make a fine pair," she commented tongue in cheek. "He likes catsup with his pancakes."

"And I like catsup with grilled cheese sandwiches." He grinned over his shoulder at her, then glanced over her approvingly. "But this isn't for breakfast. It's for lunch." And he nodded at the table, where a large picnic hamper sat.

"Lunch?" she echoed blankly.

"You forgot, didn't you?"

"Forgot?" She searched her mind frantically, then laughed a little sheepishly. "I guess I did."

Ward began to transfer golden brown chicken legs and breasts from the pan to a platter. "We," he asserted, "are going on a picnic. Unless the idea of a day out doesn't appeal to you?" He studied her questioningly.

The oddly tender light in his eyes incited a kind of restlessness deep in her body, but instead of ignoring the insidious warmth inside her, she found herself responding to it. "I can't think of anything I'd like better," she answered softly. "I'm sure it will be a day to remember."

That brief exchange seemed to set the mood for the day.

It was late in the morning by the time they loaded the Blazer with the hamper, cooler and blankets and settled Robbie in the car seat between them. The weather was bright and sunny, with just enough of a crisp October bite in the air for Jenna to decide to throw in light jackets for all of them at the last minute.

As they sped along in the Blazer, all the tension and dark thoughts of the past weeks seemed to drift away. She gazed appreciatively at the pastoral landscape just outside the win-

dow. A coat of burnished gold covered the hills, and herds of
cattle grazed peacefully beneath the noonday sun. Jenna knew
the picnic was only a temporary reprieve from the dismal days
that would follow when she left next week, but with her son
beside her—and yes, Ward, as well—*especially* with Ward—she
was determined to enjoy the day to the fullest.

There were several other cars in the small parking area Ward
pulled in to, but the park was quiet and so peaceful that she felt
a measure of tranquillity steal into her soul. Ward had no
sooner set Robbie on his feet than a pair of squirrels emerged
from behind the trunk of a huge oak tree. Robbie was after
them like a flash of lightning. His chubby legs pumped furiously in an effort to catch them, and Jenna laughed at his for-
lorn expression when the squirrels quickly scurried up the tree
and scampered across an outstretched branch to stare down at
him, their bushy tails madly whipping the air.

They ate their lunch on an outspread blanket beneath a towering cottonwood tree. Replete from the salad, chicken and
crusty bread Ward had packed, Jenna leaned back on her elbows and watched as an eagle looped gracefully through the
vivid blue sky until it seemed no more than a lone speck in the
distant ceiling overhead.

"Ducks, Daddy! Look!" Robbie called in high-pitched excitement. He pointed and began to run as fast as his legs could
carry him.

Both Jenna and Ward followed. There was a small pond at
the bottom of a gently sloping hill, its glasslike surface glinting silver in the sunlight. Trees and wildflowers lined its edges,
and Ward caught up with Robbie just as he was about to plunge
headlong into the water after the ducks, who were halfway
across the pond by now.

"Oh, no, you don't, young man," he emphasized firmly.
Swinging Robbie high in his arms, Ward leveled a stern look at
his small son. "You can watch from here as long as Daddy or
Jenna is with you, but you are not to go into the water."

"It's a good thing you remembered to bring along an extra
set of clothes," she murmured. There was a flicker of concern
in her eyes, however. Children as young as Robbie knew no
fear, and she shivered a little as she looked at the deceptively
smooth surface of the pond. It was impossible to tell how deep
it was, but then, it wouldn't have to be deep at all for a child as
small as Robbie to invite trouble.

Ward cocked an eyebrow at her. "That was one of the very first rules I learned as a single parent. Never go anywhere without at least one change of clothing."

He sounded so nonchalant, almost blasé, that Jenna found herself looking for the now familiar darkening of his expression, or perhaps a flicker of pain in his eyes. Granted, no mention of Meg had been made, but she still half expected it. Instead she found herself on the other end of a gaze so warm and affectionate she felt as if a hundred tiny fireworks had just exploded in her veins.

She hurriedly dropped her eyes. "I wonder if there's anything left over from lunch we could feed the ducks," she muttered. "I think I'll see."

When she returned, Robbie was standing by the water's edge, though Ward had crouched to curve a protective arm around him. Ward looked up when a crackle of twigs announced her presence.

"Find anything?"

She held out a small sack. "Just some bread crusts and the popcorn we were saving for later."

"Popcorn?" He raised both eyebrows.

Jenna laughed. "If ducks are at all like sea gulls, they'll eat anything."

She smiled to herself over his skeptical look and moved closer, watching as he gave a few of the crusts to Robbie. There were six ducks in all, and they were apparently used to being fed. The water rippled as they swam toward Robbie, who laughed delightedly when they began to gobble up the pieces he eagerly threw out one by one.

Ward wandered a few yards away and, apparently on a whim, threw out some of the popcorn from the bag he still held. One duck swam toward him, wasting no time in swallowing all the kernels.

He rolled his eyes heavenward as Jenna flashed a triumphant grin. "There's no accounting for taste," he said with a shake of his head.

"That's exactly what I thought this morning when you told me you liked catsup with grilled cheese sandwiches," she retorted promptly. She nodded toward the duck that had separated itself from the others, its tail feathers wagging prettily as it seemed to wait for another treat. "I'll bet that's a female."

Ward grinned over at her. ''I guess I'm the kind of person that dogs and children adore.''

''And ducks,'' Jenna added dryly. Her eyes dropped meaningfully to the first duck, who had been joined by the rest of the flock, apparently deserting Robbie's bread crusts for Ward's popcorn.

Ward's eyes twinkled. ''Maybe it's my cologne.'' Robbie scowled indignantly when his newfound friends scuttled away, but promptly joined his father and dug a small hand into the bag to come up with a fistful of popcorn.

When the ducks' appetites were more than satisfied, Jenna took Robbie over to a small play area near the spot where they had picnicked. His back propped against a rough tree trunk, Ward watched while Jenna pushed Robbie on the swings and merry-go-round. The sound of their mingled laughter drifted to his ears as the pair came sailing down the slide together, Robbie perched on her outstretched legs.

Not for the first time, he was struck by how warm, how patient, how loving she was with Robbie. Yet this time was different. He felt he was seeing her—and his world, as well—in a different light, unclouded by the doubt and uncertainty that had colored his perception for so long. She was an immensely sensitive woman whose capacity for love made her vulnerable—as he had learned for himself.

Leaving her son wasn't going to be easy for her. He felt a stab of pain in knowing the anguish it would cause her. Nor did he want her to leave. She had stayed because he had asked. Because he needed her. And he did, God knows he did. She had brought so much into his life, made him feel as if he were slowly gaining back a part of himself he had lost.

He remembered how he'd felt the night Robbie was sick with strep throat, the night he'd come home and they were gone. He'd been afraid, yes—but underpinning that fear was something else, something that had nothing to do with Robbie. Jenna had brought light where before there had only been darkness, and he didn't want to think about how empty his life would be when she left. His hand clenched as he thought of her fiancé. She didn't love him. She didn't. Otherwise she couldn't have stayed in Plains City so long.

His eyes softened as they rested on her. The sun caught the reddish highlights in her hair as she flipped it back over her shoulder with a careless hand. He remembered its silky texture when he had run his hands through it, and the warmth of her skin beneath his fingertips, and the taste of her mouth under his. A shudder of longing wracked his body, but he knew that desire was only part of what he felt for her.

"Is that your little boy over there?"

The voice startled him from his thoughts. Ward looked up to find a woman standing before him. A little girl of perhaps five held her hand. He recalled having seen them in the playground with Jenna and Robbie.

"Yes, he's mine," he said with a nod. There was a flash of pride in his eyes as they rested on his son.

The woman laughed. "It wasn't hard to figure out who he belonged to." Her gaze sharpened for a moment on his face. Then she nodded toward the playground. "Although I think he favors his mother a little more."

Ward smiled. "I think you're right. He definitely has her eyes."

It wasn't until the woman had wandered off again that he realized what he had said, and more, comprehended the scope of his thoughts. For the first time, he had let himself think of Jenna as Robbie's mother, and it hadn't hurt at all. In fact, quite the opposite. He felt something soar free and easy within him.

"His mother," he said aloud, as if testing the words. "Robbie's mother." He felt his lips curve upward. "My son's mother—*our* son." He hoped no one was listening to his muttering—they'd think he was crazy.

As it happened, Jenna dropped down on the blanket just seconds later, winded from running with Robbie as he chased the bright yellow ball he'd brought along. "What's so funny?"

"Wouldn't you like to know." Ward's eyes, warm and intense, lingered on her face before he impulsively bent over to brush his mouth lightly across hers. The kiss was brief and sweet, tender with just a hint of passion. Her heart fluttered like the wings of a butterfly, and she thought she almost felt it skip a beat.

A warm flush tinted her cheeks as Ward chuckled. His eyes dropped meaningfully to where her breasts heaved beneath the thin cotton fabric of her pale blue shirt. "Because of me, or our son?"

Our son. This time her heart did skip a beat; she was sure of it. "Robbie, of course," she murmured breathlessly. "Just remember, your turn's next."

"Of course," he echoed somberly, an almost wicked glint in his eyes. Then he laughed. "I'm used to the way he wears me out. That's why I'm letting him run you ragged for a change."

"That's big of you," she grumbled good-naturedly. Sitting cross-legged on the blanket, she propped her shoulder against the tree trunk. Suddenly very glad they had come, she breathed in deeply of the crisp, clean air, drinking in the sights and sounds around her. She chuckled as Robbie ran in raucous circles around the blanket. "Where does he get all his energy? Although I guess that's a silly question when he's been cooped up inside for so long with chicken pox and strep throat."

Aware of the two pairs of adult eyes that followed his every move, Robbie's antics grew more winsome by the moment. "And what would he do without his adoring public?" Ward murmured, grinning. He glanced at Jenna, who responded with a brilliant smile then again turned her rapt attention to Robbie, who was now intent on somersaulting across the emerald field of grass. Ward's heart swelled at her tender expression and the look of sheer pleasure on her face, but there was a poignant longing in her eyes, as well, that tore into his soul.

They had come such a long way in the past three weeks, he thought to himself, suddenly overwhelmed by the feeling of closeness, the feeling of togetherness, the undeniable knowledge that the three of them were so right together. He reached out a hand and laced his fingers through hers, breathing a sigh when she didn't draw back as he half expected her to. Instead she smiled a little shyly, he thought, as he rested their clasped hands upon his denim-covered thigh.

Tiring at last, Robbie finally came over and sat between them, and it wasn't long before he was sound asleep, his head pillowed on Jenna's lap. From the direction of the pond he could hear frogs croaking throatily and the steady drone of crickets nearby. Slanting afternoon sunlight enhanced the faint yellowing of the trees and proclaimed the coming of autumn. The pond reflected the golden color of the surrounding landscape.

She lifted her head, letting the utter peace and tranquillity of the setting fill her senses and her being. But it wasn't so much the place as the company that filled her with contentment.

Company? She smiled to herself. It was perhaps an odd word to apply to her son and her son's father. A rush of pleasure swept through her. She could hardly believe that Ward had actually called Robbie *their* son. The comment inexplicably filled her with happiness, and she wanted to pinch herself to see if she was dreaming.

But the warmth of Ward's hand tightly enfolding her own was real, as was the pressure of Robbie's head on her legs. Jenna slipped her fingers through his tousled dark curls, marveling as she had so often at how long and dark his eyelashes were against his flushed cheeks. A feeling of love, sweet and pure, bubbled up inside her.

Aware of Ward's eyes on her, she finally looked up. "It's beautiful here," she murmured. "Did you come here often with Meg?" Too late she realized what she had said. Her breath suddenly stopped for fear of shattering the mantle of contentment and companionship that had settled over them.

Ward was silent for so long that she began to think this was exactly what had happened. But then he turned his head slowly to look at her. "It's funny you should say that," he remarked, "because this is the first time I've come here since she died."

Jenna was almost afraid to look at him. But there was no animosity in his expression, nor were his eyes shadowed with pain, as she had expected.

His hand tightened almost imperceptibly around her hers. "Jenna—" he spoke in a very low voice "—would you mind if we talked about her for a while?"

Her. There could be no doubt who he meant. For a wild, panicky moment, she almost refused. She had wanted to know for so long, but understanding the heartache it would cause him, how could she make him discuss Meg? Then she remembered Eileen's having said that Ward never talked about Meg to anyone, not even her.

"Why, Ward?" she asked, unable to prevent either the words or the faint catch in her voice. "Why now?"

Squirrels chattered in the branches high above. A breeze whispered through the trees. "You were right, Jenna," he said softly. "I've been tied to the past. But now... maybe it's time to close the door...."

"It may not work, Ward. Believe me, I know." She swallowed the ache in her throat. For three and a half years she had tried to banish the memory of her son. And she had never succeeded. But now...now she didn't *want* to. "Memories are precious," she said unsteadily. "Don't let them go. Don't let anyone take them away from you, not when they're all you have."

He was quiet for a time. "Perhaps that was a poor choice of words. What I'm trying to say is that I think it's time I stopped dwelling in the past. It's time I went on with my life." He paused. "It's what Meg would have wanted," he finished softly. His fingertips grazed her chin, and he looked deeply into her eyes. "I want to tell you, Jenna. Please."

Something in his quiet entreaty made her hurt inside, even while she fought an inner battle. Suddenly she didn't want to hear how much Ward loved Meg, how he would love her forever despite his avowal to go on with his life. Her lungs burned with the effort it took to control her own selfish longings, but she sensed that his need to purge himself was as strong as her instinct to protect her own emotions.

Her fingers tightened around his as she silently gave him her answer.

The quiet was marred only by the sound of his voice as he talked. And talked. Once he started, he couldn't seem to stop. And Jenna thought despairingly that she'd been right, after all. Ward was purging himself. Much of what he said she had already learned from Eileen. That he and Meg had grown up together, had been childhood sweethearts.

But wisely she said nothing. She only listened, or tried to, with her head and not her heart.

She almost lost control when he spoke of the day she died.

"It was such a shock." He shook his head as if he still couldn't believe it. "I thought she was a little pale, but I never dreamed... Then when I came home—" His words trailed off, and it was a very long time before he could speak again. When he did, his voice was low and tense, seemingly ready to crack. "I knew right away something was wrong. Robbie was wet, crying hysterically.... Meg was lying on the floor, unconscious. I felt..." His eyes closed and his tone was almost violent. "God, I've never felt so helpless in my life! I called an ambulance, but somehow even then I knew... By morning—" he paused, faltering "—by morning she was gone."

The silence that followed seemed like the deadly calm before the storm. Before Jenna could say a word, Ward's eyes opened, two pools of darkness. "She was pregnant, Jenna. Pregnant!'' He had almost spit the word. ''Ironic, isn't it,'' he said, his mouth twisting bitterly, ''that the very thing she wanted for so long should end up killing her. We'd been told by countless doctors that she could never even hope to conceive. And she didn't even know.''

Jenna's mind whirled. *Pregnant! But how . . . ?* Comprehension suddenly dawned. *A tubal pregnancy . . . She hemorrhaged. . . .* Jenna was almost afraid to speak because of the bitterness etched across Ward's features. ''You didn't know, either, did you?'' she whispered. ''Until . . . later.''

Ward nodded.

Unthinkingly she wrapped her other hand around his. Tubal pregnancies are dangerous and difficult to diagnose. She recalled a few cases. The problem is that unless they are diagnosed very early, the enlarging egg can rupture the fallopian tube and the patient will likely hemorrhage. And that was apparently what had happened to Meg.

In the same instant, another realization swept through her. ''You blamed yourself, didn't you? You felt responsible because she was pregnant.''

His mouth was a grim slash on his face. ''I *was* responsible. She hadn't been feeling well. She was pale and she'd been having some abdominal pain. I tried to get her to go see a doctor, but she thought it was just a flu bug.'' He inhaled deeply. ''I guess I didn't try hard enough.''

Jenna shook her head, her eyes beseeching. ''You couldn't have known. No one could have. You can't continue to take the blame for something you had no control over.''

After a long time he said quietly, ''I suppose you're right.'' He leaned his head back wearily against the tree trunk, and Jenna's heart went out to him. She would have given anything to be able to take his pain as her own, to erase all the heartache and months of unhappiness. She felt helpless, as helpless as Ward must have felt when he'd lost Megan.

But all she could do was murmur tremulously. ''I wish there were something I could say. . . .''

Ward's face suddenly softened. ''You don't have to say anything. Just the fact that you're here with me is enough.'' He turned his head to look at her and groaned at the glistening emerald of her eyes. ''Oh, God, Jenna, I've done it again. You said this would be a day to remember, but I don't want it to be because I've made you cry again.'' He lifted a hand to brush the dampness from her cheeks, but at the delicacy of her skin beneath his knuckles, he felt something give way deep inside him. Slipping his hand beneath the silken fall of her hair, he tugged her gently forward.

Their lips met with the lightness of a feather, the caress so gentle and sweet that Jenna felt another tear slip from beneath her closed eyelashes. Yet the tear she shed wasn't only for Ward, but for herself—part for the anguish he had suffered and part for the gift he had just given her without even being aware of it. Her heart threatened to burst with tenderness for this man as she realized how special the day really was. Ward had trusted her, trusted her with a part of him that he had shared with no one, not even his sister. With a sigh, she looped her arms around his neck and gave herself over to the moment.

"Are you guys gonna get married?"

They drew apart as if they'd been burned, both glancing down at the same time. Jenna looked embarrassed, while Ward's eyes lighted with amusement, and Robbie looked utterly delighted as he stared up at the two adults.

"That was a very short nap, young man." Ward reached for his son just as Robbie bounded up. He ruffled the little boy's hair, then stood up. Robbie's gleeful laughter filled the air as he was tossed skyward several times and caught in Ward's strong hands. Holding the youngster securely in one arm, he turned to look down at Jenna.

With the blazing sun at his back, his dark hair appealingly tousled by the wind and a smile softening his craggy features, he made a very captivating picture. Jenna felt her heart surge with a heady, powerful emotion as her eyes traveled from father to son.

She had loved Robbie even before she had met him, loved him without knowing him. And now that she did, she loved him for the sweet, bubbly child that he was. She loved him because he was a part of her...and she loved him even more because he was a part of Ward.

She took the hand Ward extended and let him pull her up. For a moment, the three of them were linked. A feeling of infinite tenderness welled up inside her. She had once thought she would never be a part of the closely knit circle between father and son, but at that moment she was.

She heaved a lonely sigh. For beyond these precious few days in her life, a family was the one thing the three of them could never be.

THE COMBINATION of fresh air, sunshine and Robbie's short nap made for a very sleepy little boy later that evening. It was shortly after seven when Jenna did up the final snap of his pajamas. Noting how short the sleeves were becoming, she glanced at Ward, who was busy gathering the discarded clothing. "He's going to need new pajamas soon," she said, lifting Robbie's sturdy body into bed. "It won't be long before these are outgrown."

Good-night kisses were given and Robbie was tucked into bed, and he was asleep almost before his head touched the pillow. "He's going to be tall," Ward said, drawing Jenna into the hall and quietly closing the door behind them. He lifted a hand and tucked a long strand of hair behind her ear. "Were your parents tall?"

Jenna had thought the same of Robbie many times before—between her and Ward, she didn't see how Robbie could avoid it. But the words, coming from Ward, as well as the pleasantly rough feel of his fingertips as they grazed her cheek, were strangely intimate. "My natural parents, you mean?" she asked softly. When he nodded, she shook her head. "I really couldn't say."

"I suppose not." A thoughtful frown creased his forehead. "You probably don't remember much about them."

Jenna nodded. "All I really remember is a man and a woman with dark hair and being held close in someone's arms." She paused and added with a fleeting smile, "A feeling of being warm and cosseted, a feeling of belonging." *A feeling much like what she had felt today.*

"It's probably just as well," he murmured—a little absentmindedly, she thought, "that you remember only the good things."

They had moved toward the stairway, and he halted at the landing.

"It just occurred to me," he said slowly, "that I've never said thank-you for my son."

Jenna stood motionless, scarcely able to breathe from the lethargy that suddenly invaded her limbs. The last faint em-

bers of the sun drifted in through the stained glass window
above the stairs, subduing Ward's sharply angled features and
making her achingly aware of the softness in his eyes. She was
almost unbearably conscious of the warm weight of his hand
resting on her shoulder.

She moistened her lips. "There's no need," she murmured
breathlessly.

"There's every need." The quiet intensity of his voice
stunned her. "I don't know how I'd have made it through this
past year without him. And I'm beginning to wonder how I
ever got along without you." There was something faintly
alarming in his last statement, but for the life of her, she
couldn't think what it was. All she could do was stare at him
at the oddly humble expression in his eyes. "Thank you, Jenna.
From the bottom of my heart, thank you."

He bent his head and kissed her, a kiss as gentle as a light
summer breeze on a warm moonlit night. Jenna was touched
beyond words at the profound emotion in his voice. When he
lifted his head, she looked up at him with shining eyes. A lump
began to swell in her throat. "Oh, Ward," she whispered, "you
make me feel so...so proud. And yet I almost feel as if I don't
deserve this." Her voice trembled. She turned her head ever so
slightly and pressed her lips against his palm where it lay cradled against her cheek.

At the feel of her lips against his skin, any thought of restraint that Ward might have entertained fled like dust before
the wind. He simply wasn't capable of holding back any longer.
He wanted to hold her, protect her, touch her and claim her for
his own. He ached for her, ached with a longing he had never
known before. His fingers wandered over her mouth and the
curve of her cheek before he tipped her face to his. For an endless moment he held her gaze, unable to believe the emerald
flame glowing in her eyes.

With a groan that was part joy, part relief, he folded her into
his arms, glorying in the feel of her yielding softness, in the intoxicating scent of her hair and skin, the way she clung to him
as if she would never let him go.

And that was exactly how Jenna felt. Her lips parted without any urging from his and she knew a moment of nearly un-
controllable joy at the tenderness of his touch. She couldn't
hide from herself any longer; she couldn't hide her feelings
from Ward, either, and she didn't want to. All her pent-up re-

ponses to him rose to the surface and blocked out all else. She
had never felt closer to him, never felt more a part of him, than
at this moment, and she longed to share herself completely and
utterly.

Ward's arms dragged her closer yet, stroking the tender line
of her back. Jenna gave herself up to the fiery urgency of his
mouth, of his hands as they caressed her.

His breathing was as ragged as her own when he finally lifted
his head. "Oh, Jenna—" he whispered her name "—I want
you so much...I don't think I can stand much more of this."

His expression was so tortured she knew only that she had to
find a way to erase it. "Then make love to me, Ward," she insisted recklessly. Her fingers smoothed the lines beside his
mouth. "Make love to me now."

For a timeless moment their eyes locked. Wordless mes-
sages passed between them, communicating the depth of their
need, the longing neither could contain any longer.

A feeling of heady excitement raced through her when he silently took her hand and led her down the hall. It wasn't until
they were standing in the bedroom, Ward's room, that reality
came crashing down around her. She couldn't help but remember that other painful night when they had almost... Meg
had come between them then. Would it happen again? And if
it didn't, would Ward be subconsciously thinking of her? Perhaps even pretending she was Meg?

Ward caught her by the shoulders just as she was ready to
whirl and run from the room. In the shadow of the lamp that
glowed dimly in the corner, he could see the fear in her eyes.

And he, better than anyone, knew what caused it.

Jenna's breath came jerkily. "Not here," she muttered,
vaguely aware she probably wasn't making any sense. "Please
not here."

Ward's arms slid down and pulled her taut unyielding body
up against his. His hand slid soothingly up and down her back
until he felt her relax against him. With a finger under her chin,
he guided her eyes to his.

"It has to be here, Jenna," he said quietly. "Not just for me,
not just for you, but for both of us. It's time to let go. You
showed me that."

"I—I don't want any ghosts between us." Her eyes were
cloudy, never wavering from his.

His fingers slid with lingering gentleness down her throat. "There won't be," he promised gently. "You were so right when you said that memories are precious," he said softly. "Let's make our own magic, Jenna. Let's make our own memories." His arms tightened around her. "I've brought you so much pain, Jenna. Let me bring you something else. Let me bring you pleasure."

Suddenly that was all that she wanted, too. Blindly her mouth sought his, and in seconds the kiss deepened to quench a ravenous thirst that consumed them both. Clothes were a barrier that neither would tolerate, yet Ward's touch was incredibly gentle as he undressed her. He seemed totally entranced when at last he gazed at her slender bared body in all its glory, and Jenna felt near to bursting with emotion. His eyes slid over her with heated intensity, kindling a warmth that spiraled like wildfire through her body.

Her fingers trembled as she slipped his shirt from his shoulders and undid the clasp of his belt. Her heart beat thunderously when she drew her to him on the bed with nothing between them but heated flesh. At first Ward only kissed her, but deeply, longingly, as if he couldn't get enough of her. The endless, drugging kisses sent her pulse spinning madly and she reached for him, digging her fingers into the taut muscles of his shoulders.

He seemed to know instinctively what would please her the most. Jenna moaned, gratified, when his mouth finally closed over the throbbing nipple of her breast, his tongue swirling hotly around first one aroused peak and then the other. A welter of excitement whirled inside her as his hands and mouth caressed and explored every inch of her skin until she was on fire for him.

It wasn't until she caught a glimpse of his eyes, dark and burning, that she realized how much he was holding back. Wanting desperately to drive him wild with the same searing pleasure he was giving her, her hands moved restlessly over his body. Her hands glided across the fluid contours of his back and her fingers slid around to the lean planes of his abdomen, loving the silky feel of the dark hair that matted his chest.

But when his hands feathered over the inside of her thigh, the gnawing ache deep inside cried out for him to possess her. And somehow Ward knew it, too.

"Look at me, Jenna."

His compelling tone blended with the mesmerizing touch of his hands. Helplessly she lifted her eyes to his, knowing her own reflected all the yearning and hunger she felt for him. The tenderness she saw there only intensified her longing to feel their bodies joined together as one.

"I've dreamed of seeing your face at this moment," he whispered raggedly against her cheek, then raised his head to look at her. "Let me see you...now."

And Jenna held nothing back as his legs parted hers. She cried out her joy when, with a surge of power, she at last received the bold strength of his essence, mindless of everything but him and knowing that nothing on earth had ever seemed so right. Sensation after exquisite sensation rippled through her as she found herself caught in a wave of spiraling delight that carried her ever higher. Together in mind, body and spirit, they soared, stealing out and away to a realm of glory that knew no bounds.

Long minutes later, weak, satiated and overwhelmed by lethargy, Jenna was swept by a wave of utter peace and she sighed. A pair of hard male arms tightened around her, and warm lips brushed fleetingly against hers. Ward turned her on her side and drew her back into the warmth and security of his embrace.

"I don't know why I fought against this so long," she murmured sleepily against his chest.

Ward pressed a fleeting kiss on her mouth. "Neither do I," he whispered, smoothing an idle pattern down her spine.

Through half-closed eyes she gazed up at him. There was a lazy half smile on his face, a glimmer in his eyes, a glimmer she had never before seen. But Jenna was simply too tired to be capable of analyzing either that or the experience that had shaken her so deeply.

Tomorrow. There would be time tomorrow. For now, all she wanted was sleep. With a sigh of contentment, she burrowed her face in Ward's shoulder and let slumber overtake her.

CHAPTER THIRTEEN

JENNA AWOKE to the sound of a heartbeat drumming steadil beneath her ear and a sense of being uncommonly warm Caught in a world halfway between sleep and wakefulness, sh was for a moment incapable of orienting herself to her sur roundings. She began to stretch, and found one slender leg in timately tangled between a pair of hard male thighs. Everythin came back to her in a shattering rush of awareness. She ha made love with Ward. *Ward.*

With absolutely no thought of Neil.

Her mind swam dizzily. She turned her head to where War still slept peacefully beside her, his hair dark and tousled again: the pillowcase. A wave of guilt swept through her. How coul she have been so foolish as to allow things to go so far? Wha had she done?

Ward chose that moment to finally waken. Stark surprise wa registered in the sleepy brown gaze that met hers, and for a instant Jenna suspected he was just as confused, just as wai as she.

"Good morning," he murmured. His eyes flitted away, onl to return again almost immediately. "Are you—okay?"

Almost unbearably conscious of the naked male body so nea to hers, Jenna was feeling embarrassment enough for both c them. Yet at Ward's tentative question, a little of her shyne: crept away, along with all thoughts of Neil.

She nodded faintly, unable to take her eyes from him. Ward hair was mussed from sleep, and his jaw was dark with a night growth of beard, but Jenna felt every nerve ending in her boc quiver to life. "You need to shave," she finally blurted out.

Ward rubbed a hand over the bristly line of his jaw. ' know." His smile was a little sheepish as he propped himself c his elbows to look down at her. He seemed to hesitate. The: as if compelled, he slowly leaned over to touch his lips ever s ghtly to hers. When he lifted his head, he glanced over at the ock—the hands pointed to nearly eight-thirty—then back to er.

"You slept late." His words were accompanied by the gentle ouch of his fingers brushing her cheek. "Big day yesterday?"

Jenna felt herself go weak from his kiss. She couldn't help ut respond to the hint of amusement in his voice. "No." She aused, then added very softly, "Big night."

Ward's smile deepened. "I know the feeling." Leaning over, e kissed the tip of her nose, his expression warm and more ender than she'd ever seen it. "Jenna, last night . . . I can't tell ou what it meant to me."

Her self-consciousness vanished at his declaration, and she hispered, "Oh, I think I do know." Her hand drifted up to radle his lean cheek. Suddenly it seemed the most natural thing the world to be lying there with him, reveling in the heat of is body next to her own. It seemed just as natural to lift her ead and rain gentle kisses on his jaw and mouth. She felt omething blossom and grow inside her when she sensed his lips miling beneath hers. As she deepened the kiss, his mouth pened to accommodate the gentle glide of her tongue. Her eart jumped erratically, and she wanted nothing more than to ose herself to the heightened impatience already claiming them oth.

"God, Jenna." Ward's breath came raggedly and his arms ocked around her as he pulled her above him. Jenna's eyes rew smoky with passion as she felt the burgeoning heat of his rousal nudging her belly. She sighed with delight . . . and heard mall feet hit the floor with a thud at the same instant.

"Robbie!" she gasped.

For an instant Ward's arms stayed tightly around her. Then, ith a resigned sigh, he put her from him and sat up. "Much s I hate to say this," he muttered, running a hand through his ousled hair, "there are some definite disadvantages to having three-year-old in the house on a lazy Sunday morning."

Jenna couldn't have agreed more, though she didn't say so loud. The tiny voice of reason inside told her that Robbie's ming couldn't have been better. Clutching the sheet to her reasts, she sat up and swung her legs over the side of the bed, fraid that Robbie would soon make an appearance in Ward's edroom.

"I—I think I'll head for the shower." To her utter embar
rassment, her voice wobbled a little, and she felt a rare blus
appearing at the sound of a soft masculine chuckle behind her

She fled toward the bathroom while she still had the chance
It wasn't until she was safely in her own room again, a towe
wrapped turban-style around her still damp hair, that she re
alized she had relegated Ward to yet another cold shower.

A slight grin edged her lips as she pulled the towel from he
hair. She could still feel the imprint of his body on hers.

BOTH JENNA'S and Ward's warm, buoyant mood persiste
throughout the day. She marveled that she had grown so clos
to him in so short a time, and knew a sense of sheer, unadu
terated bliss that he seemed to feel the same. How many time
he touched her that day, smoothed her hair away from her face
dropped a fleeting kiss on her cheek or lips, or simply sent
speaking glance across the room, she couldn't have said. Sh
knew only that he made her feel giddy, alive and so full of jo
she felt she would burst.

She should have known her newfound happiness was simpl
too good to be true.

With the evening dinner dishes done, she wiped her hands o
a dish towel and gazed out the kitchen window. Robbie wa
busily playing in the sandbox, and Ward was in the barn, tir
kering with the engine of the Cessna in preparation for his tri
to Tulsa tomorrow. Her smile faded for the first time that day
She would miss him—miss him terribly, she knew—but to thin
about that would mean that she would also have to face up t
what would come after his return home. And that was some
thing she wasn't yet ready to do.

Squaring her shoulders, she pasted the smile firmly back i
place and decided to check on Robbie and Ward. She had n
sooner stepped out the back screen door than she heard th
doorbell ring. The insistent peal was heard again just as sh
backtracked and reached the dining room.

"Coming!" she yelled, shaking her head and wondering wh
the impatient caller was. But her welcoming smile faded whe
she opened the door.

"Neil!" she gasped. "Wh-what are you doing here?"

"I could ask you the same thing!" he snapped. He brushed by her and closed the door, his eyes sweeping around the empty living room. "Are you alone?"

Still stunned by his appearance, she could only nod. He moved into the room, and Jenna eyed him, suddenly very uncomfortable. He looked tired, a little disheveled—and very angry.

She wet her lips nervously. "I had no idea you were coming. You haven't called—"

"Because all we do is argue," he cut in. "And I had the feeling I'd be waiting forever if I waited for you to call."

Jenna frowned. "That's not true, Neil."

"Isn't it? In case you've forgotten, we *are* engaged!"

His sharp tone made her wince, and she sat down heavily on the sofa. "No, I haven't forgotten," she said in a low voice. And she hadn't. She simply hadn't wanted to think about it, and now more than ever, she was beginning to realize why. She should have been elated at seeing him once more. Instead she felt nothing, no warmth, no responsiveness, just a niggling sense of unease.

"Do you have any idea how long you've been here?" he demanded. "It's been nearly a month. I thought you were only going to stay a few days—just long enough to see your son!"

"It just didn't work out that way." Her eyes dropped to where her hands were tightly clasped in her lap, then lifted. "Why have you come, Neil?" she asked again.

"Isn't it obvious? I think it's about time you came home."

His high-handed attitude was beginning to get to her. Her eyes narrowed speculatively as he paced to a halt in front of her. "I'm perfectly capable of coming home when I'm ready, Neil," she announced a trifle forcefully.

"Really?" His laugh was brittle. "And just when might that be? We're getting married in less than three weeks! Think you'll be back in time for the wedding?"

Her steady gaze faltered at his sarcastic tone. She opened her mouth, but to her horror, she had no ready answer. Her future was with Neil—not here. But she *was* here, and heaven help her, she didn't want to leave. She was with her son and she wanted it to go on forever. *Her son.* How could she disappear from his life once more with no regrets? But it wasn't only Robbie; it was Ward, a tiny voice reiterated firmly in her mind. Her feelings were just as deep—perhaps deeper, than those for her son.

Her heart in turmoil, she gazed at Neil. Was this the man she wanted to spend the rest of her life with? She'd met Neil within a year after Robbie was born. Could it be possible that when she and Neil had started dating and become engaged she had simply needed someone in her life? Needed someone to love who would love her in return? Someone to make up for the child she'd lost? She drew in a deep, quivering breath.

What she needed was here. What she needed was her son. And she needed Ward even more.

She could still feel Neil's eyes on her face, hard and accusing, when Robbie ran into the room. "See what I picked for you, Jenna? Flowers!" he cried proudly, and thrust a handful of bedraggled dandelions at her.

"Aren't they lovely?" contributed a dry voice. "I didn't have the heart to tell him not to bother."

Over Robbie's head Jenna saw Ward framed in the doorway. Her expression was unknowingly stricken, and two pairs of eyes focused sharply on her face, one in concern and the other in tight-lipped scrutiny.

Dimly Jenna saw Ward's eyes drift from her to where Neil stood in front of the fireplace. Recovering quickly, she made the necessary introductions.

"Robbie, why don't you go put the flowers in the kitchen sink and then play outside for a few more minutes? Jenna and I will find something to put them in later."

Ward's voice was very soft, but held an undercurrent that sent Jenna's eyes flying to his face. His expression was grim as he studied Neil, and there was a tightness about his mouth that sent a flutter of alarm racing up her spine. With a curious look at Neil, Robbie skipped happily from the room.

The words had no sooner left Ward's mouth than Neil pulled himself taller. "I'm afraid Jenna won't be around later," he said coolly, leveling a faintly challenging look at Ward. "She's coming back to Houston with me tonight."

Ward's gaze swung to Jenna. She saw a flicker of something that might have been disbelief in his eyes. "Is that true?" he asked her quietly.

His expression was questioning but steady, and somehow bolstered her courage. "No," she said firmly, then looked at Neil. "I'm staying, Neil."

"Like hell you are!" Neil's face contorted into a mask of rage. "Damn it, Jenna, I don't know what's gotten into you—"

"She said she's staying. Didn't you hear?"

At the crackling animosity that flared between the two men, Jenna felt like an unwelcome spectator at a three-ring circus.

Neil took a step forward and thrust out his chin belligerently. "This is between Jenna and me, so why don't you butt out?"

Jenna gasped at his rudeness, paling when she saw Ward's hands ball into fists at his sides. He seemed so big, all raw masculinity and hard muscles, and he towered at least four inches above Neil. She jumped to her feet and quickly moved to stand between them.

"Ward, please... Maybe you should go with Robbie. It really is best if Neil and I settle this alone." Her tone was pleading as she turned to him.

His eyes bored into her as he considered her request. "Are you sure?" he asked finally.

She nodded and he left the room, but not before sending another gritty look at Neil. Taking a deep breath, she met Neil's angry gaze unflinchingly. "I'd like to explain, Neil," she said quietly. "I've already told you about Robbie's chicken pox—"

"He didn't look sick to me."

"He isn't, not anymore. But Ward is going to Tulsa tomorrow, so he's asked me to stay with Robbie until he gets back later in the week."

"And then you're coming home?"

Her eyes faltered. "I—I'm not sure."

Neil snorted. "That's what I thought. You might as well tell me right now who it's going to be. Me or him?"

Her temper began to prickle at his sneer. "Would you deny me this time with my son? It's the only time I'll ever have to be with him—"

"I'm not talking about your son. I'm talking about his *father!*"

Shock held her motionless. Her heart almost stopped beating. "What do you mean?" she asked faintly.

"Oh, I think you know exactly what I mean!" he flung at her viciously. "Did you think I wouldn't notice the way he looked at you? There's something going on between you two, isn't there?"

The charged silence that followed threatened to choke her.
"Yes," she whispered. She dropped down into the chair that
was nudging her legs.

"Exactly how far has it gone? Has he ever touched you?
Kissed you? Held you?"

Jenna nodded, feeling utterly miserable.

"I see," he said coldly. "Quite a little family affair you've
had going here. No wonder you weren't anxious to return to
me. Have you been to bed with him, too?"

She didn't answer. She couldn't. Neil was furious, as he had
every reason to be. She had betrayed him, betrayed his love.

"Have you, Jenna?"

She closed her eyes against the drilling sound of his voice.
But her heart remembered. Her heart knew. "Yes, I made love
to him," she whispered, and knew with every ounce of her being that it was true.

Her eyes flicked open and she stared into Neil's blazing blue
eyes. "Damn it, Jenna," he burst out. "I trusted you."

Her heart ached for him. "I'm sorry, Neil. It just—it just
happened. Neither one of us planned it . . . I don't know what
else to say."

"Don't say anything," he said bitterly. "Just so we understand each other this time—the wedding's off." He started toward the door, then changed his mind and turned back to her
with a cutting look. "In fact, maybe I should be grateful. Your
sudden attack of conscience doesn't say a lot for you, you
know."

Sudden attack of conscience? He wasn't making any sense.
"What do you mean?"

"Oh, come on, Jenna. You gave away your baby, your own
flesh and blood. And then, when you finally decided to come
back for another look, you were determined to walk away
without a backward glance *a second time*. Who but a cold-
hearted bitch could do something like that?" His laughter was
without mirth. "Like I said, maybe I should be grateful. I'd
hate for you to do the same thing to a child of ours. Children
aren't very tolerant about a mother's desertion, and let's face
it, you don't exactly have a good track record."

Dimly she heard a car door slam, an engine roar, followed by
squealing tires, and knew with a vague sense of relief that Neil
had gone. Emptiness grew steadily around her and her head

began to whirl. She was barely conscious of footsteps echoing hollowly across the kitchen floor.

She didn't realize she had covered her face with her hands until she felt Ward gently pry them away and clasp them tightly in one of his own. He was kneeling in front of her. "He doesn't understand," she muttered. "He doesn't understand!"

"Who doesn't understand?" he asked sharply. "Neil?"

"Yes." Her whisper was barely audible.

"Is he gone?" Ward searched her face as she nodded, noting how she looked. He took a deep breath. "What happened, Jenna?"

But Jenna wasn't paying any attention. She was still too numb with reaction. "I did it for love," she said in a whisper that tore into his heart. She lifted pleading eyes to his face. "I did it for love, Ward!"

"Jenna, for God's sake, tell me what happened!" This time there was a sharp edge of anxiety to his voice. "What did he say that upset you so much?"

"We're not getting married," she announced in a high, tight voice. "He—he broke it off." Her eyes were vague as they fixed briefly on his face.

Fear clutched at his insides. Was that what had sent her into this state? No! He refused to believe it.

Warm hands closed around her shoulders. "You don't love him, Jenna." The words were both a plea and a demand.

There was no response. She scarcely heard him, for Neil's words echoed through her mind, slicing into her heart like the lightning thrust of a rapier. *You gave away your baby, your own flesh and blood.* Her lips began to tremble and her face crumpled. "Oh, God," she whispered. "What have I done?" She buried her face in his neck as he pulled her forward into his arms.

"Jenna, please . . ." He smoothed her hair, feeling the tension coiled in her body as she drew long, shuddering breaths. "Will you tell me what's wrong?"

He felt a hand at his shoulder, and saw Robbie standing beside them, his small brow furrowed in concern, his green eyes wide with uncertainty as he sensed that all was not right. Jenna saw him, too, and with a ragged breath reached out and drew him to her, needing to hold him close to her as much as he needed to be reassured. He responded by throwing an arm around both Ward and her and smacking each of them wetly on the cheek.

Ward was relieved to note that the haunting vacancy in her eyes was gone and her smile, though shaky, was genuine. "Time for bed, young man." He stood up with Robbie in his arms and sent Jenna a look that seemed to say the subject wasn't closed yet.

She was in the kitchen making a pot of coffee, or trying to, when Ward came back downstairs. There were more grounds littered around the base of the percolator than in the paper filter lining the basket. He didn't say a word, merely came up behind her and stood... waiting.

Jenna stiffened. Then her shoulders sagged defeatedly as she stared unblinkingly downward. "Will you look at this," she murmured. "I've made such a mess...."

The catch in her voice didn't go unnoticed by Ward, and he knew it wasn't the scattered coffee grounds on the counter she was talking about. He laid his hands on her shoulder, his thumbs kneading the tautness he found there. "You might have fooled Robbie," he said very gently, "but you don't fool me. I'm here if you want to talk about it. If not—" he hesitated "—then let it go."

"Let it go!" She felt hysteria rising in her and fought to battle it down. In its wake came a wealth of anger, frustration, disgust and, strongest of all, guilt.

"Don't you realize what I've done?" she whispered hoarsely. "I gave away my baby, my child, a part of me! And I planned it—*we* planned it! What kind of woman would give away her own flesh and blood and then walk away forever?" She wanted to scream, to cry, but as always when she desperately needed the release, the tears refused to come. She turned then, naked heartache evident in her eyes.

Ward felt her anguish as if it were his own. It had been his selfish need, his and Meg's, for a child of their own, that was now tearing her apart. And just as surely, seeing her so distraught was tearing him apart. With trembling hands he reached out and cradled her against his chest.

Slowly, with jagged phrases and disjointed words, the accusations Neil had hurled at her came out. Ward closed his eyes and muttered harshly under his breath, and when she was finished, he lifted her chin and looked deeply into her pain-clouded eyes. "You didn't walk away forever, Jenna."

She shook her head. "But I wanted to," she said miserably, her voice filled with self-loathing. She held herself stiffly away from him, as if by touching him she would somehow poison him, as well. The knowledge that her gift of life had made Megan and Ward the happiest people on earth was the only thing that had sustained her during the months following Robbie's birth. And though that hadn't changed, for the first time she couldn't forgive—or forget—what she had done. "I tried to walk away. I really did. I just—I just couldn't." Her eyes darkened further. "And you didn't want me here, Ward. You can't deny it."

He was quiet for a moment. "No, I can't," he said bleakly. Then his voice hardened. "But I was wrong, and I can disagree with what that bastard said to you." With a gentle smile, he pressed a hand over her mouth to stifle her protest. "Through Robbie, you gave Meg and me so much, more than I can ever say. Please don't hate yourself for that. There's no shame in giving, and no shame in loving. You said it yourself, Jenna. You did it for love. Meg knew it, and I know it, now more than ever."

"Oh, Ward," she choked out, and flung herself against his chest. "I don't deserve this."

His fingers slid down her cheek to her chin, raising it until she was looking directly into his eyes. "What you don't deserve is the torture you're putting yourself through. You gave a part of yourself, Jenna, and I can't imagine a more loving gift. You are the most warm, sensitive, caring person I have ever known, and I pray to God with every day that passes that Robbie grows up to be like you."

An ache filled her throat. Did he realize how much that meant to her? The words were priceless, more precious than silver and gold. She slipped her arms around his neck and buried her face against his chest. "Oh, Ward." A hoarse cry rose from deep in her soul. "What will I do without you?"

Framing her face in his hands, he gazed down at her, his own expression a reflection of the joy and pain that filled her heart. "I've been asking myself that same question for days already," he whispered. "And I wish I had an answer."

His eyes revealed the depth of the emotional scars he carried, but there was also a faint light of hope there. With a sigh, their lips met in a passionate fusion of mind and body. Her senses were acutely attuned to his nearness, and the heat of his lips on hers drew from her a response that only he aroused. His hands skimmed her back as he swept her into his arms and held her as if he would never let her go.

Was it wrong of her to want this man so much that nothing else mattered, to long to share again the sweetness they had experienced last night? In his arms she could find forgetfulness, no matter how fleeting. In his arms she could find forgiveness . . . and love.

"Make love to me, Ward," she whispered pleadingly. "Please."

His arms crushed her against him. "You're so soft," he moaned into the dark cloud of her hair. As fiercely possessive as his hold was, his mouth grazing her cheek was unbearably tender. "I want you, Jenna. It makes me ache inside just to look at you, let alone touch you."

"Then make love to me," she begged again. She pulled his dark head down to hers, threading her fingers through the thick hair just above his nape. "Make love to me now."

Ward lifted her in his arms and carried her up the stairs. Jenna murmured a protest, saying she could walk, but he refused to let her go. Even when her body glided down the length of his as he lowered her to the floor, he kept one hand anchored on her waist as the other went to the buttons of his shirt.

It was exquisite torture to watch him undress with deft movements. With every inch of muscular flesh that was revealed to her, she ached for the moment she would be able to touch and caress him at will. When her own clothes had been disposed of, she stood in a soft circle of amber light.

His eyes roamed over her small firm breasts, lingering there before moving down over her flat abdomen, gently swelling hips and slender thighs.

Ward breached the distance between them with a single step and gazed down at her, his eyes lighted with desire. After spanning her waist with his hands, he trailed his fingers over the hollow of her abdomen, and commented softly, "You don't look as if you ever had a baby."

Jenna smiled rather shyly up at him. "Not just a baby," she whispered, "your baby." Her voice trembled as she added, "*Our* baby."

He smiled then, and Jenna felt her heart turn over at the tenderness in his eyes. He drew her to him, and she gasped at the feel of his male desire, bold with hunger for her as he laid her down on the bed. While his tongue probed the receptive caverns of her mouth, his palms slid coaxingly across the pink swelling tips of her breasts. Then he carved a pathway to one rosy nipple, taking it gently into his mouth. His tongue circled slowly, teasing the ripe peak to exquisite hardness and sending a current of desire racing through her. Gentle hands roamed over her hips and legs, tickling the soft skin of her inner thighs and sending waves of heat pouring through her veins.

Her hands stroked the muscles of his back, then slid to the taut hips pressed against her own, conveying her need to him with a subtle pressure of her fingertips.

For an instant Ward lay poised between her thighs, gazing down at her with a fevered intensity and a clear delight that left her breathless. "You're so beautiful," he whispered with awe.

Knowing that she gave him pleasure was far more important and precious to her than the fulfillment of her own desires, yet a sob of pure joy escaped her lips as he slid his hands beneath her and guided her to him. She arched upward, surrounding him with her warmth and surrendering herself completely in her eagerness to share herself.

Responsive to every slow, sure thrust, every endearment murmured hoarsely in her mouth, every soothing caress of his hands on her aroused flesh, she felt herself floating higher and higher in a glorious tide of well-being. She loved this man, loved him as she would never love another, and with each rousing motion of love, her body expressed the overwhelming depth of her feelings. Together they climbed to a pinnacle of fulfillment, then floated gently as a feather back to reality.

Later Jenna lay on her side, her head pillowed on Ward's shoulder, her legs still entwined with his. Overcome with a drowsy lethargy, she dimly heard him chuckle as her lashes fluttered closed. Utterly exhausted, she fell asleep vowing that tomorrow she would tell him . . . tell him that she loved him.

CHAPTER FOURTEEN

BUT TOMORROW CAME too soon, and with it, all the uncertainties of the days just passed. Jenna didn't doubt that she loved Ward; there was no question that she did. Yet there was no joy in the admission, no comfort in the truth, for theirs could never be a healing kind of love, a joyous kind of love. It was a love that could bring only hurt, a love that was tinged with sadness.

Morning crept in slowly, first in a hazy gray spear of light, then in errant shafts of golden radiance. Ward slept peacefully beside her, his dark hair tousled on the pillow next to hers, his breathing deep and even. He lay on his stomach, one arm curved over her slender waist. Awake since dawn, Jenna turned on her side to stare with vague fascination at the smooth expanse of his back, the tanned skin stretched across the vibrant muscles she had caressed and explored so eagerly.

They had made love again the previous night, and while it had taken only a single caress from him to set her on fire, the memory was bittersweet. Ward hadn't made love to a woman since Meg; despite the fact that he'd said the thought of making love with his head and not his heart left him cold, weren't there times when physical need overruled all else? No. *No.* Her mind rebelled at the thought. He felt something for her, she was sure... only was it enough?

She sighed, and when she did, Ward opened his eyes to gaze at her drowsily. "Good morning," he murmured. As he yawned, his arm tightened around her and his fingers traced an idle pattern on the small of her back. "Back to your old habits again, I see," he observed dryly. "Awake at sunup again, weren't you?"

Jenna made a halfhearted attempt at a smile. With a pang, she realized just how much she loved him, and her heart throbbed to know that her feelings weren't returned in full measure. But she could never be satisfied with anything less.

And Ward would probably never be truly satisfied with any-one but Meg.

"Jenna—" His fingers caught at her chin, cupping her face lightly in his hands. Her eyes dropped swiftly against his gent-ly probing gaze, and closing her eyes, she buried her face in the hollow between his neck and shoulder. She knew he was aware that something was wrong. But though Ward's eyes darkened at her oddly vulnerable expression, he said nothing. His fin-gers fell away from her face to sift gently through the long strands of hair that spilled across his chest like a midnight cur-tain of silk. "I like your hair," he said softly. "It's so long." He smiled rather crookedly. "Almost as long as the rest of you."

Jenna felt her cheeks redden. Though neither his tone nor his words implied any criticism, she wondered fleetingly if he was mentally comparing her to Megan. She had been so petite, with short blond hair swirling softly around her face. Had he com-pared the two of them last night when he held her in his arms? Had he enjoyed making love with Megan more than her? Swiftly she put the brake on the disturbing escalation of such thoughts.

"I'll get the coffee on," she said hurriedly. Sitting up, she started to slide from the bed.

Ward wasn't yet ready to let her go. Moving with amazing speed for having awakened only moments before, he banded his arms around her waist and drew her back against the naked warmth of his chest. "There's no hurry," he said after glanc-ing at the bedside clock. "It's barely seven." With unerring accuracy, his mouth nuzzled the acutely sensitized skin just below her ear.

"But—you're going to Tulsa this morning. And you have to pack yet."

"That won't take long." His gravelly whisper echoed in her ear. Her breathing quickened as he trailed a line of searing kisses across her shoulder. The feeling of his soft chest hairs pressing against her bare back kindled a fiery warmth inside her, and she ached to turn in his arms and lose herself in the hot desire already coursing through her.

The next moment she did exactly that. Currents of electric-ity raced through her as he stretched out beside her once again, the heat of his body a brand she sought to imprint fiercely upon her own. His mouth captured her breathless moan of passion, and when at last he released her lips, he gazed down at her with an elemental blaze in his eyes. Jenna shivered with pleasure, and reached for him.

At precisely that moment a cheerful voice demanded, "Are you guys gettin' married again?"

Startled, they both looked over to find Robbie at the side of the bed, his chin propped on his elbows and a pair of impish emerald eyes gazing at the two of them.

"Robbie..." There was an odd catch in Ward's voice as he stared at his son, but his lips twitched as he pulled the quilt higher over Jenna's bare shoulders. The horrified embarrassment he'd glimpsed in her face before she buried it against his shoulder was too precious for words. But somehow he made his voice sound suitably stern. "Robbie, it would be nice if you knocked before you came in."

Robbie's small black brows drew together in a frown. "Never had to before," he announced matter-of-factly, then looked at Jenna. "Will you fix pancakes for breakfast, Jenna?"

Ward smiled as Jenna's unintelligible mumble was lost somewhere in the vicinity of his chest. "Tell you what," he said, winking at Robbie. "If Jenna doesn't, I will."

When he finally scooted Robbie off in the direction of the kitchen, he tugged playfully at a strand of Jenna's hair. "It's safe to show your face again. He's gone."

"I suppose you think that was funny," she said, raising her head to glare at him.

"Funny?" Ward's lips quirked. "It wouldn't have been if he'd come in five minutes later." He laughed as her cheeks pinkened even more. "He's only three. He doesn't have any idea what was going on. And he associates kissing with marriage."

"Thank heaven for that," Jenna snapped, and began to gather up her clothes. With the sound of his laughter ringing in her ears, she stalked from the room.

When the time came for Ward to leave, however, she could only cling tightly to him. They were standing on the front porch, and Ward kissed the trembling lips she offered. "With this kind of a send-off," he murmured when he finally lifted his head, "I can't wait to see the kind of homecoming I get."

"When will you be back?" To her shame, she felt her eyes blur. She blinked rapidly, but she knew he saw the overbright shimmer of her eyes.

Ward tightened his arms around her and rested his chin on her shining head. "Wednesday evening," he answered absently. He drew back to look into her face. "You're not making it any easier for me to leave," he chided gently.

All she could manage was a tremulous smile. "I know." The smile faded. "I wish you didn't have to go," she whispered.

His breath caught at the depth of emotion reflected in her eyes. "So do I." The kiss he gave her was long and deep. His breathing was ragged when he finally raised his head. "I'll miss you." He pressed a last, lingering kiss on her parted lips, then reluctantly disengaged himself from her arms.

IT DIDN'T TAKE Jenna long to realize that the emptiness she'd felt that morning was only a prelude to what was to come in the days ahead. She tried telling herself that things would work out, but the little voice inside sounded just as uncertain as she felt.

When Ward returned, she knew she would have to leave, if for no other reason than to take care of the wearisome job of canceling the wedding. She was glad that an elaborate celebration hadn't been planned. Nevertheless, there were still numerous tasks to be taken care of. What she wasn't looking forward to were the inevitable questions about why the wedding was being canceled in the first place. She could only hope that people would be understanding enough not to pry unduly.

She knew now, more than ever, that she had never really loved Neil, not in the way she should have. She hated herself for hurting him, yet she knew she would never have been truly happy being married to him. While she was pregnant, she had tried so hard to suppress any maternal instincts she might have felt because she knew she would have to give up her baby. But she suspected it was the longing for a family of her own that had led her to believe she loved Neil in the first place, a need she had only fully realized during these past weeks with Robbie.

Early Monday evening Dr. Reynolds stopped by. Jenna was sitting on the porch with Robbie when he drove up, and Robbie promptly frowned at him, then took off in the direction of the swing set.

Steve Reynolds laughed as he sat down beside her on the top step. "Looks like I'm not exactly his favorite person."

"I guess not," she agreed, smiling at him.

He glanced toward the front door. "Is Ward around?"

Jenna shook her head. "He's in Tulsa for a few days. He'll be back Wednesday."

"That's just as well." The look he gave her was piercingly direct. "Actually, it's you I wanted to talk to." He cleared his throat. "You see, I've finally figured out why you've looked so familiar to me all along."

"Oh?" She smoothed a strand of hair away from her face and smiled. "I'm sure we haven't met before."

"No. We haven't."

Something in his tone brought her eyes to his in a flash. She found him gazing at Robbie. "Plains City is a small town and—well, people do talk. Surrogate motherhood is still the exception rather than the rule when it comes to a woman's infertility." There was a brief pause. "Most of the people in town don't know that Robbie is really Ward's son."

"I'm not surprised," she said quickly—perhaps a little too quickly. His eyes traveled from Robbie to her, and remained fixed on her face unwaveringly. Her heart began to beat with thick, uneven strokes. "You know, don't you?" she whispered.

Steve Reynolds nodded. "I'm only surprised it took me so long to figure it out. The resemblance is really amazing."

Jenna swallowed. "And I suppose you think I shouldn't have come."

He hesitated for a moment. "It's not my place to judge. I'll admit that as a physician I'd have advised against it—" he shook his head, then smiled a little wryly "—but if Ward hasn't minded letting you stay with him all this time, then that's good enough for me."

A grateful smile spread across her face. "Thank you," she said softly. She reached out and squeezed his hand. "That means a lot to me."

Steve Reynolds looked a little embarrassed, but then he grinned. "It would mean a lot to me," he said emphatically, "if you would seriously consider coming to work for me. I still haven't found an office nurse. An old country doctor like me can't afford to pay big city wages." He raised an eyebrow. "I have a feeling we'll be seeing a lot of you around here."

She smiled rather wistfully. "I doubt it. I'll probably be heading back to Galveston when Ward returns."

He studied her gravely before rising to his feet. "If you change your mind, you know where to find me." He extended his hand, and they exchanged goodbyes a minute later.

It wasn't until after he'd left that she realized just how tempting the offer was. Her mind began to race. Now that the wedding to Neil was off, was there really any reason she couldn't stay here—permanently? Mentally she ticked off the advantages. She suspected she wouldn't mind working with Steve Reynolds; it would be a change from the hectic pace in E.R. She liked the quiet, small-town atmosphere and found the wide-open plains soothing and restful. She would be only too happy to call this sleepy little town home. And of course there were two very obvious attractions—Robbie and Ward.

Ward. Her shoulders slumped as she climbed the stairs to ready the tub for Robbie's bedtime bath. What would he say when he came home from Tulsa and she told him she'd found a job here, that she was set on moving lock, stock and barrel to Plains City? Would he think it was to be near Robbie? It was, partially. But her mind suddenly froze. Perhaps he would think she had an ulterior motive—to inspire his trust and then someday run off with his child. Considering his conduct since his arrival, and even very recently, all the signs pointed in that direction. For that matter, could she watch Robbie grow up, and remain uninvolved, a spectator on the sidelines?

She was far too involved already, she realized sadly.

And yet there wasn't only Robbie to consider; there were her feelings for Ward, her love for him. Even if he approved of her moving to Plains City right now, what about tomorrow? Next month? Next year? Even if Ward's feelings for her did indeed blossom and grow, would they ever be enough for her? He had loved Meg all his life, *still* loved her, in fact. Her thoughts grew bitter. How could she, the mere mother of his child, ever hope to compete with fifteen years of marriage and love everlasting?

She was immediately ashamed of the thought. It wasn't fair to any of them; nor was it fair that for the first time in her life she felt utterly out of control. Her future held nothing but a series of question marks.

The only thing that Jenna was certain of was that nothing would ever be the same without Ward. Nor did she want to jeopardize or tarnish the memory of what little happiness they had shared together.

THOSE BLEAKLY distressing thoughts stayed with her throughout the night and much of the next morning. She had only to look at her son or pass by Ward's bedroom to be reminded of her problems. She felt as if she were caught in a whirlpool, being pulled inevitably downward, with no hope of ever surfacing.

The weather matched her mood. The sunshine of the past week had disappeared, and the sky was a dark, leaden gray as gloomy storm clouds swirled and churned their way north. Her one small reprieve came when Eileen burst in the back door shortly after lunch that day, her face wreathed in smiles. "Guess what?" She threw her arms around Jenna, who was just emerging from the dining room. "I did it!" she cried gleefully. "I actually did it!"

Jenna couldn't help but smile at her air of infectious excitement. "You actually did what?"

"I got a job!" Eileen's voice rang out exuberantly. "And not just any old job, the *perfect* job! I'm the newest staff photographer for the *Abilene Herald!*"

Jenna's eyes widened. "That's wonderful!" She hugged the older woman. "Didn't I tell you not to give up hope?"

"You certainly did!" Eileen laughed. "In fact, I owe it all to you. It was your idea in the first place, you know. Remember the day you said it was too bad I didn't live in New York or Los Angeles, because then I could work for one of the scandal sheets?" Jenna nodded, and Eileen added triumphantly, "Well, that's when I decided to check with some of the newspapers in the area. Although I think the reason I got the job is because the editor got tired of taking my calls every day."

"Oh, I think you deserve a little credit, too," Jenna teased. "A little persistence never hurt anyone, and after all, you're the lady with all the talent, you know." She moved to the cupboard to remove two cups, as well as a glass for Robbie, who had scampered in to give his aunt an enthusiastically sloppy kiss. Jenna smiled at the sight and asked over her shoulder "When do you start?"

"Next Monday." Eileen sat down at the table, only to get up the next minute, too excited to sit still. "Although I'm not sure how I'll ever get through the next week." She laughingly groaned. "I'm not sure I can wait that long."

"What did Frank have to say?" Jenna placed a steaming mug of coffee in front of her and joined her at the table.

"He was nearly as excited as I was." She grinned happily. "As I *am*," she corrected.

They chatted for a few more minutes before Eileen suddenly jumped up. "I almost forgot. I left something in the car." She returned a moment later with a huge leather-bound album in her hands. Placing it on the table in front of Jenna, she smiled. "This is for you."

Frowning, Jenna reached out to trace the gold binding, but the look changed to one of budding delight when she opened it. "Oh, Eileen," she exclaimed. "I can't believe you did this." The album was filled with dozens and dozens of pictures of Robbie.

"I found most of them in a box in the linen closet," Eileen said. She shrugged, looking a little embarrassed. "And I thought you might like to keep them."

Jenna smiled and flipped back to the first page, where she saw that one was of her and Robbie, the first day Eileen had visited during his bout with chicken pox. His arms were thrown around her neck and she was smiling radiantly down at him. In it, Eileen had captured all the love she felt for her son.

"This is precious," she whispered, genuinely touched. "Thank you, Eileen. I'll treasure it always." She leaned across the table and hugged Eileen once more. When they finally drew back there was moisture shining in both their eyes.

"Sentimental old me." Eileen laughed shakily, taking a handkerchief and wiping her eyes. "Frank always says he dreads the day Katie or Tim gets married, because anyone looking at me will likely think it's a funeral, instead."

Eileen was still visiting when the phone rang a short time later. Jenna heard it as she was descending the staircase after putting Robbie to bed for his nap, and Eileen held out the receiver when she returned to the kitchen. "It's for you," she said. "Long distance."

Neil. Jenna's heart sank, but she took the receiver and spoke into it cautiously. "Hello?"

"Jenna, thank God I reached you!"

It wasn't Neil at all, but her mother. Recognizing the unfamiliar sound of strain in her voice, Jenna instinctively tensed. "Mom! What is it? What's wrong?"

"It's your father, Jenna." Her mother sounded terribly distraught. "He's been hurt...."

"Hurt! How?" she gasped.

"The hurricane...he was in the shed this morning...a branch of the cottonwood tree crashed through the roof."

Stricken, Jenna looked through the window over the sink. Even this far north, the wind was blowing gustily. As she watched, several large raindrops splattered the window. She should have known there was a storm raging on the Gulf Coast. "How is he, Mom?" she asked hurriedly.

The line crackled and it was a moment before Marie Bradford's voice could be heard. "Not good, Jenna. He's in the hospital. They'll be taking him into surgery in just a few minutes." Marie's voice broke treacherously. "He—he's in critical condition."

"I'll be home as soon as I can." With that urgent promise, she hung up the phone. Dazed and ashen, she buried her face in her hands.

"Jenna?" Eileen touched her shoulder anxiously. "Jenna, what's wrong?"

Jenna looked up into Eileen's concerned face and shook her head to clear it. "My father," she muttered hoarsely. "The hurricane on the coast...he's been hurt. I have to go. I have to pack." On leaden feet she began to move toward the stairway, gathering momentum as she took the steps two at a time. Eileen followed and watched Jenna heave the suitcase onto the bed, as if she were scarcely aware of what she was doing. But suddenly Jenna stopped and pressed hot hands to her cheeks. "Oh, Lord," she muttered. "I completely forgot about Robbie. What will I do with him? Ward won't be back until tomorrow...."

"Don't worry about Robbie. I'll stay here with him until Ward gets back." Eileen's voice came from directly beside her, and Jenna saw that she had already scooped up some underwear from the dresser drawer and was folding it neatly into the suitcase.

Jenna opened her mouth. "But your job—"

"Doesn't start until Monday, remember?" She guided her firmly onto a chair and directed Jenna to stay put and gather herself together. In an amazingly short time, Eileen had her suitcase packed and sitting by the door. "The only thing that bothers me," she said with a deep frown, "is how you're going to get home. If Ward didn't have the plane—"

"I'll be fine," Jenna said with a valiant attempt at a smile.

"I don't like the idea of your driving all that way by yourself," Eileen said quietly. "If I didn't have to stay with Robbie, I'd go with you myself." Her eyes brightened. "Maybe Frank—"

"Eileen, really, I'll be okay." She held her hands out, palms downward, and gave a forced laugh. "See? Steady as she goes."

Ward's sister glanced skeptically toward the window. "But what if the weather worsens?"

Jenna squared her shoulders. "A little rain and wind won't stop me." Eileen's face still wore a worried expression, and with a sigh, Jenna moved toward her. "Eileen, the best thing you can do for me is to stay here and take care of Robbie. He'll likely be upset when he wakes up and I'm not here." She smiled a little wistfully. "Or maybe that's just wishful thinking." She couldn't help but think of Ward, as well. What would his reaction be when he arrived home and found she wasn't there?

Eileen's smile was halfhearted. "No. It's not. He'll miss you, Jenna. We'll all miss you." The smile faded. "This is goodbye, isn't it?"

Jenna nodded, her throat suddenly tight. There was no need to lie, to pretend she would be back. She wouldn't. She couldn't. It would be much too painful. Perhaps what she regretted most of all was not having the opportunity to say goodbye to Ward, to see his face just once more....

Eileen made Jenna promise to call and let her know when she'd arrived safely back in Galveston, no matter what the hour, and to let her know how her father was doing, as well. Jenna was surprised to see tears sparkling in Eileen's soft brown eyes, and she hugged her one last time.

"Thank you again for the album," Jenna said softly. She squeezed Eileen's hand. "I think I'll look in on Robbie before I leave."

In his room, Jenna's eyes rested quietly on her sleeping son. How she loved him—loved him because he was a part of her, but more because he was so much his father's son. He possessed the same square chin, the same straight nose. His lashes fanned out like dark crescents on his face, and she lovingly traced her fingers over the soft curve of his cheek, knowing that never again would she touch her son. Never again would she hold him in her arms or listen to the bubbly sound of his laughter. Her fingers memorized the silkiness of his hair. Then she bent slightly and pressed a whisper-soft kiss on his mouth.

There was so much pain swirling inside her that she wasn't sure which was worse—the agony of leaving Robbie and Ward or the desperate fear that clutched at her heart in knowing that her father lay weak and ill in a hospital bed so far away.

Finally she drew back to look down at him one last time. The tears slipped unheeded down her cheeks as she said a last goodbye to her son. "Think of me sometimes, Robbie," she whispered to the sleeping little boy. "Think of me and remember that I love you, that I'll never stop loving you though I can't be with you."

CHAPTER FIFTEEN

THE WEATHER JENNA had so blithely dismissed to Eileen had her nerves stretched tautly by the time she was even halfway home. The wind howled eerily through the cracks in the car windows. The highway was wet and slippery, and she passed more cars than she cared to count that had careered out of control and lay abandoned in the ditch.

It was the middle of the night when she finally pulled into the hospital parking lot. It was nearly deserted, and she dodged the puddles pooled on the asphalt as she ran through the entrance. Her steps never wavered until she passed through the double doors of the intensive care unit.

In her father's room, her legs threatened to buckle beneath her when she first glimpsed him. Her fingers curled tightly around the metal side rails of the bed for support. The hospital setting was her work environment, one she was well used to, but unaccountably the antiseptic smell, the tangle of IV tubes and monitors attached to her father's inert form almost gagged her. His skin appeared lifeless, almost as pale as the stark white of the sheets and pillowcase, and an array of mottled bruises darkened the left side of his face and one arm.

Her hand trembled as she touched the shock of tangled gray hair that lay on his forehead. He didn't stir, didn't move a muscle. He just lay there, his breathing deep and labored beneath the oxygen mask clamped to his nose and mouth.

One of the night nurses came in then. Jenna recognized her and nodded abstractedly, all her attention focused on her father's gaunt form. The nurse gave her a brief rundown of his condition, but all Jenna really caught were snatches of phrases—"internal injuries . . . punctured lung . . ."

Her head was whirling as she stumbled toward the ICU waiting room off the hallway. Her mother's voice as she rose from a cramped position on the sofa brought Jenna out of her trance.

"Jenna. Thank God you're here! Have you seen your father yet?"

She nodded, and mother and daughter embraced. Jenna took a deep breath. Then her eyes moved over the worry lines etched in her mother's forehead. "Mom," she said in some concern. "You shouldn't be here. You should be home in bed!"

Marie shook her head. "I couldn't leave him. I didn't want him to be alone in case..." Her lips trembled and she broke off.

"He'll be all right," Jenna said with a surety she didn't feel. Her heart ached for her mother, and she wished she had been there to comfort Marie during the long, lonely hours that day. "He has to be," she said fervently. "He just has to!"

"It doesn't look good," Marie said sadly. "He's weak and frail and... he's just not as young as he used to be. He's been out of surgery for hours already and he still hasn't regained consciousness. The surgeon—" her voice faltered "—he says it's touch and go."

But Jenna refused to give up hope. She couldn't convince her mother to go home and snatch a few hours rest, but with morning's first light, she was relieved to note that a little of the strain had left her mother's expression. Jenna's heart was heavy, but she was glad she was there to lighten the burden on her mother's shoulders.

Nonetheless, the next twenty-four hours were a nightmare she cared never to repeat in her life as both she and her mother silently prayed for a miracle.

WHEN WARD ARRIVED HOME Wednesday evening, he had no idea that Jenna was in Galveston, standing vigil at her father's bedside. He could hardly wait to see her. Two days away from her had made him realize what he'd already begun to suspect. Since Meg had died, even though he had Robbie, there were so many times when he'd felt alone and so empty. But he knew now, beyond any doubt, just how much Jenna had given to him, how much she meant to him.

She meant the world to him.

His stride was light as he took the porch steps two at a time. He grinned as he remembered Jenna's parting kiss, thinking of the welcome he knew was only seconds away, impatient to feel her soft lips beneath his once more.

He stopped short when he found Eileen in the kitchen instead. Seeing his father, Robbie flung himself at his legs. Ward lifted him and kissed the chubby cheek his son offered. Then his eyes sought Eileen's. "Where's Jenna?"

The anxious look on Eileen's face when she saw him in the doorway sent a cold shaft of fear through him. His arm tightened around his son.

Eileen made a helpless gesture with one hand. "She's gone, Ward—"

"Gone? Gone where?"

Eileen darted him a tentative glance. "Back to Galveston." He looked so wounded that for an instant she felt they'd both been hurtled backward to another time, not so very long before.

"Ward, she had to leave," she said. She moved closer and laid a hand on his arm, looking up into his taut features. Shooing Robbie into the living room, she hurriedly explained what had happened to Jenna's father.

"Have you heard from her?" he asked tersely when she was finished.

Eileen nodded.

"How is her father?"

She shook her head. "Not good, from the sound of it."

"Jenna," he said abruptly. "How is she? How did she sound?"

Eileen hesitated. "A little tense," she said in a low voice. "Though she told me she was fine and not to worry about her."

A grim little smile curved Ward's lips. That sounded like Jenna. She was probably scared as hell, even while stubbornly insisting she was fine. She would be brave even while her heart was breaking. She was so strong, so independent—and so damned vulnerable. He cursed softly beneath his breath. The smile faded. "I guess it's a good thing I didn't bring my suitcase in. Looks as if I'll be needing it tomorrow." At his sister's puzzled gaze, he said quietly, "I don't want her to be alone, Eileen."

She looked up at him. "You're going to Galveston?" When he nodded, she reminded him, "She does have her mother with her." She hesitated. "And her fiancé."

"I want to be with her. I have to know that she's all right." His voice hardened. "And she no longer has a fiancé."

He ignored Eileen's soft gasp of surprise and brushed by her into the other room. "Ward, wait!" She practically ran after him. "I...I understand, really," she said breathlessly when he stopped. "You see...Robbie said something today...." She glanced away when Ward's eyes narrowed questioningly. "He mentioned seeing you and Jenna in bed together. And at first I thought I must have misunderstood. But I didn't, did I?"

"No," he stated baldly.

She met his gaze levelly. "I'm glad," she said quietly. "I loved Meg, but I've always hated the thought of your spending the rest of your life alone."

"I don't intend to." His voice was very low, but his meaning was clear. Eileen smiled as their eyes met in silent understanding.

TWO DAYS without sleep had left Jenna feeling numb and weary to the bone. She had finally persuaded her mother to go home and rest Wednesday night, but only by issuing strict orders that she was not to show her face at the hospital until at least eight o'clock in the morning. Jenna had also assured her mother that she wouldn't leave until she returned the next day.

It was getting harder and harder to sit by her father's bed, watching his still form. She hated the feeling of helplessness that plagued her, knowing there was nothing she could to help him. If there was consolation to be found, it was in the fact that while he was no better, neither was he any worse.

"Jenna." She looked up to find Neil in front of her, holding a cafeteria cup and saucer. His smile was tentative. "I thought you could use some hot tea."

"Thanks, Neil." She had been lying on the narrow couch in the waiting room. Family members of patients in the intensive care unit had been filtering in and out all morning and well into the afternoon, but she'd been alone for the past fifteen minutes. Straightening up, she accepted the cup appreciatively.

"Any change?" Neil shoved his hands into his trouser pockets and looked at her.

"No," she said quietly. "He's still unconscious."

"Where's your mother?"

"In with Dad." Jenna took a sip of the clear amber liquid and leaned her head back. Only one visitor at a time was allowed, and then only for a short time.

Neil glanced around the small room, then took the armchair across from her. She was too tired to notice the uncomfortable look that flitted across his face, but after a time he cleared his throat and said, "Jenna, we need to talk."

She sighed and turned her head to look at him. Neil had stopped in to check on her father several times since her arrival, but neither Jenna nor Neil had mentioned their last disastrous meeting. Jenna had been too worried about her father to give it much thought. Neil had offered kindness and a shoulder to lean on, and she had accepted it gratefully, if not lovingly. In reality, it was Ward she longed for, Ward she ached to confide in, Ward's arms she wished would hold her and soothe away her fears.

"Neil, please." She gestured vaguely. "This isn't the time or the place."

"I know," he said. "But with your father ill, we haven't had much time to ourselves." He hesitated. "I suppose we should postpone the wedding."

Jenna looked at him numbly. "The wedding?" she repeated. "There isn't going to be a wedding."

"I was angry and upset when I said that," he told her quickly. "I said a lot of things I didn't really mean."

"Neil—"

"No, please, hear me out." He ran a hand over his smooth brown hair, obviously speaking with difficulty. "I won't pretend it will be easy," he said finally. "I hate the thought of you with another man, but I think the best thing for both of us is to forgive and forget."

Forgive and forget? Did he really think she could dismiss either Ward or her son that easily? She shook her head. "It's not that simple, Neil."

His mouth tightened. "Why not? It was hard for me to accept that you had another man's child, but I've come to terms with it. As for Ward Garrison, I know you well enough to accept that it won't happen again after we're married."

Jenna clasped her fingers tightly in her lap. She didn't want to hurt Neil any more than she already had, yet what could she say? That she didn't love him—that she never had, not really? Compassion stirred in her.

"There's no use pretending anymore, Neil," she finally said heavily. "You and I—we're just not right for each other. Our marriage would never stand a chance. Don't you see that?"

"No, I don't. You said you loved me!"

"I thought I did." Helplessly she lifted her eyes to him. "Only I know now that what I felt wasn't love. That's not to say that I don't care for you, because I do. Only—only I can't marry you," she concluded miserably.

A muscle worked angrily in his jaw. "Damn it, Jenna! You can't possibly have changed that much in the few weeks you were away!"

"No, I haven't," she agreed quietly. "I'm simply seeing things differently, more clearly. My feelings for you aren't what I thought they were—they were what I *wanted* them to be.... It's over, Neil. Accept it. Please." Her eyes pleaded with him.

"Accept it!" He jumped to his feet. "Damn it, Jenna, I won't let you do this! It's not going to end like this, do you hear? It isn't!"

He strode angrily from the room, and Jenna stared after him silently. It had ended a long time ago, she acknowledged wearily. She was exhausted, both physically and mentally. The interminable hours of waiting were finally exacting their toll on both body and mind. She thought of her father, lying still and unresponsive, though both she and her mother willed him to live. But as she did so, the lingering thread of hope she had clung to so stubbornly these past two days began to fray at the ends, and she felt herself coming apart.

The walls of the small room, whose neutral blue-and-gray color scheme was meant to be soothing, suddenly began closing in on her. She stumbled into the hallway, but even there, as she took deep gulps of air, a wave of despondency swept over her. She had never felt so alone. And she was tired, so tired of trying to pretend that everything was going to be fine, when in reality, *nothing* would ever be right again.

If only Ward were here, she thought desperately, sagging against the pale green walls of the hallway. He would know what to say, what to do. God, how she needed him! Her throat felt raw with the effort to keep from sobbing.

Her head jerked up at the sound of footsteps echoing in the long, dismal hallway. A man had just stepped off the elevator and was walking straight toward her, his steps firm and purposeful. He was dressed in dark slacks that clung to powerful thighs. The pale gray shirt he wore emphasized the muscled width of his shoulders. Her eyes widened as the tall spare figure drew closer.

Finally the man drew to a halt, an odd half smile lifting his lips as he stopped and stared directly at her. Her heart fluttered as she stared back, unable to believe her eyes.

"Aren't you even going to say hello?"

It was that deep, gentle voice that finally prodded her into action. With a strangled half sob, she threw herself straight into Ward's arms.

"How did you know?" she murmured shakily. "How did you know I needed you?" She rubbed her cheek against his shoulder, reveling in the feel of his arms around her, strong and secure, and of his heart beating steadily beneath her ear.

He didn't answer at first, at least not directly. His fingertips glided over her face as if to memorize her every feature. Then he bent his head, and the roughness of his cheek grazed hers as he gathered her closer in his arms. "I wanted to be with you," he said softly.

Jenna drew back to gaze up at him through shining emerald eyes, her hands still linked with his. Somehow those few, simple words meant more to her than anything else he could have said.

Ward noticed with concern the faint mauve shadows beneath her eyes. "Are you all right?"

"I am now." She smiled up at him.

"And your father?"

Jenna sighed and briefly described her father's condition. Ward slid his arm around her shoulders and brought her gently up against his lean strength. "When was the last time you ate?" he asked with a frown. "Or slept?"

She flushed a little. "I had some tea a little while ago," she said quickly.

They had been walking toward the waiting room as they spoke, and now they stopped in the doorway. "And I suppose you've been sleeping on that." His tone was stern as he waved a hand at the narrow couch along the wall.

Jenna sighed and looked away.

"That's what I thought," he said grimly. "The first thing I'm going to do is get some food inside you and get you home and into bed."

"Ward, wait!" she protested as he took her firmly by the shoulders and began to march her into the hall once more. The idea of going home and snuggling into the warm comfort of her bed sounded heavenly. But she bit her lip guiltily and glanced toward the imposing double doors that led into ICU. "I hate to leave my mother alone here. It's been so hard on her...."

His face immediately softened. He lifted a thumb to stroke the curve of her cheek. "What if I take you home and then come back here to be with her? I won't be able to stay very late though. I'll need to pick up Robbie in Houston before nine tonight."

"Houston?" Her eyes widened. "Robbie's in Houston?"

"He's with an old college buddy of mine," Ward explained "He and his wife have a little girl about Robbie's age, so he's in good hands." He smiled a little at her stunned expression. " brought him along because I didn't want to burden Eileen, now with her starting her new job. I also thought your mother might want to see him. Do you think she'll mind?"

In answer she stood on tiptoe and lifted her lips to graze his cheek. At the last minute he turned so that her mouth met his instead. The kiss they shared was brief, but Jenna felt herself drawing strength from the warm touch of his mouth on hers "I'm glad you came," she whispered shakily. "And I'm glad you brought Robbie."

Ward's hand on her waist guided her gently back to the tiled floor. "There's no place I'd rather be." His tone was grave, but his eyes were lighted with an oddly tender expression.

Shyly, softly, she kissed him once more. With that fleeting caress, she felt the knot of pain inside her begin to uncoil. "I'll let Mom know I'm leaving," she said, then disappeared through the double doors.

Inside the intensive care unit, she beckoned to her mother They spoke in hushed whispers near the doorway.

"Oh, Jenna, I think he's better." Marie's eyes were shining "He opened his eyes once, only for a second, and he squeezed my hand while I was talking to him."

They clasped each other tightly. "He's going to be all right Mom," Jenna said in a choked whisper. "I know he is."

Marie squeezed her hands and stepped back. "I think you're right." Her eyes scanned her daughter's face. "Why don't you go back to your place for a while? If there's any change, I'll call you."

Jenna nodded. "That's what I came in to tell you." She paused, then said softly, "Mom, Ward's here. And Robbie is with him."

A look of surprise flitted across Marie's face. Then she smiled. Jenna had few secrets from her mother, and she had confessed her feelings—and her fears—about Ward, and her doubts about Neil, as well.

"On second thought, why don't you plan on staying at home with me for a few days?" Marie suggested. "There's plenty of room for all of us. It will be less cramped than your apartment and it's closer to the hospital."

"That's a good idea," Jenna agreed, then frowned. "Though I'll have to check with Ward to see if he's made other arrangements. I think he's planning on staying tonight, but after that I'm not sure."

He would, he assured her a few minutes later, be staying as long as he was needed. *I'll need you forever,* she told him silently. The only thing that prevented her from blurting it out was the realization that he might not want to hear that from her.

"How did you get here?" she asked curiously as they began walking down the dimly lighted corridor.

"I flew." He reached out in front of her to press the Down button on the elevator.

Jenna gasped. "You flew? With Robbie? In this weather?"

Ward shook his head and sent her an admonishing glance. "You haven't been outside the hospital at all in the past two days, have you?"

"No." Her tone was a little sheepish as they stepped into the elevator. A moment later she saw what he meant. The autumn sky was a brilliant blue, and white puffy clouds floated high above. It seemed almost indecorous to come from the stifling atmosphere of the hospital to the freshness of outdoors, where a warm scented breeze blew in from the Gulf on such an achingly beautiful day.

Still, the signs of violence from the recent hurricane were readily apparent. Crews were still hard at work cleaning up the downed tree limbs that lay scattered throughout the city as Ward and Jenna drove to her apartment, where she picked up some clean clothes. When they finally pulled into her parents' driveway, she couldn't prevent her heart from leaping into her throat. It took a conscious effort to prevent her eyes from lin-

gering on the pile of faded bricks and torn shingles that ha·
been the shed.

Ward saw the look and wasted no time in pulling her into th·
house. Less than an hour later, she had been briskly and effi
ciently fed, showered and dressed in a white linen nightgown.

Drawing the covers back on the wide double bed in the roon
Jenna had occupied throughout her years at home, Ward mo
tioned her into it. "Remember the time you said I was always
trying to put you to bed like a child?" His grin was a trifl·
wicked.

"This is your big chance, then." She smiled as she obedi
ently slid into bed.

Ward laughed and plumped the pillow under her head. "·
remember thinking there wasn't a chance I'd put *you* to bed lik
a kid."

"And I've always thought you were a very capable man."
When he pulled the covers over her, an impish smile curved he
lips. "Do you tell bedtime stories, too?"

"Not at three o'clock in the afternoon," he said promptly
His eyes ran appreciatively over her slender curves, outline·
beneath the lightweight blanket. He placed his hands on eithe
side of her body and looked down at her. "Right now bedtim·
stories are the last thing on my mind."

Jenna smiled her satisfaction. Despite her fatigue, her bod·
responded to the dark flame in his eyes. So she sighed when h·
straightened and briskly tucked the loose ends of the sheet an·
blanket snugly beneath the mattress. "Just like my mother,"
she grumbled good-naturedly. But her eyes lighted up as sh·
turned on her side and snuggled beneath the blankets. "Ex
cept she always kissed me good-night," she murmured, look
ing up at him from beneath her lashes.

Ward's eyes darkened as they ran over the silken tangle of he
hair, fanned out behind her on the pristine whiteness of th·
pillowcase. "I think that could be arranged," he said, and ber·
down to give her a deep, lingering kiss that had Jenna smoth·
ering a frustrated groan when he finally lifted his head.

"That wasn't a very motherly kiss—or a fatherly one, e·
ther." The protest was made as she looped her arms around h·
neck. "Maybe we should try it again till you get it right," sh·
suggested throatily.

"If I do, you'll be getting more than just a kiss. You don't exactly inspire maternal *or* paternal feelings where I'm concerned."

Ward smiled down at her and shook his head. He was indeed sorely tempted to sink down beside her and love the breath from her. "You need to rest right now," he decided. "And I need to get back to the hospital and your mother, and then pick up Robbie later this evening."

"Then I suppose I'd better sleep now while I'm able to." Her eyes sparkled rather mischievously. "Maybe we should have stayed at my apartment, instead. Because I doubt I'll sleep tonight, knowing you're in the next room with Robbie instead of me."

Ward smiled and pressed a kiss on her mouth. "There will be other times," he said softly, then gently disentangled himself from her arms.

CHAPTER SIXTEEN

IT WAS NEARLY NOON when Jenna finally made it downstairs the next day. The memories of the previous night—her father, Ward, Robbie—rushed into her mind, and she hurriedly showered and dressed.

She wasn't quite prepared for the sight that met her eyes in the kitchen. Ward was at the sink, his forearms plunged into soapy dishwater, while Robbie was sitting in her mother's lap contentedly stuffing his mouth full of homemade chocolate chip cookies.

It was Ward who finally looked up and saw her wavering in the doorway. "Well, well," he said lightly. "Look who the wind blew in."

Marie and Robbie glanced up at the sound of his voice. Robbie wasted no time in scrambling off Marie's lap and hurtling himself at Jenna. Scooping him up in her arms, Jenna received a damp kiss on the mouth and returned an equally warm one of her own.

Jenna's smile encompassed all three of them, but it was Ward she spoke to. "So," she said, eyeing the sinkful of dirty dishes, "my mother's put you to work already."

"Oh, I'm not complaining." His eyes were affectionate as he glanced over his shoulder at her, then traveled to her mother. "At least not yet," he added dryly.

Marie laughed, and Jenna couldn't help but notice the look of shared amusement that passed between them. The thought flitted through her mind that it was almost hard to believe they had met for the first time just last night. It wasn't until Jenna moved toward the table that a slight frown found its way between her dark brows. "How's Dad today?"

"Well—" Marie paused, then broke into a wide smile. "—why don't you ask him yourself? He's been waiting for you all morning."

Jenna stood stock-still. Her arms tightened around Robbie. "Do you mean it?" she breathed.

Marie nodded, her eyes lighted with the same vibrant delight as her daughter's.

"Well, then." Jenna set Robbie on his feet, her face transformed by a brilliant smile. "What am I doing here?"

"I was wondering the same thing myself," her mother said, laughing as Jenna moved toward the door. Robbie grinned as Marie tweaked his nose and lifted him into her lap once more. "You can tell him I'll be up shortly," she called after Jenna. "Right now I think I'll get acquainted with this young man."

JENNA WAS MORE than pleased that her mother, Robbie and Ward took to one another so well. Ward took over the household chores in his typically capable manner, leaving both Jenna and Marie free to visit the hospital whenever they wanted.

The next evening after dinner, Ward and Marie lingered at the kitchen table over their coffee. Jenna had darted over to her apartment to check on things and had taken Robbie with her.

Marie placed her spoon on the table and gazed across at Ward, her expression rather speculative. "You and Jenna have grown very close, haven't you?"

The corners of Ward's mouth turned up in a fleeting half smile. "I certainly hope so. Jenna means a great deal to me." He hesitated. "Has she ... said anything to you?"

"Yes, she has." Marie's look grew thoughtful. "But even if she hadn't, there are times when Jenna doesn't have to say a word for me to know exactly what she's feeling." Her brows lifted. "You know she's adopted, don't you?"

Ward nodded.

"Losing her parents was very hard on her," Marie went on to say. "Her first year with us wasn't easy for any of us. She scarcely uttered a word, but those huge green eyes said it all, and I don't think she was even aware of how much she was communicating." She sighed and shook her head in remembrance. "I used to think she would never open up, never let us help her. It used to break my heart to watch her, knowing she was hurting inside and not letting any of it out. It sounds crazy, but Jerry and I used to pray that she would cry or scream— anything to let go of her grief."

Ward's eyes darkened. His heart ached for the child his sweet, loving Jenna had been. So scared. So alone. And so damnably brave. "She was lucky to have you," he said very gently.

Marie's smile was pensive. "Jenna was an extremely quiet, sensitive child. Even once she began to warm toward us, there was still so much she kept bottled up inside herself." She paused. "Do you know that to this day I have never seen her cry?" she added quietly. "She had the usual scrapes and bumps, just like any other child, but I never once saw her shed a single tear."

Ward's throat tightened, remembering the night he'd surprised her going through the picture album, and the ensuing flood of tears. Tears shed not for herself, but for Meg. And then later, she'd been just as confused and afraid as he was of the tumultuous feelings that had sprung up between them. But despite her fears, she was so strong, so giving, so alive to the feelings of everyone around her.

He loved her. With all that he possessed, with every ounce of feeling in his soul, he loved her.

"I'm glad you've been here for Jenna." Marie's quiet voice broke into his thoughts. He looked up at her, his expression rather dazed. Then he smiled.

"Jenna is one very strong woman," he said softly. "Like her mother."

AFTER THOSE CRITICAL first days, Jerry Bradford's condition improved daily, though the doctors anticipated he would be hospitalized at least another week. He was moved from intensive care to a regular room Sunday morning, so both Jenna and Marie wore radiant smiles when they returned home Sunday afternoon.

Ward grabbed Jenna by the shoulders and seemed just as heartened as she by the news. It wasn't until her mother and Robbie withdrew from the room that a shadow passed over his face. When he drew her quietly toward the sofa, her heart began to pump fearfully.

"What is it?" Her eyes anxiously scanned his face.

"Jenna—" he squeezed her hands "—I have to head back home soon."

"Wh-when?"

"I should leave tomorrow. Tuesday at the latest," he said quietly. "My partner called while you were gone. Something's come up and I'm needed back at the office as soon as possible." He paused, his dark eyes gauging her reaction.

"I—it's all right." She spoke hurriedly at his guilty look. He'd said there would be other times, and she had to believe that. Her eyes lifted to his as she took a deep, steadying breath. "Ward, we—we need to talk before you leave."

"Yes," he said slowly, "we do." His eyes roved over her pale face. "Jenna..."

But whatever he was about to say was cut off abruptly by the sound of the doorbell.

It was Neil.

She heard Ward's indrawn breath behind her and saw Neil's face tighten at the same time, and half turned to see the two men sizing each other up. She knew a fleeting sense of déjà vu and quickly positioned herself squarely between them.

"Hello, Neil," she said quietly.

He nodded in response to her greeting and stepped inside. An uncomfortable look flashed across his face as his eyes swung between Ward and Jenna before he finally addressed her. "Do you think we could go for a walk or something? I'd like to talk to you," he added hastily on seeing Ward's frown.

Jenna stilled Ward's displeasure with a pleading look as their eyes met and communicated. Then, to her relief, Ward's eyes softened. He silently retreated, leaving Jenna alone with Neil.

The atmosphere was strained as Jenna pulled a windbreaker on over her pale blue blouse. The temperature wasn't all that cold, but the day was cloudy and there was a cool nip to the breeze. Neither she nor Neil spoke as their steps carried them down the sidewalk edging the wide, tree-lined street.

Finally Neil pulled her down onto a bench in a nearby park where Jenna had played as a child. For a long time he just looked at her. Then at last he spoke.

"It really is over, isn't it?"

It was more a statement than a question, yet Jenna found herself searching for an answer. She jammed her hands into the pocket of her coat and looked straight ahead. "Yes, Neil," she said quietly. "It is."

"It's him, isn't it?"

She turned to look at Neil then. She had no trouble discerning his meaning, but surprisingly, there was no trace of anger on his handsome features, only an oddly pained resignation lurking in his eyes. "You mean Ward?"

He nodded.

"It would have happened, anyway," she told him very gently. "Even before I left for Plains City, I'd begun to have doubts." In the tumult of the past few days, she hadn't realized she still wore his ring. Now she removed it and very gently pressed it into his hand. "Let's not lie to ourselves, Neil. We weren't right for each other. And it's better that we discovered it now, before we made each other miserable."

Neil gave a short laugh. "You think I'm not miserable now?"

"Neil, please." Her eyes were shadowed. "This is hard enough as it is. Don't make it worse."

"I suppose you're right." He sighed and stretched his long legs in front of him. "I didn't take the job at Bates-McKinnon," he said after a moment.

"Because of me?" Her eyes widened.

"Partly," he admitted. "But then I started thinking... Maybe you were right, after all. It would have been like going over to the enemy camp."

She touched his arm gently. "I'm proud of you, Neil," she told him softly. "I think you did the right thing."

"I hope so." A grim smile curved his lips as he stood up. "I hope it works out." His blue eyes flickered as his smile faded. "And I hope things work out for you, as well."

The sound of children's laughter drifted to her ears as they retraced their steps. In the driveway of her parents' house, Neil gently touched her cheek, his eyes roaming over her face. On impulse, Jenna reached up and touched her lips gently to his, then murmured a last goodbye, unaware of a watchful pair of brown eyes glued to her every movement from inside the house.

She should have been relieved, she realized as she watched him drive off, that he had finally accepted the end of their engagement so calmly. She was free, as free as she had once proclaimed Ward to be, free to love whomever she chose.

But there was a part of her that was almost afraid to believe...

Her mind was suddenly filled with Ward. His laughter. His smile. The feel of his arms, strong and secure as he held her against his chest. Those dark brown eyes soft with love...

For his son. For Meg. For her? Yes. Yes! He did love her! She clung to the thought before a fleeting despair nipped at her.

But was it enough? She wanted all that he had to give, all his love—as he had given Meg. Was that so selfish of her?

Suddenly the front door opened and Ward stood there. For a long time they stared at each other. Ward's face was somber, his eyes dark and unreadable. His taut stance in front of her only served to further her apprehension, to tighten her stomach into a cold hard knot as she moved inside.

The tense atmosphere increased when he finally stepped inside and closed the door behind her.

It was Ward who finally broke the brittle silence between them. "Which is it?" he asked in a very low voice. "Congratulations or condolences?"

She sent him a deep, searching look. "Why? Are you waiting to pick up the pieces?"

"As a matter of fact, I am," he returned very quietly. "If it comes to that."

If it comes to that? She was almost afraid to read too much into his words. Her eyes were dark with uncertainty, the color of jade as she tipped her head to the side.

Ward approached her. His fingers encircled her wrist and he lifted her hand to stare at it, his eyes on the bare spot where she had so recently worn Neil's ring. "Does this mean what I think it does?"

His tone was hushed, his eyes guarded as they met hers. She felt a flicker of awareness that Ward was just as uncertain as she. "It means," she said in a voice that wasn't entirely steady, "that I have a wedding to cancel. But—you already knew that."

His look grew more intense. "Are you sure you want to do that?"

Jenna shook her head, her eyes glued to his. "I—I don't love Neil, not in the way I should, not in the way he deserves. I could never be happy with him."

"And what about me, Jenna? Could you be happy with me?"

The moment stretched out endlessly as Jenna stared at him. "Ward," she whispered, "what are you trying to say?"

"I think you know." There was a heartbeat of silence. "Don't you, Jenna?"

The tenderness in his eyes did not disguise the hint of anxiety in his voice. The combination sent Jenna's mind racing and her heart thudding wildly. The flame of hope burning faintly in her heart began to grow stronger.

Ward could hold back no longer. With a shuddering breath, he started to reach for her, but her sudden gasp brought him up short. Jenna was staring intently at his hand.

"Your wedding ring!" Her eyes flew upward to his. The flame burned brighter yet. "It's gone—"

"I should have stopped wearing it a long time ago," he said quietly, his expression reflective. "It belongs to another time." He paused, and then continued. "You brought light into my life, Jenna. You showed me that I've been living in the shadows, and for that I'm grateful."

"I—" Her hair swirled around her face as she shook her head. Gratitude? She didn't want his gratitude; she wanted his love—all that he had to give and more! "Ward, please—what do you want from me?" Her hands lifted in an almost pleading gesture.

The next thing she knew she was caught in a rough embrace that was all the more precious because of its urgency. Ward took her mouth in a scorching kiss that was both tender and demanding, sending a torrent of desire rushing through her veins. She sagged against him weakly when he finally tore his mouth from hers and drew back from her.

"Oh, Ward, I wish you didn't have to leave tomorrow! I wish—" The words came from deep inside her, but suddenly she stopped, aware of his eyes boring into hers.

"What, Jenna? What do you wish?" His fingers tangled into her thick hair and brought her face to his.

Under that intent, scorching gaze, she felt as if he were reaching into her soul. And she could no longer deny to him what she had never denied to herself since she had first discovered it. "I wish..." She struggled for breath, her heart thundering painfully in her ears. "I wish we could be together forever." Her voice caught painfully. "I—I love you, Ward."

His eyes searched the dark green depths of hers. Then his arms tightened around her in a fierce embrace that nearly crushed the breath from her. Yet Jenna reveled in the contact, the heat of his body, the strength of his arms around her. She buried her face against his chest.

"Oh, God, Jenna." He drew in a harsh, rasping breath and rested his chin on her bent head. "I didn't realize how desperately I needed to hear you say that until I actually heard the words." He tugged her head back so he could look directly into her eyes. "I love you, Jenna," he said very softly. "I love you."

Her heart melted beneath the velvet of his voice. She felt herself being slowly drawn into the warmth of his eyes and she knew a moment of brief spiraling joy, but suddenly her eyes were filled with torment.

"Oh, Ward." She pulled away from his arms and sank onto the sofa, weak-kneed and shaken. "How can you be sure?" she whispered. She focused her vision on her hands, willing them not to shake.

He sat down beside her and took her hands in his. His hands were warm, comforting, immeasurably gentle despite their strength. "Don't you think I know what I feel?" he asked very quietly.

"I think you know what you *think* you feel." Still she refused to look at him. She desperately yearned to believe him, and yet she was afraid.... "You just said you were grateful. And maybe—" her voice was a halting whisper "—maybe you're mistaking gratitude for love. Maybe it's because of Robbie! And not only that, you've been alone for so long—"

"No." There was no mistaking the firm conviction in the voice that cut through hers. "I was in love for years, Jenna. Believe me, I know the feeling."

"Oh, Ward!" His name was a cry of pure agony on her lips. "You're still in love with Meg! Don't you think I know that? Maybe it's selfish of me, but I want to be loved for myself. I— I don't want to play second fiddle to Meg!"

She started to lurch to her feet, but Ward's relentless grip on her hands wouldn't let her. The seconds ticked by. The room was steeped in silence. The pressure on her hands increased until she felt her bones would be crushed. Then, abruptly, he released his hold and his hands came up to cradle her face. Gently he turned her toward him. "A part of me will always love Meg. I can't deny it," he told her quietly.

A raw pain throbbed in her breast as she felt the words clear to her soul. She opened her mouth to speak, but he stilled the sound with a finger on her lips.

"But that doesn't lessen what I feel for you. That doesn't mean there isn't room in my heart for you. You fill my heart, you fill my soul, in a way I've never even dreamed of, in a way that's never happened before, even with Meg." His voice dropped, and his eyes moved over her face tenderly. "As for Robbie, he's only one of the reasons—not the only reason— that I love you. He looks like you, he has the same sweet, loving nature, and nothing could please me more. Looking at him and knowing that he is a part of you fills me with so much pride, so much love, I can't begin to describe it.''

His hand feathered over her cheeks, her eyes, her trembling mouth. "Oh, Ward," she whispered. "I can't believe this is happening. I'm afraid that if I close my eyes I'll open them and find it's all a dream."

With infinite gentleness, he bent and pressed his mouth to hers. "Never doubt that I want you," he whispered against her mouth. "Never doubt that I need you. And *never* doubt that I love you."

Jenna's eyes clung to his, but she could not speak. All the uncertainties, the doubts, all the anguish of the past weeks were banished as she slipped her arms around his neck and held him with all the love she felt in her heart. Ward gathered her close and took her lips with a kiss that spoke of need, of passion, of boundless love that sent a surge of aching sweetness through her veins.

It wasn't until Jenna felt herself being lifted, cradled in strong, tender arms and borne toward the stairway that she realized his intentions. "Ward," she murmured weakly, "my mother . . . and Robbie . . ."

"Have gone out for ice cream." He flashed a triumphant smile. "I very politely requested that they not hurry home too soon."

He carried her with surprising ease straight toward her bedroom. She hid her smile in his shoulder. "And what did she say to that?"

His eyes glinted as he set her on her feet and very deliberately closed the door behind them. "Your mother," he said, pretending a thoughtful air, "is a very wise and obliging woman." Then he grinned. "She said she would be more than happy to see that Robbie doesn't disturb us until morning."

"Rather sure of yourself, weren't you?" Jenna retorted, a sparkle lighting her eyes.

Ward's eyes sobered, and Jenna realized in that instant how very uncertain of her he had been. "You scared the hell out of me when I saw you kiss Neil," he admitted.

"I never really loved him," she told him gently.

His hands settled possessively on her waist. "It doesn't matter anymore." He drew her to him once more and kissed her lightly, then more deeply, with ever increasing ardor.

And then there was no more time for words. His hands shook as he slowly removed her clothing, and allowed Jenna to do the same for him. Her fingers moved over his skin with the same lingering tenderness, the same caressing touch that he had used on her, arousing a flame of passion in both of them. Ward moaned his compliance as they stretched out on the bed, his body molded against her curves.

His hands traveled a searing path, grazing her throbbing nipples, wandering over her stomach, and lower. His mouth followed, warm and tormenting, as he paid homage to first one ripe peak and then the other. Weak and yearning, Jenna clutched at his shoulders and, with a breathless moan, began to incite him to the same fevered pitch she had reached, stroking and sliding her fingers over his back, reveling in the smooth texture of his skin beneath her fingertips.

And then they were one, fused in throbbing delight that carried them ever higher, ever upward, to the heavens and beyond. Jenna breathed his name as waves of heat poured through her, and she reached her quivering release as Ward took his own with a driving compulsion that was all the more precious for the pleasure she knew she gave him.

The shadows of early evening found their way through the narrow opening in the curtains. His tender arms held her gently as she floated back to earth, basking in a warm cocoon of contentment. She snuggled drowsily against Ward, a smile of serenity curving her lips as she ran a lazy hand over the dark mat of fur on his chest.

Ward stilled the motion of her hand, lifting it and planting a warm kiss in the palm before he settled it on his stomach once more. His eyes were lighted with affection as he turned his head slightly to gaze down at her.

"I suppose it will mean going to the expense of a new and bigger water heater," he whispered, a smile on his lips that sent a warm glow radiating through her, "but can we finally tell Robbie we *are* getting married?"

Her hand ceased its restless exploration of his flesh, still warm and faintly damp from their fervent lovemaking. Jenna propped herself on an elbow and stared down at him. A tinge of uncertainty crept into her voice. "Are you sure that's what you want?"

His eyes, warm and glowing, captured hers. Jenna waited, almost without breathing, for his answer.

"Oh, Jenna." Her name was half laugh, half groan as he threaded his hands in her hair and brought her mouth down to his. "That is what I want, more than anything in this world. I love you, and I want you beside me, as my wife, for the rest of our lives."

The heartfelt emotion, the raw conviction in his voice, touched her deeply. Joyously she cried his name, and was rewarded as his lips took hers in a deep, soul-wrenching kiss that had them both breathing heavily when he reluctantly drew away to look at her.

He sighed as he saw that her cheeks glistened. Overwhelmed with happiness, Jenna was helpless as her eyes filled and tears slid unchecked down her face.

Softly he kissed away the lingering traces of dampness from her face, then pressed her back on the pillows and gazed down at her with loving eyes. "Just promise me one thing," he requested.

"Anything," she told him tremulously. "Anything."

She smiled through her tears, and Ward felt his heart turn over. He framed her face with his hands and ran his thumb beneath her misty green eyes. "Please, Jenna. It breaks my heart to see you cry. No more tears. Ever."

Her eyes once again burned, her throat ached, but she was so full of joy she felt she would burst with it. "I can't promise," she whispered against his mouth. Then she smiled, a beautiful, brilliant smile, and kissed him with every ounce of feeling she possessed. "But I'll try...."

SHE HAD NO TROUBLE keeping her word—until a glorious day the following autumn. That was the day Christina Marie Garrison was born. Wasting no time in letting the world know of her arrival, she let out a loud wail and was promptly handed first to her radiantly smiling mother and then to her beaming father, who was garbed in drab green surgical attire. The sight of her husband, so big, dark and strong-looking, tenderly cradling his tiny daughter with love and pride shining from his eyes, filled Jenna with such profound emotion that she promptly burst into tears.

The days sped by, filled with love and laughter and a wealth of happiness. At the tender age of nearly four months, Christina still occasionally woke her mother for a midnight feeding, and a particular night a week before Christmas was one of those times.

Jenna sat in the rocker near the fireplace while Christina nursed contentedly. She had carefully crept downstairs with the baby so as not to awaken Robbie and Ward. Outside the world was crisp and cold and dark, but inside the gaily decorated house the atmosphere was warm and welcoming, despite the midnight hour. A lamp burned dimly in the corner, casting just enough light in the room that Jenna was able to see both the tiny figures of the Nativity scene spread out on a silky blanket of angel hair across the mantel and the huge Christmas tree in the corner.

She brushed her fingers lovingly across the fine dark fuzz that covered the baby's head, noting that her long feathery lashes were beginning to droop. Already her eyes were beginning to darken to the same warm, golden brown as her father's.

A rustle of movement caught her attention, and she looked up to see Ward standing at her side, his hair tousled from sleep. Her breath caught in her throat at the tenderness in his eyes, resting hungrily on her upturned face. She would never cease to be moved by the love and warmth that filled his eyes whenever he looked at her.

Yawning, he rubbed a hand across his chest. "You're spoiling her rotten," he said, dropping down beside her. Leaning over the arm of the chair, he brushed his lips across the baby's chubby cheek.

"Feeding her is spoiling her?" Jenna wrinkled her nose at him. "Now if you said that her grandma and grandpa and Aunt Eileen and Uncle Frank spoiled her, I might be inclined to agree."

He grinned a little ruefully. "Guess I'm just jealous." His expression was indulgent as he touched the tiny dimpled fist that lay curled against her breast, and his eyes feasted on the expanse of bare skin that lay open to his gaze. Glancing down, Jenna noticed that the baby's small mouth had dropped away from her nipple.

"I hope you didn't do that on my account." Ward laughed as she frowned good-naturedly and modestly covered her bare breast with her nightgown once more.

He followed along behind her as she silently padded up the stairs. When she bent to lay Christina in her crib, he brushed aside her hair to drop a warm kiss on her nape.

Once they were cozily ensconced in their own bed, Ward wrapped his arms around her and tucked her head into the hollow of his shoulder. "By the way, I forgot to tell you. I saw Steve Reynolds this afternoon. He wanted me to ask if you would be interested in filling in for Marianne this summer. She's taking a two-week vacation in August."

Jenna smiled. Dr. Reynolds, who had delivered the latest addition to the Garrison family, had lamented long and loudly when he was forced once again to hunt for an office nurse, his latest having abdicated in favor of her husband, son and newborn daughter. He had hired Marianne only the day before Christina was born.

"I don't see why not." She pressed a kiss on Ward's beard-roughened chin. "Unless you have something planned."

She felt him smile against the soft skin of her temple. "I don't have anything planned for August," he murmured. His hand drifted below the hem of her nightgown to trespass on the satiny skin of one bare thigh. "But I do have something planned for the next few minutes."

She playfully slapped away his hand as he started to mold her tightly against one lean hip. "You've already had your fun for the night," she reprimanded tartly.

He laughed softly. "I wouldn't count on it."

Before she knew it her nightgown had been whisked neatly over her head and dropped in a heap next to the bed.

"Again?" She laughed a little breathlessly, then shivered as his hands traced a lazy, erotic pattern on her full breasts. "This is beginning to become a habit—and not at all in keeping with the image of a forty-year-old man." They had celebrated his birthday last May.

Tender fingers traced the outline of her lips. "It's funny you should say that," he answered thoughtfully. "Because I feel as if my life is just beginning."

Then he took her lips in a long, drugging kiss that sent a feverish excitement swirling throughout her body, and Jenna's last thought before she was drawn into a whirling vortex of love and passion was that he was right.

The best was yet to come.

He only wanted a child—
until she offered him a package deal.

EVER SINCE EVE

Pamela Browning

Chapter One

"I'm really sorry, Ms. Triopolous. You seem well qualified, but we've already hired someone else."

Eve swallowed her disappointment, put up a brave-enough front to shake hands with the employment interviewer, and escaped into the bright spring sunshine. She had hoped that this particular job in the public relations department of a large advertising agency might be exactly suited to her, and, in fact, it was. But she'd lost out on this position, just as she had lost out on so many others.

"You're overqualified," they'd tell her, or, equally exasperating, "Your experience is excellent, but unfortunately we don't have an opening right now." Which could be true, of course. With the competition from foreign imports, local textile mills were closing at an alarming rate. Two people fought for every textile-related job in this textile-oriented city. Even for skilled jobs, like the ones for which Eve, a magna cum laude graduate of the University of North Carolina, applied.

The sound of her heels on the pavement was muffled by the rundown condition of her shoes, a defeated sound that produced no echo, just a dull pounding. She retreated past houses with signs declaring Rooms for Rent. Well, that was one thing she and Al, her father, hadn't tried yet—renting out the extra room in their tiny mill-owned house. It was, she reminded herself, something she could keep in mind as a last resort—that is, if they weren't evicted first.

By the time she reached the park not far from the ad agency's building, she admitted to herself that she had no other options but to find a lodger, and even the meager rent derived from renting a room wouldn't help much. She wished fervently that she would land a job, but she'd tried every ad in the newspaper, all to no avail. And she'd been searching for a job for months.

Had today's advertising-agency job really been filled by someone else? Or had the fact that she'd been summarily dismissed from her prized job as public relations director at Wray Mills had something to do with it? There was an old-boy network in Charlotte; its members had brushed shoulders at the same colleges, communicated through civic clubs, and their lives were inextricably interwoven through their families. Maybe the word was out: "Don't hire Eve Triopolous. She stirred up trouble at Wray Mills."

Eve eased herself down on a convenient park bench next to a bed of purple-and-yellow pansies, their quaint, kitten-like faces upturned toward the sun. She'd always been partial to pansies; she agreed with Emily Dickinson that violets and roses were too flashy, too showy, too intense. I'm like a pansy, she thought with pleasure. Quaint, quiet, calm. Not flashy.

Nearby a small blond boy tossed bread into the water. Three white ducks paddled furiously across the tiny pond, racing each other for the food, furrowing the sparkling blue ripples into shimmering wakes. The boy squealed in delight and ran to beg more bread crusts from his mother, who tousled her son's curly hair before he danced out of reach. Eve smiled and inhaled a breath of balmy, fragrant air. The sun felt warmer than it had all winter and warmer than it would feel any other day of the year. The soft breezes of spring were sweeping away a long, cold winter, and she was glad.

Dire rumblings from the region of her stomach reminded her she was hungry. She shook a solitary plastic-wrapped sandwich from a brown paper bag and unfolded the newspaper to read while she ate.

The ad fairly jumped out at her from the Personals section of the Charlotte *Courier-Express*. In stark contrast to the other ads set in small type, this one captured her eye with bold capital letters:

Surrogate Mother Wanted. Couple will pay $12,000 plus expenses to healthy woman to bear their child. Replies confidential. Call 425-4272.

Intrigued, Eve lowered the newspaper to her lap and thoughtfully bit into her bologna sandwich. Twelve thousand dollars!

Did it really say twelve thousand?

She set the sandwich carefully on the brown paper bag from which she had so recently removed it and scanned the ad again.

Yes, it really did. Twelve thousand dollars! That was a lot of money to Eve Triopolous at this low point in her life.

With twelve thousand dollars, she could move her father out of the mill-village house that they had been ordered to vacate by Wray Mills's management.

With twelve thousand dollars, she could pay a hefty portion of Al's considerable medical expenses.

With twelve thousand dollars—but wait. Maybe it wouldn't be that easy.

She'd heard of surrogate mothers. She wrinkled her forehead, trying to remember what she knew about the subject. As she recalled, surrogate mothers were hired by couples when the husband was fertile but the wife couldn't become pregnant. The surrogate was artificially inseminated with the husband's sperm, which united with the surrogate mother's egg. The surrogate's job was to carry the baby to term, surrendering it to its father and his wife soon after delivery.

Could Eve become pregnant? As cautiously as she would test her footing on a crumbling red-clay bluff, she tried the word on for size. *Pregnant*. She'd never been pregnant, but she didn't see why she wouldn't be fertile. Eve met the only qualifications stated in the ad. She was a woman, and she was healthy.

Oh, she was very healthy. She had not caught so much as a cold in the past five years. Her body hummed along, breathing, digesting, doing all the things a body was supposed to do, even when she fueled it on a diet composed largely of cheap bologna sandwiches, peanut butter and junk food. Presumably, her body could become pregnant, too. Pregnancy was, after all, just another bodily process. And bodily processes were nothing to be afraid of. They were natural, normal.

And she'd might as well face it; Eve had tried everything else. Today, basking in the warm sunshine, sliding her tired feet surreptitiously out of her shoes because they were sore from walking from job interview to job interview to save gasoline, Eve was feeling truly desperate. Desperate, and to some extent hopeless. She remained unemployed even after applying for every job that seemed within the range of her wide capabilities, and her responsibilities at home weighed heavily on her narrow shoulders. And not the least of all, she was sick of bologna sandwiches.

Eve didn't stop to think about what Al, with his Old World ways, would say. And at this point she didn't care what anyone else would say, either. She wasn't afraid of being pregnant, and she didn't look for reasons why she shouldn't be a surrogate mother. At the moment, desperate as she was, there weren't any.

Twelve thousand dollars could be hers, but first she'd have to produce a quarter for the phone call. She fished through her purse, digging into the lining, scrounging for loose change. Then, recklessly tossing the bologna sandwich in a nearby trash can, she raced lightly on tiptoe across grass spring new with green, her tread bright with renewed hope, her short black hair gleaming with blue highlights in the bright spring sunshine. She dropped her quarter in the public telephone with a resounding *clink*.

Wombs for rent, she thought wryly to herself, and then she dialed the number.

IT WAS ONLY FIVE DAYS after she made her phone call that Eve met the Langs.

A nervous Eve, still surprised to find herself there, waited in the cool, crisp, air-conditioned reception room of the Queen City Infertility Clinic, leafing distractedly through an elderly copy of the *Ladies' Home Journal*. She tapped her foot impatiently. She had polished her shoes that very morning, using the last of the navy-blue polish. She'd dressed conservatively in a navy-blue suit and her best white blouse with the lacy frill at the neck, the same suit she had worn to all those job interviews.

Who were the Langs, anyway? That was the first question she had asked Diane Holtman, the clinic counselor, when Diane had called with the news that an infertile couple was interested in Eve and wanted to meet her.

"Mr. Lang is a textile executive," Diane told Eve over the phone, "and Mrs. Lang is the holder of a degree in music and a volunteer for several of the city's worthwhile charities." Other than that, all Eve knew was that like all couples who consulted the Queen City Infertility Clinic, the Langs were desperate to have a child.

Of course, Eve hadn't dreamed that she'd be called back so soon after taking a comprehensive psychological test and filling out the interminable eight-page form, a form that had made her squirm with its in-depth questions.

"Why do you want to be a surrogate mother?" had been one of the questions. Eve thought about that one for a long time. Finally, she'd written, "For the money." And then, because it was equally true, she added, "Because I want to help somebody." Eve liked the idea that she and the couple for whom she would carry a child would be mutually helping each other.

"Eve?"

Eve looked up. The receptionist beckoned.

"Follow me, please."

Eve did, twitching surreptitiously at her skirt, worrying that her slip showed. She wanted to be perfect. She wanted the Langs to like her. And because her future, if they chose her, would be inextricably intertwined with theirs for as long as it took to create a baby, she wanted to like them.

Diane Holtman was waiting for her at the door to her office.

"Eve," Diane said, clasping her hand warmly. She drew Eve inside.

"This is Eve Triopolous," Diane said to the couple sitting on the couch. "Eve, Derek and Kelly Lang."

With a nervous smile, Eve turned toward the couple, and the moment she saw them, her nervousness melted away, and she thought, *They're beautiful!*

For the Langs were, if any couple could be said to be, a golden couple. Derek Lang was poised and perfect in his well-tailored pin-striped suit. Kelly Lang was blond but not brittle, *au courant* without being annoyingly so. Derek's coarse butternut-brown hair was combed back from his face in a conservative style, neither too long nor too short. Kelly had that indefinable look of the well-to-do, the jewelry and clothes and bearing of the typical Junior Leaguer.

While she was taking their measure, the Langs were taking hers. Kelly Lang thought in surprise, *Why, how sincere and open she looks!* Kelly had been initially concerned about what kind of woman would volunteer to be a surrogate mother. But thirty-four years of living had taught Kelly to trust her native intuition, and Eve's natural dignity reassured her.

Diane Holtman began to guide the three of them skillfully through the crucial interview, but all the while Diane was talking, Derek Lang paid little attention to what she was saying. His eyes were summing Eve up. Unlike his wife, who was thinking of the internal woman, Derek dealt solely in externals. He was uncommonly pleased with what he saw.

Eve Triopolous's black hair was straight and sleek and shiny, and above all, it looked healthy. She wore it in a haircut shorter at the nape than at the sides, as precise and neat as the haircuts of Japanese schoolchildren. In fact, everything about Eve Triopolous was neat and precise. High cheekbones. Milky-white skin. A small nose, honed to a fine point at the end, with nostrils that did not flare or spread even when she smiled. Eyebrows naturally dark and smooth and kempt, feathering acrosss her brow like the tips of ravens' wings. Huge brown eyes, eyes you could burrow into, they looked so soft. He'd read on her personality profile that she was twenty-eight years old and had never married.

"The thing is," his wife was saying earnestly to Eve, interrupting his perusal of her, "that the child would not be yours at all. We would be using my egg and Derek's sperm, which would be fertilized in a laboratory, and then the resulting embryo would be implanted in your uterus."

"I didn't know that was possible," Eve said. "I had assumed that it would be my egg and the husband's sperm, and that the embryo would result from artificial insemination."

"Often artificial insemination is the way it's done when perhaps for some reason the wife isn't producing a viable egg," explained Diane. "But in the case of the Langs, their infertility problem is that Kelly has had a hysterectomy—she has had her womb surgically removed. She still has ovaries, and she can produce the egg. Kelly's egg can be fertilized with Derek's sperm in vitro, but Kelly, of course, cannot carry a child because she has no uterus. That's where you come in, Eve."

"The embryo would be implanted in my uterus?" asked Eve in surprise.

"Yes. The baby would be what is often referred to as a 'test-tube baby.' The implantation in your uterus would be done at a hospital by a local gynecologist who is an expert in infertility. And you would carry Kelly and Derek's child to term."

Eve's head spun. But this was even better than she had thought! The only misgiving she had harbored about this whole idea involved her mistaken assumption that the baby would result from her egg, would be half hers, part of her, and that she might very well develop emotional ties to it before it was born.

Now, because of the Langs' unusual situation, even that worry faded away. It would not be Eve's baby at all. She would shelter the test-tube child inside her body for nine months, she would bear it, she would turn it over to the Langs. And she would walk away from the experience virtually unscathed, pleased that she was doing a good deed, and not only that, but she would be twelve thousand dollars richer.

And then she would pay their bills, buy a little house where she and Al could live, and she would find a job.

Eve swung her head around to study the Langs. She watched them thoughtfully, studying every detail.

Derek Lang leaned slightly forward in his seat, his clear gray eyes fixed on her in silent entreaty. Eve took in all aspects of him—the broad shoulders, the fine fabric of his suit, the ready intelligence of his expression. He must be a very special kind of man, she thought, to go through this painstaking process in order to have a child. A spark of empathy passed between them in that moment, unmistakable to the two of them. In that moment, Eve recognized the qualities she always looked for in a man—but never found. How fortunate his wife was to have him for a husband!

Kelly Lang gripped her husband's hand so tightly that her knuckles shone white in the glare of the overhead fluorescent light. And Kelly was special, too—several cuts above the ordinary. It was clear to Eve that the Langs were a fine couple, the kind of people who deserved to be parents. Any child of theirs would be a fortunate child indeed. And she knew that all their bright hopes of having a child of their own were pinned on her.

Her decision was made. She didn't have to think about it twice.

With an air of impeccable calm, Eve smiled at the two of them and said softly, "I'm willing if you are."

She was immediately gratified by Derek's beaming smile and the happy tears pooling in Kelly's sky-blue eyes.

So WILLING were the Langs that Eve found herself in a gynecologist's office that afternoon. After a routine physical, Dr. Perry informed Eve and the Langs that he had discovered nothing to indicate that Eve could not carry a child to term.

"I'm so happy," Kelly Lang confided, impulsively hugging Eve when they said good-bye in the parking lot.

Eve hugged Kelly back. She'd only met Kelly that day, but with all their talk of fertility and infertility and babies and bodies, she already felt that unmatchable woman-to-woman closeness that often develops between dear friends. Eve knew instinctively that Kelly was the kind of woman who would be a wonderful mother, who would tirelessly chair committees on the PTA, who would make sure that a child saw the pediatrician regularly and had all the right inoculations.

Moreover, Kelly was a woman who loved her husband; Eve could see that in the way she reached for his hand from time to time, resting her fingers trustingly in his. She was capable of loving a child deeply, the way a child should be loved. And Derek—well, Derek was obviously the kind of man to whom everything came easily. So would fatherhood.

"I'm happy, too," Eve said slowly and with some surprise. She had not expected to feel so delighted. She had expected to feel emotionally removed from the situation. But the Langs were so warm and enthusiastic that their happiness was infectious. Eve already felt as though the three of them were inexorably bound together as they set off upon an adventure of the first magnitude. She drew a deep breath. Having this baby was going to be a wonderful, uplifting experience; she just knew it was.

"I'll have my lawyer draw up the papers," Derek Lang said, smiling widely and shaking her hand briskly in farewell. His hand was firm, his grip reassuring.

"And I'll call you and let you know when the papers are ready," Kelly said with a cheerful smile before folding the crisp white linen of her exquisitely cut dress around her and ducking into their silver Mercedes sedan.

It's almost too easy, Eve thought in amazement, watching their Mercedes until it was swallowed up in the rush-hour traffic on Independence Boulevard.

And then, still slightly stunned by the staggering events of the day, she drove her own unassuming Volkswagen Beetle fifteen miles home to Wrayville, the level of her optimism falling lower and lower with the passing of every mile.

Because now she was going to have to explain this whole strange business to Al. And telling her father, Eve knew, would not be easy at all.

"OH, DEREK, Eve is everything I had hoped," Kelly Lang said later in their bedroom, twining her fingers together behind her husband's neck. She gazed at his handsome face, at his wide eyebrows, which were a bit too short, at his nose, which would be ordinary if it were not blunted at the end.

He nuzzled her forehead. "She's perfect," he said, slapping his wife affectionately on the rump before moving to the closet and removing his tie. He hung the tie on the specially built rack, straightening it until it hung neatly.

"She has a matter-of-fact look about her, doesn't she?" Kelly offered. "As though she wouldn't go into a dither over anything. And that's good, Derek, because I've been reading about babies before they're born, and the experts think they can hear while they're still inside the mother. I wouldn't want our baby to be carried by somebody who was noisy and quarrelsome and—"

"I don't think you have to worry about that with Eve Triopolous," Derek said, picturing Eve's intelligent face in his mind. And not only her face but the rest of her, too—the white skin, the narrow shoulders, the waist not as small as it might be. And her hips, wide hips, hips that would spread to bear a child with no trouble at all, from the look of them. Wide hips swelling gently from waist to thigh, fertile-looking hips, hips that could easily accommodate a baby for nine months, and no doubt a pelvis that would cradle that baby in comfort until the time of birth.

His eyes softened on his wife. Kelly glowed, she sparkled, she looked happier than he had seen her in a long, long time.

Slowly, he unbuttoned the top button of his shirt, and then he unbuttoned the next.

Kelly caught the meaning in his eyes.

"Do you think we have time to make a baby before dinner?" Derek asked softly, moving to take her in his arms. It had been too long since the last time; with his busy work schedule, he was always so rushed.

Kelly lifted her lips to his. So many times Derek had initiated their lovemaking with those very same words back in the days before she had had to have her hysterectomy. The words brought back fond memories of a time when she had still hoped that they *could* conceive a child of their own, and today that hope had been rekindled in the person of Eve Triopolous.

"Oh, darling, this time let's pretend we're really making a baby," she breathed, because in her heart she knew—she *knew*—that soon, soon their baby would be conceived, not inside her body but in a dish in a laboratory, but that didn't matter; it didn't matter at all.

The important thing is that there would be a baby, hers and Derek's, and in her heart she would hold close the comfort that it *could* have been this act of physical love that created their baby; it *could* have if things had been different.

AT THAT MOMENT, Eve was parking her VW under the chinaberry tree in front of a white frame house with a green shin-
gled roof, a house that was identical to every other house in
what was known as Cotton Mill Hill, the mill village of Wray
Mills. She spared a quick glance toward the cotton mill itself,
a sprawling brick building with two tall smokestacks that
dominated the scene from its location on the hill. Dominated
the scene, the people, the town government, the police force,
everything, by virtue of its employment of at least one member of every family in Wrayville. Wrayville would not have existed if it were not for Wray Mills.

But because of her agreement with the Langs, the mill would
not dominate the Triopolous family any longer. Eve rejoiced at
the thought of it.

The odor of fatback hung in the humid air. Mrs. Quick
across the street was boiling up a mess of collard greens, no
doubt, for that big family of hers. The smell of food cooking,
even the greasy smell of fatback, made Eve's mouth water. She
had skipped lunch again today.

"Al?" She swung inside, her heart sinking. She hoped he'd
had a good day. But there was no sign of her father in the small
comfortable living room, a room that Eve had delighted in
furnishing in soft restful colors with her own salary from the
mill.

"Al?"

"In the kitchen," she heard, and Eve peered around the door
frame to see her father, in his customary chambray work shirt,
standing in front of the sink, washing salad greens.

"Thought I'd get a start on dinner," he said, his voice
wheezing. "Have any luck looking for a job today?"

Eve paused. "Let me do that," she said gently, taking the
lettuce from him. "You sit down and rest."

"Don't boss me, daughter," he said playfully, but she noticed that when he sat in the kitchen chair, he sank into it as
though he had little energy. Out of the corner of her eye she
noted the sallowness of his skin. She'd thought his breathing
had sounded more labored than usual last night, and it worried her.

What to tell him about her day? She'd never answered his
question about looking for a job. With luck, maybe he wouldn't
ask it again. Yes, that was the thing to do—ignore the question. She still didn't know how to tell her family-oriented father, so set in his old-fashioned ways, that she had hired herself

out as a surrogate mother. He worried about her too much as it was.

Which was what he was doing at the moment. *Poor Eve*, Alexander Triopolous thought as his daughter blended lemon juice and olive oil for salad dressing. *She tries so hard*.

"Eve, you know, I can sympathize with you being out of work," he said, thinking she might want to talk about it. After all, he himself had been a long time without employment in his own youth.

Eve swished the salad dressing in its cruet before answering. "It's different now from the way it used to be," she said carefully. "This isn't 1947. It's not a post war economy. I thought I'd have an easier time getting a job."

"This area depends on textiles," he said. "And with all the foreign imports—well, foreign imports are kind of like the red tide. They're killing jobs around here."

He meant it to be a joke. But after he'd returned from France in World War II, when he'd gone back to his family home in Tarpon Springs, Florida, and expected to resume his profession of harvesting sponges like many of the other members of families of Greek heritage who lived there, red tide had been no joke.

Red tide, a microscopic malady, began destroying the sponges on the floor of the Gulf of Mexico in 1947, and sponge fishing died out. The Greek-American spongers in Tarpon Springs moved on to other lines of work as bankruptcies flourished and stores closed their doors. In desperation, Al had contacted his army buddy, Joe Rigby. Joe hailed from Wrayville, North Carolina. Did Joe know of any jobs there?

"Yes," Joe had enthused, phoning long distance over a crackling wire. "Get up here. The cotton mill is hiring."

And so Al Triopolous had hitched a ride to the little town outside Charlotte, and best of all, he had gotten a job in the card room of Wray Mills, a cotton mill that manufactured gauze and diaper fabric that was much in demand because of the post war baby boom.

The handsome Greek-American had appeared breathtakingly exotic to the local girls, who were entranced by his un-Southern accent and his flashing brown eyes. Still, he had managed to elude all of them for seven years until he met blond, petite Betty Simpson. And then he had fallen, and he had fallen hard. It wasn't the austere, restrained courtship it would have been under the stern Greek traditions in Tarpon Springs. Al married Betty within three months of meeting her.

Al Triopolous never left his job in the card room, the place in the mill where cotton, straight from the bale, is fed into carding machines whose wire teeth separate and straighten the fibers. He grew accustomed to the cotton dust hanging thick in the air, leaving an ever-present coating on his clothes, on his wavy black hair and in his lungs. There was nothing unusual about the coating of cotton dust, because loping down the hill after work to the little house he and Betty rented from the company, Al looked like most of the other mill hands. Covered with lint, they were called "lintheads." Al never minded being called a linthead. What he would have minded more was being unemployed.

He hated to see his daughter going through the same hell he had gone through back in '47. Coming home day after day after looking for work, Eve looked exhausted. It had been going on for months now, this job search of hers. It was all his fault she had lost her prime public relations job in the mill.

Eve would have held that job forever if it hadn't been for him. A high school honor student, Eve had attended the University of North Carolina on a scholarship provided by Wray Mills. And when she'd "made trouble"—the mill's words—about Al's workmen's compensation claim, they had fired her with angry diatribes about being an ingrate after all the company had done for her. Eve was not one to compromise her principles, and that made Al proud. But he'd filed the claim, and then she'd felt she had to stand behind it. He'd never get over the feeling that it was his fault that Eve was out of work.

"Did Nell Baker stop by today, Al?" Eve asked him casually as she dished up their dinner, leftover lamb stew, from a pot on the stove.

"Can't you tell? She dusted and vacuumed, and she drove me out of the house. It was good for me, I guess, because I managed to walk down to the corner and back." He shook his head. "She's a whirlwind, that one." But Eve noticed that he was smiling.

"She likes you," Eve said teasingly. She smiled and flipped her short hair back from her face as she sat down beside him. "In fact, I think she has a crush on you."

"Ha!" her father said. "Nell Baker just wants somebody to push around. I remember how she used to treat poor old Bud. 'Do this, do that,'" he mimicked. "Drove the fellow to his grave, if you ask me."

Eve's smile faded. Bud Baker had died over a year ago of what was termed "acute chronic respiratory disease." Bud had worked in the carding room, too. He'd displayed the same symptoms her father had.

"Say," her father was saying, realizing it was time to change the subject, "I heard a rumor today when I was out walking. Somebody told me the mill's going to be sold."

"Sold?"

"That's right. Nobody's saying who the customer is yet, but the word is that it's a big conglomerate that owns several mills. What do you think of that?"

"I wonder how the sale of Wray Mills to a big textile conglomerate will affect your claim," Eve said darkly, unable to eat any more stew.

"No telling. I'm not saying I believe the talk. There've been rumors before."

"That's true," Eve said, the tension easing in her stomach. "Lord, I can't wait to get out of Wrayville."

Al shot her a shrewd look. "How can you say that?" he asked. "You've never known any other home."

Eve shoved her plate of stew away. "On the day they fired me from the mill, I was glad, *glad*, because I knew I'd be leaving," she said fervently.

She got up and rinsed her plate off in the sink, willing her heart to stop pounding. She couldn't help the resentment that she felt against the mill. Not after what the management had done to her father and to her.

Al began to cough, and she turned in alarm. She should have known not to talk about getting fired; whenever Al became emotionally upset, he coughed.

His skin looked papery and old, and the coughing was wearing him out. Eve rushed to her father's side and held his hand until the coughing spell had spent itself at last.

"Ah, Eve," he said, his voice no more than a whisper. "Maybe you're right. You need to get out of Wrayville, away from the mill. You'll get a job soon—sure you will—and then maybe in a couple of years you'll meet a nice man, get married and have babies. You know, that's the one thing that would comfort me in my old age. Some grandchildren, Eve. I've always loved kids. Wanted more of my own. You'd be happy, Eve, settled down with a husband and some babies."

He smiled at her wistfully, and Eve pressed her cheek against his so that he couldn't see the despairing expression in her eyes.

As old-fashioned as his hopes for her were, she knew he wanted only the best for her, and the best for Al Tri-op-olous since his Betty had died had been his relationship with Eve, his only child. Eve couldn't tell Al now—she didn't dare tell him—that she was going to bear a child, that the child wasn't even going to be hers and that she would have to give it up in the end. He wouldn't understand. He wouldn't even appreciate the irony of the situation.

The anguishing question tormented her: if she couldn't tell her father she was going to be a surrogate mother, how in the world was she going to manage it at all?

Chapter Two

Charlotte, North Carolina, is named after Queen Charlotte of Mecklenburg-Strelitz, wife of King George III of England, and the city bills itself today as the Queen City. If Charlotte is truly the Queen City, thought Eve as she steered her Volkswagen down shady tree-lined streets on this unseasonably warm May afternoon, then Myers Park must surely be the many-faceted jewel in her crown.

It was a section of town where big houses sat far back from the street, so far back that all Eve could tell about them was that they were large, and in some cases palatial. Here the very air was rarefied, and the breeze slipping through the leaves overhead whispered ever so discreetly, "Money, money, money."

The Langs' house turned out to be a Georgian structure of old brick with an imposing front door, a neatly manicured garden and a look of old money. Textile executive? Derek Lang must be the scion of one of the area's well-known textile families, the product of prep school and Davidson College and Harvard Business School for his MBA. This wasn't the home of any middle-management type.

Eve didn't know why Kelly Lang had insisted that she sign the papers relating to their employment of her as a surrogate mother at their home. She would have preferred the cool formality of the lawyer's office. But it was too late now to insist upon that.

Eve smoothed her hair and checked her face in the mirror before walking swiftly up the brick walkway to the front door. As she raised the brass lion knocker and let it fall, she realized how hollow her stomach felt. She wasn't sure if the hollow feeling was due to nervousness or if it was because she hadn't been able to face the thought of another bologna sandwich for lunch and so hadn't eaten anything since breakfast.

"Come in out of the heat," bade Kelly, answering Eve's knock, wearing a rose-red sundress and dangling white hoop earrings. When Eve hesitated inside the door, Kelly immediately put an arm around her waist and drew her across the hall to the study.

"This is Harry Worden, our attorney," Kelly said, indicating a florid-faced white-haired man who spread papers on the desk. He looked up as they entered, gave Eve a curious once-over, and apparently deciding that she passed inspection, he stumped over to shake Eve's hand.

"And of course you know Derek," Kelly went on.

Derek nodded. Today, in the face of a hot late May day, Eve wore a simple white short-sleeved cotton dress of some soft, petallike material, severely tailored except for white embroidery on the collar. With her coloring, the effect of the white fabric against her pale skin and dark hair was stunning.

"If you'll just sign here...and here," Harry Worden told her and without a word, but gripping the pencil tightly in her nervousness, Eve signed and sat back in the big wing chair.

The papers were shuffled to Derek, who scrawled his name quickly and with a flourish, and then to Kelly, who signed and then flashed her husband a radiant smile.

It's legal, Eve thought with a sense of amazement, *just like that. Three signatures and I get pregnant. When I pass go, I'll collect twelve thousand dollars...twelve thousand dollars...twelve thousand dollars....* The sum throbbed inside her head with each beat of her heart.

The attorney handed each of them a copy of the contract and snapped his briefcase closed. "Now if you'll excuse me," Harry Worden said with a brisk nod, "I'll be going back to my office." Kelly left with him, presumably to see him to the door.

Eve rose from her chair. She had just signed away at least nine months of her life, but the reality had not hit her yet. The enormity of what she was doing, the impact of it—when would she believe it? When the embryo was implanted in her uterus? When her body began to change from the effects of pregnancy? When her pregnancy was so unmistakable that she finally had to tell Al, or worse yet, that he guessed? She grabbed the back of the chair in sudden dizziness as Kelly returned.

"Eve?" Kelly's worried face wobbled in front of hers; Derek's strong arms held her up and then eased her onto a nearby couch.

"I—I'm all right," Eve said.

"Are you sure?" Kelly felt her forehead.

"It's just the heat. Or something," Eve said, struggling to sit up.

"Umm," Kelly said uncertainly with a quick glance at her husband, "there was something Derek and I wanted to talk over with you. If you feel up to it, that is. Are you hungry? That is, would you join us for lemonade and a snack?"

Eve's stomach manufactured unseemly noises at the mention of food. She managed to look mortified.

"Yes," she said with as much dignity as she could muster. "Actually, I forgot to eat lunch today."

"Oh, in that case," Kelly said, summoning a sweet-faced black woman wearing a gray-and-white uniform, "we'll have some of my aunt's chicken salad sandwiches. Louise, make sure some of Aunt May's sandwiches are on the tray, will you, please?"

"Now, wouldn't we be more comfortable on the terrace? It's shady there this time of day." This was Derek. He regarded Eve seriously and with concern as Eve passed a hand over her face, trying to brush away the light-headedness.

At Derek's suggestion, the three of them naturally gravitated without discussion through the French doors to the adjoining terrace overlooking a tranquil rose garden and sat down at the small wrought-iron table. Eve tried to restrain herself from eating too many of the delicately assembled chicken-salad sandwiches, but they were so *good*.

"Are you feeling better, Eve?" Kelly inquired after Eve had polished off at least half a dozen of the little triangles, and Eve smiled and nodded and reached for one last sandwich.

"Then perhaps we should talk about—" And here Kelly looked at her husband for help.

Derek cleared his throat. "Kelly and I thought that—or rather we *hope* that—you will consider moving in with us after the baby is conceived. That you'll live here, with us, until the baby is born."

Wide-eyed, Eve looked from Derek to Kelly, who nodded to corroborate the invitation.

"Our contract stipulates that we take care of your living expenses," Kelly reminded her.

"But—"

"We would still pay you a generous allowance," Derek interrupted, mindful that she had replied in part to the form's question "Why do you want to be a surrogate mother?" with

"For the money." It hadn't escaped Derek's attention that Eve had looked hungry when she arrived here, looked as though she were used to being hungry, and he didn't want his child to be deprived of the proper nutrients while it was *in utero*. If she lived here, she would eat properly; Kelly and her Aunt May would see to that. He didn't mind paying her an additional allowance, not at all. Kelly had convinced him that it would be worth it to ensure a healthy baby.

"Please say you will," Kelly said softly but persuasively. "It would be fun for me to watch the baby grow, to go with you to Dr. Perry for the checkups."

Still undecided, wondering if Al could manage without her, if Mrs. Baker would look after him, Eve only stared.

"Would you like to see your room?" Kelly stood up, taking Eve's answer for granted. Eve found herself being propelled up the wide stairs, past the majestic grandfather clock on the landing, down a hall carpeted in jade green, to a guest room that was a charming vignette of antiques. A French needlepoint armchair waited elegantly before an English lady's writing desk. Pink Scalamandré velvet print swooped into graceful swags over her window. A Schumacher print covered the walls, and the same print cunningly adorned the coverlet on the dainty brass bed.

"It would make my wife happy if you'd stay with us," Derek said, sliding an arm around Kelly's shoulders and pulling her close.

Eve loved the room. It was beautiful. "I'll think about it," she said, feeling as though she'd been inserted unawares into a fairy tale of her own imagination. She felt like a princess, and a bogus princess at that. What had she done to deserve such beautiful surroundings? She peered into the corners of the room and regarded the closet door with trepidation. She fully expected a frog to leap out wearing a sign demanding Kiss Me.

"You wouldn't have to move in, you know, until you're actually pregnant," Kelly said anxiously, totally unaware of Eve's feelings of unworthiness.

"When—when will that be, I wonder?" Eve asked as the three of them walked downstairs together.

Kelly's face shone. "That's the other thing I wanted to tell you. Oh, Eve, I spoke with Dr. Perry this morning," she said. "We're going to try next week." She smiled lovingly up at her husband.

Next week, Eve thought with wonder. *I might be pregnant next week. Pregnant. Me!*

The thought awed her.

THE PROCEDURE had been simple. An egg extracted surgically from Kelly's ovary united with Derek's sperm in a Petri dish, and in an incubator set previously at the temperature of body heat, the fertilized egg shivered and shuddered and clove in two. In sudden bright bursts of energy, nuclei split, chromosomes energetically aligned themselves, and the unique design of a new baby was irrevocably created. And once again, in a process as ancient as the ages but no less miraculous for all that, a fertilized egg became a new human being, child of Kelly and Derek Lang, citizen of the universe.

When it was several cells in size, the tiny embryo was injected into Eve's uterus by Dr. Perry, using a syringe with a soft plastic tip. Kelly had been present in the room when it was done, clinging tightly to Eve's hand.

"Are you all right?" she'd kept asking Eve, her blue eyes intent on Eve's face.

Eve, lightly sedated, barely felt the embryo when it entered the mouth of her womb. "I'm perfectly all right," Eve reassured Kelly. She was glad that Kelly was with her, holding on to Eve's hand for dear life. Kelly's presence made the tiny morsel of life in her uterus seem more like Kelly's baby. And she must remember, Eve told herself fiercely, that it *is* Kelly and Derek's baby. She, Eve, was merely providing a temporary home for it.

If they were lucky, the embryo would embed itself in the lining of Eve's womb, and Eve would be pregnant. *If.* That one little word with its myriad possibilities had never seemed so big to any of them before now.

Afterward, the three of them settled down to wait, Kelly and Derek in their big Georgian house in Myers Park, and Eve, nervous despite her calm front, at home in Wrayville with Al.

If the pregnancy didn't take, they would try again. And again. They would try every month for a year, if necessary.

But an elated Eve knew by the end of the first week that they had been successful. Her breasts began to swell, and she knew from her recent reading that this was one of the first signs of pregnancy. Eve understood her own body too well to believe that this new swelling and tenderness was a sign of anything other than what it was.

Eve cautiously told Kelly, who called every day, that she thought she was pregnant.

"On the first try? Oh, Eve, I can hardly dare to hope!" Kelly's voice quavered with emotion.

"Neither can I," Eve replied, her heart in her mouth. She wanted this to be the real thing, hoped for it more than she ever thought she would.

Al answered the phone one day when Kelly called. "Who's that?" he asked when Eve had hung up.

"A new friend of mine," she said casually.

"Oh," said Al, who was engrossed in a tired rerun of *Gomer Pyle* on television. "I didn't think I recognized her voice." And he said no more about it.

Eve agonized. She almost wished Al had been more curious, because she'd never kept secrets from him before. When would she tell her father what she was doing? What would he say? How would he react?

For Al Triopolous was the product of an old-time Greek culture where marriages were arranged, where husband and wife didn't kiss in front of the children, where girls did not date, where old traditions were preserved. True, he had broken those traditions himself when he had left Tarpon Springs, never to live there again, and when he had subsequently married Eve's mother. But what would Al think of a woman, his own daughter, who deliberately impregnated herself with the child of a couple she hardly knew? And for money, at that? Though her motives were pure and would benefit both of them, Eve dreaded telling Al with all her heart.

Nights, lying awake and listening to Al's labored breathing next door, Eve stared into the darkness and worried the problem in her mind. She hugged her secret close in the dark, running her hands over her breasts, her midriff, her hips, searching for some sign that her body was betraying her to Al. But no, her stomach was still flat. And so she still didn't tell him.

"WELL LADIES, how does February sound for your baby's due date?"

Kelly and Eve, side by side in Dr. Perry's office after his examination of Eve, turned to each other in glee. Eve never knew who held her arms out first, she or Kelly. She only knew that she was happy, joyful, ecstatic, on behalf of Kelly and Derek.

Kelly pulled away from Eve and wept into a daintily embroidered handkerchief. "I can't help it," she said sobbing, "I'm just so *happy*! And oh, Derek will be, too!"

Eve was happy, too, but that wasn't why she wept. She wept because she still didn't know how she was going to tell Al.

"AND SO THEY WANT ME to move to Charlotte," Eve said carefully.

"This 'textile executive' you're going to work for—he doesn't mind that you were dismissed from Wray Mills?" Al asked sharply.

"We've never actually discussed it," Eve said, moistening her lips and hating herself for being so evasive.

"Ah," Al said, and he paused to cough. "It must be a pretty good job, eh? What exactly will you do?"

"I'm going to be a sort of personal assistant," Eve said, getting up and rummaging in a drawer for her father's inhaler. "Have you been using your inhaler, Al?" she asked. "I don't like the sound of that cough."

"Don't worry," he said.

"I'd worry a lot less if I thought you were taking good care of yourself while you're living here alone," she told him firmly, setting the inhaler within Al's reach.

"Mrs. Baker will be glad to take care of me," he retorted. His dark eyes sparkled at her.

"Oh, Al, you know what I mean," she said.

"I'll miss you, daughter. But we'll still have the weekends."

"Yes," Eve said, trying not to wince as her swollen breasts chafed against the fabric of her too-tight bra. "We'll still have the weekends."

But for how long? she wondered. *How long will it be before I start to show?*

IT TOOK ONLY A WEEK of living with the Langs to turn Eve's act of self-survival into an act of love.

Yes, the hefty allowance that Derek gave her made it possible for Eve to tackle the tall stack of Al's medical bills. Yes, the contracted agreement that she would receive twelve thousand dollars when the baby was born ensured a brighter future for her and Al. But after being with Kelly and Derek and Kelly's Aunt May, who lived with them—well, Eve would have been an emotional cripple if she hadn't loved them.

"Eve," Kelly would say, popping into her room after breakfast, "I'm going shopping. Won't you come with me? Oh, please say yes," and Kelly would bear Eve away in the Mercedes, drive to Eastland Mall or Southpark Mall or any of the other wonderful shopping places Kelly knew, and they would shop for baby furniture or baby clothes or maternity clothes for Eve, giggling and carrying on like two teenagers.

Or Eve would say after she had been there a few days, "Kelly, play something on the piano, will you, please?"

And Kelly would sit dreamily at the piano, playing tune after tune while Eve listened attentively and with admiration for Kelly's considerable talent.

Eve loved Kelly for her lack of pretense. Kelly was easy to be around; she was a good conversationalist; she possessed a voice that rolled forth rapidly at times and at other times proceeded in fits and starts as she stopped to catch her breath and then rattled it out in words.

The two of them talked and talked, Kelly of her upbringing in upper-crust Charlotte, Eve of her childhood in a cotton-mill town. Their backgrounds were dissimilar enough to be interesting to each other, and they had the common ground of the baby now growing in Eve's womb. After only a few weeks, Kelly was the sister Eve had never been privileged to have.

Aunt May was nearly seventy, a spry type with a great cloud of curled white hair sheened with lavender. Her plump figure, because of her addiction to frivolous shoes with absurdly high heels, reminded Eve of a pouter pigeon wearing stilts. A box of chocolates was never far from hand, and Aunt May was deplorably hard of hearing and kept misplacing her hearing aid. She pronounced herself "tickled pink" about the baby.

"I don't think much of space flights and laser weapons and all that," she confided loudly to Eve on Eve's first day in the Myers Park house. "But I do approve of modern technology that lets somebody have a baby for somebody else. Now that's progress. Here, dear, have a chocolate-covered cherry. No? You're not into bean curd and health food things, are you? What's that? What?"

Eve, who had only been trying to tell Aunt May that she was determined to eat properly for the baby's sake, gave up. It was enough that Aunt May liked her.

And Derek. The unfailingly methodical Derek, who rose at the same time every day, dressed in a well-cut three-piece suit before going outside to retrieve the paper and then read it carefully front to back before driving off to work at his job in one of the new gleaming glass-and-chrome office buildings on Tryon Street. Who always kissed his wife as soon as he walked through the front door, whose love for Kelly beamed from his gray eyes, which could sparkle with humor or darken with empathy.

Was there ever so perfect a husband as Derek? Did he ever fail to compliment his wife on her appearance or neglect to hold her chair for her at dinner or listen when she spoke? Eve's admiration for Derek grew day by day. *If I ever marry,* she thought more than once, *let it be to a man like him*. But this was only daydreaming. Such men, Eve had decided long ago, were few and far between. Even the one man she'd ever been serious about, and that was more than two years ago, had had a few rough edges. And Derek had none of those, at least none that Eve could see. *I'm glad Kelly has Derek,* Eve thought on several occasions. The best part was that Eve knew that Kelly understood her own good fortune. .

A thoughtful host, Derek even took time to inquire gravely after Eve's health.

"You need to eat regularly," he had chided her one day when she admitted that she'd skipped lunch.

Eve shrugged. "It's an old habit."

"Seriously, Eve, the baby's health depends on what you eat. Or drink."

"I don't drink. Not even wine with dinner."

"I know." His eyes, slate-gray now, rested on her fondly. "That's one of the things that Kelly and I picked out of your personality profile. You don't drink, and you don't smoke. That was important to us."

"I never cared much for drinking. And smoking—well, I tried a cigarette once. I hated it."

Derek laughed. "I tried it once, too. And hated it." He smiled warmly.

"Now junk food's something else again," Eve admitted with a grin. "I love to fill myself full of potato chips, pretzels—"

"Have you ever eaten cheese doodles dipped in Pepsi?" asked Derek with a rare look of mischief.

"Don't tell me you're a junk-food junkie, too!" said Eve, shocked to amazement. Junk food simply did not fit in with what she knew of the ultraconservative Derek Lang.

"Don't tell anyone. It wouldn't be good for my image," he whispered.

"I won't," Eve whispered back conspiratorially. "If you won't tell anyone that I still occasionally snitch a potato chip behind Kelly's and Aunt May's back."

Derek laughed again. Then he became more serious. "I can keep a secret. *If* you'll promise me not to skip any more meals."

Eve sobered. "I promise," she said, meaning it. "I want this baby to be healthy, too, Derek."

It was shortly after that when Derek intercepted Eve on one of her secret solitary forays into the pantry at midnight.

"Aha!" he said, flicking on the light. "Caught you!"

Although she was startled, Eve's mouth curved upward in a smile, which made her look like a happy chipmunk, for she had just crammed it with a double handful of caramel corn.

Derek relieved her of the bag of caramel corn and stuffed his own mouth, and they stood solemnly munching until Eve swallowed hers and burst into laughter.

"Do you raid the pantry often?" Derek asked curiously when he could. He had just returned from an eighteen-hour day at the office and was wearing his customary three-piece suit; Eve was clad in her nightgown with an old bathrobe over it. He stared down at her bare feet.

"Umm—well." She curled her toes under so that the hem of the long robe covered them.

"The truth, Eve," he said sternly.

"No," she said boldly, looking him straight in the eye. "Because if I did, you would have caught me long before this."

He stared at her, then threw his head back and laughed long and loud.

"Shh, you'll wake everyone up," Eve said in consternation.

"And that would be a terrible mistake. They'd eat all our caramel corn."

The episode had ended with their sitting at opposite ends of the breakfast-room table, coconspirators passing the caramel corn back and forth until it was all gone. When, at one in the morning, yawning, they both traipsed off to bed, she and Derek were friends.

Eve was pleased that Derek cared about her. And she was happy that, like Kelly and Aunt May, he had accepted her temporary presence in his home as part of his life.

Yet despite the easy camaraderie, on the third week of Eve's residence in the Myers Park house Kelly confided that Derek was distracted by problems at work.

"I just thought I'd mention it, because we don't want you to think he's not interested in you and the baby. But Lang Textiles is going through growing pains." And Kelly shook her head ruefully. "Derek feels responsible, because since he took over as president after his father retired, it's his management concept, and he wants it to work. Anyway, Derek's job is going to gobble up a lot of his time for the next few weeks," Kelly said. She lit up with a brilliant smile. "That's why I'm so glad you're here, Eve," she said, linking her arm through Eve's and making Eve feel more a part of life in this house than ever.

Eve knew without a doubt that this baby she carried, this baby who was now no more than the size of Eve's thumbnail, was the luckiest baby in the world, being born to Kelly and Derek.

Still, even the most perfect couple were bound to have disagreements. Nevertheless, for Eve it was a surprise when she finally encountered one.

On a warm summer evening five weeks into her pregnancy, Eve lingered alone in the study, thumbing through a book Kelly had suggested she might like, when she heard Kelly and Derek talking on the terrace. She started to leave; it was almost dusk, and if she had stayed, she would have had to turn on a light, which would draw attention to herself.

"But Derek, I just thought if you felt like talking about it, I—"

"Kelly, no. I'm tired when I get home at the end of the day, and as for talking about the mills, well, I'd rather not. We're so bogged down in negotiations that I wonder if I ever should have been so hardheaded about acquisitions, if maybe the others were right." Derek's voice was tight with worry.

"With the baby on the way," Kelly said slowly, "I know I haven't been exactly attentive to you, and that worries me. I haven't meant to ignore you. It's just that I'm so excited, and I love having Eve here, and maybe I've been spending too much time with her. I have to confess that I—I was lonely before Eve came, with you so busy."

"Lonely?"

"Yes, Derek. There are so many things I've wanted to talk about, and—"

"Don't I talk with you? Don't we do things together? Didn't I call you this afternoon and ask if there were any errands that needed doing downtown so that you wouldn't have to go out in the heat?"

"Of course, but that's not what I mean. Oh, Derek, with the baby coming, we should be closer than ever, and we're not. You know we're not." Her voice lowered a half tone. "We haven't made love in weeks!"

"You know how tired I've been!" Derek snapped. Then, wearily, he said, "Oh, hell, Kelly, I'm sorry. I love you—you know that—and I'm happy about the baby."

"I know," Kelly said, sounding anything but happy herself.

A long silence. Then Derek said tenderly, "Come over here," and that was when Eve, very disturbed by this time that she had eavesdropped on this highly personal marital discussion, crept quietly out of the study and upstairs to her room. It was nothing. Of course it was nothing. So why did she feel so unsettled by it?

Naturally there was no mention of Kelly's discussion with Derek when Kelly knocked gently at Eve's bedroom door the next morning.

"Eve?" Kelly said.

Eve, still wearing her bathrobe, lay on her back on the brass bed, fighting nausea. Eve hadn't told Kelly that she'd begun to have morning sickness. It would only worry her. The nausea only lasted for a short time right after breakfast, and besides, it was just a slight queasiness.

"Come in," Eve said, sitting up. She wondered, a little guiltily, how Kelly and Derek's discussion had ended last night. She hoped—but then, it was none of her business.

"You're not sick, are you?" Kelly asked in concern.

"No, no. Just a little tired. You know, I asked Dr. Perry about it, and he said it's usual to be tired during the first couple of months."

"I was going to ask you if you wanted to come with me this morning," Kelly said with a grin. She looked normal and happy and also very pretty in her pastel plaid skirt with the sky-blue blouse that matched her eyes. "But I've just changed my mind. If you're tired, you'd better rest."

"No, I—"

"I'm going to the printer's. My music club is staging that benefit concert next month, and I'm going to order the programs this morning. I'll only be gone for an hour or so, so it's hardly worth your getting up and getting dressed. I'll be back before you know it." Kelly cast a look out the window. "Anyway, it looks like rain. One of those summer storms is probably brewing. We can't have you traipsing about in the wet, little mother!"

Eve fell back upon the pillows with a wry grin. "Well, as long as you put it that way," she said.

Kelly laughed. "See you later. And if for some reason I'm not back before lunch, look after Derek for me, will you? In his present frame of mind, he's not able to take Aunt May for more than fifteen minutes at a time."

"Will do," Eve said, and Kelly jingled her car keys at her as she cheerfully waved goodbye.

Moments later, Eve heard the Mercedes backing out of the garage, and shortly afterward the pitter-patter of raindrops began. A distant rumble of thunder rattled the window. Soon the melody of the rain on the roof lulled Eve to sleep, and she slept until almost twelve.

When she awoke, she was amazed that she'd slept so long. She went downstairs to ask Aunt May or Louise if Kelly was home yet, yawning in spite of her long nap. She'd be glad when this phase of her pregnancy was over, she thought. She'd never expected to be so tired.

A car reeled recklessly into the driveway, and Eve peered out the hall window at it through the steady downpour. Oh, it was Derek. He was home for lunch as usual, and she, slugabed that she was, hadn't even dressed yet. She turned to go back upstairs.

But something about the way he angled out of his low-slung Corvette stopped her. He hurried through the rain without a raincoat, which was peculiar in a man as meticulous as Derek. Derek was never without an umbrella; when it rained, he always wore a tan Burberry raincoat, even for the slightest shower. His shoulders seemed oddly slumped.

And now he was striding toward the house, his suit coat flung open, his tie flying up against his shirt, and his face was the face of a man demented.

Something was wrong, terribly wrong. Eve froze, unable to move.

Derek threw the front door open and saw her standing there, cringing now like a frightened rabbit. His eyes were rimmed in red, and in a heart-stopping moment, Eve was positive that the water on his face wasn't rain.

His face, his handsome face, crumpled before her very eyes. He held his hands out to her in supplication. They trembled, flinging raindrops on her feet.

"Eve," he said, his voice hoarse with anguish. Petrified, in horror, she didn't know what to do.

"Eve, there's been an accident. A terrible accident. Eve, oh, Eve, Kelly is dead."

And then Derek collapsed in her arms.

EVE NEVER KNEW afterward how she got through the next few days. The turgid July heat clamped down on the house in Myers Park even more oppressively than usual, and the heat intensified the smell of the flowers, the flowers that were strewn everywhere, disgorged by florists' vans and florists' trucks until it seemed that all the flowers in the world had converged upon this spot.

Aunt May was literally prostrate with a grief that, for the first time in her life, she could not assuage with chocolates. Derek was unable to function, and this so surprised and angered him that he wasted no time on the usual bromides or niceties required by the occasion. Heartbroken, he moved through the rituals stony-faced, rigid and uncommunicative. And so the bulk of what needed to be done fell on Eve's shoulders.

Derek's father came from South America, accompanied by his elaborately bejeweled wife, who was young enough to be his daughter, and Derek's mother arrived from Virginia and remained glassily tranquilized throughout the ordeal. Derek's sister, an angular woman with no warmth to her, who was quite clearly there only because she felt it was an obligation, flew in from Grosse Point on the morning of the funeral and rapidly flew out again that evening. Kelly had only one relative, Aunt May. So when people wondered who Eve was, she merely said she was a friend of the family. No one knew, no one guessed, what her true mission in the household was.

Eve's main concern was for the baby she carried. Her mourning was for the baby's mother. And for the baby's father she felt compassion. She had never seen anyone as grief-stricken as Derek Lang.

But she—she must remain strong. For the baby's sake. For Kelly's sake. And for Derek's sake.

Because when all this was over, when the mourners had gone home, the baby would be all that Derek had left of Kelly.

And so the night after the funeral, when the house was finally silent, when darkness fell, when the only sound in the house was the muted tick-tock of the grandfather clock on the stair landing, Eve knocked on the door of Derek's study.

He didn't answer, so she pushed the door open.

Derek sat at his desk, one small lamp lit, and the green-shaded light picked out the golden highlights in his butternut-brown hair. His face was buried in his hands, and he didn't look up when Eve walked in.

She cleared her throat. "Derek," she said softly, "I don't mean to be a bother. But we need to talk."

He raised his head, and his face seemed engraved with new lines of tragedy, his gray eyes reflecting the agony of his loss. He didn't speak for a long moment, just stared at her as though he had never seen her before. For a moment he wondered who she was, what she wanted. Then he remembered, and with the memory came even more sorrow.

"Eve," he said, and his voice was raw. She saw his throat muscles working, and she thought he would break down. But he didn't.

She felt a foreshadowing of doom, but she knew she was headed straight for it and that it was too late to stop.

"Eve," he said, more clearly now that he had regained control of himself. "I've been thinking about it. I think the best thing for you to do under the circumstances would be to have an abortion."

Chapter Three

The air felt leaden. Eve couldn't breathe. Her eyes dimmed, and she had to grip her hands together tightly to keep them from shaking. She sank into a chair across the desk from Derek. Had she heard him correctly? No, she couldn't have! But from the way he was measuring her reaction, she knew she had.

She was taking it calmly. He might have known she would. Hadn't Kelly said that Eve wasn't the type to go into a dither about anything? Eve sat squarely in the chair, her hands folded neatly in her lap, and his eyes lingered for a moment on her hands. Her fingernails had wide half-moons at the base and were cut sensibly short and unadorned by anything but clear nail gloss. Everything about her was neat and precise; she was a symmetrical person. Eve. A symmetrical name, even. He liked symmetry in furnishings, which is why he had chosen this Georgian house, but also in people and in life. Only life wasn't always symmetrical, was it?

"No," she said firmly.

He closed his eyes and reopened them. He was not in the mood for an argument.

"It would be best," he repeated. "Best for all of us."

Eve shook her head. "I can't believe you mean that."

"I do."

"Derek, you're very tired. You're overwrought. I can understand. In fact, it would be better if we talked in the morning." She started to get up, groping for the support of the chair arm. She was falling apart with weariness.

"Yes, I am tired," he acknowledged heavily. "In fact, I'm exhausted. But I assure you that I'm thinking clearly and that I am not drunk or stoned or under the influence of anything else that would distort my thought processes."

"But to destroy the life that Kelly wanted so much, to destroy part of her and part of yourself—"

"That's enough!" he said sharply. And then, more kindly, he said, "Look, it's not your fault. You were dragged into this by us, and I apologize for that. You—"

"I was not dragged into anything!" Eve protested, her temper flaring. "I wanted to have this baby for you and Kelly. I wanted to help you and—"

"You wanted the money," he said wearily. "I read the application. Look, you'll get your twelve thousand dollars. I'll pay you, anyway."

Eve swallowed. Her mouth felt dry. "I did it partly for the money," she said slowly. "But that wasn't the whole reason. Derek, I loved Kelly. She was like a sister to me."

Derek leaned back in his chair and blinked at the ceiling. A sigh tore from his body, a sigh of anguish. "Don't talk about her," he said brokenly. "I can't stand it." He pressed the heels of his hands to his eyes for a moment, then lowered his head to look at Eve.

Tears dampened Eve's lower eyelashes. She looked so hurt, so vulnerable. God, what a scene to put her through! First Kelly and now this. Eve had suffered too many shocks lately. Derek knew in that instant that he could have handled the matter more sensitively, and he wished he had.

He stood abruptly and walked to the window, gazing out over the moonlit terrace with its memories of his wife. Just a few nights ago the two of them had stood there.... He clenched his hands and stuffed them deep in his pockets before he turned to face Eve, who was surreptitiously brushing at her damp cheeks with the edge of one hand.

All through this whole ordeal, Eve had been a quiet, comforting presence, handling all the small details that he and Aunt May had been unable to manage. Derek hadn't seen her cry at all until now. Too late, his heart flooded with gratitude. He was ashamed of himself for hitting her with this at the wrong time.

He walked slowly to where she sat staring down at the carpet.

"Eve, look at me."

Slowly, she raised her eyes to his, those soft brown eyes. Deep inside them he saw the hurt.

He spoke gently. "Eve, this isn't the time to discuss this. I'm sorry. I shouldn't have startled you with it. But time is important. If it's going to be done, it should be done soon. You're how far along?"

"Six weeks," she whispered, sick at heart.

"Six weeks."

She squared her narrow shoulders, and looking down at her, he noticed that one was slightly lower than the other. Her shoulders looked so fragile, as though any burden would be too great for them. But when she stood up, he realized suddenly that he had miscalculated her reaction.

"There will be no abortion, Derek," she said, looking him straight in the eye. "Even if I have to raise the child myself."

Now her shoulders rose in anger, like hackles, and she reminded him of an angry swan he had once seen, a fierce black Australian swan that had spread its wings and attacked him with a frightening hiss when he wandered too close to its nest. But Eve simply stared at him, her gentle brown eyes glinting with determination, and then she turned swiftly and walked out of the room.

Bring the child up herself? He couldn't believe she would even consider it. It was out of the question.

Slowly, Derek returned to his chair. He had made a mess out of this; no doubt about it. He asked himself in anguish, *What would Kelly do?* And because he knew the answer right away, he let his head sink to the desktop, the cool polished walnut surface soothing his hot forehead.

Oh, Kelly, Kelly, he thought. And then, finally, now that everyone had gone, he felt alone enough to loose the floodgates of his own grief.

"NEVER," Eve muttered to herself as she flung off her clothes and slipped into her nightgown. "Never."

She slid between the sheets of the dainty brass bed and stared up at the ceiling. She knew she wouldn't sleep tonight.

There was no way Derek could make her get rid of this baby. Ultimately, it was her body; feverishly, she had examined her copy of the contract with the Langs. Although their attorney had not foreseen this contingency, as far as Eve could determine, the contract they had all signed gave Derek no right to insist that she terminate the pregnancy.

Abortion was against Eve's principles. It would always be against her principals. She would never, as long as she still drew breath, allow anything to hurt this baby, the baby Kelly had wanted so much.

For now Eve knew that she wanted the baby, too. The baby was part of Kelly, and that part of Kelly deserved to survive.

Tears trickled out of the corners of her eyes, and she pressed the palms of her hands to her abdomen as if to shield the unborn child. In wonder she realized that her abdomen was beginning to swell ever so slightly with the baby's presence. Suddenly she was overcome with an emotion that she recognized as unmistakably maternal: she loved this baby, this baby that was part of her and yet not, and this baby needed her. As much as Kelly and Derek, she was responsible for its existence. Without Eve, this baby could not have been.

No matter what Derek said, the baby would be born.

Even, as she had told Derek, if she had to raise the baby herself.

"DID YOU SLEEP WELL, Aunt May?" Eve asked Kelly's aunt the next morning.

Aunt May trickled another spoonful of sugar into her coffee and stirred it lackadaisically. "Need curls?" she replied. "I should say I need curls. In fact, I have a hairdresser's appointment this morning."

"Not need curls, Aunt May," Eve said more loudly. "I asked if you slept well."

"Oh," Aunt May said in a slightly disappointed tone. "That pill the doctor gave me put me right to sleep. Do you have anything to take at night, dear? You're looking tired."

Eve hadn't slept last night, not a wink. "I wouldn't take any medicine, because it might affect the baby," Eve reminded her gently.

"Oh, I hadn't thought of that. You do have to be careful, don't you?" Aunt May raised blue eyes to Derek as Derek entered the breakfast room. "Good morning, Derek. Did you know Eve can't take any sleeping pills because of the baby?"

Derek shot Eve a sharp look, which she returned levelly. Eve *did* look tired, he thought. But she wasn't taking sleeping pills because of the baby. What was the point when soon the baby wouldn't exist anymore?

Louise, her eyes downcast and swollen with crying, brought a serving dish of scrambled eggs and retreated to the kitchen. Derek helped himself before passing them to Eve, who passed them on to Aunt May without taking any.

"Aren't you eating breakfast?" Derek asked sharply.

"I'm not hungry," Eve hedged. She was barely managing to keep morning sickness at bay.

"I'm not hungry, either," Aunt May declared, pushing her chair away from the table. "I don't have any appetite. Anyway, Louise is driving me to the hairdresser in an hour or so, and I want to get dressed." She smiled wanly at Derek and Eve before weaving off down the hall in a pair of impossibly high heeled satin bedroom slippers.

"Eat something," Derek ordered, pushing the scrambled eggs in Eve's direction.

The very sight of eggs sickened Eve.

"I—I can't!" she managed to gasp before lurching to her feet and running for the powder room nearby, where she slammed the door closed and, with a peculiar sense of retribution toward Derek, proceeded to be sick to her stomach.

"Eve? Eve!"

Eve ran the water in the sink and dashed some over her face. She stared at her reflection in the mirror. Her face looked back at her, a chalky gray-white. If only Derek would stop making that ungodly racket outside the door, she would feel much better. Trembling, she threw the door open and with a great deal of effort walked out with her head held high.

"Are you all right?" Derek didn't like the look of her, and he didn't want to worry about her. Didn't he have enough to worry about with his wife dead and the mills to run and poor old Aunt May? And yet he *was* worried about Eve, her normally pale skin so white that he could see the minute blue veins threading her eyelids like a natural eye shadow. Did her eyelids always look like that? He couldn't remember.

"Morning sickness," she explained unnecessarily. It surprised her that he was so upset. It gave her hope that he was so upset.

"I didn't know you were having morning sickness."

"It just started about a week ago." She forced a smile.

"Can I get you anything? Are you all right?"

Surprisingly enough, she was hungry—ravenously hungry.

"I think I'll eat breakfast, after all," she said, sounding stronger than he had expected. And then she sat down, and to Derek's utter disbelief, she devoured not only a huge mound of eggs but also sausages and biscuits complete with butter and orange marmalade.

"You said you didn't want me to skip meals," she said by way of explanation.

"That was before—" And then he stopped because of the warning look in Eve's eyes.

A biscuit and its accompanying marmalade sat heavily on her tongue. With effort, she swallowed. "Before you decided that this baby wouldn't be born?"

Derek nodded. "I'm hoping you'll come to your senses about this, Eve."

"No, Derek, I meant what I said."

Louise, sniffing loudly, came in to clear the table, and they remained silent until she left.

"Eve, you're only adding to my grief by being stubborn."

"And you're adding to mine by being stupid."

No one had ever, in all his life, called Derek Lang stupid. He flushed, and then he rose from the table and threw his cloth napkin on the table. With one last unfathomable look at Eve, he slammed out of the house, and in a few moments Eve heard the Corvette roar out of the driveway.

Eve sat in the toile-papered breakfast room and stared grimly out the bow window at the woodpecker that was finding its own breakfast in the bark of the tree outside.

She managed to remain numb for five minutes. Then the phone rang.

STUPID. Was he being stupid?

As he drove to work, Derek forced his mind to flip through the gut-wrenching scene in his study last night.

I was stupid, he realized with a start. Stupid to have thought that Eve would fall right into his pattern of thinking, stupid to have flattened her so suddenly with the idea of an abortion. Well, maybe not stupid. He was grieving for his wife, and perhaps he hadn't been thinking as clearly as he thought he had. If he'd been thinking clearly, he never would have approached Eve in that manner, never.

He parked his Corvette and fielded the startled gaze of the parking attendant as he set off at a swift walk for the nearby entrance to his office building. Probably no one expected him to come to work the morning after his wife's funeral. Well, why shouldn't he? There was nothing to stay home for now.

"Good morning, Mr. Lang," was the subdued but surprised greeting of the receptionist.

Derek nodded briskly and proceeded with what he considered appropriate speed down the gray-carpeted hall to his office. Returning to work was turning out to be an ordeal of the first magnitude, he thought to his chagrin. But then, it would have been an ordeal no matter when he did it.

A group clustered around the water cooler murmured morning greetings, which he returned a bit too heartily. He walked on, aware that they were all staring at his back. He clenched his teeth.

"Good morning, Derek," said his secretary, Maisie Allen, hanging up the phone. Obviously she had been forewarned that he was on his way, probably by the goggle-eyed receptionist.

He nodded, less briskly this time, and fairly ran into the sanctuary of his office, shutting the door firmly behind him. He stopped for a moment, feeling oddly out of breath as he stared at the wide-window view of Charlotte below, and wondered why there was no fresh cup of coffee on his desk. Maisie always had coffee waiting on his desk when he arrived.

"They didn't think I'd come in," he said out loud, and then he jumped when the door behind him opened unexpectedly.

"Just delivering your coffee," Maisie said, trotting briskly to his desk and setting his cup down on it. An inadvertent picture of Maisie's moon face surmounted by a tall and pompous hat at the funeral sprang into his mind. They had all been there, though, taking part in his tragedy. All the employees. His office manager must have given them yesterday morning off.

"Thanks," he said in as normal a tone as possible, though to himself his voice sounded as though it were pitched incredibly high.

Maisie, a no-nonsense matronly woman with an immense bosom and an equally huge derriere, trotted back out again. Derek walked slowly to his desk and sat down at his chair with a sigh.

Well, why shouldn't he come to work today? Work was the only thing that would take his mind off Kelly and the accident. Work and its attendant problems—the worry about what foreign textile imports were doing to the industry, the acquisition of the new mill—would occupy his mind, if not assuage his grief.

He ventured a tentative sip of the coffee. It was very hot. He set the cup down on his desk again. In the summer the weather was too hot to drink coffee. That's what Kelly always said. Kelly....

With difficulty, he forced himself not to think about her. Think about something else instead. Perhaps he should give up coffee; someone else had given up coffee recently. His brain fogged up like a windshield on a rainy night, and when the fog cleared, he could hear Eve, as distinctly as though she were sitting beside him. In fact, when she'd said it, she'd been sitting beside him at the dining-room table. "I'm giving up coffee until after the baby's born, because I'm worried about the effect caffeine will have on its growth." Kelly had smiled in approval, and so had he. Eve had smiled back, revealing that one bicuspid, turned slightly sideways, the only feature that offset the symmetry of her face but only showed when she smiled.

Eve smiling, Eve crying. Eve crying the way she had cried in his study last night, the glistening tears drooping momentarily from her lower eyelashes before spilling down her pale cheeks.

He knocked his coffee cup over and jumped up before the brown liquid could stain his navy-blue suit. Swearing, he blotted at the mess with a monogrammed handkerchief. He could have called Maisie to clean it up, but—well, he didn't want to talk about anything right now. He snatched the oval gold picture frame up before the coffee inundated it, then dabbed ineffectually at the desktop and replaced the picture frame. The picture, of course, was of Kelly, an exuberant Kelly on the day they had climbed Mount Mitchell, the highest peak in North Carolina. It had been one of the happiest days in their lives, the first day of a wonderful vacation they'd taken six years ago, right after she'd found out for sure she was pregnant. He had snapped the picture himself.

Six years ago. That baby would have been almost five and a half by this time if it had lived. Five years old and no mother. But would Kelly have been in her car at that precise time four days ago, in the path of the other driver, if she'd had a five-year-old child at home? Maybe not. Then again, maybe, and maybe the child would have been with her, in which case he would now be mourning both his wife and his child. Who was to say what would have happened had some turning point in life arranged the choices differently? Who knew beforehand what twists of fate would affect us? The myriad possibilities loomed before him in a kaleidoscope of combinations: you travel this road, and other roads branch off it; you select a different road, and you're presented with other roads, other choices.

It was what he would have to make Eve see, he knew. That the road he had chosen when Kelly was alive was not the road he would choose now. That it wasn't too late to backtrack and start over again, taking another route.

Was Eve capable of comprehending?

He pictured her soft brown eyes, her intelligent face. Yes, she was capable. He was sure that eventually he could make her see the folly of continuing this pregnancy.

Who would have thought that Eve could be so stubborn?

"AL, DON'T BE PIGHEADED!"

Eve's patience with her father was wearing thin. She didn't want him to get upset; if he did, he'd only have another coughing spell, which would sap his fragile energy. And it was obvious to her that Al was going to have to muster all the energy he could. Today, this very morning, the management of Wray Mills had ordered them to vacate their house by the end of the week. They'd known they'd have to move eventually. But by the end of the week? Impossible.

"Eve, dear, I'm going to walk over to the mill first thing in the morning and talk to them. I'll ask them for a month's extension. I've lived in this house for thirty years; another month wouldn't hurt. Anyway, they don't have a waiting list. No one wants to move in. I think they'll listen to me."

Eve shook her head dubiously. "You're a thorn in their side. They want to get rid of you, probably so they won't have to find your 'lost' workmen's compensation claim before they sell the mill. You know, every time you walk past the mill, they probably feel guilty for what they've done to you."

"Done to me? You mean this lung problem? I know, I know, but Wray Mills gave me a job when I was desperate. I've never forgotten that."

"Oh, Al. They gave you a job that made you sick in the end. And they say that the disease you have can't be proved to have been caused by conditions in the mill. That's hogwash, and you know it!" Eve paced the floor of the small living room, wrapping her arms around herself in her agitation. On the floor a fan hustled the stale heavy air of a Piedmont summer, but it wasn't the fan that chilled her. It was her father's unwarranted respect for Wray Mills.

"Let me talk to them tomorrow," Al insisted. "You're staying the night?"

Eve gestured toward her small overnight bag. Al's phone call with the news that he was about to be evicted had brought Eve back to Wrayville immediately, and she had packed enough clothes so that she could stay for a few days. Anyway, she had needed to get out of the Myers Park house. She hadn't wanted to talk to Derek, because she knew he'd only pressure her.

"I'm glad you're staying," Al said, his features brightening with his first smile since Eve's arrival that morning. "It'll be like having you living at home again."

But of course it wasn't. Could you ever go back home? Eve wondered as she walked down the narrow Cotton Mill Hill street after dinner, waving to the neighbors, most of whom she had known all her life, and stopping now and then to chat with those she knew well.

Yes, she said over and over, she was enjoying her new job. Yes, she told an interested Nell Baker, she liked living in Charlotte. She sensed that their friends were being cautious about what they said about living arrangements, perhaps because everyone knew by this time that Wray Mills had ordered them to vacate the company-owned house. People sympathized, Eve knew. It was just that they were wary of saying much about the situation for fear of reprisals from the company, especially now that everyone's job was in jeopardy because of the rumored takeover of Wray Mills by a large textile conglomerate.

At the bottom of the hill, she recognized the lanky jean-clad figure of Doug Ender. He hailed her with enthusiasm, smiling as she approached. Doug was one of the few people in Wrayville who was not dependent on Wray Mills for a living.

He'd grown up here, and his family had been mill people, but they were all gone now. Doug, a bachelor, had worked his way through law school at the University of North Carolina and had returned to Wrayville to start his modest practice. He handled wills, lawsuits, and defended local toughs who got into trouble with the law. He and Eve had known each other since they were children, and he had done her a favor by agreeing to take the case in Al's claim for workmen's compensation.

"Eve," Doug said, his face lighting with pleasure. He looked genuinely happy to see her, and she was happy to see him. "I heard you found a job." He fell into step beside her.

Eve nodded. She was unsure whether to discuss her "job" with Doug; she worried about his reaction. She and Doug were close—close enough, she'd thought on various occasions, for their relationship to deepen into something more. But it never had, mostly because Eve had always held back, waiting for that special chemistry to happen. And now, with her pregnant— well, if the chemistry was going to happen between them, it would have to wait.

"Any news about my father's claim?" she asked him, partly to change the subject but partly because she wanted to know.

Doug's expression became serious. "No, I'm afraid not. The mill management is in chaos, not knowing if the mill is going to be sold or not."

"Then it's true? Somebody is talking about buying Wray Mills?"

Doug nodded. "It looks like it. Eve, I don't know what that would mean in regard to Al's claim."

"I suppose it depends on the buyer," Eve replied. "Whether or not they have a record of settling byssinosis claims or not."

"Some of the textile companies deny that it's a legitimate disease. They say they're not sure conditions in the mills cause it."

"No one who has ever seen the inside of a card room at the mill could say that all that flying dust isn't detrimental to the people who work there."

"Not everybody has seen the inside of a card room," Doug said with irony. "You and I never would have if we hadn't grown up here."

"We're just lucky, I guess," Eve said ruefully.

"Yeah," he said. Then, quickly, he suggested, "Say, Eve, let's have dinner together tonight."

She looked up at him, surprised. It was entirely natural that he ask her out, and a few weeks ago she would have accepted. But now, with her mind in a turmoil about Derek's demand that she have an abortion and with her worry about Al's possible eviction, how could she say yes?

"Oh, Doug," she said, "I can't. I'm only here for a few days, and I should spend my time with Al. He hasn't been feeling well at all."

"I understand," Doug said evenly, and Eve could tell at a glance that he really did understand. He was a nice-looking man, tall and dark, with hazel eyes that crinkled at the edges when he laughed; she'd always thought Doug was attractive.

They reached her house, and he walked her up the front path.

"I'd like to see you some other time," he said, looking down at her and smiling that wide comfortable smile of his. "Maybe we could go to a movie. Or we could have dinner together in Charlotte. I have to go into the city sometimes."

"Okay," she said carefully.

She told Doug goodbye and hurried inside the house, feeling a little sad. She hadn't really counted on this apprehension about Doug's attitude toward her pregnancy. Did her feelings mean that she cared more about him—and in a deeper and more meaningful way—than she'd ever admitted to herself?

She peered into the mirror over the bathroom sink. Despite the sorrow of the past week, she looked better than she'd ever looked; her cheeks had rounded with this pregnancy, and her swelling breasts strained against the fabric of her simple cotton blouse. She wondered if Doug had noticed. If he had, he hadn't let on.

After dinner, Eve said to her father, "I'll clean up the kitchen while you rest." Al gratefully went to sit on the rusty green metal glider on the front porch where he watched the fireflies and chatted idly with a few old cronies from the neighborhood.

Eve couldn't help feeling nostalgic as she worked in the familiar kitchen. How many of these blue-willow-patterned dishes had she washed in this sink as she was growing up in this house? She traced one of the willow-tree branches with a fingernail and thought she had washed more dishes than most little girls, because her mother had died when she was eleven. She'd taken over the responsibility of running the house at an early age, arranging the dishes in shining rows in the kitchen cabinets, taking pride in managing the household money, seeing that the mops and buckets and the Electrolux were lined up neatly in the broom closet.

But of course the real responsibility hadn't hit her until Al had to quit his job prematurely at age sixty, when his doctor had diagnosed him as totally disabled due to chronic lung disease. Then, at the age of twenty-six, financial responsibility had fallen squarely on her, but she'd been proud of her ability to support the two of them and support them well.

By that time, she'd progressed through the mill's manager-trainee program into which she'd been hired after receiving her B.S. in business administration at UNC. She'd been handling the coveted job of Wray Mills's public-relations director with considerable aplomb for over a year. Eve Triopolous was one of the few salaried women managers employed at the mill. The year she'd been fired was the first year she'd drawn an executive bonus. Oh, she had loved her job, all right. But that was in the past. Right now she had to figure out what to do about her future.

Sighing, she declined to watch television with her father and went early to bed where she ran her hands over her abdomen again, exploring the expanding world of the baby who remained a secret to most of the world, to her father, to Doug, to everyone who didn't live at the house in Myers Park. Eve couldn't help smiling into the darkness. It was exciting, feeling her body change shape to accommodate a new human being. Never again would Eve wonder why some women seemed to revel in their pregnancies.

The next morning, over Eve's worried objections, Al walked, huffing and puffing from the effort, up Cotton Mill Hill. She couldn't go with him; she was *persona non grata* around the offices of Wray Mills since her dismissal. And besides, Al's absence would give her a chance to get over her morning sickness in private. Eve stood edgily on the tiny front porch, arms folded tightly over her stomach, anxiously watching Al and worrying about him as she watched his tortured progress up the hill.

"Don't do this!" she'd begged in vain. To her, confronting the very officials who had decreed that they move was too much like throwing himself at their mercy. Where was her father's pride, his self-respect? But she hadn't figured on his misplaced loyalty to the company for which he had toiled for thirty-eight long years.

"Don't worry," Al had insisted, patting Eve awkwardly on the shoulder. "I have to talk to them. I have to. I'm sure as soon as they realize what a hardship it is for us to move in a week, they'll soften their attitude."

Like they softened their attitude when you filed a claim for compensation and they fired me? Eve was tempted to ask, giving way to shrewishness.

But she held her tongue. She knew as well as Al that he didn't have any place to go if they were evicted. So she stood by helplessly, wishing there was some other course they could take, while Al labored his way up the hill to beg for time from the management at the mill.

"Eve! Eve?" Derek stomped through the lower hall, calling up the stairs. Where was she, anyway? He had expected her to be right there, the way she always was, standing silently in the background, a gentle presence watching him greet Kelly with a kiss.

"She's not here," Aunt May's voice quavered. "She's gone home for a few days." Aunt May came and peered down at him, her round, wrinkled face hanging over the upstairs banister. "Is everything all right?" she ventured.

"Yes. I mean, no, how can it be all right?" he shot back impatiently. What a question to ask someone whose wife had just been killed! The old girl didn't have much sense, never had. But she was Kelly's aunt, and he'd always been polite. It was going to be difficult without Kelly to act as a buffer between them. Well, perhaps Aunt May hadn't heard his remark.

It was too much to hope for. "Oh. Well. I see," Aunt May said, sniffing. She pulled her head back in from the stairwell, like a turtle. Now he knew he had hurt her feelings. He could hear her retreating down the hall toward her room. She was probably in tears. Oh, God, was anything ever going to be all right again?

He ran upstairs and burst into their bedroom, the pale blue haven he had shared with Kelly. He had to find Eve, and he'd forgotten where Eve said she lived before she moved in with them. He sat down at Kelly's small secretary desk and started pulling out drawers and digging in cubbyholes. Where the devil was Kelly's tan leather address book?

He dragged a bunch of papers out until they all sat in a heap in front of him. Bills for Kelly's charge accounts, a bunch of personal correspondence, but no address book. The book would have Eve's address in it, neatly inscribed in Kelly's round handwriting; he knew it would. But he couldn't find it.

Kelly's raw silk jacket, the one she had worn when they went out to dinner last Saturday night, hung over the back of the chair where he sat. When he'd decided that the address book wasn't in the desk after all, he fingered the silk fabric for a few moments, lost in memory. A hint of Kelly's favorite fragrance wafted from it, bringing her back to him in a strangely haunting way.

"When does the hurting stop?" he asked himself brokenly, and then he buried his face in the raw silk, wishing he had Kelly, wishing he could find Eve, wishing that he could still look forward to fatherhood, wishing without hope that everything could be the way it was before the accident.

"AND SO THEY GAVE ME a week to stay here while I look for another place to live!" Al declared triumphantly, but never had Eve heard so hollow a victory. What had the mill management so graciously bestowed? Just another week. And after that, then what?

"I'll look for a place in Charlotte where we can both stay," she told him. Al thought she was living temporarily with a girl friend while searching for an apartment for herself in the city.

"Evie, I never wanted to be a burden to you," Al said quietly, his expression clouding over. Eve knew what a blow to Al's Old World pride it was to have the woman of the house taking care of him. In Greek families, it was customarily the other way around.

"You're not a burden," Eve told him firmly and with a smile that she hoped did not look forced. She patted him awkwardly on the shoulder, like a parent comforting a child. When had he become the child and she the parent?

Eve knew she could remain at the Myers Park house with Derek and Aunt May for the next week. She needed that time to bargain with Derek, to talk him out of this idea he'd had about her getting an abortion. Surely when the first pangs of grief had faded, he'd realize what he was doing and agree that the baby should be born and that he should be its father. He *was* the father, after all; nothing could change that.

But it was going to be difficult. And she couldn't stay at the Myers Park house with Derek after she'd convinced him that the baby must be born; it would be better for everyone if she moved out. She and Al could find a place to stay in Charlotte.

There was one problem, though. Money. She had a couple of hundred dollars in her savings account, a cushion against hard times, and if these didn't qualify for hard times, she didn't know what did. Her small hoard probably wasn't enough to rent a place, and she knew that Al didn't have as much saved as she did. If she could get a job—but she'd already tried that, and she hadn't been pregnant at the time.

Actually, there was more than one problem. If she and Al lived together, she'd have to tell him even sooner about her pregnancy. It would be very hard to hide so telltale a sign as morning sickness from her father.

"Don't worry, Al," she said, trying to sound more confident than she felt. Even as she said it, anxiety gnawed at her stomach. She knew, in that moment, that in trying to alleviate their problem, she had only added to it. Things had been bad before; their future had been bleak. But now, now! They were being evicted, and she was pregnant besides. She still didn't know how she was ever going to tell Al.

And yet, given the same chance all over again, Eve knew she would do exactly what she had done—contract to bear a child for Kelly and Derek Lang.

That was what, despite everything, she still intended to do.

Chapter Four

Eve, dragging her feet but determined to tackle Derek once more, went back to the Myers Park house on Monday.

"Oh, Eve, it's so good to see you," said a mournful-eyed Aunt May when Eve tentatively tapped on her bedroom door and announced that she had returned. Aunt May pursed her lips. "I know how hard it is for Derek right now, but he's been absolute hell to live with."

Eve smiled a sad smile. "I can imagine" was all she said.

"Well," Aunt May said, rallying. Today she wore her hearing aid; that was a relief. "I'm glad you're here, Eve. I wanted to bake some cookies today. Will you help?"

Eve was surprised, then glad. Baking cookies with Aunt May would get her mind off her own problems, and it would give her something to do until Derek came home and they embarked on their inevitable discussion. She knew that Derek would not postpone it; he would want to get it over with.

"I'll be glad to help," she told Aunt May warmly.

The two of them chased Louise out of the kitchen, and Louise gladly relinquished the space, smiling, Eve realized, for the first time since Kelly's accident.

"What kind of cookies are we making?" Eve asked as she helped assemble the ingredients.

"Chocolate chip," Aunt May said. "They're Derek's favorite. Now Kelly, she always prefers—" And then Aunt May stopped, her round pink face dissolving into distress.

"That's all right, Aunt May," Eve said, choking up herself. "It's hard to realize that she's really gone, isn't it?"

Aunt May nodded before turning her back and busily sifting the flour. Eve allowed her the privacy of silence for a while.

"Here, Eve, you measure the chocolate chips," Aunt May finally said, and Eve did.

"Does it bother you to talk about Kelly?" she asked Aunt May.

"Some," Aunt May said. Her faded blue eyes rested on Eve's face, and there was sorrow in their depths. "You know, Kelly was always so *good*. She let me mess around in the kitchen. She made sure Louise wouldn't mind my cooking before she hired her. Kelly turned down three perfectly fine maids because they didn't want to allow an old lady in their kitchen. Considering how hard it is to get good help these days, that shows how much Kelly cared about me, don't you think?"

Eve nodded, unable to speak.

Aunt May relieved Eve of the cup of chocolate chips and dumped them into the stiff dough. She stirred the dough rapidly, then stopped in mid-stir. "Kelly kept me from being a lonely, dried-up old woman. Now I don't know what will happen to me. I really don't know." After a moment she smiled shyly at Eve. "But with you here, I won't be lonely, will I?" she continued with forced briskness. "Now hand me that spatula, will you, please?"

Eve put the spatula in Aunt May's wrinkled hand, sorrow welling up inside her. This wasn't the proper time to defeat Aunt May's expectations. And yet she doubted that she would be living at the Myers Park house much longer.

In midafternoon, Derek called to tell Aunt May brusquely that he wouldn't be home for dinner and to go ahead and eat without him, only Aunt May thought he said he had his feet about him and hung up, vaguely puzzled, the thought never occurring to her that Derek hadn't given her a chance to tell him that Eve had returned.

That was why Derek was surprised to stumble upon Eve unawares at nine-thirty that night when he arrived after several hours of misspent time at the country-club bar. Eve was sitting in the comfortable wing chair in his study, knitting what appeared to be a yellow bootee. The sight of her, looking so domestic and content in the pool of light from the desk lamp, irritated him.

"Knitting little garments, I see," he said with annoyance. He was more than a little drunk.

Eve started at the sound of his voice. She hadn't heard him come in. The color drained from her face. This wasn't the Derek she knew; he was in his shirt-sleeves and had tossed his

suit jacket carelessly on his desk, and his eyes were bloodshot.
He didn't appear to be in a good mood.

"They're for the baby," she said firmly, knowing that this
would be a perfect lead-in for the conversation that was to follow. She didn't see any sense in postponing it no matter what
kind of mood Derek was in. It was a problem that needed to be
confronted head-on, full-out and immediately.

"There isn't going to be any baby," Derek said just as firmly.

"Derek—" Eve began. She drew a deep breath and rested her
knitting in her lap. "Now that you've had a few days to think
it over, you must see that you can't destroy Kelly's and your
baby. It's part of both of you, and there's no reason why you
can't approach fatherhood with the same eagerness you had
when Kelly was alive. You wanted this baby. You know you
did."

Derek set his lips in a grim line. "I wanted it then. I wanted
it because of Kelly. But I don't want it now."

Eve spoke slowly, and her voice flowed, mellifluous and un-
afraid, into what had been a menacing silence.

"I think you do, Derek. You're denying it right now, but I
think you want this baby."

She was wise and so sure. He resented her intrusion into what
should be his decision and his decision alone. "It wouldn't be
fair to bring a baby into this world without two parents," he
said gruffly. It was what he truly believed.

Too late, she realized from his slurred speech that he'd been
drinking, but she didn't see anything to do but go on with it.
"Derek, it's all you have left of Kelly," she reminded him
gently. "This baby, this child, that she wanted so much. You
know how she longed for a baby; she spoke of her yearning to
have a child so often. She was overjoyed about the baby. I'm
sure that after you think it over, you'll change your mind."

A lump rose in Derek's throat, choking off words. Why did
Eve insist on making this so difficult? Why didn't she just have
the abortion and be done with it? It was cruel of her, cruel and
heartless, to remind him of his beloved wife's longing for a
child. Damn, damn, damn! Why didn't she just go away, this
woman who was gazing at him so implacably, gazing with soft
brown eyes as gentle as a gazelle's, the black pupils so large that
they gave her face a kind of openness that Kelly had remarked
about, that Kelly had liked.

"Oh, God," he said, clenching his hands into fists and
throwing a look of pure anguish in her direction. He wished

he'd had more to drink. To Eve's despair, he threw the French doors to the terrace open and flung himself out into the night.

Eve dropped her knitting and ran after him. She didn't trust him now, didn't trust the misery he was feeling, didn't know what the misery would make him do. For she knew that he was mourning his wife, and she knew that if she missed Kelly, Derek missed her a hundred times more and in many more ways. It was pathetic, seeing this strong man, to whom everything had apparently come easily, in pain over this. She wanted to help him. She wanted him to be the way he had been before Kelly's death, neat, methodical and organized, not sad and disheveled and drunk. In a burst of suffering, she realized that she had not only lost Kelly; she had lost Derek, the *real* Derek, the one who had joked with her and laughed with her and been her friend, too.

Cautiously, she tiptoed out into the night, expecting Derek to be on the terrace. But he wasn't there.

Where was he? She peered into the gloom. It was a dark night, and there was no moon. Finally, she saw his white shirt—at least she thought that's what it was—in the rose garden. Her heart beating rapidly, she descended the brick stairs and walked briskly toward the rose garden, where the sweet and heavy fragrance of the roses made her stomach lurch. Her morning sickness was threatening to become morning, afternoon and evening sickness. Any strong odor seemed to bring on the nausea, and Eve had no earthly idea what to do about it.

"Derek?" she said softly.

"Leave me alone," he said gruffly, and she could tell from the roughness of his voice that he was either in tears or perilously near them.

"No," she said, her stomach churning so that she could barely speak. She tried not to smell the roses, tried to ignore their cloying fragrance. "Leaving you alone would be the worst thing I could do," she said. "You don't have to lock your grief inside you. It helps to talk about it."

"How the hell would you know?" he said, his back toward her. He was tall, much taller than she, and she realized with a start that she hadn't ever seen Derek in anything but a business suit. He never wore sport shirts, and tonight his white long-sleeved shirt, which he wore to work every day despite the summer heat, displayed his shoulders to advantage, shoulders that Eve now realized owed little to the shoulder pads in his suit jackets.

"I know about losing a loved one," she replied evenly, although her stomach was still roiling. "My mother died when I was eleven."

Silence. Then Derek said in a quieter tone, "I'm sorry. I didn't know."

"It—it was a long time ago," she said.

"When does it stop hurting?" Derek's voice was no more than a whisper.

"I'm not sure it ever does. You go along day by day, learning to live with it, and after a while you're able to think about other things. Time is a healer. It's a trite thing to say, but it's true."

He turned to look at her, to gaze down at her eyes, the whites of which seemed luminescent in the darkness. Her skin, so fair for a brunette, glowed with a dewy freshness, and her cheeks were more rounded than they had been when she first moved in with them. Suddenly his senses were filled with her, with the way she looked as she returned his gaze with so much empathy. But no, he shouldn't be leaning toward her this way, closing the distance between them, wanting to touch her, wanting her to hold him in her arms and soothe away the pain. He shouldn't, and he wouldn't.

Stiffly he said, "Perhaps it is as you say. Maybe time really is a great healer; I don't know. At any rate, I'm not going to change my mind about the baby."

"But—"

"Please don't argue with me. I've opened an account at the bank for you; I've deposited three thousand dollars in it. That's in addition to the twelve thousand I was going to pay you after the baby was born. I'll pay you the twelve thousand when you've shown me evidence that you've had the abortion." He thrust something into her hands; incredulously, she looked down and saw that it was a passbook.

Derek's words gouged Eve's very soul. She wanted to cry out in agony with the pain. What kind of woman did he think she was, to accept payment for the killing of his and Kelly's child? What kind of man was *he*? Had he always been this monster, or had he really been the loving, thoughtful man she had observed with Kelly? Thoughts swam through her mind, swelling and ebbing, churning, churning the way her stomach churned....

With great economy of movement, Eve leaned over and threw up beneath a perfectly shaped rose bush.

"Oh, Eve," Derek was saying in horror, and she closed her eyes so she wouldn't have to look at him. His voice descended upon her as from a great distance. "Eve, you poor thing. Eve?" He sounded stone-cold sober now.

His arms folded around her, and she wanted to die of embarrassment, wanted to sink into the soft mulch at their feet and never see him again. She retched once more, but this time Derek was holding her head; tears streamed down her face, and Derek was wiping them away with his handkerchief.

"Eve, can you stand up? Shall I carry you inside?"

Her head spun dizzily, crazily, on a rose-scented merry-go-round. Only there was nothing merry about it. "No," she managed to say finally, "no." And then Derek was brushing the hair away from her forehead, was gently rubbing the back of her neck, and she realized that they were sitting on the hard ground. Derek was sitting on the ground with utter disregard for his clothes, and she was cradled against his chest.

"Are you sick? Should I call a doctor?" The worry in his voice surprised her. She wouldn't have thought he could surmount his pain to care about her, especially when they had just participated in such an unnerving discussion.

"No, please," she said, "it's just the morning sickness carried over to the evening. Any strong odor seems to set me off, and when I smelled the roses . . ." Just thinking about it set off a new wave of nausea, and she struggled for control.

"Have you been vomiting every day?" Derek sounded flabbergasted, and when she looked at him, she knew his concern was real.

She nodded. "It will pass soon," she said, not too confidently.

Eve was aware of the crickets in the shrubbery, creaking out their raucous song, and she suddenly felt the smooth, fine cotton of Derek's shirt against her cheek, and she became aware of the warmth of his body close to hers. She struggled to sit up straight.

One lock of Derek's usually perfect hair fell over his forehead. "You won't have to go through this much longer," he said, and if his words were meant to be soothing, they were not. His meaning was unmistakable.

Stunned that he would say this to her when he knew how she felt about the abortion, Eve pushed him away. Shakily, she rose to her feet, brushing Derek's hand away when he tried to help her.

"An upset stomach is a small price to pay for a baby," she said with dignity, and she turned and walked swiftly away. Quick tears stung the inside of her nose, and Eve knew she was dangerously close to breaking down in front of him. But that, after her embarrassment in the rose garden, she was determined not to do.

"Eve," she heard him call, his voice urgent, but she paid no attention. She had meant to change his mind tonight, but she had failed; she had failed utterly.

Late that night, when she was in bed and her light was out, she heard Derek's heavy footsteps in the hall. They paused outside her door, and she tensed, holding her breath, waiting for him to knock. But he didn't knock, and shortly thereafter she heard the door to his room close gently, and then, thoroughly exhausted, Eve slept.

The next morning she realized why Derek hadn't knocked. She found the bank passbook on the floor just inside her door. When she'd heard him pause outside her door, he'd been pushing it underneath. Folded inside was a note.

"Eve," it said in Derek's large and neat script, "take the money. When it's over, I'll see that you get the twelve thousand. I'll be out of town for the rest of the week on business. It would be best if it were over with when I return." He had signed it simply "D."

"It would be best if it were over with when I return," Eve repeated out loud to herself. How unfeeling, how uncaring!

Angry now, she ripped the curt note into little pieces and tossed them in the wastebasket. Maybe it was good that Derek didn't want the baby. Would she really want this child to have a father who was so unmoved, so emotionally detached, that he could write such a note?

Trembling, she sank down on the bed and buried her face in her hands. Derek Lang could keep his three thousand dollars, the bonus he was paying for her to commit murder. She wouldn't touch it. She had told Derek she was prepared to raise the child herself. Well, in spite of everything, she still felt that way. She didn't know how she was going to support her father and herself, and she certainly didn't know how she would support a child. But if she had to, she would.

In the meantime, she required a place for Al to live. For herself and Al, she corrected herself. It was clear that she could no longer stay here. This house was no longer a safe haven.

She squared her shoulders and steeled herself to make the best of these changed circumstances. She went downstairs, found the newspaper where Derek had left it so precisely folded and flipped through the For Rent ads. Before long she had carefully weeded out the ones that were clearly unsuitable for her, which left her with a list of possibilities. After telephoning most of them, she gave up in discouragement. Everything was so expensive! Landlords wanted the first month's rent and a security deposit. "I'd like to see the house," she said more than once, "but we can't afford it."

Thoroughly disheartened, Eve decided on the spur of the moment to ride over to Wrayville to visit Al. She wanted to check on him, to make sure that he was getting along all right, and besides, she needed the lift that seeing her father would bring. She called a goodbye to Aunt May, who was murmuring things to herself as she puttered around the daylilies on the terrace, and she told Louise not to expect her back in time for dinner.

Before long, she was in her sturdy Volkswagen, heading out of the city. The day was bright and hot, and as the red clay road banks skated past her car window, Eve's spirits lifted for the first time since Kelly's accident. Derek was being unreasonable, and his position on the abortion was unconscionable, but the baby was safe, and the silver lining in this dark cloud was that she and Al would be together again when she finally found a house for them. *When* she finally found a house? *If* she finally found a house. It was proving to be more difficult than she had anticipated. And she still didn't know what she was going to do about a job.

When she pulled her car beneath the chinaberry tree, she was surprised to see Nell Baker peering anxiously out the window. Nell smiled widely at the sight of Eve and ran outside.

"Eve, I'm so glad to see you," Nell confided, sliding an arm around the younger woman's waist. "Did your boss let you off work today?"

"I'm glad to see you, too," Eve replied, ignoring the question. "How's Al?"

"Oh, Eve, not good. Doug Ender stopped by, I understand, and afterward Al had a real bad spell. In fact, I thought that was why you came home. Didn't Al call you? No? Well, I came over to stay with him after I stopped by and saw he wasn't well, and I can tell you that he hardly slept all night. He's upset about leaving Wrayville, you know. And, of course, his claim against the mill." The little woman, so robust and full of energy, peered up at Eve through silver-rimmed glasses.

Eve concealed her alarm. "Is he all right now?"

"He's asleep, and a good thing, too. Oh, Eve, it worries me. You know how he is. He thinks he can fight this sickness all by himself, but he can't; he can't. I saw it happen with my Bud."

"And the company claims that the disease doesn't exist," Eve said bitterly.

"Maybe if Wray Mills is being bought by that big textile group, maybe it will make a difference in your father's claim. Maybe they'll admit that working in the mill caused Al's byss—byss—Oh, how do you say that word?"

"Byssinosis," Eve replied. "Byssinosis. Just say brown lung. It's easier, and it means the same thing—that a man worked in cotton-dust levels that were dangerously high and that he got sick and may die because of it."

"It killed my husband," Nell Baker said dully. "I know it did." With visible effort, she changed the subject. "Eve, have you found a place for Al to live? I already have one boarder, you know. Al could board with me if he likes."

Eve shook her head. "That's kind of you, Nell. But Al and I want to be together if possible. I've been looking for a place." Today she longed to pour out her story to Nell, who had been wonderful to her ever since her mother died. But she knew that Nell would be shocked if she knew that Eve carried another couple's child, and she thought that Nell might even tell her father. And in his present state of health, telling him would be disastrous.

At Nell's urging, she peeked in on her father. He was lying on his bed, and his breathing was tortured and difficult. He had to fight for every breath he took, for every bit of life-giving oxygen. It broke her heart, as it always did, to see her once-vigorous father reduced to such a painful state.

"If you'll stay with Al, I'm going to walk over to Doug's office," she told Nell. "I have to know what Doug said to get Al so upset."

"I'll be here," Nell assured her.

Eve's nostrils twitched at the customary cooking odors emanating from the Quicks' house across the street. No longer did such aromas stimulate Eve's appetite. She stepped up her speed until she was well past.

Doug's office was located in a small brick building at the bottom of the hill.

"Eve," Doug said, looking uncommonly pleased to see her. He hurried around his desk to clasp her hands in his. His eyes clouded with concern at the expression on her face. "Are you feeling well? You look so pale."

"Oh, Doug," she said, sinking into the chair across from his desk.

"Something's wrong," he guessed, pulling a chair up beside her. Then, with alarm, he said, "You're not sick, I hope?"

She lifted her eyes to his. She could talk to Doug; she could trust him. She'd known him all her life. He was one person whom she could turn to for advice. "I'm not sick, Doug," she told him. "Just pregnant."

His face reflected shock and surprise.

Quickly Eve poured out her story. Doug listened incredulously, then intently.

"Can Derek make me have the abortion, Doug?" she asked urgently.

"Eve, I—" He stopped, then stood up and paced around the room, thinking. He shook his head and smiled at her, but his hazel eyes were troubled.

"I don't think he can make you have an abortion. As far as I know, no case like this has been tested in the courts, and I admit this is outside my area of expertise. But it's your body, and since there are no provisions in the contract you signed, well, I don't think Lang has a leg to stand on."

Relief flooded her. "Thank God," she whispered.

"Eve, if I can help you in any way..." Doug began.

"I'll be all right," she told him. "The best way you can help me is by doing as much as you can for Al. Nell told me you stopped by to see him."

"I had to tell Al that we may have to sue Wray Mills for his compensation."

"Oh, no," Eve said. "Al would hate that." Anger surged through her at this news. Conditions in the cotton mill had ruined her father's health so that he'd had to quit work before retirement age, and then Wray Mills refused to pay back wages and compensation. Yet Al would recoil from the thought of any legal action against the mill, to which he had felt loyal for thirty-eight years. If they were forced to sue Wray Mills, what toll would that take on her father's health?

"It might be a good idea to file the lawsuit before the rumored sale of the mill occurs," Doug said.

"Rumored? You mean it's still not a sure thing?"

Doug shook his head. "The mill management is trying to keep a lid on rumors. So far, I've heard so many big textile names mentioned as possible buyers for the mill—Spring, Cannon, Burlington—that I don't know what to believe these days."

"Don't file a lawsuit, Doug. Not yet. I don't think Al could take it."

"All right, Eve. I won't. I'll try to think of something else we can do instead." Doug's voice was gentle.

She rose to go.

"And Eve," he said in parting, "keep in touch."

Eve nodded before walking blindly out of his office, through the tiny waiting room and outside. She kept her head down as she walked the short distance back to the house. It had been hard to tell Doug what she'd been through, but she felt better for it. And she knew she could trust him not to discuss her situation with anyone else.

She visited with Al for a short while after he woke up, fighting tears as she watched Al struggle for the breath to talk.

"I talked with Doug," she finally said, feeling it necessary to bring the subject up.

"He told you that we might have to sue the mill to get my compensation?"

"Yes. I asked him not to do that yet. He said he'll try to think of something else we might do."

"Good. Good. I don't want to sue the mill. I just want what's rightfully mine."

"Well, don't worry about it," Eve said soothingly.

"I won't. It's nice that you have a good job now, Evie. We don't have to worry about money so much."

"I love you, Al," she said, bending over to kiss his cheek before she left, hoping he could not read the despairing expression on her face.

"I love you, too, Eve," Al told her.

Oh, what was she going to do? How was she going to manage? After a quick farewell to Nell Baker, she fled the mill-village house, trying to organize her thoughts.

Riding along the country highway toward Charlotte, Eve thought, *I've got to get a job.* If she had a job, she'd know how much rent she could afford. It was pointless to continue searching for a place to live if she didn't know how much money she'd be making. At the moment, everything seemed to be caving in on her at once. Al's obvious setback made her ache inside, and then there was Derek and the baby and even Aunt May to worry about.

She'd filed a job application at the big computer plant in northeast Charlotte, but that had been months ago. They'd never called her, but it would be a place to start. She could go by and check on the status of her application today. She glanced at her watch. It was past one in the afternoon, and she hadn't eaten lunch.

I promised Derek I wouldn't skip meals, she told herself. Then she realized that Derek couldn't care less. It wasn't Derek to whom she had to keep promises now; it was the baby. It wouldn't be good for the baby if Eve fell back into her haphazard eating habits. She checked her face in the small rearview mirror. She looked presentable, but she knew of a small restaurant at Dugan's Crossroads up ahead where she could order a hamburger and use the rest room to make any major repairs to her makeup. She wanted to look her best when she tackled the computer company's employment office.

She slowed in front of the neat clapboard house adjoining the restaurant's parking lot. The parking lot was filled, but Eve finally found a place to park beneath a rusted Coca-Cola sign featuring a woman wearing 1950s makeup.

What is going on in here? she wondered when she stepped inside. The place was packed. It was a small restaurant, once a country store, and every booth was filled. The patrons were mostly men in work clothes. Perhaps there was a big construction project nearby. She worked her way to the counter and edged onto a just-vacated stool.

It was a good ten minutes before a harried fellow wearing an apron appeared in front of her.

"Take your order?" he asked, whipping out an order pad.

"I'd like a hamburger and a glass of milk," she told him, and he disappeared into the kitchen where she could observe him through the pass-through. He seemed to have more arms than an octopus as he slapped a circle of hamburger on the grill, mixed a new batch of cole slaw and shot whipped cream onto a hot-fudge sundae.

Didn't he have any waitress help? Apparently not, because not only was the guy doing all the cooking, but he waited tables, too.

Her hamburger was delicious, and she wolfed it down. She wanted a glass of water, though, and when she tried to catch the eye of the restaurant's jack-of-all-tasks, she failed. Well, she could get it herself. This was hardly the kind of place where it was necessary to stand on ceremony. The glasses and water were on the other side of the counter. She got up and poured water into her glass, only to be confronted by the fellow, whose shirt was embroidered with the name Lenny.

"Gee, thanks," he said, breaking into a broad grin. "Mind getting some water for those fellows next to you at the counter?

Say, you want a job for the next two hours? I'm swamped," he said. "Pay's good, plus you get tips."

"But—" she started to say, and then stopped. Nell Baker always said that a bird in the hand is worth two in the bush, and this would be a way to pick up some extra cash. "I've never waitressed," she said uneasily.

"Come on; it's no big deal. Here," he said, thrusting the order pad into her hand. "Got to get the orders of those people who just came in. Sure, go on!" With a challenging grin, he bustled away.

Instead of being annoyed, Eve found herself amused. A waitress! Well, it was a job, if only for the next few hours, and at this point she wouldn't turn down anything that would bring in money. So she obediently wrote down orders, carted food to tables and cleaned them with a Clorox-soaked towel after the customers left. It was four o'clock before the restaurant cleared out enough for her to talk with Lenny.

"Say, you're good," he told her admiringly. "Thought you said you never waitressed before." He was the possessor of a jaunty smile and a mobile mouth; it would be hard not to like him.

"I haven't," she said. Coins weighted her skirt pocket. She'd made out pretty well in tips.

"Want a job? Permanent. I need someone. Got this construction job about a half-mile up the road. Big new hot-water-heater plant. Got construction workers coming in for breakfast, break, lunch, another break; then the shift's over at three, and they come in for a snack. Listen, I've never been so busy in my life, and my last waitress quit yesterday to run off to California with her boyfriend."

"Well," said Eve, her mind racing. "This location is awfully far from the city. My father and I are moving from Wrayville to Charlotte, and I *am* looking for a job. But to drive all the way out here every day to work—I don't know."

"What kind of job are you looking for?"

"I used to be in public relations. I wasn't counting on being a waitress."

"Public relations? This job'll teach you to *really* relate to the public!" Lenny's grin faded; then he shrugged. "You find a place to live in Charlotte yet?"

"No, I—"

"Look, you want to work here, you can stay in the house next door. It's my house, two bedrooms, but with a wife and four kids it got too small. Inherited it from my folks; this restaurant used to be my dad's store. Built it up myself, doing real good. Anyway, the house is empty. You want to live there, we can work out something on the rent and your salary.''

"You'd let us live in your house?" Eve was stunned at the offer.

"Sure. Better for people to live in it. Keeps vandals away, and you'd be close to your job."

She'd like that. She'd be able to keep an eye on Al. He'd enjoy coming to the restaurant, chatting with the construction workers. He wouldn't be lonely.

She didn't have to think twice. Lenny's offer was a solution to two immediate problems.

"It's a deal," she heard herself say, and without further ado, she and Lenny shook on it.

Chapter Five

Derek steered the Corvette around a huge puddle in the middle of the road. Tropical storm Dondi, downgraded last night from a hurricane, had moved in from the coast and was dumping torrential rains on the North Carolina Piedmont.

He shifted uneasily in his seat, his damp shirt sticking to his back, and wished longingly for the cool, crisp weather of October. This was the last week of an unusually humid September; approximately four weeks to go until relief arrived in the form of the first frost.

He slowed the Corvette to a crawl as he approached the L & D Cafe at Dugan's Crossroads. The Corvette's windshield wipers scrambled frantically, barely able to keep up with the deluge.

Believe it or not, there was a woman actually walking alongside the road in this horrendous weather. He noticed her, tried not to splash her, then cast a backward glance toward her in utter disbelief.

She wore a loose, nondescript beige raincoat over a white uniform, and she held an umbrella over her head, which didn't help much to protect her from the rain. But her hairstyle—he'd never seen anyone else with that particular hairstyle, geometrically precise, black hair short in the back but longer at the sides.

"Eve," he muttered, wishing he could get a better view of her. But a van loomed behind him, riding his bumper, and the last he saw of her, someone was holding the door of the restaurant so she could duck inside.

He'd come home to the Myers Park house from his business trip three months ago and found Eve gone. He discovered the bank passbook with its untouched three thousand dollars placed in the exact center of his desk, a silent rebuke.

Still, he'd fully expected Eve to turn up after the abortion and ask for her twelve thousand. When she didn't, he wondered why. But he couldn't find Kelly's address book to contact her, and he didn't want to try to locate her through the Queen City Infertility Clinic—too many unhappy memories there. So he never did. He was sure that after he'd left on his business trip, Eve had seen the light and had the abortion. He figured she'd find him when she needed the money.

But she hadn't. He hadn't heard one word from Eve, not one. After Kelly's death, Derek had fiercely attacked the many problems of adding Wray Mills to the Lang Textile empire, trying to find solace in his work, and so he'd never followed up on his obligation to locate Eve. Moreover, when she'd left, he was wallowing in the depths of his grief, indulging in boundless self-pity. Only recently had he begun to take mild pleasure in the things he'd enjoyed before—a round of golf, a quiet dinner with old friends, and sometimes he couldn't face even those.

Could that have been Eve going into the L & D Cafe? No. Why would Eve be at that little restaurant at Dugan's Crossroads? Still, the memory of her teased him, and the nagging idea that he'd been derelict in his duty toward Eve wouldn't let him rest. A week later, when he had to go to Wrayville for another round of interminable secret negotiations, he stopped at the L & D Cafe. No reason not to stop there, anyway. It was lunchtime, and he was hungry.

He realized as soon as he stepped inside that he was out of his element. His pin-striped suit was clearly out of place among the yellow hardhats and worn blue denim shirts and jeans. But he slid across the red vinyl seat in a vacant booth and scanned the neatly typed menu. From the jukebox in the corner blared the sound of John Denver whining for his old guitar. Derek drummed his fingers impatiently on the scuffed Formica tabletop. The service was slow.

Where was the waitress, anyway? He didn't see one. There was a guy with Lenny written across his chest who seemed to be everywhere at once.

"I'd like to place my order, please," Derek said when the guy breezed by.

"Sure," Lenny said amiably before disappearing again.

And then, and then . . . he saw her. His heart fell to his gut when he recognized the crisp, neat hairstyle, the high white cheekbones, the brown eyes that seemed larger than ever and could belong to no one but Eve, Eve Triopolous. She seemed to float ethereally behind the counter, treading on air, a graceful woman in white who, with her long swanlike neck and her air of calm composure, looked altogether too aristocratic to be working in a place like this. But there was no doubt in his mind as he watched her slide a sandwich plate onto the counter from her tray and favor the man who sat there with her unique smile, that she indeed worked here. He held his breath. He hadn't remembered Eve Triopolous as being so beautiful.

She turned on her heel and walked around the end of the counter, and it was then that he realized. He gasped with the impact of it, and the room tilted, bent in two. For when he saw her gently rounded abdomen beneath the skirt of her uniform, he knew.

He shut his eyes tight, then opened them again. Eve was still pregnant. She was something like four or five months pregnant; he didn't know which because he had never been very good at determining such things.

The buzzing in his ears reached monumental proportions, and when it stopped, she was standing beside him, marking something efficiently on her order pad, and then she inquired crisply and impersonally, "May I take your order, please?"

His hand clutched her wrist, and her eyes widened in alarm as she looked up, completely unawares. She hadn't paid any attention to him; he was just another customer.

When she recognized Derek, her knees went weak. They stared at each other for a long moment, startled brown eyes converging with steely gray ones. Eve felt her world, the one she had constructed so carefully in the past few months, crumble slowly to dust.

"What are you doing here?" was the best he could manage.

She wrested her arm away. "Working," she said evenly. "Did you want to order something?"

"My God, Eve, how can you be so blasé?" he said tightly.

She lifted an eyebrow. "I'm not. Now are you ordering or aren't you? I have a job to do."

"We have to talk."

"We don't have anything to talk about."

"You can stand there with my baby in your belly and say that we don't have anything to talk about?"

A curious glance from one of the construction workers made him lower his voice at the end of his sentence.

Eve flushed. "Please, Derek. Don't embarrass me."

That brought Derek to his senses. He didn't want to embarrass her; it was embarrassing enough, he was sure, to have to work in a place like this, with all these men looking at her day in and day out, watching her pregnancy progress.

One thing he knew—he couldn't eat anything. "Look," he said wearily, "can I come to the place where you live?"

"No," Eve said quickly, thinking of Al. Her father was still struggling to understand the forces that had compelled Eve to volunteer as a surrogate mother. His attitude toward her unmarried pregnancy was touchy enough without the baby's father appearing on the scene.

"Then you come to my house," he told her. "Please."

"Why? Have you had a change of heart?" Her tone was sarcastic. Maybe he deserved it.

"If you don't agree to meet me somewhere, I'll be back here again and again until you do," he said through clenched teeth.

"Eve? Eve!"

It was Lenny, calling her from the kitchen.

"I can't have you coming here," Eve said, glancing worriedly over her shoulder toward the kitchen and feeling something akin to panic. "You'll jeopardize my job."

"You shouldn't have a job like this, on your feet all the time; it's not good for you. And the work's hard."

Her features stiffened into an impenetrable mask. Her eyes were full of disdain. "This job is going to enable me to support your child, Derek," she said tightly, flipping the pages of her order book over and stuffing the book in her uniform pocket.

He tried to avoid looking at her bulging abdomen, but it was right in his line of vision. Guilt washed over him.

"My office," he said with effort. "Tomorrow. Eleven-thirty?"

"Tomorrow is my day off," she said. She wondered at the bleakness in his voice, the pain in his eyes. What was she getting herself into? She would be a fool to agree to see him, to risk upsetting her life again for him.

No, said a voice deep inside her. *Do this for Kelly.*

It was what Kelly would have wanted; Eve was sure of that. If there was any chance that Derek would accept his child, any chance at all, Eve would have to take it.

"Eleven-thirty," she said quietly. "All right, Derek. I'll be there."

He nodded slowly. There was a faint dusting of dark hair on her forearms. He'd never noticed that before.

Without speaking, aching inside, he handed her his business card in case she didn't know where he worked. Then he got up and walked out of the restaurant. He knew she was watching him from the window as he unlocked the Corvette and slid inside. As he drove onto the highway from the gravel parking lot, he couldn't remember feeling this despondent since the day Kelly died.

It was clear to Derek as he drove back into the city that something had gone terribly wrong with his life. He'd always had a plan for everything. Things came easily to him, he was convinced, because he had made an overall plan for his life when he was still in his teens.

This was the result of having a mother who would say to him when he was six years old and on the way out the door with his playmates, "Derek, what's the plan?" Early on, he got the idea that there must be a plan for everything. Get an education, find a suitable wife, get married. Have two children, a boy and a girl, who would go to prep schools and then to good, prestigious colleges, not the state university, and who would grow up to have plans that would include summer visits to their parents who would by then be stooped and gray haired and retired according to plan.

All was guided by the plan. But then Kelly had the problem about not being able to have babies. That had certainly not gone according to plan. After Kelly's hysterectomy he'd thought, *Oh, well, sometimes you have to alter the plan; we'll adopt.* And so Derek had consoled Kelly with that. He hadn't realized how much she wanted his child, his and hers, a child of their very own, until she'd come up with the surrogate-mother plan.

Derek hadn't known much about surrogate mothers. Oh, he'd heard something about it on a television news show once. But then Kelly had presented the surrogate-mother idea to him as a plan, and that is what convinced him. There was a plan. They'd find a suitable surrogate, Kelly's egg and his sperm would unite, and not too long afterward, the baby would be born. Kelly would, of course, manage the whole thing in her own efficient way.

And then, most inefficiently, she had died. It wasn't fair, leaving him with all of it; it wasn't fair for Kelly to disrupt the plan. He felt a quick stab of anger toward Kelly, which subsided immediately, leaving him feeling foolish about being angry about something over which she had no control.

The only thing to do, thought Derek unhappily, was to make a new plan. His grief had prevented that until now. But since he had seen Eve, had come face to face with her unmistakable pregnancy— Oh, damn. The situation was preposterous. How the devil was he going to make a plan that would accommodate it?

EVE'S MIND was not on accommodation as she dressed to meet Derek the next morning. It was on her pregnancy and what she might do to convince Derek, in one more last-ditch effort, to shoulder responsibility for the child he had fathered.

"Daughter," Al said as she leveled steady brown eyes at her reflection in the mirror beside the door of Lenny's little house. "Are you sure you know what you're doing?"

"No," she admitted, fluffing out the silken strands of her straight dark hair with her fingers. "But I have to take the chance."

Al heaved a wheezing sigh. "Stay home, Eve. Derek Lang has shown the kind of man he is. He never even tried to find you."

"You'd understand if you knew what kind of shape he was in after his wife died," Eve said firmly.

"But Evie—" Al began, but Eve refused to listen. She pecked Al quickly on the cheek before escaping out the door. She didn't want any more advice.

Al was better now, but it had been rough going when she'd had to inform Al of her pregnancy and the circumstances surrounding it. She never wanted to deliver a blow like that again, ever.

She had chosen a quiet moment a few days after she'd started work at the L & D Cafe. She'd prepared Al's favorite Greek dish, moussaka, and had even spent precious money on a bottle of the imported resinated wine that Al loved so well. When Al was mellow with good food and spirits, she'd taken the plunge.

"I have something to tell you, Al," she'd said gently, in her most direct manner.

Al had had a good day. He was feeling expansive, and his brown eyes glowed with fondness.

"Eh? So what is it, Evie?"

She swallowed the lump in her throat.

"I—" She could not continue.

"Something that's hard for you to tell me?" A shadow of foreboding passed across Al's face.

Eve drew a deep breath. "I'm pregnant, Al. I'm going to have a baby."

Al stared at her. His face fell. He looked old, tired.

"It's not what you think," Eve hurried on. "I'm not involved with anyone. I hired myself out as a surrogate mother."

"A surrogate mother," Al said in disbelief. "I've heard of such a thing. But you—" And he stopped and stared at her again in disbelief. "You let your body be used that way?"

"I wanted to. They were going to pay me twelve thousand dollars. And they were a lovely couple, Derek and Kelly Lang, and they wanted a baby." Tears sprang to her eyes as she remembered Kelly's longing for a child.

"Ah, don't cry, Eve," her father said, his voice breaking. "I can't believe you let them do that to you, but don't cry about it."

Eve blinked back the tears. "There's more," she whispered.

"More? What more could there be?" Al's eyes flashed with anger, but when he saw the effect this had on his daughter, he clamped his lips tightly together.

"I was going to bear the child for the Langs. There was no job in Charlotte, Al. I wasn't living with a girl friend; I was living with the Langs. I'm sorry I lied to you, but I lied because I didn't want to tell you about it. I shouldn't have lied— I wish I hadn't—but at the time I thought it was for the best." She stopped and swallowed. "Mrs. Lang—Kelly—was killed in an automobile accident. It was awful, Al. She was my friend. And then—and then Derek said I should have an abortion."

Al sank back in his chair. He had paled, and his breathing was labored.

"Al, are you all right? Shall I get your inhaler?"

Her father shook his head grimly. "Go on," he said. "Tell me the rest of it."

"I refused to have the abortion. I ran away instead. I'm going to have the baby, Al."

With a curse, Al struggled to his feet. Eve followed him as he paced heavily into the living room.

"We needed the money," she said desperately to Al's back as he stood, his shoulders heaving, his head resting against one arm raised against the doorjamb.

"We needed the money," he repeated, his voice barely audible. "But we didn't need it so much that you had to sell yourself."

"I wasn't—" But she couldn't go on. She'd known all along that her father, with his Old World ways, would see it that way.

"Come sit down, Al," she said, going to him and turning him gently by the shoulders. He let her propel him to his favorite chair.

"I know how you must feel," she said, clasping his hand in hers. "But it will be all right. I've got a job, a real job this time, and I've found a place for us to live."

"The man," her father said. "This Lang. He won't help you?"

She bit down hard on her lip and shook her head. "I'm afraid there's no chance of that."

"He must be a real jerk," Al spat out contemptuously, "to leave you all alone with this responsibility."

"He was so devastated by the loss of his wife—" she began.

"Don't tell me that! He fathered a child and walked away from it! What kind of a man would do something like that! If I ever got my hands on him— Don't expect me to have any sympathy for the man." Al stuck out his lower lip belligerently.

"Aren't you glad I found us a place to live? Don't you want to hear about my job?"

Al regarded her balefully. "Tell me," he had said.

And so Eve had told him haltingly about the little house Lenny had offered, about her job at the restaurant.

"A waitress? You, with your college degree, are going to work as a waitress?" Al began to cough.

"It's a job, Al. A way to live. And I like working for Lenny. He's a nice guy."

Al had had no choice but to let Eve remain in control. He had moved out of the mill-village house where he'd lived all those years and had made an effort to be happy in Lenny's little house. He'd made friends among the construction workers, who jollied him along, and if they weren't the cronies he'd had in Wrayville, well, at least they were company for him. He liked Lenny, too. Eve, maneuvering now through downtown Charlotte traffic, supposed Al's adjustment was the best she could hope for.

She found a place to park in a lot not far from Derek's office building and hurried inside. At the front desk, she gave her name to the receptionist.

"Mr. Lang is expecting you," the receptionist informed her in dulcet tones.

At the receptionist's direction, Eve stepped into the elevator and rode to the twelfth floor. She walked down the gray-carpeted hallway, her eyes wide. Lang Textiles, the sign on the door had said, with a list of mills in smaller gleaming gilt lettering underneath. The executive suite occupied the whole twelfth floor of this building.

"Ms. Triopolous?" said the secretary when Eve presented herself at Derek's office. Maisie Allen was openly curious, but she cut short her stare. "Mr. Lang is expecting you. Walk right in, please."

Hesitantly, Eve pushed open the door to Derek's office.

He sat at his desk with the wide window at his back. Outside, the air looked heavy with smoky mist, blurring the blue of the sky.

Derek was on the phone, but he looked up when he saw her. "I'll get back to you on it," he said into the phone, and then he hung up abruptly.

Eve stood, her chin held high, regarding him with that cool expression on her face. Her hair swooped into the hollows beneath her cheekbones, hollows that had filled out since her pregnancy but were hollows nonetheless. Her eyes watched him warily from beneath eyelashes short and straight as the bristles in a blunt paintbrush, the kind of eyelashes that were too short to cast a dusky shadow on those perfect high cheekbones, a fact for which he was suddenly and absurdly grateful, for it occurred to him in a flash that those cheekbones should never be hidden in shadow but splendored in light.

"Please sit down," he bade her, only to discover that his heart was hammering in his chest like a wild tom-tom, making a jungle creature of him, and he'd never been anything but civilized in his whole life. While he was recovering, she spoke.

"Derek, I agreed to meet you because I hope that there is some chance that you'll accept the baby as yours," she said.

His eyes rested for a moment on her breasts, so full above the mound that was the baby. Her breasts were round and full, not cone-shaped as they had been before.... But how had he known that her breasts were supposed to be cone-shaped and widespread? He must have noticed at some time in the past, but he had no recollection of it.

He pulled his eyes away from her body, poised so carefully in the chair across from him. He cleared his throat. "You're how pregnant now?" he asked.

"Four and a half months," she said, and he thought he detected a trace of pride in her voice.

"Too late for an abortion?"

"It was always too late for that," she shot back.

His eyes flew to meet hers, and he was surprised that there was no animosity in their brown depths. He sighed and decided to be direct.

"Eve, why? Why did you run away? Why didn't you have the abortion? I thought you had. I thought—"

"Didn't you believe me when I said I wouldn't?" Her voice was deeper now, stronger.

He didn't take his eyes off her face. "No," he said quietly. "I guess not." Then he was silent for a moment. "I should have guessed when you didn't take the passbook with the three thousand dollars with you. That should have tipped me off."

She crossed her legs, and Derek found himself mesmerized by the exposed white skin on the inner part of her calves.

"No amount of money could convince me to get rid of Kelly's baby," she said.

"It's my baby, too," he said before thinking.

Her gaze was level. "That's exactly what I hoped you'd say. The baby belongs to you when it's born. I told you I'd take care of the baby if you won't, and that's still true. I love this baby, have grown to love it, carrying it under my heart all this time—" Her voice broke off, and he was amazed to see that her eyes glistened with tears.

Poor Eve. She'd been through so much. He got up and walked around his desk until he stood in front of her.

"How long have you worked at the L & D Cafe?" he asked, and his voice was low.

"Since I left your house." She dared not look at him, or she would begin to sob. She hadn't minded the work, the feet that swelled until she wore a shoe a size larger than she had before, the lower back pain that had become almost constant now that her center of gravity had shifted forward. It hadn't been easy, although she'd never complained, not even once. But now, with Derek Lang standing before her, so handsome and unchanged by the series of events that he and Kelly had set off, events that had changed everything for Eve, the burden she carried seemed heavier than it had ever felt before.

"All that time you've been working at the L & D Cafe so you could afford to have my baby?"

He had called it his baby again. "Yes," she said, staring down at his wing tips.

He touched a finger to her face and slid it under her chin. Her skin felt like velvet. He tipped her face toward him.

"Eve, let me take care of you," he said gently. "I'm ready to accept responsibility for getting you into this fix. Let me."

"I'm not sure what you mean," she whispered.

He reluctantly allowed his finger to fall away from her face and walked back around his desk to hide his pain at the situation that should never have happened. He fiddled with his letter opener to hide his unaccustomed confusion. He and Kelly had ruined Eve's life, perhaps ruined it permanently. Now that she sat so quietly in his office, asking nothing for herself, the fact was brought unavoidably home to him. To be blunt about it, he felt like a cad. He had to think what to do about it, and it wasn't easy. He didn't have a plan.

He shot Eve a glance of assessment. She looked as though she were concentrating on keeping herself pulled together, maintaining a stiff upper lip. Something about her in that instant seemed very courageous. For some reason another picture of her leaped to his mind, a picture of Eve sitting at the opposite end of the breakfast-room table from him as they both gobbled caramel corn.

"Do you still eat junk food?" He shot the question at her, not knowing why he asked.

The shadow of a smile tugged at the corners of her mouth. "More than I should. But since I've been working in the restaurant, Lenny sees that I eat the right things. He and his wife have four children."

She shrugged, finding it impossible to explain how the gregarious Lenny had taken her firmly under his wing the day she'd vomited at the smell of bacon sizzling on the grill. It was the second day she worked there, and Lenny had sized her up shrewdly and said, "Pregnant, huh?" She'd wanted to die of embarrassment, but all he'd done was pat her on the shoulder and say, "Let me know if you need time off to go to the doctor or anything," and he'd asked no questions. After that she'd tried even harder to do a good job.

"You're not still skipping meals, then?" Derek's gray eyes were unfathomable; she couldn't figure out what he wanted.

"No, it wouldn't be good for the baby," she said.

"Good. Then you'll go to lunch with me." And he picked up the phone and said, "Maisie, call the Versailles Room and make reservations for two for twelve-fifteen."

Eve gasped. "I can't. I'm not dressed for it. I didn't—"

"You're dressed just fine," he assured her, noticing for the first time what she wore. Her tent-shaped dress was fashioned of a light nubby material in a sort of rose-beige; the print scarf at her neck was folded artfully into the vee where two buttons were unfastened.

Derek tried to remember what kind of clothes Eve had worn before, but he couldn't for the life of him recall any of them. She'd favor something unobtrusive, no doubt, the kind of clothes that might have come from anyplace from Belk's to K mart. He was reasonably sure that she'd never worn anything of the superior cut and quality you found at Montaldo's. Kelly had bought most of her clothes at Montaldo's. Suddenly, he had the rash urge to hustle Eve over to that particular store and buy her something, anything.

"Well, come on, let's go," he said, suddenly wanting to be out of the office and in the fresh air.

Eve stood up, wishing she knew how to get out of this situation. She felt bloated and big and definitely not up to walking into the Versailles Room, the fanciest restaurant in downtown Charlotte, with Derek Lang looking so suave and debonair in his executive suit. People would think—but then, did it really matter what people would think? She'd stopped worrying about what people would think when she decided to become a surrogate mother.

She trudged doggedly after Derek down the gray carpeted hall until he slowed his step to match hers and tucked a proprietary hand under her elbow. His hand there made her skin jump; she didn't know how to react.

They walked to the restaurant, which was only a few doors away from the office building. Eve sent halfway-frantic glances at Derek, who kept his hand firmly cupped around her elbow. Once she tried to shake his hand away, but he demurred.

"In case you should stumble," he offered by way of explanation, waving at some nearby sidewalk construction.

The restaurant was crowded, but they were ushered quickly to their table by a maître d' whose attitude toward Derek could only be described as obsequious.

Derek gave their order to the waiter, hesitating over the wine list as his eyes seemed riveted on Eve's stomach.

"No wine for me," Eve said, and when Derek didn't shift his eyes away immediately, she blushed.

After the waiter disappeared, Eve tried to regain her customary composure. So she wouldn't have to look at Derek, so sophisticated and handsome across the white linen tablecloth, she looked around. She'd never eaten in the Versailles Room before, with its inverted waterfalls of glittering crystal shimmering with light and its creamy gold-rimmed china and its fresh flower centerpieces on every table. The room was filled with well-dressed matrons dripping with real pearls and with dapper executives in stylishly tailored suits conversing earnestly over martinis.

"It's not much like the L & D Cafe," she explained when Derek's quizzical glance intruded on her observations.

His expression darkened at that, and she knew she had said the wrong thing. "It can't be pleasant working there," he said, looking uncomfortable.

"It's not so bad," Eve retorted, her defenses up now. "Lenny has been good to me. He lets me stay in the house nearby. It's his house, and he could rent it, but it's mine now for practically nothing, and—"

"You live there alone?" he asked sharply. He and Kelly had talked about Eve's private life, but it had been so long ago. He didn't remember much about her family. Or about her, really. Memory had been lost, set adrift on the sea of grief in which he had been floundering for the past three months.

"My father lives with me," she said.

"I see." He was immensely relieved. What if she had been living with a man, a boyfriend? At the moment he couldn't have imagined anything worse, although he supposed that for Eve at this time in her life, such a situation was unlikely.

Eve said, "How's Aunt May?"

"Lonely, and as daffy as ever."

"I never found Aunt May daffy," Eve objected seriously.

Derek raised his eyebrows. He hadn't expected Eve to stick up for Aunt May. Eve's defense reminded him of Kelly; that was something Kelly might have said and which Derek would have attributed to family loyalty.

"Really?" he said thoughtfully.

"Aunt May's lonely, as you say. And her hearing problem makes communication difficult. But that's no reason to put her down. She was nice to me," Eve said reflectively and with more than a little sadness. She'd hated not saying goodbye to Aunt May. She'd left a fond note, because she couldn't have faced Aunt May's questions.

"She misses you," Derek told her. "It was a mean thing you did, running off like that. Aunt May cried for days. And on top of Kelly—"

"Stop," Eve said fiercely. Her eyes flared with a brief spark of anger; then, like a snuffed candlewick, it went out.

"Sorry," Derek said, looking down at the tablecloth. He paused. Lately his wife's aunt had been rubbing him the wrong way more than usual. It felt good to be able to open up about it to someone who might understand.

"Aunt May drives me crazy," he went on a little desperately. "Remember how Louise used to serve roast beef on Sunday and things like chicken breasts and veal cutlets on weekdays? Well, Aunt May buys oddments like hot pickled sausages and Twinkies and something called tofutti and expects Louise to make a meal out of it. Aunt May says she sees people eating these things on her favorite soap opera. I never get a decent meal anymore."

"That shouldn't pose a problem for a closet eater of junk food," Eve pointed out.

"But it's not fun to eat junk food if you don't have regular food to compare it with," Derek said. "Actually," he went on in a more controlled tone, "I think the old girl needs something worthwhile to do with her time. Planning for the baby gave her that. Did you know she sewed a complete christening gown by hand, all daintily embroidered? The gown, the bonnet, everything. She showed it to me after you left. She worked on it in her room every night. She'd wanted it to be a surprise for Kelly, she said. And after—afterward, she wanted me to have it. I—I had to tell her that you'd had the abortion, because I thought you had."

"Oh," Eve said in a small voice, feeling as though the breath had been knocked out of her. She ached at the thought of Aunt May thinking that she, Eve, would have actually allowed such a thing to happen to this baby.

"I was wrong to have told her that," Derek said heavily. "But at the time..."

"Oh, Derek, please tell her—tell her the truth," Eve said, her voice breaking.

"You could tell her yourself. *Show* her yourself. Come back home, Eve," Derek said softly. "Come back where you belong."

His eyes, so compelling, would not release hers.

"I can't," she said, wishing he wouldn't look at her like that.

The waiter served their food, providing an untimely interruption.

The waiter left. "Why can't you?" Derek asked just as Eve, striving for normalcy, was about to delve into her fruit salad. His tone of voice was so commanding that she didn't think she'd be able to eat a bite.

She set her fork back down on the table. She inhaled a deep breath, trying to be as rational as possible. "Aunt May aside, it would be wrong of me to accept your hospitality, Derek, when you don't even want the baby. Besides, my father lives with me now, and I can't leave him. I'm his sole support." She picked up her salad fork again, only to find that her hand was shaking.

"Eve, I'm reassessing this whole situation, but I need time. I'm sorry, but I still don't think I can take the baby, for more reasons than I want to go into right now. But, Eve, you shouldn't be working that waitress job. I want to take care of you. I feel responsible for you and for the baby; you must understand that."

"You didn't feel too responsible for us three months ago," she pointed out.

A white line bisected the space between Derek's eyebrows. "Do you know what it was like for me then? Losing my wife and then faced with rearing a child all by myself? Don't you have one iota of understanding for how I felt?" His expression was agonized, and with a shock Eve thought, *Why, he's felt this more than I ever dreamed,* and her thought was followed with a rush of unexpected compassion for this man who spoke with such anguish and such passion. Never had she expected to feel so sensitive to Derek Lang and his heretofore incomprehensible emotions.

"Maybe I do understand," she said slowly and with great surprise.

"At least if you were under my roof I'd have the comfort of knowing you were eating properly—"

"I am eating properly," Eve insisted. "I told you that."

"Knowing you were eating properly and that you didn't have to work in that restaurant. And it would be so good for Aunt May to have someone around the house; you got along with her well."

Eve remembered the two of them baking cookies together; it was the kind of thing she had always imagined she would have done with her mother if her mother had lived. She would like showing Aunt May how to make Greek pastries. Aunt May would like it, too. It was true that she had missed Aunt May.

"I have my father to think about," she reminded Derek doubtfully. "I can't just up and leave him, you know."

"Your father could come with you. There's plenty of room in that big barn of a place, plenty of room for all of us. It's so empty now, so empty."

Eve picked at her lunch, nudging morsels of broccoli quiche around her plate. Al, feeling as resentful as he did, would never move into Derek's house.

"Will you think about it at least? Will you, Eve?" Derek couldn't understand why she didn't jump at this chance to make things easier on herself. The world was filled with women who would hang on to a man as though they had a problem with static cling—and not in their panty hose, either. Obviously Eve Triopolous was not one of those women.

Thoughts whirled through Eve's head. If she lived at the Myers Park house with him, wouldn't he begin to feel a curiosity about and perhaps an affection for the baby she carried? She'd pegged him as a warm, caring person—or at least as one-half of a warm caring couple—before. Couldn't Derek Lang become that person again if he were given the chance? Didn't he deserve that chance, for the baby's sake as well as his own?

Again she thought of Kelly, of this much-wanted baby who was the product of a union of Kelly and Derek. Eve loved the baby, did not doubt that she loved it enough to take care of it for the rest of its life if need be. But a child belonged with its biological parents if possible; she utterly and with all her heart believed that, and she, Eve, would never be this baby's biological parent. It was Derek, only Derek, who was the sole surviving biological parent of this child, and father and child belonged together.

The piece of broccoli quiche she was toying with broke apart. She lifted her eyes to his once more. "I'll think about it, Derek," Eve said slowly. "I'll think about it." It was all she could promise at the moment.

Derek smiled, the slow smile lighting up the depths of his silvery eyes, illuminating his handsome face. She didn't know how it happened, but his hand found hers on the tablecloth, was warm as it covered hers, and as his fingers curved around her hand to press against her palm, her back stiffened, and she uttered a single involuntary "Oh!"

"Eve," he said, not yet knowing the import of what had just happened. His voice was warm honey flowing over and around her, and all at once she wanted to get up from the table and throw her arms around his neck, to laugh, to sing, to let everyone in this big fancy restaurant experience her boundless joy.

She smiled, a big smile that revealed her quirky bicuspid, and it was a smile that brightened her eyes and warmed his heart quite unexpectedly.

"Eve, what's wrong?" he said in alarm when he saw the moisture collecting in the corners of her huge brown eyes. But she was smiling; she was smiling with such brilliance that she couldn't be in pain.

"Derek, oh, Derek," she said, pressing her free hand to the gentle mound only partly concealed in the folds of her flowing rose-beige dress in a gesture that he found strangely endearing. "I think I just felt the baby move. For the first time!"

And he couldn't breathe with the wonder of it, he couldn't speak, he couldn't do anything except squeeze Eve's small white hand tighter and tighter, and she was squeezing back, their energy flowing back and forth, one to the other, conveying their awe and reverence and amazement at this irrefutable evidence of the baby's existence and its reaffirmation of life. And they sat like that, unaware of clanking silver and glassware, of passersby brushing the sides of their table, unaware of anything at all, clasping hands across the linen tablecloth and clearly shaken at their sharing of this special moment.

Chapter Six

"And so your mind is set, daughter?" Al regarded her over the apple cobbler that reposed on their dinner table that night courtesy of Lenny at the L & D Cafe.

"Yes," she affirmed. "I've given Lenny notice, but he says you can live here as long as you please. I'm moving into the Myers Park house, and Derek is very happy. Al, please understand—this is something I have to do." She watched him anxiously, hoping that this new direction wouldn't send him off into another coughing spell.

"I'm sure Derek is 'very happy,'" Al huffed. "You moving into his house like that. In my day it would have been a scandal, and I still think it's highly improper. I never thought to see the day that a daughter of mine would be pregnant with a man's child and not even married to the man." He fixed her with a baleful look. His blatant disapproval broke her heart.

"Al, Al," she said, running nervous fingers through her short hair. "Nothing improper has ever taken place between Derek and me. You know that. You know how I contracted to bear a child for him and his wife; you know everything. I haven't done anything wrong, Al. And now I'm convinced that moving into the house with Derek would be *right*, the right thing to do under these very unusual circumstances. Please understand!"

Al shoved his chair back from the table and walked to the window. It looked out on the highway, and down the road the neon lights of the L & D Cafe were just flickering on.

"Understand? You ask a lot, Eve. You've always been a good girl, taking care of the house when your mother died, getting top grades in college, then being hired on as public-relations director at the mill. I've always been proud of you. And you've been loyal, and you've taken care of me. You never ran around with men or acted wild like some of the girls we knew. But Eve, this surrogate-mother idea is out of character for you. I don't know why you ever did it. I can't believe you didn't ask me first."

"Ask your permission? Oh, Al, I'm a grown woman. I didn't require your permission. And we needed the money."

"In the old days, the daughters in Greek families didn't date, didn't marry, without their fathers' permission."

"In the old days, there was no such thing as *in vitro* fertilization," Eve reminded him gently. "Couples who wanted babies had to do without them, because infertility could not always be cured. Isn't the new way better?"

Al looked sad. "Maybe." He reflected on this for a moment. A car's headlights illuminated his face, and then Eve drew the curtain across the window. She sat down on the sofa and beckoned Al to sit next to her. She placed one hand protectively over her abdomen, hoping she might feel the baby move. She sat like that often these days.

"Did I ever tell you, Eve, that your mother and I wanted more children?" Al said so suddenly that it startled her.

"You've said you wanted a bigger family," she told him.

"Well, we did. A big, big family, as big as the Quick family who lived across the street from us in Wrayville. We never had any children after you. Your mother never became pregnant again."

"Do you know why?"

"No. Her doctor couldn't tell her why. It just never happened. I've often wished we'd had more children, lots of children, like the big Greek families I knew when I was growing up."

"So you see, Al," Eve said, encouraged by this revelation, "what I'm doing is a sign of progress. Of modern medicine. There's no stigma attached to being a surrogate mother, at least not among people who are well-informed."

"Still, you're going to live with this man, the father of your baby." Al was stubborn, just as she was. His lower lip stuck out, underscoring his implacability.

"Only until his baby is born. And you could come live with him, too," Eve said. "You're perfectly welcome. In fact, you and Aunt May would be the perfect chaperones."

"No," Al snorted. "That's where I draw the line. I'll not go with you, Eve. I cannot stop you from doing what you will do. But I needn't put my seal of approval on such goings-on."

She'd known he'd react this way, but she'd felt bound to repeat Derek's offer. "If you're going to be that way, well, I know you'll be happy here in Lenny's house. You can still go over to the restaurant and talk with the construction workers. And I can visit you a few times a week if you like."

"No," Al said obstinately. "You have taken matters into your own hands once too often. You assume too much, daughter. I won't live in Derek Lang's house but I'll not presume on Lenny's generosity, either!"

Eve was dumbfounded. She'd thought she'd arranged everything so perfectly; if Al wouldn't go to Derek's house, he'd stay here at Lenny's. She couldn't believe he wouldn't go along with it.

"What will you do?" she asked.

"I'm going," Al replied loftily, "back to Wrayville. I'll rent a room from Nell Baker. She offered it, you know. She rents a room to one other widower, Vernon Platts, so I won't be lonely with the two of them around. My social security check will cover the expense."

"But Al—"

"I miss my friends from the mill. I miss Wrayville. I didn't want to tell you that before because it tore me up to see you working so hard so that we'd have a place to live and food to eat—" Al's voice broke.

"Oh, Al," Eve said, on the verge of tears herself. "Oh, Al."

"Anyway," Al went on, recovering, "maybe this is for the best. I can go back to Wrayville, and you won't have to work so hard in the restaurant, eh?" In that moment Eve sensed how difficult it had been for her father to be so absolutely dependent on her.

"I wish you'd go with me," Eve whispered, knowing it was hopeless."

"No, that I cannot do, Eve," Al said, heaving himself up from the sofa.

"I'll miss you," Eve said, trying not to burst into tears which seemed to be precipitated these days by any little emotional crisis.

"I'll miss you, too, daughter," he told her, but his face was set in an unyielding expression, and she knew that however much Al loved her, he was not going to change his mind.

"Eve?" It was Derek, home from work for the day. Tonight, her first night back, he was early.

In her room, Eve set aside the book she was reading and pulled herself to her feet with the aid of one of the brass bedposts. The bigger she got, the harder it was to stand up on her own. The baby turned a somersault; with a grin she patted the hard mound of her belly.

"We're going to go see your daddy," she whispered to the baby.

Derek saw her as she rounded the landing, the big grandfather clock chiming six times in welcome as Eve slowly made her way down the flight of stairs, her white hand barely skimming the banister. She looked so beautiful that she took his breath away.

There were two spots of color high on her cheeks, which was unusual in itself. But it was her eyes, her eyes sparkling in her bright, intelligent face, that captured his attention. And she was smiling in welcome, showing those tiny white teeth, so perfect except for the one bicuspid, and she was rounder in places than she had been just a couple of weeks ago. He was so happy to see her that he felt like scooping her into his arms and whirling her around, which of course would never do.

He fell back on the mundane for something to say.

"You're all moved in? Everything is comfortable?"

"Everything is lovely," she said honestly. "Lenny helped me move my things in his truck, and Aunt May was so happy to see me that she baked my favorite kind of cookies. Peanut butter."

"My particular favorite is chocolate chip. But should you be eating cookies? Are cookies junk food? Don't you have to watch your weight or something?" He looked so boyish despite the dignity of his conservative but elegant suit. He looked like a suitor come to call, which was ridiculous, considering that it was his foyer in which they were standing, gabbling like idiots about inconsequentialities, and she was the guest, not he.

"Peanut butter is very nutritious, Derek," she assured him solemnly. "So I'm sure it's okay to eat peanut-butter-cookies."

"Ah," he said, rocking back on his heels. "Will you join me for a drink before dinner? No, you won't. Bad for the baby."

"I could have tomato juice," she suggested, suddenly wanting very much to sit down with Derek, to watch his face as his expression changed in response to her.

"Tomato juice," he said with satisfaction. Louise appeared in the hall.

"Please get Eve a glass of tomato juice, and a bourbon and branch water for me," he instructed.

"I'm so glad you're back," Louise whispered, squeezing Eve's arm as she passed her on the way to the kitchen. She flashed Eve a wide white-toothed smile. Louise's reassurance made Eve feel good, as though her presence here was desirable in and of itself, not just because she was gestating the Langs' child.

"Your father never changed his mind about moving here with you?" Derek asked carefully once their drinks had been served and they sat in the living room, Derek on a Chippendale couch, Eve in an armchair with her feet resting on a footstool upholstered in needlepoint.

She shook her head. "I'm afraid not. He's renting a room from a former neighbor, and he seems happy with his decision."

"Why didn't he want to live here?" Derek asked, wrinkling his brow.

Eve shrugged. She didn't want to offend Derek. "You have to understand my father's background. He's very Greek, very Old World. He doesn't approve of my being unmarried and pregnant. He doesn't approve of our living together."

"Good God," Derek said before tossing down a long draft of his bourbon and branch water. He stared at Eve. "And so he thinks you're some kind of scarlet woman? Letting your body be used for pay?" There was irony behind Derek's voice, and something more, too.

"More or less," Eve said, and she couldn't look at him. Why did she always cast her eyes down when caught in his intense gaze? Why couldn't she return his look with one of her own, one that told him she was proud and strong and could handle any circumstances that came along? Was it some Old World ploy, learned subconsciously from her black-garbed grandmother so long ago on those lengthy family visits every summer to the Greek community in Tarpon Springs?

"How awful," Derek said. "How terrible that this should come between you and your father." His words were heavy and oppressive, falling as they did like dead weights into the tightly strung atmosphere of the room.

Eve tried to speak around the lump in her throat. She would never understand how she managed to cope when she was on her own, and then when Derek came along and put his thoughts about her situation into words, she always choked up.

"It's not your concern," she said unhappily. "It's not your worry. Anyway, my father and I are on good terms. I'll visit him often."

"But he'll never understand why you did this," Derek offered.

"No. Probably not."

"Eve." She couldn't avoid his eyes when he spoke in that authoritative tone of voice. And when she looked at him, his expression was tender and compassionate.

"Eve," he went on, speaking slowly and distinctly and watching her with total absorption, as though he wanted to get inside her head and hear his words from the inside out, as though he wished he could *be* her for this short moment in time and therefore hear what he had to say solely from her point of view. "Eve, please accept my apologies. I am sincerely sorry that Kelly and I ever started this, that we ever got you into this—this mess. If I had it to do over again, I would never agree to it. Never."

"But—"

"Never, Eve," he said with heart-stopping earnestness.

"Let me say what I was going to say," she said softly. She became aware of the glass in her hands, of the dampness from it running down her palms. She set it carefully on a coaster on the burled-walnut cocktail table in front of her. She stood and walked to the fireplace where she stared at the huge gold-framed oil portrait of Kelly over the mantel, summoning the words she wanted to say. She drew strength from the sweet expression in Kelly's blue eyes.

"I'm glad that I'm pregnant," she told him, turning to look at him. "I love the feeling of a child within me. And if I hadn't decided to be a surrogate mother, I might never have had the chance. So don't feel sorry for me. I'm happy, Derek; I'm really happy."

Derek shook his head and lifted his eyebrows in disbelief. Her pear shape was starkly outlined against the white of the wall behind her. Eve was absolutely, unmistakably pregnant, her neat, compact body forced into new lines by the baby. He couldn't imagine that she actually enjoyed the process. Though he had to admit that from the healthy look of her, pregnancy seemed to agree with her. Still, he said in a quiet voice, "Don't be silly. You would have eventually married some nice fellow and settled down to raise a bunch of kids."

Eve shook her head vigorously. "I'm not so sure. I'm twenty-eight, Derek, which is closer to thirty than I like to think about some days. I've never dated much—only one serious romance, which ended when the man left Wray Mills for another job far away—and after that I concentrated on my job. I was a good Greek daughter, taking care of my father, never planning to do much else. I might never have borne a child. Now I will. I'm not sorry."

"This man of yours—did you want to marry him?" He was way out of line, asking. But somehow he had to know.

Eve took her time answering. She and Burke Whitlaw had gone through the manager-trainee program at Wray Mills together. What they'd experienced was more a commonality of interest than anything else. They had shared some good times. Yet when Burke had left Wrayville, there'd really been no great sadness. In fact, Eve had been aware only of a sense of moving on, of growing. Marry Burke? She'd never considered it seriously. They hadn't been right for each other.

"No," she said slowly. "I didn't want to marry him. Or anyone."

"But you're so pretty, Eve. A woman like you—" he left his sentence unfinished, thinking about men competing for her warm smiles, wanting to touch her body, to kiss her slim and elegant neck, the nape of it where the hair was so short and sleek, to kiss the insides of her milky-white wrists. Oh, there should be men flocking around Eve Triopolous. He couldn't believe that there weren't.

Eve blushed slightly. She was glad when Aunt May chose that moment to descend upon them in a fit of unbecomingly girlish enthusiasm, and Eve sat down again so that she could prop her feet up.

"You know what I did today?" Aunt May asked, bounding without pause into the conversation. "I planted the pansy beds. Oh, they're going to be so pretty in the spring! I planted lots of those big yellow ones with purple petals. Do you like pansies, Eve?"

"Oh, yes," said Eve. "They always remind me of little faces, upturned toward me and smiling."

"Now that's a sweet thought. I never thought of them as faces. My grandmother used to call pansies heartsease. They do kind of ease the heart just to look at them, don't they?"

Aunt May prattled on, but Eve welcomed her ramblings. She was irked that Derek looked as though he could barely tolerate them, and she was uncomfortable under his frank and undisguised gaze, but it was only a short time until Louise announced dinner.

Aunt May insisted on lighting tall candles, which cast the wainscoted dining room in a mellow glow, and Eve took her customary place to Derek's left, with Aunt May at the foot of the table. Eve was conscious that the three of them avoided looking at the place to Derek's right, where Kelly used to sit. Other than that, dinner was unremarkable except for a warm, familiar sense in Eve's heart that she was happy to be back.

"AND HOW DID YOUR VISIT to Dr. Perry go today?" Derek asked when he came home the next night.

"Fine. I'm fine, the baby is fine, and when the weather is fine, I'm supposed to do lots of walking." Eve smiled at him as she pulled on a loose cardigan that she kept hanging in the foyer closet.

"You're going for a walk now?" Derek seemed surprised.

"Of course. The leaves are changing color, and the neighborhood is beautiful."

"I'll come with you. That is, if you don't mind."

For one long, terrible minute she seemed taken aback, and he was afraid she was going to say no. But then she nodded briskly. "All right," she acceded.

They stepped out into the crisp, cool air. Derek inhaled deeply; this was the kind of weather he liked.

"Let's stop and look at Aunt May's pansy plants," Eve said on impulse. Aunt May had not only planted huge beds of them but had bordered a long brick walkway alongside the house with little green plants, flowerless now.

"They seem so fragile," Eve said, staring down at the tiny green sprouts. "As though they won't make it through the winter."

"Oh, they'll make it," Derek said confidently. "Aunt May has a wonderfully green thumb. I employ a gardener, of course, but she loves to work with the flowers herself. She's the one who created the rose garden for Kelly, you know. Those pansies will come up blooming in the spring; wait and see."

Wait and see? It was not likely. The baby was due in February, and she would be gone by the time the pansies bloomed. But the baby, if Derek kept it—surely she could persuade Derek to keep it—would be able to see the bright colors of the pansies, their nodding little faces.

"Heartsease," she murmured, wondering how her heart would be eased if she had to leave the baby. She didn't dare think about it, not now. She turned and walked swiftly down the path, so swiftly that Derek, with his longer strides and without the handicap of being off balance, could barely keep up with her. She didn't slow down until she reached the sidewalk.

They strolled down the tree-lined street. Dogwood leaves had already turned various shades of red—carmine, ruby, scarlet. Lagging just behind were the leaves of the ginkgo trees, bright bursts of yellow now.

"What else did the doctor say today?" Derek's eyes fixed on her with interest.

"I'm gaining too much weight. And I should remember to take my vitamins."

"Gaining weight? How dangerous is that?"

"Not as dangerous as they used to think it was, but if I gain a lot, I'll have trouble losing it after the baby is born."

"I see."

"I didn't know you'd be so interested," ventured Eve, casting a curious sidelong glance at him.

"Of course I am," he said quickly. He shoved his hands down in the pockets of his suit trousers. A little girl in a smocked dress ran out of one of the houses across the street and stood staring at them.

"I wonder what she's staring at," Derek said, amiably.

"You, probably." Eve smiled. "You strolling down the street for a casual before-dinner walk, relaxed and comfortable in your three-piece suit."

Derek pulled his hands out of his pockets and looked down at himself. "Honestly? Do I look out of place?"

This brought a peal of soft laughter from Eve. "Yes, Derek. Most people take off their ties and vests and suit jackets when they come home from work, and then they put on something more comfortable."

"Comfortable? You mean a sweater?"

"A sport shirt, a sweater, a turtleneck. Don't you have any?"

"Well, of course," he said, sounding miffed. "People give them to me for gifts. But I feel perfectly comfortable in what I'm wearing."

"Don't you ever unbend? Have fun?"

"Well, I don't openly cavort, if that's what you mean." He had stopped sounding miffed and was looking down at her with laughter in his eyes. "It's sort of like eating junk food. Bad for the image."

"Oh, Derek. Is the image so all-important?" She spoke in a teasing tone, but he chose to answer her seriously.

"I became the president of a Fortune 500 company when I was only thirty-one. I never thought people would take me seriously if I showed up at the office looking less than dignified."

"And at home?"

There was a long silence, and then he said very quietly, "I wasn't home much."

The way he had spoken made her bite back the light retort on the tip of her tongue.

"I'm getting winded," Eve said after they had walked another block in silence. "Do you mind if we sit on that wall for a minute?"

"No, of course not."

She rested her hand on the stone of the wall for a lingering moment. It was cold, but she sat down anyway, and Derek sat beside her, staring moodily into space. Leaves freed by a stirring breeze overhead drifted down. One landed on Derek's shoulder.

Without thinking, Eve reached up to flick it away. So did he. Their hands touched.

Eve quickly pulled her hand away and clasped it with the other in her lap. The buoyancy of their mood had vanished, fading during their conversation, disappearing entirely when their hands had brushed each other. Eve shivered.

"It's getting chilly now with the sun going down," Derek said abruptly. "We'd better be getting back to the house."

Unhappily, Eve stood up, avoiding his eyes, and they headed toward home. Derek didn't speak, and neither did she. In the houses along the way, lights were winking on, and it was dark enough for windows to cast geometric shapes onto the spacious grounds of the houses they passed.

"I had so much responsibility at work," Derek said suddenly. "There was always so much to do."

With a start, Eve realized that Derek was talking about his absences from home, the effect they had had on his life with Kelly. Her cheeks colored when she recalled the conversation she had overheard when he and Kelly had been on the terrace and she had been in Derek's study.

"I—I'm sure there was," she said, wondering why he was telling this to her.

"Most of the time she understood, I think. If only I hadn't become president of the company when I was so young! But there wasn't any help for it. Dad groomed me to be president from the time I was a boy, in the manner of all the old textile barons. If you had a son, he would one day take over the mills. I never dreamed that my father would decide on early retirement and run off to Rio de Janeiro with a woman younger than I am."

"Is that what happened?"

Derek nodded grimly. "And that left me holding the Lang Textiles bag. Not that I didn't relish it at first. Putting my ideas to work was—and still is—a challenge. But I should have known what a toll it would take on my marriage."

What was he telling her? That his marriage hadn't been as perfect as it seemed? That he and Kelly weren't really the "golden couple" she had imagined? Eve groped in her memory for something Kelly might have told her that would help her to understand. As close as she and Kelly had grown, Kelly had never revealed any problems with her marriage. Kelly had always been cheerful and smiling, delighted about the baby, supportive of Derek. The only sour spot Eve could remember was that scene on the terrace when she had run away before they'd detected her presence, and even that had ended in tenderness between Kelly and Derek.

Derek's words bewildered Eve. But she knew by the deeply etched line between his eyes that he was tormented by something, something she knew very little about and perhaps never would. She didn't need to know, really. It was enough to know that Derek was flagellating himself for some real or imagined problem in his marriage and that he needed someone to talk to.

"Do you want to tell me about it?" she asked softly, forgetting her chill, forgetting everything but the human being who walked beside her and who seemed so lost and alone.

The faraway look in his eyes disappeared and was replaced by one of guardedness. He studied Eve's face, upturned toward him in the dusky shadows of early evening. Then his eyes dropped to the round protrusion of her belly, more noticeable than ever now that her hands, tucked into the cardigan's pockets for warmth, pulled the sweater fabric taut. He seemed to come to his senses.

"Not now," he said unhappily.

A chastened Eve walked faster, trying to keep up. Had she overstepped her bounds by asking Derek if he wanted to talk? But she could have sworn he'd been asking her, in his own oblique way, to listen!

Eve knew that only if Derek felt whole and well would he take this baby. *Let me find the best way to help him,* Eve thought fervently as she preceded him into the brightly lit foyer. And inside her, his child stirred, reminding her that time was growing short.

Chapter Seven

The telephone rang bright and early on this Saturday morning. Eve, who had been awake since seven and had just come in from retrieving the newspaper from its accustomed place beneath the boxwood hedge, scooped the ornate gilt receiver off the hall phone.

"Eve?"

She recognized the male voice immediately. "Doug! How in the world are you? I haven't talked with you in weeks!"

"I know, and we're going to remedy that. How about dinner tonight?"

"Nothing's wrong, is there? Al's not sick?"

"No, no. He's looking chipper, in fact. I think living at Nell's house agrees with him. But, well, do I need an excuse to see an old friend?"

Eve sank down on the bottom step, then regretted it. How would she get up again?

"Eve?"

"You don't need an excuse to see me, Doug, but I'm very pregnant. I'm not sure—"

"I have nothing more strenuous in mind than sitting in a quiet restaurant and lifting our forks to our faces. Anyway, you can't turn me down. I have something important I want to talk with you about."

"Important?"

"Important. To the mill workers who have been disabled by cotton dust. They need help, and no one knows it better than you. I need to discuss a couple of matters with you. Now how about it?"

"Since you put it that way, how can I refuse?" She smiled into the phone, picturing Doug's warm hazel eyes. She'd like to see him.

"I'll pick you up, say, at seven?"

"Could we go earlier? Since I've been pregnant, I don't like to eat that late. I mean, would you mind?"

Doug's voice was warm, caring. "Have I ever minded adjusting my plans for you? Remember the time I gave up a junior high school track meet to stay home and help you nurse a sick hamster? I was a sure bet to win the hurdles in that particular meet, too."

"I remember, all right! The hamster gave birth to a fine, healthy litter." Doug had been so gentle, so genuinely interested, that day. He hadn't changed a bit. That was the way he was now. Those qualities were what made him a good lawyer as well as a good friend.

"So after I gave up a track meet, picking you up at six o'clock instead of seven seems minor. I'll see you then, Eve."

"Okay," she said before replacing the phone carefully, thoughtfully.

"How's this for a casual weekend at home?"

Eve looked backward up the staircase to see Derek descending with a sheepish grin on his face. He wore a silver-gray pullover sweater with a white shirt under it.

"Very nice," she murmured approvingly. "Are you wearing that to work?"

Derek noticed that Eve, perched on the bottom step, looked strangely reflective. As usual, not one hair on her head was ruffled or out of place, and he was impressed all over again with the precision of her. Something leaped inside his chest, and for a moment it threatened to distract him. But he recovered when he recognized the warm interest in Eve's eyes.

"I," he announced, parading in front of her and giving his reflection in the hall mirror a thorough once-over, "am not going to work today."

"You always work on Saturdays," she pointed out, trying in vain to lurch off the bottom stair to a standing position.

"Yes, but not today. It's my favorite month of the year. And it's time for Oktoberfest. You and Aunt May are going with me. Aren't you, Aunt May?"

"What's that?" Aunt May said, wandering in from the kitchen. Eve thought it doubtful that Aunt May was wearing her hearing aid. Her expression was too dreamy.

"The Oktoberfest," Derek said loudly. "I've invited you and Eve to go with me."

Aunt May made a face. "That big German festival in the park? Where they have this big band with tubas blaring away so that I have to turn my hearing aid off and where everyone drinks beer? Derek, you should know by now that beer isn't my cup of tea." She fluttered her fingers in distaste and tottered through the living room toward the sun room.

Eve wrinkled her brow, trying not to laugh at Aunt May's mixed metaphor.

"Eve? How about you? Oktoberfest is really not as bad as Aunt May says it is. Instead of walking around the block again, why not come with me and do your walking in the park? You must be ready for a change of scene." His smile was engaging.

"They really should go," Aunt May quavered loudly from the sun room as though she were talking into a void. "Derek so seldom gets away from work. Eve ought to go with him." Louise was humming to herself in the kitchen, so Eve knew Aunt May was talking to herself. It was hard to get used to hearing herself be talked about to no one. This habit of Aunt May's annoyed her this morning more than usual. And not being able to get herself up from the bottom step annoyed her even more.

"If I can't get up from this step, how am I going to manage Oktoberfest?" Eve said irritably. "Derek, could you lend me a hand?"

Derek knit his brows at her. He hadn't noticed that she'd been trying to get up. "Why didn't you say something?" he demanded, hauling her to her feet.

"Well, it's embarrassing not to be able to do things for myself," she answered scowling.

He'd never seen her disgruntled. For a moment, this new demeanor startled him. Then he grinned. Of course. All pregnant women got this way. Isn't that what the popular literature said? He was lucky she hadn't asked him to go out in the middle of the night to buy pickles and ice cream. But that was silly. Eve would never do that, although it was something wives asked of their husbands. But their situation was not that of husband and wife.

He cleared his throat. "If you get stuck somewhere at Oktoberfest, I'll help you up. Promise," he said, sketching an absurd "cross my heart and hope to die" across the chest of his new gray sweater.

And so, cajoled by Aunt May, urged by Derek, Eve went upstairs and dressed in a pair of rust-colored maternity slacks and an amber-colored mohair sweater with a big cowl neck that almost covered the lobes of her ears. It was the shoes that were a problem. None of her shoes fit, her feet had swollen so. She finally settled on a pair of black corduroy bedroom slippers that looked exactly like black corduroy bedroom slippers and would fool no one. She, who always wanted colors to match or at least complement each other, who winced when people wore sandals with tailored suits or white shoes with a black dress, didn't really care about this today.

When she was ready, she found Derek waiting outside in the driveway, noisily warming up the Corvette's engine.

"You look marvelous," he said as she opened the car door, and then his eyes fell to her feet as she folded herself downward into the low-slung sports car and tucked her feet in after her.

"It's probably out of line for me to mention this," he said, "but haven't you forgotten to put on your shoes?"

"Unfortunately, these *are* my shoes," she said. "They're all that fits anymore." She regarded her ill-clad feet as though they belonged to someone else.

"Your feet are *that* swollen?" Derek looked aghast.

"I'm afraid so. It's all right. These are comfortable."

"But Eve, you have to have shoes," he said, trying to reason with her.

"I do," she insisted. "These." She grinned at him just to show him that she didn't think her swollen feet were a serious matter, at least not as serious as he seemed to consider them.

"Mmm—" was all he said, and his mouth was set in a grim line as he rammed the car into gear and backed out of the driveway.

Minutes later they rolled to a stop in front of a porticoed shoe store, one in which Eve had never dared even to browse because the prices were so high.

"Derek?" she ventured as he slammed his car door and came around to her side, yanking the door open.

"Come on," he said, and then his eyes softened as he looked down at her. His voice was gentle when he spoke again. "We're going to buy you some shoes."

"I don't need—"

"Yes, you do." He leaned down and lifted her hand off the edge of the seat. "Need some help getting up?"

A gentle tug, and Eve found herself rising out of the seat, found herself being hastened inside the store, found herself sitting in a blue velvet chair, being fitted with butter-soft leather shoes, pair after pair, by a saleswoman with a well-modulated voice.

"I don't need all these," Eve stage-whispered frantically when the saleswoman disappeared to look for another size in one of the styles. Derek still held her hand, she realized belatedly.

"I'll decide what you need," he said firmly.

The saleswoman returned.

"She'd like to try another pair like those suede ones. No, not those, the others. In brown. Or rust, if you have it."

"Certainly," the saleswoman said, sliding a shoe on Eve's foot. It didn't fit. The saleswoman disappeared again.

"Derek!" Eve's eyes were round, her expression one of amazement. The saleswoman came back and inserted Eve's foot into another pair.

"Walk in those," Derek commanded. Finally, he released her hand, as if he'd just noticed that he held it. He dropped it as though it burned him.

Eve stood up and trod gingerly across the well-padded blue carpet to the mirror. They were beautifully made shoes of Italian workmanship with hand stitching. She could never afford them in a million years.

"I can't buy these," she hissed at him.

He pulled his eyes away from her feet and lifted them slowly to her face. Then he lowered them to take in her legs, slim beneath the rust-colored slacks, and the way her sweater fell loosely over her wide hips, and the contour of it so gently cupping her breasts.

"I'm buying them for you," he said, but the words wanted to expand in his throat, choking off air, hurting him.

Before she could object, he handed over a credit card and signed a sales ticket.

"She'll wear those," he said, pointing to a pair of rust-colored gillies, and then the shoes were being laced on her feet, and she was still speechless.

"You shouldn't have done that," she said when they were back in the Corvette, speeding through streets where defrocked trees raised spindly branches to a piercingly blue windswept sky. "My slippers were all right."

"Not if we're going to dance the polka at Oktoberfest," he said, slanting a look at her out of the corners of his eyes.

"Polka! Dance the polka! Derek Lang, you must be joking!"

"It's part of the festival. A tradition," he said as though that explained everything. He slid the Corvette neatly into a parking space between a Ford and a Chrysler.

"Wow, that's a nice car, mister," said an admiring kid whose eyes were round as saucers in his coffee-colored face.

"Thanks," Derek said, slamming his door and hurrying around to Eve's side. He handed Eve carefully out of the Corvette before he knelt to address the child.

"Do you live around here?" Derek asked in a conspiratorial whisper.

The boy nodded shyly, pointing at a neat red-brick house across the street.

"Well, do you think you could keep an eye on my car for an hour or two?"

"Sure!" the boy exclaimed, overwhelmed.

"Then here's a couple of dollars. Maybe you could buy a Matchbox car with it—a Corvette model."

"Sure!" The boy's whole face lit up.

"Good." Derek stood and slapped the boy on the back—good buddies now.

"Why did you do that?" Eve asked curiously as they wound their way through the crowd. "Your car doesn't need watching. Not here. It's a safe neighborhood."

"He was cute," Derek said, dismissing the subject.

You were so good with that little boy, she wanted to say. But she didn't. Only it was hard to understand why Derek wouldn't want his own child, who loved perhaps be a little boy who loved Corvettes and liked being slapped on the back by a father like Derek Lang.

The brass band blared out German tunes, bravely rather than skillfully, but no one cared about the musicians' lack of skill. The colorful milling throng surged around the park bandstand, two thousand barrels of specially imported German beer flowed freely, and young men in lederhosen abounded.

"You didn't wear your short pants," Eve murmured, looking down at Derek's legs.

"Short pants? Ha! You just got me out of a three-piece suit, Eve. Don't expect short pants until next year!" He laughed down at her, looking genuinely happy for the first time in a long time.

Without asking her if she wanted it, he bought Eve a plate of apple strudel.

"I shouldn't eat this." She sighed before digging into it, and her gusto in eating pleased him.

For himself, Derek bought a bowl of sauerkraut from a vendor, trying to eat it neatly but unable to stop the strings of it from dripping down his chin, and Eve laughed so hard at the sight that she had to clutch her abdomen.

"You're all right, aren't you?" he asked anxiously, and she nodded, wiping tears from her eyes. The ever-meticulous, everproper Derek Lang, wearing a sweater and allowing sauerkraut to drip down his chin!

A fat lady yodeled. A dance club climbed up on a wooden platform and performed a German folk dance with lots of hollering and knee slapping. Afterward couples drifted onto the platform and began to dance. This festival, so ethnic, reminded her of Greek festivals attended in long-ago years with her mother and father and assorted aunts, uncles and cousins.

"Are you watching them dance? Getting some pointers?" Derek asked her, taking in the sparkle of her eyes, the tapping of her foot in time to the music. The cool, crisp air had brought a bloom to her cheeks, and she looked as though she fairly itched to dance. Was she a good dancer? He would find out.

"Yes, I'm watching, but don't expect me to get up there and make a fool of myself," she told him tartly.

"How about a waltz?" he said when the band began a new piece, a swirling Viennese number.

"A waltz?" she said doubtfully.

"Come on; let's try it," he said, pulling her to her feet. "We might as well test-drive those new shoes of yours."

Against her better judgment, she let him propel her toward the dance floor. It was with misgivings that she let him surround what was left of her waist with his arm and hold her hand high with his other hand, moving her to meet the music surely and smoothly.

And it was amazing how her new bulk flowed along with him, how easily he guided her around the floor, gently, soothingly, making her feel dainty and feminine and, well, like a young girl again.

"You dance nicely," he said in his best dancing-school voice. Of course he had gone to dancing school. It was what young gentlemen of his social stature did.

"I have a good partner," she replied easily. He held her far away, not close, which was the correct position for the proper execution of the waltz. As far as her stomach protruded, it did not touch him. She would have been embarrassed if it had.

"Let me know if you get tired. We can sit down any time you like."

She smiled up at him, the tree branches above them reflecting in the starry irises of her eyes as they whirled around the dance floor. "I wish Aunt May had come," she said.

"I'm glad she didn't" was his reply, and it was uttered with an intensity that surprised her. But there was no time to answer, because the band jumped without pause into an earsplitting, foot-stamping polka. And before she knew it, she was doing the polka, too, slightly out of breath, her face flushed, hanging on to Derek for dear life and loving every minute of it.

"Are you okay?" he shouted at one point, and she was; she was light on her feet, buoyant in his arms, laughing back at him with an energy imparted by crisp air, good food and energetic music. When the dance was over, Eve, caught up in the spirit of the moment, dropped Derek a ridiculous little curtsy.

Someone shouted, and a little girl standing at the edge of the dance floor, waiting for her parents, let go of her helium balloon and began to wail over her loss. Derek, seeing what had happened, stopped the balloon man and bought the child a shiny new silver one. And Eve thought, *He's sensitive to children. He likes them.* And she wondered why he didn't want his own child, the child who even now floated free in her womb, dancing to the music that was her heart.

They ate big, soft, hot pretzels with mustard on them, and Derek drank a beer. Eve listened happily to the oompah-pah music, and she, who had been burdened with problem after problem for longer than she cared to remember, realized that she had never had such a good time in her life.

Then, when the sun dropped behind the lacy branches of the trees and the air cooled accordingly, Derek said, "Let's go," and he held her hand as he led her through the crowd to the car. She knew he held her hand so that she wouldn't get lost, so that he could blaze a trail through the crush of people for her, but she liked the connectedness of it, and when he let go of her hand, she missed its warmth.

The little boy they had seen earlier was perched on a tree stump, steadfastly watching the Corvette.

"Hi, sport," Derek said, tousling the boy's fuzzy hair. The boy regarded Derek as though he were nothing less than a god.

"Do you know what I want you to do?" Derek asked him.

"Uh-uh."

"Go over there—" he pointed to a balloon seller on the edge of the crowd "—and tell that man to give you the biggest, reddest balloon he's got." He slipped a five-dollar bill into the boy's pocket.

The boy clutched his pocket and broke into a wide grin. "Gee, thanks, mister. Gee, thanks." He scampered away across the dun-colored grass.

The Corvette hummed toward Myers Park, and Derek slipped a cassette into the tape deck. "It's not oompahpah music," he apologized, "but it's not bad."

"Not bad," she agreed, leaning her head back against the headrest. "Thanks for taking me, Derek. I had a wonderful time."

"It's not over, you know. I'm treating you to dinner."

She didn't speak for so long that he knew something was wrong.

"I—I can't, Derek. I have other plans."

It hadn't occurred to him that Eve might have something else to do. She was such a homebody; she never went out.

"I'm sorry," he said. "I didn't think you'd be busy."

"Well, usually I'm not. But an old friend asked me to go out, and I said I would."

"That's all right. We can make it another time." But he knew it wasn't all right, and another time wouldn't be this time, with their euphoria coasting them along on a natural high for the rest of the evening.

"I wish we could," she said lamely.

"It's all right," he repeated a little too sharply. If he couldn't be with Eve, he'd have to stay home alone with Aunt May. The prospect did nothing to cheer him.

Eve remained silent, staring out the window, her shoulders hunched down in the seat. The joy in being together had evaporated, and the atmosphere seemed depressingly flat. Well, he could call up someone, go out, anyway. The Kleinsts—but they'd only try to push Debby Kleinst's sister off on him. Jay Stanley—although Jay would have a date, no doubt, on a Saturday night.

They barely spoke, and at the house Eve hurried directly upstairs—to dress for her evening out, he supposed. Derek mixed himself a drink and sat in the darkening living room, staring gloomily at Kelly's picture over the mantel, waiting for the ring of the doorbell, suspecting that Eve's "friend" would be a man. Why was he so sure of this? Why didn't he think she'd be going out with a girlfriend?

In due time the doorbell rang, and Louise answered it. The male voice that greeted her, that sounded pleased when Eve came down the stairs, was no surprise. Derek knew that he should go out to greet Eve's visitor, but he remained rooted to his chair. When the door closed after the two of them, he listened for Eve's clear laughter floating back on the wind, but he didn't hear it.

When the sound of the car was gone, he got up and poured himself a healthy splash of bourbon. Then he slumped in his chair again and lifted it to his lips.

"She's a good dancer," he told the gold-rimmed picture of Kelly, and then he realized he was doing what Aunt May was always doing—talking to thin air. He hoped Louise hadn't heard him, sitting here in the dark, talking to a picture of his wife. She'd think he was loony for sure.

Why should he find it so depressing that Eve had gone out to dinner with another man?

And he wondered if she'd worn the shoes he'd bought her.

As THEY WAITED for their dinner to be served at Hearthside, a steak house on Albemarle Road, Doug said, "It's like this, Eve. If we don't do something for brown-lung victims, who will?"

"Not the companies, evidently." Eve's tone was bitter.

"Not the companies. They're dragging their feet even though they've been told by the federal government to clean up the cotton dust. In the meantime, we need to educate the workers. There are people in Wrayville who have valid claims. Our job is to find them."

"And once we find them?"

"Many of these workers don't know how to go about filing a claim. Some of them are too sick to care. But they can be helped, Eve. We can help them, you and I."

"How?"

"When we locate people who have valid claims, we'll get all the claims together and file them with the state industrial commission instead of Wray Mills. It's a viable option, you know. If a company disputes a claim and refuses to reach a settlement, we're entitled to seek an award from the commission. Wray Mills has been uncooperative, to say the least, so why not go to the industrial commission? It'll be hard for the commission to ignore so many claims filed in a bloc, especially if I threaten legal action."

"I can come to Wrayville one day a week. Would that help?"

"Sure. I've had a special phone line installed in my office, a sort of brown-lung hotline. Your father and Nell Baker take turns coming in to answer it and to field questions workers have about the disease. I need someone who is good at working with people to help workers fill out forms, to help decide if they have a case. That's you, Eve, if you'll do it.'' His eyes burned into her with the fervor of one committed to a cause.

"You know I will." She smiled at him warmly. This was something she wanted to do. It would ease her feeling that she had given up on the problem of byssinosis when she undertook this pregnancy, and that wasn't what she had meant to do at all.

"Thanks," Doug said. "Can you come to work Monday?"

"I don't see why not. I could come every Monday, I suppose."

"Of course, if you have something else planned—"

"No. My days are free."

Doug considered her for a long interval, carefully keeping his eyes far removed from the rising mound beneath her loose smock. For a moment she felt a twinge of sadness over what might have been between her and Doug if things had been different. Her pregnancy—and its effect on her life—had changed the way she responded to Doug. Now she couldn't imagine his being anything more to her than he was at this moment—a very close and very dear friend.

"Do you mind if I ask you something, Eve?"

She was surprised. "Of course not."

"Are you happy there? Do they treat you well?"

"Doug! You make it sound as though I was kidnapped, as though Derek and Aunt May treat me like a—well, like a servant!"

"Do they?"

"Oh, Doug. Of course not. Derek is—pleasant," she said lamely, wondering how else she would describe him. Pleasant? He had been more than that today, for instance. But she had no reason to go into that now with Doug. She plunged on, mindful of the way Doug's eyes assessed her. "And Aunt May is a dear."

"There's been no more talk about an abortion?"

"No," she said, and drew a breath to say more, but then she stopped.

"What is it, Eve?" Doug knew her too well; he sensed that there was more to this story than he'd been told.

"Derek still hasn't said he'll keep the baby." Her eyes, sad and anxious, met his over the expanse of blue tablecloth.

"So what happens to the baby when it's born?"

"I don't know. I don't know." Eve bit her bottom lip.

"If he doesn't want the baby, do you still intend to raise it yourself?"

"Yes," she whispered. She let her shoulders rise, then fall helplessly. "I don't know what else I could do."

"Put it up for adoption," he said gently. "That's one alternative you should consider."

She shook her head slowly. "I couldn't. Not now. Not after it's been a part of me. I can feel this baby, Doug. It turns somersaults inside me. Its tiny knees poke me in the ribs at night. It hears my voice, is lulled to sleep by the music I play on my radio. Oh, Doug, the only person I could give this baby up to is its natural father."

"And he's said nothing about keeping it?"

"Nothing. And he's good with children, Doug. You should have seen him today with the children at the park. He was—"

"You went to the park with him?"

"To Oktoberfest. He had to practically drag me, but Aunt May insisted, and I—" How could she explain what a wonderful time she'd had with Derek? "He's—he's a good man, Doug. I don't want you to think he isn't."

"If he is as good as you say he is, he won't let you undertake the raising of this child by yourself." He spoke softly; he truly cared about Eve. He couldn't stand for anyone to take advantage of her.

"Somehow I'll make him see that he wants this baby. Somehow I will." The fierceness of her words startled Eve herself.

"How?" Doug wondered out loud.

"I'm not sure," she said carefully, but she remembered the close feeling she had shared with Derek that afternoon. As they grew to know each other better, perhaps he would listen to her, would begin to see reason. They couldn't go on avoiding the topic indefinitely, after all.

A discussion was inevitable. But apparently it was going to be up to Eve to bring it about.

"Good luck," Doug said softly.

"I'm going to need it," she replied, not knowing at the time how true her statement was.

Chapter Eight

Derek cast about in his mind for the thing to do next, but for the life of him it wouldn't come to him. There was no plan.

God knows he had tried to make one, but every time he thought he had it figured out, something happened to distract him. Like stumbling upon Eve in the L & D Cafe. Like her dazzling smile when she danced the polka with him. Such events made all plans irrelevant.

This baby. There it was, like it or not. It was amazing, really, to think that the impersonal globe of fullness under Eve's clothing was a living, growing child.

Aunt May made such a fuss over Eve's pregnancy. She was always worrying about whether Eve napped every day or wore her boots with the nonskid soles when she went out on damp days. "I wish she'd eat more," he heard Aunt May say to no one in particular when she was out poking around in the pansy bed one day. "I wish he'd *talk* about the baby."

Derek, on this occasion, had ducked guiltily beneath the grape arbor, bare of leaves now and affording little concealment, before Aunt May detected his presence. He had little doubt that she was speaking of him and his refusal to even mention the child.

Well, what was he supposed to do? He didn't want the baby now; that was all. He felt responsible for it, and for Eve. He'd sheltered her under his roof, hadn't he? And here she was, a small, bright presence to whom he had become ridiculously attached in so short a time.

Those children at the festival in the park—the little girl who lost her balloon and the kid who'd watched the Corvette for him. Cute. He liked kids. But the responsibility! Their illnesses! Their education, their clothing needs, their table manners, for goodness' sake! PTA meetings. Sewing pink satin ribbons on a girl's toe shoes. Making a pinewood derby race car for Cub Scouts. How could he take all that on by himself? With Kelly it would have been fine. Kelly managed things so well. But a child needed two whole parents, deserved to be brought up by two parents rather than a busy textile executive and an eccentric great-aunt. And Kelly was gone.

Instead, there was Eve, who stared at him with her big brown gazelle eyes and left so much unsaid. He thought about the things she might have said at times when he was away from her, for instance at work, when he should have been concentrating on working up his presentation before the governor's task force on textiles.

Eve—she'd stayed out late with that fellow, that friend she went out to dinner with. And at a time when she needed her sleep, too. It angered him when she'd wandered in after midnight. Where had she been all that time? At the guy's apartment? In a bar? Both of those seemed unlikely places for Eve to be.

He'd started working straight through lunch in the days after Kelly died so he wouldn't have to go home, as he always had before at lunchtime. But on the Monday after Oktoberfest, he'd careened home in his Corvette, only to be disappointed that Eve wasn't there.

Aunt May found him in the kitchen, staring out the window at the driveway where Eve's Volkswagen should have been parked. Aunt May brightened immediately.

"Why, what are you doing home, Derek?"

"Looking for Eve," he said moodily.

"Well, you can't *leave*," she said in annoyance. "You just got here."

"Not leave. *Eve*."

"Oh, Eve. She's not here."

"Ye gods," he muttered under his breath before freeing himself of Aunt May and rushing off to a drugstore lunch counter where he disconsolately made do with a soggy cheeseburger.

What was this private life of Eve's about which he knew so little? Where did she go? Whom did she see?

"I don't think you should be driving yourself places," he told her seriously that night after dinner. They had been watching television, with Eve in charge of the remote control. He spoke during a commercial featuring a bald man whose shiny head was being sectioned off with Magic Markers. To his relief, Eve clicked the TV set off just as the man turned around with a whole new head of hair.

The silence was deafening.

"Dr. Perry says I can drive right up until the last minute unless something goes wrong," she said at last and with a cheery smile.

"But I worry about you," he said, as though that should be enough to make Eve hang up her car keys for the duration.

"Do you, Derek?" She regarded him calmly with a level gaze.

"Well, of course," he said, wishing suddenly that he hadn't begun this.

"I'm glad to hear it. Because that must mean you're concerned about the baby, too."

"I suppose so," he allowed cautiously. He didn't like the glint in her eyes.

"I'm concerned, too, Derek. About what's going to happen to the baby after it's born."

"I think it should be put up for adoption. There's a shortage of babies, and somebody out there is looking for a healthy infant."

"You would put Kelly's baby up for adoption?" Her voice was softly incredulous.

"Do we have to talk about this?" Impatiently, he stood and walked to the window. Outside, cars whooshed silently by the house. The air hung heavy with the smoke from neighborhood fireplaces. He'd have to lay a fire in the fireplace soon himself. He felt a definite chill in here.

"Derek, how long are you going to avoid this issue?"

"Eve, I—"

"This baby was a wanted child once," she reminded him in a troubled tone. "Your and Kelly's child. Your firstborn, Derek."

She almost didn't catch the murmured words he spoke. "Not my firstborn," he said.

"What?"

"Not my firstborn. Kelly was pregnant once. Didn't she tell you?"

"N-no," Eve breathed, sinking down on the couch. "No."

He turned to face her, his eyes dark. "She was pregnant. Oh, it was before her hysterectomy. She lost the baby in her seventh month."

"I'm so sorry. I didn't know." She sat perfectly still on the couch while Derek paced the floor, agitated now.

"She was so happy to be having a baby. *We* were so happy. And I went to the Far East on a trade mission for the textile board, and Kelly was here with Aunt May, and she tried to lift a heavy chair to move it, and she felt pains and was rushed by ambulance to the hospital. If I had been here, I would have done that lifting for her, but no, she couldn't wait. I could have come home a week early. I wanted to, in fact, but at the last minute the coordinator of the mission had to put a report together and I stayed to help him. I knew Kelly was all right at home; I mean I *thought* I knew it, and she wasn't. And she had the miscarriage all alone, with no one but Aunt May, and I wasn't even in the country. Didn't get home until days afterward." He lifted his hands helplessly, and there was no mistaking the anguish in his eyes.

"Derek, chances are you could have done nothing to prevent it," she said comfortingly.

"That's what they all said. But I still felt responsible. Because I had the chance to come home, you see, and I didn't take it. Because I wanted to be the boy wonder, not just a tagalong on the trade mission. I wanted to show my stuff and prove that I could wheel and deal as well as the rest of them, even though I got my position and my power by inheritance, not because of anything I did to earn it." His mouth curled downward at the edges in self-disdain.

"Oh, Derek" was all she could say. He sank down on the footstool and stared up at her, his voice hollow.

"And afterward she had the hysterectomy because of complications; she was never all right again after that miscarriage. Poor Kelly. It was very hard on her. But she never changed; she was always cheerful and happy, and I tried to forget by burying myself in work, and I neglected her. Work was a convenient excuse—I was never there for her."

Eve's hand moved slowly of its own volition to touch his bowed head ever so gently. "It's all right, Derek," she said soothingly, softly. "It's all right. You can't go on blaming yourself." She couldn't comprehend the weight of guilt under which Derek Lang had lived for so long. But maybe she could alleviate it.

"It's not all right," he whispered as her thumb began to caress his jawline. He closed his eyes under the comfort of it. It had been so long since anyone had touched him in tenderness. He lifted his own hand and held hers where it rested against the lean, hard planes of his face, and the inside of his arms ached with the yearning of wanting more of her comfort, more of her touch.

He had loved Kelly so much that he didn't think he could love another woman that way again, but suddenly he wanted to. It was more than an awakening of desire. It was a longing for all the other things love meant to him, for companionship, for parallel thoughts, for caring and nurturing. But he didn't want to mix these longings up with Eve, with the way he felt about her, with his wistful wish for her gentle, abiding warmth.

Still, his arms reached out to her, went around her slim, fragile shoulders, and his head came to rest on her broad, curving breast. The scent of her was fragrant and sweet, filling his nostrils and lingering at the back of his throat. The skin of her cheek was as soft as a butterfly wing upon his, and a swinging arc of silky hair, black as midnight, feathered across his temple. His heart was eased by her.

She murmured something, lots of things, but the words were only shapes and not real. The comfort was real, the comfort of Eve, and she herself was real. Without thinking, he sought her lips. They were pliable beneath his, sensitive, responsive. He could have gone on kissing her—it would have been easy—but as he drew even closer to her, the hard, round knob of her pregnancy pressed against him. Startled, he pulled away. He hadn't expected the child to feel so hard. He thought it would be soft, like Eve herself. But there it was, between the two of them, implacable in its presence.

"I'm sorry," he said with dignity. "I shouldn't have done that."

Eve's eyes were round and soft and vulnerable. "Derek, it's—"

"No," he said harshly. "No." He whirled away from her and walked swiftly from the room.

It was only afterward that he wondered what she had been about to say.

"Evie, Evie, you look like a million bucks!" Her father held her away from him, his eyes sparkling.

"Thanks, Dad," she said, laughing. It was so good to see him again, and he wasn't wheezing as much as he had been; she was sure of it.

"Look, this is where you'll work," he said, showing her a scuffed gray metal desk that had somehow been wedged in between the door and the table in the waiting room of Doug's office where her father and Nell took phone calls on the brown-lung hotline.

"Where'd you get the desk?" she wanted to know.

"Oh, Nell dragged me to a garage sale Saturday," he said sheepishly. "We paid ten dollars for it."

"It's a bargain," she told him, sitting down in the swivel chair and opening and closing the metal drawers.

"Claim forms, pencils, pens; everything you'll need is right there," Al said proudly. "I've got two people coming in this afternoon just to talk to you. I told them, 'My daughter will know if you've got a claim or not.'"

"And if she doesn't, I will," Doug added, ambling in from the inner office and perching on the side of Eve's desk.

The outside door swung open with a blast of chill November air. "Excuse me, is this the place to go if you know about a case of brown lung?" The woman who stepped inside rubbed raw red hands together; she wore a defeated look.

"Yes," Eve said, smiling encouragingly. "We can help you."

"It's about my brother," she said worriedly. "I keep telling him, 'Sam, you've got some of that brown-lung disease.' But he ain't so sure. Says its a cold that hangs on and on. But a cold shouldn't last over a year, should it?"

Doug and her father discreetly withdrew. "How long has your brother worked in the mill?" Eve asked briskly, poising her pencil over a yellow legal pad.

"All his life. Since he was fifteen. Like all the rest of us."

And so Eve jotted down the details of a life story that was to become depressingly familiar in the next few weeks. A job in the mill, entered into in good faith when the employee was young. A surfeit of cotton dust, dust everywhere, dust that clung to clothes and nostrils, eyebrows and eyelashes, ingested and inhaled until the body rebelled.

Byssinosis. Brown-lung disease. A malady that many textile manufacturers claimed did not exist. A disease for which even some of the biggest, best-known textile companies refused to acknowledge responsibility.

"It's depressing," Doug said later over a cup of coffee in the nearby Wray Cafe. "I wonder how long the mill management can go on ignoring it?"

"A long time," Eve said. "No one makes them comply with government regulations. The textile industry wields so much clout that government officials are discouraged from insisting on safeguards in every mill, everywhere. In the meantime, many workers get sick and die without ever getting around to filing a claim. It's sad.''

"We're making progress, though," he said, looking optimistic. "Thanks for helping, Eve."

"I couldn't *not* help," she confessed. "Not the way Al is. Whatever we do, whatever progress we make, it's bound to benefit Al. He looks so much better, Doug. I think it's because he has something important to do, answering that hotline."

Doug laughed. "I'm not so sure it's the hotline as much as it's the widow Baker. You should hear them in there when she arrives to take over his phone shift. She always shows up early, and they sit in my waiting room and laugh and talk like two kids."

"Really? That's amazing!"

"Yeah, I know. Nell and Al have known each other for years, but I don't think they ever *really* knew each other until Al moved in with her."

Eve grew suddenly quiet. It was much like her situation with Derek, she thought. She was getting to know him so well, now that they lived in the same household.

Getting to know him well but not yet well enough. Not well enough to convince him to do the right thing by this baby.

"WHERE IS SHE?" Derek fumed, pacing up and down the foyer. It was Monday, and Eve wasn't home yet. She was never home when he got in from work on Mondays.

"He wants to know where she is," Aunt May explained to the air.

"She should have been home before this storm started. The roads are icing up."

"What did you say?"

"The roads are icing up," Derek said, peering out one of the sidelights.

"Rising up?"

"*Icing* up," he repeated, none too patiently. Then, more kindly, he said, "Why don't you help Louise get dinner on the table, Aunt May?"

Aunt May teetered off obediently, and Derek resumed his vigil. He supposed he wouldn't worry so much if it weren't for what happened to Kelly. Now he distrusted damp pavements.

He interrupted his pacing to switch on the TV in the den. The program was interrupted by a weather bulletin.

"Motorists are warned to drive carefully," the patent-haired announcer intoned. "With temperatures below the freezing point and a light drizzle falling on Charlotte tonight, ice will be a hazard on area roads."

Morosely, Derek opened the front door and stood framed in the doorway for a moment, as if such action would conjure up Eve's VW at the end of the street. When it didn't, he went back inside and slammed the door, hard.

"Is that Eve?" Aunt May called from the kitchen.

"No," he replied.

He considered phoning the police to see if any accidents had been reported in the area. Which was ridiculous. She wasn't late, not in the strictest sense of the word. How could she be late when he never knew what time to expect her home? Well, he could hardly impose a curfew on her. But didn't he have a right to know, when she wasn't there, where she was and whom she was with?

He supposed not. Still. The very fact that she lived in this household gave him some right to know that she was safe. Didn't it?

He dug in the bow-front chest on which the hall telephone sat and surfaced with a dog-eared phone book. He looked up Hospitals in the Yellow Pages. He considered calling an emergency room. Which one, though?

Not a very good idea, so he shelved it and the phone book, as well. He could just imagine calling an emergency room and telling the answering nurse, "I'm looking for Eve Triopolous," and the nurse would say with annoyance, "What relationship, please," and he'd answer blankly, "What do you mean?" and the nurse would say impatiently "What relationship—sister, wife, mother, niece, grandmother?" and he would hang up. Because she was no relation.

Mother of my child. The words came out of nowhere, focused on the deepest recesses of his mind and branded themselves there. For the first time, he confronted the fact that his tender feelings for her were more than that.

Eve was the mother of his child, and he panicked with the fear of one who had already lost the most important person in the world to the whims of the weather. The weather had been responsible for the accident that had taken Kelly's life, and he could not bear the thought that Eve was endangered in any way by the capricious weather.

"I'm going to go out and find her," he said, reason eroded by his terror.

"I'm not sure that's such a—" Aunt May ventured with startled blue eyes. "Why don't you just—"

But he'd already yanked on his Burberry raincoat. He raced out the back door through the garage to where his Corvette was parked in the driveway.

He'd forgotten the key, so he had to run back inside, all the way upstairs, where his car keys reposed in blessed unknowing innocence on his dresser. He grabbed them and took off down the stairs, taking them two at a time all the way down.

Out the door again, then fumbling with the lock on the Corvette. It was iced over, and he cursed. Dropping his keys, scooping them up off the slick pavement of the driveway, his fingers shook.

And then the distinctive metallic chatter of the VW's engine. He looked up through the misty drizzle illuminated by the headlights. A rainbow surrounded the car for a brief moment until Eve shut the lights and engine off and stepped blithely out into the rain.

She was surprised to see Derek there.

"Oh," she said, and he could have sworn that the simple one-syllable word wore shades of disappointment it had never worn before. "You're going out."

"No. Not now. I was going to go looking for you." Mist beaded on her eyelashes. It glittered in the overhead outside light.

"Looking for me? What on earth for?" She stared at him through the mist.

His eyes dropped to the gourdlike shape beneath her raincoat.

"I was worried," he said.

"Oh, Derek. You shouldn't have been." She gestured at the bag of groceries in the back of the Volkswagen. "I stopped off at the store. I've taken over the grocery shopping. You'll be pleased to know that I've bought a beef roast for Sunday dinner. No more pickled sausages, I'm afraid. And guess what—I bought you a package of cheese doodles." She smiled, then laughed. "And here we stand out here in the rain like two people who don't have enough sense to come in out of it." She whirled, light on her feet, and his heart flew to his throat.

"Careful," he said tightly, grasping her arm above the elbow. "Don't prance like that! You could fall. Do you have on your boots with the nonskid soles?"

"Prance! Derek, my prancing days are over. And yes, these are the proper boots for the weather. Honestly, you're getting as bad as Aunt May! Look, why don't you carry in that bag of groceries?"

But thinking about what might have happened to her, about how worried he had been, Derek remained serious all through dinner, all through the evening, when he barely left Eve's side while she watched television and then dozed.

Eve couldn't help dozing, but she wasn't really asleep. She was only resting. It had been a difficult day for her in Doug's office. Two people had showed up who clearly had no brown-lung claim but were obviously trying to take advantage of what they perceived as a possible cash handout. It turned out that one had had asthma ever since she'd been a small child and the other one was faking entirely. It had taken more than an hour in each case to wheedle the real information out of them, and then she'd been angry. Because, as she told Doug afterward, such people were harming the chances of workers who really had contracted brown-lung disease. Plus, advocates of help for brown-lung victims didn't need any fakers. There were enough residents of Wrayville who were sick with the real thing.

"Anybody want to play Trivial Pursuit?"

Eve jerked awake to see Aunt May standing in front of her, holding the two blue Trivial Pursuit boxes and playing board in her hands.

"Not now, Aunt May," Derek said peremptorily. "Eve's tired."

"Oh, but Derek," Eve said gently as a look of disappointment slid over Aunt May's pudgy features. "I think I'd like to play Trivial Pursuit. Yes, I really think I would." She gazed mutely at Derek, and he knew she was tired but was thinking of Aunt May's feelings.

His heart softened. "Just a short game, then," he said, and warmth crept into his voice in spite of himself.

They set up the board on the card table that Kelly had prized so much, a cherry-wood antique with inlaid ivory marquetry. Aunt May hummed as she distributed the markers and the single die with which the game was played.

Derek studied Eve covertly as they took their places around the table. Her dark hair shone blue-black under the light from the lamp, and her fingers, with their fine white skin, were so smooth as to look disjointed, like the fingers of a porcelain doll, until she moved her marker along the playing board and proved that her fingers had joints, after all. Derek sat close enough to her to sense a scent reminiscent of white violets. Surely white violets had a scent? Or if they didn't, this is what they would smell like, this heady sweetness that permeated her hair and filled his nostrils and tasted so good when he kissed her.

Kissed her. He had actually kissed her. It had been crazy to do that, crazy. *He* had been crazy. It never should have happened.

Her low laugh at something Aunt May had said, something that wasn't all that funny, chimed with the mellow timbre of English church bells.

It was his turn, and he tossed the die. And she asked him the next question, her voice cool and flowing, draping syllables over the air rather than stabbing through it like Kelly's.

"What?" he had to say, pulling himself with great effort out of his reverie.

"Your question is 'What baseball player advised, "Avoid running at all times"?' "

He had to stop and think. He wasn't with this game, not at all.

"Well," he said, because he had heard the quotation before. But now all he could do was listen to the echoes of Eve's soothing voice asking the question, and he couldn't for the life of him think of the appropriate answer.

"Do you give up, Derek?" Aunt May asked eagerly.

"I give up," he said.

"Satchel Paige," Eve said triumphantly, dropping the question-and-answer card in the back of the box. "Your turn, Aunt May."

Satchel Paige. Of course. Satchel Paige had been one of Derek's favorite philosophers, and a great pitcher to boot.

What else had Satchel Paige said? Something like "Don't look back. Something may be gaining on you."

Yeah. The old fellow was right, and he hadn't been talking only about baseball.

Something was gaining on Derek, all right. Contentment sitting here with Eve and Aunt May so cozy in the haven of his home, with the weather surging against the window in sheets of rain and rattles of wind, a chill November night pressing in upon them in all its fury. Contentment had settled on this house, and peace, and, yes, more than that. And it had come in the person of Eve Triopolous.

Was it disloyal to Kelly to feel contentment in Eve's presence? His mind grappled with the thought, but as generous as Kelly had been, as loving, he knew she would have approved

She had loved Eve, Kelly had. She had chosen Eve, after all, to be the mother of their child until it could be safely born.

Whatever it was that was gaining on him, Derek thought in a flash of perception, it was something good.

"Your turn, Derek," Aunt May said again.

"Yes," he said, but he wasn't talking about Trivial Pursuit. He was talking about a pursuit that was, to him, anything at all but trivial.

At long last, a plan began to take shape in his mind.

Chapter Nine

If the early December weather was any indication, Charlotte was in for a severe winter.

Snow seldom intruded into the mild climate of that Southern city; when it did, it usually made its brief appearance in January or February. But by mid-December of this year, a few random flakes had already fluttered halfheartedly down from gray windswept skies.

Eve spent a Christmas divided between Wrayville and Myers Park, between Aunt May's dainty Christmas cookies and Nell Baker's more robust homemade fruitcake, between the elegant beef Wellington Louise served on Kelly's graceful Rosenthal china and the baked ham offered by Nell on her new ironstone dishes from K mart. The contrast of Christmas celebrated in the two households was striking in the extreme, but oddly enough, this Christmas satisfied Eve as no other had.

In Wrayville she did not feel the weight of home and its responsibilities settling slowly on her narrow shoulders. The burden was lifted now that she perceived Al's well-being as held firmly in the capable hands of Nell Baker. Somewhat to Eve's surprise, she found herself feeling enfolded and protected by each of her two separate families. By this time, living in such close proximity, bound by their shared memories of Kelly, she had definitely grown to think of Derek and Aunt May as family.

"Maybe it will snow for Christmas," Derek remarked hopefully on Christmas morning after he had exclaimed over the soft blue sweater Eve had knitted for him and after Eve had thanked him for the neat cosmetic case he had given her.

"Snow?" Aunt May snorted gently. "It's never snowed on Christmas, at least in my memory."

And it didn't snow on Christmas. But it did snow the next day, the snowflakes stealing softly down upon them in the night when the weather forecasters had assured them that there was no chance of it.

Eve awakened early the morning after Christmas and blinked her eyes against unaccustomed glare beaming onto her drawn draperies. When she parted the fabric at the window, the mantle of just-fallen snow glistened from garden and garage, from branch and fence post. The world was quiet and new, the sere buffs and browns of winter gracefully hidden by the sparkling white blanket that covered everything in sight.

"I'm going out," Eve declared after a hurried breakfast with Derek and Aunt May.

"But it's *not* snowing out," Aunt May insisted loudly. "That was last night, dear."

"Eve said she was *going* out, Aunt May," Derek said, drawing his eyebrows together at the sight of Eve arranging her down jacket over her bulky form. "And Eve, I don't think you should."

"Nonsense," she said briskly. "I love the snow. And we've seen precious little of it the last couple of years. Just a walk in the snow and I'll be back in, safe and sound." She smiled at Derek reassuringly.

"Well, if you insist," Aunt May said doubtfully. "I'll ask Louise to put on a pot of hot cocoa for you for afterward. Nothing like hot cocoa to warm a person, I always say." She wobbled toward the kitchen on impossibly high red heels, a holdover from Christmas Day.

"No one's shoveled the walks. They may be icy. I don't even know where our snow shovel is. Be sensible." Derek stood up the way he always did when he wanted to exert his authority in this household of women.

He'd been so thoughtful of her lately that Eve hated to deny him anything. But she would find the outside so invigorating; it would feel so healthful. Aunt May kept secretly nudging up the thermostat so that the temperature in the house was hot to the point of stuffiness.

"Why don't you come outside with me?" Eve invited Derek on the spur of the moment. "It's a mere four inches of snow. Hardly a threat for me or for anyone else. Come on, Derek; it will be fun." She fairly glowed with well-being.

Derek looked distinctly uncomfortable. He ran a finger under the collar of his shirt, a new flannel one he had bought recently and which was so casual that he still felt out of place when he wore it.

"Me? Out in the snow? Why?" He looked so puzzled that Eve almost laughed.

"To feel it. To scuff your feet in it. To throw it, for heaven's sake, Derek. Haven't you ever thrown a snowball?"

He thought for a moment. "Well, not since I was a child. Snow is for kids."

"Derek, Derek." She laughed, tugging his jacket from a nearby coat tree. She tossed it at him, and he caught it with a startled look. "Come on. You're going to throw a snowball. You're going to make a snow angel."

Reluctantly, he slid his arms into the sleeves of the jacket.

"What's a snow angel?" He looked so genuinely perplexed beneath that well-groomed thatch of butternut-brown hair that Eve laughed again.

"I know you're a Southern boy, Derek, but you must know what a snow angel is. I grew up around here, too, and I've made whole flocks of snow angels."

"The process sounds fairly vigorous," he remonstrated, throwing her a look of pure concern as she pulled him out the back door and down the wide steps. He held her hand tightly in case she slipped on the icy bricks. "Are you sure you're able to make snow angels?"

This time her laughter echoed off the rooftop, tinkled like bells in the crystalline air. She took a few giant steps, and snow crunched beneath her boots. She left dark footsteps in her wake, and dead sprigs of grass popped up in the middle of them. She inhaled the freshness of the crisp, sweet air and flung her arms out wide, spinning in place with the glory of this beautiful winter morning.

She bent, graceful in spite of her clumsy contours, and scooped up a handful of powdery snow. She tossed it at Derek.

And he, because she looked so young and so carefree and so beautiful that he could hardly stand to look at her, hid his feelings by tossing a handful of snow at her. And then they were yelling and laughing and chortling into a veritable blizzard that they stirred up themselves, until Derek yelled, "Uncle, or whatever it is I'm supposed to holler when I give up!"

"Oh, Derek," Eve gasped. "If you only knew how you look. Like a little boy all lit up with happiness." And he did, too. His hair fell boyishly over his forehead, and he seemed to have shed a weight or a burden so that his expression reflected a light-heartedness she had never noticed about him before.

"I've suddenly remembered how to build a snowman," he announced to Eve's delight. His smile spread wider and shone bright as the sun.

"Let's!" Eve said. "We'll build one where Aunt May can watch us from the bow window in the breakfast room!"

But Derek's idea of a snowman was not simply ordinary balls of snow rolled to graduated sizes and stacked one on top of the other. Derek's version of a snowman was an elaborate snow sculpture.

They worked together to stack the snow as high as a man, and then Eve stood back and offered sprightly commentary while Derek molded it with his hands so that it had legs, feet and gently curved arms bowed gracefully over its stomach.

"That's not a snowman," Eve said, puckering her forehead in consternation. "It's a snow woman! And a pregnant one at that!"

Derek stepped back and judiciously regarded his creation. He clapped a hand to his forehead. "You're right! But it was a subconscious creation."

He patted the belly of the figure into a more rounded form. Eve watched his gloved fingers, so strong and sure as they lingered upon the shape of the woman, and suddenly she felt so embarrassed that she had to turn away.

But Derek seemed pleased with what he had wrought.

"Be back in a minute," he tossed back over his shoulder as he galloped toward the house, and true to his word, he appeared a short time later with a fluffy organdy-draped hat in his hands. He tilted it to the side of the figure's head, stepped back and squinted his eyes critically, then produced a black lace scarf from his pocket and wound it around the snow woman's neck, leaving the ends to flutter in the slight breeze.

"And she needs a nose," he said, embellishing the face with a red radish. With a flourish, he produced two chocolate bon-bons. "Eyes, donated to the cause by Aunt May."

From the window, Aunt May waved her smiling approval.

"Isn't our snow woman gorgeous?" he asked Eve with a twinkle.

"Lovely, Derek. You've outdone yourself."

"You're right. And I'm more than ready for Louise's hot cocoa. But first you're going to teach me how to make snow angels!" Derek grinned at her, more carefree than she'd ever seen him. He seemed to have shed completely the veneer of sophistication and perfection, seemed to have relaxed in her presence, seemed to be having fun.

"We have to find the right patch of snow," she said, unthinkingly grasping his hand in hers. She led him to a likely spot. "And then lie down in it." Which Eve awkwardly proceeded to do, flat on her back, much to Derek's consternation. Inside her, the baby battled for a position at this new angle, jolting her, but pleasantly.

"Do I have to lie down, too?" Derek looked as if it would hurt to shed his last invisible shred of dignity.

But Eve didn't laugh, although she wanted to. "Sure," she told him. "Right next to me."

He did, albeit reluctantly.

"And then," she said, demonstrating vigorously, "you move your arms up and down."

He sat up straight, frowning down at her. "Good heavens," he muttered. "How ridiculous."

"Well, maybe," Eve admitted, pumping her arms harder than ever. "But this makes the angel's wings." With one last dubious look at Eve's face, framed so cunningly against the snow by the red knit cap she wore, Derek lay down again.

Derek waved his arms up and down in the snow.

"Like this? Am I getting the technique right?"

"Well, you don't have to do it so hard. You're throwing snow clear over to that dogwood tree."

Derek slowed down.

"Now what?" he asked, stopping and turning his head to look at her. Locks of short curved hair had escaped her cap, enclosing her face in parentheses.

"We do the same thing with our legs." Eve concentrated on moving her legs. That was a little harder, especially since her abdominal muscles seemed to have migrated northward.

But Derek managed all right.

"When are we finished?" he asked, as though begging for mercy.

"Now. We can stand up—carefully now; you don't want to mess it up—and look at them."

Derek loomed over her, hands on hips, looking askance at the angel he had made.

"It's not bad for the first snow angel I ever accomplished."

Eve lay on her back, admiring the shape of his head against the brilliant blue sky. He was a handsome man, was Derek.

"You mean you'll make more sometime?"

"Every time it snows," he said soberly. "Now that you've taught me what to do with it."

Eve snickered. "You've openly cavorted, Derek. Do you realize that?"

Derek pretended to look horrified. "I'll never live it down if they find out at the office."

"Your employees probably think you were born wearing a three-piece suit."

"Yup. And a pair of wing tips."

They laughed together. Their laughter swooped upward and out, startling a blackbird on the telephone wire. The bird winged across the sky, air bound. Eve lay in the snow, earthbound.

"I hate to have to ask you, Derek, but I can't get up. Help me, please."

"What's wrong? Is anything wrong?"

His anxiety was touching, almost comical.

"No, what I mean is, I can't get up without rolling over onto my side, because I can't sit up from this position, and if I rolled over on my side, I'd mess up a perfect angel. Just give me your hand, please."

Derek reached down for her, she placed both mittened hands inside his gloved ones, and he lifted her neatly to her feet. He stood so close that there was scarcely any space between them, so close that she smelled the clean, fresh evergreen scent of him. She was enfolded in his misty breath.

"I'm sorry," she said by way of unnecessary explanation. "I just couldn't get up." His lips were full and slightly parted, and they slowly drifted down toward hers.

"Don't apologize to me for your condition," he said fiercely, an unnamed emotion gleaming behind his eyes. "Ever."

If she hadn't broken away in confusion, they would have gone on standing there, and he might have kissed her. But she said, with an attempt at gaiety, "I'm ready to go in and see what Aunt May has to say about our handiwork," and she walked rapidly away over the snow. Oh, what if he had kissed her again? She remembered very well that time in the living room—how soft his lips had felt against hers, how warm. How delicious they had tasted....

"Hang Aunt May," Derek mumbled under his breath, but she couldn't hear him, and after he said it, he was ashamed of himself and glad Eve hadn't heard.

Eve had reached the middle of the steps by the time he thought of it, and unwilling for this time with her to end, he said suddenly, "My mother used to make snow ice cream."

Eve half turned, a gently curving smile upon her lips. "Oh, my mother did, too."

"Could you remember how to make it?"

"Maybe. I think so."

He smiled, pleased that he had thought of this one more thing they could do together. "I'll bring in the snow," he said, heading for the garage and a space of snow that was unsullied by their antics.

"I'll help—" Eve said eagerly, swiveling around, and then it happened.

Her feet flew out from under her on a patch of snow-covered ice, she grabbed wildly for the handrail and missed, and she thumped down all five steps before landing in a wildly skewed position at the bottom of the stairs.

Derek watched, unable to reach her in time to do anything. His heart flew to his throat. Suddenly the blue sky, the glistening snow, the joy in his heart—all were gone, and in all of his consciousness only Eve was left. Eve, sprawling in the snow and lying so still that he dared not breathe.

It took less than two seconds for him to reach her. He fell to his knees, his arms enfolding her without thought, his eyes wildly searching the pale face beneath the red knit cap.

"Eve— Oh, my God!" He brushed snow from her cheek; it melted and left a wet trail down her cheek, a trail that might have been traced by tears.

"Is she all right?" cried Aunt May, who had come running awkwardly outside on her high heels. "Is she hurt?" Aunt May hugged herself against the cold.

Eve's eyes fluttered open beneath those remarkable winged brows. "I'm fine," she said breathlessly, aware only of Derek's panicked face in her field of vision. "Just a little shaken up."

"I thought you were unconscious," Derek said unsteadily.

"No, just had the wind knocked out of me. Whew!" she said, pushing him away. "Let me up."

He held her gingerly by the elbows once she was safely on her feet. "I should never have left you on those stairs alone. I knew they might be icy."

"It's okay," she insisted. "It could have happened whether you were with me or not."

"I should never have left you," he repeated. "Never."

Eve took the stairs one step at a time, pausing for a moment on each, with Derek holding on to her the whole time as though she would break if he let go.

"I won't have you feeling guilty," she murmured softly, with a meaningful look that was not meant for Aunt May to see.

But Derek did feel guilty, overwhelmingly so, and even though he relinquished Eve to Aunt May's fussing ministrations and Louise's anxious queries, he continued to watch her as they unwrapped her from her coat and brought her a towel to dry her face, waiting for a sign of trouble. Pregnant women weren't supposed to fall down flights of stairs, and she'd had a pretty hard fall.

"Are you sure you feel all right? Do you want me to call Dr. Perry?" he kept asking even when Eve was ensconced on the couch with a heating pad for her feet and a mug of cocoa steaming color into her cheeks. "Are you sure you don't feel any pains?"

"I'm as strong as a horse," she reassured him. "And after all, I landed on a pretty well padded portion of my anatomy. Except for a few black-and-blue marks, I'm going to be fine. Really."

"I'm calling the doctor," he said, "just to be on the safe side."

When Derek had Dr. Perry on the line, he asked to speak with Eve, who answered the doctor's questions briefly and then hung up.

"What did he say?" Derek demanded.

"He said not to fall down stairs again," Eve told him demurely.

"Eve—"

"No, honestly. He told me to watch for warning signs, but I feel okay. I'll stop by his office tomorrow and have him make sure everything is all right."

"Eve, can I get you anything?" Aunt May hovered so close that she gave Eve claustrophobia.

"No, and I believe it's time for *Love of Hope*. You don't want to miss it. Today's the day the hockey player's dachshund digs Susan out of the cave she's been hiding in since October."

"It is? Oh, indeed it is! And the hockey player's ex-fiancée is going to decide whether to marry the lead singer of Purple Madness, who's been in the hospital waiting for a kidney transplant! Well, if you don't mind . . ." And Aunt May wobbled away in her red shoes. They heard her in the sun room, ruffling through the wrappers in her almost-empty box of chocolates and muttering to herself, "I wonder why they named the hockey player's dog Albert. That's such a funny name for a dog, and I wonder what the baby's name will be; Eve hasn't mentioned anything..." And then the rest of her solitary conversation was lost in a loud torrent of words from Aunt May's currently favorite soap opera.

Alone with Derek, sure of his undivided attention and grateful to Aunt May for unwittingly supplying an opening, Eve said meaningfully, "That is a good question, you know— what to name the baby." Kelly had told Eve what names she had chosen; did Derek know what they were?

Derek felt distinctly uncomfortable and somehow betrayed. He was so worried about her that he could hardly sit still, and *she* wanted to talk about a topic that he'd been deliberately avoiding. He'd gone so far as to make a plan, sure, but the plan Derek had made did not include discussions of the baby. It would have to, eventually, he supposed, but Eve's remark left him at a loss for words.

Nevertheless, he figured there was nothing to do but answer her somehow. "I guess it depends on if the baby is a boy or girl," he said carefully after a long time.

"I guess it does." And Eve watched him over the rim of her mug as the melodramatic theme music from *Love of Hope* enveloped them in its crashing refrain. She was ready to tell him Kelly's choice of names, but as usual he seemed unwilling to talk about anything concerning the child she was to bear.

Oh, why won't he confront the problem of the baby, Eve thought impatiently. She hadn't pushed him for any answers; she had waited as quietly and as patiently as she knew how. But soon—the baby's birth was little more than a month and a half away—she would have to know if Derek planned to keep this baby.

He was softening. She knew he was. As they became better friends, she saw the kind, thoughtful man that Derek Lang really was, and she didn't think he had the heart to give away his own flesh and blood. But the way his mind worked, with the guilt about Kelly's miscarriage all mixed up in his feelings about this baby, she knew he felt unworthy of being a father. And if his own unworthiness was all that was preventing him from accepting this baby, she'd have to make him see that he was wrong.

"Derek, you'd make a wonderful father," she said softly.

His head, which had been bent low over his folded hands, shot up sharply.

"That's what Kelly said," he told her.

"Kelly was right."

"Kelly was right about a lot of things." His eyes were clear now, not troubled. "She was right that you were the proper person to carry our baby to term. But today I feared for you, Eve. Seeing you like that, in a heap at the bottom of the stairs—" He gestured helplessly with his hands, then folded them beneath his chin and leaned forward, elbows on his knees.

"But everything is all right." Her eyes regarded him seriously. He could scarcely look into their depths, because to do so would reveal too much too soon. Why this reluctance for her to know what he felt? Was it because he was afraid of rejection? Or was it because of their business agreement, that he felt constrained because the baby was between them?

It wasn't the baby he was thinking of; he didn't care about the baby. He simply couldn't think of the baby, because it was so seldom real to him. But Eve was real, Eve was here, Eve was Eve, and ever since Eve had moved back into this house, he'd felt like a new person. Eve filled him up, leaving no room for anything else.

"It was not the baby I feared for, Eve. It was you." He said this firmly.

What an inappropriate time for the phone to ring! It was like a scene from one of Aunt May's soap operas, the phone barging in at exactly the wrong time in order to keep the man and the woman apart. Exhaling sharply when Louise brought the telephone and plugged it in so Eve could speak without having to get up from her warm spot on the couch, Derek stuffed his hands deep in his pockets and walked to the window overlooking the snow woman they had built.

Funny how he had sculptured a pregnant woman, all the while unaware that he was doing so. Funny and Freudian, as though he were aware of the baby on some deep psychological level even though he could scarcely stand to acknowledge its existence most of the time. He didn't want to think about it, didn't want to talk about it. He only wanted to think about Eve, of her sweet laughter, of her gentle touch, a touch he wanted to know more of and didn't know how to get.

Behind him, Eve laughed and said, "I'll meet you at two o'clock, Doug, on Friday as planned. Don't worry. No, I'm fine. Stop worrying, I said! Give Al and Nell my love."

That man—it was that other man that Eve went out with. A surge of jealousy washed over Derek in a giant wave, jealousy such as he had never known. Who was the guy? What was his role in Eve's life? How often did he phone her? Where did she meet him? Was he some fellow she'd known before to whom she'd return once the baby was born? And Eve would be twelve thousand dollars richer, he thought cynically. Let's not forget that.

The television noise from the sunroom ceased abruptly, and Aunt May wandered through the breakfast room, yawning. She popped a malted milk ball into her mouth and said through it, "Why don't you offer Eve some more cocoa, Derek?"

"You do it," he growled in as sour a mood as he'd ever known, and while Aunt May clamped her mouth abruptly shut at his surliness, he stomped away upstairs and slammed his bedroom door hard.

He stared at his image in the mirror over the dresser. His chest heaved beneath the flannel shirt—a flannel shirt, for Pete's sake! If it weren't for Eve, he wouldn't be wearing a flannel shirt, even though it *was* specially ordered from L. L. Bean. She'd probably have him wearing gold chains around his neck next.

He had rearranged his life, changed his mode of dress, the way he spent his time. All for Eve, and why? Abruptly, he realized that she had a whole life apart from his, had always had a life apart from his, and he knew nothing about that life.

He furrowed trembling fingers through his hair, leaving it uncharacteristically rumpled.

Once the baby was born, Eve would go back to the life she had left, although it appeared that she hadn't ever left it. Her previous life trailed along after her, humming along on phone lines, luring her somewhere on Mondays, a persistent but apparently welcome force.

So what should he do? Ignore it? How could he? She had a past, and well he knew the influence of the past on the present and the future. Okay, so he'd have to learn about her previous life. Should he hire a detective? No, that smacked of invasion of privacy.

He'd get her to talk about it, then. Find out what kind of home she came from. Who her friends were. What kind of job she'd before she had decided to become a surrogate mother.

He couldn't believe he'd ignored all these things for so long. But of course there'd been no reason *not* to ignore them. Because you always ignored things that were not relevant, and Eve had not been relevant. Until he had grown to care for her.

"I DON'T KNOW, Eve. I want to buy Nell something nice for her birthday, but I'm not much good at choosing presents for women. That's why I wanted you to help me." Doug poked through a rack of women's sweaters in the small specialty shop. He held up a pink angora pullover and studied it. "Does this look like something Nell would wear."

Eve shook her head at the idea of Nell's rotund figure encased in pink angora. "Not really. How about a nice cap and matching scarf?" She shook them out for his inspection.

"No, she has something like that already. Come on; let's walk over to Belk's."

He offered Eve his arm, and she took it companionably. Crowds had thinned out; the after-Christmas sales at Eastland Mall were almost over, but several days after Christmas there were still bargains to be had.

"I can't imagine having a birthday so close to Christmas," Doug said. "Poor Nell. At least mine's in July. That means I get presents at two different times during the year."

"The baby's birthday will be in February," Eve told him. "Kelly and I planned that well, didn't we?"

"Mmm, you certainly did. Say, let me know if I'm walking too fast. I'm still worried over that fall you took."

"It caused no permanent damage, although I've got a bruise you wouldn't believe. Anyway, I visited Dr. Perry to reassure myself and everyone else, and everything is okay."

"I'm glad." They walked on, stopping to look in windows, pausing once to watch workmen removing a giant Rudolph the Rednosed Reindeer display.

"I keep thinking of the baby," said Eve as they watched Rudolph being carted down the mall concourse. "Next year it will be having its picture taken with Santa. Somehow it's hard to imagine."

"It is, isn't it?" They walked on a few paces. "Has Derek decided to keep the baby, or don't you know?"

"I think he's working around to it. He seems to find it difficult to discuss. I was going to ask him if he would go to Lamaze childbirth classes with me. I want to do prepared childbirth, but I don't think Derek's ready for that. Oh, Doug, I don't know."

Doug gazed down at her and gently patted her hand where it rested on his arm. "If you ever need me for anything, Eve, I'm here. To drive you someplace, to take you to the doctor, even to go to Lamaze classes with you. You're not alone, Eve. I want you to know that."

"Oh, Doug, that means a lot. You've been the most supportive friend." She swallowed the lump in her throat, touched by what he was offering.

In Belk's, Doug bought Nell a warm cardigan. "It's for her to wear in my office when she's on duty answering the hotline," he said. "It gets chilly out in the waiting room sometimes."

"How are things going with the filing of the new brown-lung claims?" Eve asked Doug as they left the store.

"That's one of the things I wanted to talk with you about today. Wray Mills's management found out what I'm doing, and they've asked me not to file claims with the industrial commission until after the takeover by the conglomerate is complete."

"You mean they've finally admitted that another textile firm is buying Wray?"

Doug nodded. "Yeah. But they're not saying who it is. Apparently the deal is so far along that the Wray Mills's management doesn't want the conglomerate to know that it's acquiring workmen's comp problems along with the mill. Until money actually changes hands, management wants to soft-pedal any claims, and they're very nervous that we're signing up brown-lung claimants. They don't know how lucky they are that we're not suing anyone—yet."

"Well, who's taking over the mill? Have they told you the name of the firm?"

"No. Nobody's talking. It's hush-hush, like a lot of these big takeovers often are. Everybody's keeping quiet so as not to get the employees upset. You know as well as I do that a takeover by a conglomerate often means a layoff. And Wrayville's economy can't take massive unemployment right now. Local people look at Lincolnton, at Greenville and at Roanoke Rapids where workers are unemployed due to plant cutbacks and closings, and it doesn't look good."

Eve shot him an exasperated look. "So what are we going to do? Stop signing up brown-lung claimants?"

Doug's lips drew into an uncompromising line. "No. I've got at least twelve good solid claims, claims you helped me get, and I may have more."

"Those people worked hard for the mill, and the mill owes them something," Eve said.

"I've been thinking about sitting on these claims until I find out who's buying Wray Mills. I'd much rather deal directly with the company than with the commission, because the commission is notoriously slow in settling. When new management takes over Wray Mills, maybe they'll have a heart. Not all mill owners fight workmen's comp claims or government regulations. There's a mill owner in Loomsdale who has spent at least three million dollars on new equipment to cut down on the amount of cotton dust in the air at his plant." Doug opened the outside mall door for Eve, and she walked ahead of him into the cold air toward the parking lot.

"If only—" she said, and then gasped. At first she thought the pain was due to the frigid blast of December wind she inhaled into her lungs, but when it happened again, she knew it was more than that.

She clutched at Doug. "Doug," she managed to breathe.

And she knew at that moment with agonized certainty that something was wrong, something was terribly, terribly wrong.

Chapter Ten

What is happening? What? Am I having a miscarriage? Why does it hurt so much? Derek! Derek!

Had she called Derek's name out loud? She didn't know, didn't know anything except that it was cold and it hurt, and she knew that the ambulance attendants didn't mean to be rough, but there was this spasmodic knifing pain in the small of her back. She was absolutely terrified.

"Eve, don't worry; we're rushing straight to the hospital," Doug said with unflappable calm, holding her hand tightly once they were inside the small confines of the ambulance.

The hospital! She tried to block out the wail of the ambulance siren, but it was impossible not to hear it, impossible. She clenched Doug's hand hard and fought the worst panic she had ever known. The pain wouldn't let her think about much else; her whole being was focused on the pain streaking through her body. Was it going to get worse? What was happening to her body? It always functioned at optimum efficiency, doing what it was supposed to do, walking, breathing, getting pregnant, everything, but her body seemed alien to her now, a thing apart. *She* could not be in such pain— The worst pain she'd ever felt in her life before this was from a broken collarbone, but this was terrible!

She heard the ragged sound of someone sobbing and realized it was she who cried; out of sheer terror or pain, she didn't know which. Doug's familiar face, so worried, swam woozily in front of her, but it shouldn't be Doug; it should be Derek. Where was he?

She didn't know if she asked for Derek, but she must have, because Doug said gravely, "I'll call Derek as soon as we get to the hospital. I promise," and she sank back on the pillow and somehow found her other hand and pressed it instinctively against the baby, trying to comfort the child she had carried within her all these long months, worrying that their journey together was ended, was over, and if that was true, it was not good.

The hospital—noise and white uniforms blurring in front of her, the pervasive hospital smells and sounds, the strange vocabulary—"Ritodrine? You want ritodrine?"—and then someone yelling "Stat!" too close to her ear, and a sexless being looming over her in a mask, and Doug letting go of her hand, which felt like a lifeline being snatched away.

It wasn't what she had wanted, this chaotic way of entering the hospital. She had wanted peace and serenity for this baby, but this scene was neither peaceful nor serene, and the unfamiliar faces around her made her feel lost and misplaced.

"What week of your pregnancy is this?" a rasping voice behind her demanded. Without ever seeing who it was, Eve replied automatically, "Thirty-fourth week." The voice said crisply, "She's thirty-four weeks, six weeks from her due date. Has anyone palpated the fetus for size?" and then she heard, blessedly, Dr. Perry's familiar deep voice asking questions, and she fought the tears of pain and panic, wanting to keep her wits about her so that she could help him with whatever he had to do.

He examined her quickly but thoroughly.

"The baby's head is in position, and your cervix is dilating, Eve," he said somberly when he had finished. "The ritodrine doesn't seem to be stopping your labor. It looks like you're going to have this baby."

"But it's too soon!" she cried.

"We have a wonderful neonatal intensive-care unit at this hospital," he soothed. "Your baby is premature, and it's small, but it will have a good chance at survival."

A good chance! Only a chance? But this baby was important, damn it, important for Kelly's sake, and because she had sheltered it under her heart, *in* her heart, this baby *had* to live!

She had a sudden mental picture of the baby the way she had envisioned it, a roly-poly cherub with fat rosy cheeks, an upstanding tuft of blond fuzzy hair like Kelly's, with eyes that could not change from the new-baby gray color but would remain gray, the color of the irises lightening until they were small replicas of Derek's eyes. And then the vision dissolved in a racking pain that was much worse than any of the previous ones.

Oh, Derek, why weren't you with me? she cried inwardly when the pain had passed, and as they wheeled her through the wide swinging doors to the delivery room, she thought with a jolt, *What if Doug forgot to call him?*

DEREK WHEELED recklessly into the parking lot of the hospital in his Corvette, damning the lack of parking spaces, damning the elderly flower-laden ladies who blocked his way, damning hospitals and life in general.

The phone call had interrupted an important meeting about the acquisition of Wray Mills, a meeting in which they were tying up all the loose ends, but none of that mattered to Derek. He'd startled all the managers and lawyers by leaping out of his chair in the conference room as soon as he scanned the note Maisie slipped to him, by letting Maisie to provide inadequate explanations, by running from the building as though the Furies were after him. Which perhaps they were; he recalled from his study of Greek mythology that the Furies punished the perpetrators of unavenged crimes, and in his own eyes Derek was guilty.

It was as though this crisis with Eve were Kelly's situation all over again, with Eve being rushed to the hospital too early. Only this time, he, Derek, was going to be there, no matter if work had to wait, even if his rushing to be with Eve in her hour of need scotched the new mill deal. This was his chance to make reparations for his absence when Kelly had miscarried; at least that's how it shaped up in his own mind. Silly, maybe, because he knew it was too late to ever make anything up to Kelly. But it wasn't too late to do something for Eve. And he was convinced deep in his heart that he had a lot to make up to her.

"Eve Triopolous?" he said briskly to the pink lady, or whatever they called the volunteer workers, and she looked Eve's name up on a list, slowly running her manicured finger down the column of names until Derek wanted to scream with anguish at her uncaring, lackadaisical attitude.

"Third floor," she said sweetly and with a smile. "Room—"

But he didn't hear her. He was running down the aisle to the elevator, was staring at his distraught reflection in the stainless-steel walls of it as it slowly climbed, stopping interminably on the second floor for a group of orderlies and student nurses who giggled over something stupid one of the orderlies said and then he was out and running again, but was stopped by a guy in a white coat with a stethoscope around his neck.

"Where do you think you're going?" the doctor demanded.

"Third floor, Eve Triopolous—she's pregnant," he blurted out.

"Well, if she's pregnant, you're on the right floor, the maternity wing. Don't recognize the name, though. If you'll—"

And then Derek spied the wiry fellow in blue jeans glowering at him from the waiting area, and he knew somehow that this was the fellow Eve sometimes met, Eve's friend, the guy who took her out.

"Derek Lang?" the fellow said.

"Yes," he said, pulling himself up to his full height and appraising the other man.

The guy stuck out his hand. "Doug Ender. I'm the one who called your office."

"Where is Eve?" he demanded. "What's going on?"

"Actually, I suppose her doctor could tell you more about it, but he's with her in the delivery room now."

"The delivery room!" Derek rocked back on his heels, stunned.

Doug Ender regarded him coolly and without liking. "She's giving birth prematurely, Lang."

"Oh, God," Derek said, and sank down on the nearest chair.

Silence engulfed them, and surprisingly, Doug felt sorry for the man. He had expected to feel antagonism, anger, anything but sympathy. But it was clear that Derek Lang was deeply stricken by this news.

Doug cleared his throat. "I was with Eve when she felt the first pain," he began.

"She was in pain? How much pain?" Derek's words sliced jaggedly through the air, and his eyes were red and filled with a silent pain of his own.

Doug straddled the straight chair beside him. "I rode with her in the ambulance, and they did everything they could for her. They tried to stop the contractions, but they couldn't, so they wheeled her into Delivery half an hour ago."

"The—baby?" Derek whispered hoarsely. "They can save the baby?"

"I don't know," Doug said slowly. "The doctor didn't have time to talk to me, and I'm not directly involved, so I don't know if he'd tell me, anyway."

Derek closed his eyes, tight. If anything happened to this baby, Eve would be shattered. If anything happened to this baby—well, it was unthinkable, but he *was* thinking about it, and he wondered how he could ever have wished this baby dead.

"How could I have been so stupid?" he mumbled as if to himself. "How could I have been so blind?"

"I beg your pardon?" Doug looked genuinely confused.

"I didn't want her to have this baby," he said slowly, his desperation making him uncharacteristically talkative. "I wanted her to have an abortion."

Doug didn't speak for a long time, but finally he thought that he had been mistaken about Derek Lang. If he, Doug, was any kind of friend to Eve, he would also be a friend to this man, whom Eve liked and admired. It was clear that Derek Lang had suffered, was still suffering.

"She told me about it," he said to Derek reluctantly. "We've been friends since we were kids; we grew up together, and I'm an attorney. It was natural for her to talk to me about her situation." He shrugged. "I didn't have such a high opinion of you, to tell you the truth." His clear eyes assessed Derek. "But now—"

"Now?"

Doug shrugged. "I see what Eve meant. You don't mean her any harm."

"No, I never did. I wish she'd never been dragged into this mess, had never become—" He stopped abruptly. He had been about to say that he wished Eve had never become pregnant, but was that true? Eve herself had said that she was glad she was pregnant in spite of everything. Derek searched his mind, searched his heart, and in them he found gratitude.

This baby that was being born now, this very second, was his flesh and blood. Eve could so easily have gotten rid of the baby when he pressured her, but she hadn't. She had gallantly and valiantly refused to have the abortion, and she had taken care of herself and the baby, as well as her dependent father, before Derek had found her again. How could he, Derek, have been so stupid, so foolish, so confused? It must have been his grief over Kelly that had kept him from thinking straight. For now, with the impact of a blow to his solar plexus, he saw that the baby was worth her protection, was worth something in his eyes. It would be more grief for him if it didn't survive, because the child was his own—and Kelly's.

"She insisted on saving the baby," he said softly. "She was right." A fierceness came upon him when he thought of the defenselessness of the child, and adrenaline surged through him. He would protect the baby now, if only he could. He couldn't bear the thought of anything happening to it. But how like him, he thought bitterly, always too little too late.

"I should have helped her up the stairs; then she wouldn't have fallen," he said helplessly. He stared into space, seeing Eve's crumpled body lying so forlornly in the snow only a couple of days ago, when they had built the snow woman.

A nurse in a stiff white cap arrived silently on crepe soles and looked from one of them to the other. "Which one of you is Mr. Lang?" she asked.

Derek sat up straight. "I am," he said.

"Dr. Perry will speak with you now. Follow me, please."

IT WAS DARK outside when Derek finally crept into Eve's hospital room.

Her body scarcely mounded the white bed coverings; the bed seemed so large it almost swallowed her up. The covers rose and fell with the steady rhythm of her breathing, and Derek paused in the doorway to collect himself, to steady himself after the events of the day. He sagged with the burden of his weariness; his gray eyes were smudged shadows beneath his brows. Nervously, he twisted the bright bow attached to the vase of flowers he had bought in the hospital gift shop; they were carnations, which he would have preferred not to buy for Eve. She wasn't a carnation type, but carnations were all they had, and so carnations they were. He would have to find out what her favorite flower was.

"Derek?" she said fuzzily, turning her face toward the door. His heart turned over in his chest at the sight of her familiar winged eyebrows, the generous mouth, her dark hair cupped so perfectly to her head. She looked pale and wan after her ordeal; one hand was attached to tubing running to an IV hanging from a chrome stand.

"Yes," he replied, shutting the door silently behind him and not knowing where to go.

"You can sit down," she said, lifting her free hand as though with great effort. "Over here." He saw an orange plastic chair beside the bed.

"Eve—"

"I heard the baby cry," she said softly, her eyes huge and velvety. "He cried. That's a good sign, don't you think?"

The thought of what she'd been through hung like a weight on his heart. "I hope so. I hope so, Eve." He set the vase of flowers carefully on the radiator cover in front of the window, hiked his pants legs by the creases at the knees and sat down in the chair.

"Oh, Derek," she said, looking at him, and her voice sounded sleepy like a young child's. "Your tie is perfect, and your vest is buttoned. Not even rumpled. How like you."

"Eve, I've been frantic with worry. I didn't want anything to happen to you or the baby." His eyes searched her face urgently.

"I knew. I don't know how I knew, but I did."

He swallowed. "And now, if the baby doesn't live—" he began, but he couldn't continue.

Her hand crept across the counterpane, found his and nestled into his palm. Slowly he lifted his eyes to hers, and he saw that hers glimmered with tears. But there was courage in the set of her chin.

"The baby will live, Derek," she said, because it was what she had to believe. The tears spilled over and trickled down her cheeks, dropping to the white coverlet, where they left small damp patches.

And he couldn't speak, because his mouth ached from holding it so stiffly, but he knew it was right to gather her in his arms, to hold her close to his heart, and so he did, being careful of the IV apparatus taped to her hand. And when he saw her eyes closed, the shadow of her damp feathered eyelashes dark against her cheek, his heart was full. She was so beautiful and brave and strong that he should have admitted his love for her long ago.

He had almost lost her—Dr. Perry had made it clear that he had almost lost Eve—and he couldn't have borne that loss. And if they lost the baby... But Eve did not believe the baby would die. She had been right about a lot of things, and perhaps she was right about this, too.

Derek had a son. And he wanted that son to be part of his life as he had never wanted anything, except Eve herself.

BLESS DOUG, Eve thought the next morning. He had taken it upon himself to go to her father and to break the news that the baby had been born prematurely. And Al had withstood the news well, considering his concern about Eve. His voice had sounded stronger than Eve had expected when he called Eve first thing in the morning.

"You take care of yourself, Evie," he cautioned. "Don't be up and around too quick, now."

"I'll be all right," she assured him. She was sitting up in bed this morning; she was regaining her strength.

"I'll come see you as soon as Nell can drive me," her father told her. "Probably this afternoon during visiting hours."

They hung up, and Eve lay back on her pillows, thinking. She knew how much her father had looked forward to grandchildren. She could only imagine what he must be feeling over his own daughter's risking her life for a child that was not even hers.

But the baby felt like her own; that was the thing. Intellectually she knew it was Kelly's and Derek's—but emotionally she was bound to the baby as though it belonged to her.

"Ready to go see your new baby?" caroled a nurse as she maneuvered a shiny wheelchair through the wide hospital doorway. The nurses didn't know the circumstances of this baby's conception. That secret rested solely with Dr. Perry.

"Oh, yes," Eve said eagerly. This morning she had eaten well and was feeling much less groggy. Dr. Perry had stopped by; so had Dr. Ellisor, the pediatrician. He had been serious but not unencouraging.

"The baby is very small, Ms. Triopolous," Dr. Ellisor had told her. "Only four pounds. And we can expect him to lose some of that birth weight—all babies do."

"But otherwise he's normal?" She held her breath while waiting for the answer.

"As far as we know," he had replied. "But of course," he cautioned, "he's not out of danger yet. Barring any unforeseeable circumstances, though, I'd say you have a healthy infant who will pull through this."

Eve found the pediatrician's words encouraging despite this cautionary note. And now she was to see the baby!

The helpful nurse installed her in the wheelchair with a blanket tucked around her legs for warmth and Eve's IV attached somehow to the back of the chair; then she wheeled her cheerfully down the hall and around the corner. The neonatal intensive-care nursery was separate from the regular newborn nursery, which they passed in transit.

A proud grandmother stood at the window of the newborn nursery, tapping the glass and cooing to a pink bundle being held up for her inspection on the other side. In their Isolettes lay sturdy babies with fuzzy heads, red faces howling mercilessly, tiny ears as pink as seashells and dimpled fists experimentally flailing the air. The healthy babies, born at or near term.

Eve's heart beat faster as they approached the intensive-care nursery, where the most advanced technology aided premature babies, all of whom fought for every heartbeat, every ounce of body weight, every precious breath.

But no one had prepared Eve for what she would see there—for the immense room, all intimidating stainless steel and glass, for the tiny babies cradled in something called Ohio beds with tubes and wires crisscrossing their wizened bodies and the air filled not with lusty cries but with the hums and bleeps of monitors.

The picture of a rosy-cheeked baby faded forever in Eve's mind when she first glimpsed the child she had carried inside her for the past seven and a half months.

His face was wrinkled and red, and his eyes were swollen shut. A scattering of brown fuzz was the only hair on his head. He lay naked in the position the nurses had placed him, and he did not respond to Eve's presence.

Then, completely without warning, she burst into tears. Before she had been sure that the baby would live. She had been, she thought, unshakably sure. But that certainty was gone now that she had seen him. He was so little, so helpless.

"There, there," comforted the nurse, but the words were no comfort at all.

Why hadn't anyone told her how he would look? Why hadn't she been better prepared for the neonatal intensive-care unit? Clucking like a mother hen, the nurse wheeled her swiftly back to her room, Eve sobbing into her hands all the way, eliciting concerned looks from each person they encountered in the hall.

Eve huddled in her bed afterward, refusing lunch.

And then Aunt May descended upon her, bringing Eve's toothbrush and offering chocolates and solace of a sort, and Aunt May asked her if she had seen the baby yet, whereupon Eve cried and cried. And then her father and Nell came, fast on the heels of Aunt May, and her father caressed her shoulder, and Nell maintained a chirpy one-sided conversation, and Eve cried some more.

Where was Derek? Why didn't he come? They would let Derek see the baby; they wouldn't let Aunt May or her father or Nell, but Derek, as the baby's father, would be allowed to see him. And then she would have someone who understood. And then she would not feel so utterly alone.

THE INTENSIVE-CARE NURSERY was not an encouraging place. The baby was not a beautiful baby. But nothing could describe the thrill that Derek Lang felt when he first laid eyes on the small scrap of humanity that was his son.

"My son," he said out loud as though he could not believe it.

"Yes indeed," said the nurse who had brought him there before she discreetly bustled away.

"My son," he said again humbly, knowing that the world was not a place worthy of this child, that life would be harder than a child could know, that this baby deserved the guidance and care of his father in order to make his way through it all. And he would have that care and guidance, no matter what.

"I love you, my son," he whispered over the hum of the machinery that kept his baby alive, and his eyes filled with sudden tears.

EVE WAS SLEEPING when he entered her room, and he sat for a long time beside her, feeling thankful that he and Kelly had chosen Eve and not some other surrogate mother. For Derek well knew that many another woman would have bowed to his wishes for the abortion. The thought made him shudder.

At long last, she opened her eyes, instantly awake.

"I saw the baby," he said. "He's beautiful."

"Beautiful?" was all she could say, and then her eyes clouded with tears that she could not stop.

He held her again, hugging the warmth of her body against his. "Shh, everything is going to be all right. He's going to make it."

She managed to stop crying. He handed her a tissue, and she blew her nose. "I wish I could be like the heroines in books and cry without looking awful," she said shakily.

He laughed. "You look beautiful," he told her.

A nurse's aide came in with a bouquet of flowers. Then she hurried away.

"We need to decide what to name the baby," Derek said, walking to the window and then turning to face her. "He should have a name."

Eve stared at him, the afternoon sunlight slanting through the blinds and marking his face with a pattern of light and shadow.

"But that must mean that you're—that you're going to—" She stumbled over the words as the full impact of what Derek had said hit her.

"That I'm going to keep the baby. Yes." He smiled at her, but his smile was serious and not frivolous.

"But that's—that's—" She had been going to say that it was wonderful, but the words wouldn't shape themselves. If Derek kept the baby, then she would not be able to. *If* the baby survived, that is. And she could not imagine being parted from this child, could not imagine, after all the two of them had been through together, giving him up. She would have gladly died for this baby, who had been part of her but not of her; because of her pain he was even more indelibly hers than Derek's. She began to cry, not bothering to hide her face, just letting the tears slip down her cheeks.

"Now, Eve," Derek said, hurrying to her side, and his touch was gentle upon her face, drying the tears.

"It—it's normal to have postpartum crying jags," she said when she was able to speak. "Perfectly normal."

"What should we name him, do you think?" he said, reasoning that if he could get her thinking about the name, she wouldn't feel like crying. "Naming him is an act of faith," he explained as he eased himself down on the edge of her bed. "Somehow he will know that we expect him to live if we give him a name."

Eve pleated the sheet into accordion folds, avoiding Derek's eyes. She had once tried to get Derek to talk about names. It had been fruitless then. His willingness to do so now signified his change of heart. It should have made her happy, but it didn't.

"Kelly wanted to name the baby after you if it was a boy," she told him, her memory conjuring up the night she and Kelly had stayed up to watch *The Late Show* on television because Derek was working late. They had propped the popcorn bowl on a cushion between them, and Kelly had confided that she wanted the baby to be Derek if a boy and Elizabeth if a girl. "Kelly wanted to name him Derek Robert Lang, Junior. She said he would be called Dob."

"All right," said Derek. "Derek Robert Lang, Junior, is his name. Would you like to go see him?"

How could she say no, with Derek gazing at her so expectantly? After all, she had hoped for so long that he would recognize the baby as his, and he had. Now she would have to nurture that relationship and make sure bonding between father and son took place. It was the last thing she could do for the baby, after all, before she left him. It was the last thing she could do for Kelly.

She remained silent as Derek wheeled her to the intensive-care nursery himself. As they stood together—well, actually only Derek stood; Eve sat in her wheelchair—looking at little Dob, Derek's hand rested lightly on Eve's shoulder.

"Look, Eve," he pointed out, his voice eager. "He has Kelly's mouth! Doesn't he?"

Eve nodded, nervously biting her lip in frustration that this baby didn't look like the healthy newborns. But she had to admit that Derek's son's skin looked a little pinker this afternoon and that he reacted to the noise when someone dropped a metal pan in an adjoining room.

"I think he smiled," Derek said in an awestruck voice. Eve leaned forward in her wheelchair, straining to see. And yes, even though Dr. Ellisor might have denied it, she *did* think Dob smiled.

Yet after Derek had wheeled her back to her room and kissed her elatedly on the cheek, declaring that he was going to pass cigars out in the hospital lobby, Eve sank even deeper into devastating depression. On top of her failure to accomplish the carrying of this baby to term, she had to deal with the fact that he was no longer hers in any way.

Dob was Derek's child. Irrevocably, undeniably, scientifically and for all time. Nothing in the world could alter that irrefutable fact.

Chapter Eleven

"Eve, dear, imagine my surprise when Susan turned out to be the sister of the lead singer of Purple Madness. You know, *he's* the one who's been waiting for a kidney transplant, and now they're all putting pressure on her to donate one of her kidneys to her long-lost brother so he can marry the girl who used to be engaged to the hockey player, but Susan doesn't want to donate her kidney because her brother was so rotten when he was a kid, but he's reformed, and I really think that Susan ought to be nicer to her own *brother*. I don't care if she's been living in a cave for the past three months; she still has her suntan, so she's probably very healthy and all—" Aunt May continued loudly on and on in this vein, filling Eve in on what had transpired on *Love of Hope* since Eve went into the hospital.

I suppose it's too much to wish that Aunt May came equipped with a volume knob, Eve thought wearily as Aunt May plodded through the plot of her favorite soap opera. As though she could care about the hokey problems of Susan and the hockey player or the surly lead singer of Purple Madness while Dob, poor little Dob, lay helpless in his crib.

Five days after Dob's birth, Eve had gone home from the hospital. Dob had not. He would not be allowed to leave the hospital until his weight reached four and a half pounds and he was able to take nourishment by mouth.

Nell had invited Eve to come home to Wrayville where Nell would care for her, but Eve insisted that she wanted to visit the baby three times a day, and Wrayville was too far for that. And so she went home to the Myers Park house where Aunt May and Louise cosseted her and catered to her more than she had any right to expect.

"Ready, Eve?" Derek's smiling face appeared around the arch leading into the sun room.

"Yes," she said gratefully, glad to be spared any more of Aunt May's interminable saga. Derek helped Eve with her coat, solicitously suggested that she wear her gloves, and held the door for her as they trooped out to his car.

"Aunt May driving you crazy?" he asked with an understanding sidelong look at her profile once they were headed down the street in the Corvette.

"Not exactly," she said, staring straight ahead with a distracted air about her.

In the old days she would have defended Aunt May. Derek concentrated on his driving, worrying about Eve. She wasn't the same person since the baby had been born, and he missed her cheerfulness, her optimism, and most of all, her willingness to converse with him. They had had some interesting and spirited conversations in the old days.

Derek drove to the hospital to see Dob three times a day, once in the morning, once in the afternoon and once at night. His work schedule was suspended for the time being. Whenever it was possible, he went in to the office, but when it was not, he delegated his duties to subordinates, new mill or no new mill. Acquisitions, foreign textile quotas, the governor's task force on textiles—all seemed of little importance. For now, Derek wanted nothing more than to be with Eve and his son.

"Dr. Ellisor called just before we left the house," Derek told Eve.

Eve snapped her head around, clearly surprised. She had heard the phone ring during Aunt May's recitation, but she had felt too weary to break the long monologue to go answer it. Louise would answer it, or Derek would answer it. Phones were not part of her world these days. Nothing was important to her except Dob.

"What did the doctor say?"

"Just a progress report. Dob is doing fine."

She sank back into the Corvette's bucket seat and blinked rapidly. Her forehead ached from dammed-up tears. Surely the doctor had said more than that. Maybe Derek was keeping something from her. She wished now that she had spoken to Dr. Ellisor herself, just to reassure herself that Dob was all right, really all right. In spite of all the attention and sympathy, day by day Eve sank even deeper into a morass of depression. Seeing Dob three times a day, watching him helplessly as he lay here, did not help matters.

"Don't worry," Derek said when they finally stood in the intensive-care nursery looking at Dob. He couldn't help but be concerned about Eve these days. This Eve was so passive, so quiet, so unlike the Eve he had known before the baby was born. Failing to rouse any response in her, he turned his attention to the baby.

"Hi, Dob," Derek said gently, as he always did. "Hi there, fella." Dob wriggled in response to Derek's voice.

"See that? He knows you," the nurse said, smiling in satisfaction.

Eve leaned anxiously over the baby, watching him intently. Derek thought, *If only she would talk to the baby, speak to him!* But she never did. She always left the talking to him.

Eve tried to ignore the noises coming from the monitors, the screens that told their tales of the preemies' health. She kept her arms tightly folded across her stomach, the place where she had once carried Dob close to her heart, gripping her elbows with her hands. Her arms ached to hold this baby, but she knew she never would. And she didn't know if she could stand not holding him.

A loud beeping noise startled her, scared her out of her wits, and when she realized that the warning signal emitted from Dob's monitoring equipment, a hundred raw nerve endings transmitted the shock to her brain. The blood rushed from her head, and her legs turned to water.

Dob is dying was her first desperate thought, and she screamed and then began to cry, to cry so loudly that the nurse who rushed to take care of Dob, saying, "There, there, my little man, you've just rolled over on one of these wires and set if off; now let's just move you a bit," motioned Derek to take Eve away, and he slid his arm around her, half supporting her as he eased her out of the nursery and maneuvered her through the nearest door, one that led into a large supply closet. He closed the door after them so Eve wouldn't be subjected to the curious stares of passersby.

"Oh, God, Derek, I thought he was dying. I don't want him to die!"

"He's not, Eve. He's gaining weight, and he's better every day," Derek said desperately, trying to figure out a way to tell her that the danger was mostly in her own mind. Because Dob *was* better; the doctor said so.

But Eve was hysterical, pushing him away when he tried to hold her against his chest so that he had to grab her wrists and force her back against the gurney that was stored in the room.

for emergencies and wrap his arms around her when she began to flail wildly at him, completely out of control, so unlike Eve that he didn't know who she was.

Finally, she had no more strength left and lay sobbing against his shirt. She was so different from the calm capable person she had once been that he knew she was sick from the strain of the past weeks, that she had been living under more tension than she could take and that she needed him as much, if not more, than his son, who had others who could take care of his specialized needs.

Eve's heart drummed madly against her ribs. She wanted to run. But she was too weak to run, and there was nowhere to go. There was no place where she could be rid of the guilt over what had happened to make Dob a premature baby, where she could feel free of the constant tormenting anxiety about his future, his health.

She was a daughter, had once been a child. She well remembered being securely held in the circle of her father's arms, and she recalled with longing the days when her mother had been alive and would smooth her hair to comfort her at all the odd little moments of childhood when comfort was needed. Would Dob have that? Had she brought a child into this world only to surrender him to a life of pain and loneliness?

When she had decided to become a surrogate mother, she had thought she was helping two deserving people, Kelly and Derek. But the way it had turned out, she was saddling Derek with a lifelong responsibility that perhaps he even now did not really want, and she had produced a child who could not yet survive on his own.

He needed machinery and medicine to survive, and if he made it, then what? Was his life going to have the quality that Eve had been so sure of in the beginning, when everything had looked bright and optimistic, before Kelly's accident, before Dob had been born too early? Would it have been better to have had the abortion?

"Eve," Derek said as from a distance, and her name echoed and reverberated inside her head. He was so much stronger than she that she knew that there was no point in fighting anymore, in fighting any of it. She stumbled against him, and his arm was beneath her knees, swinging her up on the soft padded surface of the gurney. Her arms were around his neck, and she was sobbing into his shoulder, tears dissolving into the impeccable navy-blue silk of his tie. He was murmuring "hush" and brushing her hair back behind her ear and dabbing at her streaming eyes and nose with a soft towel from one of the shelves.

His fingers soothed her, stroked delicately at her hair, traced the jawline between ear and chin, until she stopped sobbing and the tears ran silently down her cheeks. His little finger caressed her collarbone beneath the blouse she wore, the bone so fragile and birdlike. He kissed her eyebrows and gave her a hand to hold. She couldn't stop herself from gripping it tightly, hanging on to his strong fingers as though they were some kind of anchor to reason. Holding his hand comforted her somehow. How could she have hated him only moments ago, Derek, who had been so kind, who cared so much? She was an ungrateful wretch; she didn't deserve him. Why didn't he leave her here in this awful supply closet and go away? The tears stopped, and her eyes drifted closed, shutting out the glaring overhead fluorescent tubes, shutting out Derek's worried face, leaving her in blessed darkness.

"Eve," he said, knowing that she had no strength left to fight, that all the fight in her had dissolved in guilt and misgivings. He smoothed her cheek reflectively, watching over her as he would watch over a child, as he would watch over Dob. Eve needed him. Eve needed him as much as Dob, maybe more. And he could help her because he had faith now, because he knew that Dob was going to survive and was going to get out of this hospital and go home to the Myers Park house. Where Derek would be waiting and where Derek hoped that Eve would be waiting, too.

"You were there for me when it was my darkest hour," he said, his voice no more than a whisper. "You took care of me, and you made sure no harm came to my child. Do you know how grateful I am to you for that? Do you?" He didn't know if she heard him; her chest rose and fell evenly, and she lay perfectly still. He thought she had fallen asleep on the gurney, exhausted by the mental and physical strain of the past half hour. But even if she were asleep, perhaps she heard him. And so he kept talking to her, because he wanted her to know.

"If you had listened to me, Eve, I would be alone now. Utterly alone. Without Dob. Without you. I didn't know what that would mean to me at the time. I thought that without Kelly my world had ended. I loved her so much, and I felt so sad that I hadn't been the kind of husband I should have been. You showed me that my life could go on, Eve, and I can never thank you enough for that. Never, never. And so, darling Eve, I will take care of you now."

Her eyelids fluttered, but they didn't open. Derek pressed a thumb along the long swanlike whiteness of her throat; her pulse throbbed steadily against it.

He dropped a kiss on Eve's right temple, and her grip tightened on his hand.

"It will be all right," he told her firmly. And he meant those words as he had never meant anything in his life.

"GET HER AWAY from home, from the hospital from all the reminders of what she considers her failure," Dr. Perry said, running a hand through his white hair until it stood on end like ruffled feathers.

"Her father lives in Wrayville," Derek said. "Eve could go here, I'm sure."

"Good. Send her. Don't let her visit the baby in the hospital or—oh, let's say at least a week."

"She'll worry," Derek said with certainty. "She'll see this as banishment of sorts, as if it's her fault she went to pieces and so you sent her away."

Dr. Perry shot Derek an incisive look. He nodded his head. "She might. But she needs time to pull herself together in a place where she won't be seeing Dob three. times a day. She's tearing herself apart with this insistence on going in to see him so often when there's really nothing she can do to help him."

"If you'll talk Eve into it," Derek said, "I can take her to the mountains. I have a cabin there. Aunt May could come with us, even Eve's father if he would like, and his friend Nell, and it would be a support group for her. All the people who love her gathered around, and she would feel that love and concern. We can be in touch with the hospital and with Dr. Ellisor by telephone every day, and we could be back in the city in a couple of hours if necessary."

"Dob is doing very well according to his pediatrician. He weighs over four pounds now, and he may be well enough to go home at the end of the week. And as for Eve, don't worry. I'll talk her into this mountain vacation of yours." Dr. Perry regarded Derek thoughtfully. "It sounds like the best medicine in the world for both of you," he said.

"I WISH YOUR FATHER could have come," Derek said conversationally as he skillfully steered the Corvette around a huge pothole in the dirt road on the outskirts of the Pisgah National Forest in the Great Smoky Mountains. "Your friend

Doug assures me that your dad feels no hard feelings over you
pregnancy anymore.''

"Mmm,'' Eve said listlessly, staring out at the bone-bar
winter branches flailing at the scudding gray sky overhead. He
hands lay inert in her lap, like two fallen birds. The sight of he
usually animated hands lying so still tugged at Derek's heart
strings.

"I'd like to know your father,'' Derek went on. "Worked i
a textile mill all his life, did he?''

"Mmm,'' Eve said again, not at all interested in talking
Each revolution of the car's wheels took her farther away fron
Dob, as if she wouldn't be leaving him for good soon enough
and now they had made her leave for a whole week. She didn'
have the strength to fight it, though, and Dr. Perry had beer
adamant. She would not be allowed to see Dob, so why not le
Louise pack her bag? Why not let Derek bundle her into the ca
and take her on this godforsaken trip into some wintry moun
tain wilderness? At the last minute, Aunt May came down wit
a cold and couldn't go along, but Eve suspected that it was les
the cold's fault than the fault of Derek's cabin, which didn'
have a television set and where Aunt May would miss the up
coming kidney transplant operation on *Love of Hope.*

Damn, why wouldn't she talk to me? Derek despaired, grip
ping the wheel tightly in his hands. He turned suddenly into th
deeply rutted road that wound up the mountain to the cabir
hoping that his neighbor had followed Derek's directions t
open the place up, do whatever needed to be done to the frac
tious plumbing and make sure the fireplace flue wasn't blocke
by a bird's nest or something.

Smoke snaked upward from the high stone chimney, Dere
noticed with satisfaction when they reached the clearing
"Good old Farley,'' he said to Eve. "He's never let me dow
yet. Look, he's got a fire going in the fireplace for us.'' H
eased the Corvette to a stop next to a stack of fresh firewood

"Come on,'' he said to Eve, assisting her unresisting figu
from the Corvette. "Got to get you inside and warmed u
Aunt May made me promise to make sure you ate somethin
hot as soon as we got here. Are you hungry?''

Eve regarded the gray cedar-shingled structure and shook he
head. "No, I'm not hungry. Not at all.'' The place was b
enough—huge, in fact. The Langs always did everything on
grand scale. A mountain cabin, Derek had told her. This plac
was a mansion. You could house three or four families fro
Cotton Mill Hill in this place.

"What's wrong? Don't you like it?" Derek looked genuinely disturbed. He wanted her to be happy. It was touching, really.

"It's—it's lovely," she said lamely, taking the steps heavily, as though each was a major obstacle. Derek's hand remained at the small of her back, guiding her. At the door he dug a key out of the pocket of the shearling jacket he wore and inserted it in the lock. Eve stared down at the flagstone porch beneath her boots. Little pockets of snow nestled in the corners. Fresh snow covered the sloping front yard. Beyond, she saw leafless deciduous trees and a bank of evergreens. There were no close neighbors.

"Here we are," Derek said, ushering her inside. He flipped a light switch, and a wagon-wheel lamp overhead threw the place into a mellow glow.

He set her bag down on the bottom step of a sturdy staircase and rubbed his hands together.

"Now for something hot," he said, raising his eyebrows inquiringly. He smelled of the cold, of the outdoors, of woodsmoke from the chimney.

"I really don't—"

"I promised Aunt May," he said. He slid an arm around her slim shoulders and drew her through the hall, through a large dining room, into a huge kitchen. "Even if it's only hot tea," he began, rummaging in a cupboard.

"Hot tea would be nice," she said when she realized that he wasn't going to give up until she ate or drank something. Anyway, it would give him something to do. He seemed so nervous, and what were the two of them going to do, rattling around in this big place by themselves all week? She wondered dully if she could get by with retiring to bed and pulling the covers up as high as they would go and not coming out for seven whole days. Or ever, preferably.

"Milk?"

"What?" She tugged herself into the present time and place.

"I was asking if you wanted milk in your tea," he said patiently.

She shrugged. "It doesn't matter."

"Milk, then. That's what I'm having. That's the way my grandmother always drank her tea. Must have been the English influence. Did I ever tell you my grandmother was English? Well, she was."

Eve sat down on a cane-bottom straight chair that Derek pulled up to the scarred kitchen table for her.

"I forgot to take your coat! Here, Eve, let me get it for you."
When she didn't stand up, he lifted her hands from her lap and
pulled her up. He unfastened the buttons for her and slipped the
coat off her shoulders. She stood unresisting, like a child,
sinking back onto the chair when he left the room to hang her
coat in the hall closet.

"I make tea the English way, you know," he told her as he
set the kettle on to boil. "Just the way Grandmother taught
me." A glance over his shoulder told him that Eve's face was
pinched and white and that she couldn't have cared less about
his grandmother. She barely looked up when he set the cup of
tea in front of her.

"Go on, try it," he encouraged with a friendly smile. He had
to keep up the conversation. They couldn't just sit here staring
at each other. He couldn't allow her to drag him down into the
emotional depths where she was; it was his job to keep her mind
off Dob any way he could. To make her hopeful, to pull her out
of this awful depression. And so he talked, asking her questions, but not too forcefully, telling her little bits and pieces
about himself, but not too intrusively.

And it worked, if only a little. She favored him with a bleak
half smile once, exposing her quirky bicuspid, and he almost
fell out of his chair in relief. He had been telling her about a
prank he and some buddies had pulled back in his high school
days; they had unfurled a roll of pink toilet paper all over the
red maple trees in the neighborhood fuddy-duddy's yard. He
supposed that her view of him—the ultraconservative Derek
Lang—didn't jibe with the picture he was painting for her. But
the tiny smile made him hope that somewhere inside this bare
husk of a woman was the Eve he had known, the Eve he loved.

He carried her suitcase upstairs and showed her the room she
would occupy; it was a cozy guest room rustically decorated in
frilled unbleached muslin curtains and an antique pine canopy
bed surmounted by a huge feather bed covered in red-and-white
striped ticking. The floors were bare oak, and an immense
fireplace banked with glowing embers dominated one wall.
Framed embroidery decorated the walls; some of it was in poor
taste—fat little girls wearing sunbonnets so you couldn't see
their faces, a pig inexplicably embroidered in bright blue—but
some of it was very pretty. All in all, Derek found it the most
cheerful bedroom in the house.

"So I've shown you the bathroom. Don't forget, now, that
the bathtub faucet handles are reversed; the cold one is the hot-
water faucet, and the one labeled hot is really the cold. My fa-

ther had a hard time finding any local fellows who could do plumbing work when he built this place, with the result that the plumbing here leaves a lot to be desired. Anyway, is everything okay?''

''Um-hmm,'' Eve said listlessly, staring out the window at the snow. It was so white, so quiet, so peaceful. A peaceful, quiet place. She wanted to lie down and sleep, to sleep for a long, long time.

She felt Derek's strong hands on her shoulders. He turned her around to face him, and his eyes searched hers. He wanted something from her, she thought wearily. He wanted something she couldn't give him.

''Well, then, I'll leave you alone for your nap.'' His hands dropped from her shoulders, a gesture of defeat.

She nodded, staring at his face, at his neat eyebrows, at his blunt nose. She knew that face now. It had become part and parcel of her life, and soon she would have to say goodbye. Thank God she no longer felt anything. Thank God she was numb. Because if she felt anything, if she allowed herself to feel, she would only hurt inside.

Eve crawled into bed and burrowed deep into the thick warm feather bed. She didn't bother to take off her clothes or put on her nightgown. She didn't even think about it, because she was beyond thought.

All she wanted to do was sleep. And sleep. And sleep.

Chapter Twelve

Derek let her sleep, and she slept more than fourteen hours. He looked in on her once before he went to his own room that evening, saw that she was sleeping peacefully and stole away without waking her. He reminded himself that she was not only suffering in Dob's behalf, but she was also still recovering from a difficult childbirth.

He awakened early, before she did. He knew this because he lay in bed, listening for sounds of her moving about. But he heard none, so he got up and showered and shaved in the little bathroom adjoining his bedroom, wondering if she were lying deep in her feather bed and listening for sounds of him.

"Good morning," he said to her, ready to start anew when she finally appeared in the kitchen.

"Good morning," she replied, not smiling. She wore a wraparound wool skirt of Wedgwood blue with a white sweater. She had regained her figure since having the baby, although her breasts were fuller, rounder. But her stomach was flat beneath the front wrap of the skirt. As always, she looked neat and precise. Her hair was a glossy black cap hugging her head. The nape of her neck beneath the short, sleek hair appeared white and vulnerable.

"I'm putting together a breakfast for us," he told her cheerfully. "Not as good a breakfast as Louise makes, of course, but I'm pretty good at whipping pancakes together from a mix. How many pancakes can you eat?"

He was looking at her expectantly. Eve shrugged and shook her head. "I don't know."

"If I can eat six, you can surely manage three, don't you think? I've got real Vermont maple syrup. I dug an unopened tin of it out of the pantry. Kelly had a thing for real maple syrup ordered from Vermont, not that watered-down sugar water they sell in the supermarket."

"You came here with Kelly?"

A spark of interest; that was good. And it didn't hurt to talk about Kelly anymore, the way it had in the beginning, when the very utterance of her name felt like a dagger piercing his heart.

"I came here with Kelly often, especially in the first days of our marriage. She loved the mountains."

"Did she," Eve said, but it wasn't a question. It was more of an observation.

"Look, do you think you could set the table? You'll have to find the plates and cups and silver yourself, because I'm not sure where everything is. I haven't been here in a couple of years."

Obediently, Eve moved to the cupboards, opening and closing them like an automaton as she tracked down the requisite supplies.

She didn't feel Kelly in this house at all; everything here seemed so impersonal. "Kelly didn't pick out these dishes," she said when she was setting them on the woven place mats. The dishes were ugly brown-and-yellow pottery, chipped and worn.

"No, those are left over from when I was a boy. They're pretty old, I guess, and probably came from the local pottery, which tried to make a go of it and failed. This place wasn't Kelly's and mine, you know. It belonged to my parents. We came up here every summer when I was a kid, and occasionally in the winter. Then, after their divorce, I inherited it."

"But you don't come here?"

"Well, not anymore. Before Kelly's miscarriage we came often." He wondered if he should be talking about this; perhaps, considering Dob's premature birth, miscarriage was an uncomfortable topic for Eve. But he felt no compunction about speaking of what had been a sad time in his and Kelly's life. It had happened so long ago that it was part of the past. He thought of Kelly and everything concerning her with a strong feeling of loving nostalgia. Eve had been right about that, too; time was a great healer.

"Oh" was all Eve said. The topic was closed, so maybe she didn't like to be reminded. He'd have to feel his way very carefully, try not to tread ground that would make Eve retreat even more into herself. Since the support group he had envisioned for Eve hadn't materialized when her father and then Aunt May couldn't come, he would have to be her support group. He was well aware that one person could hardly take the place of two others, but he intended to try.

Eve managed to eat two pancakes and to sip some canned grapefruit juice, but Derek couldn't persuade her to eat any of the little sausage links he had prepared.

When he was through cleaning up the kitchen, he went into the big living room and found Eve sitting in a rocking chair by the window, staring out. She rocked slowly to and fro. In the white north light from the window, her skin shone so translucent that he saw a tracery of blue veins at her temples.

"What shall we do today?" he asked her, rubbing his hands together.

She swiveled her head and looked at him, wishing he didn't look so enthusiastic. She didn't want to do anything. She wanted only to sit here and rock and watch the snow, avoiding all thought.

"I don't care," she said politely, and then returned her attention to the outdoor scene.

It would be easy to become exasperated, he said to himself, raking his fingers through his hair and standing undecided for a moment. Then he turned abruptly and sat down on the floor in front of the coffee table where someone had long ago started piecing a dusty jigsaw puzzle together. The mindless fitting of the pieces would require no creativity or thought. He would work on the puzzle, pointless as it seemed, because he could talk to Eve while he did it. He didn't know what would get through to her; he only knew that he had to keep talking to her, trying to make some impression on her, giving her something to think about when she refused to think.

And so he talked about his boyhood and asked questions about her childhood as he worked on the puzzle picture of a red covered bridge.

Eve responded when he asked her about her Greek heritage; evidently she was proud of it. He asked her about Tarpon Springs, and she told him about her vacations there. She even ventured information about her grandmother's recipe for honey cake, and he told her she should teach Aunt May how to make it. For some reason, Eve seemed to shrink inside herself at the suggestion. Just when he thought he had established a connection between the two of them, she fell strangely silent again, answering him with monosyllables and staring out the window.

That night after she had gone to bed, he stepped out on the front porch and stared at the silver-white sickle of a moon holding the sky in the curve of its arms. He wondered if the reddish-colored body near it could be the planet Mars. No, not Mars. It must be Venus. He'd never been much good at astronomy. Something skittered through the underbrush, and he tried to think what kind of animal would be abroad on a night like this, when the ground was covered with snow and the air so cold.

He would like to bring Dob here. He could imagine it someday, his son following him into the woods, his own old field glasses slung around the boy's neck, and he'd enjoy pointing out the different birds to Dob, who would love bird-watching as much as he, Derek, had loved it when he was a kid. At night they'd figure out the constellations together. They'd camp out, too, just beyond the clearing. Derek wondered if his old tent was still usable. He'd have to get it out and see. And there would be family picnics in the summers, with cold fried chicken and deviled eggs and ripe red tomatoes from the mountaineers' gardens. He and Dob and Eve.

But that was in the future. First Eve would have to snap out of this depression. He wished he had taken the time to get to know her better before the baby had been born. He had resolved to do that, to find out what kind of life she was used to living, to find out where she was from, what she liked to do. But he hadn't thought of it until it was too late. And now, when he needed to know Eve in order to help her, he didn't know her very well at all.

Oh, why didn't I insist that Aunt May come with us? he agonized. Whatever else bothered him about the lady, Aunt May was good for one thing: filling in silences. And there were so many of those between him and Eve. Why wouldn't she talk? Why wouldn't she talk to him?

There was nothing to do, he thought unhappily, but to keep at it.

But the second day was like the first, and the third like the second. Eve remained heavy with depression and unresponsive to him or anything he suggested. The only times she ever rallied was when he called the hospital for the daily progress report on Dob, and afterward she sank into lethargy again. And she slept for such long periods of time that secretly he worried that she was physically sick as well as mentally exhausted.

Eve awoke on the fourth day and went down to breakfast as usual.

"Good morning," Derek said as he always did. He was inexpertly lining up bacon slices in a frying pan; his big hands looked so clumsy at the task! Something stilled inside Eve. She had taken Derek for granted, and in her zombielike state she had not recognized his efforts. He'd talked, cooked, hauled firewood for the greedy fireplaces. She'd lived off him like a parasite—she, who had always been so independent. She was ashamed of herself.

To Derek's immense surprise, after breakfast Eve sat word-lessly down beside him and began fitting pieces into the jigsaw puzzle. He didn't comment on her presence. As he watched her with her hair swinging forward across her pale cheeks, he was overwhelmed by the clean, sweet fragrance of her. Once their hands touched by mistake, and his skin burned where her milky-white flesh met his.

After a couple of hours of silently working on the puzzle, the Seth Thomas mantel clock, which Derek had carefully wound the day before, struck noon. It startled both of them, that brassy intrusion of metallic sound.

"I'll fix lunch if you like," Eve offered, much to Derek's surprise.

"Fine," he said, his heart flipping over. It was the first time she had volunteered anything, the only time she had spoken without his speaking to her first.

Eve found a tin of tuna fish, opened it and deftly mixed the contents with mayonnaise. Derek brewed tea, covertly watch-ing Eve and admiring her grace of movement.

When they sat down at the old kitchen table to eat, Eve was startled to find that Derek was staring at her.

"Is the sandwich all right?" she asked quickly.

"It's fine," he said, but he continued to watch her. She chatted with him, and although she was not by any means lo-quacious, he sensed that she was trying hard to open up and be some company for him. Good; maybe she was feeling better. He would think of something to keep them busy this after-noon. He had come to the conclusion that Eve's constant brooding wasn't good for her.

After lunch Derek stood up and stretched and said ever so casually, "Would you mind coming down to the basement with me, Eve? I need you to hold the flashlight for me while I poke around down there." He held his breath, waiting to see if she'd continue being communicative or if she'd sink back into her all-too-familiar listlessness.

To his immense relief she nodded her agreement, and he handed her the big flashlight to carry. They descended the steps carefully.

"No telling what's down here," he cautioned. "I haven't ventured into this basement since Kelly and I replaced the old furnace with electric heat. Careful, there's a cobweb!" and he brushed it away with his fingers before it could trail across her face.

"It's a big basement," Eve said.

"It sure is." Derek nudged at a cardboard box with his toe. "Wonder what's in all these boxes." He bent over and looked. "Oh," he said on a note of surprise, "it's all my old Hardy Boys books. I remember reading those. I used to bring a shopping bag full of them up here every summer."

"I read Hardy Boys books when I was a kid," Eve told him. She was making an effort to rouse herself from her lethargy. It was difficult, but Derek, with his constant encouragement, was clearly trying to ease her way back to normalcy. She wanted to meet him halfway.

"I would have pegged you for Nancy Drew," he said grinning. "Or Judy Bolton."

"Oh, I read those, too." She managed to grin back.

"Train the light on this corner, Eve," he told her. He tugged at a large bundle.

"What are we looking for, anyway?" she asked, her curiosity aroused in spite of herself.

"My tent."

"Your tent? You're not planning on a camping trip in this weather, are you?"

"Heavens, no. In the future sometime. Now where could it have gone? I know it's down here somewhere."

Eve circled the light around the basement. It fell on an object hanging on the wall.

"There's something we could use now," she told him. "A sled. Why don't you wait and look for the tent some other time?"

"My old sled!" Derek said in amazement. "I wondered where that was."

"And all the time you told me you didn't know how to play in the snow," Eve said.

"Well," Derek said sheepishly, "I had forgotten. And now, here's old Rosebud."

"Rosebud? Your sled is named Rosebud?"

"I saw this movie once," said Derek. "*Citizen Kane.* And he had—"

"I know. A sled named Rosebud."

"I guess I should have been more original. But at the time it seemed like the perfect name for my sled. Of course, I didn't get to use it much because we hardly ever had snow. But I did love that sled."

"I wish you would find the tent," Eve said with a sigh.

"You're getting tired, aren't you? You should have said so. Here," he said, taking the light from her, "I'll finish this. You go upstairs and rest."

"I'm fine," she objected. "Really." But he noticed that she was shivering, and he urged her ahead of him up the steps.

"I can get the tent later. In fact, it probably isn't any good anymore, anyway. When Dob is big enough to go camping, I'll let him help me pick out a new tent."

"You were looking for the tent for Dob?" Eve said with a woebegone expression on her face. They stood in the kitchen now, facing each other in the too-bright daylight.

Derek nodded. He wished she wouldn't look that way, so vulnerable. It was his mention of Dob; she always looked that way when he spoke of his son.

"It's time to call the hospital," Derek said gently. "They'll give us a progress report on Dob."

Her face lit up all at once. "Is it time? Oh, good."

So Derek dialed the hospital's number and managed to catch Dr. Ellisor there. He passed the phone to Eve. And when she talked to Dr. Ellisor, Derek's heart softened at the glow shining within her deep, dark eyes. *She loves Dob so much,* he thought with wonder, amazed that she loved this child, who was, after all, no child of hers.

But then, being male, he couldn't imagine it, harboring another human being within his body, breathing for it, eating for it, until you thought of it as part of yourself. And then having to part from it in the painful process of childbirth and, in Eve's case, having to leave it in the hospital when it was time to go. Eve had been through so much; no wonder she was not herself. He kept forgetting what she had suffered.

"Dob's taken an extra ounce of formula, Derek," Eve said with barely suppressed excitement after she replaced the receiver in its cradle. This *was* good news.

"That's great. That's wonderful." Derek beamed down at her.

Her expression faded to wistfulness. "I wish—" And then she stopped and stood forlornly staring into space. He knew she wished she had been there, had been the one to coax him to take more at his feeding.

"I know," he said, yearning to take her in his arms. "Say, Eve, we can't be there, but let's celebrate. Let's drive down the mountain and have dinner someplace. How about it?"

"But—"

"I won't take no for an answer. Anyway, I'm tired of eating things out of cans."

She sighed softly. "It's nice of you, Derek. But I just don't want to go out. You go; I don't want you to stay because of me. I can heat up a can of soup or something."

He would not surrender her to inertia; he refused to let her talk him out of it.

"Wear something pretty," he told her impulsively when she started reluctantly up the stairs to change clothes.

"But I don't have anything pretty," she said, and then her cheeks flushed.

He had forgotten; she'd worn nothing but maternity clothes for months. "Then wear something comfortable," he said gently, and he watched her as she walked up the stairs, her legs slim beneath her skirt.

He should give her some of Kelly's clothes. But no, that wouldn't be right. Anyway, they wouldn't fit Eve. Kelly had been bustier, slimmer-hipped. He could hardly remember Kelly's size; how strange it was! He could only think of Eve, the narrow shoulders, the sturdy hips, the slim legs. He'd love to see her wearing bright colors—coral, jade green, crimson, aquamarine. Eve should have new clothes of her own.

She appeared wearing a beige sweater dress with a turtleneck; it was fuzzy, as if made of lamb's wool or, less likely, cashmere. He could tell it wasn't new, but the light behind her rimmed her in gold so that her figure appeared to be haloed. Her earrings were simple gold discs flashing beneath the arc of hair at her cheeks. He thought she looked beautiful.

He took her to a restaurant called the Juniper Inn near the Blue Ridge Parkway. The restaurant was in an old house and was renowned for its good food. When Eve didn't seem to know what she wanted to eat, he ordered for her with confidence.

After the wine arrived, he held his glass up and waited for her to raise hers. She did, a bit hesitantly. He had never seen her drink wine or anything alcoholic before; she had been pregnant as long as he'd known her.

"To Dob," he said softly, because he knew that was the only thing Eve would want to drink to.

"To Dob," she murmured, and when she tried to pull her eyes away from his, his sheer force of will prevented her.

"Derek?" she whispered, setting her glass on the table. The wine sloshed back and forth; her hand was unsteady.

"What would it take to make you happy, Eve?" he asked her gently.

"For Dob to be well," she said with feeling.

"He's going to be," Derek said. "My son is a survivor, Eve."

Eve looked somber. "If only I hadn't gone out in the snow that day—" she began.

"No," Derek interrupted. "We both have enough to feel guilty about. I could have stopped you from going out. I should have been there when you went up the steps, not running over to get fresh snow for snow ice cream."

"But you—"

"The point is, Eve, that either of us could feel guilty about that day. And yet Dr. Perry has said that he doesn't think that the fall had anything to do with your going into premature labor. Don't you see? We could go on hating ourselves forever if we wanted to. We could blame ourselves for Dob's being premature, but it won't do any good. I ought to know. I blamed myself for years for Kelly's miscarriage. And my guilt did more harm than good in the long run. I should have let go of my guilt and been a better husband for Kelly when I had the chance." His eyes burned into her.

Eve traced a circle on the tablecloth with one finger. She raised troubled eyes to his. "I don't know how to get to where you are," she admitted. "You've grown through that setback, you've forgiven yourself, but the guilt I feel is like a net trapping me. I know there's a way out, but I can't find it. I just keep floundering around in my thoughts, wishing…wishing…" She could not go on.

"I'll help you find your way," he said. "If you'll let me."

She only stared at him unhappily.

And yet it turned into a pleasant evening somehow. Not just for him but for her, too. He made a deliberate attempt to cheer her, calling upon his considerable repertoire of repartee. The wine relaxed both of them until Eve actually laughed once at something he told her about work, and he thought that his work would be something they could talk about, not just now but during the next few days. His eyes lingered on her mouth, the lips curved upward for once, and he was struck with the thought that it was a passionate mouth, and at that moment he wanted to kiss her very much.

He hesitated when they said good-night at the foot of the stairs. He longed to sweep her into his arms and had an absurd picture of himself carrying her up the stairs like a movie hero, but that was ridiculous. This was Eve, practical, down-to-earth Eve, and she was sad, and he was sorry, and when he kissed her, it would have to be real, not a replay of something he once saw in a movie.

But she surprised him. She lifted one hand slowly and touched the palm of it to the lean plane beneath his cheekbone, curving her hand to fit. Her hand trembled, and for a moment he thought about actually sweeping her up into his arms, but he couldn't move when he looked deep into her bottomless brown eyes and saw the tenderness in their depths.

"You are a good friend to me, Derek," she whispered, and his heart lightened, because he hadn't known what he was to her, and friendship was a start.

And then she was gone, moving swiftly upward, leaving him to stare after her, feeling breathless and hopeful and so much in love with her that his heart ached.

DEEP IN HER WARM FEATHER BED, Eve remained wakeful. She closed her eyes, only to find that they sprang wide open again to stare into the darkness. She tossed; she turned. She could not find a comfortable spot.

She would have been a fool not to know what was wrong with her. It was Derek, Derek Lang. She felt close to him, closer than she ever had to any other human being, even her father, even Doug.

Well, was that so surprising? They had been through so much together—first Kelly's death, then finding their way back to each other. Not that finding their way back to each other had been for their own comfort; Derek had taken care of her out of guilt, and she had accepted his care because she had the welfare of the baby at heart. She had hoped that Derek would come to want the baby eventually, and that had happened, thank God. And then there had been the heartbreak of poor Bob's being a preemie and therefore at risk, and they had shared that pain. Derek had been so kind to her. It was only natural for her to feel grateful to him.

And yet . . . and yet. The way Derek's soft gray eyes beamed comfort over dinner, the compassion he felt for her and which he took no pains to conceal. The *liking* she felt for him, for the person he was.

He'd spoken to her so kindly in the restaurant tonight. And slowly, slowly, what he had said began to pierce her consciousness. If he, Dob's father, did not hold her accountable in any way for what had happened to cause his son's premature birth, if he didn't hold himself responsible, then perhaps she could let go of her own overwhelming guilt. And yet when she thought of poor little Dob and all the needles and machines that he had to endure in order to stay alive, it was hard not to blame herself. Still, she knew in her heart of hearts that Derek was right—blaming herself didn't help anyone, not Dob, not Derek and certainly not Eve Triopolous.

Derek had comforted her with his words. When they had said good-night at the foot of the stairs tonight, she had longed for Derek to comfort her even further by gathering her in his arms. She'd wanted nothing more, just his sweet, warm, gentle comfort.

Was that so odd after everything they'd been through? After all, they were the only ones who could understand the pain of seeing Dob in the intensive-care nursery. It was only natural for them to turn to one another in their need.

But Derek was Kelly's husband. Eve had loved Kelly.

Derek had loved Kelly, but Kelly was gone.

Derek had kissed Eve once.

She imagined his kissing her again, his lips sure and smooth against hers, so silky as they trailed from her lips to her neck to the space between her breasts and then beyond. To join her body to his would be the pinnacle of sharing and giving, the ultimate expression of—but what was she thinking? With difficulty, she pulled herself back from her thoughts and made herself think rationally. Or as rationally as possible, anyway.

With wonder, she admitted to herself that she could love him so easily. *Love.* She whispered the word into the darkness, unfamiliar with the set of it on her lips. A beautiful word, one that opened its heart in acceptance and closed its eyes in peace.

Love.

The word eased her into a jumbled sequence of scenes, all mixed up and yet somehow too clear. Derek, his mouth warm upon her lips. Her lips reaching up, up, toward his, and the sweetness of his mouth. His hands upon her body where they had never been before, feeling natural and right. Her legs entwined with his and murmuring his name over and over until it became a moan in her throat. The heat in her breasts, cooled by his kisses. Finally, his head pillowed on her shoulder, his hair against her cheek. Sleeping, the two of them, together.

Love.

She whispered the word in her dream, and then she slipped to a deep, deep sleep.

HE PHONE RANG shrilly early in the morning before he woke , and Derek lurched out of bed, momentarily confused, be- re shrugging into his robe and running downstairs where the ly telephone was.

It was Maisie Allen, his secretary, on the line.

"Just a few points to clear up on that contract for the new ill," Maisie said, and he was so relieved that he sagged down to the couch nearby. He had thought it was the hospital lling. He had thought something had happened to Dob.

And Eve had, too, for she appeared at that instant, pulling the familiar old bathrobe over her nightgown, her eye- ows winging upward, startled.

"Dob?" she whispered urgently, her face tense with strain. s it Dob?"

He slid his hand over the mouthpiece and smiled reassur- gly. "No," he whispered, "it's my office."

Her shoulders slumped in relief, but when she turned to pad vay on her bare feet, he caught her hand in his free one and ould not let it go until she sat down on the arm of the couch xt to him.

"Fine, Maisie, I'll agree to that. Sure. This has dragged on r the better part of a year now, and I just want to get it over th. Yeah. Okay, call me if you have any questions." He hung .

"I'm all right," Eve said tremulously, pulling her hand away.

"Are you?" His eyes searched her face.

She inhaled a deep shaky breath and attempted a smile. es."

"Let's have a cup of coffee. Or tea. We've both had a scare."

"All right."

He noticed her bare feet again. "You'd better go put on some ppers."

She smiled. "I will. You know those old black corduroy ones u didn't want me to wear to Oktoberfest? I still have them."

He grinned at her, remembering that day with fondness. It s the first time he had felt good, *really* good, after Kelly died. 'll have the water boiling before you get back," he said, get- g up and heading for the kitchen.

When she returned, he noticed that she had run a brush through her hair and that her face had a fresh-scrubbed look. She competently poured the tea he had brewed and sat down across from him, the old black corduroy slippers peeping out from beneath her long robe. There was a sense of familiarity about sitting across a breakfast table from her now; the ease of it warmed and heartened him.

"Actually, that phone call was about a new mill Lang Textiles is acquiring," he told her. He wanted her to be interested in his work; he had made up his mind to talk about it when she seemed ready to talk.

"Oh?" she said. "So how many mills do you own now?"

"Twenty-two," he said with satisfaction. "Eleven of them acquired since my father retired."

"So many!"

"One thing I learned at Harvard Business School is that you either grow or stagnate. I'd rather grow." His eyes sparkled at her; she was captivated by his dynamism when he spoke of his work.

"And where is this new mill of yours?"

"Wrayville," he said. "That's where you grew up, isn't it?"

Oh, what had he said wrong? He didn't like the white line around her lips or the way she had clamped them shut, nor did he like the way her dark eyes narrowed.

"Yes," she said shortly, dropping her eyes to her teacup. "I grew up in Wrayville."

"And your father worked in a mill most of his life, right? He worked at Wray Mills, then?"

"Yes," she said, whispering the word, her head in a whirl. She had never in all this time dreamed that Derek's company would be the one to buy Wray Mills. She should have guessed, she supposed, but so many other big names in the textile business had been mentioned as rumors swept Wrayville that she had never given Lang Textiles a thought.

Her stomach did a dive, turned over. This man, Derek Lang, who sat across from her and who was her friend—this man had the power to right the wrong done to dozens of textile workers in the past and to make the future of present workers free of the crippling brown-lung disease! Did he know the working conditions at Wray Mills? Did he care? He was a caring man—she knew that—but she also knew that he was a hardheaded businessman who needed to make a profit because he still felt the need to prove himself worthy of his inherited position.

Should she take him into her confidence? Should she tell him about the workmen's compensation claims waiting for him when he finalized the takeover of Wray Mills?

She shoved back her chair. "I—I think I'll get dressed now," she stammered, fighting for composure and avoiding Derek's eyes. She almost overturned the cane-bottom chair in her haste to get away.

Derek's gray eyes reflected hurt and rejection. But Eve couldn't stop to think about that; she needed to be alone. She had to think about other things. About what to tell Derek—if she should tell him anything—about the effect the Lang Textiles' takeover would have on the claims she had worked so hard with Doug to file, about—oh, about all sorts of things.

She had retreated from the real world long enough. Now she had been yanked back into it by Derek's revelation, and the shock of it bent her mind, overshadowing her anguish over Dob and her grief at having to give him up.

Running upstairs, fleeing to the privacy of her room, she knew that she couldn't afford the luxury of self-pity for Eve Triopolous any longer, not when the quality of life for hundreds of mill workers was at stake.

What should I do? she agonized, sinking down on the edge of her bed. *How much should I tell him?* Questions hurled themselves back and forth in her mind as she searched her soul for the right answers.

It was at least two hours before Eve appeared before Derek, who was in the living room halfheartedly working on the jigsaw puzzle. He didn't understand why she had fled, especially when things were going so well between them.

He looked up to find her standing quietly beside him. She was tastefully dressed in a long-sleeved dress the color of burgundy; it had a stand-up ruffle at the neck instead of a collar. She carried her small suitcase in one hand.

Eve's velvet-brown eyes met his directly. He rejoiced to see that she looked like the Eve he remembered.

"I've decided," she said in her clear firm voice, "that it's time for you to meet my father."

Chapter Thirteen

Wrayville in winter hunkered spare and bleak in the shadow of Cotton Mill Hill. Weak January sunlight glinted off the dirty windows of the two-storey brick building that dominated the scene, and a chill wind whipped around the corners of street after street of identical mill-village houses.

In the middle of Nell Baker's block, children with runny noses played in the street. They ran away at the car's approach and stood wide-eyed on the curb, staring at Derek's Corvette. One of them yelled something derisive.

"Here it is," Eve said suddenly. "Fourth house on the right." Derek slowed his car to a stop in front of the white frame house.

He shot her a dubious look. "Are you going to tell them I'm the new owner of the mill?"

"No," Eve said. "Since there's been no public announcement, they won't know yet. If your name is connected to the mill, it will seem like just another rumor. To Al and Nell, you'll just be Derek, Dob's father."

Derek felt ill at ease, but he could see that Eve did not. She sailed confidently up to the front door and knocked. The door swung open to reveal a round, ruddy-cheeked woman wearing glasses with silver frames.

"Eve!" The two women embraced, and Derek felt even more awkward than before.

But Eve turned to him quickly and drew him forward. "Nell, this is Derek."

Nell smiled an uncertain greeting as she ushered them into a minuscule living room. It was tiny, but the furniture had been polished to within an inch of its life, and the blinds at the windows were raised to let in the maximum light.

"You'll want to see your dad right away," Nell said with an inquiring look.

"Yes," Eve said.

"Vernon's gone to the barbershop, and your father's out on the back porch watching television. I'm so glad I had the porch closed in last summer; it's made a wonderful TV room. Al stays out there most of the time. Thank goodness for the sports network. Al and my other boarder both love it."

Al, resting in a reclining chair with a plaid blanket over his lap, looked up as Eve paused in the doorway. On the television set in the corner, men in baggy shorts ran back and forth on a hardwood basketball court.

Derek's first impression of Eve's father was of a sick, elderly man. But Eve's father wasn't elderly; she had told him that he was only sixty-two! And these days, that wasn't old. It wasn't even retirement age. But hadn't she said her father was retired from Wray Mills? Or had she said that he used to work at Wray Mills? Derek couldn't recall.

Al tried to struggle to his feet, but Eve put a restraining hand on his shoulder.

"Don't get up, Dad," she said gently. Nell quietly turned down the volume on the TV set. The men continued running around on the basketball court; without the sound, the game looked like pointless scurrying.

"I—I—" Al said, and then began to cough. Finally, the cough subsided into an agonizing wheeze that punctuated every breath. But Al held up his hand to shake Derek's, and there was a welcoming light in his brown eyes, which were so like his daughter's. Derek gripped Al's hand with his customary vigor, but he realized too late that his grip was too much for Al, whose hand lay within his, lacking the strength to do much more than make a futile effort at a proper handshake.

Derek did not know how to react. He knew, of course, of Eve's father's resentment toward him for the part he had played in employing her as a surrogate mother. And yet he knew that with time and because he had taken care of Eve and had been kind to her, her father's resentment had faded into acceptance. Still, Derek felt some embarrassment at his part in what Eve's father had so long considered the immorality of her situation. He had assumed, in the light of his discussion with Eve at the Juniper Inn, that Eve wanted him to meet her father in order to exorcise that part of her guilt, in order to put it behind her, as he, Derek, had urged her to do.

But perhaps that wasn't the reason at all.

"You're feeling well, Evie?" her father was asking.

"Very well, Al. The few days in the mountains helped."

"And the little fellow?" This question was directed to Derek.

"He's doing fine. He's eating well and may come home from the hospital soon."

Al nodded, his energy spent.

"Have you had your flu shot this year, Al? You know how important that is."

"I carried him to the doctor for it myself," Nell said, peeking around the door from the kitchen.

"She did," Al said with a smile. "She's a right pushy old gal, if you want to know the truth."

"Aw, Al. Now don't go telling Eve how much I bully you. Besides, if it weren't for me, you wouldn't be working in Doug's office. And you like working there." Nell appeared bearing a tray with a coffeepot and four cups. She handed cups around and disappeared into the kitchen before reappearing with four plates of fudge cake.

But Al couldn't eat his and only waved it away. Eve left it sitting on the end table near him. Al coughed again; Derek tried not to listen and looked blankly at the men on the television screen. The men ran off; cheerleaders in short skirts danced on. It seemed wrong somehow, cheerleaders shaking pom-poms in this sickroom. For that's what it was, all right. This man was very ill.

"Do you have your inhaler, Al?" Eve asked anxiously.

"He's got it. It's right there in the table drawer," Nell assured her. She frowned. "He does need a new refill, though."

"We can get it for you before we leave," Eve said quickly with a look at Derek, who confirmed her words with a nod. "That way you won't have to go out in the cold, Nell."

"That's real sweet of you, Eve." Nell smiled her thanks.

The cake was good, and Nell was pleasant. But the hour dragged on and on for Derek in the light of his realization that Eve's father was a chronic invalid. Why hadn't she told him? She had never mentioned anything to that effect.

Finally, blessedly, it was time to leave. Eve bent and kissed her father goodbye. Al tried to get up again, but this time Derek urged him not to. His coughing seemed to have left him exhausted. In spite of himself, Derek looked back over his shoulder one last time before he left. Al's lined face was sallow and weary, and he lay limply in his recliner chair.

"I'll be back with your medicine in a few minutes," Eve called back to Al. "Just as long as it takes us to run down to the drugstore on the corner."

Derek said nothing when they were in the Corvette. He followed Eve's directions to the drugstore.

"Come in with me?" she asked.

"Sure," he said, although he didn't understand why she wanted him to.

He followed her down the long row of merchandise to the pharmacist's section. They waited while the pharmacist, an old friend of Eve's, filled Al's prescription.

"Come here," Eve said, tugging Derek toward an alcove near the cash register. She pointed to a machine. "Do you know what that is?"

Derek shook his head. All of this was beyond him; what point was Eve trying to make?

"It's a Liberator," she said. "It weighs eighty-four pounds. It provides oxygen for people who can't breathe well. See that clear tubing? It allows the patient to move no more than twenty feet away from the machine. If the patient has to go out, for instance to church or shopping, he has to carry a portable liquid oxygen set." She looked Derek squarely in the eye, sizing up his comprehension. "That's what my father has to look forward to," she told him bitterly. "That will be the next step for him. He'll have to rent a Liberator so he can breathe, probably that very one."

"Here you are, Eve," the pharmacist said, stepping out from behind the partition. "Al doing okay?"

She managed a smile for the pharmacist, whom she had known all her life. "He's about the same, Charlie. Thanks."

Derek followed Eve out of the store. Her purpose was now clear.

"Your father has brown-lung disease, doesn't he?" They stood outside on the pavement now; wet black leaves blew against their feet and stuck to their shoes like soggy leeches. But Eve didn't move. She stared up at him, almost defiantly.

"Yes, he does. He worked in the card room at Wray Mills for thirty-eight years." She bent her head against the wind and stuffed her free hand deep in her coat pocket, walking swiftly ahead of him to the car.

He opened the door for her and went around to the driver's side. Then he threw the car into gear and drove slowly back to Nell's house. He watched Eve as she ran quickly up to the front porch and handed the medicine quickly through the front door.

She waved cheerily, called something encouraging to her father and ran back out to the car. She brought a fresh-air smell with her when she folded herself into the seat beside him.

Derek stared at her. He looked hollow-eyed, like someone in shock.

"Well?" she said.

"I don't know about you, but I think I'd like to stop somewhere for a drink," he said heavily.

IT WAS A ROADHOUSE on the outskirts of town, a working-class hangout, but Derek stopped, anyway. There was a dearth of customers; the only cars in the parking lot were a dilapidated old Dodge sedan and a rusty pickup truck with two hunting dogs flapping their tails back and forth as they nosed against the tailgate.

Inside it was dark and gloomy. On the jukebox a woman wailed a somebody-done-somebody-wrong song. None of this mattered to Derek. He only wanted to sit down across a table from Eve and let her help him sort out his feelings about what he had just experienced in Wrayville.

They ordered—for Derek, his customary bourbon; for Eve, a glass of water. She wanted to be at her clearest and sharpest for this conversation.

"I've never met anyone with brown-lung disease before," Derek said. Above the round table where they sat, a Miller beer sign winked sporadically on and off, victim of a faulty light bulb.

"The people who suffer from byssinosis are usually poor and uneducated. They're not people who travel in your circles," she told him matter-of-factly.

"I suppose not," he agreed. His eyes were dark and troubled in the flickering light from the sign.

"I'm fully aware that some people deny that brown-lung is a disease," she said carefully. "I know that two people can work side by side in a dusty room and one will develop symptoms and one will not. There's an individual variability in response to the cotton-dust irritant. And nobody has yet figured out how a patient gets to the point where the disease is irreversible chronic lung disease. But no one who has seen the effects on mill workers over a period of many years can say that the cotton dust in the mills doesn't play a part in the disease's development."

"But a lot of brown-lung patients are smokers," Derek said. "Who can say that tobacco didn't cause their disease?"

"My father never smoked. Neither did Nell Baker's husband." She sipped at her water. "Oh, Derek, I have to admit that today was one of my father's bad days. He has good days; he has bad. But we can't expect him to ever get much better. His disease is irreversible according to the doctors."

"Why didn't he transfer out of the card room when he began having respiratory problems?"

"In the old days, you were happy to have a job. You didn't tell management where you wanted to work. You worked where they sent you. And as you know, there was no union at Wray Mills to stand up for workers' rights. Tell me, Derek, have you ever been inside a cotton mill? If you have, you must know what the working conditions were like twenty years ago, ten years ago. And even now." The sputtering light from the beer sign lit her face in all its earnestness.

"I went with my father once," Derek said, "to a mill over in Cherry Grove. I was only about ten years old, but that was part of his training of me as a future textile magnate—to take me to the mills when he went. And I followed Dad into the mill and saw the workers moving around in this haze of thick white lint with the machinery making an awful noise all around them. I was intimidated by all of it, to tell you the truth. I asked my father how the people could work under those conditions. Lint was everywhere—under the looms, in the workers' hair, heavy in the air like a blizzard of cotton dust. And Dad laughed and said the lintheads got used to it."

Eve's eyes flashed fire, and two red spots appeared high on her cheeks. "Used to it! They got sick from it!" She leaned closer over the table. "The dust was everywhere. They couldn't get away from it. My father used an air hose to blow the lint off him every night before he left the mill, but he still had to keep his work clothes in a separate closet so that the dust wouldn't get all over his good suits."

"I knew that Wray Mills hasn't complied with the law in cleaning up their plant," Derek conceded. "That's something we investigated before buying. But I had no idea there were any brown-lung sufferers. They didn't tell us that."

"I know," Eve said angrily. "They deliberately concealed the information. They 'lost' my father's claim after he filed it two years ago when brown-lung disease was diagnosed and he had to quit work. And when I objected to their treatment of him and when I refused to hand out statements to the press that

Wray Mills was taking steps to comply with the cotton-dust standards set down by the state labor department, I was fired.''

"Fired!"

"Yes, fired from a very good public relations job. Why do you think I hired myself out as a surrogate mother? I'd been unemployed for months.''

"You needed the money," Derek said woodenly. "I read it on your application.''

"Yes, I needed the money to support my father.''

"My God." Derek stared at her as though she were a stranger. He'd realized he didn't know everything about her. But he'd felt close to her, had experienced the ease of friendship with her, had thought he knew *something* about her, and yet now he felt as though he hardly knew her at all. He could not have imagined the pressures Eve Triopolous had faced, and to think that he had added to them when he had insisted on the abortion made him feel sick and angry with himself.

He motioned to the barmaid for another drink. She poured it and brought it to them, all twitching hips. They sat silently until she slinked back behind the bar.

"I want you to know, Eve, that Lang Textiles has a history of bringing each of its mills into compliance with the law. We're a big company, and it's a huge capital expense, but we can afford the air-filtration equipment and new machinery it will take to clean up Wray Mills.''

She studied him. The corners of his eyes fanned with creases she had never noticed before. "Wray Mills has taken advantage of every appeals procedure available under the law in order to stave off compliance," she told him. "In the opening room, workers are breaking open bales of cotton in air six times dustier than regulations allow. The most that's ever happened after an inspection is that the labor department fines the mill five hundred dollars and gives them a year to comply. You're saying that you're going to change this?"

"You're damned right I am," he said through clenched teeth. The beer sign flared brightly as if in approval of his words.

And Eve believed him.

"We'll use remote-control bale openers at Wray Mills," Derek told her. "In every plant where we've installed air-filtration systems and remote-control bale openers, not only has the machinery reduced worker exposure to cotton dust, but productivity and the quality of the product have improved.''

"And the workers? People like my father who have brown-lung claims? There are at least twelve people with valid claims, thirteen counting my father. I helped fill out the claim forms myself.''

"You?"

"Yes, me. I spent Mondays working with Doug Ender in his office. We ran a brown-lung hotline. I donated my time, and Doug took time out from a busy practice to donate his. We canvased Wrayville by telephone. I filled out forms. We threw out the people who were faking it because they wanted free benefits.''

"You and Ender? When you were living at my house?" This news astonished him. Now he knew where Eve had gone on Mondays, why she was never there when he arrived home from work.

Eve nodded her head once, twice.

He stared at her, finally comprehending. And he comprehended more than her passionate advocacy of the rights of workers to work in a clean environment, more than her championship of brown-lung claimants. He comprehended the uncompromising high standards of Eve Triopolous and her stubbornness when confronted with what she considered wrong, whether it was the failure of a mill to comply with regulations or the shunting aside of a hearing-impaired old woman or—abortion. In a world that could be ugly, Eve never compromised her convictions. She had always been, to his knowledge, faithful, loyal, moral—and kind.

He looked at her soberly, and when he spoke, his voice was calm.

"This fellow Ender. Is he important to you?"

She considered this, and Derek found that he couldn't breathe.

"He's an old friend, and very dear to me. But we're not romantically involved, if that's what you mean." She spoke candidly, and there was a ring of truth to her words.

"That's what I mean, all right," he said, draining the liquid in his glass. He locked his eyes with hers, knowing he had never been so relieved or so happy in his life.

"Let's get out of here," he said, rising from his seat and tossing a large bill on the table.

He couldn't resist pulling the plug on the maddeningly erratic beer sign before they left.

THEY HAD TO PASS the hospital on their way back to Myers Park. Eve glanced at him as they approached it.

"Derek?" she said softly.

He swung the car into the hospital parking lot. "We'll go up to the intensive-care unit," he said. "We'll try to see Dob."

Dr. Perry had ordered Eve not to see Dob for a week, and it hadn't been that long yet. But Derek felt sure that if Dr. Perry could see Eve now, he wouldn't object to her visiting Dob, if only for a few minutes.

Derek and Eve stood side by side in the elevator on the way to the intensive-care unit, suddenly self-conscious together. A new tension existed between them, and they both knew it. Eve sensed what Derek was thinking, and her heart pounded in her chest. She knew him well enough by now to know what he wanted. Did she want the same thing? Was it *right* to want it? Was the affection she felt for him really love, or was it something else?

The nurse on duty outside the intensive-care nursery glanced up from the charts spread out on her desk. She was someone they knew from all their previous visits, and she smiled with pleasure when she saw them.

"Derek. Eve. You've chosen a good time to come." She stood up and beckoned. "Follow me."

Through the window they saw an aide sitting in a rocking chair, holding a bundle wrapped in a blue-and-white checked flannel blanket, and she was holding a bottle in her hand.

"It's Dob," Eve breathed, recognizing the unmistakable shape of Dob's head, the sparse tuft of brown hair on his head.

"Would you like to feed him?" the nurse asked with an inquiring look at Eve. "We've taken him off the tubes. He's taking all his nourishment by mouth."

"I—I—"

"You'd better put on a gown and a mask," the nurse said, producing one of each. "You, too, Daddy." She handed a similar outfit to Derek.

Once properly garbed, they entered the nursery. The aide wordlessly stood up and handed the bundle over to Eve. Eve's heart swelled with love; her chest felt so full that it hurt. Dob wriggled; he moved his legs restlessly, and his tiny seeking mouth rooted for the nipple so recently removed from it.

Eve sank down in the rocking chair, cradling Dob against her breasts, and inserted the nipple into Dob's mouth. With a sigh of pleasure, he began to suck at it, his eyes, gray and curious, fixed steadily on Eve's face.

Her own eyes filled with tears of happiness. There was no way she could have imagined the euphoria of holding Dob in her arms, to feel again bound to him as she had felt when he had still been a part of her.

His cheeks had filled out, and although they weren't plump, he was no longer wrinkled. His skin was pink and rosy, and someone had combed his hair into a peak down the middle of the top of his head. He was more than a bit of raw tissue; he was real, he was beautiful, he was *Dob*. He was a miracle.

His eyes drifted closed as the round cheeks worked at the nipple. A thread of milk ran out of the corner of his tiny rosebud mouth. Derek reached down and wiped it away with a corner of the blanket. Derek's face was absorbed, and in a quiet way, joyful. But Derek would never be bound to this baby the way Eve was. Never.

"Do you want to hold him?" she asked softly, glancing up at him.

Derek shook his head. He smiled tenderly at the two of them.

"No, not this time," he said gently. "I'd rather watch the two of you together. I've never seen a more beautiful scene."

His eyes touched her heart with gladness, and they did not speak to each other again. There was no need to talk. One heartfelt look said everything that needed to be said between them.

NO ONE WAS AWAKE at the Myers Park house when Eve and Derek tiptoed through the back door. Aunt May didn't expect them back for a few more days; anyway, it was late, and Aunt May usually retired early.

Nevertheless, Eve felt like a criminal sneaking up the stairs hand in hand with Derek.

"I don't want to leave you," he said outside her bedroom door. His hands rested lightly on her upper arms, and she found herself inclining toward him so naturally that she saw no point in stopping.

Her forehead met his chin. He put a finger beneath her chin and lifted her face until he was looking full into it. The wingswept eyebrows, the straight, sharp nose, the high cheekbones and her eyelashes, so short and dark. All were breathtakingly familiar and yet much too unfamiliar. He drifted his fingers across her features, committing them to memory so he could recall them and the way they felt whenever he chose. And then he lifted her mouth to his, the lips slightly parted, and he slid his arms around her, delighting in the rightness of it, the perfection of it.

His mouth met hers, and he was touched that her lips trembled beneath his, but they didn't tremble for long, because then everything was sure and honest, and their lips together felt right and familiar even though they had only kissed once before.

Eve's doubt melted away as Derek's lips explored hers, and happiness surged through her so that she was able only to think, *Yes, yes!* as she returned his kiss with joyful abandon. After all they had been through, after their sharing of grief and guilt and joy, after circumstances had so irrevocably blended their lives, how could she ever leave this dear and wonderful man? She couldn't.

Derek pulled her tightly against him, so tightly that he felt his heart beating in unison with hers, speeding up, urging them on, racing toward what they both knew was the inevitable result of their passion. This night, they could not be apart. It was as simple as that.

His lips released hers, and he looked down at her to see tears glazing her dark eyes. Without a word he opened the door to her room and drew her inside, closing the door softly behind him.

"Eve, I want you to know I love you. This isn't merely a—"

She placed a quieting finger across his lips. Her voice was warm and rang with a new confidence. "I know. And I love you. It's just that at first it didn't seem right. I couldn't be sure if it was real, and if it wasn't real, I couldn't admit to it, but now I'm sure, Derek. Very sure."

He smiled at her in the dark. "And so am I. We've shared so much. So much, Eve," he said and his head bent to hers again, absorbing her in a kiss that took her breath away.

When finally they broke apart, he slid his hands around to the buckle of her belt.

"May I?" he whispered.

Slowly she nodded. He unfastened the belt, then moved his hands around to the tab of the long zipper at the back of her dress. When he tried to slide it, it wouldn't budge.

"Oh," Eve murmured. "It gets stuck on the ruffle sometimes." She lifted her hands and found the tab, and his hands remained over hers as she tugged it loose. Then he slowly edged the zipper slide down and down, past her waist, over her hips until he felt the silkiness of the undergarment beneath.

Eve shrugged out of the dress, letting it puddle into folds on the floor. She stood before him, pale and white, in her slip.

He eased the straps over her narrow shoulders and kissed her shoulders one by one. Then he shimmied the slip down around her hips, letting his hands rest there for a moment as he captured her lips in a kiss, then allowing the slip to fall around her ankles.

She wore a bra that crowded her breasts, still swollen from childbirth; she had had a shot after the delivery to dry up her milk, because she would not be nursing Dob, but her breasts remained full and round. Derek knew, he understood, and he was gentle as he unhooked her bra, removing it before touching her reverently and then pressing his lips to each dark peak, one by one.

And then he slid her panty hose downward, and she gracefully lifted one leg and then the other as he knelt at her feet, and when he stood up again, she stood before him completely naked and free, and he caught his breath at the absolute beauty of her in the light from the street lamp outside the window.

Silvery marks marred the smooth white skin of her newly flat abdomen. Carefully, tentatively, he caressed one with an experimental finger.

"These?" he whispered.

"Stretch marks," she breathed, aroused by his touch. "From Dob."

"They won't ever go away, will they?" His voice sounded anxious.

"No." Her eyes on his face never wavered. "But it doesn't matter." Suddenly she felt elated; she had borne this man's child, and she was proud of it.

He knelt again and gently kissed each stretch mark. She closed her eyes against the sweet torment of her desire for him.

He stood again, holding her loosely within the circle of his arms. "It's too soon after the baby to really make love, isn't it?" he asked her gently, kissing her earlobe as he did so.

"Yes," she murmured, not at all embarrassed. She felt no modesty or shame with him, none at all. "But we can—"

"I know," he said, lifting her in his arms and striding to her narrow bed. He laid her carefully there as though she might break, and his eyes caressed her as he took off his clothes, too.

She lifted up the sheet and blanket for him to come to her, and he laid down beside her, absorbing her warmth, the softness of her body, the pleasure of their skins touching. He drew her into his arms and murmured her name over and over into her fragrant hair.

"I love you, Derek," she said, her lips hungry for him, hungry for all of him.

"And I, you," he said unsteadily. Newly wise in their love for each other, they knew better than to say all the words, so in this time and space they spoke no more of their love. The peace enveloping them was as pleasant as their caresses, as soothing and as meaningful as their love itself. With a passion so tender that Eve thought her heart would break with the joy of it, Derek made love to her until their exhaustion overcame their euphoria, and finally they slept, entwined in each other's arms.

When the morning sun broke through the trees, Derek reluctantly slipped away to his own room.

"Because," he said lovingly as he sat on the edge of her bed to kiss her goodbye, "for your sake, I want to keep up appearances for Aunt May. Until we get married, that is. Will you, Eve? Will you marry me?"

For a moment he was afraid. What if she said no? Because of Kelly, because they were from different backgrounds, because of a hundred and one reasons why he wasn't good enough for her. And he wasn't good enough, not by half.

Eve smiled and reached up to pull him down to her, sliding her arms around his neck. "Yes," Eve replied, her voice thick and warm. "Yes, my darling. I'll marry you. As soon as we can."

Chapter Fourteen

ve Triopolous married Derek Lang in March in a short pri-
ate ceremony at the home of the groom. Her father, looking
piffy in his best suit and coughing very little, attended the
edding with Nell Baker, who wore a new lavender dress for the
ccasion. Aunt May, who was touchingly overjoyed, donned
er best three-and-a-half-inch rainbow-striped high heels with
er teal-blue suit, and she even bought a new battery for her
earing aid so as not to miss any of the ceremony. Doug Ender
as there, and Derek's friends, the Kleinsts and Jay Stanley,
ame, too.

Also in attendance was Derek Robert Lang, Jr., sleeping
eacefully in an heirloom cradle under the bay window in the
ving room with Louise standing by in case he awoke.

"He's supposed to sleep through the ceremony," Eve said
rvously, glancing at her wristwatch as she and Derek took
eir places before the judge in the living room with their guests
oking on. "He just finished his feeding."

Indeed, Eve had almost been late for her own wedding when
ob spit up all over her wedding dress. Fortunately, she had
other one equally as appropriate, so she exchanged apricot
k for eggshell lace and thanked Derek for being so insistent
 buying her everything in sight the day he took her to Mondo's to outfit her with a trousseau.

"Well," Derek had said, adjusting his tie one last time and
en turning to her with a smile on his face. He kissed her
oringly on the tip of her nose, admiring once more the geo-
etric precision of her haircut, short in back and longer on the
es. "That just shows you how good it is to have a plan. And
 alternate plan, of course."

She beamed up at him. "Just be sure to let me in on what the
plan is from now on, will you? It helps." It still rankled that he
hadn't told her earlier how much he loved her. Because then she
wouldn't have thought all the things she had thought, that she
would have to leave Dob, that she would have to leave Derek.
And maybe she never would have become so depressed that she
went utterly to pieces.

But of course Derek had made up for it. He told her he loved
her every chance he got. And she thought she would never hear
it enough, even if he told her every five minutes for the rest of
her life. Which he had laughingly threatened to do as he offered his arm to escort her down the stairs to the ceremony.

"And will you, Derek, love her, comfort her, honor and keep
her in sickness and in health—"

Why, he already has, Eve thought.

"I will," Derek said, and his eyes upon her face shone with
commitment and love.

"To have and to hold from this day forward, for better for
worse, for richer for poorer, in sickness and in health, to love
and to cherish, till death do us part." Eve's eyes, shining with
happiness, never left Derek's face.

Above them, Kelly smiled in the gold-rimmed portrait over
the mantel. It was as though she blessed them in their union.

Derek drew Eve tenderly into his arms and kissed her gently
on the lips. And she clung to him, overwhelmed with happiness.

From the cradle beneath the window came a low whimper
and then a long wail.

"Oh," Eve said, pulling away from Derek. "I thought he'd
sleep through it. He always takes a long nap after his afternoon bottle." She hurried to the cradle and picked up the crying baby. "There, there, Dob," she soothed, patting him on the
back. "It's all right. Mama's here."

"Champagne in the dining room for anyone who's interested," Derek said, and with a comforted Dob reposing in Eve's
arms, they all trooped in for a toast proposed by Doug Ender.

"To Derek and Eve and Dob in their happiness," Doug said,
holding his glass high. Everyone raised a glass of Derek's favorite Dom Perignon to his lips, and Derek beamed at his wife
and son.

Louise passed dainty sandwiches and petits fours on which
she and Aunt May had collaborated, and a cornered Doug listened patiently to Debby Kleinst's glowing description of her
unmarried sister.

"I told Derek," Aunt May declared earnestly to an interested Nell Baker, "that the only thing I could possibly miss my soap opera for was this wedding. Did you see the last episode of *Love of Hope*? The hockey player told Susan about the computer hackers who penetrated the bank records, and—"

"I'm sending in a consultant to determine what measures are necessary at Wray Mills to bring it up to standard. I'm prepared to spend as much as necessary to clean up the air in the next few months—"

"Evie, you look so pretty. And the baby's a cute little fellow, isn't he? You know, it's nice to have a grandchild. It really is. I wish your mother—"

"Psst, Eve, come in here. I haven't told you I loved you since before the ceremony. It's been at least half an hour. Do you have any idea how much I love—"

"Derek, stop it! Aunt May or somebody will walk in any minute, or Louise asking if we want something to eat!"

"What do you think, Dob? If your mother won't kiss me, I'll have to kiss you. Come on, son; come to Daddy," he urged, and Derek eased an open-mouthed Dob into his own arms and stood beside the cradle, gazing happily down at his son. Then he planted a kiss on the baby's small forehead.

"Look, Eve, he smiled! He did! He has Kelly's mouth. Remember I told you that one day in the hospital?" Derek sounded genuinely pleased.

Eve gazed at her son. "Kelly's mouth but definitely your nose." And Dob *was* smiling. Definitely smiling, his eyes crinkling with mirth.

Derek laid Dob gently in the cradle and watched as his son energetically bicycled his legs. Then, after several moments of exercise, Dob yawned widely and sighed as his eyes drifted shut. In a time span as brief as the blink of an eye, he had fallen asleep.

Hand in hand, Eve and Derek watched their small son.

"You know," Derek said with a glance out the window, "it's almost time for Aunt May's pansies. See the little green sprigs in the flower beds? Remember she planted them in the fall to bloom in the spring?"

"Yes," Eve said, recalling the very day. "I wondered how those fragile little plants would ever weather the winter." To be honest, she had worried then about how *she* was going to weather the winter, how she'd manage to leave the baby behind when spring came, because at that time that was what she had hoped for, that Derek would keep the baby. Then she had never dreamed that he would keep her also. Well, the pansies had weathered the winter, and she had, too. They were both stronger than they looked.

"I love pansies," she told Derek. "They're my favorite flower. I sat beside a bed of pansies the day I saw your ad for a surrogate mother in the newspaper. I've always thought I was like a pansy. Not flashy."

He studied her face, so dear to him now. "I like that. You *are* like a pansy. And they used to be called heartsease. You've eased my heart, Eve. Ever since you came back."

She turned within the circle of his arms and rested her head on his chest. She closed her eyes and let the sweet comfort of his embrace enfold her. She felt so safe, so happy, and the feeling made up for everything that had happened in the past.

"I'm never going to leave you again, Derek. Never."

"You'd better not. It isn't in the plan. And in this case, there's no alternate plan, either."

Eve lifted her head and smiled at him, revealing her quirky bicuspid, and then they laughed together and after one last quick but heartfelt kiss, the two of them hurried arm in arm to join their wedding guests.

And in his cradle, Derek Robert Lang, Jr., slept on, blissfully unaware for the time being that his life, his existence, his very *being*, was a true miracle of love.

RUGGED. SEXY. HEROIC.

Stony Carlton—A lone wolf determined never to be tied down.

Gabriel Taylor—Accused and found guilty by small-town gossip.

Clay Barker—At Revenge Unlimited, he *is* the law.

JOAN JOHNSTON, DALLAS SCHULZE and MALLORY RUSH, three of romance fiction's biggest names, have created three unforgettable men—modern heroes who have the courage to fight for what is right....

OUTLAWS AND HEROES—available in September wherever Harlequin books are sold.

MILLION DOLLAR SWEEPSTAKES (III)

No purchase necessary. To enter the sweepstakes and receive the Free Books and Surprise Gift, follow the directions published and complete and mail your "Win A Fortune" Game Card. If not taking advantage of the book and gift offer or if the "Win A Fortune" Game Card is missing, you may enter by hand-printing your name and address on a 3" X 5" card and mailing it (limit: one entry per envelope) via First Class Mail to: Million Dollar Sweepstakes (III) "Win A Fortune" Game, P.O. Box 1867, Buffalo, NY 14269-1867, or Million Dollar Sweepstakes (III) "Win A Fortune" Game, P.O. Box 609, Fort Erie, Ontario L2A 5X3. When your entry is received, you will be assigned sweepstakes numbers. To be eligible entries must be received no later than March 31, 1996. No liability is assumed for printing errors or lost, late or misdirected entries. Odds of winning are determined by the number of eligible entries distributed and received.

Sweepstakes open to residents of the U.S. (except Puerto Rico), Canada, Europe and Taiwan who are 18 years of age or older. All applicable laws and regulations apply. Sweepstakes offer void wherever prohibited by law. Values of all prizes are in U.S. currency. This sweepstakes is presented by Torstar Corp, its subsidiaries and affiliates, in conjunction with book, merchandise and/or product offerings. For a copy of the official rules governing this sweepstakes offer, send a self-addressed, stamped envelope (WA residents need not affix return postage) to: MILLION DOLLAR SWEEPSTAKES (III) Rules, P.O. Box 4573, Blair, NE 68009, USA.

SWP-H895

WESTERN *Lovers*

Available in August

Two more
Western Lovers
ready to rope and tie your heart!

THE BEST THINGS IN LIFE—Rita Clay Estrada
Ranchin' Dads
When single dad Beau McGuire arrived at the
Carter ranch to reclaim his missing daughter, he
hadn't expected to start an instant family. But that
was before he laid eyes on Honey Carter....

MOONBEAMS APLENTY—Mary Lynn Baxter
Denim & Diamonds
Kari Kerns needed Nate Nelson's help—and the
sexy cowboy never turned down a beautiful damsel
in distress. He didn't know why Kari was on the
run, but he couldn't stop daydreaming about the
luscious body beneath her tight blue jeans!

And available in September...

HEART OF THE EAGLE
by Lindsay McKenna

THE FAIRY TALE GIRL
by Ann Major

HARLEQUIN® ▼ *Silhouette*®

WL895

As a Privileged Woman, you'll be entitled to all these Free Benefits. And Free Gifts, too.

To thank you for buying our books, we've designed an exclusive FREE program called *PAGES & PRIVILEGES*™. You can enroll with just one Proof of Purchase, and get the kind of luxuries that, until now, you could only read about.

BIG HOTEL DISCOUNTS

A privileged woman stays in the finest hotels. And so can you—at up to 60% off! Imagine standing in a hotel check-in line and watching as the guest in front of you pays $150 for the same room that's only costing you $60. Your *Pages & Privileges* discounts are good at Sheraton, Marriott, Best Western, Hyatt and thousands of other fine hotels all over the U.S., Canada and Europe.

FREE DISCOUNT TRAVEL SERVICE

A privileged woman is always jetting to romantic places. When <u>you</u> fly, just make one phone call for the lowest published airfare at time of booking—<u>or double the difference back</u>! PLUS—you'll get a $25 voucher to use the first time you book a flight AND <u>5% cash back on every ticket you buy thereafter through the travel service</u>!